The Quintessential WORLD OF DARKNESS

Kevin Andrew Murphy

William Bridges

Edo van Belkom

Rick Hautala

Jody Lynn Nye

the quintessential world of darkness	*stewart wieck & anna branscome (eds.)*
cover art	*kathleen ryan*
jacket and book design	*john snowden*
art direction	*richard thomas*

Published by
White Wolf Inc.
735 Park North Blvd. Suite 128
Clarkston, Georgia 30021
www.white-wolf.com

First printing October 1998
10 9 8 7 6 5 4 3 2 1

C⬤ntents

THE LOTUS OF FIVE PETALS
OR
THE INFAMOUS HOUSE OF LADY MIAO

Kevin Andrew Murphy

THE FIRST PETAL

"The Tale of the Black Tortoise"
A Story of Sorrow

The room swam with stale smoke and alcohol, a nimbus of ghostlight around each table votive, washing the sailors' faces as pale as the drowned men many of them would one day be. As if an omen, there were less of them than there should have been otherwise, even with the unseasonal winter rain to drive them indoors. Not that Anchalee minded. Fewer customers meant less time on stage, and the sooner she could get off her feet.

The music died an early death with the deejay's help, and Anchalee gave a languid twirl, gave one last kiss, took one last bill, then slipped back through the mylar curtain to the slightly fresher air backstage, feeling slow and ponderous as a river turtle surfacing for air. She gasped for breath, bending over, hands on her knees. The plastic streamers clung to her skin like a fisherman's net, trying to drag her back, until at last she straightened up, stumbling farther in, and they released their hold.

There was a calculated pause of ten seconds, while Anchalee caught her breath and the patrons began to bang the tables, then Mei Ling slipped past her, the pins of her headdress tangling for a moment with the curtain, and the cheers and catcalls erupted. Then the insistent backbeat of the euro-pop the Chinese girl preferred for her act.

She was the star, after all. Mei Ling, with her bananas and goldfish and razor blades. Anchalee was nothing more than the half-time show.

Anchalee brushed her hair back from her face, still sticky with sweat and the breath of a hundred drunks. What a way to make a living. What a way to live a life. But at least the Patpong clubs had better hours and better pay than the sweat shops, and while a dancer didn't make what a courtesan might, she at least could make it on her feet as opposed to on her back, and, for the most part, choose her dance partners. An option which most of the business girls didn't have, at least the ones at the proper houses.

Then, of course, there were the stars like Mei Ling. Stars dictated their own hours, wrote their own acts, and made more than the dancers and tea girls combined. Anchalee envied her the money at least. As for the act, well, being pawed by drunks and tourists was bad enough, and when money was tight, at least she could take it as a saving grace that she didn't have to engage in sexual relations with groceries and goldfish. And as for the razorblades, it was bad enough nicking her legs in the shower without having to worry about cuts in *other* places.

Mei Ling could keep her act. And her money.

Anchalee took a moment to pull the *baht* notes from her G-string, careful of where the twisted corners bit into her flesh. Mr. Chanai sat waiting in his peacock-backed rattan throne, eyes watchful as a monkey's. Silently, Anchalee straightened the bills and placed them in his palm as he counted. His tongue clucked like an abacus as he divvied up the notes, sixty/forty, his favor. Still, better than most clubs in the district.

The few notes in odd sizes and colors he set aside. Mr. Chanai kept all the foreign bills for himself. The larger ones would go to the bank or the black market, depending—American dollars were always useful for various services, and British pounds weren't far behind—while the smaller ones were used to wallpaper the back of the bar. Mr. Chanai was quite proud of his collection, which was one of the oldest and most complete in the Patpong.

There were only a few foreign bills this time, and only a few were dollars. He set aside their equivalent in *baht* notes, plus the 'dollar bonus,' and at last he sighed, handing Anchalee her share. He tucked the rest in the pocket of his old Hawaiian shirt, disappearing the foreign bills into his moneybelt. "Not as high as your usual take. And today is a Friday."

"It will be higher tomorrow," Anchalee promised. "It's winter, and the rain can't last long. There should be a larger crowd then."

Mr. Chanai pursed his lips. "I saw the crowd, Anchalee. And I saw the way you worked them. It *should* have been higher, and it would be if your mind were on your job." He grimaced. "Mei Ling was not pleased to have her warm-up act be so cool, and her take will be lower because of it unless she takes *extraordinary* measures. And we are running short of parakeets."

Anchalee bowed, humbling herself. "I'm sorry, Mr. Chanai. I've been feeling…a bit under the weather. But I will rest up."

Mr. Chanai looked at her, considering, and reached for the swizzle stick he kept in his customary glass of poison-green liqueur and melting ice. "You are too fat, Anchalee," he pronounced at last, taking the plastic wand from the glass. He sucked the emerald drop from the tip, then pointed it at her belly. "Too fat. Right *here*."

The cold plastic poked her, and Anchalee flinched back, her hands rushing to protect her belly.

Mr. Chanai laughed and went back to stirring his drink, ice rattling like funeral chimes. "Too fat," he repeated, "or maybe I should say, too *ripe*. You can't dance at night when you are sick in the morning."

Anchalee clutched the money tightly in both hands and held it to her breastbone. "I can still dance."

"What, you think you're Demi Moore?" Mr. Chanai laughed at his joke, rattling the ice against the glass. "I'm sorry, Anchalee. American boys like their dancers pretty and thin. The Japanese and Koreans are the same way, and likewise with the Europeans. You're still pretty, but you're far too ripe. I've been watching you," he sucked a few more drops of melon cordial from his plastic wand, "and this has gone on too long."

He smiled then, showing teeth brown as a peasant wife's from betel-nut chew. "Of course, if you simply need a doctor to squeeze it out, I can make arrangements. I'll advance the fee from your next week's pay if you need it; after all, you're hardly the first of my girls to get herself in such a predicament." He patted her on the rear. "I'd rather not lose one of my better dancers. Especially since this *is* winter, and better nights are sure to come."

Anchalee stepped back away from him, covering herself as much as her arms and the silver pasties and G-string would permit.

Mr. Chanai licked his swizzle stick again and waved it like a scholar's brush. "Do as you like, of course, but spare me any pretty Buddhist platitudes about abortion and the Hells reserved for it. If you were all that good a Buddhist girl, you wouldn't be in a place like this, and for that matter, you wouldn't be in the position you're in either." He shrugged. "Look at this way, Anchalee: It could be worse. You could have AIDS." He paused, the swizzle stick on the way back to his mouth, a green drop poised on the tip. "You don't, do you?"

Anchalee shivered. "N-no." She stepped back another pace. The doctors had checked. Thankfully she had been spared that.

With a sigh, Mr. Chanai went back to stirring his drink, sitting back in the rattan chair till it creaked. "Lucky thing," he remarked. "Kara had it.

She danced for me before you came here. Pretty little thing. Lovely voice. Decided to supplement her income with unspecified services, and instead of going through a reputable house, with a madame who could check the customers beforehand and a doctor who could keep tabs on her health, she thought herself clever to eliminate the middleman and keep all the profit for herself. Japanese businessmen were her specialty. She caught it from one of them, I think. Wasted away to nothing." He paused, wistful. "Tuberculosis killed her in the end. That, or pneumonia. Doesn't matter." He droppered more of the green liqueur into his mouth. "She's dead now. Hardly enough of her to put in a box. I paid for a bit of her funeral. She had some wages coming when the police took her away, and she always did like flowers."

He looked at Anchalee, rubbing his chin with one wrinkled hand in the same posture used by ancient sages and monkeys at the zoo. "But that's not the case with you, is it, Anchalee? You're not prostituting yourself. Not yet. You consider yourself above such things. You've simply taken a lover, and he knocked you up."

Anchalee looked at her feet. "Yes, Mr. Chanai."

"Is he married? Some businessman with a fat wife and a house far away?"

"N-no. He's a serviceman." There. She'd admitted it. No going back now.

Mr. Chanai sucked his swizzle stick. "American?"

"Y-yes. But he left two months ago." She paused. "He will be back. He sent me a letter only last week."

Mr. Chanai dropped his stick back in the glass and left it there. "And have you sent him a letter, explaining your...situation?"

Anchalee bit her lip. "No."

Mr. Chanai sighed, tired and world weary. "Let me give you a bit of advice, Anchalee. Yes, I would like to keep you as one of my girls, for that means you will turn me a profit, but I know that will not be forever. I will have to turn you out of the stable soon enough, when you turn up fat or old or lame, and every girl happily disposed of is an old whore whom I won't have to shoo away from my doorstep in years to come. But Asian girls and American servicemen? I have seen it before. Many times, in fact. In years past, it was very popular, and I am in some ways touched that you are so old fashioned. Dancers and sailors are very...quaint." He looked at her with his wrinkled monkey-sage face, wise and just somewhat mischievous, like Hanuman. "Well, as I've said, I've seen the dance before, and happiness does happen. Sometimes. Rarely. And never perfectly—certainly not in this business—but perhaps close enough to what you need."

He then gave her a look as hard as that of Old Bancha, the chief gossip and grocer of her village before she came to Bangkok. "But if you think that by having this child, Anchalee, you will be able to shame this man into taking you back to his homeland and making you his wife, well then, there are orphanages filled with the results of such thoughts, children spat upon and reviled as halfbreeds by their aunts and uncles." He smiled, showing his brown teeth. "Sometimes even their mothers and fathers. If they survive."

He paused then, actually picking up his glass and taking a long drink, something he did very rarely. "Well," he said, setting the glass back down on the battered rattan table, "my advice—my advice to you is to write this man and find his feelings on the matter. If the Heavens smile on you and your impropriety, well then, you will have what you desire—a marriage vow and a ticket to the West, and in that I'll wish you every happiness. But if the answer is no, well then, I advise you to get an abortion, since the fate of a halfbreed child is bad, and the fate of a halfbreed's mother is far worse. After all, a child can always be sent overseas for adoption, and the same cannot be said of you."

Anchalee bowed. "Thank you, Mr. Chanai. Thank you for your advice. But I—"

He silenced her with a gesture. "Do not whine, Anchalee. Do not plead. There is nothing that sounds more like an old whore, and nothing that irritates me worse." He sighed, then reached into his pocket and peeled off a few more bills and thrust them in her direction. "Here. Take it. But do not consider this charity. It is either severance pay or a retainer while you consider your options. In time, you will see the wisdom of my advice, but every girl seems to feel a need to discover these realities for herself."

Money was money, and Anchalee snatched it. "Thank you, Mr. Chanai." Then, blinded by tears, Anchalee ran for her dressing room to gather her things.

Thankfully, the folk of Bangkok were nowhere near as perceptive as Mr. Chanai. It was two more months before Anchalee truly began to show, and a month beyond that before anyone began to comment.

In that time, three more letters came from Howie, her American lover. Anchalee sent two more. She wrote of love. She wrote of longing. She did not write about the baby.

KEVIN ANDREW MURPHY

Her landlady was less understanding than Mr. Chanai. "I will not have a whore living in my apartment. Especially a whore who cannot pay her share of the rent." Mrs. Kritdee stood in the kitchen with a jar of salted eggs in her hands. "Where are the *bahts* you promised me?"

"Please," Anchalee begged, "I will bring you the rest next week. You know I lost my job in the Patpong. Now I'm selling curry in the street."

Mrs. Kritdee rolled her eyes and roughly shoved the jar to the back of the cabinet. "Selling curry? So *that's* what they're calling it these days." She smiled then, and it was not a pleasant smile. "As for the money, that's what you said the week before, and the week before that. I have no patience for whores or deadbeats. Take your things and get out."

"I will be paid tonight."

"For what? A few hours work? Pah!" Mrs. Kritdee spat, though she made sure to land it in the sink. "*That* for the few coins you earn now. I am not running a flop house where you pay by the night, and if I were, I would expect much more. Get out!"

Anchalee looked at her eye to eye. "You've found another boarder, haven't you? One who will pay you more money."

Mrs. Kritdee sneered. "And if I have, is it any business of yours? Something is still more than nothing. Now go away. You are no longer welcome in my house."

Anchalee stood there, her world beginning to crumble around her. "Where will I go?"

Mrs. Kritdee sneered. "To the temples or the gutter, back to your village or to Hell for all I care. I'm not having you here anymore, not serving as an example for my children. Khun!"

This last shriek was directed towards her eldest son, Khun, who lay lounging on the couch, eyes closed, headphones over his ears, hypnotized by the silent beat of the latest pop. With a start, he woke, pulling down the headphones, and yawned. "Yeah mom?"

"Take this whore out of my apartment!" Mrs. Kritdee pointed her finger at Anchalee. "I have grown sick of her, and she is three weeks behind on the rent!"

Khun sat up and shrugged his massive shoulders. "Okay." He looked at Anchalee. "If mom says you're out, you're out."

Anchalee looked silently about for help. The girls were at school, and Spun and Leong, the other two boarders, were currently at work. "Khun?"

He gave her a bland look, and Anchalee knew that he dared not oppose his mother. Khun was at the old woman's mercy just as much as Anchalee, and he knew it. "Maybe you could try down at the airport. See if your boyfriend's come in yet."

Mrs. Kritdee rounded on her son. "What? Her lover isn't even Thai?"

Khun turned his bland expression to his mother. "Well, duh. He isn't even Asian. I thought you knew, mom."

Mrs. Kritdee screamed then, and the next thing Anchalee knew, she was slapped across the face. "Out! Out of my home, you whore! You peasant who sleeps with devils, and doesn't even pay rent!"

Anchalee felt her hands balling into fists, and she almost struck the old woman right then and there. But she knew that Khun would not stand by and see his mother injured, if only from a sense of self preservation. "Allow me a few minutes to gather my things. And may the Buddha have mercy on you when he's discovered what you've done."

Mrs. Kritdee stood there, ready to scream again, but she was a woman who always got what she wanted, and right now she wanted Anchalee gone. Anchalee gathering up her own possessions would save the old woman the trouble of doing it herself and leaving them to be stolen outside the door.

Clothes were the hardest to part with, and the easiest. Since her pregnancy had progressed, most of her old favorites did not fit anymore. She quietly moved them to Leong's side of the closet; the factory girl had envied her half of them, and wouldn't mind holding the others until Anchalee could find a place for herself. If that happened.

Anchalee felt a hot tear roll down her cheek. It wasn't supposed to be like this. Howie had said he'd be back by now, but that was before, and now his latest letter said he wouldn't return for another five months.

Five months was too long to wait. The baby would be due by then, and then...

She picked up the love letters. The love letters and the little toy beanbag bear with the Coca-Cola bottle in its hand. A token, nothing more. Not a ring or fine jewelry, just a child's toy. The little white bear smiled at her mockingly, but Anchalee stopped before throwing it across the room. A pale white bear, like Howie, with his white skin and his moon-blond hair and long pointed nose. So strange when she first saw him, even for a Westerner, but oddly enough, not ugly. Even handsome in an exotic way.

She clutched the beanbag, the gesture making the stuffed bear stick its toy bottle into its mouth, and she caught her breath, remembering. The same childish gesture, the same addiction to soft drinks.... She cried more as she realized that the gift had been meant as a reminder—"For you to hug when I'm not here." That's what he'd said.

"I thought you were packing," Mrs. Kritdee said from the doorway.

Anchalee looked to her, wiping the tears off on her wrists. "I am." She thrust the bear and letters into the middle of the bundle she was making from a sheet. "Just give me a few more minutes. It will save you the trouble."

Mrs. Kritdee stood in the door, watching her as Anchalee sorted through her things. She placed her extra brushes and makeup on Spun's dresser. She hadn't needed most of them since she'd given up dancing, and if she somehow hitched a ride back to Kanchanaburi, she'd have less use for them there.

If only Howie had a telephone number. If she could just call him, just explain matters to him...

"So what did your lover say?" Mrs. Kritdee asked. "Did you tell him your shame, and did he say he never wished to see your ugly face again?"

"What?" Anchalee turned, her mouth dropping open.

Mrs. Kritdee pointed to the pile on the bed. "Those letters. You looked at them and you were crying. I can only assume that you told him, and he denied it, leaving you with a child and no legal recourse."

Anchalee paused, then hardened her face into a mask. "Yes, of course," she said. "You have guessed it perfectly."

Mrs. Kritdee smiled. She liked gossip almost as much as Old Bancha, and mostly the unpleasant kind. "How very unfortunate. I don't suppose there's any chance of me ever seeing my money?"

Anchalee bit her lip, then finally said, "Maybe in Hell."

The old woman blanched, but while Anchalee knew she had scored a hit, she could take not pleasure in it. The harridan had the last word in action, if not literal truth. Once all her things were packed in a bundle she could barely carry, the door slammed behind her with the finality of the sealing of a tomb.

Only afterwards did Anchalee think of the possible letters that might come to that address, and the glee with which Mrs. Kritdee would throw them away.

Anchalee worked all night in the curry booth, her bundle pressed back awkwardly against the wall of the building, the sheet dirtied with the dried urine of drunks and dogs and the ashes of old cigarettes.

Business, however, was better than most nights, tourists and gamblers alike out for an evening on the town. Unfortunately, unlike her time at Mr.

Chanai's club, she did not get to keep anything of what she made. On occasion, a Westerner would give her a 'tip,' and rather than correct his error, Anchalee pocketed the money. She was too poor at the moment to be proud, and while tipping was hardly the custom in Thailand, apart from the western clubs—it was hardly honorable to accept money you hadn't earned, except as charity—charity was exactly what Anchalee expected to be asking for very soon. She knew that Mrs. Polasit, who owned the curry cart, would fire her once she could no longer arrive at work clean and on time, and without an apartment, no matter how cramped or modest, and a working shower….

Anchalee thought of her options as she dished up more chicken stew and peanut-spiced noodles. She could go to one of the mosques if she got truly desperate—which she was—and while she wasn't planning to convert any time soon, she was clean, washed, and pregnant, and for the price of listening to the Muslims' disapproval and sermons, she could have a place to stay for the next few nights.

The Christian missionaries, though there were less of them, did roughly the same thing. Not that there weren't more than enough Buddhist shrines and temples—especially in Bangkok, City of Temples, and Angels for that matter—but most of the Bangkok monks were more concerned with tourists than tending to the needy, and as the city's needy went, she ranked rather low in the order of things.

Everything had its price in Bangkok, and you only got something for free if people thought they could sell you something. Which was a price in and of itself. Anchalee took a spare moment to prepare a plate of hot morsels skewered with toothpicks and set them at the top of the cart in easy reach of passersby.

The tidbits disappeared like rice in a field of hungry birds, but for the loss, she snared three more customers. In Bangkok, you never got something for nothing. The samples lured in paying customers, and the charity of the missionaries was no different. The only difference was in what they were selling.

In this case, religion. Anchalee considered flipping a coin to see if she should go to the Christians or the Muslims. She wondered whether to tell them a lie, like she had Mrs. Kritdee, or whether it would do to tell them the truth, that she loved a man whom she'd spent all of one week with, that she'd sent him letters, though not ones containing the whole truth, for fear that she'd frighten him away like a rice bird from a snare.

Or for fear of what she thought herself.

Did she really love him? Could you love a man with whom you'd spent no more than a week, with whom your only real conversations had been in another language, one which you spoke only brokenly and badly?

Anchalee had no illusions about her command of English. It was a crazy language, far worse than Vietnamese or even Chinese, and about its only saving grace was that dictionaries for it were cheap and plentiful. It took her half an hour to decipher a third of the words in Howie's letters, for all that they were very sweet and simple.

Rather like the man himself.

When she was a small girl, she had dreamed of marrying a farmer, like her father. A wealthy farmer, to be sure, but a farmer all the same. Businessmen were never home, and actors and movie stars were some place far away.

Then she had grown up, and moved to a city where there were actors and movie stars and businessmen by the thousands, so many in fact that they brought them in by the planeful and in boatloads. And in that golden city, with its bars and temples, she had met the simple son of a farmer.

Of course, when as a girl she'd dreamed of a strong, handsome farmer's son, she'd been imagining one from somewhere perhaps a bit closer. Ratchaburi or Pheteburi, or perhaps Samut Songkhram. Not Brooten, Minnesota. Wherever that was.

Somewhere in the United States, to be sure. Somewhere up at the top with lots of lakes, and snow, which Anchalee had never seen except in pictures. And big pale-haired men like Howard Hanson.

His brothers were just like him, he'd said, and the same with a lot of his friends. A Swedish settlement, Sweden being another far-away place in the far north with snow and farmers and men named Hanson.

They'd met at a bar on Leong's birthday, when Anchalee took her out for a night on the town. He'd been at the next table, attempting—if that was the right word—to order drinks in Thai. She'd wanted to practice her English, and so she'd helped him, and he'd helped her in turn. Childhood conversations, nothing more, about where you grew up and what you did. Basic schoolbook work.

His father raised pigs. Anchalee's father did too. And though it had happened half a world away, it was amazing the similarities there could be between two lives, and the opinions of children regarding pigs and what it was like to raise them.

Anchalee did not dream of raising pigs like her father, but she had dreamed of a man like Howie who could share her laughing moments. They had seen each other the next night, and the next, and the night after that, after a day spent together, they had slept together.

The hotel was wonderful, and Howie was…fun. So much fun, in fact, that the rubber had broken.

It was at his look of shock and alarm at that moment that Anchalee loved him.

Afterwards? Well, that was another matter. He was sweet, it was wonderful, she looked forward to his letters, and even more to another visit.

She was old fashioned enough in that. Love at first sight might happen in movies, but courtship was important. She worked on improving her English, since there didn't seem much hope for his Thai.

And then her period came late, and the test from the store confirmed her fears—pregnant.

What would he say? What *could* he say? That he didn't plan it either? That it had just happened? That he might love her, but it would take a bit more time, and one or the other of them getting a better grasp on a language, before they could know for certain?

Anchalee dished up the last of the noodles, sprinkling on extra peanuts that would otherwise have gone to waste. She didn't want to lose him, didn't want to spoil a chance at happiness, for all that the fairytale had already been ruined—first the courtship, then the marriage, then the children afterwards. Children before the courtship had even truly begun?

Abortion, however, was out of the question. Murder was forbidden, and much as Anchalee liked to be a 'modern girl' in many things, that was one sin she couldn't contemplate.

Besides, what would Howie say? If he did love her, then discovered that she had killed their first child, just for the sake of living some girl's fantasy of the way courtship should proceed?

If she could just talk to him, it would be so much easier. Just a phone call instead of a letter, something she could be sure would reach him, something which he couldn't run away from, at least without changing his phone.

But a seaman aboard a U.S. Navy ship did not have such luxuries, no private phone to his bunk, anymore than Anchalee had a line of her own, or even Mrs. Kritdee to take messages anymore.

Anchalee considered. Ships still had phones. Expensive, cellular phones, but ones that could still be used. Even by low-ranking seamen, if just for emergencies.

She had his name. She had the name of his ship—U.S.S. Louisiana. And she knew where the American consulate was.

KEVIN ANDREW MURPHY

She could reach him. Directly. Without having to worry about the mail. By all the Hells, consulates even had translators on staff, so there'd be no need to worry about broken English or fractured Thai. It wasn't as if she could hide anything anymore, and as Anchalee knew from her time in the Patpong, it was hard to ignore anyone if they were in your face.

Mrs. Polasit came and collected the cart just after midnight, looking askance at Anchalee's bundle.

"I'm moving," Anchalee said simply. "I didn't have time to take everything to my new place and make it to work on time, so I brought it along with me."

Mrs. Polasit nodded, not wanting any more explanation than that, then handed Anchalee her pay for the evening. "Could you come a little earlier tomorrow? It's been unusually cold, so I expect business to be good."

"Of course, Mrs. Polasit." Anchalee smiled and gathered up her bundle, glad that at least this was one situation she hadn't been turned out of—for the moment—and set off for the Embassy. If need be she could camp out on the steps.

By the Eight Immortals and their Wives—for that matter, there might even be tea and coffee. Protests against the West were all the rage, and while Anchalee didn't pay any more attention to politics than she needed to, she didn't care what sign they gave her to hold so long as she could keep warm and not be told to move along.

And tea would be a nice idea. On the side of Phrayathai Road, behind the curry cart, it was warm enough, but now that she was near the Chao Phraya, the River of Kings—dead ones, from the smell of it—it was quite a bit cooler.

Anchalee set down her bundle and undid one corner, searching about for the edge of her black silk jacket. That would be considerably warmer, and—

"What you got in the bundle, missy?"

Anchalee looked up, seeing a young punk with his hair spiked up in a fringe and bleached yellow, like an emperor penguin.

"Nothing," Anchalee said, leaning over quickly to tie up the corner.

Wrong move. She saw the kick coming out of the corner of her eye, and tried to step back, but she was fat and slow as a tortoise with pregnancy. The boot hit her shoulder, knocking her on her back, and she saw the next kick aimed for her stomach.

"No!" Anchalee wailed, curling full fetal to protect herself and her unborn child, and was rewarded by a kick, instead, to her skull. The pain exploded bright, followed by blackness and numbness.

She didn't know how long she lay there, time nothing more than shock and pain. Then she felt hands on her, vaguely aware of someone lifting her. "H—H—" She tried to speak, give some words of thanks to her rescuer, but then the next moment felt the arms release her and felt herself drop.

She dropped for a long while. Then came the splash, and the cold as the ancient River of Kings closed around her.

THE SECOND PETAL

"THE TALE OF THE WHITE TIGER"
A STORY OF WORRY

Lady Miao, the Courtesan of the Silver Claws, and owner of many other fine titles and sobriquets, was having kittens.

They fell from her robes, mewling and crawling, questing with blind eyes, then growing larger by leaps and bounds as they tumbled down the steps of the pavilion, becoming fully formed white tiger cubs by the time they came to the courtyard floor.

Phat Ho giggled and held up a long scroll. "Tony Moretto," she pronounced, "you stand accused of losing your traveler's checks, then walking into the Palace of our Mistress, Lady Miao, Courtesan of the Silver Claws, Mistress of the Bone—"

"Aighghgh!!!" screamed the man handcuffed to the iron rings conveniently set into the flagstones. One of the cubs had discovered his nose, and was biting it while pretending that his scalp was the belly of a rather mangy brown rabbit.

Phat Ho wound her scroll back around the brass rod and rapped him with it. "Stop that!" she admonished. "I haven't finished reading the charges!"

He opened his mouth, perhaps in answer, perhaps in protest. In any case, it didn't matter—the cub caught his tongue with its needle-sharp white claws.

Phat Ho giggled. "There," she said, "let that be a lesson to you in the power of metaphors. You will now be quiet and respectful while I read the charges before my Mistress?"

KEVIN ANDREW MURPHY

She prodded him with the brass rod again, but the kittens unfortunately took this as the signal to pounce. The man screamed again, a wordless gargle rising to a loud shriek as the cat released his tongue, his glasses knocked flying a moment later as the kitten became more energetic, discovering something *else* to play with, and a moment after that the flagstones were stained black. It would have been red, but the moon was only at crescent, and Lady Miao did not care for electric lights unless absolutely unavoidable.

Phat Ho rolled her eyes and looked away, pretending that what was happening was not happening. "Well, suffice it to say, we *do not* have an automatic teller machine...."

"Aighgh...." The scream became a gurgle, followed a moment later by a clatter of brass as Phat Ho threw the scroll to the courtyard floor.

"That's it!" the royal clerk shrieked. "I've had it. In the immortal words of W.C. Fields, even if he *was* a barbarian, 'Never share the stage with children or animals—they'll steal the scene every time!'"

Lady Miao laughed, lifting the hem of her robe back up so some of the kittens could return and crawl up inside her, bringing with them the delicious scarlet *chi*. "Oh, don't trouble yourself, Phat Ho. I asked you to provide entertainment and you did. Now have a little flesh before it gets cold."

Phat Ho turned demure, fluttering her long eyelashes like a proper courtesan, even if they were as fake as her breasts. "I don't know if I should."

"For me," Lady Miao said, then added as a possible bribe, "You know you'll play the better clown if you eat the fool first."

The royal clerk waved her hands in the air in the exaggeratedly feminine way common solely to transvestites and female impersonators. In the modern age, at least. In centuries past, some of the imperial eunuchs had affected the same mannerisms. "Oh, very well. If I must. But your kittens ate all the best parts."

She leaned down, taking a moment to unshackle a foot, then carefully unlaced the Nike and pulled off the sock. "Do you think *codpieces* might ever come back into style?"

"*Codpieces?*" Lady Miao asked, unfamiliar with the word.

"An old barbarian invention," Phat Ho explained. "Rather like Tupperware. To keep the best parts fresh."

"Oh," Lady Miao said simply. Sometimes it was better not to ask.

Her clerk began to play her favorite game of 'bite the accupressure points,' nibbling the foot down like it was a chocolate rabbit. A delicacy of which, in fact, Phat Ho was also rather fond, and could use as a diagnostic doll for a rather engaging—if low—comedy routine regarding the Rabbit in the Moon and a gynecological exam.

Lady Miao smiled. Her court was very fortunate to have Phat Ho. Eunuchs had gone out of fashion centuries before, and all of the *Kuei-jin* ones had long ago progressed to become prosperous mandarins in their own right.

But a female impersonator? Lady Miao wanted to thank the Muslim fanatics who'd beaten Phat Ho to death five years ago, but couldn't, because three years ago her royal clerk had eaten the last of them.

"Phat Ho?" Lady Miao asked. "Can you send hell money to Muslims?"

The female impersonator shrugged eloquently, looking up at the moon and placing one beautifully manicured hand on her breastbone. "I don't know, Mistress. How *do* you send hell money to Muslims?"

"No, no," Lady Miao corrected gently. "Not how *do* you, but *can* you?"

"Oh." Phat Ho looked pensive. Sometimes she could be quite the monkey, and it was hard to get her to take anything seriously. Then again, that's what made her so valuable as a clerk—it was heavy business being the chief minister of a court, with constant worries and petty concerns, and the occasional diversion was useful to keep the heart light.

"I don't know, Mistress," Phat Ho finally concluded, with all seriousness, then added, "Do you think Mr. Moretto is going to get his traveler's checks replaced?"

Lady Miao looked at the blood and the last bits of bone her cubs were playing with. "*That*, Phat Ho, is a very good question. But enough of levity. We've had amusement, we've had refreshments. Now down to the serious business of the evening: How goes the task of apprehending the River Prowler, that crafty little *chih-mei?*"

Phat Ho bowed in a low obeisance. "Oh Mistress, mercy! Mercy! I regret to inform you that on this night we have yet again failed, absolutely failed, to apprehend the *chih-mei*—alone."

Lady Miao paused, processing this, editing out the joke, and watching the sly grin spread over Phat Ho's artfully made-up face. "Alone? You mean you have not only apprehended the River Prowler, but another *chih-mei* as well?"

"No, Mistress…" Phat Ho said. "We have the *chih-mei*. Finally. At long last. The crazed cannibal corpse is plaguing the river no longer. But our other guest is something far worse. Something far, far more violent and terrible. A creature so awful I shudder to describe it, for fear of attracting the attention of the Yama Kings."

"What?" Lady Miao demanded. "Quit beating around the bush! What is it? A *hengeyokai*? An *akuma*? A *Kin-jin*?" She said the last and shuddered with revulsion.

"No, Mistress," Phat Ho said, still smiling slyly. "It's something far worse and more terrible than all of those. A creature ridden by the darkest *P'o*. A wailing, hungry, insatiable demon. We have apprehended," she paused for dramatic effect, "a *baby*."

Lady Miao paused. "A baby?"

Phat Ho nodded. "Yes, a baby. But not just any baby. A *dhampyr*, a little imp possessed of its *P'o* and the demon arts. A *chih-mei*'s baby. The *chih-mei*'s baby."

Lady Miao stood up, feeling the pain in her bound feet for a moment, then ignored it, taking a step down from the pavilion, her kittens falling into line beside her. "Well then," she straightened the fall of her white fur robes, "I've never heard of such a thing, but with all the ten thousand things in the Middle Kingdom, that means very little. Anything *can* exist. Anything at all. Even a *chih-mei* with a baby. But that being the case, the sooner we shock this *chih-mei* to her senses, the sooner we'll have the little demon off our hands."

Lady Miao made her way carefully down the steps of the pavilion, waving away Phat Ho's wordless offer of assistance. "I have not given birth to anything save tigers for the past five centuries, and I'm not about to start playing nursemaid now."

"I quite agree," Phat Ho said, falling into place, three steps behind. "You already know my thoughts regarding children."

"Of course. That other quote by the barbarian philosopher 'Fields' of which you are so fond."

"'I like children,'" Phat Ho giggled, "'*if* they're properly cooked.'"

Lady Miao waved the comment away, "Yes, yes, very amusing," and sidestepped the remains of the unfortunate Mr. Moretto, careful of the train of her robe. "Have the gardeners hose everything into the carp pond. It's been a while since the fish were fed, and it won't do to have anything so inauspicious staining the inner courtyard when we host the opera reception tomorrow night."

"Of course, Mistress," Phat Ho said, giggling at some private joke.

One kitten remained behind to play with the skull.

Lady Miao was certain the *chih-mei* had been sent by the Yama Kings to bedevil her. First there was the matter of its capture—six months! A record, at least for her court. Then there was the creature itself.

Pale, bloated, obviously a drowned girl, but crackling with fierce *Yang* energy to the point of imbalance. Though that much was certainly obvious. The creature had actually given birth. "You certainly have a lust for life, don't you, my dear?" Lady Miao said through the grate in the dungeon door. "Some potent reason for refusing death. Though of course the reason for that is easy to guess."

The creature only snarled and lunged at her, while behind her the baby gurgled with delight.

Lady Miao waved a sandalwood fan under her nose. The stench of a ripe *chih-mei* was bad enough, but when mixed with carrion and baby shit, it was well nigh unbearable.

So far, she had fed the *chih-mei* three individuals—a busboy who had dented an antique silver tray at the reception, an old gentleman who was doddering along the street and didn't seem to have anything better to do, and a little girl Phat Ho had lured away from the Klong Toey slum with promises of candy.

They'd given her the candy, for what it was worth.

However, the little girl seemed key. The *chih-mei* had still eaten her, but had seemed to pause for a moment, as if the child had reminded it of someone from its former life.

"Phat Ho," Lady Miao pronounced at last, "I believe what we need is a baby. A fat, happy baby."

Phat Ho paused, her inkbrush still in the air. "A baby?" She was in the process of doing the week's accounts at a little table she'd had set up outside the dungeon door. "Do you want me to steal one, or just buy one?"

Lady Miao was feeling magnanimous that night. "Oh, buy one. Give its mother enough money so she can buy rice to make a few more. Tell her it's going to a mother who just *adores* babies. That's bound to be true in one sense or the other."

"Yes, Mistress." Phat Ho dunked her brush a few times in the water jar, then scurried off to accomplish the task.

Lady Miao smiled. Good help was a pearl beyond price.

She really had to thank those Muslims.

They waited till the *chih-mei* was asleep, then had Wang Tzu open the oubliette in the audience chamber above and lower the baby, bassinet and all, into the dungeon.

Phat Ho rubbed her hands together, then held her finger to her lips, bouncing up and down on her heels like a schoolgirl. Lady Miao held up a hand for her to be still, then pressed closer for a better look through the door grate.

The bassinet touched the floor, rocking slightly, the baby still asleep, and then the grappling hook lowered further and moved aside before reeling back up. Wang Tzu was another treasure the Ministers of Hell had blessed her court with, a black marketeer and smuggler until the Cultural Revolutionaries had sent him off for 'reeducation.'

Lady Miao would have to thank them too. Burning a few of the writings of Chairman Mao would probably be appropriate. With all due ceremony, of course. Maybe she could immolate them with a monk.

The iron hook reeled back up, silent, and then a half minute later, the springs snapped back and the trap in the ceiling clanged shut.

The *chih-mei* and both babies awoke at once. After a moment of squalling, the *chih-mei* quieted her own child. It was one of the few moments when she looked even remotely human.

Then she turned, cocking her head, and looked puzzled. An expression which looked exceedingly odd on a fanged, red-eyed corpse.

But not, Lady Miao reflected, on the face of a monkey or ape. Seven centuries before, the Duke of Tsin had kept a menagerie of pet orangutans, and it was *exactly* that sort of expression the beasts exhibited when the Duke had presented them with the infant son of his unfaithful courtesan, Hwa. Hwa, of course, had fared nowhere near so well with orangutans— Lady Miao still recalled the amusing spectacle of the apes tearing her apart and wearing her bloody corpse for a hat—but the child itself had remained perfectly safe, raised up as an orangutan, until the Duke of Tsin had tired of the game and simply had him killed.

The posture, and the gestures, of the walking corpse at the moment seemed remarkably similar to those of Duke Tsin's orangutans, and Lady Miao wished she had a sedan chair and a honeyed drink to complete her pleasure as she watched the drama unfold.

The *chih-mei* approached the basket. First wary, claws upraised, then softening to curiosity as it lifted back the blanket. Then it looked back to its own baby, sleeping on the filthy rags in the corner, then back to the new infant.

Then the *chih-mei* sat down and cried, the light going out of its eyes, now no longer a *chih-mei*, a filthy, blood-encrusted ghoul, but a mere girl, though still filthy and blood encrusted.

Lady Miao signalled for Phat Ho to open the door, and her clerk did. Then, with the tiny and silent paws that were her feet, Lady Miao came down the steps into the dungeon. "Hush, my dear," she purred, "you are among friends now. Please, what is your name?"

The girl looked up, startled, but her tears continued to flow, streaking through the dirt and blood upon her face. "An—Anchalee."

Lady Miao smiled. "Like the pop star. How fortuitous."

Anchalee looked back to the baby, still crying, then started to put out a hand. She stopped suddenly as she saw her filthy, gore-encrusted nails. "I— I—" She looked back to Lady Miao, frantic for understanding, then turned away and gasped in horror, "I was going to *eat* the child...."

A snicker from Phat Ho echoed down into the dungeon, but Lady Miao ignored it. It would not do to tell this girl how many people she *had* eaten. To do so now could easily shock her back to her *chih-mei* state, and it would be unbearable for that to happen at this moment. If just because Lady Miao was fond of her white tiger robe, and didn't want to go to the expense of getting another.

"Hush, my dearest Anchalee. Hush. It's all right now. Your *Hun*, your higher soul, has taken control of your body. And while it is true you are one of the Hungry Dead, you are now in your rational mind. Now come upstairs where you can bathe and be made presentable, and I myself will see that your child is taken care of."

Anchalee stood up, and, careful of the filth, Lady Miao guided her up the stairs.

Phat Ho stood holding the door, and Lady Miao gestured with her head to the two babies, mouthing the words, *"Take care of them."*

The Courtesan of the Silver Claws then prepared herself for the inevitable jokes that would be made later, but didn't worry overmuch. Phat Ho was good help. She knew which one to keep and which one to eat, though jokes would be made about it for years to come.

It was, unfortunately, what the poets called a 'classic setup.'

A little more than an hour later, Lady Miao sat in her reception room while Phat Ho brought Anchalee in. Cleaned and perfumed, she was quite pretty, with long, straight hair, olive skin, and fine Thai features. Not Chinese, which was unfortunate, but to be expected in the barbaric south.

Lady Miao's handmaidens had dressed the girl in apple-green silk, as befit a young woman and supplicant of the court. And she looked nervous and frightened and just slightly out of place. Lady Miao guessed that this was a girl who'd done her share of grovelling in the past, and was prepared to do it again. An excellent quality in a new courtier, and a rare one as well.

"Welcome, child," said the Courtesan of the Silver Claws, gesturing to the room with her matching manicure. "Make yourself at home. I go by many titles, but for now you may call me 'Lady Miao' or 'Mistress.'"

"Where…" the girl began.

Lady Miao smiled. "Where are you? Do not fear. This is not the Yomi World. You are still on earth, in Bangkok. In my private palace in the Yaowaraj. I am from the heart of the Middle Kingdom myself, and so I find favor with the Chinese district, humble though it is."

The girl shook her head. "No…no…I meant the baby. Where is the baby?" She paused, biting her lip. "I remember a baby…."

"Your baby," Lady Miao reminded her, nodding. "Your name is Anchalee, yes?" The girl looked up and nodded hesitantly. "And your child…?" The girl gave a blank look, and Lady Miao shrugged. "Oh well. Never matter. Names are easy enough to come by. Phat Ho!" She clapped her hands. "Bring in the baby."

It seemed more for Anchalee's sake than her own that the royal clerk refrained from any jokes regarding "Which baby?" but merely exited out a gilded side door, returning a moment later with the bassinet.

Lady Miao's ancient heart skipped a beat, but then realized that Phat Ho had no doubt disposed of Anchalee's child's filthy rags, as well as the bassinet's former occupant. Practicality and a joke all at once—the essence of her royal clerk. "Look, Mistress," Phat Ho said proudly, "I have discovered a marvel known as a 'binky.' It pacifies even the most fiercely wailing *P'o* demon."

Anchalee held out her arms in a wordless entreaty, and Phat Ho came forward, presenting the child with all due ceremony. The girl reached into the bassinet's blankets and took out the child, who woke on the contact, the pacifier clattering to the tiled floors of the audience chamber.

The child began to wail and horns sprouted from its head. The girl did not flinch, this obviously a familiar sight.

Lady Miao wished there was a dignified way she could plug her ears, but merely said, "If you need to nurse him—her?—any matter, please do so. I won't be shocked. I've seen many far more shocking things in my life." *And done them, for that matter,* Lady Miao added to herself, though it wouldn't do at the moment to assault the girl's sensibilities any further.

With a dancer's grace, Anchalee sat down on one of the low cushions, then loosed the front of her robe and let the child suck. The wailing ceased and the horns subsided, and a troubled smile came over the girl's face as she watched her baby nurse, now looking like any human infant—small, pinched and monkeylike. But no longer demonic.

Best to distract her a bit. "You have lovely movements, my dear." Lady Miao lay back on her ivory divan and adjusted a pillow. "Have you ever danced professionally?"

"Y—yes," Anchalee said. "At Mr. Chanai's club. But that was before...I became pregnant." She paused then, biting her lip. "I used to dance in the village festivals. I came to Bangkok in hopes of gaining a job at the Cultural Center. I had heard they needed dancers."

"And did they?"

The girl shook her head, a bitter tear forming at the corner of her eye. "No. They asked me to put my name on the waiting list."

Lady Miao nodded. "And then you found a job with this Mr. Chanai?"

Anchalee inclined her head, and Lady Miao sat up a bit more on the divan. "What happened then? Please, tell me. There must be no secrets between us."

The girl then began to tell a story, both sordid and all too common in Bangkok—'Little innocent comes to the big city and has her dreams crushed, finally ending in her death.'

There were, of course, differences. First off, the girl wasn't some starry-eyed idiot. Young, yes. Idealistic, yes. But practical as well. She'd come to be a dancer. She had alternate plans of getting a job in a shirt factory. But when the job had presented itself at the strip club, she'd jumped at it. Half a cup was better than none, and a dancer made more than a pig farmer's daughter. And whatever the Muslims might say, pigs on two legs were cleaner than pigs on four.

The pregnancy was unplanned for, yet she had paced herself. A sweat shop would have worked her till she miscarried. A lesser job as a roadside vendor? Practical, sensible, respectable. Perfectly decent if she had already been married.

And of course she was a devout Buddhist, of the rural variety. The type who ate meat but didn't believe in abortion.

Now, of course, she'd switched the flavor of her meat. Pigs on two legs, after all, were cleaner than pigs on four, and long pork was

KEVIN ANDREW MURPHY

understandably sweeter than short pork, whatever the Buddhists might have to say on the matter.

Regardless, it all boiled down to very much the same thing: When presented with an obstacle to something she wanted, Anchalee still got it, even if it meant settling for second best, or just something a little bit different than what she'd originally planned.

Even death hadn't been able to forestall this pattern. It seemed to be the girl's karma.

"The Judges of the Dead," Lady Miao said at last, "must have looked with mercy upon you. That, or you didn't even stop for them when you rushed back to save your child."

"So I am dead?" Anchalee asked.

"After a fashion," Lady Miao replied. "And alive as well, after a fashion. We call the process 'The Second Breath.' You are one of the Hungry Dead, the *Wan Kuei*, the Ten Thousand Demons. Or you may prefer to use the modern term of '*Kuei-jin*.'"

"*Kuei-jin?*" Anchalee echoed.

Lady Miao laughed. "Yes, I know, it hardly rolls off the tongue—Chinese prefix, Japanese suffix. But it's the sort of thing that treaties and peace accords are made of. The '*Kuei-jin*,' the 'demon folk.'" She smiled then. "If it's any consolation, the word bristles the Japanese *Kuei-jin* almost as much as it does me."

Lady Miao spread her hands wide, gesturing to the room and its opulent furnishings, then brought her arms back, touching fingertips to fingertips, and steepling her fingers together. "Or I can put it in even more modern terms and explain it in the language of the cinema: You are a vampire. You drink the blood of the living, and you must do so if you wish to continue your existence. Such as it is. However," she added softly, "yesterday, it was worse. You were a zombie, a cannibal corpse with little mind or reason beyond a desperate cunning and a driving hunger. You agree that your state today is a vast improvement over that?"

The girl nodded. "Y-yes."

Lady Miao laughed again. "You have an engaging stutter. Keep it. That sort of innocent coquettishness will serve you well in my court. Oh, and by the way, you are now part of my retinue, and I am your mandarin. We Hungry Dead have laws, and that is one of them. You are hereby entering into your apprenticeship, and will not leave these walls until I see fit."

"I am a prisoner?" Anchalee asked.

"No," Lady Miao corrected, "you are a baby. And like a baby, you will be kept under close supervision until you can stand on your own two feet.

Metaphorically speaking." She paused. "You are also immortal, one of the *Wan Xian*, so the time you spend inside these walls is really not a sacrifice. I am doing this for your benefit, and while I hope that one day you will repay my kindness, that investment is far in the future. And by no means a certain thing."

Anchalee bowed her head, holding her baby close. "I understand."

"No, you do not, but you will soon enough." Lady Miao studied her for a long moment. "This is also a working house, not just my personal pleasure palace. Or, I should say, it is my personal pleasure palace, and that means it's a house of business. Though you've had no formal training in it, I believe you may make an excellent tea girl."

"Tea girl?" Anchalee looked up, alarmed.

"Does prostitution bother you?" Lady Miao asked. "Don't let it. You seem a tender sort of soul, and you probably wouldn't care for hunting on the streets. Mugging old ladies and passersby? That is what the Hungry Dead do, at least the rabble without a court. The jackal who attacked you and threw you off the bridge is no better than any of us here. But I think you would find it preferable to have your meals delivered to you, and for them to be willing victims, not strays or innocents. For you to be a courtesan, that's what it would mean."

Lady Miao ran her tongue lovingly over her teeth, then yawned widely as a tiger, letting her tongue loll out a full foot before pulling it back. "The dead," she said by way of explanation, "do not suffer the limitations of the flesh that the living do, and in this business, that is an asset. Some patrons will pay quite a bit extra for the right tricks, and once you have found your *dharma* and progressed along the path, you will find that you can suck breath and the more rarefied essences from the living and gain as much sustenance thereby as you do now from blood. Or flesh."

She sat up then, straightening her robe. "For now, however, you are a blood drinker. I think we will style you up as a dominatrix, with a straight razor and a whip. You will fulfill some businessman's perverse fantasies, then lick his wounds clean, thereby gaining your sustenance, him his pleasure, and most importantly, leaving him none the wiser. It is amazing the awful things you can sell if you just call them 'pleasures' instead of 'tortures.'"

"'Painting Aunt Polly's Fence,'" Phat Ho put in, then quickly bowed. "My apologies. I spoke out of turn. Merely the words of Twain, another barbarian philosopher."

Lady Miao looked daggers at Phat Ho. "Yes, I suppose so." She hadn't the faintest idea *what* concept she was agreeing with, but it didn't do to appear ignorant before one's lessers. And Ho's quotations tended to be spot-on when you could actually understand them.

But perhaps this was Ho's signal that a different tack was needed. "Yet if you don't care for anything so forceful, perhaps you'd care to play the sympathetic nurse who comes in to clean up *after* the dominatrix has finished? It comes to much the same thing in the end, and if you are unenthusiastic in playing the demon, the customers will tell." She smiled. "It's an engaging thought, isn't it—mortals hiring real demons to play demons from their fantasies?"

Anchalee appeared revolted by the very concept, but finally said, "Everything is for sale in Bangkok."

"Everything," Lady Miao agreed, then reached out and smoothed down the girl's hair. She did not flinch. "I believe we are going to get on very well, Anchalee. Very well indeed."

Lady Miao purred. At long last, everything was falling neatly into place.

Months passed, and Anchalee proved to be an apt pupil, and a passable, if not terribly enthusiastic, courtesan. She learned how to focus her *chi* through the various arts of the Hungry Dead, but the most important function of her training was that she progressed in her *dharma*—choosing the Way of the Resplendent Crane over the Dance of the Thrashing Dragon, to the approval of Wang Tzu and the horror of Phat Ho. But as unbalanced as the Thai girl was with *Yang* energies, it was probably all for the best.

Cranes, after all, made much more responsible mothers than Dragons, and Lady Miao was not about to deal with diapers. Especially with a child who could sprout a tail and fling them off whenever they became dirty.

Lady Miao was certain that this child was a special torment devised by the Yama Kings. The Demon Lords had decided to invent something worse than a normal cranky baby. But the girl, like most Cranes, decided that this was merely her just punishment for the sins of her life and bore it without complaint.

As for the child, Anchalee insisted on naming him 'Howard' after his father. It was a ridiculous barbarian name, but then again, the child's father was a barbarian as well, so that was to be expected. And it was in many ways appropriate, Lady Miao thought, that a demon child be given the name of a barbarian.

Thankfully, even demon children had to sleep sometime, and 'Little Howie' was resting peacefully in the next room. Probably hanging by his tail from the curtain rod, Lady Miao considered. 'Demon Monkey' would have been a better name, all things considered, but there was no reason to give the little *dhampyr* an inauspicious name to live up to, no matter how appropriate.

Regardless, Phat Ho, being a woman (or at least a transvestite) of many talents, had used the bones of the late Mr. Moretto to fashion an attractive Mah Jongg set, which she'd set out on the table in the Winter Parlor, part of Anchalee's suite. Which was pleasant since, with Anchalee, it now gave their court a fourth for play, so they didn't have to trouble with some flustered mortal taking the final place at the table and worrying about offending the Hungry Dead.

Wang Tzu shuffled the tiles, the bones fairly crackling with dark *Yin* energy, swirling with power around each *pai*, the sacred divinatory tiles. After an appropriate time, he removed his fingers from the bones and bowed, allowing Lady Miao first pick, which she took, interpreting the omens as she revealed her pieces.

First the Three of Bamboo—'The Toad,' meaning a recovery from sickness. Easy enough to interpret *that* omen. Lady Miao glanced to Anchalee, who was looking quite pretty and alive, despite the severe black silk dress she'd affected as some form of legalistic Crane penance.

The Courtesan of the Silver Claws shrugged and flipped up the next tile to stand beside the first: The Four of Bamboo—'The Carp,' meaning determination or long life. In this case, both.

Next the Five of Bamboo—'The Lotus,' signifying a baby.

There were only three suits in Mah Jongg, and so many Bamboo pieces either meant a very potent omen, or else that Wang Tzu hadn't shuffled very well. But Lady Miao had watched him, and the tiles should have been sufficiently jumbled even if she *had* just taken the ones nearest her.

She turned over the next tile. Not the Six, but the Seven of Bamboo—'The Tortoise.' Learning or illegitimacy. The latter, most likely, if the omens were telling the tale of Anchalee's life.

With hesitant silver nails, Lady Miao turned up the next piece to stand in line by the others. Bamboo again, and this time the missing Six—'Water.' Either travel or correspondence.

But to who?

Lady Miao reached for the next tile. This would cinch it. If arithmetic progression continued and the Eight or Nine of Bamboo showed up, the omen would be meaningless, except to signify that Wang Tzu hadn't shuffled very well—'The Fungus' and 'The Willow' meaning, respectively, 'eccentricity' and 'tact.' Hardly the most useful omens.

But she flipped up the next one and revealed the Two of Circles—'The Pine.' Signifying a strong young man.

Tired of the suspense, she flipped up one more. Back to Bamboo, and still with Two—'The Duck.' Devotion and partnership.

Lady Miao sighed. You did not argue with the Mandate of Heaven, or for that matter, Hell, or question the bones of the oracle. Lady Miao wondered who Mr. Tony Moretto had been that the omens his bones gave would be so helpful, or so clear, but that wasn't the question now.

She turned to Anchalee. "My dear, I believe it is time you wrote 'Little Howie's' father."

The Thai girl blanched. "Howie? But…I'm dead."

"Only in a sense," Lady Miao answered.

Anchalee paused. "I thought you wanted nothing to do with the West."

Lady Miao sighed again. "What we want and what we get are two entirely separate things, Anchalee. You know that as well as I." She rubbed 'The Duck' between her thumb and forefinger, feeling the grooves cut into the bone. "Besides, it is only proper that the child have a chance to know his father. Even if he *is* a barbarian."

"And he can change the diapers," Phat Ho put in. "This is the modern age, and we women don't have to raise the children alone."

Wang Tzu snorted.

Anchalee bit her lip. "But I no longer have his address."

Lady Miao smiled then and set the piece back down. "Wang Tzu?"

The smuggler looked up from his pieces. "I have made my investigations. I have the man's address, as well as that of his family." He paused. "He made Seaman First Class last month."

Lady Miao smiled. "And your English has also gotten much better, hasn't it, Anchalee? Phat Ho has been tutoring you. You can now write him a very nice letter."

Anchalee looked around the table, trembling no doubt at the enormity of all that had happened to her and the danger of the game she was about to play—and not Mah Jongg. "What am I to tell him?"

"The truth, of course," Lady Miao replied, then added, "selectively. It's what men want to hear. Tell him that you became pregnant, but that you did not tell him for fear that he would never wish to see you again. Tell him then that you suffered an unpleasant fall, and were delirious for months afterward, during which time your child was born. After which you were taken in by a kindly lady and her household who nursed you back to health and your proper frame of mind, and after a bit of investigation, you rediscovered his address and whereabouts. You regret that you did not contact him earlier, and you beg his forgiveness, but you did not wish him to see you while you were ill and irrational."

"She makes it sound like an opera," Phat Ho remarked.

Lady Miao tried to ignore this, but knew that she betrayed a trace of a smile. "I believe we should also take a picture of you and little 'Howie,' so that 'Big Howie' will know you're both all right."

Phat Ho smiled. "Little Howie with horns or without?"

Lady Miao stared at Phat Ho until her court secretary looked away. "What do you think?"

"'Without,' Mistress..." Phat Ho responded in a whisper, then turned to Wang Tzu. "Care to make a wager on how many rolls of film it's going to take?"

Wang Tzu did not respond, but Lady Miao could see in his eyes that the wager was on.

THE THIRD PETAL

"THE TALE OF THE CRIMSON PHOENIX"
A STORY OF THE UNEXPECTED

It was on a Tuesday three days outside of Guam that the letter came. It was almost a year, and five unanswered letters, since Howard had last heard from her. But there was the postmark—only a week ago—and there was the name on the return address: *Anchalee Selakul.*

It was a big letter too, with the spongy padded feeling of cloth inside.

"So, whatcha get?" Jim asked, reaching for the letter with one long hairy hand. He still hadn't been able to requisition a jacket that covered his wrists. "I got cookies from mom."

Howard held the letter out of the way. "None of your business, furball."

"Whoo-hoo!" Jim hooted. "It's something from a girl. You got a love letter, right?"

Howard shrugged. "Heck if I know. And I won't get a chance to find out unless you quit grabbing."

"Uh, c'mon Howie," Andre said, sitting down next to him. "Share your letter and ape boy'll share his cookies."

"Hey, those are my cookies!" Jim grabbed possessively for the tin before Andre could hand them around, dragging it back across the galley table and leaning atop it with both arms. "Mine!"

KEVIN ANDREW MURPHY

"And this is my letter," Howard said. "Hopefully from my girlfriend."

"That cute little number you met in Thailand?" Andre asked. "How much you have to pay her?"

Howard punched him in the arm, hard. "Nothing. Just your basic fling." He grinned. "I wooed her with stories of my dad's pig farm."

Jim munched a cookie. "I thought it was your uncle who had the pig farm."

"Yeah, but I still worked there in the summer. Same difference." He grimaced. "My dad did cows."

Jim snarfed on his cookie. "And you admit it?"

"Where Howie here gets that thick skull." Andre chuckled.

Howard ignored them and slit the letter open with his penknife, careful of the contents. Inside was a red silk scarf with a phoenix embroidered on the corner. He unwrapped it carefully, and the next moment a photograph fell out onto the table.

It was Anchalee, carefully posed in a black silk dress, holding what looked to be a four- or five-month-old baby.

Andre was the first to speak. "Well, I think we know why she didn't write you."

Howard paused. "Why…?"

Jim reached out from across the table and turned the picture towards himself, looked at it, then said, "Well, one of two guesses, and I don't think the first is too likely: Either she ran off and got married to some other guy, and she wanted to show you a picture of her new kid, or else face it, Howie—you're a father."

Howard unfolded the letter, and started to feel seasick as he read down, scanning for the fateful words, which he finally located:

I name son 'Howard,' after you. He very good and happy baby, except when he bad, which sometime. Please to come soon. He need his father.

The rest of the letter was more of the same. *Please to come soon.*

Howard leaned heavily against the table, stunned.

"So what is it?" Andre asked. "C'mon, Howie, you can tell us."

Jim reached out and snapped his fingers at Andre. "Earth to Watson, Andre. Buy a clue. Look at Howie's expression. Look at the letter. Then look at the picture and figure it out—Asian babies don't get light brown hair unless their dads have hair like *this*." He reached over and fingered a lock of Howard's hair until Howard swatted his monkey fingers away.

"Cut it out!" Howard pulled the photograph towards him. "It's not funny!"

Jim leaned back with a goofy grin on his face. "You see me laughing?"

A crowd was beginning to gather, and Howard heard Andre whisper, "Howie knocked a girl up!" Then a moment later the hubbub died down as Phillips, the Chief Petty Officer, pushed his way through the crowd.

"All right, men, what's the commotion about?"

Jim was the first to speak up. "Remember the bargain trip some of us guys took to Thailand last year? Well Yul Brynner here said, 'Shall we dance?' and one thing led to another, and now we've got little Tuptim."

Phillips paused, incredulous. "What the *hell* are you talking about, sailor?"

Andre translated: "Blondie here went to Thailand and knocked a girl up."

Phillips had a long pause, then at last turned to Howard. "Son, didn't I warn you about the little brown sisters?"

"Hey!" said Warren Nguyen. Everybody looked to him, and he added, "Uh, respectfully, sir. But still, 'Hey.'"

This time Jim translated: "He meant the 'vertically challenged melanin-enhanced sororital wombyn,' Nguyen."

Phillips glared at him. "Shut up, sailor. Nobody can figure out what in the hell you're talking about." He glanced around. "The rest of you, clear out. This is none of your damn business. Hanson, in my ready room in five minutes. This is serious, and you need some space."

Everyone cleared out, even Jim and Andre, and Howard just stuffed the photograph and the letter and the scarf back in the envelope. In a daze, he stumbled off to Phillip's ready room and sat down.

Good God. What in the hell was he supposed to do?

First thing was get the letter back out. He read through it fully this time, gathering all the gist of it, despite the broken English. Anchalee'd been really sick. Some accident with falling off the bridge and nearly drowning.

Howard had seen that river. It made the Mississippi look clean in comparison. God, falling into something like that.... No wonder she'd been laid up.

She'd also been crazy, she said, or at least that seemed to be what she was getting at. Probably one of those nasty tropical fevers they were always talking about.

But the point of everything was that she was fine, the kid was fine, everything was fine.

Except it wasn't. Fucking broken rubber.

That sort of thing happened. Happened to his cousin. Only difference was that his cousin was thirty and married for five years. One more kid was not so big of a deal.

One kid, period, when you're twenty-two and in the navy—now that was the big deal.

And Jim was right, him and his fucking Sherlock Holmes routine. The kid had really light hair for an Asian. And a heck of a lot more nose and cheekbones, and Howard knew *exactly* where he got that. If Howard hadn't been blond and under ninety, he could have impersonated Bob Hope. Or at least the guy's nose.

There was a *click*, and Howard looked up, seeing Chief Phillips latching the door of the cabin. "Rough day, sailor?"

Howard nodded, starting to stand up, but Phillips gestured for him to stay seated.

"At ease, Seaman. Let me see." Phillips put out his hand, and Howard handed him the letter and photograph. Phillips studied both of them for a long while, then handed them back. "Well, she got pregnant, so she can't be one of the little brown sisters. At least not one of the professional ones." He leaned back against the desk, his arms folded across his chest. "Who was she?"

Howard sighed, feeling his knees turn to water, and he was glad he was sitting. "Just a girl. We met in a bar. She was really cute. We hung out for a few days, had a great time, and then we had sex." Howard looked up, not really knowing how to say it. "And, uh, the rubber broke."

Phillips paused, digesting this. "Asian rubbers are shitty. And too small. Can't trust 'em." He looked Howard up and down. "Did you have yourself checked out?"

Howard nodded. "Yes sir."

"Well then, she can't be one of the little brown sisters. You'd definitely have caught something from one of them." He looked as if he spoke from personal experience. "Don't worry, sailor. I'm not here to pass judgment, just to make sure this ship runs properly. You have any shore leave coming up?"

"In about a month, sir."

"We'll be in to Osaka next week. Take it then. I'll give you the authorization. You can catch a flight to Thailand from there and sort things out." He looked at Howard straight on. "Listen, Seaman, there are a lot of sailors who have wives and girlfriends back home. Some of them with kids. This isn't any different." He shrugged. "Just a little more unexpected. But it's the sort of thing that happens. You can use my phone to make arrangements, and if anyone needs to, they can call me back. Just keep it short."

Howard sighed, glad he'd been spared a court martial or whatever they did with seamen who screwed up like this on shore leave. "Thank you, sir."

Chief Phillips nodded. "You can stay in here until you're ready to face your crewmates, sailor. Best of luck." He clapped Howard once on the shoulder, then left the cabin.

Howard sat and just looked at the photograph.

Singapore Airlines Flight 243 docked at Gate 10. Jim and Warren were with him. Jim as moral support, Warren as native guide.

For what it was worth. "I tell you, man, Bangkok is Party Town! Saigon sucks," Warren said, waving to the airport. "If I wanted to commune with my ancestors, I'd just show up for Thanksgiving."

Warren was a study in opposites. On one hand, he was short and flat-nosed, with classic Vietnamese features, like a good quarter of the people in the airport. On the other, he talked like a California surfer boy. Which he was, in the modern sense. It was like someone had taken the soundtrack of *Endless Summer* and swapped it into *Apocalypse Now*.

"I thought Vietnam had some good waves," Jim said.

"Good," Warren agreed, "not great. Great you go to Australia for. Now there they've got some great mackin' waves."

A woman came up to Warren and said something quick and honking, to which Warren replied, "Whatever, lady," and walked on.

"What'd she say?" Howard asked.

Warren shrugged. "Either she wanted money, or she was trying to sell us a duck."

"Party town," Jim remarked. "They cater to every taste here."

Howard clutched his head with one hand and dug his fingers into his scalp. "C'mon, guys. I'm freaking out, remember?"

"Chill it, duuude," Jim said to Warren, which sounded even stranger with Jim's Boston accent on top of it. Howard walked faster, outdistancing them both for a pace, or at least Warren. Jim's gangly legs caught up in almost no time. He didn't know why he'd brought the freak show with him, except they were his friends, and he needed someone along on the trip to keep him from going nuts.

Jesus Christ, this was just too weird. He was almost out the building when Jim grabbed his sleeve. "Howie—luggage. Remember?"

Howard nodded. He'd forget his head if it wasn't screwed on right now. He hadn't even gotten a chance to speak to Anchalee, just some woman called 'Phat Ho,' and if there ever was a cruel name for someone to accidentally get, it was that.

Of course, after everyone had their laugh, Warren had to top it. He had a cousin named 'Phuq Mi.' Honest to God. Phuq Mi. Of course it was pronounced "Fook Me," but that wasn't much better. And his older sister was named 'Bich' and his father was named 'Dung.' The pronunciations were actually 'Bik' and 'Yung,' but, as Warren said, the cruel spellings were just another reason why the Vietnamese hated the French.

"Howie" probably meant something really embarrassing in some Asian dialect, but that's what you got for being named after your uncle.

"Warren means 'wombat' in Australian," Warren put in. "I found that out when I went to Sydney."

"I thought the Australians spoke English." Jim collected his duffel from the luggage carousel.

"I made that same mistake once," said a blond woman with a terribly British accent. "Could you hand me that bag there, the green one?" She pointed and Jim did. "Ta!"

"I mean Native Australian," Warren continued unabated. "Aborigine. Except there they call it 'Abo.'"

"And when the wombat comes, he will find me gone..." Jim sang in yet another non sequitur, and Howard just grabbed his duffel and shouldered it.

He walked three steps away from the loonies. "Someone shoot me now. I'm in Hell and I forgot my boarding pass...."

"Taxis are this way." Warren headed off through the glass side doors. Howard sighed, then rounded and followed.

When they emerged from the second set of doors, the heat hit them in a wave. Howard gasped, the thickness of the air almost taking his breath away. Jim just swore: "Fuck! Who turned on the sauna?"

"Welcome to the home of my ancestors," Warren replied, "or really, welcome to the home of the next-door neighbors of my ancestors' cousins. Now you know why we left."

Cabs were pulling up at the curb, as well as little three-wheeled motorized taxis. 'Tuk tuks' Howard remembered them being called.

Before, he'd taken them because they were quaint, and because you didn't need the air conditioning in winter. Now they took one because they were cheap, and this wasn't a planned vacation by any stretch of the imagination.

"Where to?" the cab driver asked.

"The Yaowaraj." Howard fumbled with the zipper of his on-board bag, finding the piece of paper with the note. "Number 476, um, however you pronounce this…."

He showed the piece of paper to the cab driver, who whistled low between his teeth. "Ah, you going *there*. I know that place. *Very* famous. No problem."

The *tuk tuk* took off from the curb, joining the jostling madhouse of traffic Howard remembered from his last visit.

"So where is this place we're going?" Jim asked.

Howard shrugged. "Anchalee just said it was the house of her benefactress. Some kindly old lady."

The cab driver laughed. "You Americans funny…."

"Why are we so funny?" Howard asked, but the cab driver just chuckled and didn't say anything more.

Jim fished out his wallet and pulled out a twenty. "Vanna, I'd like to buy a vowel." The cab driver looked back at him, obviously understanding the "buy" part, but not the rest of it, then looked at the twenty. His eyes went wide. "Colonel Jackson wants to know what you know about the place we're going."

"Yes, Colonel Jackson," the cabbie said respectfully, taking the bill from Jim and nodding in thanks. Then he lowered his voice to a conspiratorial whisper: "The place you go—that house the house of the infamous Lady Miao. Old, yes. Kindly…well, that be nice thing to say to her face. Say it. She like that."

Jim raised his eyebrows, then wiped away the sweat he'd just knocked into his eyes. "So we're going to a cat house? That's it?"

The driver laughed. "Not so simple. You want cat house? I take you. I know many. Many good ones. Lots of pretty girls. House of Lady Miao? That something *very* different. Very old. Very respectable. *Very* mysterious. Tea girls you get anywhere. There? Murderers. Thieves. Cutthroats. Politicians—and their wives! Movie stars and 'beautiful' people. You know what I mean?" He turned and winked, jerking the cab around a motorcyclist out cruising. "You know where House of Lady Miao is, you already *know* what you want. But invitation only."

"I've got an invitation," Howard said.

The cabbie smiled. "Good. Then you live. Maybe."

"What else?" Jim asked.

The cabbie turned around, his face becoming closed and unreadable. "I say too much already. You want more, you pay more."

36   **KEVIN ANDREW MURPHY**

Howard started fishing for his own wallet, but Jim stopped him, even though he was sweating even more visibly than before. "Second question's never worth it, Howie…" he said in a low undertone, "but holy fuck! Your girlfriend's part of the Bangkok underworld."

The cabbie chuckled. "I say too much already."

Warren turned back around from his seat up next to the driver. "You got any connections?"

"Shit!" Jim swore. "Closest I've got is that my sister dated one of the Capolupos from New York. I don't think that'll cut it. What about you?"

Warren grimaced. "Me? My family cut everything when they got out of Saigon. Boat people, remember? Not much clout. Howie?"

Howard wiped the sweat from his brow. "What do you mean 'Underworld'? I'm from Brooten, Minnesota, remember? We don't do 'Underworld.'"

"That's right," Jim said, "you do cows. Silly me. I forgot."

When they finally pulled up at Number 476 Unpronounceable Street, the place looked like something from…hell, Howard didn't quite know what it looked like. Kind of like a postcard he'd once got from his aunt when she'd gone to San Francisco's Chinatown, and a little like the poster of 'The Forbidden City' that Mrs. Svenson had had on her wall back in tenth grade. But a lot more impressive than either up close and personal. Pillars. Gold leaf. And those little curlicues on all the corners of the roofs that Warren had just said were sort of intended as skateboard ramps for wind dragons, to shoot them back into the sky if they ever touched down.

"Cool," Jim said. "Dragon thrashers. What'll they think of next?"

Howard got out of the back of the *tuk tuk* and uncramped his legs. As requested in the letter, he'd put on the red silk scarf Anchalee had sent him, even though it wasn't exactly his sort of thing. Thai motorcycle cowboys were wearing them all over the city, and on them it looked cool, in a Red-Baronish sort of way. But on him, with his hair and his coloring, it either made him look like a swinger from some old Seventies porn flick, or worse yet, Fred from *Scooby-Doo*.

Jim obviously had the same thought: "Look, Fred," he said, pointing up at the mansion, "isn't this the part where the bats come out?"

For once, Howard could actually follow his train of logic. "Bite me, Shaggy."

Jim just turned to Warren. "Scooby, why don't you pay the nice man?"

"All right, Raggy," he said, playing along, then added, to Howard, "Don't sweat it, Howie. Red means 'Good Luck' all over Asia. I'm sure that's why your girlfriend sent it to you." He grinned. "Though it really does make you look like Fred. Or a Swedish porn star."

"Thanks, Warren!" Howard shouldered his bag and started up the steps, getting away from the loonies. With friends like these...

They'd gotten there just as night was falling, which was good, since Phat Ho had said everyone took siestas during the day to deal with the summer heat, and Howard didn't want to wait on the front porch or wake anyone up from their afternoon nap. Jim caught up a moment later, and after they waited another minute for Warren to finish talking with the cab driver, the *tuk tuk* took off. Once Warren had lugged his bags up the steps, they were all there, standing in front of the world's most enormous teak double doors.

Jim gestured to them. "After you, my dear Alphonse."

Sometimes the man was seriously weird, but Howard didn't sweat it. He just reached for the knocker, which was pretty much what he thought Jim meant, almost having it slip out of his hand when he lifted it. It was this huge brass thing, made in the shape of some Chinese character—probably 'Good Luck.' Everything in Asia seemed to mean 'Good Luck.' That, or 'Death' or 'Demon' (probably explaining all the need for 'Good Luck'). For all he knew, it was 'Abandon hope all ye who enter here.' Asians could cram a lot into a single character.

He then released the knocker, and instead of just the usual *thud*, there also came the loud *clang-g-g-g!!!* of a brass gong somewhere inside the house, like something from an old black-and-white movie.

A moment later the door opened, ten feet tall if it was an inch, and one of the most refined and elegant Asian women Howard had ever seen stood framed in the doorway. Her hair was perfect, her manicure the same way, and her body was encased in a sheer dress studded with thousands of pale green sequins, like a mermaid. "Ah," she exclaimed, looking at the red scarf, "you must be Howard! And these are the friends you mentioned, Jim, and would it be, Warren?"

Her accent was perfect, if halting, with just a trace of British in it, and she then said something fast in what sounded like Vietnamese. Warren responded with something slower and much more hesitant, ending with, "I'm sorry, ma'am, but my Vietnamese really sucks."

"It 'sucks' in an enchanting way," she responded, "and I'd love to help you improve it," she reached out, and with one long green nail, touched the tip of his nose, "Warren."

He blushed and she took her hand back, looking flirtatiously at Jim as she placed her hand on the edge of the doorframe in an obvious pose. "I am Phat Ho," she said, "and this is the House of Lady Miao. Welcome. Come freely. Go safely; and leave something of the happiness you bring."

"*Dracula*," Jim whispered to Warren.

She caught it and tittered. "Why yes, I am glad you recognized it. I am very much a fan of the Western cinema. But I'm not bad," she said, striking another pose, "I'm just drawn that way."

"Jessica Rabbit," Jim responded. "With a color shift."

Phat Ho tittered gaily, taking one perfectly manicured hand and putting it under Jim's chin. "Why don't you come up and see me some time?" she purred, and even Howard could place the impression as Mae West. "But please, come in," she said, relaxing the pose and returning to her regular voice, "you are honored guests, and Anchalee is most eager to see you. Or at least Howard."

She opened the door wider and they were ushered in, and the next moment a half dozen uniformed servants like at some fancy hotel or military banquet were standing at attention, assuming that the hotel or banquet hall was part of an ancient Chinese theme park. She clapped, speaking quickly in Chinese, and the next moment one of the servants was shutting the door and the others were holding out their hands for the duffels and on-board bags.

"Uh," Warren said, "we were thinking of getting a hotel some—"

"Heavens no!" Phat Ho protested. "I will not hear of it! You have accepted the hospitality of Lady Miao, and my Mistress would be most offended were she to hear that she had been refused!"

That was enough for everyone. The servants instantly had the bags, and like stage hands in a conjuring show, disappeared without a sound, or even a trace after half a minute.

Phat Ho bowed and smiled graciously. "Now, if you will allow me, I will go upstairs and see if the Mistress is indisposed. She is most eager to meet with you, but I will see if there is time for you to refresh yourselves first."

"Uh, sure," Howard said, and the next moment Phat Ho was slinking up the stairs.

Once she was out of earshot, Warren whispered, "Y'know what? I think she's a guy."

"Well duh, California boy," Jim responded. "We just ran into the fucking Asian Ru Paul."

"You think so?"

"Hell yeah! 'Phat Ho'? There's a stage name if there ever was one."

Howard looked at both of them. "What are you talking about?"

"Hello, Earth to Bullwinkle," Jim flicked Howard in the skull, "we're not in Frostbite Falls anymore. We're in Bangkok. And you'll find a god in every golden cloister, and if you're lucky then the god's a she. If you're lucky," he stressed.

"What in the hell are you talking about?" Howard asked.

Warren shrugged. "I don't know what Jimbo's bag is, but shhh! Here comes Lady Chablis."

Phat Ho slinked down the gracefully curved staircase, sequins dancing with every sway of her hips, and Howard tried not to stare. A guy? Well, she was a little taller than most Asian girls, and she dressed like a high-class hooker or someone at the Oscars, but other than that?

"Lady Miao," she announced, "wishes to see you immediately. If you will pardon the lack of time to refresh yourselves, she will pardon any fault in your appearances."

"Uh, sure," Howard said, now sure more than ever that they were being taken to see the Queen of the Bangkok underworld.

The room was upstairs, elegantly appointed, like what would happen if Martha Stewart had Imelda Marcos's budget, a Chinese theme, and absolutely no morals: silk, gold, furs, jade, silver, porcelain, and an entire impound locker full of intricately carved ivory. The room alone must have been responsible for the deaths of twenty elephants.

And sitting in the middle of this monument to the death of endangered species everywhere, on an ivory throne, wearing a white tiger-fur robe and with a living white tiger cub perched in her lap, sat a woman who had to be at the top of the hit list for Greenpeace and every other environmental organization in the free world.

"Bow..." Warren hissed, and the next moment, Howard found himself doing so. She didn't have any bars or medals, but she had more than enough stripes, and Howard quickly realized that if this were the navy, she'd rank somewhere up there with an admiral. If it moves, salute it. That seemed to be a pretty good watchword.

"Gentlemen," purred the woman on the throne in perfect British-accented English, "you honor me. Please, rise, and introduce yourselves."

"James Buford, Seaman Second Class, ma'am. United States Navy." Jim actually saluted, whether out of reflex or what, Howard wasn't sure.

"Warren Nguyen, Seaman First Class, ma'am," Warren said, following but forgoing the salute for another bow.

"Howard Hanson," Howard said, "Seaman First Class. U.S. Navy. Ma'am." He also bowed.

"So formal," she purred. "So very military. That speaks well for the West, even for those," her eyes lingered on Warren, "not truly of it."

Phat Ho coughed for attention. "His Vietnamese is atrocious, Mistress. But I have offered to tutor him."

Lady Miao stroked the tiger cub, which watched Howard with intense blue eyes. "And his Chinese?"

"Nonexistent, ma'am," Warren put in. "Begging your pardon."

Lady Miao looked at him. "Pardon granted, for the moment," she stroked the tiger cub, "but do you need my pardon, or that of your ancestors? You are Vietnamese by your face and name, but in the traces about your eyes and chin, I also see Chinese ancestry. How can you honor your ancestors properly if you do not speak their language?"

Warren didn't mention showing up for Thanksgiving or sending cards at appropriate holidays, which was probably all for the best. "Dunno, ma'am."

"Look at me when you speak to me," Lady Miao said in a deceptively soft whisper.

Warren stood at attention. "I don't know, ma'am."

"I do," Lady Miao said, eyes blazing. She stroked the tiger cub. "You must study and perfect your Chinese, as well as your Vietnamese. Otherwise, your ancestors will be angry. Very angry. And trust me, but you do not wish to deal with the vengeful dead!"

Anyone else would have sounded loopy as a fruit bat making that speech, but Lady Miao looked so serious as she said it that Howard gathered that she somehow knew whereof she spoke. She certainly seemed to have made an impression on Warren, who seemed about ready to piss his pants. "Yes, ma'am!"

The lady with the tiger cub looked over the three of them, then finally sighed. "This audience is at an end. Phat Ho, take these two," she gestured to Jim and Warren, "to their chambers and allow them to refresh themselves. You," she said to Howard, "may proceed through those doors. Anchalee and 'Little Howie' await you in the room at the end of the hall. Do not deviate from the path. My young pupil is most anxious to be reunited with her child's father, and I would not wish 'Little Howie's' father to become…lost…in any of the many rooms of my palace."

And that was it. Howard knew exactly what it was like to be dismissed, and after he remembered to bow instead of salute, he got his ass right through the gilded double doors and shut them behind him.

There was a long hall in front of him, with doors to either side and little curio tables with vases and priceless whatnot, but—thankfully!—there was only one set of double doors at the end of the hallway, so there wasn't any confusion.

Howard practically sprinted to get away from Lady Miao, who probably had more bodies stashed under her throne than China had tea, since the overall impression the room gave was *I have killed twenty elephants and a tiger to provide 'decorator touches' for my reception hall. They are rare and priceless, not that I care. You are considerably less rare and priceless. Do you think I care if you live or die, except as it amuses me?*

The answer was pretty fucking obvious. Howard got as far away from her as he could, then paused at the end of the hall, sweating like a pig. *Calm down. Just calm down.* He wiped the sweat from his brow and tried to still his hands, thinking that the last thing Anchalee would want to see was her kid's dad showing up a nervous wreck. Then again, she *lived* with that crazy woman, so she probably knew exactly what it was like.

After running his fingers once through his hair, and straightening the ridiculous Red Baron scarf, he gave a hesitant knock.

A moment later, the door opened, and Anchalee was there, looking even more beautiful than he remembered her. As much from terror as anything else, he embraced her. She hugged him back, with surprising strength, and after a long moment in each other's arms, they both relaxed their grip, though didn't let go.

She cradled her head against his chest. "I miss you so much."

"I know, Anchalee. I missed you too."

After a minute more, she released him, then raised a finger to her lips. "Be very quiet," she said, "Little Howie sleeping. But come in."

Howard slipped inside, and she quietly latched the door behind him. The room was an elegant parlor, done in the same Chinese style as the rest of the place, but without the ivory and tiger fur, and with perfectly normal baby toys scattered about. Hello Kitty and Paddington Bear were cozied up in one corner of the sofa, and a Tickle-Me Elmo lay face down on the floor. And on the far side of the room was a crib with a sleeping baby.

"Anchalee," Howard whispered, "I know she's your benefactor, but that woman is seriously crazy!"

Anchalee looked about with wide eyes, as if frightened that someone might be listening, then looked back to him and whispered, "Not crazy. Very old. Very powerful. *Always* get what she want."

Howard paused. "Old? She doesn't look a day over thirty."

Anchalee's command of English seemed to fail her, but between grimaces, hands-over-ears, and throat-cutting gestures, seemed to convey the general gist. "Oh, she's had a lot of face lifts," Howard concluded. Anchalee smiled as if in agreement, but he wasn't exactly sure.

He wished that her English or his Thai were better, or that they at least had a dictionary on hand, but his was back in his on-board bag. "Baby?" he finally asked.

Anchalee nodded, leading him over to the crib with exaggerated tiptoeing gestures and lots of finger-to-lips. Howard followed, getting a good look at 'Little Howie.'

He was a cute baby. Not that much like him, but then not that much like Anchalee either. Pretty much the sort of kid you got when you had two people of very different races get together, somewhere between the two of them. Little Howie's hair was straight, which was about the one feature they both had in common, but pale brown, not black like Anchalee's or blond-white like Howard's own. But Howie Jr. did have a little bit of his chin.

Then the baby rolled over and opened his eyes, and the next moment he sprouted horns. Big black devil horns, and a screaming fanged mouth. Then a long lizardlike tail shot out, whipping his Mickey-Mouse diapers across the crib as he bounced in the air, flying like a lemur to hang from the curtain rod and scream.

Howard stood aghast, staring and staring, then finally looked to Anchalee, desperate for any sort of explanation, anything to make the world even a halfway rational place again.

Anchalee grinned helplessly, her English obviously failing her, then at last licked her lips and said, "Demon baby?"

The world then went very black as Howard passed out.

THE FOURTH PETAL

"THE TALE OF THE GREEN DRAGON"
A STORY OF INFATUATION

Phat Ho decided she was in love. The skinny sailor, the one with the permanent five o'clock shadow and the arms like an ape, had recognized every impression she'd done, even Joan Crawford and Rita Hayworth. And she realized that she had finally found another devotee of the cinema whose passion matched her own.

It was love. It had to be.

"*I feel pretty, oh so pretty,*" she sang, dancing about her boudoir and throwing open the doors of her wardrobe.

She would wear her largest breasts in his honor.

"*Pretty, and witty, and gay....*" She turned to her serving maid and pointed to the pair of huge shimmering silicon mounds that each took a shelf of its own. "It is a special occasion tonight, Jin-jin. Tokyo will tremble! Prepare Godzilla and Rodann!"

The girl bowed humbly, first assisting Phat Ho by unzipping her gown, allowing it to puddle to the floor around her ankles. Ho stepped out of it, and Jin-jin gathered the dress up, laying it over the back of a chair for the moment.

Phat Ho then ran her fingernails under each of her current breasts and invoked the flesh *shintai*, allowing the skin to part and the more modest pair of silicon globes she'd named 'Charlie' and 'Edgar' to slide out. She handed them to Jin-jin, who had a basin ready for them and the slime of blood. Then the girl went and set them aside, retrieving the larger set, first Godzilla, then Rodann. Ho wore Godzilla on the left, over her heart.

She lifted them up and the skin stretched over both monster tits, sealing to anchor them in place. Phat Ho fondled them with delight, smearing blood across her nipples, then realized the terrible mess she was making. "Jin-jin, be so kind as to finish with my toilette. I'll attend to my hair and make-up myself."

"Which dress, Mistress Ho?"

She thought a moment. "Oh, the emerald silk with the spangles. The low-cut one."

"Yes, Mistress Ho." Jin-jin bowed obsequiously, and with that, Phat Ho reached up, rubbed the back of her neck, then hooked in her nails as she slit her throat.

Flesh separated from flesh, and *Hun* from *P'o*, as she let her higher self take her head and entrails and float free while her baser nature stood there in her body, fondling those parts that suited its interests.

The dragon's breath of *chi* energy buoyed her up as she floated over to her dressing table, thinking even purer and more enlightened thoughts about what a perfect soul mate the skinny sailor might be. "*See that pretty girl in that mirror there?*" she sang, then reached out with one intestine to select a lipstick. Plum, she thought, would work well. Plum to match the color of her heart.

She checked the shade, and finding it a perfect match, applied it to her lips. "*Who hoo ha a-a-i ir e?*" It was hard to sing while putting on lipstick, but Phat Ho tried anyway, and her heart danced with glee, bobbing up and down amid the jellyfish streamers of her entrails.

"Such a pretty girl! Such a pretty face! Is that me?"

Phat Ho pirouetted in the air, at least with her head, then unwound her intestines as she selected a make-up brush. Intestines, she considered, were almost as bad as telephone cords. They were always getting knotted when you least expected it, even if you didn't do much with them.

She applied touch-up blush and green eyeshadow, then thought about something to do with her hair. A French braid? A chinois? Perhaps a radiant *Charlie's Angels* style? She tried all of them, allowing her hair to arrange itself. It was easiest to fly with the 'Angel,' but that didn't mean it would look the best.

"What do you think, Jin-jin?"

The girl glanced up from where she was dressing the body, having it pose while she adjusted the hem of the dress to deal with the new 'Oh no! There goes Tokyo!' bustline. She took the pins out of her mouth. "The chinois, Mistress Ho. The Great Lady is always pleased by that."

The Great Lady, Phat Ho considered, would also be wearing the same style, this being an occasion for a state banquet. Which meant, formal as it might be, wearing the same hairdo as the Mistress would *not* be appropriate.

The 'Angel' then. Phat Ho pulled open the top drawer and got out a large drycleaning bag which she used to swathe her entrails. Hairspray could sting, much as it might be necessary to hold up a Seventies hairstyle without elaborate *chi shintai*. She took the Aquanet and began spritzing her hair from every conceivable angle, floating her eyeballs out of their sockets both to keep them safe and so as to gain a better vantage point—mirrors just didn't work anywhere near as well.

A knock sounded on the door while she was thus engaged. "Come in!" Phat Ho cried, and a moment later old Tsing Mao entered, bowing low. "Thousand pardons, Mistress Ho, but please, you must come quickly. Mistress Anchalee is very distraught, for her barbarian gentleman has passed out."

Ho paused, hairspray still upraised. "And Little Howie is hanging from the curtain rod?"

Tsing Mao bowed again. "You are very perceptive, Mistress Ho. You have guessed the situation exactly."

Phat Ho sighed. "Tell her I'll be there in a moment. And fetch Lao Shen and maybe some opium."

"Yes, Mistress Ho."

Phat Ho gave her hair one last perfunctory spritz, set down the hairspray, popped her eyeballs back in their sockets, and turned to see that Jin-jin hadn't completed the hemline just yet. She sighed. "Jin-jin, you finish up here while I go deal with matters. I should be back in a short while. And oh yes, I'd like to be accessorized with the emeralds."

"Yes, Mistress," the serving maid said, and Phat Ho floated past her, tossing the drycleaning bag aside after using it as a condom to keep from getting doorknob germs on her intestines—you could get the damndest stomach cramps if you weren't careful.

She floated down the hall, squeezing the *Yin* poisons from her kidneys until they suffused her form, turning her white and then completely transparent. *If* Anchalee's lover somehow came to himself, then the last thing he needed to see was her head bobbing along without the rest of her. After all, it could come as a rude shock for a man to suddenly see a beautiful woman undressed. And you could hardly be more undressed than she was at the moment.

Phat Ho extended her tongue and grasped the door handle, tongues being a bit more resistant to germs than intestines, despite the drawback of the disgusting taste of brass polish. She floated invisibly into the room, checking out the basic situation. Anchalee was there, frantically trying to wake her lover up while their baby howled like a monkey and swung from the curtain rod.

First thing was first. Phat Ho used her tongue to pick up the Tickle-Me Elmo that had cost a small fortune on the black market—but worth every *baht* of it, all things considered—and constricted it around the middle as she lifted in the air, performing an apparent levitation and causing Little Howie's eyes to grow wide as he saw it. "A-ha-ha-ha! A-ha-ha-ha! That tickles!" cried the toy, like any number of the customers of the House of Lady Miao, and little Howie reached out his hands for it, absolutely enchanted.

Ho floated it closer to him, allowing him to grab it. Enraptured by the spell of American merchandising and fake fur, the child's *P'o* subsided, the tail and horn retracting, and the baby fell back into his crib to play with his favorite toy. Phat Ho happily released it—vibrating plush could be very amusing, but not in your mouth.

"Phat Ho?" Anchalee inquired, looking about upon seeing this miracle.

"I'm here," Ho replied, "or at least the rational part of me."

Anchalee was crying, hugging the unconscious barbarian. "He won't wake up."

"Men are like that, sometimes," Ho said, laughing. "Get used to it, duckling." Then on a more serious note she added, "But I expect he's had a rude shock. Best thing is to slip him a little opium to take off the edge, then let him sleep it off. Then explain it to him later while Little Howie is somewhere else. Lao Shen will be here in a moment anyway."

"I know," she said. "Tsing Mao told me."

Phat Ho smacked her lips, trying to get red fake fur out of her teeth, and knowing that at the very least she'd have to retouch her lipstick. That was the problem at times with the disembodied *penangallan* form, but at least it did allow her to be in two places at once—often a necessity in her position.

Tsing Mao arrived then, with Lao Shen in tow, a hypodermic in one hand and a bottle of rubbing alcohol in the other.

Phat Ho bobbed invisibly around them. "Can I leave this in your hands, Anchalee? I do have other things to attend to."

The girl paused, then held her lover while Lao Shen prepared the hypodermic. "Yes, Phat Ho. A thousand gratitudes."

"A-ha-ha-ha! A-ha-ha-ha! That tickles!" cried Elmo again, and Little Howie laughed.

One disaster taken care of, Phat Ho returned to her room to find another one already in progress—her lusty *P'o* had taken full control of her body, overpowered Jin-jin, and was currently disporting itself on the bed, her serving maid trapped beneath the weight of Godzilla and Rodann.

"Stop! Stop that!" Phat Ho cried. "Stop, or you'll ruin the dress!" But the lusty *P'o* continued on unheeding until Ho took the simple expedient of snaking her organs back into her body, and with her head now reattached, she let her *Hun* let her *P'o* know who was boss.

Unfortunately, the *P'o* was not wanting to listen to reason at the moment, so rather than argue, Phat Ho just let the *P'o* keep the one organ it was truly interested in and got off Jin-jin and the bed, taking a moment to smooth down her dress.

"Jin-jin," she said, "when it finally tires itself out, do me a favor and *spank* the naughty thing."

Her serving maid propped herself up on her elbows and panted, "Yes, Mistress…" before lying back down.

Phat Ho went to her dressing table to inspect the damage. Thankfully, Jin-jin had already placed hairdresser's napkins around the neckline of the gown, so she hadn't bloodied the dress when she performed the reattachment. Thoughtful Jin-jin. Phat Ho removed the napkins, then applied a little deodorant and dusting powder to take care of the worst of the sweat, retouched her lipstick, put a dab of *Murasaki* behind each ear, and attended to her jewels herself. Jin-jin was obviously tired out by her ordeal and could *hardly* be expected to be a proper lady's maid at the moment.

The needle was still hanging from the hemline, so Phat Ho also did the last few stitches herself, biting off the thread, and sitting down on the bed next to Jin-jin and finally collecting her naughty *P'o*, which in the end had tired itself out. Like all men, even demon-possessed ones. "Jin-jin, if you could get me my pale green panties and the celadon pumps?"

"Of course, Mistress Ho." Jin-jin caught her breath, then rolled out of bed and went and fetched them. Phat Ho put them on. "Thank you, my dear. You've been very kind. You may have the rest of the evening off. After you clean the room, of course."

Jin-jin tucked a stray hair back into place and bowed. "Thank you, Mistress Ho."

Phat Ho set off down the hall, fully prepared to deal with another petty emergency. She hoped James Buford would like the way she looked. She loved a man in uniform, or even out of it, and she'd always had a weakness for Western devils. Especially the hairy ones.

She did a little skip and a dance step down the hall. *"I'm in love with a wonderful boy...."*

Natalie Wood might be dead too, but she didn't stand a chance against Phat Ho.

Dinner consisted of many wonderful and lavish courses: lobster namprik, chicken satay, salted eggs and peking duck. And of course human liver, braised with onions and garlic and served with a delightful tamarind sauce.

Phat Ho enjoyed it very much. So did James Buford. He even asked for seconds. "My mom makes liver too," he said, "with bacon and apples. But it's nowhere near as good as this."

"The secret," Phat Ho said, spooning up a choice bit, "is to get it fresh. And to get the right *kind* of liver. This is the liver of suckling pig. Very choice. Very tender." Suckling long pig instead of suckling short pig, but no need for them to know that. At least not yet. "You probably do not study the Tao, but if you do, you know that the liver has many wonderful properties. It is the organ of Wood, though it is ruled by the Earth. As such, it helps to balance the Blood and the Spirit, the *Yin* and *Yang* energies. Very healthful."

"That dish takes a lot of pigs," said Warren Nguyen, sitting at the right hand of Lady Miao at the small banquet table she reserved for intimate occasions. "What do you do with the rest?"

"That," said Phat Ho, "is a question for the next course." She clapped her hands and the servants came forward with a gilded platter, placing it on the table, and on her signal, removing the delicately cloisonnéed cover. "Baby back ribs!"

The guests were suitably impressed, and Lady Miao laughed delightedly at their reaction. "I am so glad you are pleased," she said, placing one hand on Warren Nguyen's. "We have Westerners over for dinner every so often, but we seldom see them enjoying themselves like this."

"Ma'am, if this is what you serve every night, then I'm heartily surprised." Jim Buford gestured to the servants to keep piling the ribs onto his plate. "This absolutely amazing."

"You know," Phat Ho said, "if you were to step into our kitchens, I think that would be *exactly* your reaction." Mixed with shock and horror, of course, but that went without saying. "Our chefs are specially trained by Lady Miao herself. Before they come here, very few are even remotely familiar with the techniques she has perfected over many years of study."

The skinny sailor looked up from nibbling a baby rib. "Julia Childs, eat your heart out."

Lady Miao laughed, "What an engaging thought!" then turned to the white tiger cub she had sitting beside her on the table, on the opposite side from Nguyen, with its own personal plate of ribs.

Phat Ho was pleased that the evening's entertainment was proceeding so splendidly. Lady Miao was absolutely enchanted with the idea of Western devils at the all-you-can-eat cannibalism buffet, and it was allowing the Mistress and her to dine on humans, and with them, at the same time. Sort of a 'Have your cake and eat it too' situation.

Besides which there was the added bonus of being able to flirt with James Buford, or Jim, as he preferred to be called. "Would you like some longbeans, Mr. Buford?" Phat Ho held up the dish very near her plunging neckline and newly enhanced breasts, almost threatening to pour it down her cleavage, and she knew Jim was trying not to stare.

"Uh yes, please," he said. "And please, call me Jim."

"Of course, Jim." Phat Ho passed him the dish of perfectly innocent Chinese longbeans—there were reasons why truly devout Buddhists were vegetarians—after taking a bit herself.

"So, Mr. Buford," Lady Miao said, serving her tiger cub a few more tidbits of human liver in tamarind sauce, "how do you like Bangkok?"

"Um, it's very nice. I haven't seen much of it yet. Howie said he'd show us around, after…" he glanced around. "Just where is he, anyway?"

Lady Miao smiled. "I thought it best if he and Anchalee spent some time alone together, without anyone prying into their affairs."

The tension in the air raised a notch, and Jim turned back to nibbling his ribs. "Bangkok is really, uh, beautiful. And very interesting too. Great architecture. Warren told me all about the thrashing dragons."

Phat Ho paused at the mention of her *dharmic* path, and Lady Miao actually dropped her chopsticks. There was a deadly silence broken only by the sound of the tiger cub chewing bones, in the end shattered by Lady Miao: "And just *what* did Warren tell you about the Thrashing Dragons?" Her head swiveled by degrees as she said this until she was at last looking straight at the Vietnamese boy.

He suddenly realized he was on the hot seat, and set his baby back ribs back on his plate. "Uhh…" he said, "uhhh…I didn't say anything about any 'Thrashing Dragons.'" He paused, looking around. "Maybe it was 'Smashing Pumpkins'?"

"*No*," said Lady Miao, "I distinctly heard the words 'Thrashing Dragons.' *What* do you know about the Thrashing Dragons?"

Warren turned very pale and at a complete loss for words, until Jim said, "Go ahead. Tell her, Nguyen. The dragons? The skateboard ramps? You know what I'm talking about."

"No," Warren said in almost a whisper, "I don't. What *are* you talking about, man?"

The attention was focused back to Jim, who looked around, apprehensive, then said, "Uh, I don't know if it's bad *joss* to talk about this or anything, so stop me if I'm saying anything I'm not supposed to, but the rain gutters? The curly flips at the corners of the buildings? Well, Warren said they were like skateboard ramps or ski jumps for wind dragons, so they fly back up in the air if they ever touch down."

Lady Miao nodded. "That is very true. What most Westerners believe to be a mere architectural fancy is in fact an ancient *feng shui* device which allows us to channel harmful energies back into the air, where they are harmlessly dissipated." She blinked her tiger-gold eyes. "That explains the 'Dragons.' But what about this 'Thrashing' you mentioned?"

"Uh," Jim said, biting his lip, "skateboarders…snowboarders…they're called 'thrashers.' They thrash on the slopes. It's what they do. So if, uh, dragons went snowboarding off of ski jumps on the corners of buildings, they'd, uh, be 'thrashing dragons.' Natch."

Lady Miao raised her eyebrows and allowed the tiger cub to lick the long-pork grease from her fingers. "What a…unique…interpretation. I don't believe I have ever heard of such a thing."

"Um," Jim said, still glancing around nervously, "I hate to ask, but did we just accidentally say the name of a gang or something?"

"Tong," Warren put in. "They're called 'tongs.'"

Lady Miao turned her hand so the cub could lick the back of her silver-framed manicure. "I don't believe that it is any of your business, Mr. Buford. We shall speak no more of the subject, for I would be *most* displeased were I to hear of it again. Yet let me ask you another question: Does the phrase, 'A Thousand Whispers' mean anything to you perhaps?"

"Uh…is that some Goth band?"

Lady Miao did not answer, but Warren then said, "Jim, you're thinking of '10,000 Maniacs.'"

Lady Miao paused and looked back to Warren. "The '10,000 Maniacs'? What is this '10,000 Maniacs'?"

"A band?" the Vietnamese boy answered.

"Um, well," Jim said, taking the heat off his friend, "it's not really a *Goth* band. Just a regular sort of band. Modern rock. They broke up a couple of years ago anyway, and Natalie Merchant went off to do her own thing."

"Merely a group of Western musicians, Lady Miao," Phat Ho said, picking up the nearest bit of liver with her chopsticks, "nothing to do with…anything you might consider important." Such as, for example, the *Wan Xian* and the *Wan Kuei*, the Ten Thousand Immortals and the Ten Thousand Demons. Sometimes the Mistress's ignorance of pop culture could be very distressing. Not to mention amusing.

"*I* will be the judge of what interests me, Phat Ho," Lady Miao corrected her. "See if you can arrange for this 'Natalie Merchant' to play a concert in Thailand."

Phat Ho nodded. "I will contact her booking agent."

"Very good," said Lady Miao, then turned back to Jim. "You are an intriguing man, Mr. Buford. Your chance turns of phrase seem to have a habit of touching on…subjects better left unspoken. So, tell me, *what else* have you heard of Bangkok?"

After a long and uncomfortable silence, Jim looked around. "Isn't the *Jeopardy* theme song supposed to start playing now?"

"What?" asked Lady Miao. In answer, Phat Ho began to hum it.

"Bangkok for ten thousand." Jim took a deep breath and bit his lip. "What is 'cat houses'?"

In that moment, Phat Ho decided she truly loved him. "You've just won the Daily Double."

Lady Miao and her kitten both blinked, not that there was any significant difference between the two. "Yes," Lady Miao agreed, and Phat Ho put her hand on Jim's knee as her Mistress dissembled, pretending that she understood what she was agreeing with and looking disconcerted as she did, "you have won this 'Daily Double.'" She smiled, and Phat Ho could see that Jim could also tell that the Great Mistress was doing her best to save face and cover for her ignorance. "Would it surprise you, Mr. Buford, to find that this is a 'cat house'?"

He looked to the tiger cub. "Well, it's a house, and you've got a cat…."

Lady Miao smiled and shook her head. "I'm afraid not, Mr. Buford. A clever dodge, and a diplomatic answer, but try again. Would it surprise you if this house were a cat house?"

He sat there sweating, in need of a hint as to the proper answer, so Phat Ho gave him one, sliding her hand up his leg and reaching out one finger.

"Noooo…" he said slowly, "I don't think it would surprise me at all…."

This, of course, was another part of the evening's entertainments—seeing whether the Western boy could keep his composure about what was being done to him under the table, and if he could, seeing how long it took Lady Miao to figure out what was going on and tell them to stop.

"And how do you like your girls, Mr. Buford?" Lady Miao asked. "Old? Young? And if so, how young?"

"Uhh…" Jim said slowly. "I'm not into little kids."

"Really?" asked Lady Miao, picking up a baby rib and taking a delicate bite. "I think you might be surprised how young a girl you might actually enjoy. Tender young flesh might be very much to your taste and you might never realize it." She took another bite.

"I-I-I-I," Jim stuttered, "I really don't think so."

"Truly?" Lady Miao asked, amused. "How young of a girl have you ever had?"

"Uh-h-h-h-h…" he said, then quickly, "Fifteen."

"And how old were you at the time?"

Just as fast: "Sixteen."

"And you are how old now?"

Sweat was visibly starting on his face now, and he quickly blurted out, "*Twenty.*"

"So forceful," she said. "So tense. I would not have thought the subject would make you so uncomfortable. Would you, at your age now, have sex with a fifteen-year-old? Why or why not? Would you then consider a fourteen-year-old? Thirteen? Twelve?" She paused. "You seem very distressed, Mr. Buford. Would you like me to stop?"

"Y-y-y-y-e-s-s-s..."

Lady Miao watched the veins stick out on his thin, hairy face, obviously puzzled as to why this might be. "Then I will stop."

Phat Ho gave him one last touch. "*Oh thank God...*" he breathed fervently and just about collapsed on the table. Phat Ho took her nails back and quietly licked at the delicate *Yang* energy until Lady Miao noticed.

Lady Miao blinked, and then very obviously held back a laugh. Phat Ho scored a point for herself.

The evening's entertainments were going *very* well.

After dinner, they played Mah Jongg with the set Phat Ho had made from the unfortunate Mr. Moretto. Jim was quite good at it. Warren was passable. Lady Miao, of course, won.

She also read the omens in the bones, but as usual, didn't reveal what she found. Phat Ho was interested in only one question, and, with an eye on Jim, selected a tile.

It was the Green Dragon. The Chinese character *Fa*, 'Commence,' with the very obvious interpretation of *Go for it, girl!*

As Lady Miao said many times, "We do not question the bones of the oracle." Especially, Phat Ho added to herself, when they tell you what you want to hear.

All that was necessary, then, was setting the stage. He was primed. He was ready. All it would take would be the proper entrance and the right presentation.

Lady Miao gave a delicate signal that she fancied the Vietnamese lad. Phat Ho acknowledged this, and correspondingly placed him in the Silver Tiger suite, Lady Miao's chamber for her special playthings. Phat Ho signaled back that she fancied the hairy sailor, and while Lady Miao didn't even acknowledge this, it was a safe bet that she already knew of Phat Ho's choice.

She took Jim to the Chamber of the Green Dragon, her personal totem and sponsor. "Leave your door unlocked..." she whispered in his ear and nibbled the lobe once. Then she swayed off down the corridor, staggering a bit with the weight of Godzilla and Rodann, and blew him a kiss over her shoulder. He had a goofy grin on his face, and that boded very well for the evening indeed.

Phat Ho went back to her room and shut the door. It was a pity, all things considered, that she'd given Jin-jin the night off. But, ah well, it wasn't as if she needed terribly much, and before her murder, she'd done very well by herself.

But preparing for an evening was always important. She detached her head and sent her body to go shower first, since perfume and deodorant would only do so much, and she didn't want to bed Jim while smelling like a man who'd just had sex. Naughty *P'o*. Naughty, naughty *P'o*. But while the *P'o* was off washing itself, she floated about and checked through her wardrobe, selecting a jade-green peignoir and a matching pendant. Really a jade statuette, but with Godzilla and Rodann to contend with, anything less than a paperweight would get lost. Besides which, it was in the shape of a dragon, and simply bristling with sexy *Yang chi*, just in case he was up for another go-round.

Her body emerged from the shower and had sprouted demonic faces all over it, all of them singing lewd flower drum songs in various Chinese dialects. Phat Ho sighed. Naughty *P'o*. But demons would be demons, and those extra mouths *did* have their delightful uses once she got a lover accustomed to them. She waltzed a few paces with her body, letting it take the lead for the moment. After all, it *did* have the male equipment. Then she took possession of her lower half, except the unnecessary equipment, which she detached and put in the laundry hamper along with her dress, pressing the edges of flesh in to form the appropriate opening. The *P'o* spirit, however, she kept with her, since she would have need of her darker passions if she wished to enjoy herself.

Phat Ho sponged off her neck, put on a few more drops of perfume—*Zen* this time—then floated off down the hall to her midnight assignation.

And it was wonderful, as she knew it would be.

THE FIFTH PETAL

"THE TALE OF THE YELLOW EMPEROR"
A STORY OF BALANCE

Anchalee lay oranges and slices of jack fruit in the offering bowl, lighting sticks of costly civet incense, which, before being burnt, had the unfortunate faint scent of cat piss, yet produced only sweet smoke once lit.

Cat piss incense, Anchalee thought, wiping her fingers on her dress. Was this the best she could offer the gods?

The jade Buddha only smiled benevolently.

"Oh merciful Buddha," Anchalee prayed. "I am a demon, unclean and unworthy, but I pray not for myself, but for my child. He is also touched by the Yama Kings, but when I see his sweet face, I know he is also touched by Heaven, and for the sake of Heaven I pray you to help him, and to help his father, who is a good man, even if a mere barbarian. He is a sailor, and the son of an honest farmer, and for these ancient trades and my ancestors who worked them, I pray you to look with favor upon him and aid him so that he may show our son the path of virtue and righteousness, morality and benevolence, which I am too unclean to lead him upon. This I pray you." She touched the foot of the Buddha and wept, then went to the next shrine and gave the same prayer and offerings to Kwan Yin, Goddess of Mercy.

As she finished her prayer and offerings, the fine rose quartz image began to shine with an inner light, and Anchalee saw tears begin to form in the corners of the goddess's eyes. "Oh mercy! Mercy!" Anchalee cried as tears of light rolled down, one by one, to land in the offering bowl, touching the white lotus which floated there and causing the blossom to shine with its own radiance.

An almost indescribable scent rose up, like fields upon fields of lotus blossoms, mixed with roses and jasmine on a summer day, yet even more perfect, and Anchalee knew the scent to be the breath of Heaven.

My child, the voice of the Goddess spoke in her head, *you are unclean, and the Judges of the Dead have already pronounced sentence on you. But I grant you this one small mercy, for the sake of your child and the sake of your tears. Take but one petal of my lotus—one petal, no more—and take this to your child's father and place it upon his tongue. If you do this, the madness of the Yomi World will be cleansed from his mind and he will be able to look upon his child without horror, but with benevolence and rectitude, as befits a proper father. This is my mercy to you, and my gift to him, for the sake of your child.*

The light faded, but the scent remained. The scent of peace and of Heaven.

Hesitantly, gingerly, Anchalee plucked the least of the lotus's many petals, and saw the holy radiance die at her unclean touch. All except a glimmer in the one petal she had plucked. Clutching it to her breast, rushing for fear that the mere fact of her existence would snuff out the goddess's blessing before she had chance to act upon it, Anchalee ran from the room, back to the chamber where Tsing Mao and Lao Shen had placed Howard's unconscious form.

He still wore the red scarf she had sent him. Carefully, Anchalee pried open his lips and placed the lotus petal, already withering at her touch, between them.

His movements were hesitant at first, slow, but then he tasted the Lotus of Paradise, and Anchalee saw him smile, a smile of beatific radiance and peace.

"Wake up…. Oh please, wake up…." She touched his shoulder, shaking him gently, and he roused as if from a pleasant dream.

A light played in his eyes and a smile upon his lips. "Anchalee?" He sat up, rubbing his head and luxuriating at being awake. He smacked, licked his lips and swallowed. "Mmm, I just had the craziest dream…. Nice at the end though." He smacked his lips again. "What did I just eat?"

"A taste of mercy, and of Heaven." Anchalee paused, reexamining what she had just heard. "Since when did you speak Thai?"

He chuckled, rubbing the back of his neck and stretching. "What are you talking about, Anchalee?" He blinked. "Boy, your English sure got good quick. But I still don't understand what you're saying." He looked around the room then and laughed, the laugh of a man who was very drunk or very stoned. The laugh of a man who had eaten of the Lotus of Good Fortune. "I'm still dreaming, aren't I?"

She shook her head. "No. Would that you were. Then, all of this would be a nightmare and we could wake from it."

"Yeah, right." He smiled and shook his head, a drunken man choosing to play along with the sober. "So what happened?"

She sighed, realizing that this was a burden she must bear alone for the moment, and Heaven's mercies, though great, were not everything that an unworthy demon might wish for. "There is so much to explain. You understand me now because Kwan Yin, the Goddess of Mercy, granted you her benevolence. And I am here, in my unclean state, because I died, yet did not submit to the Great Wheel of Transmigrations. My desires for the world were too great—to see my baby born, to live my dream of a life with you in a wondrous, foreign land, to have oh so many good things which I then thought I deserved, but now know I am unworthy of—and the Judges of the Dead punished me for my impatience and unworthy desires by sending me back as one of the Hungry Dead."

Howie chuckled. "So you're saying that you refused to wait in line, so they kicked you out?"

She paused. "Well, yes, that would be one way of putting it."

"And Little Howie?"

She sighed. "He is tainted by my unclean state. He is what is called a 'dhampyr,' not fully mortal, but not immortal either. He has been punished for my sins."

"Well, I've heard that one before." Howie grimaced, sardonic even in his drunken state. "Nice to see we're not the only ones on the block with that concept."

Hesitantly, Anchalee placed her hand atop Howie's. He did not flinch back. "You are taking this very well."

He shrugged, beatific. "Eh, *que sera, sera*. Best way I can take it. There's not anything I can do to change it, is there?"

She shook her head. "No, I do not think so. It is simply my karma, and yours."

"Well then," he said, "answer's simple. Just good old-fashioned Midwestern stoicism. Take your frostbite and don't complain. That's what my ancestors did, and a million Swedes can't be wrong."

"Swedes?" Anchalee echoed. "It sounds very Confucianist, this suffering in silence."

Howie shrugged again. "I don't think Confucius was Swedish, but if that's the sort of thing he said, then he would have fit right in." He sighed. "Rubbers break. You deal with the consequences, and it doesn't do you any good to bitch about it, so why bother?" He looked at her, the fog of euphoria not quite lifted from his eyes. "But I wish you'd told me more of this going in. It's been…a bit of a shock."

She looked back. "Is that more of this 'Midwestern stoicism'?"

He shook his head. "No, that's called understatement. But we Midwesterners do it a lot too."

She sighed. "So what do you plan to do?"

He grimaced. "Well…for one thing, I've got to take you and Howie Junior to meet the folks. My mom will shoot me if she doesn't get to see her grandkid. I already told her, and she won't care if he's half demon." He grinned. "Well, she will, but it won't make any difference. She still won't stand for any nonsense."

"Midwestern stoicism?"

He smiled, still under the beatific thrall of the lotus. "You got it."

Lady Miao sat in her audience chamber, listening to the barbarian's proposal. She sighed and stroked her tiger cub.

"So you propose," she said at last, "to take a member of my court back to Brooten, Minnesota?"

"Yes, ma'am."

She raised her eyebrows. "You intend to marry Anchalee?"

"It doesn't appear I have any choice."

She paused. "No," she said, "you do not. Not if you wish to live. But I'm curious as to how you reached this conclusion on your own."

He licked his lips, and Lady Miao braced herself for the torrent of perfectly accented ancient Chinese syllables that were set to course through the lips of the barbarian's pasty, long-nosed face. This, she was certain, was a torment designed specifically for her, since Kwan Yin, Goddess of Mercy though she might be, also had a vengeful aspect, and could design tortures even more exquisite than the Yama Kings when the mood struck her.

Such as now. "Well," the barbarian said, not only in perfect Chinese but with the accent of Lao Tzu, Lao Tzu when he'd had too much plum wine and he laughed and spoke his mind, "if I don't marry her, my mother will kill me."

"Truly?" Lady Miao asked. "Do barbarians so casually murder members of their own families?"

"Well no," he said, "it's just that I'd just wish she'd kill me. If I went back without Anchalee, and without marrying her, she'd never speak to me again, and she'd make my life a living hell."

"Ah," said Lady Miao, "it appears that even barbarians can have proper mothers. If *my* son were to do such a thing, that is *exactly* what I'd do to him as well." Lady Miao considered exactly *which* living hell might be appropriate—the Hell of Being Boiled Alive, or just the Hell of Being Salted and Flayed? But it didn't matter at the moment. "And since you have acknowledged 'Little Howie' as your son, you are now a member of *my* family as well. We *Kuei-jin* have customs, and one of those is adoption into corpse families. Anchalee is now my daughter, and as such, her child is my grandson. And blood is blood, even inauspicious barbarian blood, and as you have honorably taken your place as the child's father, you are protected. Even more so since you will soon take your rightful place as my daughter's bride. You are, much as I might wish it otherwise, family, and so I cannot kill you without bringing the wrath of Heaven down upon my head." She paused. "Not that I haven't felt Heaven's wrath before."

"I understand, ma'am."

"No," she said, "but you will." She flipped out her ivory fan and dandled the blades in front of the tiger cub. It pawed at them. "However, you are also a military man. You are familiar with the concept of an indenture?"

He nodded. "Yes, ma'am."

"Well then," she said, toying with the kitten, "know you this: Anchalee is my apprentice, and is indentured to *my* court. She will not leave this house until I feel she is ready, and I do not care what your mother feels on this matter, any more than your commanding officer might care for her opinion."

"Yes ma'am. I understand, ma'am."

"In this, I think you do. Anchalee will not be released from my service until I am certain that she will not be a discredit to me or my court. Of course," she added, "if your mother wishes to visit her here, I would be *most* interested in meeting her. She sounds like a woman of strong opinions."

"She is, ma'am."

"I can appreciate that." Lady Miao smiled then, showing all her teeth. "I see you are still quite nervous, Mr. Hanson. And this, I can only assume, is for your friends, for *you* are quite safe here, so long as Anchalee and her child remain to keep up the links of blood between us." Lady Miao picked up the tiger cub, and then, yawning wide, swallowed it whole, subsuming the kitten back into herself.

She licked her lips. "As for your friends, they are the friends of family. Ill-favored, distant family, but family all the same. So long as they mind their manners, they are welcome in my house. And if they do not, well, unpleasant things can happen. But we are all responsible for the actions of our friends. Aren't we, Mr. Hanson?"

Howard woke up alone, which was just fine, because that was the way he'd gone to sleep. The sun was already up, squeezing a row of bright knives through the string holes in the venetian blinds. He just about screamed as it all came back to him.

He'd been hallucinating. That was it. He'd caught one of those weird Asian flus. Or he'd eaten the wrong thing on the plane and gotten Pol Pot's revenge, or whatever it was called.

The image of a baby with his chin, horns, and a prehensile tail suddenly surfaced in his mind. And then Anchalee telling him she was his undead demon bride. And Lady Miao, who'd been scary enough as the Queen of the Bangkok Underworld without being revealed to actually *be* the Queen of the Bangkok Underworld in a completely different sense of the word.

She'd eaten a tiger cub.

And Midwestern stoicism could only take so much. Short of lutefisk, he was going to need some coffee to fortify himself, and damn strong coffee at that.

He got up, pulling on the red silk robe that had been left out for him, and peeked out the door.

"Good morning, sir," said an old Chinese servant in perfect American English. "I trust you slept well?"

"Uh, no," Howard said, "but that was to be expected. Thanks for asking." He also remembered something about suddenly being able to speak Chinese, something about a gift from the Goddess of Mercy.

He grimaced. That was right—Anchalee had said, "Goddess of Mercy," not "Goddess of Solving All Your Problems and Having Everything Turn Out Perfect and Wonderful." He should be thankful for small mercies and leave it at that. Midwestern stoicism—after all, the frostbite *could* be worse.

Howard took a deep breath. "I'd like to see my kid."

The old servant bowed. "I'm afraid that—"

"Listen," he cut in, "I know about the horns and the tail and everything. Can I see him?"

The old servant paused and bowed again. "Right this way, sir."

Howard followed down the hall and into the nursery, or really the elegant sitting room that had been commandeered as a nursery. Two women, almost in tears, were trying to get the baby down off the chandelier. Somehow, the sight was no longer terrifying—just what you'd expect from any other normal six-month-old who happened to have horns and a prehensile tail.

The baby screamed upon seeing him, and Howard screamed back. "Knock it off!"

The baby paused, its yellow eyes growing wide as it seemed to understand him, which to Howard was a real first with babies. Then he remembered Kwan Yin's gift and licked his lips, remembering what *his* mother used to say. "You get down from there right now, young man! And be glad your grandmother's not here, because if she were, she'd smack your bottom so hard you'd learn what crying's all about!"

Howie Junior looked very frightened all of a sudden, probably hearing it in Rosemary's babytalk or something, and jumped down off the chandelier onto the settee, curling his tail around his feet.

Howard was shocked that it was actually working, but then if Asia had demon babies, there was no reason why the Goddess of Mercy couldn't also be the Goddess of Smacking Your Bottom So Hard Your Grandchildren Will Remember It. "Now be good!" he said. "And stop crying! There's nothing to cry about. You've still got all your fingers and toes, and, uh, a tail too."

"Waugh!!!" the demon baby wailed. "Waaugh!!! Want Elmo!"

The kid was talking really well for six months, but Howard realized that understanding baby talk might also be part of the gig too. "You want Elmo?"

"Elmo!" Howie Junior cried. "Give!"

Howard located a Tickle-Me Elmo doll, all matted with baby slobber, and held it up. "I've got Elmo here. If I give you Elmo, will you promise to be good?"

"Promise?" the baby echoed, and Howard realized that, like a bad Japanese monster movie, his lips weren't quite synching with the words. It was definitely supernatural understanding.

"Only good boys get to play with Elmo," Howard said. "Now stop crying, and put away the horns and the tail, and you can play with Elmo."

"Howie good! Howie good!" the baby cried, and the horns and tail, not to mention the mouthful of fangs and the glowing eyes, disappeared from view, leaving a normal, brown-eyed baby.

Howard pressed Elmo's stomach to prime it and handed the toy to his son. "A-ha-ha-ha! A-ha-ha-ha! That tickles!" the muppet cried, vibrating, and Little Howie cooed in delight. No translation was needed.

Howard sighed. Midwestern stoicism. You had to take the good with the bad. Bad news? He was an unwed father at twenty-two, with a Thai demon baby. Good news? He had a power that mothers all over the world would be willing to kill for—perfect fluency in babytalk. And unlike Thai, that wasn't something you could learn.

He smiled. "Howie, I'm your daddy. Do you know what a daddy is?"

The baby looked up. "Nuh-uh."

"Well," Howard said, "let me explain it to you…."

Which he did, uttering a silent prayer of thanks to Kwan Yin. Who would of course understand exactly what he meant.

Phat Ho woke in the arms of her new lover. It was day, and he would have woken first, but she had taken more than a bit of his *Yang* essence, and men tended to sleep very heavily after you did that.

Besides which, it was time to prepare for the next night's amusements, as well as this afternoon's. She leaned over and kissed him on the cheek, then got up, padding softly over to the door and letting her feminine *Yin* energies suffuse her, turning her flesh transparent as she unstrapped her peignoir and let it drop to the floor. The dragon statuette she set on curio table—she'd emptied its *Yang* reservoirs the night before anyway—and then she opened the door of the room, and shut it again, this time hard.

Jim slept on, but a bit more troubled, rubbing his face with his furry monkey arms and eventually reaching out for where she'd been. "Ho?" he asked, then just grabbed the pillow and snuggled.

Eavesdropping had never been quite so fun before death.

About fifteen minutes later, he got up, and Phat Ho watched as he paraded before the mirror. "You stud, you," he said, flexing, scratching his crotch, then tousling the hair on his shoulders, and she had to keep from laughing. He was an even more amusing man the morning after than he was as a lover. And he was quite amusing as that too. Phat Ho had never met another man besides herself who had memorized the entire ballroom scene from *The King and I*. And while she'd done the scene before herself, it was only her head waltzing with her body, and that wasn't anywhere near the same thing.

Jim found a robe, went out and wandered down the hall, asking servants where Warren and Howard had got to. They told him, and Phat Ho followed. Like well-trained servants, they of course did not comment on the cold breeze that went by after the young gentleman.

Breakfast was set up in the winter garden, so Phat Ho stepped aside to whisper a few words in the servants' ears. They nodded, and a moment later were going about pulling all the blinds and closing all the drapes.

"Hey!" Warren said from his seat at the breakfast table. "What's with the dark all of a sudden?"

Tsing Mao bowed. "Honorable sir, it becomes *very* hot in Bangkok. We shut all blinds now to conserve air conditioning." He paused, giving a wary, conspiratorial look and holding up one finger. "Besides, Lady Miao be *very* upset if prize orchids scorch." He then flipped on an electric light and went and began tending to the orchids.

Phat Ho made a note to give Tsing Mao an extra day off next week. She could appreciate his humor.

Jim sat down with his friends, helping himself to some melon. "*Good morning, good morning…*"

"Well, you're fucking chipper," Warren said. "I see you didn't have a tiger sniff *your* butt."

"No," Jim said. "What was her name?"

Warren didn't say anything, to which Jim responded, "Let me guess: It was Lady Mee-o-oo-w-w-w!" He yodeled up the range in a perfect cat screech, at which point Warren punched him and Howard looked frightened.

"Cool it, Jim," Howard hissed. "You're playing with fire. That woman's deadly."

Actually, they were both right, though Phat Ho was pleased by the astuteness of her new lover's guess. Mistress Miao was very fond of feeding while in the form of a tiger, particularly since she enjoyed the *Yin* energies that came with terror.

"Sorry," Jim said. "Forgot myself."

Howard looked at him, pale eyebrows raising. "You got laid, didn't you?"

Warren blinked. "Man, don't tell me you did the fucking drag queen!"

Phat Ho blinked at this and listened closer. "Warren, buddy, I know about fucking, but I don't know about any drag queens."

"Phat Ho!" Warren hissed. "You said it yourself! And her tits were like three sizes bigger by the time we got to dinner!"

Jim gave his goofy grin. "And you think she had a boob job in the time between? Listen, Nguyen. I saw 'em. Up close. And they're real. Not even any scars." He took a bite of cantaloupe. "She calls 'em 'Godzilla and Rodann.'"

Warren sat back, shocked. "So what are you?"

"Me?" he asked, perky. "That's easy. I'm King Kong." He grinned. "Anyway, I already asked about the dress. She had this massive corset on, but she said that's the only way a woman as stacked as she is can get into one of those slinky numbers." He poked Warren in the arm. "So what's this about tigers sniffing your butt?"

The Vietnamese boy looked around, frightened. "The lady who runs this place is *fucking nuts*." He held out his hand like a blade and underscored the last two words. "She doesn't just have tiger cubs in this place—she's got a full-size fucking white tiger walking around the halls."

Jim looked incredulous. "And it sniffed your butt?"

"Hell yeah! After we had dinner with the Last Empress, I was just lying in bed, trying to get to sleep, when the door starts to open, and I think, shit, I didn't shut it right, and I start to get up, then suddenly this tiger—this huge fucking white tiger—slips into my room. So I just lie there, scared off my ass, and it just pads up, and walks around me, and next thing I know it's sticking its nose in my butt-crack and taking a deep whiff. And I get so scared I nearly pass out. And then it walks out, and you know, man, that's just the way the vampires are supposed to do it!"

Howard just sat there, looking pale, but Jim only scratched his head. "Huh? How'd we get from tigers to vampires? I thought I was supposed to be Mr. Non Sequitur."

"Don't you remember?" Warren asked. "'Come freely. Go safely. Leave a little of the happiness you bring'? That Dracula shit the transvestite chick did at the door?"

"Transvestite? Warren, buddy, trust me, but she's *not* a transvestite. We were *dead* wrong on that." Jim was then struck speechless for a moment, jawing and gesturing wordlessly until he finally said, "And the *Dracula* quote? So what? So she's a film nut! So am I! Hell, I did that same riff in high school at my Halloween party." He scratched his head again and gestured to nothing in particular. "And what does that have to do with tigers sniffing your butt?"

"You didn't talk to the cabbie. And you're not Asian, man. So listen to me," Warren insisted. "I went and gave the cabbie another twenty for what else he knew about this place, and he said to watch out, 'cause people say there's vampires here. And not the Hollywood type, but the Asian type my grandma told me about." Warren shuddered. "Scared the fuck out of me when I was little. There's vampires all over Asia, and they don't just suck blood. Some of them steal your liver, with long razor-edged tongues. And go flapping around through the air with their heads and no bodies." He waved his hands next to his head, like a disembodied bat, and Phat Ho made sure to remember the gesture. It would amuse Lady Miao greatly when she related the story later. "And then there's ones that just steal your breath, your *chi* energy. They can suck it out of anywhere. Your mouth, your ear, your dick. Heck, they can suck it out of a hole in your little toe. And sometimes they take the shape of animals. Mostly cats."

Jim sat there, slack-jawed, and finally physically closed his mouth. "And what was your grandma smoking, Warren? Flying heads? Liver thieves? Vampire cats that get high by whiffing farts? Hey, you know what?" he said, trying to keep from laughing, "*That's* why they fed us pork and beans last night!" He puffed himself up like Bela Lugosi. "Good eee-vening! I vant to sniff your farts!"

Warren looked sheepish. "It does sound kind of stupid when you put it that way."

"Hell yeah," Jim said. "Listen, Warren, I'm not saying that Lady Miao isn't the Far East's answer to Siegfried and Roy, and Don Corleone all rolled into one, but listen to yourself...." He turned to Howard. "C'mon, help me here,

Howie. Am I right, or am I wrong? We're in cat house with Thai mobsters, and that's dangerous enough without pretending it's *Bordello of Blood* meets *The Year of Living Dangerously*. Vampires are just crazy talk we don't need, right?"

"Uh, yeah," Howard said. "Crazy talk. Couldn't have said it better myself."

Phat Ho smiled as she realized that Anchalee's lover was in on the secret. Which would make the game all the more amusing in the long while.

Howard was in the know. Jim could be kept in the dark, at least until he no longer proved entertaining with mere vanilla sex and *The King and I*. Warren, however, could probably be driven mad with hints and whispered clues. Lady Miao would delight in having tigers chase him about the house, and would have no trouble feeding from him all the while.

Phat Ho smiled to herself, very well pleased. They would have amusements and diversions for at least a week!

And if she could locate a certain cab driver, she knew exactly what the chef might prepare for dinner.

Howie came running across the playground and jumped straight into his father's arms. "Kindergarten is fun!"

His father held him and hugged him, then looked him straight in the eye. "No tails?"

Howie shook his head. "No tails."

"No horns?"

"No horns."

His father smiled, then paused. "Any biting?"

Howie bit his lip, then finally said, "Heather bit Martha. Hard. They both went home."

His father looked serious. "Then Heather's very bad and has a naughty *P'o*. And her mommy and daddy are going to be very upset with her. But you're my good boy," he kissed Howie on the forehead, "and let's keep it that way."

Howie hugged his father about the neck. "Yes, daddy. I promise."

"Good." His father set him back on the ground and held his hand. "Now let's go to grandma's. Uncle Jim and Aunt Ho are in town, and your mommy and I are going to go visit with them."

"Can I see them?"

"Maybe. We'll see. If you're good." Daddy squeezed his hand. "C'mon, Elmo's waiting in the car."

The Silver Crown

BY WILLIAM BRIDGES

DEDICATION
To my brother John.
And to my father.

ACKNOWLEDGMENTS
Thanks to Joshua Gabriel Timbrook for Albrecht and Mari,
and to Daniel Greenberg for setting the scenery.

And like a dying star is every work of your virtue: its light is always still on its way and it wanders—and when will it no longer be on its way? Thus the light of your virtue is still on its way even when the work has been done. Though it be forgotten and dead, the ray of its light still lives and wanders. That your virtue is your self and not something foreign, a skin, a cloak, that is the truth from the foundation of your souls, you who are virtuous.... And some who cannot see what is high in man call it virtue that they see all-too-closely what is low in man....
— Nietzsche, *Thus Spoke Zarathustra*

Great innovators never come from above; they come invariably from below, just as trees never grow from the sky downward, but upwards from the earth.
— C.G. Jung, *The Spiritual Problem of Modern Man*

Prologue

Mad Luna was in hiding when King Morningkill held the feast. It was ordained that all the tribe should be there, under the new moon, regardless of excuse or mission otherwise. Tonight, before all, Morningkill would reassert his kingship over the Silver Fangs, the North Country Protectorate, and all the Garou of North America. Even if only he believed such claims anymore.

Greyfist growled low, an almost inaudible rumbling in the back of his throat. The horse beneath him whinnied and rolled his eyes, nostrils flaring as his instincts told him to flee from the predator he heard and smelled so close. Greyfist came to his senses and laid his hand on the horse's neck, patting it calmly and reassuringly. "There, there, Tyre. Nothing to get worked up about."

The horse quit its nervous prancing and stilled itself at Greyfist's calm words. Greyfist steered the mount forward to continue his inspection of the bawn, the boundary between the Court of Jacob Morningkill and the world outside. He cursed himself for letting his rage get the better of him.

Damn it all if he, of all the Garou at court, could not control himself! It did no good to get worked up over things you could not change. Things other Garou—better Garou—before you had tried and failed at. No, griping would not change the king's mind and clear it of its years-old madness.

There. It was said. Mad. No other Silver Fang would dare admit that the king was mad, but that's what it surely was. *Eccentric, they would say. But mad? Certainly not. That is the talk of fools outside the tribe, envious of our position and state. Denied Gaia's divine favor, they grumble and gnash their fangs, desperate for the Fangs' divinely ordained glory. They would have to earn through hard labor the honor to which the Fangs were born.*

Greyfist spat in disgust. It was such thoughts, such arrogance, that had brought the tribe low, that had allowed a madness like Morningkill's to go so long ignored.

But to think as Greyfist did was treason.

Then gut me for a traitor, he thought. *Ah, how easy it is to speak so boldly in your own mind. But to act out this heroism? No, not I. I shall go on heeding the king, acquiescing to his strange demands. It is the way. It has been so for more years than humankind has built cities. Who am I to question such tradition? The king's Seneschal. But not the king himself. Only he can change the ancient laws. Only he can revive the tribe.*

But Morningkill...? His damn jealousy and paranoia had driven away all worthy successors. Was it to end with him? The great royal line, the ancient family of the House of Wyrmfoe? The family that had bred such heroes as were not seen in the world today? Such Garou as Aleking Axeclaw? Gorak Rules-by-Right?

The horse halted and reared back, whinnying in fear. Greyfist gripped the reins to avoid slipping off and again patted the horse's neck. "Calm. Calm. I'm at it again, fuming with anger. Doesn't do you any good, though, does it? I'm sorry, Tyre. Calm down."

But the horse still rolled its eyes and backed away from the trail. Greyfist sighed and dismounted, holding the reins to keep the horse from bolting. He stood still and slowly pulled the animal to him. The horse stopped its shying and settled, looking left and right fearfully, and finally let loose a loud sigh and stood still. Greyfist again patted its neck.

"There. That's better. What's a Garou doing riding a horse, anyway? You deserve much better. Not easy to train a horse to let a wolf crawl onto its back. But Morningkill likes horses. Morningkill demands horses. And so, we Garou ride horses. Royal pageantry. How vain. And you pay the cost."

Greyfist looked about as he stood, still rubbing the horse's neck. It was dark, with no moon to light the night. The landscape was a mass of black shapes on black shapes, vaguely formed into trees. He had reached the far northern edge of the bawn. and was now surrounded by the trees, huddling in on all sides except where the trail cut through the deep wilderness. Thanks to the laws that protected it from human despoiling, this was wilderness even humans avoided, as was much of the Green Mountain range of Vermont. The North Country Protectorate covered much of southern Vermont, but Greyfist knew that it had once stretched from Manhattan Island to the Canadian border, long ago when the Silver Fangs had first arrived on the continent to carve their territory from the native lands. From the native's hands.

Greyfist listened. Before he'd left on his patrol, he had used the Gift taught him by spirits to see, hear and smell with the senses of a wolf without actually shifting into wolf form. The only sounds he heard were those natural to the night. Insects buzzing off in the woods, the slight rustle of trees in the breeze. Somewhere farther off, the faint chattering of a brook. Nothing unusual or dangerous here.

Greyfist climbed back onto the horse and turned it around, setting off down the path, back toward the court where the feast was already starting. As he rode, he tried to still his anger. He was used to these tirades when the frustration was too much for him. He realized that he overreacted much of the time. Morningkill did have his moments, after all. He was a scion of the royal house. You could only fall but so far from that kind of pinnacle.

But Greyfist remembered Jacob from younger days, when the king had first made him Seneschal. There had been trust between Jacob and Greyfist in those days. Even today, Morningkill trusted none among the Silver Fangs so much as Greyfist. But why then did he not listen to his counselor's advice more often? Why did he insist on listening to Arkady, vain Arkady? He was enamored of the young hero, Greyfist supposed. The Garou son Morningkill had never had, perhaps. At least a son who lived up to all the traditions, not like Morningkill's real grandson.

Greyfist shook his head. He loved Morningkill dearly, remembering the man he used to be and might become again. If the king could shake off the madness. Where did this paranoia of his come from? Why were so many in the tribe cursed these days with such worries? Had the line really fallen, as the Shadow Lords claimed? No, Greyfist could not accept that. *Start thinking that way, and Harano follows.*

But then… there was the dream. The dream he had had but three nights ago. The dream which had kept him awake almost every night since, thinking it over, fighting to remember every detail of it. Was it a dream or a vision? Misinterpreting such things could be dangerous, especially considering the portents this one revealed. But after hours of consideration, Greyfist believed his dream had been sent by Falcon, the totem spirit of the tribe. But he still could not say what the dream meant for him, for Morningkill and for the tribe.

A dream of fallen kings and ones newly crowned. Of battle and pain. Of an oppressively dark, cathedral-like chamber where a single unblemished band of silver glowed bright.

Greyfist sat up in his saddle and looked ahead. Enough ruminations. He had no idea what the dream meant: it was a scattered play of images, and he did not have enough clues yet to figure it out. He thought instead of the security of the caern. While he was not the Warder, as the king's Seneschal it was his duty to ensure that the moot was safe and that the king was not threatened. So he had taken it upon himself to patrol the outlying regions, leaving the defense of the center to the Warder. Besides, he thought it best to cool his rage well away from the court happenings.

He was confident that the Warder could handle the duty, even though she was still healing a bad wound suffered on one of Morningkill's quests. He had sent Regina to fetch a tribal fetish from the Get of Fenris in the Adirondacks, and she had had to challenge one of their heroes for it. She had won, but still felt the pain of her wounds.

In addition, she now had to play Gatekeeper, at least until young Eliphas Standish could be ordained. The previous Gatekeeper, Garrick Batell, was dead, killed a week ago on a hunt. He had been lured into the Umbra alone and assaulted by a Bane; his body had been found by a wandering tribe of Fianna. That had been humiliating, watching them bring back the body. It wasn't right for a Silver Fang not to be brought home by his own pack. But Garrick had been stupid, and that was exactly what a Garou could not afford to be, with the Wyrm always waiting for just such an opening.

Greyfist rode back into the large clearing that formed the caern and court of the North Country Protectorate. He quickly surveyed the field. Tents were erected in a pattern across the meadow: those to the north were for the Lodge of the Sun, while those to the south represented the Lodge of the Moon. The northern tents were white with gold pictograms; the southern tents black with silver pictograms. Underneath both tents, and to the east, were huge wooden tables and high-backed chairs, each marked with the crest of its owner. Propriety demanded a seating order at court. The eastern table, out in the open and under no tent, was for the Armies of the King, all the Silver Fangs and court retainers who were not a part of either Lodge. The food had not yet been brought from the nearby mansion— the Morningkill estates—although the youngest from the Kin families were setting the tables in preparation.

But none were seated yet, as it was still the introductory stage of the feast. Garou and Kinfolk mingled on the field, taking part in the courtly game of greetings and gossip. Some Silver Fangs rode horses, dressed in regal display to impress the king, who dearly loved equestrian pursuits. They all wore finery, which for some meant sharp suits or elegant gowns; for others, bone fetishes or gold-laced robes. An odd mix of modern and primitive.

And at the nexus of all this activity, all the comings and goings, greetings and blessings, was the Grand Oak, the ancient tree where the throne of King Jacob Morningkill had been carved among the mighty roots. And on the throne, surrounded by both Garou and human Kinfolk of noble blood, was Morningkill himself. The king was dressed in the brightest of finery, his robe stitched in silver with ornate pictograms illustrating his family's great lineage. His arms displayed gold bracelets handed down from the treasuries of ancient human kings who, unknown to their fellow men, had been Kin to the Silver Fangs and had served only through the graces of the noble Garou. And on Morningkill's head was the crown, carved from wood and studded with jewels won from realms in the distant spirit world by previous kings.

But under all this glory was an old man with a bitter face, whose eyes darted about, watching for potential treachery from the sycophants swarming around him.

Greyfist shook his head in shame.

Kin families had the king's ear and were making full use of the opportunity. Apparently there was a dispute between the Rothchilds and the Albrechts, for Darren Rothchild and Warren Albrecht both argued before the king. Greyfist was always disgusted by such petty displays, but he had to forgive the Kin. They did not share in the full renown of their parents or children and so had to erect a pecking order of their own. The Kin were important, for they carried the blood of future Garou, but they mimicked the Fangs' own noble bureaucracy too well for Greyfist's taste. Theirs was a life of indentured servitude and arranged marriages.

But where was Arkady? Where was the King's Own Pack, his personal guard? Greyfist looked over the field, searching for any sign of them. Inconceivable that they would be late to the king's moot. Yet Greyfist had not seen them before he left on his patrol, and they were not in sight now. He would have words with Arkady when he finally arrived. He was damn tired of Arkady's irresponsibility, always off chasing renown. His place was here, damn it! There was glory and honor enough in serving the king, and Arkady would have to learn to live with it.

Greyfist's horse suddenly screamed and broke into a run, throwing Greyfist off. He hit the ground hard and heard the snap of his collarbone, followed quickly by sharp pain. He ignored it and stood up, looking for his horse, which he spotted quickly disappearing into the woods. Damn it! Was the animal so easily spooked? His anger hadn't been so harsh that time—

Four sharp knives raked into his back and he fell, grunting in pain. He looked over his shoulder to see a Garou in Crinos form standing behind him, his claws dripping blood—Greyfist's blood. The werewolf grinned wide, a sick grimace. Spittle poured from his mouth as if it welled up from deep within his throat, beyond his control. His fur was terribly mangy, and patched with greenish blotches. The ears were not those of a wolf, but rather resembled a bat's. A Black Spiral Dancer, a werewolf of the tribe of the Wyrm. He looked past Greyfist. Toward the throne.

The creature leaped over Greyfist at a run. Greyfist tried to stand, but the pain hit him hard, causing him to gasp for breath. The king! The king was in danger! He concentrated hard, trying not to panic, and began to shift forms. His muscles grew bigger and his bones followed suit, changing shape and size, forming wolfish features. Now in Crinos form, the form of battle, Greyfist stood.

All about him, a war raged. Silver Fangs fought with other Black Spiral Dancers. The insane creatures gibbered and roared, throwing themselves maniacally at the startled Silver Fangs. Court finery was stained with ichorous blood and gore as the surprise-attackers tore into the Silver Fang warriors.

Greyfist took all this in as he loped toward the throne, moving as fast as he could. He screamed to himself to run faster, but his legs wouldn't respond correctly. Blood still oozed down his back, but his collarbone had reknitted itself as he had changed.

Before him, Greyfist saw his Black Spiral assaulter fighting savagely with Regina, the Caern Warder. She had lost an arm but had cost the creature two or three ribs, which lay bloody on the ground. Its rib cage was gaping open, spilling viscera, but it didn't seem to notice. It had the upper hand and was battering Regina badly.

Behind them, sitting on his throne and staring dumbly at the fight, was Morningkill. The Kinfolk who had been clamoring for his attention not five minutes ago were nowhere in sight. Greyfist couldn't blame them. What human wouldn't flee from a Black Spiral Dancer?

Greyfist drew his klaive and rushed up behind the tainted Garou. Before the thing could hammer another blow onto the fallen Regina, Greyfist thrust the silver sword into its spine. It reared back its head and screamed, dying an instant later.

Greyfist pulled the weapon out of the steaming body and limped over to Morningkill. "Are you all right, my king?" he cried.

Morningkill looked at him, dazed. He then shook his head as if to clear it and stared at Greyfist, his eyes clear and bright. "Yes. I am fine. You have done well, Greyfist. A Half-Moon succeeded where none of my Ahrouns could." He looked over at Regina, who slowly pulled herself to her feet.

"She did her best, my lord," Greyfist said as he limped over to her.

Regina nodded a silent thank-you to him. She picked up her severed arm and held it to the stump. "Do not worry about me," she said. "We must get the king to safety."

"No," Morningkill said. "I will stay on my throne. The moot is about to start."

Greyfist stared in shock at Morningkill, who stood resolutely before the oaken throne. "My king, the moot is over! The Black Spirals have invaded the court! We must flee to safety!"

Morningkill seemed confused and looked out over the meadow. Greyfist also scanned the area and saw, far out on the field, five Silver Fangs finishing up the battle. The King's Own Pack. Arkady had finally arrived. On the field were six Black Spiral bodies, not including Greyfist's attacker. Two horses lay dead, as did three Kinfolk retainers.

Greyfist looked at Arkady, who sauntered across the field, dragging the body of one of the Black Spirals behind him as a trophy. *So cocky and confident,* thought Greyfist. *Why wasn't he here earlier?*

"You see?" Morningkill said. "My guard is here! Arkady has come! There, out on the field! The battle is over. We have won the day!" He began to laugh, but it was choked off in his throat as a figure leapt from the branches above. It hurtled into Morningkill and both of them went down in a heap.

Greyfist ran to the throne and slashed at the Black Spiral Dancer, severing its head with one expert sweep of his klaive. He quickly pulled the spasming, headless body off the king.

Morningkill lay staring at Greyfist, as if he recognized him for the first time in years. The king's guts were spread out in his lap; his blood seeped into the ancient oak. He breathed chokingly, trying to say something.

Greyfist screamed in anguish. "Healers! Healers! Damn it!" He fell to his knees and cradled the king in his arms. Morningkill whispered low and Greyfist, tears streaming down his furred cheeks, bent his ear to the king's weak words.

"My...grand...son...?" Morningkill said, his eyes rolling up to meet Greyfist's. "Bring him...home." The king's eyes shut and he slumped into Greyfist's arms, letting go his last breath.

Greyfist cried, clutching the king close to his breast. "Jacob. Jacob. Why like this? Why?"

Greyfist heard frantic footsteps approach and a sob of anguish. He looked up to see Arkady, staring at the dead king. His face bore shock and grief at once, but also a look of disbelief, as if what he saw could not be true.

"The king? Dead?" Arkady said, almost in a whisper.

Greyfist gritted his teeth and suppressed a growl. "Dead. The king is dead."

Regina fell to her knees, her head bowed, her hand dropping her severed arm before she could heal it. Other Silver Fangs now gathered round, as did Kinfolk of the court. All stared in shock and dismay at Morningkill's body.

One of the Kin cried out, beginning a wail which quickly spread throughout the crowd. Arkady threw back his head and let loose a howl. All the Silver Fangs followed, their heads back and eyes shut with grief. Greyfist joined in, and their howl mixed with the Kin's mournful wailing and was carried out across the woods to the nearby towns, where people clutched their bedsheets in terror and dug themselves deeper into their beds, trying to shut out the fearful sound.

Greyfist laid Morningkill on the ground, wrapping the king's arms across his chest in a regal pose. He rose and walked over to Arkady, who stood two heads taller than him. Arkady was an imposing figure of pure white fur and black leather battle armor. Nonetheless, Arkady's grief was no equal to Greyfist's anger.

"Why weren't you here?" Greyfist yelled. "You were his guard, the King's Own!"

Arkady looked at Greyfist and narrowed his eyes in anger; Greyfist knew something was not right. He saw into the large Garou's eyes and knew that the grief which he now threw off was a blanket easily discarded, that his sorrow over Morningkill's death was not so genuine as his howl had made Greyfist first believe.

"We tried to get here, my pack and I," Arkady said in his thick Russian accent, stepping forward and forcing Greyfist to look up to his height. "But we were attacked outside the bawn by Black Spiral Dancers. By the time we finished them and arrived, the battle had already begun."

"But how? How did they get past the guards?"

"Look! There across the field!" Arkady spun and pointed to the meadow. "See? Holes from the ground. They came from beneath us. Who knows how long they had been burrowing there, secretly and silently so that none of us would know. This was planned, yes? They knew well when to attack."

Greyfist stared at the three holes in the earth. *So that's what spooked Tyre,* he thought. *It wasn't me. He sensed those damn things moving beneath us.*

"So Garrick the Gatekeeper was killed on purpose, to make sure our defenses would be low," Greyfist said, still staring at the dark entrances into the earth.

"Yes, Seneschal. That must be it," Arkady said.

Greyfist wondered how long they had been under there, planning their attack. When he turned back to Arkady, the Garou had stepped up to the throne and was beginning to address the assemblage.

"My friends," Arkady said. "This is a great tragedy we suffer tonight. Our king is dead. But he will live on in our songs!" Silver Fang warriors cheered at that, desperate for some hope to come out of their grief. "In two nights, when the moon is crescent, we shall give him his death rite so that he may join the kings before him in our tribal spirit lands. Always will he be remembered and spoken well of."

Greyfist nodded as other Silver Fang cheered again. *Yes, Morningkill must be remembered. For his good qualities, not his bad.*

"But it is time we consider our new king!" Arkady yelled.

What is this? Greyfist thought, narrowing his eyes in anger. *This is too early! Morningkill's body still lies warm and Arkady speaks of his successor?*

"Yes, I know it is hasty, but the enemy has found us in our very court! We must swiftly have our new king!"

Greyfist stepped forward. "This is too soon! We must review the ranks. Morningkill left only one successor to the first family—"

"But he is in exile, Seneschal!" Arkady yelled to be heard. "He is unworthy, and thus a member of another royal family must rule."

"But there are no other royal families in North Country. It would take too long to summon one from another protectorate!"

"Ah, but here is where you are wrong, Seneschal. Peter, my packmate!" He gestured to a Garou in the crowd. "Tell them what we have discovered on our latest quest!"

Peter walked forward and stepped up to the throne. He was well-known here, a member of the King's Own Pack and thus highly honored. He put his hand on Arkady's shoulder and looked out over the crowd.

"We all know Arkady's story, how he came to us after traveling Europe, homeless. How he barely escaped the horrors of his mother country, Russia, when he was a small child, before his First Change. How the Kinfolk man who smuggled him from that dangerous land was thought lost and dead. But no. We have found him, the man who was a father to Arkady!

"He was old and feeble, still hurting from the wounds he had received long ago trying to defend little Arkady from the Wyrm spawn. He had told Arkady to run as the creature attacked him all those years ago, throwing himself in the way to defend the little boy, who was not yet Garou. The man had traveled ever since, trying to find Arkady again, to tell Arkady of his heritage. And all the while, Arkady had believed him dead.

"He finally found Arkady but two nights ago, and on his deathbed revealed this great news: Arkady's great-grandparents were of the Clan of the Crescent Moon! Arkady is of the Seven! He is royal, and is thus the next to succeed Morningkill to the throne of the North Country Protectorate!"

The crowd broke out into a massive howl. This was wonderful! A royal had been found, and he was one of theirs! Their own Arkady was to be king!

But Greyfist did not howl with the rest. He stepped away from the throne, where Arkady smiled jubilantly as the Silver Fangs sang his praises. Greyfist knew this was wrong. Oh, he believed Arkady was royal, all right. Who wouldn't believe it, with fur like that and that bearing of his? But Greyfist suspected that Arkady had been aware of this heritage all along, that it was not some newly discovered secret. No, it wasn't right: there was another who was in line for the throne before Arkady. There was another of the House of Wyrmfoe, the first family of North Country.

Greyfist pulled Eliphas Standish out of the crowd and walked him away from the gathering. Eliphas looked annoyed, and kept peering back at the throne, not wanting to miss anything. But he knew better than to ignore the orders of the Seneschal, who was king until Arkady was crowned.

"What is it?" Eliphas said. "What is so important that we miss Arkady's announcement? This is a great moment."

"Still your slobbering tongue, cub," Greyfist said. "I want you to go to New York City."

"What? But I am to be made Gatekeeper next week. I have many duties—"

"Next week! Not yet. You are to go to New York and bring Lord Albrecht back with you."

Eliphas stared at Greyfist. "Albrecht? I can't do that! He is in exile!"

"No longer. It was Morningkill's last request, stated with his dying breath. Are you to deny the king's final commandment?"

Eliphas looked down in shame. "No, of course not. If the king declared the exile over, then…." He raised his head and looked at Greyfist, worried. "But what about Arkady? If Albrecht is no longer denied the court, then he is next in line, not…."

Greyfist nodded. "Exactly. And Morningkill knew that. So, go and do not say a word of it to anyone. You are to speak of this only to me and Albrecht. Just so you know how important this is, I'm declaring it a Court Quest. Do you understand?"

"Yes!" Eliphas said, realizing it would mean honor for him if he succeeded. "I'll be back with him tomorrow."

"Go then." Greyfist watched Eliphas leave immediately; the boy did not even bother to say good-bye to anyone at court. That was good. The young one knew how to follow a court dictate.

Greyfist looked over at Arkady, who was now staring back at him with a frown, obviously wondering what Greyfist was up to. Greyfist smiled and nodded at the newly revealed Duke. Arkady smiled back, but it was a weak smile, full of uncertainty.

1

Albrecht was in one of his black moods. He walked down the wet street toward the triangular park two blocks away. He looked up at the gray sky, still dark with the new dawn, and blinked at the rain. *The sky is crying*, he thought. *A slow, mournful drizzle of rain falling on the city, spattering the streets with a sheet of tears. Warped reflections of our world stare up at me from the still water—a mirror, shattered with every step I take.*

God, you're really full of it today, Albrecht said to himself. *What's the big deal? It's just another rainy day.*

Then why do I feel like shit? Bad feeling, like something I'm not going to like is coming down the pike. Never been much for omens, but they seem to like me an awful lot, judging from the past few months. Even an Ahroun can get premonitions now and then. But premonitions of what? I don't have a clue. Just feels wrong, that's all. Is this what a wolf feels like before stepping into a trap?

Albrecht turned the corner and stopped to look at the small park across the street. It was not a very large park, but by city standards it was big enough. It gave Albrecht and his small pack a place to meet besides Central Park, which was crawling with too many other Garou for Albrecht's taste.

He was early by almost half an hour to meet his pack here today, but that would give him time for a smoke or two. Evan didn't like cigarette smoke, and while Albrecht normally didn't give a flying fuck, he had agreed to compromise when with the pack. Mari didn't like the smoke either, but she never said anything about it. Just fumed in that way of hers, and found other ways to attack Albrecht. She still hadn't gotten over that fight they'd had a few years ago. *Just a damn flesh wound,* Albrecht thought. *Deal with it, already.*

Albrecht crossed the rain-slick street and walked onto the wet grass. Standing on the grass was frowned upon by the law, but he didn't care. It was what grass was for, wasn't it? He walked deeper into the small, two-to-three-block-square park. When he got to the usual bench, there was a man sleeping on it with newspapers piled over him. Albrecht sat down next to him and lit up a cigarette, pretending the guy wasn't there.

He leaned back and let out a cloud of smoke. That felt better. Nothing like a good smoke. Oh, sure, some Garou said it would kill him one day, that he would be devoured by Hoga, Urge Wyrm of Smog. But he just nodded and smiled at such folly. Hell, Indians had been smoking for years before the Wyrm ever got to this continent. Yeah, their tobacco had been a lot purer, and Albrecht wasn't really sure just who owned the cigarette brand he smoked, but he figured there was no reason to worry about it. Wasn't as if his lungs didn't clean themselves out just fine, what with the regeneration and all.

He took another long drag and smiled, holding the smoke in for a few minutes and then letting it out slowly. *Screw 'em,* he thought. All the moral prigs. They had skeletons in their closets, all right. At least Albrecht wore his faults on his sleeve, where everyone could see them. Well, some of them. He knew he was prone to depressions that were not always obvious to others. Mari missed them half the time, although Evan seemed to understand. Albrecht had always had them, although there had been a real bad spell a while back, after his exile, which had ended only when he formed his own pack a few months ago.

The pack. That was something. Something Albrecht hadn't thought he'd ever be a part of again, not since his first pack all up and died fighting the Wyrm. He'd gotten famous with them, but that hadn't stopped them from getting themselves killed and leaving him all alone to face the renown and expectations heaped on him. It was worse when you were the grandson of King Morningkill and the scion of the House of Wyrmfoe.

But that crap was behind him now. Had been for years. He'd been kicked out of the protectorate by Morningkill, accused of hubris and lack of deference, the breaking of the Litany and so on and so on. The truth of it was that Morningkill exiled anyone who displayed genuine ability, anyone who might expose Morningkill's own faults. Albrecht wasn't the first. Loba Carcassone had that honor. And there'd been more after Albrecht, although he didn't know their names.

Albrecht ground out his cigarette on the benchback, shaking his head. Christ, but he was melancholy this morning.

"Huh? What?" The newspapers moved and fell away, revealing the man underneath, now blinking blearily and craning his neck around to look at Albrecht. "Who the hell…?"

Albrecht smiled. "You're sleeping on my property, pal." He pointed at a carving in the wooden back which read *Lord A.* "That's me. I don't mind you sleeping here, but once the dawn cracks, this bench is mine."

The man growled and sat up. He was dressed in an old army field jacket and torn jeans. He rubbed his face and then looked over at Albrecht. "That's kinda rude, don't ya think? This ain't exactly yours: it's public property."

Albrecht frowned and showed his teeth. The effect was more dreadful than merely that, however, as his rage bled out a little from his eyes. The bench sleeper looked terrified and stood up quickly.

"All right, all right. I'm gone." And he walked off, hands in his pockets, but looking back at Albrecht as if trying to figure out just what it was he had seen.

Albrecht frowned. He knew better than to do that. You never knew when you were accidentally putting the scare on somebody important. Not that a park-bench bum was important, but in this city he might have friends in low places, and low meant power in New York. The city was crawling with Leeches—vampires—who pulled the strings of many important officials from their sewer dens. Sure, some of them lived in high-rises, but the dark alleys and sewerways were their meeting places and hunting grounds.

Albrecht looked over at the two guys entering the park. They were talking to each other as they looked right at him and slowly headed his way. Albrecht wondered what the hell this was about. He didn't recognize the two. These guys had suits on underneath their trench coats, but designer suits, not federal-agent style. Businessmen? If so, what the hell did they want from him?

The two walked up to the bench and looked down at Albrecht. They looked nervous, as if unsure what to do. Then the taller of the two spoke. "Albrecht?"

"Lord Albrecht, yeah," Albrecht said, standing up. He stood about half a foot taller than the one who had spoken. The two men moved a bit closer. "What do you want?"

The tall one looked at his partner and some unseen signal passed between them. They both erupted into action, pulling long, sharp knives out of their coats and jumping toward Albrecht, swinging the knives at his throat.

Albrecht leapt back and onto the bench, then vaulted over it in a somersault. One of the knives caught his coat, tearing a foot-long rip in it, but now the bench was between them.

Klaives! Were these Garou? Albrecht turned to face them, and they split up to move around the bench, one on either side, moving carefully now, as if they were zoo-keepers trying to tranquilize a tiger.

Albrecht growled and shifted forms. In an instant he was nine feet tall in his Crinos wolfman form. His fur was white, the sign of pure blood among Garou. The attackers also began to shift, smoothly flowing into Crinos forms themselves. Their fur was also white, although mixed with faint flecks of gray.

"You're Silver Fangs!" Albrecht yelled in the Garou tongue. "What the hell is going on?"

They said nothing as they came at him from both sides. Albrecht pulled his own klaive from his coat; his was nearly bigger than both of theirs combined. A Grand Klaive, a much rarer and more potent weapon.

Seeing the large silver sword, one of the Garou hesitated, but the other lunged forward, his klaive aimed at Albrecht's guts. Albrecht stepped to the side and parried the knife, but quickly twisted his own blade and swiped it at the attacking Garou. It sliced across his opponent's arm and drew blood. The Garou yelled and jumped back just as the other one came forward.

Albrecht stepped back and met the charge with his klaive in thrusting position. The oncoming Garou barely managed to twist away, although the Grand Klaive still tore a chunk out of his side. He quickly recovered, and slashed at Albrecht.

Albrecht was startled at this one's skill with a blade, and he couldn't parry in time. The klaive sunk into Albrecht's left thigh and stuck there. Albrecht screamed in rage and leapt back.

The other Garou was ready and met Albrecht from behind, slicing into his back. The pain flooded over Albrecht and he felt himself losing control, giving into the anger and pain and rage. But he willed himself to calm down, to ignore the pain. The last thing he needed now was to frenzy.

He ducked down low and spun in a circle, holding the blade out, surprising the Garou who had struck him from behind. The sword bit into his legs, hacking cleanly through one but just grazing the other. The Garou fell, a howl escaping as he hit the wet ground.

Albrecht was up and moving before the other Garou could close in. He backed off as the other picked up his fallen comrade's klaive and moved after him. But the attacking Silver Fang had something in his other hand, something Albrecht couldn't see.

"Damn it, explain yourself! I am Lord Albrecht, of the House of Wyrmfoe! Heed your better, you bastard!"

But the Garou just kept coming forward, warily. As Albrecht moved left, the Garou followed and quickly wove to the right, gaining ground. Albrecht backed up against a tree and knew he had to make a stand.

The other Garou waved his hand at Albrecht, and Albrecht shut his eyes to ward off the sand which flew into his face. *Damn!* He raised his klaive to parry whatever came at him, fighting blind. But the blow came low, slicing into Albrecht's already wounded thigh.

And that was it. Albrecht had had enough and couldn't control his anger any longer. He succumbed to his rage and opened his mouth wide to let out a roar. He opened his eyes to see his assailant drawing back for a thrust, but Albrecht stepped forward with blinding speed, dropped his klaive, and wrapped his clawed hands around the Garou's face.

The Garou brought his blade up but wasn't fast enough to deal with the berserk Albrecht, who dug his claws into the Garou's head, raking furrows in his scalp. Albrecht's weight brought the Garou to the ground, and Albrecht immediately began savaging his captive with his rear claws, stomping the Garou's legs and raking away strips of flesh. The Garou screamed and hit Albrecht repeatedly with the klaive, all weak and ineffective blows with no leverage. In seconds, the Garou was dead.

Albrecht, totally lost to anger, crawled forward on all fours, slapping through the mud, still partially blinded from the sand in his eyes, heading for the smell of the other enemy. But there was another smell there now. A familiar smell. Not threatening.

"Albrecht! Calm down! It's over!" the source of the new scent yelled.

Albrecht circled around defensively, sniffing all about him for foes. None. Only the familiar smell. The non-threatening smell. The smell of a packmate.

Albrecht sat down and looked at Evan, who stood before the other Garou as if defending him from Albrecht. Evan looked like a fourteen-year-old boy, which he was. But he was also a Garou, and fourteen wasn't so young when you were one of Gaia's chosen. He was wiser than his years, thanks to spirits who favored him and taught him special powers. Evan was of the Wendigo tribe, even though he didn't look remotely Native American.

Albrecht frowned. Then he shifted back to human form. *Shit*, he thought. *Lost it. Damn.* He looked around and saw the dead Garou behind him, now a human form bleeding across the wet grass. He looked back at Evan. "That was not fun."

"Who are these guys?" Evan asked, leaning down and looking at the wounded one, still in Crinos form but moaning in half-consciousness, his severed leg lying a few feet away from his body.

"Silver Fangs. Beyond that, I have no idea. Can you fix him up?"

Evan looked over at the leg and then at the Garou's stump. "Yeah. Help me out here. I need you to hold the leg to the wound while I concentrate."

Albrecht gripped the klaive still stuck in his thigh and wrenched it out. The pain was incredible, but Albrecht was used to this kind of hurt and forgot it quickly.

He went and picked up the severed leg, then walked over to the wounded Garou. He dropped to his knees and held the leg up to the bleeding stump. Evan placed his hand over both and sat silent for a minute. Then the flesh around the stump and the severed leg began to grow, to reknit and pull itself back together. There would be a scar.

When that was done, Albrecht stood up and looked around. He wondered what kind of toll this fight had taken on the local residents. For all he knew, a cop or two had come running only to see three wolfmen duking it out. Of course they wouldn't remember it that way. They'd rationalize it away as anything else. The Veil.

As if to confirm his thoughts, Albrecht saw a police officer sitting on the grass near the edge of the sidewalk. He had his head buried in his hands and was muttering to himself.

Not exactly standard behavior for the NYPD, thought Albrecht. He turned to Evan. "We gotta clean this up and move out before that pig wises up again."

Evan looked over at the police officer. "I know. I saw him on my way in. I think he'll be okay." He looked at both the bodies. "Uh…you can carry this one, and I'll get the dead one." Evan began shifting into a larger form. His muscles grew wide and broad and his face took on a chunky, dumb-jock look—a sort of Mr. Hyde to his previous Dr. Jekyll. He walked over to the dead body.

"What the hell is going on?" someone yelled.

"You're late, Mari," Albrecht said. "You missed the action."

Mari walked around the bench, over to the scene of the battle. She was a wiry, muscled and intense-looking woman, a Hispanic-Italian from the Bronx. Her attitude alone could stop fights, but her physique and martial skill ensured that she could back it up with blows. Mari helped teach street-tough skills to battered women. It was a religious cause for her, and she never took kindly to Albrecht's mocking her "coddling of humans." But Albrecht knew that now was not the time to start sparring.

"Two Garou," Mari said, surveying the scene. "One dead, the other half-dead. Who attacked whom?" she said, turning to look Albrecht in the eyes.

"Don't start," Albrecht said, glaring back at her. "I didn't ask for this. These are Silver Fangs, damn it! I don't go carving up my tribe for the fun of it!"

"Then why?" Mari said, stepping closer to him. "Why would they attack you? What have you done now?"

"Me? This is my fault? These two just walk up and start slicing away, and you think I had something to do with it? Lady, get a clue: I am *not* out to make enemies."

"Come on," Evan said, looking at both of them, with the dead Garou on his back. "We'd better enter the Umbra. No way we're going to get these two to Central Park without being noticed."

Albrecht turned away from Mari and picked up the wounded Garou, who still moaned in pain and delirium. "Well, who's leading the way?"

"All right," Mari said. She walked over and picked up Albrecht's Grand Klaive. Holding it up over the street and positioning it to catch the reflection of the rainwater, she concentrated, staring into the depths of the mirror world. Evan and Albrecht moved up next to her and touched her shoulders. Then the world changed around them as Mari reached into the spirit world and pulled them into it, warping the Gauntlet around them.

The streetlights fell away and the rain stopped. They still stood in the park, but it was now five blocks long, and the buildings surrounding it were older than in the real world. The streets were empty of pedestrians, although occasional spider webs could be seen, almost hidden in the alleys.

Evan began walking in the direction of Central Park; Albrecht followed him. Mari looked around, double-checking to make sure they weren't followed by anything, then fell in behind them.

"The wounded one will surely tell us what this is about," Mari said.

"He better," Albrecht said.

2

Fengy wandered through the park on his daily rounds. He stopped diligently at each and every trash can, gathering up whatever leftover food he found there, regardless of its condition. A day-old candy bar or a week-old hot dog—it didn't matter to him. It was food.

He was digging into the can by the small pond where the turtles lived when he heard voices from behind the bushes. He looked carefully into the brush. He hadn't heard anyone a second ago, so he wondered where the voices were coming from.

Albrecht walked out onto the sidewalk, still carrying the wounded Silver Fang. Fengy jumped back in surprise, shocked by the sudden appearance of the Silver Fang lord. Albrecht was followed by Evan Heals-The-Past and Mari Cabrah, his packmates.

"That ain't right, ya know," Fengy said, startling Albrecht now. "Steppin' out in front of a fellow with no warning. Yer from the Umbra, right? That must be it, cause Fengy didn't hear ya before."

Albrecht looked annoyed. He had never liked Fengy. The rat was always hanging around, trying to get information or a free meal. The Bone Gnawers had no shame, and Fengy epitomized the worst qualities of his tribe.

Albrecht knew it was uncharitable of him to think that way. The Bone Gnawers of Central Park had welcomed him when he had had no home, and allowed him into their moot rites. But still, he couldn't get over their apparent lack of self-esteem. He knew the pot was calling the kettle black, but he couldn't help himself.

"Yeah, Fengy," Albrecht said. "We just had a jaunt through Umbral Manhattan. You should check it out sometime. Give you a sense of history. Where's Larissa?"

"Mother is on her errands, like any good Gnawer," Fengy said, knowing when he was being condescended to. "She's got mouths to feed, ya know. Some of us work for a living."

"Yeah, yeah. Look, we're heading over to the caern center. Let her know I'd like her help when you see her."

"Sure. I'll do it. Them some wounded friends ya got there?"

Albrecht ignored him and walked down the path. Evan and Mari followed. Mari turned to call back to Fengy as she walked off: "Enemies, Fengy. Enemies. Silver Fangs."

Fengy furrowed his brow in confusion. If they were Silver Fangs, and Albrecht was a Silver Fang, how come they were enemies? He scratched his head and then continued his duties, reaching deep into the trash can for the fast-food burger wrapper he had spotted at the bottom.

The pack arrived at the caern center, a small grove in the middle of the park, hidden from the eyes of any passersby on the paths that surrounded it. The trees grew in such a way as to provide good sound-proofing, so most conversations couldn't be heard by anyone outside.

Albrecht laid the wounded Fang on the ground. Evan placed the dead one nearby and put his jacket over the Garou's face.

"Well, Albrecht," Mari said. "What now?"

"I want Larissa to look at this one," Albrecht said, pointing at the wounded Garou. "If she can revive him, I'm going to find out what the hell he thought he was doing."

"*If* I can revive him?" an old, gravelly voice said, coming through the trees, followed seconds later by an old hag of a woman, dressed in thrift-store chic and smelling like she'd been bathing in dumpsters. "Course I can revive him, if he's not dead. Now, what's this all about?"

"Mother Larissa," Evan said, smiling at the old lady. "It's good to see you."

"And you, Evan," Larissa replied, smiling back at him; then she looked at Albrecht and grimaced. "But I knew there'd be trouble as soon as I heard the high-and-mighty lord here. Trouble follows him like white on rice."

"Good morning to you, Mother," Albrecht said with obvious sarcasm. "I would appreciate it if you could wake this guy up so I can beat the crap out of him again."

Larissa waddled over to the Garou and bent down, examining his wounds. "What's he done to you? He looks like a Silver Fang. This some sort of family quarrel? 'Cause I don't want no part of it!"

"I don't know what this is about. That's why I need him awake."

Larissa sighed and put her hands on the Garou's chest. She concentrated, singing an old song to herself, low enough that the others couldn't make out the words. Then she pulled her hands back and stared sadly at the Garou, shaking her head. She pulled her dirty shawl from around her shoulders and placed it on his face.

"Didn't want to live," she said. "He didn't have the strength to go on. Whoever he was, he was hurting bad before you tore into him. Not from any wound, but from inside."

"What do you mean?" Albrecht said. "What are you talking about?"

"She means Harano, Albrecht," Mari said, staring at the dead body. "'A weeping from within, crying for that which is not yet lost.' It seems to hit your tribe a lot these days, although they always want to deny it exists."

Albrecht looked down at the two dead Fangs. The enormity of it all finally hit him. He had killed two of his own tribemates. It had been self-defense, but nonetheless, two Silver Fangs lay dead. He let out a deep sigh and sat down, staring at the grass beneath him. The ground was still damp from the earlier rains, but Albrecht didn't care. Tears again, he thought. The world is still crying, but now I'm crying with it.

"Hey, Mother!" Fengy suddenly poked his head around a tree. "There's a Silver Fang out here to see you, real regal like! Something's up!"

Larissa looked at Albrecht with narrowed eyes. "I'll be right there to see him," she answered Fengy, and then pointed a bony finger at Albrecht. "You stay here until I see what this is about."

"What if this one wants to kill me, too?" Albrecht said.

"Not in my caern, he won't!" she said and pulled herself up. She hobbled over the way she had come and then squeezed her way out between the trees.

"Whatever this is, Albrecht," Evan said, coming over and sitting down next to him. "We're with you."

Albrecht looked at Mari, who looked back at him. "Both of us," she said.

"Thanks," Albrecht said and leaned back. He tried to listen to what was going on outside the grove. He couldn't hear anything but the general background rumble of the city. *Another Silver Fang,* he thought. *Is this one here to finish the job these two started, or is he here to warn me about these two?*

The answer came soon enough when Larissa pushed her way back in between the thick bushes, followed by the visitor.

The man was of medium height, but his posture and the way he looked at everyone told of someone used to getting his way with other people. He was young, though; perhaps no more than eighteen. He wore an expensive trench coat and leather riding boots, as if he'd just come from a horse show, and his hands were snugly fitted with leather driving gloves. He pulled off his sunglasses, revealing bright blue eyes. He looked straight at Albrecht.

"Lord Albrecht?" he asked.

Albrecht stood up and met the other's gaze. "Yeah, that's me. And who are you?"

"I am Eliphas Standish, soon to be Squire of the Lodge of the Moon and Gatekeeper for the North Country Protectorate and the Court of...of...." He seemed confused at this last statement, as if he had forgotten the name of the court.

"Morningkill. You're from Morningkill's court. You can say it here. It's not a dirty word, no matter what passed between me and my grandfather."

Eliphas' eyes widened as he looked past Albrecht at the two dead Garou. The newcomer walked past Albrecht and pulled the shawl and jacket off their faces. He looked down at them with his head bowed and then replaced the coverings. He turned back to Albrecht.

"I...I don't understand why they attacked you. Larissa told me what she knew."

Albrecht stepped up to Eliphas and stared him in the face. "Do you know who they were?"

Eliphas looked straight back, used to being treated in such a manner at court. "Yes. One was Alphonse Grayling and the other was Justin Beauchamp. Both were exiled two months ago from Morningkill's court."

Albrecht's eyes widened and he stepped back. "Exiles? Like me? Then why did they attack me?"

"I'm not sure. It may have something to do with succession rights...." He looked down at the bodies. "But how could they have known so soon?"

"Known what? Succession rights? What are you talking about?"

Eliphas looked up again and straightened his posture, his bearing becoming rather ritualistic in the process, as if he were performing a sacred duty. "I am here to bring you back to court."

"At whose order?" Albrecht said, somewhat incredulously.

"King Morningkill's. The late King Morningkill. Jacob Morningkill is dead."

3

Albrecht stared out the window at the passing landscape. The sun had broken through the clouds and bathed the trees in a golden glow. The still-damp leaves reflected the light back in intense, rich greens, oranges and reds. Autumnal Vermont was beautiful. Albrecht hadn't seen his home country in nearly three years. He realized, watching from the speeding car, that he missed it greatly. More than he had allowed himself to recognize. These colors were his colors, burned into his soul from early childhood. Gaia was everywhere, the Garou said, but Albrecht believed that she loved this land more than any other.

Albrecht turned and looked at Eliphas, who stared ahead down the road as he drove. This kid was pretty cocksure, Albrecht thought. It was obvious that he'd been born with a silver spoon in his mouth, as the humans would say. He was so privileged, he had no clue about just how well-off he was. Albrecht shook his head. This was exactly what pissed him off so much about the Fangs. They were all born to privilege, but had no humility about it.

Albrecht looked back out the window. *Of course, I used to be just like that,* he thought. *That's why I hate it so much. It reminds me of what I used to be. A vain, regal ass.*

He had noticed the way Eliphas kept staring at him when he thought Albrecht wasn't looking. The expression on his face betrayed what he was thinking: he was utterly confused about the Garou lord who sat in the car with him. A street-tough, uncouth Fang. Oh, Albrecht had the features of the Fang ideal, all right: well-chiseled face, fine blond hair. But it went down from there. Five-o'clock shadow, a near-perpetual frown, a torn and filthy trenchcoat, ripped jeans, etc., etc. What in the world had created such a creature as this? Eliphas was surely thinking. What could have brought him so low?

Albrecht sighed. He knew the routine. He'd thought those same thoughts once, whenever he'd met members of the other tribes. So wrapped up in his own glory, he couldn't understand how they could lead their lives dwelling among the scum of humanity. He knew differently now. He'd lived among the scum for some time, and had discovered that most of them were far nobler than the so-called heroes of his tribe. He'd quickly learned that appearance and economic status were the least hallmarks of character. The low-born, as his tribe called anyone of lesser status than they, had perhaps more virtues than a whole sept of high-and-mighty Silver Fangs.

Take his pack, for instance. He'd stand by them no matter the odds well before he would defend the honor of his tribe. Evan was a good kid, a better person than Albrecht was, that was for sure. He was decent, and always thought of others before himself. But the Fangs would consider the young Wendigo a half-breed and always look down their snouts at him, no matter what deeds he accomplished. And Mari. Boy, they would not take to her at all. She was too feisty, too ready to pick a fight with anyone, regardless of their station. No, the Fangs would not approve of Albrecht's new pack.

Well, screw them. His pack had proven many times how, no matter what feud was going on amongst themselves, they'd stand behind Albrecht. When he'd told them they had to stay behind in New York, that he had to go alone to the court, they'd pitched a fit. Mari had torn into him about Silver Fang assassins, and how Eliphas could be fooling them all and really have been sent to lure Albrecht off to kill him. Evan had downplayed the paranoia factor, but still mentioned that the court might not have Albrecht's best interests in mind when summoning him. What if they were trying to accuse him of a crime? On their home turf, he wouldn't stand a chance of justice.

Albrecht had thanked them for their concern, but made it clear that this was something he had to do alone. In a time like this, so soon after caern security had been breached, the Fangs would not allow any non-tribe members near the bawn, let alone the caern proper. As he got into Eliphas's Lexus, Mari had told him that, if they hadn't heard from him in two days, they were coming to get him, and just let any Silver Fang try to stop her. He'd smiled at this but hadn't said anything.

Mari sometimes really had it in for him, but when it came to issues of pack unity against an outside force, she could come off like his personal guardian and protector. She was the same way with Evan.

"Can I ask you something?" Eliphas said, bringing Albrecht out of his reverie. Albrecht looked at the road ahead and saw they were approaching a town. Middlebury. And past Middlebury, near the foot of the Green Mountains, was the Morningkill estate. They were almost there. Almost to the court.

"Sure, go ahead," Albrecht replied, sitting back and looking straight ahead.

"Why were you exiled?"

Albrecht was quiet for a while, looking out at the white birches they passed, ghostly blurs at this speed. "I guess you don't know. You're young enough not to understand what really went on. Morningkill and I didn't get along too well. He didn't like the idea of any Garou who could threaten his power, one who might make a better leader than him or who could point out his failings to others. Me? I was too big for my own britches. I pushed his button one too many times. I had come back from nearly getting my ass trashed by a Wyrm creature—the Vssh'krang, I think it was—and I did it alone, too. My pack was dead by then, so I was sort of a free agent waiting to make a pack of my own.

"Anyway, I dragged the thing's carcass back to the caern and presented it before the court, demanding they shower me with honor and glory and all the stuff heroes deserve. But Morningkill had gotten tired of these shows of mine. Yeah, I proved I could kick butt good, but Morningkill thought maybe I was too good. He aimed to feed me a fat slice of humble pie. I wasn't having any of that, and he knew it. So, for insolence before the king, he kicked me out."

"That doesn't seem right," Eliphas said, his brow furrowed in worry. "He was the king. He's supposed to reward us when we do our duty to Gaia."

"Yeah. So? The world ain't fair in that respect. It throws us all kinds of curves, like a mad, paranoid king who kicks the best and the brightest out of court."

"But all the other exiles? Surely not all of them were exiled out of vanity?" Eliphas looked very worried now.

"Who? Loba Carcassone? She opened her mouth about the Defiler Wyrm's plots once too often. Morningkill didn't want to hear that crap. If he listened to her, then he'd have to do something about the Wyrm, wouldn't he?"

"But everyone knows Carcassone is crazy, with her talk about the Wyrm hiding in little children, and some sort of generations-long conspiracy to corrupt humans—"

"Is she crazy? I'm not so sure about that. You get out of the caern more often and you'll see some truly weird shit. And as for the other exiles, what about those two who attacked me? What's the story there?"

"They were plotting against Morningkill. Arkady revealed the plot and personally chased them from the caern after Morningkill declared their punishment."

"Arkady, huh? I never liked that guy. That air of his, like he's holier than Gaia. And you said he's the one trying for the throne? Did you ever think that maybe he had those two kicked out because they discovered his kingly aspirations and were going to tell Morningkill? After all, Morningkill wouldn't abide anyone who wanted to be king in his place. Arkady would have wound up on the outside, like me and Loba. Hell, maybe he and I are in the same boat together, and he just wanted to save the Fangs from Morningkill's madness."

Eliphas didn't say anything. He drove on in silence, staring straight at the road ahead.

"Don't get me wrong," Albrecht said. "Morningkill and I used to be real close. I'm going to miss him, even after all he did to me. Hell, he was my grandfather, and he was damn proud that his grandson was a Garou. It used to be good between us. But he just kept getting more and more paranoid, and I just got cockier and cockier. There's nothing to be done about it now, though. He's dead and that's that."

They drove on in silence. Soon Eliphas pulled onto a side road, and about a mile or two down he pulled off onto a one-lane road. They passed an open gate and Albrecht saw two men in the rear-view mirror watching them as they drove past. They were dressed in black and wore long knives in their belts. Garou guards with klaives.

Albrecht looked ahead and saw the mansion through the trees. Cars were parked to either side of the drive. As they pulled into the cul de sac in front of the house, Albrecht saw that every space was taken.

"No one has left yet," Eliphas said. "From the moot, that is. Everyone is needed for the caern defense."

"Makes sense," Albrecht said, looking about. No others were in sight. "Just let me out here. I'll find my way around. Thanks for the ride."

Eliphas nodded and Albrecht got out of the car. Eliphas turned the car around and drove down the lane looking for a parking space. Albrecht walked around the mansion, staring up at his childhood home.

It had been a long time indeed, he thought, looking at the large house. The two-story, two-wing mansion stood large in his memory, and loomed over him now. It was exactly as he remembered it. Nothing had changed. The maple trees in the yard were older, but that was the only proof that time had passed. Morningkill had not liked change. He certainly made sure that it did not come to his house. At least, judging by the looks of it. But things would certainly change now.

Albrecht walked around the south wing of the house, looking in the windows. Same old rooms with the same old furniture. Classic antiques. No one was inside. He came around to the rear of the house and looked out over the large field.

The first thing to catch his eye was not the group of Garou out on the field, working to cover what looked to be tunnels. Or the empty tents, still standing from the aborted moot. The thing which caught his eye and drew his breath away was the tree. The Grand Oak. A huge, towering mammoth of an oak. And at its base was the throne. The king's throne.

But something was wrong, or rather, something was not exactly right with the throne. Albrecht had not seen it in years, but he knew it well from his youth, and he knew that the bloodstains did not belong. They were alien, intruders in the court. A sign that all was not right with the

90 **WILLIAM BRIDGES**

world. Standing and staring at the dried blood of his grandfather, Albrecht knew that this was going to be harder to deal with than he had thought.

He looked out over the field to the Garou who performed rites by the holes in the ground. *The Black Spiral Dancer tunnels*, thought Albrecht. The Garou were plugging them with dirt and shovels and using the secrets taught them by spirits to add more dirt where necessary. Albrecht figured that more Garou were in the Umbra, the spirit world, likewise using spirits to seal up the rents in their territory. Rites of Cleansing would also be performed, to remove any lingering taint of corruption left by the deformed Garou's passage.

The workers were looking at Albrecht now, some with unreadable expressions, others with looks of anger. One Garou, whose back was to Albrecht, turned to see what they were staring at. He was an older Garou, with black hair going gray and a strong physique. He saw Albrecht and his face broke into a smile. He walked quickly over to Albrecht and embraced him.

"Hello, Greyfist," Albrecht said. "It's been a while."

"Damn. I'd wondered if I'd ever see you again," Greyfist said, looking Albrecht over. "Here you are."

"Yeah. Here I am," Albrecht said, watching the Garou workers, who all stared at him in uncomfortable silence.

Greyfist looked at the workers. "Hurry up! Get those breaches sealed! What are you waiting for? Another attack?" He turned back to Albrecht. "Come on. We can talk in my office."

"Your office? Since when have you had an office?"

"Since Morningkill appointed me Seneschal," Greyfist said, leading Albrecht into the mansion and down a hall.

"You? Good lord! He really was crazy!"

Greyfist smiled and opened a door into a large room filled with wall-to-wall bookcases. "Have a seat," he said, gesturing toward a couch while he walked to a large desk and pulled a pipe from the top drawer.

"No thanks," Albrecht said, walking around the room. "I've been sitting all morning. It's a long drive here."

"Sorry. You're the one who chose to live in New York." Greyfist lit his pipe and sat in a leather chair behind the desk.

"I didn't choose. The Gnawers were the only ones who would have me. You're lucky I didn't move to Alaska or someplace equally remote." Albrecht walked about the office, examining it. He looked at the furnishings and the books along the wall. "Pretty posh place you got here."

"It's just an office, Albrecht. But I am glad you're here. We need you."

"We?" Albrecht said, turning toward Greyfist. "You mean the Fangs? What in the world would you need me for?"

"Cut it out, Albrecht. You know very well that you're next in line to be king."

"Hold on there! What about Arkady? I thought he wanted the job— I sure as hell don't! What are you thinking? The Fangs kick me out and then want me to rule over them? Yeah, that's real likely. You saw those stares out there."

Greyfist leaned over the desk and stared intently at Albrecht. "Don't be an idiot. You're Jacob's grandson. You are the first in line. You are scion of the House of Wyrmfoe, the First Family of the North Country Protectorate. Your line *built* this protectorate, damn it! Your position is the nominal head of the entire North American continent, based on rights of precedence set by your family generations ago when the tribe first came to these lands. All Garou are beholden to the king of North Country."

"Listen to you. You believe this crap! Let me tell you something: there's not a Garou in all of the state of New York who buys that! Morningkill has been a joke for years. Oh, sure, they're supposed to listen up when the Silver Fang king speaks, but since when have they ever done that? And who's going to make them? Morningkill dragged the crown down with him. No one respects it anymore."

"That doesn't mean it can't rise again."

"I don't know if it should."

Greyfist stared at Albrecht. "What do you mean? It's the throne, damn it!"

"I mean maybe it's this damn throne and all the authority that comes with it that's dragging us down!" Albrecht said, raising his arms exasperatedly and pacing about in front of the desk. "You've heard the way the other tribes talk about the Fangs. Well, I get a lot of that where I'm from. 'The Fangs are nuts. They're going to bring us all down with their silly dictates.' Maybe it's time the other tribes lived without the Fangs for a while, 'cause either it'll teach them that they can't live without us or, more likely, that they're right and we really are a bunch of inbred fuck-ups."

Greyfist looked down at his desk, rubbing his pipe between his fingers and thumb, thinking. Then he raised his head and looked at Albrecht again. "You can believe that if you want. Hell, I know most of it's true. But we will never become the leaders we are supposed to be if we don't strive for it. Just because others have failed does not mean we should cease to strive. Too much depends on us. Gaia depends on us. The king is needed."

"Then let Arkady be king," Albrecht said, walking to the bay window and looking out over the field.

"Arkady…Arkady is not fit."

"What do you mean? He's royal, isn't he? That's what Eliphas said. A Crescent Moon, even! You can't get much more royal than that. Besides, he's obviously more purebred than I am. Everyone's always known he had some breeding."

"But I don't trust him, Albrecht. I think he killed Jacob."

Albrecht spun around and stared angrily at Greyfist. "I thought a Black Spiral did it! That's what I was told. What are you saying?"

"Calm down. I can't prove it. And yes, a Black Spiral Dancer is what killed Jacob. But I think Arkady was somehow in on it. That he knew it would happen."

"That's quite an accusation."

"I know. But it's too damn convenient. Garrick is killed, leaving Regina to take over his duties in addition to her own. And she is still wounded from a mission Morningkill sent her on, one that I think Arkady had something to do with arranging. Arkady's pack—the King's Own, for Gaia's sake—arrives late at the moot, too late to prevent the Black Spiral Dancer from killing Jacob. And Arkady's newfound heritage is announced before the king is even buried. Doesn't it all seem too much to you?

Albrecht looked out the window again. "I don't know. Yeah, it sounds real convenient. But I've known odder things to happen. Maybe it's fate. Maybe Arkady is meant to take the throne."

"It was your grandfather's last wish that you be king."

Albrecht was silent for a while, staring out the window, across the field, at the throne. The bloodstained throne. "Vanity. That's all. Just vanity. Morningkill wanted the line to continue when he should have known better. The line is obviously unfit."

Albrecht noticed a woman and a boy walking out onto the field, toward the tents. He turned and walked to the door. "I've got to go. There's someone I haven't seen in a while."

Greyfist looked out the window and then back at Albrecht, who already had the door open. "They don't like you, Albrecht. Your Kin were shamed at your exile, and suffered for it. They blame you."

Albrecht looked at him, the anger in his eyes softening. He then walked out the door and back onto the field.

4

Margot Rothchild looked around the empty tent. The tables and chairs had already been removed, but the tent still stood. *Someone really should take them down*, she thought. *To stand here looking so forlorn, so abandoned…it just isn't right. Not considering what happened to poor Jacob. Someone really should take the tents down, for his sake.*

"Mother, what are they doing out in the field?" Seth said. The ten-year-old boy stood outside the tent, pointing to the Garou rite participants who worked to seal the holes. "They've got those funny sticks with feathers, the ones no one will tell me about. Are they doing magic, mother?"

Margot looked at her son and felt the fear again: the fear which always gripped her whenever he talked about the Garou. She prayed that it was boyish curiosity and nothing more. Just a boy's fascination with the strange. Not an instinctive yearning. *God, please no, not that.*

"Yes, dear," she said, hiding her fear away again. "Don't bother them. They're very busy."

"But what kind of magic, mother?" Seth persisted, his eyes wide with fascination as he watched one of the Garou raise his staff over his head and let loose a low, almost whispering, howl. "It's a ritual, isn't it? Grandfather says that spirits are always near when the Garou do a ritual. Have you ever seen a spirit, mother?"

"Yes. But it wasn't very interesting. It was just a bird. Just like any bird."

"Then how did you know it was a spirit?"

"It spoke to Morningkill and then flew away into the air and disappeared."

"In plain sight? It went to the Umbra, didn't it?"

"I suppose so. Now, let's get back to the car, dear. Your grandfather is expecting us to be there when he is done with his business." Margot reached for Seth's hand, but he tore it away and stepped out onto the field.

"But I want to watch the rite!" he said.

"Seth! Get back here! Don't go too close!"

But Seth was already running toward the Garou. Margot's fear broke free from the little place within her where she hid it. It would hide no longer. "Seth! Please come back!"

Seth turned to look at her and his eyes widened. He stopped running and stared at her in shock. After a moment she realized he was staring past her, behind her. She turned around and gasped.

He was taller than she remembered, and he stood so close she wondered how she hadn't heard him approach. "Jonas! You…you startled me," she stammered out, her eyes falling to the floor, unable to meet his gaze.

"I'm sorry, Margot," Albrecht said. He looked at his cousin, no longer the vivacious girl he'd once known, but a woman in her thirties, premature wrinkles and worry lines clearly visible. Stress had taken its toll on her face and bearing. She stood with shoulders slumped, unable to look him in the face. "How are things? How's the family?"

"They...they're all right. I...." She turned away, back toward Seth. "My son...he...he's run out. He's going to get in the way...."

"He's fine, Margot. There's nothing he can do to disrupt the rites. I'm sure they want him to watch."

"But I don't! I...I mean, I'd rather he not bother them. It's rude."

Albrecht looked out at Seth, who was now standing still, looking back at Albrecht, curiosity on his face. "Has he shown any of the signs? Do they know yet?"

Margot shuddered. "No. They don't know. They say it may be a few years."

"I hope the heritage is true. Gaia knows we need more Garou."

"I've got to go. Warner is waiting—"

"That's right, Margot," a stern voice said from outside the tent, behind them. Albrecht turned around and saw a middle-aged man in a suit standing and staring angrily at him. "I've been waiting by the car. I think you and Seth should go back there right now."

Margot said nothing and left, walking over to Seth, who had come back to the tent and was looking at Albrecht with awe. She grabbed his hand and pulled him around the tent, heading toward the mansion.

"But I want to see Uncle Jonas!" Seth yelled, his eyes still on Albrecht, who smiled back at him.

"Go to the car, Seth!" the stern man snapped, not taking his eyes off Albrecht.

Seth followed behind his mother, but looked back at Albrecht as he moved away.

"Hello, Warner," Albrecht said.

"Don't even bother, exile," Warner said, the disgust in his voice apparent. "I don't know why you're here, but I want you to leave my family alone."

"They're my family, too. Margot was my mother's friend. Her only friend here."

"I don't care about the past. I am concerned with the present, and you are a bad influence on Seth. If he has bred true, you are the last person I want as a role model for him."

"Oh, calm down, Warner," Albrecht said, shaking his head and looking away from the seething statue of a man before him. "You know my exile was politics, nothing more."

"So you say. But I know that you were banned from this protectorate by the king, and I intend to find out exactly why you have returned. I certainly will not allow you to torment my family!"

"I am here," Albrecht said, gritting his teeth, putting a mental cap on his growing anger, "because Morningkill asked it of me with his last breath."

Warner looked at Albrecht as if he didn't believe him. He then lowered his gaze. "I see."

Albrecht walked over to Warner. As he came out of the tent, Warner stepped back, obviously not comfortable standing so close to him.

"I'm sure you're anticipating Seth's Firsting," Albrecht said.

"Yes. If he is Garou."

"That will be a feather in Henry's cap, to sire a Garou. He'll get some respect for that."

Warner turned away, a look of disgust washing over his face. He then wiped his expression clean, replacing it with a stone-faced stare. "Henry is not the father. Joseph Batell is."

Albrecht narrowed his eyes at Warner. "Was this your doing?"

"I had to. You wouldn't understand. You don't give a damn for the family. But we have a responsibility. We must breed Garou, and Henry couldn't produce a child. I had to ensure the family had an heir, so I turned to a Garou. The chances were better of a true breeding."

"You disgust me! You and the whole damn pack of Kin families. Look what you've done to Margot! She used to be strong, and proud. But this? Forced to lie with a strange Garou just so she can breed a pup? And how is Henry dealing with this? He's probably a self-pitying wreck, if I know him."

"None of this is any of your business!" Warner said, his face now a mask of rage. "You can't possibly understand the pressures on us!"

Another voice broke in, from off to Albrecht's left, toward the mansion. "Of course he can't! He doesn't understand honor and responsibility. Too damn proud. That's why he got what he deserved and was kicked out!"

Albrecht turned to see an older man working his way toward them, leaning heavily on a cane. It was obvious he was having a hard time of it, but his anger was moving him forward.

"Father!" Warner said, stepping up to the old man and helping him to stand. "You were supposed to be in the car!"

"Margot said he was here. I had to see it for myself. Couldn't believe it. Come back again, huh?"

"I don't want to argue with you, Sutter," Albrecht said. "I'm just here for a short visit."

"Hah! You think you're going to get the crown, don't you? You! A low-bred mongrel! That damn mother of yours—I told her to stay away from my son. But he just had to get mixed up with her! It was a surprise to all of us that she was able to squeeze out a Garou. But when it grew up to be you, I knew I had been right all along. Damn scullery maid!"

"Father!" Warner said, shocked at the incivility of the old man. "That's enough. She was his mother, for god's sake."

Albrecht knew Warner wasn't shushing Sutter out of respect for his mother. He could see the fear in the man's face: fear from looking at Albrecht's expression, from sensing the growing anger and the impending loss of control that was a trait of the Garou. No, Warner quieted his father out of fear for their safety.

Albrecht was angry, but he could control the raging within him. This was exactly what he'd expected of Sutter. The old man was his human grandfather, the patriarch of the Albrecht line. The Albrechts were a highly regarded line of Silver Fang Kinfolk whose history with the Garou tribe stretched back to England, and to Holland before that. As such, Sutter was rabidly antagonistic to anyone who stained that line, as Albrecht had done when he was exiled. Jacob Morningkill was Sutter's father, but since Sutter had not bred true—had not been a full Garou—he was a second-class son to the king. When Sutter's son, James, had born a Garou son—Lord Albrecht himself—Morningkill was considered the boy's Garou grandfather, even though he was technically the great-grandfather. Since Sutter's son James had not been Garou himself, Sutter was doomed to be a mere footnote in the Silver Fang annals, a simple genetic bridge between Garou generations.

And he hated it. But instead of attacking the system, he defended it with all his might, living up to his role in society to an extreme degree. And he had handed these traits to his favored son, Warner, Albrecht's uncle.

"How is my father?" Albrecht asked Warner.

Warner looked down, unable to meet Albrecht's eyes. "The same. A damn fool still possessed by the bottle. He can't get over your mother's death. Fifteen years of misery he's given himself."

"And over what?" Sutter cried. "A girl he had no business with in the first place. She wasn't well-bred by any remote definition of the term!"

"Will you shut up about my mother?" Albrecht said, teeth gritted. He felt the chaotic stirring within his gut, the roiling that warned of a coming frenzy. But he shut his eyes and stilled himself. After all, these were just the bitter ramblings of an old fool.

Sutter looked at him suddenly, worried, and was quiet.

"We must be going, father," Warner said, moving toward the mansion, pulling his father along with him. But Sutter seemed to find his courage again and stopped, staring with eyes narrowed at Albrecht.

"Thank Gaia Arkady is royal! The thought of you on the throne sickens me! Arkady is a real Silver Fang. He is everything we hold high. Not like you. Look at you! A damn tramp. Can't even dress properly to come to your king's court."

"That's about all I'm going to take out of you!" Albrecht yelled, his voice rising. "You want Arkady on the throne instead of me? Tough! That's my right! My crown to wear! You know something? I didn't want the damn job, and I still don't. But if it'll piss you off, then I am sure as hell going to sit on that seat. And you're going to kowtow to me like nobody's ever seen! Or else you're outta here! Kinfolk can be banished too, you know."

Sutter looked as if he were choking on a large rock. His face was scrunched up in rage, red and growing redder by the second. He finally managed to open his tension-bound jaws wide enough to say, "You wouldn't dare! You can't be king! You're not half as royal as Arkady!"

Albrecht stared in utter contempt at Sutter. "Oh? Watch me. You are about to see the fight of a lifetime, old man."

Warner, pale and fearful for his father's health, led the old man away. Sutter continued to stare at Albrecht, unable to speak out of sheer anger. His eyes in from their sockets like windows into a furnace, but a furnace he was unable to control or cool down enough even to communicate. He hobbled off like that, aided by his son, and soon disappeared around the corner.

Albrecht shook his head. *What have I done now? I don't want the damn crown. Sure, I want to piss that old fart off big, but I don't want to be king just for that. Well, it doesn't matter; it's not like I've announced it before the court. I can always back out.*

He started back toward Greyfist's office but stopped when he noticed that the Garou workers were no longer engaged in their rite. Rather, they were all staring at him. Some with looks of confusion, some with uncertainty and some with disgust and hatred. But some were looking at him with...with pride. And approval. Some of them were nodding at him.

Oh, holy Luna! He was in for it now. Practically the entire court *had* heard him. His declaration was official. The only way out now was to crawl home in even more shame than he had arrived in.

Albrecht gritted his teeth and growled low. He'd be damned if that'd be the case.

5

Greyfist kicked the dirt hard. He nodded, satisfied. It was well packed. The hole was sealed up. It would take a bulldozer to open it again.

He walked across the field to investigate the other two holes. It was hard to believe the Black Spirals had done what they had. Tunneling under the caern for weeks, he estimated. And no one had known. That said terrible things about their alertness. But who would have believed they would come so close, would dare such a feat? And through sheer bedrock, at that! The soil was only eight feet deep here; they had tunneled ten feet under, through solid rock, and then come upwards to break through the soil in the caern field. *It's a wonder they didn't come up under the throne. But then Barktooth, the Shaman of the Lodge of the Moon, said that the Grand Oak's roots were deep and thick enough to prevent that. The Black Spirals couldn't have gotten any closer if they had wanted to.*

Greyfist kicked the dirt around the next hole and found it was as well-packed as the first. He did the same for the third hole and was satisfied there also. He nodded to Regina and headed back to the mansion. Behind him, he heard Regina tell her protectors to get about their duties. They had been pulled from their normal posts this morning to seal the holes, and the outer defenses now needed tending to. Soon, Greyfist would once again feel confident about the caern and bawn defenses. If nothing else, the attack had finally woken up the Silver Fangs and made them realize they were in a war. A war not only for Gaia, but for their own protection.

He heard the Garou talking as they headed off for their posts. The word had traveled quickly and was on the lips of every Silver Fang and Kinfolk in the protectorate: Lord Albrecht was to take his grandfather's place as king. Greyfist smiled. He didn't much care for the Albrechts and the Rothchilds, but they had succeeded where his idealism couldn't. Albrecht was now going to do his duty, and the relief Greyfist had felt when Albrecht yelled his intent for all to hear was greater than any he'd felt in a long while.

Albrecht was the one for the job; of this Greyfist was confident. Albrecht's own sense of self-worth had been worn down over the last few years, but Greyfist felt that was an asset. At least he possessed some humility—a quality lacking among most of the tribe members here. Oh, it would take a while to convince Albrecht that there really was no one better to rule than he, but Greyfist wasn't concerned about that. Detail, details; that's all that was. It was Arkady he was worried about.

The high-bred Garou posed a threat to Albrecht's ascension. Greyfist feared he really did have a claim to the throne, even though Albrecht was clearly next in line. Pure breeding was a wild card in Garou politics, and allowed the high-born to break many rules. Well, it would be decided soon enough.

As he passed by the throne, Greyfist saw the preparations already beginning for the meeting of the courts. In two hours, the Lodges of the Sun and Moon would gather and argue over the tricky issue of ascension to the crown. Ancient records would be consulted and debated, and after a few hours, the Lodges would come to a decision on just who was eligible to rule the Fangs. The problem was that many of the tribal records had been destroyed. Morningkill, in one of his paranoid fits, had set fire to the library a few months ago, and many documents had been lost before the flames were put out. Many more books had been ruined by the water used to douse the fire.

Of course, all of this precedence nonsense was hardly a problem for the other tribes, who each had their own rules for determining leadership. The Get of Fenris's leaders ruled by might: only those who could successfully defeat them in challenge combat could take their place. The Bone Gnawers valued the eldest among them, or those who had collected the most junk. The Children of Gaia chose the most diplomatic among them—at least, so Greyfist had been told.

But the Silver Fangs, overly concerned with blood precedence and membership in one of the Seven Royal Families, had to nit-pick their way to the crown.

Greyfist entered the mansion and climbed the broad staircase to the second floor. He turned down the north wing and walked to the last door on the left. After a pause, he knocked loudly. When there was no answer, he knocked again. After another pause, he opened the door and walked in.

Albrecht was sprawled across a giant four-poster bed, groggily opening his eyes and looking confusedly at Greyfist. "Uhhhh…wha…what time is it?"

Greyfist walked over to the window and threw back the heavy drapes, flooding the room with sunlight. Albrecht let out a yell as if he'd been hit by a baseball bat. He covered his face with his arm and tried to pull the covers over him. But Greyfist grabbed the blanket and yanked it off the bed.

"Oh, no. You're getting up. Now," he said. A long groan was the only answer from Albrecht. "Your presence is requested at court today. The Lodges will decide on the issue of ascendancy. As you are now a contestant for the throne, you really should attend."

"Do I have to?" Albrecht said in a moan which only happened to sound like words.

"No. But I recommend that you do. If not, those at court who disapprove of you may find a way to deny your claim."

"What's wrong with that?" Albrecht said, sitting up and rubbing his eyes. "That's exactly what I want. I don't want to be king."

"Then why did you scream that you did to everyone in listening range?"

"I was angry. I meant to take it back, but great Gaia, it's now an issue of honor. And I'll be damned if Arkady's going to come out of this shining purer than me."

"So?"

"So if the court says I can't be king, then I can't. It's got nothing to do with honor at that point."

"You think that, when they declare you unable to take your grandfather's place, people won't know exactly why? If you don't stand up and fight for your right at court, everyone will know you're just a blowhard coward. It's easy to claim the kingship, but much harder actually to get it."

Albrecht looked at Greyfist with a surly, smoldering expression. "Thank you, sir. May I have another?"

"Joke all you want. But get up anyway. Come to court. Do it for me, Albrecht, if for no one else."

Albrecht looked away and covered his face in his hands, leaning on his knees. "Okay."

"Okay?"

"Okay! Okay already! Just get out of here. I'll meet you at court."

Greyfist smiled and left the room, closing the door behind him.

A howl resounded throughout the caern. Guards at the edge of the bawn stopped their tasks and looked back toward the field. Even those out of view of the caern center could not help being drawn to the source of the howl. They all controlled the urge, the instinct, to answer the call, to pick up the howl with one of their own. This summons wasn't theirs to answer. The call went out to the aspirants to the throne, the Garou who sought the kingship of the North Country Protectorate. And all the Silver Fangs knew that there were only two who were bold—or crazy—enough to try for that position. All of them waited quietly, some holding their breath to hear better; waiting for the answering howls.

There—there was one from far off, outside the bawn, off to the east. Even distance could not hide its rich, deep-throated character.

Arkady. The leader of the King's Own Pack was far from the caern, which meant he would not be coming to court, but he answered the howl anyway. Although surprised by his absence, many Silver Fangs nodded as they heard, proud that, even away from the caern, Arkady would do his duty.

Then another howl, this one closer. Louder, even considering the closer proximity. Not as deep, but angrier, a growling, rage-ridden howl. The howl of Lord Albrecht. The Silver Fangs nodded again, this time more reserved, doubtful. Albrecht had been gone from the caern for a long time, and some were unsure whether they wanted him back. But no one could deny that his howl had been good, had rivaled Arkady's. No matter, though. It was just a howl. Wait for the challenge, they told themselves. The challenge would answer the question: Who would be king?

Eldest Claw, Shamaness of the Lodge of the Sun and Master of the Rite for the North Country Caern, sat down again, taking in a deep breath to recover from her howl. It had been a loud, long howl, as was necessary to summon the claimants. She waited to hear the answering cries. There was Arkady's, from off to the east. Eldest Claw frowned. The distance meant that Arkady would not be at court today. Was this arrogance? Did he not consider it important enough to come?

Then came Albrecht's answer, from much closer, over by the mansion. Eldest Claw's eyebrows rose. A good, hearty howl. Perhaps this cub was more qualified than the old lupus had thought.

She nodded to Barktooth, sitting across the circle from her. The lupus nodded back. They could now get down to business. She looked at Thomas Abbot, to her right, and nodded. The Steward of the Lodge of the Sun stood up and began the recitation.

"Hear ye, all in attendance and Silver Fangs of the court wherever ye be: the Court of the North Country Caern is hereby begun. Absent is our king, the late Jacob Morningkill. Hence, our business this day is the matter of the vacant throne. Two claimants have answered the Howl of Precedence. One, Lord Albrecht, grandchild of Jacob Morningkill and scion of the House of Wyrmfoe, the First Family of the North Country Protectorate. Two, Arkady, scion of the Clan of the Crescent Moon and purest of blood. We are to consider: which of the two claims is greatest? Which of the two shall inherit the throne?

"Ruling the court this day, as the matter of worldly leadership is determined, is the Lodge of the Sun. Leader of the Lodge and eldest among us is Eldest Claw, Shamaness of the Lodge. The court is begun...."

Abbot sat down, and all nodded their approval. Eldest Claw looked about the court. They were gathered in a circle at the foot of the Grand Oak, at the base of the empty throne. The sun shone down upon them; a good sign, considering the precedence of Lodge at today's court. If it had been cloudy, a gloomy fate would have been predicted. It was the Lodge of the Sun's position in court to decide on worldly matters, as opposed to the more spiritual concerns of the Lodge of the Moon. This was why the moot was taking place during the day.

On one side of the circle sat Eldest Claw's Lodge: herself, Abbot and Mountain Runner, the Squire of the Lodge. Across from them sat the Lodge of the Moon: Barktooth, the Shaman; Shining Outward, the Steward; and Eliphas Standish, the new Squire and Gatekeeper.

Gathered about them, as witnesses to the court, were Greyfist, the Seneschal; Regina, Caern Warder; and other, lower-rank Garou such as Pale Sire, the leader of a small Silver Fang pack which often roamed northern Vermont, away from the caern and away from politics. Also gathered were members of the Kinfolk families: Warren Albrecht, Desmond Rothchild, Cynthia Batell and a few from lesser families.

Eldest Claw sighed. This would be a long moot. She hoped they could finish at a decent time so they could all prepare for Morningkill's funeral that night. She looked up at Barktooth and began. "The debate shall begin with Arkady. What is his claim?"

"He is scion of the Crescent Moon!" Shining Outward said, standing and looking at all gathered. "Is that not enough?"

"No, it is not," Abbot said, also standing. "The Crescent Moon is not the First Family here. That honor belongs to the House of Wyrmfoe. Arkady is thus not eligible."

"But he has the purest blood of any among us," Barktooth said. "He is a Duke, the only representative of the Second Family. With his breeding, he is more than eligible."

And so the arguing went....

Greyfist shook his head. So much red tape! A sense of security and tradition was important, yes. But to drown in rituals and little laws such as those they argued here—it was too much. It was a sign that the Silver Fangs had lost touch with their primal, more flexible nature. What needed to be resurrected in the Fangs was the lost touch of the Wyld.

All the talk of the Seven Royal Families sometimes made his head swim. What a bog of lineage! It was a hobby of just about every Silver Fang to be able to trace the intricacies of his or her lineage down to the last Kinfolk as far back in time as possible. Some Silver Fangs could keep track better than others, either through good record-keeping or the active participation of their ancestors' spirits. The families that had the strongest hold on tradition and breeding were known as the Seven, for these were the seven families whose Garou blood was considered strong enough to rule a protectorate.

Legends said that there were once thirteen families, but six of them had been lost over time. Elaborate stories were told about the doom of certain royal families.

It was said that the thirteenth family, whose name no one remembered, came to an end in the War of Rage—the ancient war they had called and waged against the other werecreatures of the world. Successive births over the years following the war were never able to revive the line, and it eventually ceased to be.

The twelfth had been largely of lupus stock: those Garou who are born to wolves. It was said that this line had died out over time due to lack of proper breeding partners. Their name was also lost.

The eleventh family, the Conquering Claw, died due to massive infighting. A well-told epic about their fate served as both a marker to their glory and a morality tale against fighting amongst family members. Although a member of this lineage had been known to be born once in an age or so, thanks to the recessive Garou gene, none had owned a protectorate within historical memory.

The tenth family was not spoken of, and their name had been stricken from the tribal records. They had gone to the Wyrm. Those born of this blood were either killed by their Silver Fang parents or stolen by Black Spiral Dancers before the parents could act out their duty.

The ninth family, the Winter Snow, had seemed to be ominously named once their doom became clear: the entire family had succumbed to Harano, the great depression which few Garou could throw off once trapped within its gloomy embrace. Any new births of this lineage also succumbed to the curse. The source of their fate was a mystery to the tribe.

The eighth family was the most mysterious of all, however. Known as the Golden Sky, the entire family had disappeared in the Middle Ages and was never seen again. No new cubs had been born to this lineage since that time. Most Garou believed that the family went into the Umbra.

The seventh family was the Clan of the Crescent Moon, the premiere family among Silver Fangs; for they controlled the legendary Caern of the Crescent Moon in the Russian Urals, rumored to be the first caern created by the Garou back in the dawn of time. This was Arkady's family.

The sixth family was the House of Wyrmfoe, Albrecht's line and the founding family of the North America protectorate. They were the first Silver Fangs to create a caern in the New World, and had ruled over the entire continent since then, although almost no one outside the tribe still upheld this claim.

Of the other families, the Austere Howl was strong in Britain; the Wise Heart ruled in the Mediterranean and parts of the Middle East; the Blood-Red Crest held a protectorate in Asia; the Unbreakable Hearth could be found in various regions, but especially in the American mid-west; and the Gleaming Eye was powerful in Europe.

Each of these families favored flocks of Kinfolk with whom they preferred to breed, ostensibly to keep the lines pure. For the House of Wyrmfoe, this included the Albrechts.

Greyfist turned his attention to the court again and listened for a while. They were wrapping up their discussion of Arkady, and their decision seemed to be exactly what Greyfist had known it would be: Arkady, due to his breeding, was eligible for the kingship.

Greyfist looked around him. Where the hell was Albrecht? They would discuss him next, and he really should be here to defend his name if they tried to besmirch it, which he knew they would.

"Is he coming?" Regina asked, leaning over from her place to his right. She still nursed her arm, the one that had been severed two days earlier by Morningkill's assailant. It was reattached to her shoulder, but it would be a while before she could again use it fully.

"He's supposed to," Greyfist said, looking around the field. "He damn well better, or he'll find *me* challenging him instead of Arkady!"

Regina looked over toward the mansion. "Well, he needn't worry about that. There he is."

Greyfist followed her gaze and saw Albrecht slowly wandering his way over to the circle. He had a cigarette in his mouth and appeared to be enjoying it. Greyfist meet his eyes and glared at him. Albrecht took a long drag on his cigarette, threw the stub on the ground and stomped on it. Smiling, he shrugged his shoulders at Greyfist. He walked over to sit next to Greyfist.

"How goes it?" Albrecht said. "Can I be king yet?"

"They're just getting to you now," Greyfist said. "Arkady, by the way, is eligible. So, if they decide in your favor, you'll have to fight him."

Albrecht pulled out a pack of cigarettes. "So I figured. So everybody figured. Hell, they're looking forward to it here like it's bigger than a Foreman versus Tyson match. Maybe Arkady'll chicken out and disappoint them."

"Ha! Don't count on it. Seriously, though, you should worry. He's damn good."

Albrecht looked at Greyfist, smiling and shaking his head as if he couldn't believe what his friend had just said. He pulled out a cigarette and lighter and lit up. "Yeah. So? I'm better."

"Look, you haven't seen Arkady in three years. You have no idea what he's learned in that time."

Albrecht took a long drag on his cigarette, putting the lighter away. He then breathed the smoke out. "He hasn't seen me, either. I've been in New York. He's been here. So maybe he's knocked off a couple of Black Spiral Dancers and maybe some Bane-possessed deer. I've fought fucking Sabbat vampires. Now who are you going to bet on?"

"I think the odds on that bet are closer than you think. Did you know he killed a Nexus Crawler last year? Not by himself, of course. The King's Own Pack was there to help, but he led the battle and took very few wounds."

Albrecht frowned. "He did, huh? Hmpf. How'd his pack fare, though? I bet he let them get cut up while he coached from the sidelines."

"It's true that they took more wounds, but the tale they tell is that he threw just as many blows as they, and that his all connected and cut deep."

"Ahh, they're just talking. Trying to beef up their pack leader."

"You're an arrogant ass, you know that? When will you concede that he may be your equal in combat, if not your better?"

Albrecht shook his head. "Yeah, right. You don't win battles by thinking your opponents are better than you. You win by being better than them, and knowing it."

Greyfist sighed and turned back to the court. They were talking about Albrecht now. Barktooth was arguing against him, since Albrecht was, after all, an exile. Abbot stood up for him, letting it be known that Morningkill had rescinded the banishment with his dying breath. Greyfist looked at Albrecht, who seemed oblivious to all this talk about him, although it was clear he was listening.

"So his exile is over?" Barktooth said. "What does that matter? He's obviously unfit for the throne! Look at him!" Barktooth gestured with his snout toward Albrecht, and all eyes fell on him. Albrecht simply puffed on his cigarette. "Does he look like a Silver Fang to you? The evidence is in his breeding. His mother was low-born."

Albrecht frowned.

"But his Garou blood is royal," Abbot cut in. "That is all that matters."

"I disagree," Barktooth continued. "Breeding is everything to the Fangs. We are not mongrels like the other tribes. Gaia ordained that we would carry the blood of the first Garou with us until the end. From the Dawn to Apocalypse, we shall remain pure. Letting Albrecht, the son of a low-born human woman, take the throne is to ignore Gaia's will."

"I don't know what kind of brick got stuck up your ass," Albrecht said, standing up. "But I am the grandchild of Jacob Morningkill, your king up until two days ago. Is your memory so short? I've got enough royal blood to stain your fur. And I am sick of hearing everyone here dis my mother. She was a damn fine woman. She may not have been a member of one of our dysfunctional Kin families, but that's a virtue in my book."

Barktooth looked coldly back at Albrecht. "My memory is not short. It's long enough to remember your exile, called for by your own grandfather."

Albrecht stepped forward, staring hard into Barktooth's eyes. "Yeah? Well he ended it, in case you didn't hear Abbot over there. If you've got a problem with that, maybe you and I should work it out here and now."

Eldest Claw stood up and shouted, "Enough! Sit down, Albrecht. This is not the place for unfettered anger. Sit down, I said."

Albrecht looked at the elder, then walked back to take his seat. Greyfist put a hand on his shoulder, but Albrecht ignored it.

Rather than staring with anger at Albrecht, Barktooth smiled. Albrecht had won the respect of the lupus, as Greyfist had known he would. That's why he had wanted Albrecht here. The lupus did not judge people the way a homid did. Blood was important to him, but so was rage and the ability to respond to an insult. He judged people who stood flesh-and-blood before him, not simply the rumors and tales about a person. By losing his temper, Albrecht had managed to convince the holdout of the court, the last one to resist Albrecht's claim.

"I say that Albrecht has proven himself strong enough to bear the crown," Barktooth said, sitting down. His debating opponent, Abbot, seemed surprised. After a confused moment, he also sat down.

Eldest Claw looked about. "Is there any other who disagrees?" When no one answered, she said. "Then it is done. Albrecht is worthy. Albrecht and Arkady are the claimants to the throne." She let out a howl, similar to her earlier cry, but longer and quieter. The Howl of Confirmed Precedence.

She then got up on all fours and walked off. The other court members also stood up and walked away, some in Lupus form, others in Homid.

The court witnesses stood and departed, although Warner Albrecht gave his nephew a scowl before leaving.

"Is that it?" Albrecht said. "What now?"

"The challenge," Regina said, standing up and rubbing her arm absently.

"The fight. So, when does it happen? I'm itching to get it over with."

"As soon as you challenge Arkady," said Greyfist, standing up and stretching. He took a few steps into the circle.

"Me? I have to challenge him?" Albrecht said, standing up now himself.

"More likely he'll challenge you." Greyfist turned to look at Albrecht.

"When do you figure that'll be?" Albrecht said, reaching for another cigarette.

"Tonight. During your grandfather's funeral," Greyfist said.

6

The crescent moon haunted the night. The pale white birches stole its bare sliver of light, gleaming bright in the night while the rest of the landscape disappeared into black darkness. Except on one hill, removed from the Morningkill mansion, where torches burned. They were placed on poles every few yards, leading up a small path to the crest of the hill. Their red and orange flames danced at the top of the poles, throwing the shadows of the mourners marching up the hill into a chaotic frenzy.

At the top of the hill were Lord Albrecht, Greyfist, Regina and Shining Outward. They watched as the line made its way toward them, led by Eldest Claw, who loped forward in Lupus form. She was immediately followed by the King's Own Pack, who bore the body of King Jacob Morningkill wrapped in its ceremonial raiment. All of the Pack were in Homid form, including Arkady. Behind them were the rest of the Garou of the protectorate, and finally the Kinfolk families.

Albrecht looked about as he waited for the mourners to reach them. Trees, rocks, grass and dirt were all around him. *This is what any human might see if he stumbled onto this isolated hill.* But Albrecht saw it differently, as any Silver Fang would. The odd scratching on that tree was a marker, a pictogram carved there to declare who was buried beneath it: Henry "Woundgiver" Standish. That rock covered the grave of Lord Batell, the "Eye of Gaia," as was made clear by the wolf paw and circle pattern depressed into it. The mound of dirt he was standing next to was a fresher grave. The small rocks scattered about its edges marked it, and declared that Gregory Breaking Heart lay here. A member of Arkady's pack, killed in service to the king a year ago. Albrecht wondered if it was the Nexus Crawler that had brought him down. The cemetery, known as the Grave of Hallowed Heroes, was even more obvious in the spirit world, where the markers could not be missed and were often guarded by spirits.

Eldest Claw came over the rise; the mourners had arrived. They quickly spread out to take their places in the small clearing while the King's Own Pack marched forward to the hole. The bearers paused over it, and then lowered the king's body into the earth.

Albrecht watched Morningkill disappear into the ground. It was hard to believe the old man was finally gone. He had been seventy-five years old, long-lived for a Garou. Garou could certainly live longer, with their advanced healing abilities, but they usually died in battle before then. It wasn't that Morningkill hadn't been able to fight—hell, when he was young, no Garou on the east coast, perhaps the entire continent, could have bested him. So it was said, at least. Albrecht believed it. He had the scar to prove it.

He had been only one year into his Firsting, and fresh from his Rite of Passage, when he had gotten into a heated argument with his grandfather. Being new to his powers, Albrecht had believed he was the toughest thing to walk the earth. Morningkill had proved him wrong, but it had taken a scar to convince Albrecht of it. It was still there, a deep claw mark on his left shoulder. It even hurt sometimes, when it rained heavily.

Damn it, though, he was going to miss the old king. His scar was a mark of humility, a lesson Morningkill had meant him to learn for his own survival. Regardless of all the years and the enmity that had passed between them, Albrecht couldn't hold a grudge against this man. He had been the ideal at which Albrecht had long aimed. But that goal was as dead as the man.

The King's Own Pack moved aside from the grave to let the line of mourners pass by. They moved behind Albrecht, and he watched them as they passed. They were pretty tough-looking all right. Even that Ragabash— what was his name? Peter—looked like a bruiser. But Arkady looked meaner than all of them. The Garou did not look at him as he passed, but Albrecht paid attention to the way he walked. Confident, supple. This was a werewolf whose economy of movement showed he knew his body well. His stance was ready to assume a battle pose at an instant. Albrecht knew this because he had once tried to cultivate those moves himself. But it wasn't his style.

Albrecht turned back to the grave and watched the mourners. They all looked genuinely grief-stricken. Most of them were old enough to remember

Morningkill in better times, before the king had become…eccentric. He saw Garou whom he hadn't seen in years, and a few Garou from far protectorates, come to pay respect to the dead king.

But Albrecht noticed that Loba Carcassone was not among them: her exile had not yet ended. He would have to do something about that when he became king. He also wondered about poor Alphonse Grayling and Justin Beauchamp, the Silver Fang exiles who had attacked him and whom he had been forced to kill. The mystery of why they had attacked him was still not solved. But their bodies had not come back to the protectorate with him and Eliphas. They had been exiles, and thus were denied a proper burial among their fellow tribe members. Albrecht felt a pang of guilt. If he'd been able to control his rage, they might be alive today. He was sure their attack had been just a misunderstanding of some sort. Of course, if he hadn't frenzied, maybe *he* wouldn't be alive today.

The Garou had all gone past, winding their way back down the hill. The Kinfolk families were coming through now. There was Sutter, followed by Warner. They threw dirt on Morningkill's grave and walked on, not looking at Albrecht. Behind them was Warner's wife Daphne and her two daughters, the haughty and ugly Lenore and the quiet Margot, who pulled Seth along behind her. Margot looked at Albrecht but then looked away, nervous and shamefaced. Seth stared at him, though, obviously proud to have Albrecht as his uncle.

Albrecht shook his head. The kid really had no clue, did he? Albrecht was no role model to follow. Well, it didn't matter. If he didn't get the crown for some reason, he wouldn't be sticking around anyway.

James Albrecht walked up to the grave alone. He looked down sadly and threw a handful of dirt into the grave. Then he looked up at his son. Albrecht felt his throat tighten. The man looked terrible. He was only in his late forties, but years on the bottle had aged him badly. His eyes bore right into Albrecht's, swimming with tears, a look of pain and loneliness on his face. Albrecht looked away.

After all these years, he thought he had finally forgiven his father for being weak, for not being man enough to stand up to his own father and brother, for not defending his wife or son to them. Albrecht had borne great resentment for the man. He had grown up humiliated, called "low-born" and "mongrel" by other boys of the protectorate, most of whom had not bred true as Albrecht had. But their words had stung him nonetheless. He had thought the pain of the past was gone, but all the hate and anger came back as he saw his father here in the flesh again.

James Albrecht lowered his head and moved down the hill. Albrecht fought to keep from stepping forward, from calling out to his father to give the man some sort of word or sign that his son cared. His anger—no, his pride—was too great for that. He could forgive Morningkill, who had banished him from home, but he could not go to his father. The pain of that broken pride was greater than exile. He looked away from the gathering, trying to hide his self-loathing at his failure to forgive.

After the Rothchilds and the Batells and the other families had passed, the King's Own Pack came forward again. They carried shovels and began to throw heaps of dirt into the grave, onto Morningkill. Albrecht wanted to leave. He had to get out of there. But tradition demanded he stay. He was the closest family; he had to stay until the end.

He must have begun fidgeting or something, because Greyfist looked over at him and gave him a frown. He looked back at the Seneschal and shrugged his shoulders. *Man,* he thought, *what I would do for a cigarette now.*

The pack worked quickly, though, and soon enough the grave was covered and the dirt packed. Albrecht noticed that some of them had shifted into Glabro form—the near-human form—to work faster with the added strength. Shining Outward and Regina stepped forward, carrying a marble headstone between them. It was sheer vanity to use such a thing, and it would do nothing to hide the graveyard from humans, but Morningkill had insisted on a headstone for his grave.

They placed it on the ground and drove it in with their bare hands, shifting to Crinos form for the brute strength required. When it was solidly placed, they shifted back to Homid and stepped away, looking at Albrecht. He sighed and walked forward. Stopping at the foot of the grave, he looked down.

Well, he thought, *this is for you, Granddad. I hope you like it, wherever you are.*

He shifted into Crinos form, his bulk and height increasing greatly. He drew in a deep breath, held it for a moment, and then let out a long, mournful howl. He was joined by the others, who had shifted to Crinos or Lupus, and they all hung their heads back to the sky, crying out their sorrow to Gaia. Albrecht carried the howl for minutes and minutes as others dropped out, unable to continue. Finally, only one other was left howling with him: Arkady.

Albrecht frowned and a note of anger crept into the howl. Arkady was trying to make a contest out of this, when he knew that it was Albrecht's right to begin and end the Dirge for the Fallen. He felt his anger rise as Arkady also matched the growling note Albrecht had introduced. Now he was mocking him. Albrecht turned to look at Arkady, and saw that the wolf had been watching him all along, a smirk in his eyes. Albrecht's howl became a growl which choked off out of anger and frustration. But Arkady carried the original howl on for a few more seconds.

This was too much! That Arkady would dare such an insult here, at the funeral rites of his grandfather! Albrecht couldn't have cared less about Arkady's aspirations to the throne before, but this was personal now!

He marched forward on all fours in Crinos form. Arkady was already in Lupus. He matched the wolf's gaze and stared, growling deep and low, waiting for Arkady to back down. But the wolf stepped forward, staring up intently into Albrecht's eyes. It was now a contest to see who would break first, who would look away or who would lose control to rage.

Albrecht's vision narrowed. Only Arkady existed for him now. His vision grew red as his anger rose, a roiling furnace of molten bile in his gut. He longed to leap forward and throat the damned bastard before him, the wolf who met his gaze and did not flinch. Indeed, whose eyes bore deeply into Albrecht's, searching for some sign of weakness, some breaking point.

And then Arkady said one thing, all the while his gaze never wavering. One word spoken in the Garou tongue: "Charach."

Albrecht roared and leapt forward, faster than even Arkady had anticipated. The wolf tried to step aside, but Albrecht's fangs snapped shut on his right rear leg, causing him to howl in pain. He lunged at Albrecht, burying his snout into Albrecht's shoulder. But Albrecht was consumed with rage and ignored it, savagely chewing Arkady's leg. The wolf shifted into Hispo form—the prehistoric dire-wolf form—and then straight to Homid. In the second in which Albrecht's fangs opened wide to accommodate the larger leg and, before they could crash down again on the smaller human leg, Arkady pulled free.

Albrecht howled in anger and ran at Arkady, but was hit from the side and thrown a few feet away. This confused him for a moment. He smelled someone other than Arkady standing over him—Regina, the Caern Warder. Her face hovered over his, growling low and threateningly. Albrecht didn't know what was going on now. He had no desire to fight Regina, and so he bowed his head and shut up. When she saw his submissive gesture, she stepped back.

Albrecht looked up and saw that Shining Outward stood over Arkady, likewise cowing the Garou into submission. It was not hard; Arkady was obviously hurting badly and was only too glad to give up.

Albrecht stood up, shifting to Homid form, and began dusting himself off. "What's the deal? Why'd you stop me? That bastard insulted me! Here, at Morningkill's funeral!"

"That's exactly why we stopped you two," Regina said. "How dare you challenge over Morningkill's grave! Such a disrespect for the dead! I am appalled."

"I started nothing!" Arkady said, now standing in Homid form and limping over to his pack. His leg was badly mauled, but one of his pack members bent down and began to call on a Gift to mend it. "You saw it! This mad one attacked me!"

"Shut up, Arkady!" Greyfist said. "You know very well that you provoked it. I consider it a challenge."

"Ah, but Seneschal, I am Master of the Challenge at this caern. It is I who decides what is a challenge and what is not."

"Not in this case," Regina said. "Since you are a claimant to the throne, you cannot act in your normal caern position until the claim is resolved. Another must be declared Master of the Challenge in your place."

"Since you are the Caern Warder," Greyfist said to Regina, "doesn't the position fall to you?"

"I believe that is the standard etiquette," Shining Outward said, dusting the dirt that had been kicked up by the fight off the headstone.

"Well, then?" Greyfist said to Regina. "Is Arkady considered to have challenged Albrecht for the throne?"

"Ha!" Arkady said. "I did no such thing! I simply carried the howl longer than his weak lungs could."

"You asshole!" Albrecht said. "That wasn't your right! It was my right to end the howl. You stepped on my territory!"

"Albrecht's correct," Regina said, looking at Arkady. "You disrupted his grandfather's death rites. As a member of House Wyrmfoe, it was Albrecht's duty to lead the howl, but you took it over. I consider that a challenge."

"Pah!" Arkady said. "How silly. It does not matter, though. It was only a matter of time until he challenged me."

"Yeah," Albrecht said. "But *you* challenged *me*, so I have choice of weapons."

Arkady glared at him angrily. "So? What do you choose?"

"Klaives."

"Then I will carve you from chest to groin and hang your pelt on this tree!" Arkady said, pointing at a nearby birch.

"Hold on there," Regina said. "I haven't set the time or place yet. I decree that it will be tomorrow night before the Grand Oak. Be there by midnight, or forfeit your claim."

Arkady nodded and gave Albrecht a sneer. He then walked off, his leg now fully healed thanks to his packmate's magic. The King's Own Pack fell in behind him, and they soon disappeared over the ridge of the hill.

"King's Own Pack, huh?" Albrecht said. "We'll see whose pack they are once I'm king."

"Your temper is as bad as it's always been," Greyfist said, walking past Albrecht.

"Hey!" Albrecht said, following him. "You saw that. He provoked me. And why'd you break it up? I almost had him."

"You weren't close, Albrecht," Greyfist said. "It was clear that as soon as he got over his surprise, he would have won by out-thinking you. The way he slipped from your grip showed that."

"He got lucky on that one."

Greyfist stopped and spun around to face Albrecht. "Damn it! When are you going to wake up? Arkady can beat you. You walked right into his challenge—don't think he didn't plan it this way! He's a master of the klaive. He really will carve you up! You could have chosen Gamecraft to best him, a contest of wits. You're not particularly smart, but you could have overcome him at that at least!"

"Don't talk to me like that," Albrecht said. "I'm sick of it. In case you aren't aware, I am also a master of the klaive. And mine's bigger than his, besides. I've seen his klaive. It's nice, but it's no Grand Klaive. I think House Wyrmfoe's family heirloom is going to wind up flaying his ass."

Greyfist turned around and walked off down the hill, fuming. "Your ego is going to get you killed, and then the dream will be dead for good."

Albrecht watched his friend march off down the hill. Dream? What the hell was he talking about?

7

Mari hit the punching bag again. And again. One hundred, one hundred one, one hundred two…. After one hundred and ten blows in succession, she took a break and jogged around the one-room gym. She had broken a sweat but wasn't breathing heavily yet.

She ran past Evan, who sat at the small desk by the door looking bored, staring out the window onto the streets of New York. He turned from watching the passersby outside to watch Mari as she ran past. He yawned.

"Look, I think we should try to get in touch with Albrecht," Evan said.

Mari did not answer him. She kept running until she finished her lap. She then took a deep breath and sat down on the blue mat that stretched from wall to wall.

"Tomorrow," she said. "I gave him until tomorrow to let us know what's happening."

"Yeah, but that could be too late."

"He can take care of himself. I'm sure we would have heard something by now if he were in trouble."

"Not necessarily. Little word gets in or out of that place. Those Silver Fangs are true New Englanders: secretive and shut-mouthed."

"Well? What do you want to do? We don't have a phone number and I'm not sure exactly where the caern is."

"But Mother Larissa would know. She'd surely tell us."

"She's been bothered enough in this affair—"

The phone rang. Evan looked at it, then reached over and picked it up. "Cabrah's Self-Defense. This is Evan speaking."

"Don't you have school or something?" Albrecht said.

"Albrecht! Where the hell are you?!"

Mari stood up and walked over, her hand out for the phone. "Give me that. I've got a few things to say to him."

Evan turned away from her, covering the receiver. "Wait a minute. Let me find out what's going on." He uncovered the receiver and leaned back in his chair. "So what's happening? Do you know why those guys attacked you? Is the king really dead? Who's going to be the next king?"

"Hold on," Albrecht said. "One at a time. First: a whole hell of a lot is happening. Second: no, I don't know why those two attacked me yet. Third: Morningkill is really dead. His funeral was last night. Fourth: I'm fighting someone tonight to become king of the Silver Fangs."

"What? You're joking, right?"

"Nope. The guy's name is Arkady and he's a real asshole. But I can take him."

"But...king? You?"

"Hey, don't sound so surprised. I thought I'd get some support on this from you at least. Of course, king! I've told you my heritage before."

"Yeah, but I thought you had given up on that. I never thought you'd actually...you know, become king."

"King?" Mari said. "Albrecht?!" She reached out and snatched the phone from Evan. She yelled into the receiver, "What do you mean, king? You can't be king!"

Albrecht chuckled. "Yeah, that's what some of these guys tell me. But I say otherwise. What's the matter? Don't like the idea of ol' Albrecht lording it over all the tribes, including yours?"

"The day you 'lord it over' the Black Furies is the eve of the Apocalypse, Albrecht. Don't even joke about it. Are you serious about this? What are you thinking? We have a pack."

"Yeah, so? I can be king and member of a pack at the same time. It just means that you guys might have to help me out with official duties and all. Big-time stuff. Lots of renown in it."

"Shove your renown, Albrecht. I don't like the idea of you as king at all. Why can't another be king?"

"Because the only other contender is too big of a jerk. I can't let him have it. Hell, I'd never hear the end of all that talk—'The Silver Fangs are going down.' 'The Silver Fangs can't rule.' 'The Silver Fangs blah, blah, blah.' No, I'm not going to contribute to more of that."

"Really? What do you think people will say when they hear that Albrecht, lord of drunks, is taking the throne?"

"Hey!" Albrecht said, getting angry. "That's not called for. That was a long time ago."

Evan grabbed the phone back from Mari, who frowned at him but walked across the studio to the hanging punching bag. She began to throw a series of blows at it.

"It's me again," Evan said. "Don't worry. She's just surprised. We're behind you."

"Is that noise in the background what I think it is? Is she hitting the bags again?"

"Yeah."

"She's awfully weird for a Theurge, kid."

"Well…. Hey, what do you want us to do? How can we help?"

"I'll call you tomorrow and let you know how the fight goes." There was a pause. "Of course, if I don't survive, I probably won't be calling you."

"You said you could take this guy!"

"Well, yeah. But you never know. I'll see you! Bye!" Albrecht hung up.

Evan placed the receiver back in its cradle. He looked at Mari, who stopped punching the bag to look back at him. "He's in trouble."

"Of course he is. But he doesn't want us involved. We've got to respect that."

Evan looked out at the street, at the dirty buildings crowding in. "I guess." He didn't like it, though. Not at all.

WILLIAM BRIDGES

Albrecht left Greyfist's office. The call was exactly what he had expected: Evan curious and concerned, Mari ready to tear his head off. He knew she was just as worried as Evan, but she hid it well.

He had spent most of the day practicing with the klaive. He wasn't out of shape by any means, but after that fight in New York, he wanted to make sure Arkady didn't slip any blows past him. He concentrated on his defense, since his offense was not in doubt.

He also did meditation exercises to help calm himself down. He did *not* want to frenzy against Arkady. Greyfist was right about one thing: if he frenzied, Arkady would win. So Albrecht worked to calm himself with meditation.

But Mari had pissed him off anyway.

He should have called them earlier, and then exercised. But he knew the hours she kept at her gym, and he was guaranteed to reach her in the afternoon.

He walked back up to his room to meditate again. He was confident that Greyfist would alert him well in time for the combat.

The crowd was already gathered and waiting when Albrecht went out to the field. Regina's caern protectors had marked off the combat arena with small, white rocks placed one after the other in a large circle. The Grand Oak stood at the western edge of the circle.

There were no bleachers or raised seats, so spectators had arrived early to get the prime viewing spots. There weren't that many Garou or Kinfolk at the caern, so the circle was probably big enough that there would only be two rows once the battle began. But those rows would encircle the entire marked space.

Albrecht walked onto the field and examined it. Torches on poles surrounded the field, providing the only light besides the crescent moon and stars. A layer of dirt had been laid on the field and packed down, with all the rocks and pebbles cleared away. The field was clean and open, with no depressions. A good, fair playing field. That was in Albrecht's favor. He had never been one to rely on tricky distractions. He was a straightforward fighter, and this was his kind of field. From what he'd heard of Arkady and his fighting preferences, Albrecht would have the advantage.

He went over to the Grand Oak. Greyfist had set up a chair there, along with towels, a bucket of water and a first-aid kit. Thomas Abbot was also there. He had volunteered to act as healer for Albrecht.

"Hello, Thomas," Albrecht said to the older Garou as he sat down in the chair. "By the way, I want to thank you for standing up for me yesterday in the moot."

Abbot smiled and shrugged. "Certainly. I was only defending my views. You are Morningkill's heir, therefore you should be king."

"I get the idea you don't think much of Arkady."

Abbot sneered. "I suppose it shows too much, then. Well, if he does win—perish the thought—we will need a gadfly against his policies. I will be happy to fulfill that role."

"And if I win?"

Abbot smiled at Albrecht. "As long as you're on the up-and-up, you have nothing to worry about. Act like your grandfather, however, and you'll be in for some disappointments from the court."

Albrecht nodded. "Of course."

He looked out at the field again. Across from his position, the crowd had cleared away to make room for Arkady's chair. The King's Own Pack were carrying it over. Arkady's packmate, Peter, was to act as his healer.

Albrecht glanced at his watch. Quarter till twelve. He knew it was too much to expect that Arkady would be late. It appeared the fight was on.

A murmuring went through the crowd and Albrecht looked up to see Arkady in the circle, checking it out the same way Albrecht had earlier. He was frowning, as if he were disappointed with it. Albrecht smiled. *Good, you schmuck. I'm glad you hate it.*

Arkady went and sat down in his seat. He stared across the distance at Albrecht, smoldering. Albrecht smiled and nodded at him, and Arkady returned the nod, smiling also. *Bastard*, Albrecht thought. *Facetious bastard. Of course, so am I.*

"I just don't get it," Greyfist said. "Why does this sort of thing always come down to combat?"

Albrecht chuckled. "Wake up. We're Garou. It always comes down to two guys bashing each other's heads in."

Regina walked onto the field and surveyed it. She then took her place at the throne, to Albrecht's left. She addressed the crowd.

"Since both combatants are here, we can begin. The challenge combat has been declared: klaives. The conditions are, as always, to fight until an honorable surrender. If none is given, then to the death. I would remind both combatants to heed the Litany concerning a surrender. I will be harsh with any who disregards it."

Albrecht nodded, as did Arkady.

"Then let the combatants take the field."

Albrecht stood up. His armor was strapped over his trench coat: a small breastplate and epaulettes, carved with ornate pictogram sigils, and vambraces on his arms. He sauntered out into the circle and stopped, taking his place just inside the marks.

Arkady also rose, walking into the circle. His battle armor was more impressive than Albrecht's—black with an ornate breastplate and vambraces. Thick, black leather covered the rest of him. He was an impressive-looking warrior.

"Draw your weapons," Regina said.

Albrecht pulled his Grand Klaive from the sidesheath in his trench coat. The crowd recognized it and began murmuring. It was a well-known family heirloom, having been used by Morningkill in his youth, and by his Garou predecessors before him.

Arkady drew his blade; not a Grand Klaive, but one which he handled well. He swished it around in a circle and seemed to be perfectly at ease with it.

"Fight!" Regina yelled.

Albrecht immediately crouched low and moved forward, his klaive out before him, ready to parry any blow. Arkady walked toward Albrecht, his klaive swinging slowly in an arc from right to left. Albrecht began to slide to the right, trying to circle Arkady, but Arkady moved to his left, canceling out Albrecht's move.

"Well, Arkady?" Albrecht said. "Why don't you come at me?"

"I will act when I feel like acting," Arkady said, still swirling his klaive. "Not when you prefer it. Why? Are you afraid to take the initiative?"

"Ha! I just want to make this last, to give the crowd a show. If I started first, this would all be over in seconds."

"You are such a braggart," Arkady said, moving slowly and carefully forward. Albrecht stood his ground, his large sword out before him. "Why do you not back up your words with action?"

"I like watching you swing that thing around. Ever thought of taking up tennis? 'Cause that's what you look like, a wussy tennis player swinging a racket."

Arkady growled. "You had best take Crinos form, Albrecht. It will hurt very badly for you otherwise."

"You first, Rusky."

Arkady leapt forward, dropping down as he reached Albrecht and stabbing his knife up from below. Albrecht took one step back and easily parried. He then stepped to the right and swung his sword down, but Arkady rolled away and stood up straight again.

"Temper, temper, Arkady. I saw that coming a mile away."

"I was simply stretching," Arkady said, standing in place and swinging his klaive in an arc again. "I did not get all my exercises done earlier."

"Oh? Too busy jacking off?"

Arkady's face contorted into a grimace. He began growling and his shoulders grew broader, his arms bigger and his legs longer. He was shifting to Glabro form.

Albrecht shook his head. "Tsk, tsk. Can't even stay in Homid form long enough to throw a few taunts, huh?"

Suddenly Arkady was in Crinos form, a towering wolfman who came hurtling at Albrecht with incredible speed. His klaive whirled in a blur, one Albrecht could barely keep track of. But instead of stepping back on the defensive, Albrecht lunged forward, stabbing his sword into the whirling arc of Arkady's klaive. Arkady was taken by surprise and his klaive was knocked from his hand. He jumped back, dodging Albrecht's slashes as Albrecht closed the distance between them.

Arkady then slipped to the side when Albrecht least expected it and reached out with a claw to slice at Albrecht's shoulder beneath the epaulette before he could bring his klaive up to block it. Blood sprayed forth. Arkady had scored first blood.

Albrecht stepped back, bringing his klaive up and calming himself, ignoring the pain. It was just a scratch. But the distraction allowed Arkady to run off and pick up his klaive.

He's good, Albrecht thought. *He's more flexible than I am. I thought I had him, and even though he was surprised, he escaped pretty quick. I've gotta be a bit more careful. Ready for anything.*

Arkady was now smiling, his klaive again circling in his hand. Albrecht growled and began to shift forms, growing into Crinos. He was huge in Crinos, although he and Arkady were almost equal in height. Albrecht's fur was white, but Arkady's was even more purely white, the sign of superior breeding.

Albrecht stomped forward toward Arkady, tired of playing around. He wanted to get this over with. He had never been much for taunting in combat, and he didn't know why he had wanted to do it earlier. Had he been scared? Trying to test Arkady's boundaries? Screw that! Time to kick butt.

Arkady slowly backed away as Albrecht came closer, but Albrecht didn't hesitate. He kept coming. Arkady tried to slip to Albrecht's left, but Albrecht stepped over and cut him off. He was in range now and began to swing his klaive wildly at Arkady, with such powerful blows that Arkady knew he couldn't parry them and was forced to dodge.

But he didn't dodge. The Russian Garou stepped forward, past Albrecht's reach, and thrust in with his klaive. It slid down Albrecht's breastplate and sank into his stomach. He barked in pain and tried to step back, but he couldn't bring his large klaive up quickly enough with Arkady so close. But the other Garou moved in closer, twisting his knife in Albrecht's gut. The pain was incredible! Albrecht shut his eyes and forced himself not to lose control. He dropped his sword and grasped Arkady's head, driving his thumbs into his opponent's eyes.

Arkady screamed and pulled back, leaving his klaive in Albrecht's stomach. One of his eyes had been put out by Albrecht's claw, but Albrecht had missed the other one, managing only to scratch the eyebrow. Blood poured down Arkady's face, blinding his good eye. He ran back, trying to get clear. Albrecht ran forward, picking up his klaive and swinging it at Arkady's torso.

It was a clean shot. Arkady was in for it. The fight was almost over.

But Albrecht tripped and fell to the ground. The klaive in his stomach hit the dirt first, driving deeper, exiting the other side, barely missing his spine. He yelled in pain, coughing up blood, stunned and unable to move.

Arkady ran over, wiping the blood out of his good eye. He slashed at Albrecht with his claw, tearing through the back of Albrecht's trench coat and ripping a layer of muscle off. He drew back for another blow, but Albrecht leapt up and knocked him off balance. Rather than taking advantage of it, however, Albrecht ran to the edge of the circle and pulled Arkady's klaive out of his stomach. Blood poured forth from the wound and Albrecht clutched it tight. *Nothing worse than a gut wound*, Albrecht thought. *Hurts like hell.*

He looked at Arkady, who cautiously came at him. Arkady was barely hurt, and Albrecht was almost dead. Albrecht wondered how that had happened. He had had a clean shot, damn it! How had he tripped? There was nothing on the field! He had checked it out himself.

He raised his klaive at the last minute to parry one of Arkady's rakes. Arkady didn't seem to expect it and couldn't pull back in time, and the klaive cut through his forearm to the bone. Arkady gasped and pulled back. Albrecht stumbled forward, trying to take advantage of the surprise. He slashed upwards and then quickly to the side. The blade caught Arkady on the right shoulder, slicing through the battle armor and the bone. Arkady's arm fell to the ground.

Arkady screamed in rage and clutched his shoulder, running to the far side of the field. Albrecht tried to follow right behind him, but the pain kept him from running too fast. Arkady spun around then and ran right back at Albrecht. As Albrecht stopped and pointed his klaive forward to receive the charge, Arkady leapt into the air. He flew past Albrecht, who tried to duck, but Arkady's claw caught him on the scalp, tearing out a chunk of hair and opening a large gash.

Albrecht fell to the ground, stunned again. He tried to stand and turn, blindly swinging his sword behind him at the foe he knew must be there. He was right. His klaive connected and Arkady grunted, but the klaive was now stuck in Arkady's left thigh. Arkady stepped back to take a breath, obviously fighting to control his rage.

Albrecht blinked and wiped the blood off his forehead before it could run down into his eyes. He readied himself for Arkady's attack as Arkady pulled Albrecht's klaive from his thigh and smiled. He began to swing it around in a circle as he approached Albrecht.

Albrecht felt dizzy watching it. He was suffering from massive blood loss and a concussion, he was sure. And now Arkady had his klaive and was going to carve him up with it. Sure, he had cost the Garou an eye and an arm, and given him a big wound to the thigh, but he was still coming on while Albrecht felt like he was about to faint.

Arkady came near Albrecht and pulled the sword back to slash at him. Albrecht fell down and the sword cut empty air over his head.

Albrecht, too weak to continue, drew in a deep breath and said, "I surrender, Arkady."

Arkady didn't seem to hear him. He stepped forward and drew the sword back again.

"Damn it, it's over. I surrender," Albrecht said, barely able to sit up.

Arkady's eyes narrowed and he began to swing the sword. Albrecht shut his eyes, but the blow never landed. He opened his eyes, blinking from the blood running into them, to see Arkady, sword poised in mid-swing, staring past Albrecht at Regina, who was giving him an angry stare. Albrecht could barely hear her deep growl from here. Her message was clear: *You can kill him, Arkady, but king or no, I will make you pay for it later.*

Arkady stood there, seeming to weigh his options. He then dropped Albrecht's klaive and turned away, limping back to his chair. "Get out of here, Albrecht. You will be gone by tomorrow. And you won't return to my protectorate."

Albrecht sat there, staring at Arkady's back. He then shut his eyes and cursed himself.

8

Albrecht stared up at the night sky and the crescent moon stared back at him. He breathed heavily, wincing in pain with each exhalation. Thomas Abbot moved his hands over his stomach and concentrated. The wound began to seal up. Albrecht breathed more easily as the pain subsided.

"Turn over," Abbot said.

Albrecht rolled over onto his side. Blood ran down his back, staining the dirt. Abbot touched the torn muscles and again concentrated, calling on the healing power of the spirits to reknit Albrecht's ripped flesh. He then healed the scratch on Albrecht's shoulder. Albrecht felt much better, but he knew he would be sore for a while.

"Now, sit up," Abbot said, and Albrecht groaned as he obeyed. He almost fell back down as a wave of dizziness came over him. Abbot felt his forehead and then healed it. The blood stopped flowing and the wound closed up.

Albrecht smiled at Abbot. "Thanks. I feel like a million dollars."

Abbot didn't say anything. He just stood up and walked away. "Try to get some rest."

Albrecht sighed. He got up and looked around. Most of the spectators had left, following Arkady and his pack. Arkady's wounds had been healed and he had declared a victory party by the edge of the bawn. Most of the Garou had gone to party with their new king.

Greyfist and Eliphas stood nearby, talking quietly between themselves. Eliphas looked worried, and Greyfist was frowning. Albrecht walked over to them.

"Hey, no need for long faces," he said. "I'm fit as I ever was. And you won't have to put up with me as king now. You should be celebrating."

Greyfist looked gravely at Albrecht. "We need to talk. In my office."

Albrecht looked at Greyfist as the Garou walked off to the mansion. He turned to Eliphas, who had begun to follow. "What's up with him? Sore loser?"

Eliphas stared at Albrecht as if he couldn't believe what the man was saying. "I think you need to hear this," he said and followed after Greyfist.

Albrecht pulled out a cigarette, lit it, and followed. As he entered the office, Greyfist was standing by the window and Eliphas sat on the couch. He closed the door behind him.

"So what's up?" Albrecht said, getting a bit worried now.

Greyfist didn't turn from the window as he said, "Arkady cheated."

"Oh, come on now," Albrecht said. "You saw it. You were right all along; he really is better than me."

Greyfist turned around. "No he's not. You had him dead by rights with that one blow. Then you fell."

Albrecht flushed with humiliation. "Yeah, well...." He puffed on his cigarette. "Do we have to have a blow-by-blow? I know my mistakes. He got lucky on that one and was able to turn the tide from there."

Greyfist looked solemnly at Albrecht. "Eliphas, tell Albrecht what you told me."

Albrecht turned to the young man, who seemed very worried. "What? What is it?"

Eliphas leaned back on the couch, not meeting Albrecht's eyes. "I...I was given my accouterments as Gatekeeper yesterday. But I have not completed the training yet, so I can't be sure—"

"Don't bandy words," Greyfist interrupted. "You know the fetish was correct."

Eliphas nodded, swallowing nervously. "Yes. It can't be wrong, can it?"

Albrecht sat down next to Eliphas. "What can't? Tell me what the hell happened."

Eliphas looked at him now. "I have a fetish, the Spirit Ward of the caern. It has been used by every Gatekeeper of North Country for three centuries now. Its purpose is to alert the Gatekeeper to intruder spirits who enter the caern. It detected one during the fight. There was an alien spirit on the field. It was what tripped you."

Albrecht leaned back, his mouth open and his head shaking. "You mean Arkady brought in a spirit to cheat?"

"That's not all," Greyfist said. "It was a Bane."

Albrecht growled. "No. That can't be. Not even Arkady is that stupid."

"But the fetish does not lie," Eliphas said, exasperated. "When it warned me, I didn't know what to do. I've only just become the Gatekeeper, and Garrick is not around to train me. I went into the Umbra to see it with my own eyes, but it had fled by then. However, the area...stank of the Wyrm. It had left the scent of its corruption behind."

"Wait a minute," Albrecht said. "That could have been the smell of the Black Spiral Dancers from a few days ago."

Greyfist shook his head. "No. Rites of Cleansing removed those yesterday. Regina saw to it personally. This was a new scent."

Albrecht shook his head, staring into the corner of the library.

"Why is this so hard for you to believe, Albrecht?" Greyfist asked. "I've suspected for some time that he was behind the Black Spiral Dancer attack. He's obviously made allies among the Wyrm."

"That bastard," Albrecht said, gritting his teeth. "I would have won. I would have had him."

"Quit being so damn selfish!" Greyfist snapped.

Albrecht looked at him, surprised. "What do you mean? He caused me to lose the fight."

"Don't you understand what this means? Arkady is king now! He has brought the taint of the Wyrm onto the throne!"

Albrecht shuddered. His guts turned. It was his fault. If he'd been able to beat Arkady, the throne wouldn't be in danger of corruption. He had to do something. Albrecht stood up, heading for the door.

"Where are you going?" Greyfist said.

"To take this up with Arkady," Albrecht said, reaching for the doorknob.

"You can't!" Greyfist yelled. "You've just lost a challenge to him. You can't challenge him again; he doesn't have to accept it. The others would turn against you, and your accusation would be assumed false."

Albrecht stopped and looked down at the floor, thinking. "We've got to reveal this! He can't get away with it."

"I've already thought through all the options," Greyfist said, turning toward the window again. "Eliphas cannot bring forth the accusation because he is too new at his position, too low in rank. He has no tangible proof by which to accuse the sept's Master of the Challenge, only the faint evidence of the spirit's tracks, and no definite connection between that spirit and Arkady. Arkady is fresh from his victory and has many allies. The sept wants a king, and he has proven his right by combat to be king. Arkady would ridicule Eliphas, and force a physical challenge." Greyfist paused. "No. I have to challenge Arkady."

"What?" Albrecht said, walking back to the center of the room, staring at Greyfist's back. "You will do no such thing! He'll tear you to pieces in seconds. Hell, you know I can beat the crap out of you, and if he can get me, you don't stand a chance. Besides, what if he cheats again?"

"There is always Gamecraft. I can easily best him at that."

"But you are the one bringing the challenge. The form of resolution will be his choice. He'll choose klaives—you know it."

Greyfist sat down at his desk. "You're right. We have a treacherous secret and we can't even reveal it. Damn this whole system of rights and challenges! If only the mighty rule, then the mighty can bring us down."

"But only the mighty can protect us from the Wyrm," Albrecht said, "Or so the theory goes."

They all sat in silence for a while. Greyfist looked out the window and seemed to be struggling with heavy thoughts. Then he looked at the other two. "There is one hope."

Albrecht looked up at him. "What?"

Greyfist looked down at the desk nervously. "It...it's a bit preposterous, really. It came to me in a dream. I've been struggling to figure it out over the last few days. It's made me think a lot about our tribe's situation."

"A dream?" Albrecht said. "What makes you think this one was special?"

Greyfist looked straight at Albrecht. "I believe this dream was sent by Falcon."

Albrecht didn't say anything, but looked back at Greyfist, waiting for him to continue.

"Have you ever heard of the Silver Crown?"

Albrecht frowned. "It's an old legend, isn't it? Something about the first crown worn by a Silver Fang king? Back in the Dawn Times?"

"I have heard the story," Eliphas said. "It's the crown of kings, the true test of rulership. It is said that only those worthy to rule the tribes under Gaia and Falcon can wear the crown. The unworthy who attempt to wear it die."

"That's right," Greyfist said. "Many believe the crown is an ancient fetish artifact, not just a myth or a figment of the imagination. I saw this crown in my dream. I saw Morningkill try to wear it and perish. But I saw another—I don't know who—take it up and survive. I believe the Silver Crown still exists, that Falcon showed it to me for a reason. It's our only chance, Albrecht. If you can get the Silver Crown, you can be proven a true king, one fit to rule over Arkady."

"Wait a minute," Albrecht said. "For one, you said it kills whoever is unworthy. That could be me. Two, we have no clue if it does exist, and if so, where it is."

"I've done some research on this," Greyfist said, "with what little is left of the protectorate's records. I think it's in the Umbra, Albrecht. Waiting in some realm for a true king to come claim it. That king is you."

"Here we go again. What if I'm not worthy? I'm supposed to go off on a dangerous Umbral quest because it *might* be there? And if I get it, it *might* not fry me alive? This sounds a bit farfetched."

"What other hope do we have?" Greyfist said.

Albrecht couldn't answer that.

"I have spoken with Antonine Teardrop, a Stargazer in the Catskills who has extensive records of tribal legends. He claims to know something

WILLIAM BRIDGES

called *The Lay of the Silver Crown,* a saga composed by a Silver Fang Galliard years ago. He thinks it has clues to the crown's location."

"Look, I like Antonine and all—I mean, he saved my butt once—but he *is* a bit cracked. He tends to believe a lot of things just because they're mystical."

"Isn't my dream mystical, Albrecht? We are Garou. We are beings of spirit as well as flesh. You're an Ahroun, so I know you've never paid a lot of attention to spiritual matters; but I have. You need to believe me, Albrecht. The Silver Crown exists. And you must find it. Otherwise, the North Country Protectorate is doomed to corruption."

"All right. I believe you. I've got to get this crown. Hell, I guess I've gone off on crazier quests for less. But where do I start?"

"You return to New York, gather your pack, and then visit Antonine. He will tell you the *Lay.*"

"My pack. Great. They are going to love this."

"You need to go now, Albrecht. You have to get the crown and return with it before the cusp of the next full moon. That is Arkady's auspice, and the day he will be crowned. After that, not even the Silver Crown can break a kingship rite."

"So that's…what? Eleven days starting tomorrow? Great. I've gotta trek across the Umbra to who-knows-where, pick up a lost fetish, and get back here in less than two weeks?"

"Yes," Greyfist said. "Eliphas will drive you home."

9

Dawn touched the highest towers of New York City, but in the streets below it was still night. In the early-morning gloom, Albrecht and Eliphas drove through the awakening streets. People were coming out of their apartments and getting into their cars to head for work. Buses roared by, stopped to drop off and pick up people, and roared off again, speeding to the next block's stop.

Albrecht rubbed his eyes and put his hands back on the wheel. He looked over at Eliphas, asleep in the passenger seat. Albrecht had been too worked up after last night's revelation to sleep, so he had taken over the driving duties. Eliphas had protested, experiencing visions of massive dents appearing on his Lexus, but Albrecht was hard to resist when he was fixed on something. So Eliphas had made the best of the situation and crashed out for the journey.

Albrecht pulled up outside Mari's gym. There was a space open, probably left by someone who had just gone to work. It was a bit tight, and it had been a while since he had parallel-parked, but he was confident. He pulled forward, put the car in reverse, and backed into the space. He was looking back over the seat, doing a good job of swinging the car in, when he heard the sound of metal grinding from the front bumper. *Shit*, he thought. *Scraped the car in front.*

Eliphas sat upright and looked forward. His face fell, an expression of confirmed doom on it. He then sat back again and closed his eyes.

Albrecht straightened out in the space and shut the engine off. "Sorry about that. You took it better than I thought you would."

Eliphas didn't say anything. He just frowned with his eyes shut, looking like he still wanted to sleep.

"That's okay. Just go back to Nod. You wait here while I run in and inform the crew."

Eliphas nodded and rolled onto his side. Albrecht shrugged and got out of the car, then went up to the studio door. The large window next to it looked in on the gym. Painted in large letters were the words: *Cabrah's Self-Defense.* And in smaller letters, beneath it: *Martial Arts Classes for Women. Karate, Judo, Tae Kwon Do.* Albrecht took out his key and unlocked the door. Stepping in, he shut the door behind him and walked across the room.

As he walked, he looked at himself in the full-length mirror that ran from wall to wall on one side of the gym. Gaia, but he looked terrible. Abbot had done a good job of patching him up, but he still had a large bruise on his forehead. His coat was torn and dirtier than usual. He hadn't shaved since the meeting of the Lodges: his stubble was almost a beard. He shook his head, opening the door on the far wall, and walked up the stairs beyond it.

He came into a small hallway with two doors opening off it. He went down to the last door and knocked. He heard someone walking around on the other side and listened carefully. *Let's see*, he thought. *Judging from the sound I'd say it's Evan. Not heavy enough to be Mari.*

The door opened and Evan's face lit up with a smile.

"Hey! You're back!" Evan said. "Come on in! What happened? How'd the fight...go." His enthusiasm trailed off as he noticed the bruise on Albrecht's forehead and his tattered coat. "I guess it didn't go well. Since you're here so quick and all."

Albrecht stepped past him into the apartment. "You think fast on your feet, kid. I like that. I got my ass whupped."

"That's too bad," Evan said. But then he smiled. "I guess that means you're back here with us now."

"Hold on, now. I thought I said on the phone that just because I was going to be king didn't mean we weren't a pack."

"Okay," Evan nodded, obviously not buying it but not interested in fighting either. That was what Albrecht liked about Evan. He was the only one Albrecht knew who wouldn't immediately jump into an argument with him.

"Where's Mari?" Albrecht said, looking around the small apartment. They were in a living room with a kitchen opening off it. A hallway was to the right, leading to the bedrooms.

"She's out on her morning jog," Evan said, walking to the small table by the window. "Breakfast?" he asked, picking up a box of Captain Crunch.

"No thanks. I'm more of a Crunch Berries man myself. When do you think she'll be back?"

"I don't know. Ten minutes, maybe?"

"Well, I've got someone waiting out in the car. I don't—"

"I'm here, Albrecht," Eliphas said, coming in the door. He looked annoyed. Mari walked in behind him, glaring suspiciously at him. "Your friend here did not like me waiting in front of her establishment."

"Do you vouch for him, Albrecht?" Mari said.

Albrecht laughed. "Yeah. He's all right. You can ease off him, Mari."

She nodded at Eliphas, who nodded back. He then rolled his eyes and went to sit down across from Evan, who handed the cereal box to him. He stared at it for a minute, as if he didn't know what it was, then nodded again and took the box.

"So, Albrecht," Mari said. "What's the story?"

"You might want to sit down for this one," Albrecht said, leaning against the wall and pulling a cigarette out of his pocket. Mari's brow wrinkled in disgust, but she didn't say anything or move to sit down. He lit the cigarette and took a drag on it. "On second thought, you better stand. You're a pacer, anyway, aren't you?"

"Just spit it out," she said.

"Well, I lost the fight. I got trashed pretty good."

Mari smiled at that. "The mighty Albrecht taken down? No!"

"Oh, but wait. Here comes the good part. My opponent, Arkady, cheated. It appears that he had a little Bane ally waiting in the Umbra to trip me up. Literally. I had a killer blow on that bastard, but this Bane interceded and screwed it up."

"A Bane? So this Arkady is Wyrm-corrupt. What did the Fangs do to him when they found out?"

"Now that's the really good part. They don't know yet."

"What?" Evan said, still chewing his cereal. "Why not? You've got to warn them!"

"Hold on. It's not that easy. And that's the crux of the matter, really. You see, we can't prove it. And with the laws of challenge the way they are, we don't have anybody who could successfully bust on Arkady."

"Just point him out to me and I'll take him down!" Mari said, her fists bunching up.

"Ah, it's not that easy. Believe me, I really wish I could. But he's guarded by a damn good pack. And if I were found to be siccing my pals on him, that would be considered conspiracy against the throne. You gotta realize, he's king now."

"King!" Mari yelled. "You let a Wyrm-fetid Garou take the throne of the Silver Fangs and the rulership of the thirteen tribes?!"

"Wait a minute here! Just the other day you were singing a different tune there. Something about the day the Fangs ruled over the Furies being Apocalypse night?"

"That was *you*, Albrecht. I said that the day *you* ruled would be the eve of the Apocalypse. But apparently I got it wrong. You've let a Wyrm ally onto the throne. If that's not a step toward the Final Days, I don't know what is."

"Well, damn it! I'm trying to do something about it! I'm the only one who can take the throne from Arkady. If we just get someone to kill him— assuming they succeeded—the crown might go to a regent, one of his packmates. They could be corrupt also."

"But they might not know," Eliphas cut in, crunching cereal. "We don't know for sure that they are aware of Arkady's treachery."

"That's true. But we have to assume they're just as culpable all the same. Now, here's the plan...."

Mari raised her eyebrows, waiting.

"There's this ancient artifact called the Silver Crown. If I can get it, I can be king. I think."

Mari nodded. "Of course. The Silver Crown. If you don't kill yourself putting it on, you will be proven fit to rule the tribes."

"Yeah," Evan said. "That's a good plan. Do you know where the crown is?"

Albrecht was looking in surprise at both of them, as was Eliphas. "You mean you've heard of the crown?"

"Of course," Mari said. "Who hasn't? It's only the greatest treasure of the Silver Fangs."

"Wait. Wait," Albrecht said, throwing his hands up. "I've only heard vague rumors of this thing, and it turns out you guys know all about it? Is it just me?"

"I have only heard references to it in other legends, myself," Eliphas said.

"Unbelievable," Mari said. "You've forgotten your own treasure! No wonder the Silver Fangs are said to have fallen. Everyone knows about the crown except the Silver Fangs! And we thought you had it in hiding from the other tribes for all these years! The Furies and the Uktena would do anything to get it. But no one's looked for it because everyone knows it's being guarded by a Silver Fang sept somewhere. But now! Once this news gets out, everyone's going to be searching for it."

"Then it doesn't get out," Albrecht said, glaring at her. "'Cause we're going after it. We've got some clues. We can do this. We *have* to do this."

Mari nodded. "Yes. I wouldn't dare miss such a quest. The renown alone would be considerable, let alone the chance to see this great artifact."

Albrecht's eyes narrowed. "We need to make something clear here. We do this so the Fangs can get the crown, not the Furies. Got that? This crown needs to be among the Fangs, not sitting in some Fury stronghold on a remote Greek island."

Mari glared at him and was silent for a while. "All right. The crown goes to the Fangs. But if I think it will be misused, I will not hesitate to liberate it and place it in the keeping of our crones."

"Don't worry. If I get it, it'll be in good keeping."

"I will judge that for myself when the time comes."

"Guys!" Evan said. "Stop it. Look, Mari, we've got to do this for Albrecht. For the Fangs. For the entire Garou nation. If you can't make that promise ahead of time, it's not in anyone's best interest to involve you in the quest."

Mari's eyes widened as she looked at Evan as if he had just put a knife in her back. "You're taking his side!"

"I have to look at the greater good in this," Evan said. "You know the Furies don't need the crown. Come on. Be realistic. You're letting ego get in the way."

Mari frowned at him and then threw up her hands. "All right! The crown will go to Albrecht."

Albrecht nodded. "Thank you. Now we've got to leave. Antonine Teardrop knows some lore about the crown that'll give us a pointer in the right direction. Eliphas will drive us to the Catskills."

THE SILVER CROWN

The dome sat on a rise, poking out above the fall foliage. Evan pointed it out to them as they drove along the small back road that wound its way to the Stargazer's home. Albrecht had never been here before, but he had heard about it. Antonine Teardrop lived in one of those weird Buckminster-Fuller-designed geodesic domes. He had telescopes pointing out of windows along the top so he could glean omens from the stars. Albrecht was a bit skeptical about such things, but he knew that Antonine was considered a very wise Garou, albeit one with a foot in the twilight zone.

Albrecht admonished himself for being uncharitable about another tribe again. Antonine had saved his butt. He had saved the entire pack, back when Evan had had his Rite of Passage and the Wyrm had been after him. Antonine had been the only one to read the proper omens and to act to get Albrecht, Evan and Mari to the holy site where the spirits could instruct Evan in his heritage: that of a Wendigo prophet and warrior.

But Albrecht had not seen Antonine since then. The Stargazer stayed in his home for the most part, occasionally showing up at a Garou moot here and there to tell of a new omen. Most of the time, the rest of the Garou didn't like his omens. They were uncomfortable prophecies, pointing out insidious Wyrm plots that no Garou wanted to believe could exist. Lately, Antonine and Loba Carcassone had been working together, realizing that they had both separately come across the same Wyrm plot—if it was a Wyrm plot. Their "plot" was probably the freakiest conspiracy theory Albrecht had ever heard, linking generations of child abuse to a conscious plot by near-immortal Wyrm servitors. To untangle such a chaotic thread and put a cause-and-effect label on it seemed a bit much even for Antonine.

But they did have some scary evidence at times.

Albrecht looked at the dome as they drove closer. Loba's Wyrm plot did not concern him now, however. The crown was what was important here.

Soon they pulled into the gravel drive outside the dome. Antonine was patiently waiting on the porch that encircled the dome, obviously expecting them. He was a middle-aged man, fit and healthy-looking with deeply tanned skin and a face which had seen much of the outdoors. He wore a red-checked flannel shirt, blue jeans and brown leather shoes.

As the pack got out of the car and walked over to him, Albrecht looked around. It was quite an impressive spread. Trees surrounded the dome and grew up right next to it, leaving a nice, shady canopy over the drive and the porch.

"Greetings," Antonine said as they reached the porch. "Hello, Albrecht and Mari. And how are you doing, Evan?"

"I'm fine, Antonine," Evan said, shaking the Stargazer's hand. "I want to thank you again for all your help during my Firsting."

Antonine smiled and nodded. He looked at Eliphas. "You must be Standish. Greyfist told me about you. Congratulations on your new post as Gatekeeper."

Eliphas looked unsure of how to respond. He was obviously a bit awed to be meeting the famed Stargazer. "Thank you. I…I am very pleased to meet you. I have long respected your wisdom."

Antonine's eyebrows raised at that. "Then you are a rare Garou." He turned back to the others. "Why don't you all come in? I have prepared a meal. Standish, I have a bed you can sleep on to rest for your journey home. The rest of you will not return with him. You have another place to go, a journey you must make on foot."

It was evening. The crescent moon was at the end of its waxing, close to becoming a half moon. The Philodox moon. The pack was gathered in Antonine's living room, at the center of the dome. Rooms opened off to the side, leading to bedrooms and a kitchen. Above them, encircling the ceiling, was a walkway. Windows lined it, each with a telescope and a small table with odd devices.

They sat on cushions on the floor, facing Antonine, who had a stack of books and scrolls before him. He had a pair of reading glasses on and was looking through some of the scrolls. The Garou had eaten a fine meal, some sort of exotic Indian dish, the recipe for which Antonine said had been given to him by a friend named Shakar, an excellent cook.

Albrecht wanted a cigarette, but he wasn't about to insult Antonine's hospitality by lighting up inside the dome. He sat back and tried to relax. Antonine seemed to notice his restlessness and put his scroll down.

"Let's begin," Antonine said. "Greyfist and I have spoken about the crown before. Frankly, I was surprised that it is actually lost. I am sure you are aware of the rumors that it has been well-hidden by the Silver Fang leadership?"

Albrecht rolled his eyes. "Uhm…can we just talk about where it is now?"

Antonine smiled. "I have done some reading. It is not easy to find written Garou records, but every once in a while an enlightened Garou scholar emerges who records what lore he can for those of us who are interested. I was sorry to hear that the North Country lost most of its records in a fire.

But I believe I have discovered a source, a recent one, relatively speaking, which points to the possible fate of the crown."

Albrecht leaned forward. "Is this the *Lay of the Silver Crown* that Greyfist mentioned?"

"It is indeed. It was written in the late Renaissance by a Silver Fang Galliard...."

"I thought you said this was a recent source."

"I said 'relatively.' Understand that most of the written lore for the Silver Crown is truly ancient, older than Rome. It has fallen into common lore and become the source of many rumors and legends among the other tribes since then. But this *Lay* seems to be authentic and written by the last person to have seen the crown. At least, the last who has told of it. The author's name is Vassily Hearthcenter."

"I have heard of him," Eliphas said. "He is somewhat famous. Wasn't he a chronicler of the Clan of the Crescent Moon?"

"As far as I can tell, yes," Antonine said. "I will read you the *Lay*, but I am going to have to paraphrase much of it. The actual written language is a bit hard to understand if you're not familiar with its idiom. So, in the tradition of oral storytellers, I am going to take his story, mixed with what other lore I have concerning the crown, and tell my own tale. One which I believe aims sure at the truth."

Evan and Mari nodded. Albrecht said, "All right. Let's hear it."

Antonine took off his reading glasses and placed them in a case on the floor next to him. He folded his legs under himself and seemed to be meditating, centering himself for the tale.

"It begins, like all things, in the Dawn Times.... Long, long ago, before humans learned to think and their Weaver tools were but a dream unborn, the tribes of the Garou warred among themselves.

"There were few tribes then, but those there were had only come to their status recently. They had become separate from their brethren through migrations away from others of their kind, and the changes made on them by time and place. There was the blood of the original wolf, the Silver Fangs, and then many children who had strayed. The Children of Gaia spread far and wide and loved all which walked and crawled on and in the earth. The Get of Fenris went to the chill north to mold themselves into Fenris's hammer. The Fianna moved to the west, following the faint but beautiful music of the fae. And so on with the other early tribes.

"But it happened that they began to fight among themselves, either for right of territory, right of breeding flock, or simply for glory. They had fallen far from their first ways. The Silver Fangs, leaders of them all even then, tried to stop them, but the others would not listen. The Silver Fangs, purest of the pure, ordained to rule the Garou by Gaia, knew not what to do. They went to their totem, mighty Falcon, and asked of him a solution to their problem.

"Falcon's eyes gazed down at them, judging them. Finally, he spoke. 'One among you must choose to travel the road of sacrifice. On this road are four gates, and at each gate is a guardian who must be passed. If all gates are passed successfully, this one shall be given a boon greater than any given unto a mortal being before. He who bears this gift shall be king over all, and shall command all things of the earth to stay their proper courses, as is the will of Gaia.'

"The Fangs talked among themselves and finally decided that there was one among them who was best suited to travel the road. They went to him and told him of Falcon's words. He thought for a while, and then said, 'I shall undertake this quest. I so choose.' In the morning, he left.

"He walked for a long time, following the portents Falcon laid before him. Soon, he came to the first gate. It was but an opening in a rocky pass, with no portal to bar the way. The Garou looked about and saw no one, so he walked through the pass. But before he could get there, a beast leapt down upon him from the rocks. It was a Garou, a tribeless one, mad and snarling with rage. The Silver Fang shifted forms and fought with the ronin for a while. This was a strong ronin, one who ignored his wounds and kept fighting as a mad thing with no control. Finally, the Silver Fang killed it, although he was hurt. He left its body there and went through the pass.

"The next day, he came to the second gate. This was a wooden fence with a door between two posts. There was a beautiful woman there, a human female. The Garou had never seen one so pure before, so perfect. He knew that she would birth many Garou if given the chance. Remembering Gaia's desire that the Garou spread their seed across the world, he got down to lie with her. He then saw a falcon fly high overhead, past the fence, and he remembered his quest. He stood up again and walked through the door, knowing that the comforts of hearth and family would not be his as long as the world was in danger."

"Is that really a part of the legend?" Mari said, her eyes narrowed.

Antonine chuckled. "Yes, I'm afraid so. They saw things differently back then, Mari."

"I'm not so sure. I know many legends where the hero was a female and only changed to a male by a later storyteller. This could be the case here."

"Perhaps. But I have no evidence for it. So I shall continue my tale based on what I do know.

"The following day, he came to the third gate. It was constructed of stone, but well made. It was an arch, with a gate under it. A spirit waited at the gate, holding a bag, out of which light glowed. It was looking in the bag as the Garou came up. When it saw the Garou it quickly sealed the bag, shutting up the light. The Garou asked what was in the bag, what the source of the wonderful light was. But the spirit said it was a secret, and that only the truly enlightened could look in to see it; otherwise the secret could destroy the world. The Garou said that he was the representative of his tribe, and thus the most enlightened among them. He asked to see into the bag. But the spirit said that he had to prove his enlightenment first, that he would have to come to the spirit's home and pass an initiation.

"Now, the wonderful glow within the bag had awakened a great curiosity in the Garou. He desperately wanted to know what was in it. Perhaps it was something that could help his people? Perhaps it was the gift Falcon had spoken of? He had forgotten whether he had been through two gates or three. He was afraid that if he did not take the spirit's offer, he would be denied the special wisdom forever.

"Then he heard, from far ahead down the road, barely audible, the cry of a falcon. And he remembered his quest. He opened the gate and walked past, realizing that he would never know the secret but that others one day might.

"The day after that, he came to a great city. There was a huge portal before him, with two doors which opened outward when a large wheel inside was turned by ten men. Humans could be seen in the windows above, looking down at the Garou as he approached. He looked up at them and asked to be let in. They laughed and said that his kind did not belong there. They told him to go home and chase deer. He persisted, asking what he could do to get in. The humans talked among themselves and then said, 'You must give us your pelt.'

"The Garou was horrified. But he knew his quest. He knew he had taken the road of sacrifice. And so he nodded and said yes. The great doors opened, swinging slowly out at him with a rumbling, grinding sound. The humans came out with silver knives and carefully approached him. They stopped before him and said, 'We can't take your pelt if you have claws. We must cut them off first, to protect ourselves.' The Garou nodded and put out his hands. The humans chopped off the tips of his fingers, leaving him clawless.

"Then the humans said, 'You might still fight back as we take your pelt. You might bite us with your fangs.' He opened his mouth, and they took tongs and pulled out all his teeth. He was fangless. They then began to carve into his flesh, flaying off his hide. Soon, he was skinless and red, exposed to the world.

"They stared at him in awe, however, impressed with his resolve and wondering at his mission. They led him into the city, closing the great doors behind them. They placed him on a chair and lifted it up, marching it to the center of the city, to a great palace. They walked him up the stairs and led him into a room where the sun shone down from a hole in the ceiling above.

"There, on a dais in the center of the room, was a gleaming crown, made of pure silver. Its brilliance under the sun nearly blinded the Garou, but he knew that this was the gift he sought. He asked the humans if he could have it, and they nodded, motioning him to the crown. He took it in his hands and placed it on his head.

"He screamed with the pain as its silver burned into his raw skin. He tried to yank the hurtful thing from his head, but it would not move. It had burned into him, and become a part of him. He cried in pain, tears blinding him, and he begged Falcon to save him.

"He heard a voice, one commanding him to open his eyes, and he did so. He was standing in a field at night. The city was nowhere to be seen, although he knew that he was still standing in the same place. The pain was gone, and his pelt had regrown, along with his fangs and claws. His head felt uplifted, drawn to the heavens by the lightness of the crown. Falcon stood before him, his wings wide.

"And Falcon said, 'You now know what the Garou must sacrifice to be more than beasts. But you also know that it is a painful sacrifice, one many will not be able to bear. Return to your people and rule them wisely. All Garou will follow you now. Know that the pain of sacrifice is only because your people have forgotten the ways given them by Gaia. Were it not so, sacrifice would not be necessary. Whenever your people forget, remember that one among you must bear the burden of pain to help them remember.'

"The Garou thanked Falcon and returned to the Silver Fangs. When they saw the radiant crown on his head, it was as if they recognized it immediately, and they knew again what they had once known: Gaia's covenants of behavior. The Garou, now known as king, traveled to the other tribes, and the sight of him brought remembrance of the old ways back to them all, and they ceased to fight among themselves and knew the Wyrm for what it was."

Antonine sat back. He shut his eyes and seemed to be resting.

Albrecht coughed. "What was the Silver Fang's name?"

Antonine slowly opened his eyes. "It is lost. He is simply the first king."

Albrecht nodded.

"That's quite a story," Evan said. "Very rich in symbolism."

"Deceptively so," Antonine said. "It seems very simple and obvious at first, but it actually touches some core meanings."

"Is there more?" Albrecht said. "What about the current location of the crown?"

"Yes, there is more. Let me get some drinks and I'll begin again." Antonine stood up and went into the kitchen. Soon he brought a tray of drinks out and placed it on the floor in the midst of them. "Help yourself. It's herbal tea."

Albrecht rolled his eyes. "Don't you have a beer?"

Antonine sat down again. "Yes, but you'll have to get it yourself."

Albrecht got up and went to the kitchen., where he opened the fridge and saw a six-pack of Samuel Adams. *At least the guy has taste in beer,* Albrecht thought. He took one and twisted the cap off, tossing it in the garbage can. He went back into the living room and sat down. "Thanks. Good beer."

"Of course," Antonine said. "Now, I'll finish. There are some other legends that I'll skip because of time. But there's one from somewhere around 300 B.C. or so that I think is important.

"A Silver Fang king named Ranix Hammer Claw ruled over a protectorate in what used to be called Gaul—France, today. He was known far and wide as a terrible leader, one who had squandered many of the treasures of his kingdom. So badly had he ruled, it is said, that even the spirits fled their fetishes when he touched them, fearful of being poorly used. His own warriors stayed away from him unless he commanded otherwise, for they feared his dictates.

"He often sent his Garou off on dangerous quests for little return. While the Wyrm grew all around his kingdom, he was unaware, so busy was he sending his warriors out in search of new treasures. One day, his warriors returned with a chest. They placed it before him, and he looked suspiciously at it, still chewing on the boar's hind leg upon which he was feasting. They said that it was by far the greatest treasure yet seen in any kingdom, and they had been astonished at how easily they had won it.

"They told the tale of its winning, of how they had come upon a dark glade in a sunny wood, and how three beasts attacked them there. One was a chimera, the legendary lion with the head of a dragon and a goat besides its own lion's head. The other was a great serpent with the head of a panther, whose eyes caused fear in all who met them. The third was a falcon.

"The men drove the other beasts off into the woods, but they were afraid to attack the falcon, since it was the child of their totem. It ceased its attack against them and spoke: 'Since you have honored your vow to my father and left me unharmed, I shall give you something.' It led them to a rock in the glade and told them to lift it. When they had it up, they saw a chest in a hole. They pulled the chest out and placed the rock back. The falcon was gone. When they opened the chest, they were all stunned by what they saw, and knew they had to bring it back to their king.

"The king sat forward on his throne of wood and leather hide, still chewing on his dinner, and told the warriors to open the chest. They did, and a silver brilliance shone forth from it. The king's mouth dropped wide; his half-chewed meat fell to the floor. He dropped the boar haunch and reached his greasy hands into the chest to pick up the Silver Crown, the long-legendary artifact of his tribe. He knew that if he wore it, everyone would obey him and would have to do as he wanted.

"He cackled and placed the crown on his head. But then he screamed in pain as it welded itself to his skull. And he kept on screaming, for the burning did not stop. His very flesh began to melt about the crown, and he tried to pull it off. But as with the first king before him, the crown was now a part of him, and could not be separated. His flesh ran down his face in molten gobs, and his bones began to burn. The smell of it revolted all the Garou near him, and many fled the tent. He screamed for someone to help him, but none would dare. Soon his body fell to the floor, dead, his head a pool of ashes and sizzling grease.

"The warriors stared at their dead king. The crown was missing from his head, gone. But they remembered what they had long forgotten: Gaia's covenants, the Litany, which included the right to overthrow unfit rulers. They were ashamed that they had so long followed such a fool, and swore they would not do so again."

Albrecht and Eliphas stared uncomfortably at the floor, aware of the parallels to their own situation.

Antonine continued. "The last part of the *Lay* which I will tell you is from Vassily Hearthcenter's own experience. It concerns Dmitri Spiral Slayer, the last known Silver Fang to wear the crown. There had been a terrible Wyrm uprising in Russia. Remember, this is the late Renaissance, probably the late sixteenth century or so. King Dmitri led a pack of Silver Fangs against the queen of the deformed Garou, leaving all his other warriors behind to defend their caern. He admonished them before he left not to follow him, for if the caern fell, their future generations would fall with it.

"Vassily went with the king's pack, to glean the tale of their heroism. After many harrowing adventures, they fought their way to the throne room of the Black Spiral queen. But the hag fled into the spirit world, and Dmitri followed, alone. He followed her trail through the hell hole that surrounded her Umbral throne and finally cornered her before a pit of bubbling ichor. They fought, tooth and claw, each tearing the other to bloody pieces. Finally, the queen reached out to crush Dmitri's skull. When her hands touched the Silver Crown, she screamed in horror and yanked her hands back, but it was too late: her hands had been burnt to a crisp by the crown, and she pulled back stubs instead.

"Dmitri shoved the surprised and pained queen into the pit of boiling Wyrm's blood. That was the end of her. But Dmitri was sore wounded, and lay dying. He cried, for he knew that he had failed in one thing: the Silver Crown would be lost in this Wyrm place, fallen into the hands of the enemy.

"But then Vassily arrived, having followed the scent of his king here. He had also entered the spirit world, but it had taken him longer to thread the Gauntlet. The king, seeing his loyal vassal, wept tears of relief, and commanded Vassily to take the crown and hide it far away where no evil could reach it. All of the royal line were dead, and there were none of the Seven to take the crown after him. But Vassily hesitated to touch the great treasure, fearful it would burn him. Dmitri put his bloody hand on Vassily's shoulder and said, 'Fear not. You are but its bearer. Do not try to place it upon your head, and you shall not be harmed.' Vassily nodded and removed the crown from his king's head, whereupon Dmitri died.

"Vassily left that place, crying because he had to leave the body of his king behind where it could be defiled by Banes. But he had a duty. He traveled far, searching for a place to hide the crown. After many days, he found it. He hid the crown at the Dawn, in the Wyldest Garden."

Antonine shut his eyes, meditating again.

Albrecht sat up from his slouching. "That doesn't tell us anything. Where the hell is the Dawn? I've never heard of it as a place. Or of any Wyld garden."

Antonine slowly opened his eyes again. "It is what Vassily left behind. It is his only clue. I think I know what place he is talking about."

"Where?" Albrecht said.

"Pangaea," Antonine replied.

"That makes sense," Mari said. "It is the most primordial place in the spirit world. It has the magic of the earliest times in it. All Garou are said to revert back to an earlier form when they enter it."

"What? Sort of like in the film 'Altered States'?" Albrecht said.

Mari scowled at him. "No. I mean that the laws of reality work differently there. Things are more primitive, less formed. The Wyld is stronger, and the Weaver is but a shadow."

"I see. The Wyldest Garden. A sort of Garden of Eden for Garou."

"Exactly," Antonine said. "If you'll remember the first story, it took place in a Pangaea-like environment, except for the Weaver gates and city. I think Vassily was trying to hide it where it had originally come from."

"Don't forget," Mari said, "it's a very dangerous place. The only rule is that everything there is hungry, and there are bigger things on the food chain than Garou."

"Sounds like a challenge," Albrecht said. "So we go to Pangaea. How do we find the crown from there? It's a pretty big place, isn't it?"

"It's huge," Mari said. "As big as this continent, at least."

"Great! We're supposed to spend years finding this thing?"

"These are the only clues I have," Antonine said, standing up. "I believe that you will find the legends I told you instructive along the way. Simply look for the gates, or their metaphorical equivalents."

"Well, I guess that makes sense," Albrecht said. "Look, thanks for everything you've done. I know we couldn't have gotten this far without you."

"My pleasure," Antonine said. "I think we should rest now. You're going to need a lot of sleep; you've got a long walk ahead of you. I advise you to leave tomorrow night. The Moon Paths will be faint by day, making travel dangerous."

They nodded and went to the guest bedrooms, each of them reflecting on the tale they had heard. Only Albrecht remained in the living room, stretching out on the floor cushions. There weren't enough guest beds, so he had volunteered to take the floor.

He stretched out and looked at the ceiling as he heard the bedroom doors shut and saw the lights go out. There was a window right above him, and the stars could clearly be seen. He hoped he had what it took to wear the crown, and made a silent prayer to Gaia for Her to look favorably upon him. He then rolled over to sleep, but he was plagued by nightmares the whole night. Visions of his hands burning off, or his skull igniting, and a sharp band of pain around his head.

10

"You take care of yourself, Eliphas," Albrecht said, looking down at the young Silver Fang who sat in the driver's seat of the car.

Eliphas smiled at him. "Good luck, Lord Albrecht. I hope you succeed. For all our sakes." He turned the ignition key and the engine purred to life.

Albrecht stepped back and waved. "So do I. Don't worry. I always come through in the end."

Eliphas nodded. He accelerated down the gravel drive and drove off into the darkening day as the sun went down. Moments later, he was gone. Albrecht walked back into the dome. The others were gathered in the living room, packing for the journey. They had all brought backpacks, rations and changes of clothes with them. They had been on long jaunts in the spirit world before and knew what they needed to survive. Albrecht went over and sat down with them. Pulling his own pack over, he began taking inventory.

Antonine was walking around the room, searching through the bookcases which lined the walls. He had a stack of books in his hand. When he seemed to have found everything he needed, he went into his study, a room near the kitchen.

"What's he up to?" Albrecht said.

"I think he's making a map," Evan said.

"To Pangaea?" Albrecht said.

"Yes," Mari said. "I have been there before, but it was by a…longer route than we need now. Antonine is trying put together a good map of signposts to look for."

"Like what?" Albrecht said. "I thought the Wyld nature of the place prevented mapping."

"True, the closer you get to it. But we have a ways to go before reaching the realm itself. Any shortcut we can find will help greatly."

Albrecht nodded. "You're the Theurge. I'll trust that."

Mari nodded. "Finally thinking sensibly."

Evan smiled at both of them. He was glad they weren't shouting at each other yet. He knew that would come later, but for now they were getting along.

Albrecht zipped up his pack and placed it before him. "Done. Clothes, sleeping bag, food, water. Do we need anything else?"

Evan was also finishing his pack, and Mari had already finished hers. "I can't think of anything," he said.

Mari shook her head. "I think we've got it covered."

Antonine came out of his study with a parchment. He walked over and sat down next to them, handing the paper to Mari. "This is the best I can do. It's based on some accounts I have of journeys to Pangaea, along with hearsay from friends of mine. You should do okay by it. Remember, though, that you're departing under the half moon, so the Moon Paths will be somewhat faint and incomplete, and the Lune spirits will not be guarding all of them. Travel will be dangerous at times. However, I believe this place here"—he pointed at a spot on the map—"is a Lunae, a crossroads of Moon Paths, where you should be able to rest for the day. You will need to find as many of these as you can along the way. I don't recommend taking shelter in a realm, since you might not know the laws under which it operates before entering. The last thing you need is to get caught in a sub-realm and waste a few days trying to get out. However, it would be worse to stray off the paths; you'd easily get lost without them to guide you."

"Thanks," Mari said. "It's pretty self-explanatory. I can use this. A very complete job in such a short amount of time."

Antonine nodded and stood up. "The sun's almost set. I think it's safe for you to leave now."

The pack stood up and shouldered their bundles. Antonine led them outside and around behind the dome to a small field. He looked about and stopped, turning back to them. "This is a good spot. I've used it many times before. Mari? Do you want to lead us in?"

"Certainly," Mari said, stepping next to him. The others followed her and gathered around in a circle, all touching her. She held a small mirror up and looked into it, moving it about to catch the final rays of the sun peeking through the trees. When she was satisfied with the reflection, she stared into it. She reached out with her spirit to connect to the spirit world. Once she touched it, she pulled herself toward it. Or did it pull itself to her? Many Garou had argued that point. In any case, the Gauntlet wrapped about them and then parted as it passed. They all stood in the Penumbra, the spiritual shadow of the physical world.

The field looked very much the same on this side as on the other. It was darker here, since the sun did not shine at all. The half moon was clearly visible in the sky.

Albrecht looked around and saw part of Antonine's house beyond the trees. It looked different. Webs were spread across it, but in a very beautiful, almost chaotic pattern, as if the spider creating it had had an aesthetic purpose when weaving it. *That is weird*, Albrecht thought. *The Weaver and Wyld in balance. Quite rare.*

"I think that path is best," Antonine said, pointing down a small, one-person-wide path that disappeared into the woods. "If you follow it long enough, it leads to a Moon Path. At least, it used to. In the physical world it leads to a small pond, but I've never found the pond from this side. Just follow any signs of brighter moonlight. The Lune spirits will be there. Remember, stick to the Moon Paths: without Luna's guidance, you may never find Pangaea."

"Thank you again, Antonine," Mari said, shaking his hand.

"Yeah, you've been a lot of help," Evan said.

"Don't think anything of it," Antonine said. "I am doing what is important."

Albrecht walked up to him and put out his hand. "If this crazy plan actually works, then I'll certainly remember your help when I'm king."

Antonine smiled and shook his hand. "Just be a good king, Albrecht. Remember the *Lay of the Silver Crown*. Heed it."

"Of course. I'm kind of fond of my skull."

Antonine chuckled and walked off. "You had better get going. You have little time."

"We're off," Albrecht said, turning to the path. Mari was already ahead of him, and Evan had stepped in between them. Stopping at the edge of the woods, Albrecht looked up at the moon. *Well, Luna,* he thought. *Don't get crazy on me here. Help me out. All right?*

He then turned and walked into the woods, falling in behind Evan.

Greyfist looked up at the half moon and felt the strengthening of his spirit, a gift from Luna on the night of his birth auspice. He was a Philodox, and the half moon was his moon. He thought about Albrecht and his pack. He hoped Antonine had been able to help them. Had they left yet? Were they walking the spirit world now?

There was a knock at the door. Greyfist turned from the window and sat down at his desk. "Come in."

The door opened and Arkady appeared. He walked into the room and shut the door behind him. "Good evening, Seneschal."

Greyfist was surprised, wondering what the king-in-waiting wanted with him. "Greetings, Arkady."

Arkady walked across the room and stood before the desk, looking around the room. "I have never been here. It is a nice office. You have many...books. Have you read them all?"

Greyfist tried to hide his look of annoyance. Non-readers always asked that stupid question. "No, I haven't. They are mostly for reference. It is what remains of the protectorate's library after the fire."

"Ah, yes," Arkady said, sitting down on the couch. "I had forgotten. It is good you have saved them. You are very loyal."

Greyfist did not respond. He simply looked at Arkady, waiting for him to reveal his purpose in coming.

Arkady sat back and smiled. "You are wondering why I have come? I should not…what? Mince words? I am here to find out what Lord Albrecht's plans are since losing our combat."

Greyfist's eyebrows rose. "Plans? You made it clear that he is no longer welcome. He's gone back to New York, to whatever life he had during the exile."

Arkady looked at Greyfist, not saying anything. Then he sat forward. "You must understand my position, Seneschal. He was a threat to my ascension. I did what I had to. I bear him no personal ill will."

Greyfist opened a drawer and pulled out his pipe. He knew Arkady was lying. A bald-faced lie. As a Philodox, the spirits had gifted him with the insight to tell truth from fiction.

"But I am worried," Arkady continued. "I suspect that he will try to sabotage my rule on the throne."

Greyfist lit his pipe. "Why do you think that? It was hard enough convincing him to try for the throne in the first place. Why do it again after losing so ignominiously?"

"Yes, why?" Arkady said. "That is what I have asked myself. It makes no sense. There is no way he can take the throne by law. And to break the law is not to be king. So what could he be attempting?"

Greyfist sat back and puffed on his pipe. "I would say that he is attempting to get shit-faced drunk right about now. As he probably did last night."

Arkady's smile disappeared. "I heard that Eliphas Standish drove him back. But Eliphas has not returned yet."

"Albrecht probably dragged him out for a night on the town before returning to the caern."

"I doubt that. The Gatekeeper is a very dedicated young man. I cannot see him willingly forsaking his new duties here for a simple drunken binge."

Greyfist did not say anything. He just puffed on his pipe.

Arkady stood up. "I know that you had both Albrecht and Eliphas in here after the combat. What did you talk about?"

Greyfist's eyes narrowed. "Personal business. Why are you so curious, Arkady? If you have a problem with Albrecht, why don't you go to New York and take it up with him?"

"Because he is not in New York, is he?" Arkady said, stepping forward and putting his hands on the desk. "Where is he? Where has he gone?"

Greyfist stood up. He did not like the looks of this. Arkady was beginning to look flustered. Greyfist recognized the signs of a frayed temper: Arkady was close to losing control of his anger. Was he really so paranoid about Albrecht?

"Get out of here, Arkady," Greyfist said. "Come back when you can control your rage."

"You cannot order me around, Seneschal," Arkady said, leaning forward, eyes glinting.

"Yes I can. I am Seneschal, and you are an uncrowned king-in-waiting. You will do as I say, cub."

Arkady stood there, breathing heavily, his shoulders shaking. He was obviously trying to control his anger. Greyfist walked around the desk, toward the door. Arkady grabbed his shoulder and pulled his face inches from his own.

"You *will* tell me what conspiracy you and Albrecht have thought up!" Arkady said.

Greyfist put his hand on Arkady's and pried it off his arm. "Get out!"

Arkady exploded into action. His fist slammed into Greyfist's chin, knocking the Philodox to the ground. Arkady was in Crinos form before Greyfist could react, jumping on Greyfist, bearing him down. Arkady's weight knocked the wind out of the Seneschal, but he concentrated and shifted to Crinos form. Arkady still had leverage and size over him; Greyfist was pinned down. Arkady held his right claw to Greyfist's throat while he reached into his pocket for something with the other hand.

"Get off me, Arkady," Greyfist said through gritted teeth. "Before you bring a rite of censure upon yourself!"

"Shut up," Arkady said, pulling a bug out of his pocket. The creature looked like nothing Greyfist had ever seen. It flexed its tiny, chitinous legs as it dangled from Arkady's fingers. Arkady then grabbed Greyfist's chin and pulled it open. Too quickly for Greyfist to stop him, Arkady thrust the bug into Greyfist's mouth and down his throat. He let the Philodox go, jumping away from him.

Greyfist coughed violently, straining to vomit up the bug. His body began to shift back to Homid form, even though he tried to stop it. What the hell was Arkady doing? What had he put into him? He could vaguely feel the thing moving—crawling—down his throat. He choked out a few words, "You…will…suffer…for this!"

"Tell me, Seneschal," Arkady said, standing behind Greyfist. "What plot are you and Albrecht hatching?"

Greyfist stood up and started to speak, to tell Arkady to go fuck himself. But the words would not come out. Instead, he felt a quivering in his gut, which traveled up his spine and into his brain. He couldn't help himself as he said, "Albrecht is after the Silver Crown."

Arkady's eyes slowly opened wide. "But that is a myth! A legend! No Silver Fang has worn the crown in…in ages!"

Greyfist tried to move toward the door, but he couldn't. His legs wouldn't work. "What…what the hell is this thing?"

"It is a gift from an…ally," Arkady said. "One who knew you would not tell me what I needed to know. Conspiracy against the throne is a very serious charge, Seneschal."

"Damn you! No one has conspired. You are not king yet!"

"Oh, but soon. Soon," Arkady said. "Now, where has Albrecht gone?"

"To Antonine Teardrop."

Arkady's face fell into a frown. "Why did you involve him? He will tell Loba! She is an exile! You are delivering protectorate secrets to outsiders."

"You know that's not true," Greyfist said, feeling dizzy. "You're fishing for accusations. It won't work. You've attacked the Seneschal in his own den. I will have a rite against you, Arkady."

Arkady growled. "We will see who wields more power here, Seneschal. Where is Albrecht going from Teardrop's?"

"I don't know," Greyfist said, feeling sick to his stomach. He collapsed onto the floor.

Arkady looked worried. "What do you mean, you don't know? Surely you know where the crown is, if you sent him off for it? Why are you on the floor?"

"I…feel…terrible. What the hell did you put in me?"

Arkady looked very worried now. "Put your finger down your throat! Throw the thing up!"

Greyfist growled in pain, clutching his stomach. "It's a Wyrm creature, isn't it?"

"No!" Arkady said, leaning down over him. "It's just a fetish to make you answer my questions. It had no Wyrm scent on it."

Greyfist looked at Arkady angrily and then growled low and menacingly, looking past the Silver Fang. Arkady turned around to see a large Crinos Black Spiral Dancer step from the Umbra, grinning madly.

"Damn you!" Arkady yelled at the Dancer. "What is your fetish doing to him?"

"Killing him slowly and painfully," the Black Spiral Dancer replied, sauntering over to them.

Greyfist grabbed the fur about Arkady's throat and pulled his head around. He locked eyes with Arkady. "You bastard! You've betrayed the throne to the Wyrm!"

Arkady looked surprised. "No…. No! He was not supposed to come here. I did not intend this!"

Greyfist growled and tried to dig his claws into Arkady's throat, but a sudden pain washed over his body. He grabbed his gut again and howled as blood broke forth from a wound opening out of his stomach. The Wyrm bug crawled its way out of the wound, chewing the flesh around the edges. Arkady stared at it in horror.

Greyfist's eyes rolled up into his head and he collapsed. With the last of his strength, he whispered to Arkady, "You are doomed. Albrecht will find the crown and become the true king."

Arkady stared in shock at the Seneschal. He carefully put his hand on the Garou's shoulder and shook it. But there was no response. Greyfist was dead.

Arkady turned around to see the Black Spiral Dancer smirking down at him. "Dagrack! How dare you? We had a bargain! You have betrayed me!" He rose and pointed a clawed hand at the Garou.

Dagrack shrank, assuming Homid form. He stood about five foot eleven, with black hair streaming over his shoulders. He had a long, thin face, but a smile which spread practically from ear to ear. He held up his hands, cautioning Arkady. "Now, now, ally. You misunderstand. I am only helping you in ways you have not yet realized. Did you really think you could interrogate the Seneschal like that, and not have to kill him afterwards? I'm only saving you from him."

"But why did you come here? If the others see—"

"Calm down your wayward temper, O king," Dagrack said. "The Gatekeeper is gone, remember? No one saw me pass over. We will now proceed to stage a scene. You came to talk with the Seneschal, and things were going just fine, when a horrible Black Spiral Dancer—me—came leaping from the Umbra. Using its forbidden and unholy Wyrm powers, it killed the Seneschal. And cut you up badly before fleeing, wounded by your mighty blows."

Arkady clutched his fists and stared angrily at the wall. "No. I do not like this one bit. You think you can take control of me now because we have bargained. It is not so. I will not allow it. I did not wish the Seneschal dead. He was loyal! He would have been loyal to me!"

"Untrue," Dagrack said, walking over to Greyfist's body. He reached down and picked up the bug, putting it in his pants pocket. "He was trying to dethrone you before you had even worn the crown! You call that loyal?"

"I will not listen to you!" Arkady shouted.

Dagrack walked up and looked him in the eyes. "Oh yes, you will. Who was it who saved you all those years ago from the fomori slavering for your blood, back in the Motherland? Who helped you escape to this new land, a land where you have built yourself a base of power? You are to be king! And you have gotten here because of my aid. I have told you before, our goals are not dissimilar. It is because of the Fangs' witchhunt against my tribe that we cannot work together to heal the damage to Gaia, to war against her true enemies."

"Stop it! I do not want to hear this. Lies! You think your stupid logic will convince me?"

"If you don't believe it, why have you accepted our aid for so long? It wasn't my Garou who failed to kill Albrecht. If your two exiled flunkies had done their job, you wouldn't be in this mess now, and I wouldn't have to bail you out."

Arkady fumed, silent. He stared at Greyfist's dead body.

"Enough of this," Dagrack said. "We must bloody ourselves, and I must escape, before more Garou come."

"What if I do more than bloody you? What if I kill you and show the trophy to the tribe?"

Dagrack smiled. "Then my packbrothers and sisters will do everything in their power to reveal your treachery against the Silver Fangs. You will become a pariah, worse than your hated Albrecht. No Garou will trust you then. At least Albrecht has the Bone Gnawers to feed him. You…you will feed only with the lost."

Arkady glared at Dagrack as if trying to decide his course. He then lowered his head.

"What do I need to do?" Arkady asked.

"First," Dagrack said, opening his shirt as he walked up to Arkady, "slash me across the chest. And then across the thigh. Oh, and a head wound would be good, too. After that, I'll rip you up a bit, so you'll have some wounds to show for it. I'll drip the blood all over before I leave."

Arkady slashed out at Dagrack, hard and fiercely, cutting open his chest. Blood sprayed forth.

"Oh," Dagrack said, his eyes rolling up with what seemed like pleasure. "A bit more than necessary, but good anyway. Now, the thigh."

Arkady was disgusted. He stepped back from the Dancer. "No. There is enough of your blood here now. They will believe me."

"Not without this, they won't," Dagrack said, reaching his claw out quickly and slashing Arkady across the shoulder. Arkady grimaced, but didn't move. "One more." He slashed Arkady's left thigh, where a scar from the challenge combat two nights ago was still visible. Arkady winced and stared coldly at the Dancer.

Dagrack smiled. "Well, I'm off. Don't worry, I'll dispatch some packs to hunt down Albrecht. He won't get far." The Dancer stared at his spilled blood on the floor, leaning down close, looking for reflections within it. He stared so for nearly five minutes, and then faded out of view, into the Umbra.

Arkady kicked a chair and cursed. He looked down at Greyfist. "I am sorry, Seneschal. I never meant this. Take this condolence: I will not be pushed around so for long. I will turn the tables. It has always been my plan. It is hard to understand, I know. But…you have no idea of the horrors in Russia. How hard it is to escape. Can you think? How many have slipped past the Shadow Curtain besides me? None. I am the only one. But…a bargain was required. I will turn the tables, Seneschal. Believe that."

He then walked to the door, opened it, and howled long and hard. The Warning of the Wyrm's Approach.

11

The pack traveled down the curve of the shining road. The Moon Path reflected the radiance of the half moon above them, faint near the edges, but brighter in the center. In certain places along the road, the path actually broke up, forcing them to walk on the dark, nondescript ground between the shards of moonlight. The unformed ephemera—raw spirit—was all that could be seen in every direction around them. Their only marker was the path.

Occasionally they passed a Lune, one of the guardian spirits of the Moon Paths, gliding by on its mysterious errand. The mobile strips of moonlight spun slowly around and around as they moved past, in some unfathomable form of communication. Even Mari, who knew the language of the spirits, was puzzled. Lunes were among the most enigmatic of spirits, especially during a crescent moon. But even under a half moon, the Lunes were strange.

The pack let the Lunes pass and kept on their way. They traveled for hours, each chewing on his or her own thoughts, not sharing them with the others. The Moon Path cut through many small domains, but the pack stayed their course. As long as they remained on the Moon Path, they were relatively safe from whatever spirits laired in the domains into which they trespassed. Safe also from the odd laws of nature which were often different in each domain or realm of the spirit world. Reality was a local phenomenon here, not the shared fact known in the material world.

In one domain—a chimare, a mortal's dream given reality—they saw a man leap from a skyscraper. He fell for a long time—longer than the height should have allowed. His family and friends gathered on the street below, staring up at him and gossiping about his predicament. Before he hit the ground, the chimare unraveled and became featureless ephemera again.

The pack kept walking. Later, after passing through a mountainous mini-realm, Mari stopped and consulted the map. "I think the Lunae is just ahead. Maybe forty minutes at the most."

"I hope so," Albrecht said, pointing to the horizon. "The moon has almost set. It'll be dark in half an hour. I don't want to be out here much longer after that. Once this Moon Path goes, we're lost."

"The paths soak up light, though," Evan said. "This one should hold the light, like one of those glow-in-the-dark toys, for at least long enough for us to get to the Lunae."

"Well, let's get moving anyway," Albrecht said, walking again. "The Moon Paths are our only fixed geography. Everything else here changes so much, we'd never find our way to Pangaea in time without them."

Mari nodded, folded the map, put it in her pocket and moved on, with Evan behind her.

Half an hour later, the moon had indeed set and all was dark, except for a slight radiance from the Moon Path. Albrecht shifted into Lupus form, his backpack shrinking to conform to his new shoulder width. He had performed the Rite of Talisman Dedication on all of his equipment, allowing it to change shape to accommodate his various forms. Mari and Evan followed suit and each of them walked down the path on four legs. They made better time that way, and soon Albrecht could see a light over the next rise. As he came over it, he saw a large, glowing circle of light. Bisecting it crossways to their Moon Path was another Moon Path. A crossroads.

"This is it," Albrecht said. "The Lunae. Antonine was right."

"Let's go," Evan said, sprinting forward.

"Wait," Mari said. "Let me go first. There may be other spirits there. We don't want to pick a fight just by walking in."

Evan slowed down and let Mari pass him.

"Let us know when it's okay to go in," Albrecht said.

"I will," Mari said, shifting to Glabro form. She stepped into the circle of light, disappearing from view. Albrecht and Evan shifted back to Homid form and waited at the edge. The Moon Path was fainter, as was the other one bisecting the circle, but they weren't worried now. If worst came to worst, they'd step into the Lunae and deal with whatever was there.

Regardless of the spirits there, the Lunes would intercede in any fights. But no one wanted that. That kind of intercession could lead to anything: most often the antagonists popping up in some strange realm far away, transported there by the angry Lunes.

Mari, now in Homid form, poked her head out and motioned them in. They stepped into the circle and blinked at the brightness. When their eyes had adjusted, they saw a large, silver-white glade, with a single white tree and a lawn of white grass surrounding it. Three Lunes glided slowly about, like helium balloons set loose on a random course. A crow perched in the tree and cawed at them as they came through.

"That's Ivan," Mari said. "He's a naturae spirit taking haven here for the day while traveling the airts. Don't worry about him."

Albrecht nodded and walked to the base of the tree. Shrugging his pack off, he sat down, pulled out a cigarette and lit it up. Slowly taking a drag, he leaned back, smiling, then let out a cloud of smoke. *That's the ticket,* he thought. *Nothing like a good smoke after a long walk.*

Evan walked over and dropped his pack. After untying his sleeping bag and spreading it out, he lay down and rolled over. He was asleep in seconds. Mari was watching the Lunes, trying to fathom their movements. She gave up after a few minutes and came over to the tree, sitting down next to Albrecht.

"I haven't done a walk like that in a long time," she said.

"Me neither," Albrecht said, still smoking. "It's hell on the feet. I think we should travel in Lupus more often."

Mari sighed. "I guess. I prefer Homid or Glabro, however. I fight better that way."

"You can always shift if you need to."

"I know, but…I'd like to be ready for anything."

"You're pretty paranoid, aren't you? I don't mean in the conspiracy-theory sense, but in the…distrusting sense. You seem to think there's always someone out there ready to pop you one."

"So? In my experience, there is. The world is cruel to the unwary, Albrecht."

"Yeah, I guess it is. But going around always expecting the worst…I don't know. It seems like a waste of energy to me."

"And sucking in toxic fumes, like that cigarette you have there, isn't? Someone in this pack has to be ready in case of attack."

"Okay, okay. Don't bite my head off. Just trying some small talk is all. I'm going to crash. See you tomorrow."

"I'll take first watch. I'll wake you for the second."

"Watch? We don't need a watch. The Lunes'll warn us if anything dangerous approaches."

"We can't depend on that—"

"Yes we can. We are in a Lunae, Mari. A crossroads of Moon Paths. Luna herself protects these. If something were to happen here, believe me, we'd have enough time to deal with it. So go to bed. And don't wake me up for a stupid watch." Albrecht lay down on the grass. He rubbed his cigarette into the ephemeral dirt and put the stub in his pocket. He then rolled over and was snoring in less than five minutes.

Mari looked around for a while. When she was satisfied that the place was safe, she spread out her bedroll and lay back on it. Even with her eyes closed, it took her a while to get to sleep. Every time the crow on the branches above moved, she started, expecting danger. But she finally forced herself to ignore it, and was soon asleep.

As the moon rose the next evening, they packed up their bags and left the Lunae. The crow was already gone, presumably having left at the first crack of moonrise. They traveled down the same Moon Path, but this time they were in Lupus form from the beginning of their journey. It did make for better time, and they traveled farther than they had expected by the next morning, when the sun rose in the material world and the moon set in their world.

An hour before moonset, they had seen no sign of another Lunae.

"I think we've got to take the next domain we find," Albrecht said. "We can't stay out here. It's too unpredictable."

"And a domain isn't?" Mari said.

"Less so than the barrens between realms with no Moon Path," Albrecht said, looking at her.

She stared back at him. "What do you suggest?"

"The first thing we come upon, that's what," Albrecht said.

"Hey!" Evan called. He was a few paces ahead of them, bending to the ground. "There are some tracks here. Rabbit, I think."

Mari brightened up. "There must be a Glen nearby. I can't imagine a rabbit wandering so far otherwise."

"Let's keep our eyes out then," Albrecht said, continuing on down the road. The others followed him.

Ten minutes later, they saw the Glen. It was thirty yards to their right, off the Moon Path. It was unmistakable. The scent of grass and pollen wafted across the barrens to them. They could see the vague outline of trees from the path. After looking carefully around, they set out for it, stepping off the path, staying close to each other. Soon, they were within the boundary of the Glen, a sub-realm within the spirit world, a pocket reality which followed the laws of nature known in the material world. Of the many geographies in the Umbra—realms, domains, sub-realms, Moon Paths—Glens were perhaps the most normal; a welcome respite from the weird rules of the spirit world.

They all breathed a sigh of relief and looked around. It wasn't a very big place, perhaps five acres square, but it was lush. Trees grew up around a small clearing in the center, and a babbling brook ran across it, entering from nowhere on one side and exiting to nowhere on the other. Albrecht wondered what would happen to something that was placed in the stream. Where would it float to?

Signs of small fauna could be seen, such as rabbit tracks and mice prints. They walked around the place, making sure that everything smelled right, that the scent of the Wyrm was nowhere to be found. Satisfied with the purity of the place, they gathered in the clearing by the brook.

"I wonder what created this place," Albrecht said. "It's awfully weird to find it here."

"It was planted on purpose," Evan said.

"How do you know that?" Mari said, looking around for signs of intention.

"That tree over there," Evan said, pointing at the largest of the trees surrounding the clearing. "It has a pictogram on it. It says that this place was planted by a traveling pack of Children of Gaia."

"Well, that was awfully nice of them," Albrecht said. "Now we know it's all sweet and cozy here. That explains the cute bunny rabbits."

"Albrecht!" Mari said. "It's because of their forethought that we have a place to rest tonight. They don't deserve your mocking."

Albrecht nodded, holding his hands up toward Mari. "I know, I know. I'm just a cynical bastard, that's all. I'll shut up."

They ate their dinner in silence and then pulled out their packs and went to sleep. This time, however, Mari took the watch. She woke Albrecht in the middle of the day to tell him it was his turn. He nodded and got up, not bothering to argue with her. Surprised, she crawled under her slight covers. Although she was suspicious of danger, she knew she needed sleep for the next leg of their journey, and soon went to sleep. She slept lightly, though, having taught herself to wake at a moment's notice.

Albrecht sat by the brook, thinking about their journey. He had no clue where to start looking once they reached Pangaea. And if the crown wasn't there, what would they do then?

He heard the scuffle of a small creature moving through the underbrush on the other side of the stream. The rabbit came out and stared at Albrecht. Albrecht nodded at it. It quivered its nose and hopped back into the brush.

Albrecht looked up at the sky. He could see stars, which surprised him, although they were faint, as if they were very far off. Albrecht realized that this Glen looked up into the Aetherial Realm, the realm where the sky spirits resided. The place where Moon Bridges crossed. He wondered what Garou were now passing through those stars on their way to caerns all over the earth.

He sat thinking about such things for the rest of the day, until the moon rose again.

They took to the Moon Path again that night. After they had walked for many hours, the path began to curve wildly, and the ephemeral landscape around them started to change. Hills rose up and down; fields rippled and moved under a nonexistent wind. Wisps of cloud floated past them, ephemera that couldn't decide if they were clouds or fog banks.

"We are very near," Mari said. "The signs of the Wyld are all about us."

"How far do you figure it is?" Albrecht asked, looking about nervously. The Moon Path had already broken up twice. He hoped it could stay together far enough to get them to Pangaea.

"Who can say?" Mari said.

They kept walking. The moon was low on the horizon when they came around a large hill, and stepped into sunlight and a primordial jungle. They looked around, surprised. They had seen no sign of the realm, but suddenly they were there, standing in Pangaea. The musky jungle smells overwhelmed them after the day's walk in a largely scentless environment.

"Wow," said Evan. "So this is it?"

"Yes," Mari said, stepping forward to peer through the thick stand of trees before them. "Look here! Between these trees."

They all stepped up and looked. Beyond the trees, the landscape fell downwards, a vegetative cliff face. The vista from here was astonishing.

Laid out before them was a land from an earlier time, a primal forest of Jurassic plants. A place humans could only imagine. But here, for the pack, it was real.

Pterodactyls glided far out over the huge sea which encompassed the horizon to their right. Herds of prehistoric antelope could be seen farther off, roaming across a grassland plain. Behind the pack, through the stand of trees that now hid the Moon Path, the land rose up, and they could see mountains with timber forests along their bases. The clash of geographical regions was remarkable.

And the marks of civilization were nowhere to be seen; not a hint or clue of them. No roads, no buildings, no litter. No sound of cars or machines in the distance. Only far-off bird cries and the hum of insects. The thrashing of huge beasts in the forests. Nothing but nature, pure and untrammeled.

"Gaia…." Albrecht murmured. "It's incredible. It really is as amazing as they say." He turned to look at the other two and saw them staring speechlessly at the landscape. Something deep within him—within them, too—was stirring. Something ancient and primal, some deep sense of wonder and belonging. He had a sense that, somehow, regardless of his city ways, he was home. They were all home.

"Do you feel it?" Albrecht said. "I don't know, some sense of…belonging."

"Yes," Mari said. "All my senses are awake, even in Homid form. It's as if all my instincts were alive, as if they had finally found an outlet."

"It's great!" Evan said. "Far more real than any Boy Scout outing."

Albrecht looked at him and shook his head. "If that's all you've got to compare it to, you need to get out more."

"I *am* out," Evan said. "I think I can truly say, as none of us have ever been able to say before, that I am *out*. I am outside!"

Mari laughed. She looked about them, at the trees and the ground. "Look here. Dinosaur tracks."

Albrecht looked and saw what indeed looked like dinosaur tracks, although small ones. *One of those egg-stealers*, he thought. *But if the small ones can be here, so can the big.* "You know, I just thought of something. The legends about this place say there are dinosaurs. Big dinosaurs. Dinosaurs who eat Garou."

Mari and Evan looked at him.

"I mean, we need to be careful. It's fine and dandy to enjoy it all, but we've really got to be on our toes here. This is primal. That means dog-eat-dog. What Mari said about the food chain here is right: we're not the highest point on it."

"Correct," Mari said. "We should not let our guard down. It *is* dangerous here."

Evan looked disappointed, but nodded.

"Now," Albrecht said. "We've got to figure out where in this jungle to look for the Silver Crown."

"I've been thinking," Evan said. "We should start with the legends about this place. What does the Silver Record say?"

"I don't know," Albrecht said. "I thought you were more familiar with that. It's a Philodox and Galliard thing, isn't it?"

"It's our history," Mari said, staring scornfully at Albrecht. "We should all be familiar with it. Especially a king."

"I think there is something," Evan said. "I'm not sure. There's a line about the Litany. How does it go? Uh…. 'A Grand Moot of all Garou was called at Table Rock. All gathered from all over the world in a night's time where they were one Tribe, and the Galliards chanted the first Litany. From sunrise to sundown they repeated the words until all present could remember.'"

"That's pretty good, kid," Albrecht said. "How'd you remember all that?"

"We live in an oral culture, Albrecht. It's our duty to remember these things. Not everyone can keep records like Antonine."

"Well, what do you think it means? I didn't hear a mention of Pangaea there."

"That's just it: there's no direct reference. But that line about 'where they were one Tribe.' At a place called Table Rock. I think that's here. Don't you remember the other stories, the ones that say that all Garou are of one tribe when they enter Pangaea?"

"I've heard those, but I don't believe them. How can we lose our tribehood? It's inherent."

"But this is the Umbra, Albrecht," Mari said. "Anything can happen here. Landscapes and identities are fluid. Nothing is set."

"Fine. Let's assume Table Rock is here. What then?"

"Well, it seems to me that it would be a good place to hide the crown," Evan said. "If the record is correct, that is the place where Garou civilization began, with the Litany, Gaia's covenants. If it's not there, then surely a clue will be."

Albrecht nodded. "All right. Sounds like a starting point. Where do we go? Where is Table Rock?"

"I don't know," Evan said, looking around. "I don't have the slightest idea of where to start."

"Well," Mari said. "Where would Garou gather? Table Rock has to be someplace hospitable for Garou."

Albrecht looked out across the vista behind them. "Do you see that? Way out there, to the…north, I guess it is? It looks like a timber forest. I think that's where we'll find wolves. And where there are wolves…."

Mari nodded. "Let's head that way."

"How long a walk do you figure?" Evan asked.

"At least a half-day," Mari said.

"Assuming no interruptions," Albrecht said, walking off into the forest.

Their wonder increased as they went. After a while, the woods grew so thick they were forced to take Lupus form to get through the brush.

"Albrecht!" Mari said in the Garou tongue. "What happened to your fur?"

Albrecht looked at his pelt and barked in surprise. It was no longer white, but gray, like a common wolf. "My fur!" He looked at Mari and Evan and saw that their fur had also changed. "Mari, your black pelt is gray! Evan, yours is grayer than usual."

They all looked at each other.

"What's going on here?" Albrecht said.

"One tribe," Evan said. "We're all one tribe. No marks of breed to distinguish us. You're no longer a…a…. I can't remember what tribe you were."

Albrecht thought. "I can't either. I don't even know what tribe you guys are!"

Mari smiled. "Good. Maybe now you'll learn some humility."

"Perhaps you will, too," Evan said. "You're not a…well, you know. You're not your tribe anymore either."

"I don't need my tribe to know who I am," Mari said, and sauntered off ahead into the forest. The others followed.

Even in wolf form, the going was still slow. They had to stop many times to get their bearings. The environment changed from hardwoods to pines. After a few hours, Albrecht caught the scent of wolves. He stopped and looked around, sniffing.

"Territory," he concluded, turning to Mari and Evan. "We're in a wolf pack's territory. They've marked it in various spots," he said, pointing to a tree and a rock. "Think we should announce ourselves?"

"I don't think it can hurt," Mari said. "Go ahead."

"What's a good howl? I don't want to scare them off."

"A simple Howl of Greeting will do."

Albrecht sat back on his haunches and howled. A long, one-note howl. He looked about, waiting for signs of approaching wolves. Soon he smelled a wolf off to the left, still a ways off, but approaching them warily. Then, to the right, another smell. Also to the front now. They were approaching from all sides.

Ahead, a wolf stepped from behind a tree, obviously the alpha. Albrecht couldn't believe its size—it was a prehistoric dire wolf, akin to the Hispo form of the Garou. Then, even more surprisingly, the wolf spoke in a broken Garou tongue. It wasn't a wolf; it was a Garou.

"What…want…here?" it said, glaring at the pack.

"We seek Table Rock," Albrecht said. "I am Lord Albrecht of the…well, a Garou. My packmates are Mari Cabrah and Evan Heals-the-Past."

The alpha cocked his head. "I…Rake-to-Death. Lupus. This my place!"

"We don't want your territory!" Albrecht said. "We just want to pass through, to Table Rock."

The alpha seemed to be torn. He paced around, growling low. Then he turned to them and said, "Follow." He whirled and headed to the north.

Albrecht, Mari and Evan followed. The Garou alpha's pack could be seen and heard running along with them, a few paces away to either side. The land rose up, and they were soon running up a hill, struggling to keep up with the alpha. They finally came to the top of the rise, and looked down into a bowl-shaped valley. In the center of the valley was a large, flat rock, resting horizontally on top of a vertical slab.

"Table Rock," the alpha said, watching them as they came over the rise.

"Thanks," Albrecht said.

The alpha moved back into the woods, and the pack moved down into the valley. As soon as the wolf was out of sight, they all shifted into Homid form.

"I don't think he liked us," Albrecht said.

"We're too civilized for him," Evan said. "I don't think he's native: he doesn't seem like a spirit. He's obviously trying to get back to nature. Our reminders of civilization—our backpacks and all—probably don't help."

They reached the bottom of the valley and walked carefully up to the rock. Painted Garou pictograms adorned it, faded with time, wind and rain. The ashy remains of many fires were scattered about.

"Well, here's a sign of fire at least," Albrecht said, kicking some of the ashes. "That's civilized."

"It's probably the only concession to tool-use we'll find here," Evan said, roaming about the rock, looking into every small fissure he could find. He tried to read the faded pictograms, but few of them made any sense. "These writings are old. I can't make out most of them. Those I can read seem incomplete. None of them has anything to do with a crown, or even leadership."

Albrecht explored the valley, looking for signs of any buried objects or caves. He came back to the rock, where Evan and Mari were searching, and threw up his hands. "Nothing. There's nothing here. We're not going to find anything."

"Don't be so defeatist," Mari said, sitting down. "Maybe we need to wait. Something might show itself."

"Yeah, like a big Tyrannosaurus Rex." Albrecht sat down and fumed.

"Look," Mari said. "Maybe some Garou will show up who know this place better than we do."

"Yeah, real likely. We could be waiting weeks for that."

"I think we should camp here tonight," Evan said, coming over to sit with them. "We can figure out our next step in the morning."

Albrecht looked up at the sun. "It's weird to see the sun again. It's really throwing off my hours. Been used to night travel for a while."

"Look," Evan said. "This place is sort of like a caern. You never know what could show up under moonlight."

"All right," Albrecht said. "We'll wait here tonight. Tomorrow morning, we'll figure out a new plan." He stretched out and looked up at the shifting clouds.

Mari moved her bag to the base of the rock. "I think we should camp close to the rock. There are no animal tracks around here, almost as if they know better than to come here."

Albrecht sat up and looked around. "I hadn't thought of that. Interesting. Now, what could be driving a bunch of wild animals away from here?"

"I doubt it's the rage of the Garou," Evan said. "Maybe it's something spiritual. There may be a ritual in effect here."

"How would we go about finding out?" Albrecht said.

"Normally we'd look for signs of a ritual, such as pictograms. Those are already here. Maybe it's just the strength of successive rituals. Maybe it's the fact that fires have been lit here. That may be bad mojo for the inhabitants. Remember, Albrecht, these animals may act like animals, but they're really spirits."

"I keep forgetting. Seems so real," Albrecht got up and pulled his bags closer to the rock. "Well, I'm going to get some shut-eye. Do you want me to help you light a fire first?"

"We can manage," Evan said. "Besides, I got more sleep than either of you. You should both sleep. I'll stay up for first watch."

Mari nodded and lay down. Soon, she and Albrecht were both asleep. Evan sat for a while, listening to the sounds of the primordial world. He swatted more than a couple of times at some very large insects. *These are going to get annoying,* he thought. He wondered if there was anything he could do to ward them off, but decided that there wasn't. Except for a fire, perhaps.

He walked to the edge of the valley and started gathering what old wood he could find. He found mostly pine, which he knew didn't burn well, but there were few hardwoods in the region. He soon had a stack of wood in his arms. After carrying it back, he dug a shallow fire pit, then walked around again, this time gathering twigs and dry pine needles for kindling. These he brought back to the gathered wood and pulled out a box of matches from the sealed plastic baggy he carried them in. *Be prepared,* he thought wryly. He struck the match and held it to the kindling. It flared into life, catching on the dry twigs and growing bigger.

Evan sat back and readied himself for a long afternoon. He thought about the quest they were on and the metaphors in the fable they had heard from Antonine. He tried to figure out if these things had any meaning for them, on this quest. *Four gates,* he thought. *Have we passed any yet? Or, more importantly, has Albrecht passed any of them? Does he need to? That was just one story. The other story, about the bad king, didn't have any gates to pass. Is the quest different for everyone?*

The sun was beginning to set. Standing up and stretching, he figured he should wake Mari up and get some sleep himself. The fire was dwindling. Twice already he had had to go in search of more wood. One more trip would probably be enough for the rest of the night.

He walked into the woods again—and froze in his tracks. A loud bellow came from beyond the grove before him: a sound which tapped something primal in him, making him want to flee in terror. He shivered, but gathered his will not to move. He was a Garou, after all; his rage was his courage. After a few moments of silence, he crept forward and peeked around a large tree.

A dinosaur tore at the flesh of its fresh kill. It chewed at the bloody remains of the deer, every now and then peeking about, bird-like, to make sure nothing else was near. It stood on two legs and had sharp claws on its small forearms.

Oh shit! Evan thought. *It's one of those raptors from that movie. That means more of them must be around.* He slowly and quietly shifted to Crinos form and concentrated on his surroundings, using his near-lupine senses to discover if the dinosaur had friends nearby. But he smelled and heard nothing. The dinosaur appeared to be alone. Evan breathed a sigh of relief and backed up, turning around to head back to camp.

He heard the noise before he saw it. Only his Garou senses and speed saved him, as he jumped to the left in time to avoid the rush of the raptor. It sped past him, crying in anger and spinning around.

Evan shifted to Hispo form, the dire wolf, and ran forward, hoping to throw the thing off by attacking it. The raptor shifted to the side and slashed at Evan as he ran by. Its claws tore off some fur, but Evan's adrenaline was pumping too much for him to feel the pain.

He kept running, hoping to make it back to camp to get his packmates' help. He was afraid that he was no match for this natural predator. He heard it moving in the woods to his right, running to head him off. Suddenly he saw the Table Rock clearing ahead and put on an extra burst of speed. The raptor lunged from the trees as he sped past, then stopped dead in its tracks.

Evan ran into the open clearing and turned around to face his attacker. But it stood at the fringe of the woods, looking edgy, nervously tramping the ground. Finally it honked in frustration and slipped back into the cover of the trees.

Evan let out his breath and collapsed. After long minutes of thanking Gaia for his life, he stood up and shifted back to Homid form. His wound was only a scratch. He was also pumped up, and knew he wouldn't be sleeping anytime soon. But his guess about the supernatural nature of the clearing had been right; it did spook the natural inhabitants.

He walked over to Mari but stopped before he got to her. There was a shimmering light on the other side of the rock, growing bigger by the second.

What now? he wondered as he ran to the edge of the rock and peeked around. In the empty air, a hole had opened, silvered moonlight flowing out of it. A wolf leaped out of the hole and looked around.

Evan ducked back behind the rock and ran to Mari. He shook her awake and covered her mouth before she could speak. "There's a Moon Bridge on the other side of the rock. Someone's come out of it."

Mari bolted up. She instantly assumed Glabro form, growing larger and more muscled, but uglier and more brutish also. "Wake Albrecht," she whispered, and crept over to the corner of the rock.

Evan shook Albrecht awake, clamping his hand down on the other's mouth before he could say anything. Albrecht frowned up at Evan. "Shhh,"

Evan said softly. "There's a Moon Bridge behind the rock, and a Garou came out of it."

Albrecht's eyes widened and he stood up. "What the hell is a Moon Bridge doing here? I thought they couldn't open into this realm." He drew his Grand Klaive out and went to where Mari was standing. Evan followed him. They all poked their heads around the corner and saw more strangers come out of the Moon Bridge.

There were now six wolves, each looking and sniffing about. The Moon Bridge closed up, and the shimmering light was cut off. One of the wolves seemed to pick up a scent, and it barked at the others.

Albrecht raised his eyebrows. "They've found our scent. They seem to have been expecting it."

The new arrivals spread out, three around the far side of the rock, while the other three headed for the corner where the pack was watching. Albrecht pulled Evan and Mari back.

"Who the hell are they?" he asked. "They're obviously looking for us."

"We've got to leave," Mari said. "Now."

Evan started to run back to his backpack, but Albrecht grabbed him by the shirt collar.

"No time for that," he said. "We leave now."

Evan looked disappointed, but followed Albrecht and Mari as they ran to the edge of the forest. Behind them they heard a howl which immediately became multiple howls as all seven wolves picked it up. They had been seen. The chase was on.

Albrecht shifted to Crinos, as did Mari. Evan began the shift while he ran, but he was having trouble concentrating. He looked over his shoulder and saw the wolf pack nearly on his heels. Yelling out, he called on his rage. In an instant he was in Crinos form, and he took to four legs, catching up with Albrecht and Mari.

The wolves howled and barked, spreading out through the forest, trying to overtake the pack.

Albrecht led the pack to the left, along a ridge that apparently went to the mountain pass. If he could get to a tight pass, they could fight the wolves one-on-one.

One of the wolves caught up with them and snapped at Mari's heels. Mari spun around and slashed at it, spinning back again and continuing her run. Her claws had connected: the wolf's snout had opened up, and blood sprayed onto the pine-needle blanket that covered the ground. The wolf yelped and stopped the chase, but the other wolves ran past him.

Mari's brief attack had lost her some ground. She ran after the rest of the pack, but she was off course, running to the right where they had gone left. Too late to compensate for her mistake, she yelled out to them, "Keep running! I'll meet up with you!"

Albrecht growled back in acknowledgment. He kept the pace up, slowing himself slightly when it looked like Evan might fall behind.

The wolves split up. Three of them—the wounded one among them—went after Albrecht and Evan, while the other three went after Mari.

Mari broke through a thick stand of pines and slipped down a hill, sliding on the needles but managing to keep her balance. Ahead, to the left, was a cave mouth big enough for only one person to stand in it. She ran for it, hearing the wolves still behind her. As she entered the cave, she saw a light glowing from deep within, around a far curve. She ran forward, hearing her pursuers enter the cave behind her and abandoning her plan of holding them off at the entrance. As she came around the curve, she stopped short, staring around her in shock.

The cave was gone. She now stood on a muddy field under gray skies and roiling clouds. In the distance she heard moans of pain and, farther off, screams of horror. Barbed wire snaked through the field, and she thought she saw human limbs—hands and feet—buried in the dirt.

No! she thought. *This can't be. I've left Pangaea. This is another realm. Gaia, please let it not be what I think it is.*

She heard howling behind her and turned to see the wolves appear one by one. They stopped and stared at her, grinning evilly. Their gray fur began to change, to grow blacker. On two of them the fur began to fall off in patches, revealing mangy hides underneath. The pursuers began cackling. As the laws of Pangaea faded, they once more assumed their tribal aspects. Their ears grew to ugly proportions, with interior ridges—becoming the ears of a bat, not a wolf.

Mari growled at the Black Spiral Dancers and centered herself, ready for their charge.

12

Albrecht and Evan ran through the crevasse. They had managed to outdistance the wolves in the twisting, turning gully, but they still heard the howls behind them, just out of sight. Albrecht was trying to find a good place to make their stand. He didn't like the numbers they were up against. Evan wasn't a great fighter, and Albrecht didn't want to have to worry about him while he took on two of the wolves himself, leaving the other to attack the boy.

The ground was on a steady incline, and Albrecht could hear rushing water ahead. Albrecht prayed the water was a river running parallel to them; if it ran crosswise, they would have to make their stand, backs to the water.

They came out of the crevasse onto a ledge above a raging river which rushed from their right to their left. Albrecht cursed. They were trapped here. He looked around, trying to find some advantage to the ledge. Shoving Evan to one side of the ledge, he set himself on the other side. Their only hope was that the wolves would be running fast enough to have to fight to slow their momentum before they fell into the river below. Albrecht and Evan could then take them from behind, perhaps using their unbalance to shove them off the ledge.

The howls were mere yards away. Albrecht hunkered down against the rock and motioned to Evan to do the same.

The first wolf ran past them and scooted to a halt at the lip of the cliff. Before the next wolf appeared, Albrecht leapt at the first and kicked him in the back. The wolf somersaulted forward, over the lip, waving his limbs spastically as he hung in midair for a moment. He then fell into the water and was carried away by the current.

The second wolf vaulted onto the ledge and slammed into Albrecht, who had to pivot to keep from going over. The she-wolf was at his throat, sinking in her fangs. Albrecht grabbed her torso between his arms and squeezed her with all his might. That seemed to knock the wind out of her, since she let go of Albrecht's throat, coughing. Albrecht lifted her up and threw her over the ledge. She yipped and scrambled in the air, as if trying to swim back to the ledge. But Albrecht's throw had been good, and the wolf flew into the river.

Meanwhile, the third wolf had slunk around the corner and chomped into Evan's left leg while the boy was watching Albrecht. Evan cried out and slashed his claws at the wolf's neck, but the wolf lithely dodged and jumped in for another nip. Evan stepped back, dangerously close to the edge. When the wolf leapt in for a third bite, Evan stumbled backwards and fell off the cliff. At the last second, he reached out, grabbing for anything to keep him from falling. His hand closed on the wolf's thick pelt. The wolf tried to step back, but Evan's momentum took them both over and into the river.

"Evan!" Albrecht cried out, trying to catch sight of him once he disappeared under the water. Down to the left he resurfaced, struggling to stay up. He was already yards downstream and traveling faster. Albrecht cursed and leapt in.

The water was freezing, run-off from the mountaintop snows. Albrecht concentrated, knowing he couldn't allow the shock to stun him. He swam as fast as he could downstream, trying to catch up to the struggling Evan. He passed one of the enemy wolves crawling onto the far bank, exhausted.

As he looked ahead for Evan, he saw curls of white water. Rocks jutted out of the stream, and the water rushed around them at incredible speed. As he maneuvered around the boulders, Albrecht hoped the kid hadn't slammed into one of them.

Far ahead, he heard Evan yell.

"I'm coming, kid!" he shouted. "Try to grab a branch or a rock!" Then he saw Evan.

The boy was in the middle of the current, heading for a large spray of mist. Albrecht couldn't figure out what it was until he registered the great roar that drowned out Evan's yells. Albrecht shook his head, trying to deny it. *That can't be a waterfall*, he thought. *It's too quick a change in landscape. But this is Pangaea. Anything can happen here.*

He howled out in grief as Evan disappeared over the edge. Albrecht quit looking for things to grab onto, resigned now to his fate—he was going over. He steeled himself, and then he was no longer in water, but falling through air. He looked down and saw miles and miles of falling water, disappearing into a huge cloud of mist far below.

This can't be happening, he thought, as he shut his eyes.

Then he landed. It was a hard landing, on solid ground, but he knew instantly that no bones were broken.

That was not a mile-long fall, he thought. *Felt more like forty feet.* He opened his eyes and looked around.

He was sitting on a Moon Path. Water spray was all around him, and he could still hear the roaring of water, but it sounded farther off, as if there were a wall between him and the falls. It was dark, with no sun or moon, but faint light seemed to be coming from somewhere. He turned around and saw a rent in the night sky. Light and water were filtering in from Pangaea.

Then someone groaned. He spun around and ran over to Evan, who was lying farther up the path. He was unconscious. Then, the groan again. It wasn't coming from Evan. Albrecht looked up the path and saw one of the wolves, lying mangled. One of his legs was bent the wrong way, and it looked like a rib was sticking out of his side.

Albrecht pulled out his klaive and walked forward cautiously. As he got closer, he saw that the Garou's fur color had changed from gray to black. The hide was scarred in many places with bizarre pictograms. Unholy pictograms. The signs of the Wyrm and corrupt rites.

Albrecht spat. This thing was a Black Spiral Dancer.

He looked up at Albrecht and tried to move, but he seemed to lack the energy even for survival. His eyes half-closed, he seemed to smile at Albrecht, as if congratulating him.

"Who the hell are you, and why the hell did you attack us?" Albrecht snarled, leaning over the Dancer and placing the klaive at his throat.

The Dancer took in some heavy breaths and then sighed. "My master sent us to you. An easy kill, she said. She lied."

"Who the fuck is your master and why does she want us dead? Besides us being on the wrong side and all?"

"Queen Azaera, She of the Uncracked Egg. She demanded your death or capture. She will have it. Not from me or my pack, but from others. You live on borrowed time, Silver Fang king...."

"King? Not yet, pal. Or is that why you're trying to stop me? Did Arkady put her up to this?"

The Dancer cackled. "Oh, the Duke fumes over you. And for his petty power struggle, I'm dead. Fuck him! Fuck you! Fuck Gaia! Fuck the Wyrm! FuckFuck—"

Albrecht cut him off by slicing open his throat. The Dancer still tried to curse, but empty air escaped from the gash in his throat, never making it as far as the tongue. The Dancer grimaced and died.

Albrecht walked over to Evan and examined him. He seemed all right, just knocked around a little. His leg was gashed, but that was minor. Albrecht gently slapped him in the face, trying to wake him up.

Evan's eyes slowly rolled open and he looked around. He quickly sat up. "What happened? Where are the wolves?"

Albrecht put his hand on Evan's shoulder. "Calm down. They're dead. At least, that one is. The other two aren't here. One got to shore. I think the other one missed the gate. He's probably still falling."

Evan looked around, confused. "A gate? We're back in the Umbra! Weird."

Albrecht stood up and put his klaive back in its sheath. "Got any idea where in the Umbra we are?"

Evan shook his head. "Not in this blackness. Once the moon comes up, I might be able to figure it out. If there are any landmarks. This is more Mari's kind of thing."

"Mari!" Albrecht yelled. "Damn! She's still back there, being chased by the Black Spiral Dancers!"

"That's what they were? Black Spirals?"

"Yeah. Pals of Arkady. If we didn't have enough suspicions before, we do now."

Evan looked back at the rent into Pangaea. "We've got to go back for Mari."

"We can't," Albrecht said. "That gate opens in mid-air. It's a long drop on the other side."

Evan looked worried. "But she could be in trouble. She might need us."

"Kid," Albrecht said, taking Evan's shoulder and guiding him down the Moon Path, away from Pangaea, "She can take care of herself. She's proven that many times. We'll just have to hope she'll find us again."

Evan nodded, but didn't say anything else. Albrecht looked ahead. Far off, there was a pinpoint of light on the horizon. "What's that?"

Evan followed Albrecht's gaze and saw the light also. "I don't know. It's too far away."

"Well, looks like we got someplace to go now. Let's check it out."

"It could be dangerous."

"Yeah? We got nothing better to do." When he saw Evan's face fall, he quickly added, "At least, there's nothing we can do right now. Don't worry, we'll find her. We will."

"I know. At least, that's what I'll try to believe. Let's go to the light." Evan walked on down the almost pitch-black Moon Path, and Albrecht followed.

The Black Spiral Dancer crashed into Mari, but she pivoted and redirected his force off to the right, pushing him in that direction. She then lashed out with a quick punch to his exposed back. Bones cracked and the Dancer fell to the ground, alive but injured.

Mari turned to face the others. They were more wary than their packmate and had assumed Crinos form also. One was taller than the other and clearly female. She hissed slowly as she moved around, trying to circle Mari. But Mari backed up, allowing neither of them to get an easy opening on her. The way she had handled the first one showed them that she clearly knew how to fight. Reckless bravery on their part would only get them killed, and they knew it.

The Dancer on the ground slowly stood up. He had obviously just used a Gift to heal himself of a cracked spine. He glared at Mari, but there was a wary fearfulness in that look.

The screams came over the hill again, and they seemed to rattle even the Dancers. It was clear that they did not know where they were; but Mari did. And she was afraid.

The Dancers all turned to look at her again, and the landscape shifted. Mari blinked, and they were no longer on a muddy battlefield, but in a dirty, garbage-strewn alley. Glaring hungrily at her, no longer in Crinos form, the Dancers were now humans in black leather with knives out.

Mari shook her head. *This isn't right,* she told herself. *Those are Black Spiral Dancers, not gang members.* She backed up and hit a wall. Looking up quickly, she saw a sign above her: *The Urban Jungle.*

She stepped back, sweating. She knew this place. It was a nightclub she used to sneak out to as a teenager. It all came back to her in a rush. The nightclub, the alley, the gang. She shuddered.

The gang was approaching her, sensing her dismay, smelling the fear. She gritted her teeth and growled. She flexed her claws and looked at her hands in surprise. She wasn't in Crinos form anymore; she was in Homid. She concentrated, drawing on her anger to shift forms. Nothing happened.

She cursed. *It's this place,* she told herself. *It's this realm. It's trying to get at you, to scare you. You can't let it.*

One of the gang lunged forward and cut her across the stomach with his knife. Not a deep cut, but a painful one. Right on the scar Albrecht had made two years ago in their fight. The one for which she had yet to repay him.

Another member, the female, ran forward and swung a crowbar at her head, but Mari was thinking straight now. She easily blocked it with her forearm—although it hurt to do so in Homid form—and followed up with a right-arm punch to the girl's abdomen. The girl doubled over, clutching her stomach. Mari continued the attack and slammed her foot into the girl's head, driving her face into the oily pavement. She then kicked her with her other foot, and the girl flew back, her neck flexing more than it should have, with a snapping sound. She fell to the ground, her neck broken.

The other two gang members grabbed Mari from behind, and she moved to slip free. But one of them sank a knife between her ribs. Mari screamed in pain and fell over, blood gushing from her side. The thugs stood over her, laughing as she bled. Then they looked down the alley fearfully and ran away.

Mari tried to move her neck to see what had scared them, but she couldn't. This was so familiar. The damn gang members and their taunting. But what had really happened all those years ago was that she had freaked out and gone berserk before they had ever touched her. She had undergone her First Change and torn the gang to pieces. When she had come to, she had been covered in their blood. Their dead eyes had looked up at her, accusingly, and she'd run away, crying at the cold-blooded murder she'd just committed. Over the years, as she looked back, she had managed to convince herself that they had been going to rape her, that she was justified in killing the scum, that she had been cleaning up the streets.

But that was a lie, and she knew it. A lie around which she had built her whole identity. She had killed them. They had been just kids—younger than her—and not even a gang; just a bunch of kids hanging around together, out past their bedtimes. They had teased her, called her names, and she—sheltered girl that she was—had overreacted. They were dead because of her inability to control the Change. So what if she had never done it before, hadn't even known she was Garou? Did they care? They had never touched her except with hurtful words.

A police officer walked over and looked down at her. And she remembered him. She had forgotten him until now. The cop. Yet another thread in the weaving of Mari Cabrah's self. He had been the fuel behind her self-defense-course fire, her attempts to teach women to fight for themselves and not to rely on authority.

And she remembered what he had done that night, when he'd found a teen-age girl alone in a back alley with a bunch of dead bodies.

She closed her eyes. *Give it to me*, she thought. *Go ahead and do it. The kids have already gotten their revenge, through the Black Spiral Dancers. Finish the job.*

The police officer brought his club back and swung it down hard on Mari's head. Everything went black. Mari thought one last thing: *So this is death....*

13

The moon had risen when Albrecht and Evan cautiously approached what they had realized could only be a campfire. They had even heard someone singing from the vicinity. But they were taking no chances, so they approached silently and carefully.

Their walk had taken almost an hour, during which time Evan told Albrecht about his encounter with the dinosaur. Albrecht was impressed but said he could have taken the thing. Evan fumed in silence for a while after that. He was getting a bit tired of being treated like a child. So what if he was no match for a dinosaur? Albrecht would have been clueless in Pangaia without some of Evan's suggestions. Brawn wasn't always a match for education.

Albrecht motioned to Evan as they approached the fire. He was about to whisper for Evan to cut to the right while he cut left when he heard a low, wolfish growl behind him. He turned around and saw a thin, almost jackal-like wolf standing a few feet behind him, staring at him threateningly.

Albrecht could see markings—tattoos—on its fur. He breathed a sigh of relief. The symbol for the Silent Striders was burned into its haunches.

"We're friends," he said, putting his palms out. "I'm Lord Albrecht, of the Silver Fangs, and this is Evan Heals-the-Past, a Wendigo."

The wolf cocked its head, seemingly surprised. Then, from mere feet behind them, someone spoke. Loudly.

"Lord Albrecht? I've heard of you!"

Albrecht turned slowly around again and saw a short, red-haired man dressed in a Pogues T-shirt and torn blue jeans. His arms were laced with tattoos, and Albrecht recognized the Fianna symbol among them: the mark of the Celtic tribe of Garou. Albrecht's eyebrows rose. There were also quite a few honor and wisdom marks there, badges of merit. Standing behind the Fianna—towering over him in fact—was a blond-haired Crinos Garou, who eyed Albrecht suspiciously. This one carried a huge, two-handed hammer. Judging from the size of his muscles, it wasn't at all too heavy for him.

The red-haired man put out his hand and spoke in a heavy Irish brogue. "Pleased to meet you! My name's Jack Wetthumb!"

Albrecht shook the man's hand. "It's damn good to see some friends here."

"Oh? Troubles you've been having, is it?" Jack said. He looked at Evan and extended his hand to him as well. "Your name's a bit familiar also, but I can't place it."

"I'm Albrecht's packmate," Evan said.

"Right," Jack said, looking at him, trying to remember how he knew him. He wagged his finger at him. "You were that kid in the Amazon a few months back. The one the Nexus Crawler came after." He turned to Albrecht. "And you were there, fighting it! It all comes back now."

"Were you there?" Evan asked. "In the Amazon War?"

"Yeah, sure was. That's where I got all these scribbles on my arms. They give out medals like candy down there. All you gotta do is survive."

Albrecht nodded and glanced at the big guy. "Who's your friend? And the Silent Strider?" he asked, turning around to look at the wolf, who sat on its haunches now.

"She," Jack said, pointing at the wolf, "is known as Parts-the-Water, a damn fine Theurge. Invaluable when you're hiking the Umbra. And this fella," he said, motioning with his thumb at the large Garou, "is Ivar Hated-by-the-Wyrm. I think you can figure out just by looking at him how he got his name. He's a Get of Fenris, and my best pal. Ain't that right?" he said, looking up at Ivar. Ivar didn't say anything, but neither did he deny the accusation.

Albrecht smiled. "What about your name? How'd you pick that up?"

Jack laughed. "You ever heard of Finn Mac Cool? He's our most famous Fianna of old. Once, to get wisdom, he caught this magic salmon. To make a long story short, the eating of it gave him the smarts, but he had to suck his thumb for it—the thumb where the juices of the cooking fish had burned him. Well, I found just such a fish myself, and went through the same experience. Now," he said, holding up his right thumb, "when I sucks on this weasel here, I get the smarts, just like ol' Finn."

"He's just saying that," Ivar said. Jack looked up at him, annoyed. "He didn't eat any magic fish. He's as dumb as ever when he sucks his thumb. He just wants you to think otherwise."

"Uh…don't listen to Ivar," Jack said. "He's got a cracked sense of humor. Hey! Why don't we take you to the camp and introduce you to the rest of our bunch?"

Albrecht and Evan nodded, and they followed Jack and his friends to the campfire. There was a man sitting with a guitar, smiling at them as they came up. He looked to be Indian, from the subcontinent, rather than a Native American like the woman next to him. She was dressed in a buckskin vest and blue jeans and had long black hair falling down her back and shoulders. Albrecht stared, surprised: he knew her. She stared back, enigmatically and with faint embarrassment.

"Greetings," the man with the guitar said. "And who are our travelers?"

"This here," Jack said, "is Lord Albrecht, from Central Park. Surely you've heard of him."

"Most certainly," the man said. "It is a pleasure to meet the mighty Wyrm-slayer."

"Thanks," Albrecht said.

"And this," Jack said, "is Evan Heals-the-Past. You remember about him? The boy from the Amazon who was the talk of the jungle for that one week when we had R & R?"

"Ah, yes," the man said. "The one with the Nexus Crawler problem. I am glad you resolved that issue and are here to visit with us today."

"Thanks," Evan said. "It's really nice of you to say so."

"This fella," Jack said, pointing at the man, "is Pramati, our songster and Stargazer. Weird combo, huh? It makes for some thought-provoking fireside sing-alongs."

Pramati bowed and smiled.

"And last, but certainly not least among us," Jack said, pointing at the woman, "is Mary Black Fox."

"We've met before," Albrecht said, meeting her eyes and smiling. "But I didn't know you were Garou. What tribe are you?"

She seemed uncomfortable and looked at Jack, who glanced at Ivar, eyebrows raised, as if they were sharing a private joke.

"I'm Cherokee, actually," she said.

"I meant—" Albrecht said.

"She's not a Garou, lad," Jack said. "She's a witch. At least that's what her people call her. She's more properly a Dreamspeaker."

Albrecht's eyes widened. "A mage? Really? You didn't tell me that before either. I haven't met too many of your kind."

"I...wasn't a mage then," she said. "My Awakening was yet to come. And you're lucky you haven't met many of 'my kind.' They don't like Garou. My Tradition excepted, of course. The Dreamspeakers are the only ones among our order to understand what you guys are all about."

"I've heard of Dreamspeakers," Evan said. "You're shamans, right?"

"I suppose that's the best way to describe us," she said. "We're not like the hermetic mages, or the scientific ones for that matter."

Evan nodded. Albrecht smiled at her again. She looked away.

"Well, why don't you fellas find a spot and have a sit?" Jack said, sitting down himself and eyeing Mary with a smirk. "We've got vittles here, if you're hungry. Since you don't have any provisions on you, I assume you're on hard times. So sit down, eat up and tell us about yourselves."

Albrecht and Evan gratefully sat down and ate. The meal was beef stew from a pot over the fire, mixed with vegetables. Albrecht wondered where they had gotten the ingredients for this out in the Umbra, but didn't care enough to ask. He was too busy eating.

After they finished, Jack pulled some bottles of Guinness from a cooler behind him and offered them. They had both gratefully taken the beers and drunk when Albrecht stopped and looked at Evan.

"Hey!" he said. "Should you be drinking yet?"

"Legally?" Evan said. "No. But just try and take it from me." He took a long chug, and Jack rolled over laughing.

"The kid's gonna turn out all right," he said. "Don't worry about him. Nothing wrong with a little sip now and again."

Albrecht shrugged and drank his beer. Ivar and Parts-the-Water did not sit down, but instead stood at the edge of their circle, watching for possible danger. They listened in, however.

"So what do you call yourselves?" Albrecht asked.

"We're the Screamin' Trailblazers," Jack said. "Or that's what they called us down in the jungle, anyway. We've been thinking about shortening it to just 'Trailblazers.' What do you think?"

"I like them both," Albrecht said.

"Well, that's no help," Jack said, leaning back against his bed roll. "All right, lads, so what are you doing way out in the middle of nowhere?"

Evan looked at Albrecht. Albrecht sighed. "You deserve to know, although I really need to ask what you guys are doing here first."

Jack frowned. "It's bit rude, since we asked first.... But you're well spoken of in Central Park, so I'll trust you have your reasons for asking.

"We're after the skin of the Wyrm."

Albrecht blinked. "The what? The skin?"

"That's right. The skin of the Wyrm. You see, we heard this story down in the Amazon from an elder who was dying. He had this nice tidbit of knowledge he wanted to hand on before meeting his maker. So he handed it to us. You see, it seems that the Wyrm, being a giant snake and all, used to shed its skin regularly, back when everything was in balance. As a matter of fact, it was this shedding of the skin that helped keep the balance. Well, things got all screwed up, for whatever reason—we all know that's a matter of debate among the tribes. Well, one of the reasons things went wrong is that the Wyrm quit shedding its skin."

Evan nodded. "So the cycles were broken. It refused to grow and die and grow again, like everything is supposed to."

Jack sat up. "That's right. It hasn't shed its skin in ages, you see. So it's getting awful itchy and scummy, uncomfortable-like. That's one reason why the Wyrm is so pissy. It's wearing a damn uncomfortable skin."

"If that's the case," Albrecht said, "then why do you want to find it? It seems to me that, if you find the skin, you find the Wyrm."

"Yeah, but we're not looking for its current skin. We're looking for the old skin, the last one it shed. We figure like this elder in the jungle did, that if we can find it—somehow, someway—we can convince the Wyrm to shed its current skin. And if that happens, things might go all right."

Albrecht nodded. "That's quite a quest. Sounds like a wild goose chase; but if it's true and you do get the skin, it could mean a lot."

"That's exactly what we say!" Jack said.

"So, you got any leads?" Albrecht said.

"Yes," Pramati said. "There are many tales that speak of this skin. The trick is to find it. We have...some ideas."

"But you can understand us wanting to keep them secret," Jack said.

"Yeah," Albrecht said. "No problem. It's your quest."

"And what's yours?" Jack said.

"We're looking for the Silver Crown."

Jack looked confused, but Pramati whistled.

"That is a real quest," he said. "But I do not understand. Is not the crown hidden by the Silver Fangs?"

Albrecht looked down. "Uh…no. That's just a rumor. A false one."

Jack and Pramati exchanged glances.

"That's big news, you know," Jack said. "There are a lot of folks who'd be looking for it if that word got out."

"I know," Albrecht said. "I'm just going to have to trust you, with your honor badges and all, not to tell anyone."

Jack was silent for a while, looking at Albrecht. "Ah, you're a wise one. You know just where to push the buttons. I respect honor and all, and since you called me on it, I'll take up your challenge. Mum's the word, lad. At least from me and my pack. But I'll have to ask you to do the same about our quest."

"Done," Albrecht said.

Jack sat back again, smiling. "So, you got any leads on it?"

"We were just in Pangaea," Evan said. "But we got chased out before we could really look."

"Pangaea?" Jack said. "Beautiful place! But damn dangerous. Things are primal there. So, just what chased you out? A T-rex? A smilodon?"

"Black Spiral Dancers," Albrecht said. "My…cousin…doesn't want me to get the crown. He's guaranteed to be king of the North Country Protectorate otherwise."

"I don't get it," Jack said. "What's a Silver Fang king got to do with Black Spiral Dancers?"

"He's working with them. He used them to murder King Morningkill."

"Morningkill's dead?" Jack exclaimed, looking at the rest of his pack. They all looked surprised and dismayed. "We've been in here too long. When did this happen?"

Albrecht thought for a minute. "Nine days?"

"Ah…that recent then? I'm sorry. My condolences. You were his grandkid weren't you? That's what they say."

"Yeah. I was. Thanks."

"So who is this rat bastard who's taking over for him?"

"His name's Arkady."

"Huh. I'll have to remember that. You realize, of course, that I can't just sit on this piece of information. I gotta warn others."

"I know. Just don't talk about the crown. I don't mind—hell, I want—others knowing about Arkady."

"I get it now. You're after the crown 'cause it's the only way you can dethrone him."

"Yep."

"Well, you didn't tell us we were supping with the king-to-be! Not every day we get to hang with royalty."

Albrecht smiled but looked down. "That's assuming the crown…well, accepts me."

Jack nodded and sat back, thinking.

"Look," Evan said. "We've lost one of our packmates. Mari Cabrah. She was in Pangaea, being chased by Black Spirals."

Pramati shook his head, putting his guitar down, and said, "Why did you not say so before? We can help with that." He began searching in his bag for something.

Jack looked worried. "Hey, Pram, I don't think we should…."

"Nonsense," Pramati said. "We are with the potential king of the North Country Protectorate. Of course we can share our fetishes."

Jack looked at Evan, embarrassed. "Sorry, mate. It's just that…well, when people find out you've got neat stuff, they want to take it."

Evan nodded. "I understand."

Pramati pulled a box out. He smiled at them all and opened it. Inside was a leaf. A simple green leaf.

"What is it?" Albrecht said, leaning forward. "A leaf?"

"Yes," Pramati said. "But not just any leaf. It is a leaf from the One Tree. The first tree to grow in the world at the Dawn. It is Gaia's leaf. We were all born under its boughs. It is our center, our *axis mundi*. The tree ever calls to us."

"What does it do?" Evan asked.

Pramati took the leaf out carefully and handed it to Evan. Evan took it, holding it as if it were precious gold.

"Hold it in your palm. Go, stand away from the fire. Think of the loved one you have lost who is in the spirit world. Call out to her. Open your spirit in the calling, remember the tree. If you can do this, your friend will hear you and, if she chooses, will come to you. Distance does not matter, for the tree is always there, everywhere. It is the center. We all stand under it, even though we cannot see it."

Evan stood up and went a few yards from the fire. He looked at the leaf and thought of Mari. He thought of how she could be wounded somewhere, dying alone. He thought she might be dead already, but then stopped himself. *No,* he thought, *I won't accept that. She is alive. She is under the tree with us. She is here.*

"Mari!" he cried. "Where are you?"

He felt the leaf move gently in his hand, as if stirred by a breeze. He called her name again, with all his heart. And he looked up. Above him, towering and huge, was a tree, climbing to the heavens. On each branch were thousands of leaves, but they were all different—leaves from a million different trees on one tree. He saw a squirrel crawl down the trunk to look at him. Its nose quivered.

He heard a groan at his feet and looked down. Mari was there, lying among the roots of the tree.

"Mari! You're here!"

She opened her eyes and looked up at him. "Evan? Are you dead, too?"

"You're not dead, Mari! Just far away. Take my hand, come to where we are!" He held his hand out to her. She reached out and took it. The tree disappeared, and Mari was lying on the ground next to Evan, the light of the campfire dancing across her.

"It worked!" Evan yelled.

Albrecht got up and ran over. Bending down next to Mari, he examined her. "What happened? You're pretty beat up."

She looked at him as if she couldn't believe he was there. "Albrecht? What...?"

Jack came over. "Hello, miss. Don't worry, we'll fix you up." He waved Mary over. She got up and came to examine Mari.

"I'm going to heal you," she said. "This won't hurt a bit." She put her hands on Mari's wounds and concentrated. The wounds began to heal themselves, as if time were accelerated around them. In seconds, they were fully cured.

Mari looked at her, confused. "Thank you. I...I am surprised to be here."

Evan helped her stand up. "Come on, we'll go to the fire. You can tell us what happened."

Albrecht stepped in and helped support her on the other side. As they walked, she seemed to find her strength, and eventually shook them off. Standing on her own, she went to the fire and sat down.

Albrecht and Evan sat themselves on either side of her, looking concerned.

"You want to talk?" Albrecht said.

"I…I remember now," she said. "I was in Atrocity."

Jack grimaced. Pramati looked very concerned. Mary put her hand on Mari's, but Mari shook her head and withdrew her hand.

"I'm all right. It was just rough, that's all. I had forgotten that the only way out of Atrocity is to die to it."

"So the legends say," Pramati said. "I have never been there myself, thankfully. It must have been hard. They say that shadows of every crime ever committed live there."

"They don't feel like shadows," Mari said. "They come off like flesh and blood. The place gets you in its grip, forces you to become an actor in its play. You can't do anything about it."

"So what happened to you there?" Evan said.

"I'd rather not talk about it. It's personal."

Evan nodded.

"Well, it's over now," Jack said. "You should have some of this stew. Strengthen you up."

Mari looked at him. "Excuse me, but who are you?"

Jack laughed. "Friends of your friends here. We'll catch up as you eat."

Pramati handed Mari a bowl of stew and she ate. She was hungrier than she could ever remember being in her life. As she ate, the other pack introduced themselves to her, and explained their quest.

When she was done, Jack told them they could sleep for a few hours, until the next night, when they would break camp and move on. Albrecht volunteered to keep watch, but Jack wouldn't have any of it.

"We've just been walking for days, lad—no real action for us. We're pretty well rested up. It's you who need sleep. So get some shut-eye. We'll wake you before leaving."

"Thanks," Albrecht said. "I owe you."

"And you better believe that ,if you get that crown of yours and become king, I'll be calling the favor in."

Albrecht laughed. "All right. I'll be expecting you." He lay back on the blanket Pramati had put out for them. Mari was already asleep. *That's not like her,* Albrecht thought. *She's usually one to prowl about for danger first. Ah, she's just tired.*

Evan was soon snoring. Albrecht rolled over again. He had a feeling that they had better catch as much sleep as they could; they might not get another chance for a long time.

14

Albrecht woke in pitch blackness. He sat up and looked around. The fire was still burning, but very low now. Ivar sat between it and him, blocking most of the light. The moon was gone. It was day in the physical world, but night in the spirit world.

He stood up, stretching as he walked over to the fire. Ivar was eating the leftovers from the stew pot and nodded a greeting at Albrecht, but kept on chewing. Parts-the-Water was curled up on a blanket, fast asleep, and Jack was snoring nearby. Albrecht looked around and saw Pramati sitting a ways off, watching the dark landscape around them. Mary was on the other side of the camp, also watching outward.

Albrecht walked over to her. She looked up at him nervously as he sat down beside her.

"What's going on?" Albrecht said. "You act like you don't know me. Was I such a jerk?"

"Look," Mary said. "You were a short fling. That's all."

Albrecht furrowed his brow. "I didn't have to be, you know."

"I'm...not comfortable seeing you. I've changed a lot since then. I'm a mage now. I've found an identity."

"An identity? And you didn't have one before?"

She turned and looked at him, bewildered at his ignorance. "No. I didn't. I thought that was obvious. I was a girl who'd run to the big city to see what life was like off the rez. I met those Garou friends of yours and became fascinated with them. I thought they were just urban primitives, and you were the coolest of the bunch. Of course I was attracted to you. But was I really anything more than a fling to you? When I found out about the Garou later, and that you were one of them, I knew long-term relationships weren't your style. They're not mine, either."

Albrecht looked off into the darkness. "Huh. That's quite a mouthful. All right, it was just a fling. But you're a mage now, a mover and shaker in the supernatural world. Hell, in my book, that means it would've worked out well for both of us. Me being Garou wouldn't have mattered that much."

Mary shook her head, smiling now, as if Albrecht were a child who had inadvertently said something funny. "You are a Silver Fang, Albrecht. I've talked with Pramati. I know about your Kinfolk. I'm not the breeding type. I don't want children."

"So? Who said anything about kids?"

"You are a Garou. You've got to spread your seed. Otherwise your race dies. I know that. I accept that. But I don't want a relationship with it."

Albrecht frowned again.

"You've never had a one-on-one equal relationship, have you?"

"Sure I have."

"Don't fool yourself. You're a Garou. You've got to be the alpha in any social situation. You're trying to be king, for christsakes."

Albrecht was silent.

"I'm sorry if I come off harsh, but as soon as I saw you, I knew I'd have to rehash my past. Realize this, for me: *I don't like what I used to be.* Don't get me wrong. I'm glad I ran into your friends. They led me to this pack, which is the greatest thing that ever happened to me, short of my Awakening. But that girl I used to be.... She's a stranger now. There was never anything between you and me, Albrecht. Nothing of any substantiality. You tell yourself in your memory that I was special, but is that really true? Have you tried to look for anyone else, or have you wallowed in self-pity? I'm not that girl of a few years ago. You might as well forget her."

Albrecht nodded. "Fine. No problem. Look, I gotta…check on my pack." He stood up and walked away, not looking at her.

Mary watched him go. She felt sorry for him. It wasn't easy for a Garou to forge a relationship; nobody wanted to put up with that kind of rage. All someone like Albrecht had in the end was his pack. She did not envy him. She felt guilty about being so cruel to him, but skirting the truth here would only have made it worse.

Albrecht walked over to where his pack was sleeping and walked past, over to Pramati, to sit down next to the Stargazer.

"Greetings," Pramati said.

"Hey," Albrecht said. "So, where do you guys go next?"

"We are going back to our caern in New Mexico. We need to rest and plan our next journey. It will be our hardest yet."

"Well, luck and all. Say…Mary over there. Is she really fit for this kind of work?"

Pramati looked back at Mary, who sat turned away from them. "She is excellent, Albrecht. We could not have gotten this far without her. Mages have powers we can't imagine. Most helpful powers."

"Yeah? That's good. She's just…kinda young and all."

"So is Evan. So are most of us when we undergo our Firsting. Gaia does not care about age when she calls us for duty. I know you are hurting from a pained heart—"

"Wait a minute—"

"Let me speak. Please. It is obvious. It is the fate of the Garou. It is so rare for us to find a mate, we who are forbidden to breed with our own kind. Our rage drives others away. It is a scary thing for them to live with. Gaia asks much of us. Many sacrifices. But this is perhaps the greatest. Take strength in that, Lord Albrecht. Every lost lover is a sign of our commitment to Gaia."

Albrecht looked at Pramati. "You're right. I don't even know why it bothers me so much, either. I mean, she's right. We were just a fling and all."

"Ah. That is simple. It is the most common wound in the world, but also the deadliest. Bruised ego. If we had no ego to injure, just think what a peaceful world this would be!"

Albrecht put on a humoring smile for Pramati. "Uh…yeah. I guess."

"Ha, ha. I see your real face beneath that smile. Do not worry, I am not offended. You are wondering, how could I travel so far with a crude man like Jack if I have such a sensitive heart?"

"You're damn perceptive, you know that?"

"I am a Galliard. Luna pays me to notice such things. They are the stuff stories are made of."

Albrecht smiled and sat for a while in silence. Then he said, "This is kind of funny, you know? The chances of me meeting up with her now were real slim, but here she is. I've been thinking about the *Lay of the Silver Crown*, and what it means for me now. None of it has seemed to work out so far, but…I don't know. I just got the whole hearth and home thing slapped away from me. That happened to the guy in the story, too. Makes me wonder how much of this is coincidence…."

"Legends indeed live in us today. But in what way? Who can say? We may ask the Theurges, but I have a feeling that we must each find the answer for ourselves."

"All this deep-thought stuff is out of my league. I'm an Ahroun, damn it. This is Evan's job."

"It is the job of each and every one of us. A warrior with no awareness of his place in the spiritual order is merely a raging animal."

Albrecht sat in silence for a while. Pramati watched him as if wondering whether his lesson had gotten through.

"Tell me," Pramati said. "Where do you go next?"

"I have no idea," Albrecht said. "We didn't find clues in Pangaea. I don't know where to start."

"Why Pangaea at all?"

"A friend of ours, Antonine Teardrop—one of your own—dug up a legend about the crown. Seemed to point to Pangaea. But that was centuries ago. It could be anywhere now."

"Hmm. The crown is a powerful symbol, you know. It represents all of Garou civilization. I know that will sound strange to you, but we really do have a civilization. The Litany proves that, as do our rites and traditions. It is said that civilization began in Pangaea. The Dawn Times. That is the past. We stand in the present. But what is the future? What lies in store for civilization? Where does it lead?"

"I have no clue whatsoever. Where are you heading with this?"

"We know that our ways are dying. We need to revive them. That is what the crown represents—the resurrection of the old ways, making them new again. Now, assume that the ways are not revitalized, that they become stagnant and weary. Where does that lead? We know the beginning of civilization. But what is its end? Its inevitable conclusion, if it is not continually remade?"

"Uh…ruin? Anarchy?"

"No. That is a state of chaos upon which new forms will be built. I speak of the world as it is now if it is allowed to stay as it is, without changing. Think, my friend. What is it that lies at the heart of a meaningless life? For that is what our ways, devoid of change, have become."

"Nihilism. Emptiness. Darkness."

"Yes. Emptiness. Void. It is the inevitable future to which civilization is drawn. It is where the Silver Crown, forgotten for so many years, would be drawn to. It is a place, Albrecht. A real place now. Here, in the spirit world."

Albrecht looked at Pramati, his eyes narrowing. "The Abyss."

Pramati nodded. "It is where you must go to seek the crown."

Albrecht shook his head. "Then I might as well just stop now. I don't stand a chance in that place. No Garou does. Hell, it's the end of everything. You walk in, but you don't walk out again."

"Untrue. Many have survived to tell the tale."

"But they all shudder when they do. Most barely escape alive, with or without their sanity intact. That place'll chew us up and spit us out."

"Nonetheless, it is the only place the crown could be. Everything lost goes to the Abyss. Lost heroes, lost children, lost fetishes. It must be there, Albrecht."

Albrecht nodded. "It makes sense, but…Gaia! I can't drag Evan and Mari into that!"

"Are they not here by their choice?"

"Yeah, but they're doing it for me. Hell, Mari's already been through a lot of shit. Did you see her last night? Wasn't like her at all. And Evan…. He has no idea what he's getting into."

"I am not so sure of that, my friend. That boy has strengths you can't imagine. He may be your savior in this quest."

"Look, he's smart and all, but he's just a kid. His rite was barely a year ago. He's not ready for the Abyss."

"I believe the decision will not be yours to make."

Albrecht stood up. "Thanks for the advice. I really do appreciate it, but…I gotta think about this."

"Certainly. Please do not hesitate to ask me anything else you wish."

Albrecht nodded and walked back to the fire, his head swimming. *The Abyss!* He'd be a fool to go there. But he'd be a fool not to, if that was indeed where the crown was.

He bent down and shook Evan and Mari awake. "Hey. It's getting near moonrise. I've got to talk to you guys."

Mari and Evan stood up. Mari began stretching, her morning martial exercises. Evan yawned and scratched his head.

"You…uh," Albrecht said. "You're going to have to go back to New York."

Mari stopped her exercises and shot him a mean glance. "What are you talking about? We don't have the crown yet."

"Yeah," Evan said. "It's certainly not back in New York."

"Look…I've got to go somewhere pretty fierce. I don't want you guys coming. It's such a long shot that…. Well, I don't think it's worth risking us all for. This is my quest. I gotta go it alone."

"Oh no you don't!" Mari said, stepping up to him, her face inches from his. "I am *not* turning around now! I don't care where you're going, I'm coming along, if it's to Malfeas itself!"

"Me too," Evan said.

Albrecht looked at both of them and shook his head. "You guys are great. You really are. But I'm not kidding. The Abyss is—"

"The Abyss?!" Mari said. "What got that in your head?"

"I've talked this over with Pramati. It's the only logical place to look."

"Logic is not always the best course in the Umbra," Mari said. "We could try the Aetherial Realm first. There are wise Garou there. They might know."

"Look, guys," Albrecht said. "If it were anywhere else, it would have been found by now. It's lost. It's got to be in the Abyss."

"What about the Silver Fang Homeland?" Evan said. "Each tribe has its own spiritual realm. Maybe it's there."

Albrecht shook his head. "I think Greyfist would have known if that were the case. Besides, it's said that the homelands are sub-realms of Pangaea. We didn't have any luck there."

Mari walked off a ways, thinking. Evan began pacing, thinking also.

"The Trailblazers are going back to New Mexico," Albrecht said. "You can go with them and catch a Moon Bridge from there to New York."

"Stop it, Albrecht!" Mari said. "I told you we weren't giving up on this. It is *not* an option. Put it out of your head. If we have to go to the Abyss, then we shall."

Albrecht threw up his hands. "All right! All right! But if you go stark raving mad there, I will not feel one ounce of guilt. Because I did not choose to take you there."

"Good. I wouldn't want something like my sanity to weigh heavy on your conscience, Albrecht. Gaia forbid that!" She walked over to the fire, snarling, and sat down next to Ivar.

Albrecht looked after her, puzzled.

"I think you've pushed it one time too many," Evan said, looking after Mari. "She's been through a lot, and I guess she's sick of your condescending attitude."

"Condescending? She usually starts it! She can't get over that tussle we had a couple of years back!"

"Let's just drop it now," Evan said. He walked over and sat down next to her. Albrecht remained where he was. He pulled out a cigarette, lit it and stood there, staring out at the dark plain.

Within the hour, the moon rose over the horizon. It was a gibbous moon, a Galliard's moon. Albrecht knew they had only a few more days until the full moon. Once the full moon hit its cusp, the midpoint between waxing and waning, their quest would be over regardless of whether they had succeeded or not. Arkady would be crowned king then, with all the rites of the Silver Fangs, and no artifact of old would be able to change that truth.

The Trailblazers were packing up their camp. They seemed to have an efficient system for it: they were all packed up within ten minutes, with everything distributed amongst their backpacks. Ivar seemed to be carrying more than the rest of them.

Jack came up to Albrecht. "Well, lad, it's been fine meeting you. I wish you the best."

Albrecht put out his hand. Jack shook it.

"I hope you find the skin," Albrecht said. "Regardless, drop me a line now and then and let me know how it's going."

Jack smiled. "You got it. I will. And let me know how it all turns out for you. You can find us at the Painted Coyote Caern, in New Mexico. I wish you could come with us. Pram told me about your talk. I don't envy you. The Abyss is…bad news."

"Don't worry," Albrecht said. "Others have done it before us."

"Yeah, that's the spirit!" Jack smiled. "Well, we're off. Oh, by the way, Parts-the-Water gave Mari a couple of electric torches. They should help you in that dark pit. They're fixed up special, with spirits and all. Shouldn't go out on you anytime soon."

"Thanks," Albrecht said. "Happy trails."

"And to you!" Jack walked back to his pack, who were standing by the Moon Path now. It glowed bright under the gibbous moon. They all turned and waved at Albrecht, Mari and Evan, then walked off down the Path.

Albrecht watched them go until they took a curve in the path and were gone behind a rise. Then he sighed and walked over to Evan and Mari.

"You guys ready?" he said.

"Yeah," Evan said.

"I've been thinking," Mari said, handing a flashlight to each of them. "The best way to get to the Abyss is to find a break in a Moon Path, and follow that."

"Won't be many of those," Albrecht said. "The moon's gibbous now."

"If we keep looking, we'll find one. It doesn't take too long to find the Abyss."

Albrecht and Evan didn't say anything, but headed toward the Moon Path. Mari followed.

They walked for the entire night without finding a break in the path, and so decided to give up for the night and begin looking for whatever haven they could find to rest in during the day. About an hour before moonset, they discovered a small, abandoned, Weaver realm.

The place resembled a city block, with office buildings rising to the sky. Strands of old Pattern Spider webs hung from them. They had not been tended for a long time.

"This appears to have once been a Glen," Evan said as they walked down the street. "Until the Weaver spirits got ahold of it."

Albrecht pointed at some grass bursting through the cracked pavement. "It looks like Gaia is reclaiming the place. I wonder what drove the spiders off."

"They weren't driven off," Mari said. "Look there. They were eaten."

Albrecht and Evan looked over to where Mari was pointing. In an alleyway, the desiccated and gnawed bones of a Pattern Spider were scattered about.

"Wonder what the hell eats Weaverlings?" Albrecht said, stepping up to examine the remains of the dead spirit.

"Whatever it was," Mari said. "There's no sign that anything's been here for a while. Not enough food, I suppose."

"Then I guess it's safe to camp here," Evan said.

Albrecht nodded. "I don't think we should go into the buildings, though."

"There's an alleyway over there that looks defensible," Mari said. "The Moon Path resumes on the other side of the fence, allowing us an escape route, and the alley entrance is thin enough to keep attackers coming one-on-one."

"Good," Albrecht said.

They planted their camp in the alley and set watches. It took each of them a while to get to sleep between watches, but when they did, none of them dreamed.

When the moon rose the next night, they set off again. Another long night of travel with no sign of breakage in the path. Albrecht was tempted to grab the next Lune—they had been few and far between on the path—and force it to bust up the path. But he knew that would be more trouble than it was worth. Lunes didn't normally listen to reason.

About two hours before moonset, they came across a gap in the path. The pack stopped and looked at each other. Then Albrecht took the first step forward and boldly strode into the gap, while Mari and Evan followed. The ground there was featureless ephemera. Albrecht then walked off to the right, crosswise to the path. They walked in that direction for a while.

Then, rolling mists began to move in from both sides. The fog never came close enough to touch the pack, but it created a corridor leading straight ahead. The pack followed it. Soon the mist walls moved back, and they could see a crevasse appear in the ground ahead. It started small but widened with distance, disappearing into the fogs ahead.

When they came to the edge, they looked down.

And saw nothing.

They each gasped and stepped back, looking away from the yawning gulf, the void below. They all felt drawn down, as if gravity here pulled them harder. But they resisted it.

They each shuddered, considering what they had seen. Utter darkness, and within…the end of everything. Annihilation incarnate.

They each stepped back from the edge to consider the next move.

"What now?" Albrecht asked.

"There are tales of three paths here," Mari said. "One, called the Golden Path, is fraught with danger. It is said to be treacherous going, but great treasure awaits whomever gets to the end of it. I have never heard of anyone getting to the end. The Silver Path is the most enigmatic. I'm not sure where it leads, but some say great wisdom waits for those who brave it. Now, the Iron Path, it's the easiest. It leads to many caverns lacing the sides of the crevasse. However—and this is the catch—lots of nasty things live in those caverns. Including a creature named Nightmaster."

"What kind of creature?" Albrecht asked.

"He used to be a Shadow Lord, a Garou. Now he is said to be a child of the Abyss: its avatar. He's in charge of some of the things that live down there."

"You said caverns," Albrecht said. "I hear that's where fetishes show up."

"Yes, collected by the inhabitants. But if the crown is there, it's surely guarded by someone. Or something."

"Well, time's running out here. Let's find the Iron Path and get down there."

Mari nodded. "If we continue along the crevasse a little longer, I think we'll see the beginning of the path."

They walked along the edge, although each kept well back from it. The silence of the place was unnerving to all of them. Not even the sound of wind could be heard, although the tugging of the air could be felt, pulling down toward the darkness.

Soon they came across a path that led to a ledge down the crevasse. Precious gems could be seen along the rock wall, embedded in it. Veins of precious metals also appeared, especially gold.

"The Golden Path," Mari said. "We don't want that one."

They kept walking until they encountered another ledge, leading down. A cave opened off it about thirty yards down.

"This is it," Mari said. "The Iron Path. The Silver must be ahead, but we want this one."

Albrecht headed toward the ledge. "I'll go first. You two follow. Be careful."

"You, too," Evan said, following after him. Mari took up the rear.

The ledge was wide enough for them in Homid form, but it would be tricky if they had to take Crinos form. About fifteen yards down, it began to get dark.

"Damn," Albrecht said. "Moon's going down."

"Turn on your flashlight," Mari said.

Albrecht fished into his trenchcoat and pulled out the flashlight the Silent Strider had provided him. It was painted with pictograms, but otherwise appeared to be a regular flashlight. He clicked it on, and bright light flooded out of it. He aimed it at the path ahead and began walking again. Evan and Mari turned on their lights and followed.

When he got to the cave mouth, Albrecht carefully stepped in, shining the flashlight all around first. Bones littered the floor, some of them appearing to be the skulls of Crinos Garou. The rear of the cave disappeared into darkness. Albrecht motioned the others to follow him as he walked farther into the cave.

"I think we should start here. I bet it leads down, just like the ledge. But if the crown is here, it's in one of these caves, not just sitting on the path."

"I agree," Mari said. "Proceed."

They continued on. Far ahead they heard the dripping of water, apparently condensation from the cavern walls. They walked in the darkness with only their flashlights to guide them for what seemed like hours. The cave broke off into many different passages, and Albrecht took whichever seemed to lead down. It was too dark for them to map their way, and they had no paper anyway. Occasionally Mari would scratch a mark into the rock wall at a crossroads. Except for these faint marks, they left no sign of their passage.

Sometimes they found items scattered across the cavern floors, as if someone had dumped them there and forgotten about them. These objects varied from carved wooden toys to computer screens. The detritus of many cultures gathered in the dark.

In one small side cavern, Mari turned off to investigate a reflection from her waving flashlight. In the dirt, half-buried, was an ornate klaive. She called the others over to see it.

"It looks quite old, but very well preserved," she said. "It's got some interesting carvings on the pommel...."

"Don't touch it!" Albrecht said. "It might be cursed."

Mari moved away from it. "Anything here could be cursed. I wonder…what if the Silver Crown is also cursed from this place?"

Albrecht did not respond. He continued on down the passage. Mari and Evan followed.

Soon they heard scratching noises up ahead, faint and intermittent. They moved cautiously forward, and came to a large cavern. Albrecht swung his flashlight to the right and then back again as it passed over something unusual.

In the center of the room was a cage. And in the cage was a little girl, plaintively clawing at the lock with her pale hands.

Albrecht hurried forward, but Mari put her hand on his shoulder. He turned back and saw her cautious look. She didn't trust this situation. He walked forward anyway.

The girl did not seem to notice them or the light of the flashlight.

"Hey! Girl!" Albrecht said as he reached the cage.

The girl did not respond. She just kept scratching at the lock. Her fingers were bleeding.

Albrecht shone the flashlight in her eyes. Her pupils did not respond. He turned to Mari, who was also at the cage now.

"She's deaf and blind, I think," Albrecht said.

"Be careful," Mari warned. "She may not be what she seems."

"Don't worry," Albrecht said. "Evan! Shine your light at the lock. I'm going to try to break it."

Evan did not respond.

Albrecht swung his flashlight around. There was no sign of the boy.

"Evan!" he yelled.

Mari was running around the room now, shining her light in every corner. "Evan! Where are you?"

"When did you last see him?" Albrecht asked.

"He was right behind me before we entered the cavern," she said, running back to the passageway by which they had entered and swinging her light up it. She turned back to Albrecht.

"He's gone," she said.

15

Evan stumbled along in the darkness, weak and dizzy. He felt around. The rock walls surrounded him on both sides, getting narrower. He didn't remember this place. He had come the wrong way.

He tried to calm down, to keep from panicking. He thought back, retracing his steps to figure out how he had come here. He remembered walking behind Mari, and then something had grabbed him from behind. Something which smelled awful. Its clawed hand had covered his mouth to keep him from crying out as it dragged him off into another passage, taking his flashlight from him.

He had tried to resist, shifting to Crinos form, but his abductor was stronger. Then, it had let Evan go. Evan had run, back toward Albrecht and Mari, crying out for them. But the passageways weren't the same. He couldn't see anything, and was forced to rely on touch and smell. But everything here smelled the same—a musty, moist cave.

His abductor was gone without a sound or scent. Evan was puzzled. He carefully walked back the way he had come, but each step seemed to take something out of him. He felt spent, the way he did after using Garou magic, after expending his own spiritual energy.

He leaned up against a wall and thought about his predicament. He thought about the tales and legends of this place.

And then he knew. He knew what was happening to him. His spirit was being drained against his will. And he knew the person behind it.

Nightmaster.

Evan shivered, but he summoned all his courage and spoke: "I know you're there, Nightmaster. I've heard the stories. I know it has to be you."

He heard a step, not more than ten feet away down the passage ahead of him. He caught the scent again: the scent of ancient musk, of a very old animal. He heard low, raspy breathing. And then a voice.

"Who is this boy? Who calls me by name?"

Evan swallowed. "I am Evan Heals-the-Past, a Wendigo."

A grunt, mere feet away. Nightmaster was closer. "Why has the boy come? The boy knows of his enemy. Yet he has trespassed into his lair."

"We have no quarrel with you. We are just seeking an artifact."

"We? The boy has packmates. Who are these packmates? The boy will tell us."

Evan gasped as he felt hot, rancid breath against his cheek. Nightmaster was standing inches away from him now.

"Please. I can't see anything. Can I have my flashlight?"

Another grunt. "The light? The boy knows this place devours the light. Yet the boy begs for it. Begs for what is unnatural to this place. Why?"

"I...want to see what you look like."

"The boy wishes to see Nightmaster, leader of the Society of Nidhogg? Nightmaster, extinguisher of the sun? The boy has humor. Yes, the boy shall see Nightmaster."

Evan felt the flashlight being thrust into his hands. He flipped the switch, and light flooded the passageway. Standing inches away from him, looming at least three or four feet taller than him, was a Crinos Garou. At least, it had once been a Crinos Garou. The fur was oily and the skin parched and dried, looking almost mummified. Evan looked up into Nightmaster's eyes and saw the empty chasm there, a reflection of the empty void he had witnessed outside. The end of everything stared back at him through two wolfish eyes.

"Is the boy scared? Does he tremble before the mighty Shadow Lord?"

Evan nodded, unable to speak.

"The boy will now say what his packmates seek."

"Uh...we...ah.... The Silver Crown. That's what we're looking for."

Nightmaster stepped back and cocked his head at an angle. But Evan was not sure whether that was meant as a gesture of confusion, coming from this shell of a Garou.

"The Silver Crown. The hated crown. Crown of my enemy. Crown of the wrongful kings. The crown which was created as a joke against the Shadow Lords. The crown which stole the leadership of the pack from them. The evil crown. Why does the boy want the crown?"

"To...uh...crown my packmate king."

"Packmate is a Shadow Lord?"

"No. A Silver Fang."

Nightmaster roared in anger, lunging at Evan with his snout. Evan cringed back, knowing he was helpless before the more powerful Garou. But Nightmaster's jaws stopped just short of Evan's muzzle, as he stared into Evan's eyes, a chaotic movement deep within his own. Evan stared back, seeing that raging emotion in Nightmaster's eyes.

Evan decided to take a gamble, although he knew it would probably get him killed. "You're not as empty as I thought," he said.

Nightmaster stepped back and cocked his head again. "The boy is going mad. Seeing things. Untrue things."

"In your eyes, when you got angry. There was rage there. Not just the abyss."

Nightmaster growled low and moved toward Evan, but then stopped, confused. "Anger. Nightmaster has anger. Nightmaster always has the anger. It is part of the emptiness."

"But if you've got something, such as anger, then you can't be empty. By definition."

Nightmaster reached out and snatched Evan by the neck. He spun around and marched down the passage, dragging Evan with him. Evan struggled to breathe as the grip began strangling him. As he thrust his fingers between his throat and Nightmaster's hand, the grip loosened. Not enough to let Evan drop, though.

"The boy is wrong. The boy knows not the Abyss. The boy will know the Abyss. Like all the children. The boy will learn the Abyss. Will learn the darkness. Will be devoured by darkness. Will be a child again. Child of the Abyss."

Nightmaster stormed through passageways, jogging now. Evan was slammed into the walls as his captor hurriedly turned corners. He struggled to right himself, to get his feet under him so he could at least keep pace with the mad Garou, but Nightmaster moved too quickly and made too many surprise turns.

Then Nightmaster came to a sudden stop and tossed Evan through the air. Evan tried to twist so he would land on his feet, but then slammed into a metal cage. He yelped at the pain, and hit the ground hard, knocking the wind out of himself. As he lay there, stunned, he saw light, and heard voices calling his name....

Albrecht and Mari stood in the cavern, arguing about what to do. Albrecht wanted to pick up Evan's scent and chase it through the tunnels. Mari claimed that the scent would disappear and they would be lost; that their best hope was to wait there for Evan to reappear. As Albrecht was about to give up in disgust and take to the passageway, they heard something large and heavy hit the other side of the cage.

Albrecht ran around the cage and saw Evan lying there in Crinos form. "Evan!"

Mari came around the other side. "Thank Gaia! He's here! But what brought him here?" She swung her flashlight around the room but saw nothing.

Evan groaned, trying to speak, but he was clearly stunned and having trouble coming to his senses.

The cage door loudly unlocked itself. Albrecht pointed his flashlight toward it as the door swung wide, but no one was there. The little girl stopped scratching, although she seemed not to understand that the door was open.

A voice appeared in the cavern, coming from all directions. "The boy will get in the cage, where all children belong."

"Who the hell?" Albrecht barked.

Mari stood up, instantly in Crinos form, looking for something to attack.

Evan sat up, coughing. "It…it's Nightmaster…."

Mari's eyes narrowed and she scanned the corners of the room. Nothing.

Albrecht helped Evan to his feet. "The Shadow Lord?"

"Yes," Nightmaster said, nowhere in sight. "The true lord. Not the usurper. Not the pretender. Not the Silver Fang."

Albrecht looked around the room. "Oh, yeah? I'm not the one living in a cave, pal."

"Impudent Fang. Idiot Fang. Seeks the crown. Nightmaster will give him the crown. He will rule. King of sacrifices. Sacrificed to the Abyss."

The spirits within the flashlights screamed as the lights went out, plunging the cavern into darkness.

Albrecht drew his klaive and assumed a fighting stance. He was in Crinos form and so he opened his senses, trying to catch any sign of Nightmaster. He could see, hear and smell nothing.

A claw ran up his back, not breaking the skin or tearing his coat; but it sent a chill through him. He swung his klaive around to hit the spot Nightmaster had to be standing in. Nothing.

"The boy will get into the cage. All children into the cage. Learn the Abyss."

"You put that girl there?" Mari yelled. "You bastard! What for? She's just a girl."

"Lost girl. Wanders to Abyss. Gift for Abyss. But must be trained. Must learn to accept Abyss. Must see nothing. Must hear nothing. Must feel nothing. Must be nothing."

"You fucking asshole!" Albrecht yelled. "You don't like Silver Fangs? Well, come and get me!"

A claw slashed at Albrecht's leg, but he felt the slight stirring of the air before it struck, and was able to move aside before the full force of the blow hit him. He swung his klaive down and it struck something in mid-darkness. A grunt was heard.

"Taste of your own medicine, asshole," Albrecht said. "So the mighty Shadow Lord is not perfect. Of course not. Otherwise he would be wearing the Silver Crown himself. But then, I bet he's afraid to put it on. Aren't you?"

"Silver Crown? Give it to Nightmaster and he will put it on. Become king over more than Abyss."

Albrecht frowned. "Tell me where it is and I'll give it to you."

"No. You have it! You will give it to Nightmaster!" Something crashed into Albrecht, forcing him to the ground.

Albrecht concentrated, drawing on the power given to him by the spirits, and his fur lit up into a bright white glow, flooding the cavern.

Standing next to the prone Albrecht, revealed in the intense light of Gaia's power, Nightmaster screamed and clutched at his eyes. Albrecht slashed at the Garou's legs with his klaive, and hacked off one of them. Nightmaster crashed to the ground, trying to crawl away.

Mari ran at him from the other side and kicked him in the head, knocking him back toward the glowing Albrecht.

Albrecht grabbed him by the throat and held his klaive inches from the Garou's gut. Nightmaster blinked, trying to adjust to the light.

"Where's the Silver Crown, damn it?!"

Nightmaster looked at Albrecht, awareness of a sort dawning on his face. "The crown is here? Nightmaster has not been told! Nightmaster must punish his legions!"

Albrecht rammed his klaive into the Garou's stomach and Nightmaster screamed in pain, coughing up a pool of oily, brackish blood before he fell over dead.

Albrecht pulled out his klaive and wiped it on the dead Garou's fur. The blood was sticky, however, and did not come off easily.

"Well, this was a load of shit," Albrecht said. "The crown's not even here."

"Albrecht!" Mari cried.

Albrecht looked down at Nightmaster in time to see him get up and run off, hopping on one leg. Albrecht took off after him, but the other Garou reached the passageway first. When Albrecht came around the corner, he was gone.

"Damn it! He's got a lot of lives!"

Evan walked over to him, looking in terrible shape. His eyes barely focused. "All I know is, he scares the shit out of me. He's what we'll become if we stay here. He's probably gathering his legions now. We've got to go."

Albrecht nodded, staring worriedly at Evan before going back into the cavern. He had never seen the kid looking so ragged before. Mari was standing by the door of the cage. She looked up at him as he came near, and he saw tears in her eyes.

"She's dead," Mari said. "He cut her throat. Probably when everything was dark. What kind of sick—"

"Let's just go, Mari," Albrecht said. He turned back to the passage and walked out. Mari bowed her head and followed him, knowing there was nothing she could do. And it hurt like hell.

Evan joined them in the passage and they followed Albrecht out, his glowing fur lighting the passage for them.

"I'll say this for the Silver Fangs," Mari said. "Your spirits teach you good Gifts."

"The Lambent Flame was created for just such a situation as this," Albrecht said, marching forward. "When the First Wolf encountered the Greater Darkness to free Gaia from its clutches, the Darkness devoured him. But he learned the secret of death while in that cold embrace. And he learned how to combat the darkness with his own light. Our legends say that the Abyss is the body of the slain Greater Darkness. I didn't believe it until today."

Mari's wall scratchings helped them to orient themselves, but they took many wrong turns on the upward ascent. The passageways actually seemed to change their features at times, and Mari swore that she saw her marks on crossroads she had never been through before. These false marks invariably led them back down into the caverns. They would then have to backtrack and find those passages which inclined upwards.

What disturbed Albrecht more, however, was that he and Mari had to keep Evan from wandering off by himself down strange passageways. Whenever they stopped him, he seemed to start as if waking from a dream. Looking around, his eyes would show a despair greater than he had a right to claim for his years. Albrecht knew they had to get out of there before the place claimed Evan.

They heard noises far off, scratchings and floppings, wet slaps of flesh on stone, as if things were moving in the walls. Scuttlings before and behind them. But nothing could be seen.

They hurried their pace and readied their weapons. They were all in Crinos form, and their nervousness had begun to tell on their self-control. Mari was jittery, and Evan shivered. Albrecht was a rock, a pillar of immovable determination. His seething anger at Nightmaster and the fact that, once again, the crown had eluded him served to focus his energy on one goal: escape.

"The Fang will hurt," Nightmaster's voice came out of the darkness, from no place, indeterminable. "Yes, he will experience much pain."

Albrecht did not stop, but kept moving forward. Mari growled. She hated this baiting by the Shadow Lord. Evan concentrated and drew upon Gaia's strength to still his nerves and allow him to think straight. His purpose renewed, he began to search through the dark for any sign of the hollow-souled Shadow Lord.

"The pack will join the Abyss. The pack will welcome the Abyss. Become empty to it. One with it. Nothing with it. Legions…attack!"

A howling erupted all around them and shapes appeared before and behind: large Crinos Garou. Albrecht didn't hesitate, but immediately tore into the three attackers before him with his klaive. Surprised at the ferocity and speed of his attack, two of the Garou whimpered and disappeared, their blood trailing into the walls. The last remaining enemy swept his claws out and scraped them against Albrecht's chest. They barely broke the skin, and Albrecht lunged forward with his snout, clamping his teeth into his foe's neck. Blood sprayed across the passageway as the Garou tried to pull out of the hold, ripping his own throat in the process. The body hit the floor with a thud, and was still.

Behind the pack, Mari faced four attackers. She lashed out with her leg, meeting one of the attackers full in the face and knocking it back into the others, who were all trying to edge past him to get to Mari. She stepped back and held out her hands, calling on her Gift. Her claws shot from her hand like wasps and tore into the Garou, who screamed in pain and whimpered back down the passageway, seeking refuge in the dark. Only one remained, panting eagerly for the kill.

Mari waited for him to come and swept his feet out from under him with her left leg while leaping up with her right. She landed on his stomach and flexed her toes, driving her sharp claws into his gut. She then twisted in place, tearing a circular gash into his stomach. He howled in pain and she rammed her fist into his snout, breaking his fangs. He crumpled, unconscious.

Evan suddenly bolted past Mari and ran after the fleeing Garou.

"No, Evan!" Mari yelled and went after him.

Evan had a good lead on her, though, and reached the Garou before she could get to him. Mari had visions of Evan becoming one of them, of Evan as an empty-eyed zombie Garou. She screamed. "Evan! No!"

But Evan did not slow down. He howled in rage and leapt onto the closest Garou, which was clearly startled at Evan's ferocity and barely got his hands up in time. It did him no good. Evan tore the limbs from their sockets and threw them behind him. He drove his snout into the Garou's chest, splitting open the chest bone and rib cage, and then savagely tore out the Garou's heart with his teeth.

The other Garou disappeared into the darkness, whimpering. Mari stopped cold, staring in horror at Evan. He was frenzying, and she knew that to stop him could cause him more harm than the Abyss Garou now could.

Evan sat on top of the Garou and stared into its slowly dying eyes. As the red haze of anger cleared, he saw a spark of emotion in those eyes. He saw fear. Then the eyes shut forever, and the Garou expelled its last breath.

Evan began to cry as it all came at him at once. The horrors of the journey had finally become greater than his ability to withstand them. Sobbing, he shifted back to Homid form.

Mari approached and put her hand on his shoulder. Albrecht slowly walked up, unsure what to think. He had just seen the kid freak out for only the second time in his young Garou life; the other had been during his First Change. A frenzy was not a nice thing to witness. It stripped a Garou of all identity, making him a bestial killing machine.

"We've got to go," he said.

Evan nodded and stood up.

"Are you all right?" Mari asked.

"Yeah. It…it just got to be a little too much. You know?"

Mari nodded.

"I know, kid," Albrecht said. "It ain't pretty, but we all lose it every once in a while. For some of us, that time comes more often."

Evan walked past Mari and nodded at Albrecht. "Let's go."

Albrecht turned back the way they had come and led them forward. "You know," he said as he walked, "Nightmaster's legion are a bunch of cowards."

"Don't be so sure," Evan said. "You didn't see Nightmaster up close like I did. The sooner we're out of here, the better."

"I agree," Mari said, flexing her now-regrown claws. "We need to keep moving."

The ground rose more quickly now, and they knew they were almost back where they had begun. They also heard a whistling noise, low, almost indiscernible. It grew in volume as they walked, and soon they felt a breeze tugging at their fur, pulling them forward, as if air were rushing out of the cave in the direction they were walking.

"Strange," Evan said. "The wind is really stirring. But there are no spirits here."

"Walk now. Talk later," Albrecht said.

They came into the first cavern, stepping on bones as they went. The brittle bones cracked underfoot, but the noise was nearly drowned by the wind. The wind was a gust now, drawing the air past them and out of the cavern entrance. Albrecht stepped out onto the ledge, and immediately jumped back in.

"Damn!" he said. "Watch your step. That wind gets fierce out there. Almost sucked me into the crevasse."

From deep in the caves behind them came Nightmaster's voice: "All are drawn in. None can escape. Silver Fang will feed the beast."

Albrecht growled. "All right. Follow me. We'll hug the wall. Move slowly and carefully."

Mari and Evan nodded, and Albrecht stepped out again. His fur whipped furiously in the wind, but he was unmoved. He slowly stepped to the side, moving back up the ledge. Evan followed, swaying for a moment as the wind hit him, but he leaned against the wall and retained his balance. Mari slipped around the corner right behind Evan, but she was well-balanced and kept her place easily.

They moved slowly up the ledge toward the top, the wind whipping about them. A horrible moaning sound rose up from the dark pit. They all shivered, unable to help themselves. The wail touched a deep part of their souls, an immature, fearful place. Almost unconsciously, Albrecht felt himself being drawn to the edge, but he fought the urge and clung to the wall, moving step by step upward. But he had caught a glance into the pit, and knew the sight would be with him forever. The sight of raw emptiness, deeper than before—a yawning, hungry gulf desperate to be filled yet devouring everything which fed it; impossible to describe truly. His mind nearly shattered trying to think about it. It was only with a great effort that he could force it from his thoughts and concentrate on walking.

He staggered forward, but gained strength with every step. Each step got him closer to the top, closer to safety. Evan followed, looking away from the pit, hugging his face against the wall.

Smart kid, Albrecht thought. *If I'd done that, I'd have saved myself from seeing that—Shit! Don't think about it! Think about what's ahead. Only what's ahead.*

As he got to the top, the wind brought a scent to him: the smell of Garou. Many Garou. He poked his head around the corner and saw fifteen Black Spiral Dancers waiting there, all staring straight at him.

"Shit," he said.

198   **WILLIAM BRIDGES**

"Albrecht!" Mari yelled over the wind. "Move it! There's a pack of Black Spirals moving up the path behind us."

"Calm down, Mari. There's a lot more up here." He walked up and stood at the head of the path, his klaive out and ready. The wind stopped as soon as he was off the ledge. Evan came up behind him.

Mari heard a scream behind her and turned to see one of the five Black Spirals fall off the ledge. The Dancers had crawled out of a cave far below and were working their way up to her. The fallen one vanished in the darkness of the great pit and his scream was abruptly cut off. The other Black Spirals stared after him in horror. One of them began to laugh hysterically, walking to the edge while his companions tried to pull him back. He fought them for a moment, then seemed to come to his senses. They began to climb the ledge again. Mari grimaced and reached the top.

A Black Spiral walked over to Albrecht's pack, holding his hand up to the others to keep them away. He was a tall man with a thin face and long black hair.

"Let's not be hasty here, Lord Albrecht," he said. "We outnumber and outgun you here. But we don't want you dead." He stopped, smiling as if he misspoke himself. "Well, to be more precise, our queen does not want you dead. In fact, she has requested an audience. Would you please come along? It would not do for the would-be king to deny the queen of a neighboring kingdom."

"You know me, but I don't know you, pal," Albrecht said.

The Black Spiral Dancer feigned surprise. "You mean Duke Arkady never mentioned me? How rude. And after all I've done for him. Well, he's left it up to me to do the introductions. I am Dagrack, war chieftain of the Dank Well Hive in the Adirondacks. We're neighbors."

Albrecht stared hatefully at the Black Spiral Dancer, but sheathed his klaive. "Don't fight them," he said to Evan and Mari. "We'd lose."

Dagrack smiled, nodding.

Mari fumed at Albrecht but then looked away. Evan seemed worried.

"Don't worry," Albrecht said. "They want us alive. At least for now."

Dagrack motioned to the path on which the pack had originally traveled into the realm. "After you. There is a Moon Bridge waiting just outside the borders of this realm."

Albrecht, Mari and Evan walked away from the crevasse. The Black Spiral Dancers, eerily silent, flowed after them.

16

More fucking caves, thought Albrecht. *These ones're worse than the others.*

Albrecht, Mari and Evan walked through a winding passageway. Other tunnels broke off from it in various places, leading off into darkness. The host of Black Spiral Dancers trailed behind them, except for Dagrack, who led the way.

The tunnels stank. Not just in an unpleasant way, but in an overwhelming, poisonous way. Albrecht had coughed up phlegm twice already, and Evan was doing worse. Mari seemed to be handling it better than either of them, although she did have a nauseated look on her face.

Throughout the tunnels, growing from the floors and walls, were giant, bloated fungi. The massive black and yellow growths seemed to pulsate at times, but it could have been a trick of the light from the sputtering torches placed along the main passage.

Far off down one tunnel, Albrecht saw a greenish glow emanating from one of the walls. He tried to hurry past that tunnel as quickly as possible. Balefire. Pure, toxic radiation. The excretions of the Wyrm, it was said.

Figures shambled along on either side of their marching party: wretched creatures that looked like deformed Garou. Metis—the result of Garou inbreeding. Albrecht looked at them closely. He knew most Black Spiral Dancers were metis, since they found it hard to keep flocks of Kinfolk with whom they could breed. He also knew that their perverted society had a caste system: breeders on top and non-breeders on the bottom. But these things crawling along…. They must be the rejects, those born so deformed that they were barely viable. They were obviously performing the role of worker drones.

Albrecht shook his head and refused to watch them anymore. *Look too much at the Wyrm's works*, he thought, *and you might start pitying them. And that's the last thing they deserve.*

A howling and screaming could be heard from one of the tunnels ahead, along with grunting and heavy breathing. As they passed, Albrecht looked in, and immediately looked away again.

I did not need to see that, he thought. *I could've gone the rest of my life without seeing Black Spiral Dancer sex, thank you.*

Dagrack turned into a side tunnel, a larger one than most, and led them to an oak door placed at the end of the tunnel. It looked as if it barely fit the passage, since light flooded out from within through the large cracks on the sides. Dagrack slammed his fist into the door and waited.

A voice came from within: "Enter."

Dagrack pushed open the door and walked in, motioning them to follow. The room was circular and inlaid with marble. Polished marble. This room was different. Special. Albrecht looked across the room and saw why.

A woman sat on a chair on a raised dais, staring at them with glee. She was naked, and Albrecht could clearly see three pairs of breasts on her, one under the other, like an animal. She smiled, revealing her fangs. She had short blond hair and pale, pale skin.

The throne she sat on was a carved marble block with a depression large enough to fit a Crinos Garou. Albrecht shook his head. It was a mockery of his tribe. His protectorate. Many of the Silver Fangs of Vermont were marble barons, making their fortunes on the many marble deposits in the southern portion of the state. For this Black Spiral to deck her throne room out in it…it was pure insult.

Dagrack bowed on bended knee. "My queen. I have brought the would-be king and his pack."

The woman nodded. "Lord Albrecht. It is a pleasure to entertain royalty."

"Who the hell are you?" Albrecht asked.

She frowned. "Such manners for gentry! I am Queen Azaera."

"Never heard of you," Albrecht said, looking back at Mari and Evan. Mari was giving him a warning look. He frowned. She seemed to know who this lady was. Did Mari think it wasn't a good idea to insult her? *If so, I better back off,* he thought.

Azaera stood up and walked down the dais toward her guests. She was no longer smiling, but had a cold, hard look on her face. "We will stop this idle chatter, then, and come to the point. Where is the Silver Crown?"

"Why do you want it? I thought Arkady was your horse to bet on."

"Arkady does not recognize that he would only serve as a regent for me. I need the crown to cement my power, to expand my kingdom."

"What?! Are you nuts? It'll fry your head off!"

"Don't be so sure, deluded Gaialing. Your legends have lied before. Never has there been a ruler like Azaera. The crown will have to accept me. My ancestors say so. They have seen it before. They know its power."

"Your ancestors are just as cracked as you are, you freaking bitch."

Azaera walked up to him. He was taller, forcing her to look up, but her arrogance did not seem diminished by this. She ran a claw along his chest, playfully. "I appreciate pride in a king, but you go too far. I am queen here. You need to show proper deference, or I will be forced to make—" She stopped speaking as she felt the bulk of his klaive in its sheath underneath Albrecht's coat. She jumped back, screaming.

"Idiots! You did not disarm them!"

Dagrack shrugged his shoulders. "Slipped my mind. Surely they cannot threaten such a queen as you."

She spun on him, hissing as she began to shift to Crinos form, a huge, terrifying aspect. Drawing back her hand, she slashed at Dagrack's forehead. He grunted as the claw opened a gash, spilling blood down his face. But he did not move or try to defend himself.

"Churl!" Azaera yelled.

Dagrack sighed. "Yes, my queen."

Azaera seemed satisfied and walked back up the dais. "Disarm them."

"Over my dead body," Albrecht said, reaching into his coat and gripping his klaive.

Azaera turned and looked at him, eyes narrowed. "You will die, then."

"And you will never find the crown."

Azaera's eyes widened. "Ah…diplomacy. Now we are royal." She turned to Dagrack. "Take the packmates. Leave us! We speak of state secrets."

Dagrack rose and grabbed Mari's shoulder, beginning to pull her toward the door. She slipped from his grip and hit him on the back with both hands, sending him tumbling to the floor.

The rest of the Black Spiral Dancers howled and pounded toward her, then stopped dead in their tracks at a screech from Azaera.

"Stop! They are prisoners. Do not kill them. They are our détente." She looked at Albrecht.

He ignored her. "Mari, summon a Wyldling! Get out of here!"

Mari was standing ready to take any attack, with Evan at her back. "I can't. I can only do that from the Umbra."

Albrecht looked down. "We're fucked."

Dagrack got back up and glared at Mari. He motioned toward the door. "Make it easy on yourself and me. Just go."

Mari stepped toward the door, Evan next to her. They both looked at Albrecht as they left, but said nothing. The Black Spirals fell in behind them, and Dagrack left last, glaring at Albrecht, but then giving an angry glance at Azaera. He closed the door behind him.

Azaera walked seductively up the dais and sat on the throne, her legs spread wide. "Do you find me attractive?"

Albrecht looked away. "Not in the slightest."

Azaera frowned. "You do not know how to play the game well. So we will quit with games. You will tell me where the crown is or I will kill your packmates. No! Worse…I will make them walk the Black Spiral, dance the labyrinth. They will come to know the Wyrm as we do…as benevolent father and tortured victim of Gaia."

"Would you believe me if I said I don't know where the crown is?"

Azaera seemed to think for a minute, examining Albrecht. "Yes. But it's not what I want to hear."

"Well, I don't have any other answers for you."

Azaera looked away and seemed to be thinking to herself. "Curses. Shit. This ruins everything."

Albrecht stood watching her, wondering what weird logic was working through that demented brain.

Azaera looked at him again, smiling. "You can leave. Fly away little falcon."

Albrecht just stood there, not saying anything.

"I'm serious. Leave. I don't want you here."

"You mean I can just walk out of here? With Mari and Evan?"

"No. You can walk out of here, but they can't. Détente, lord. Détente. If you happen to find the crown, you can come back here and exchange it for them. I'll keep them around for a few days at least. After Arkady takes the throne…. Well, I think you understand political misfortunes. Don't bother coming back after that. I'll kill you then, impudent cub."

Albrecht didn't say anything. He sat there, measuring his options. He could take out his klaive and chop her up. He could then track his pack through the tunnels and rescue them, carving their way out together through a mountain of Black Spiral Dancer bodies. But he knew that was suicide. And if he did that, he would never find the crown. He had maybe two days to find it.

He felt like an ass. *Chasing after a damn heirloom rather than rescuing my packmates.* But they had known the risks when they signed onto this quest. They knew that he had to finish what he had started.

He sighed. "How do I get out of here?"

"Down the passage you came. You will recognize the Moon Bridge room when you see it. Tell the Gatekeeper that Azaera gives you leave to go. He will believe you; my Banes will inform him beforehand. Tell him where you wish to go, and he will deliver you there."

Albrecht nodded and turned to leave the room.

"Farewell, O king," Azaera said.

Albrecht did not respond. He opened the door and walked out, closing it behind him. He couldn't stand the idea of her watching him walking off down the tunnel. He marched back the way he had come, smoldering with barely suppressed rage, ignoring the crawling drones around him.

As he passed a side tunnel, he heard Mari call out. "Albrecht!"

He turned to look at her. She and Evan were being led down the passage toward whatever fate awaited them. Evan looked scared, but Mari looked furious, ready to frenzy.

"I…I'm sorry. I can't do anything," Albrecht said, watching them be pulled away.

She glared at him. "Asshole! I should have known better than to join you! You've always been a self-obsessed asshole!"

Evan looked at Albrecht, nodding. "I…understand. Just get the crown, Albrecht."

Albrecht stood there, watching his packmates disappear into the darkness. He trembled in rage, but fought to control it. Mari's accusations he could understand. He expected that from her. But Evan…. He gave up too easy. He thought of Albrecht before himself. *That's not right*, Albrecht thought. *I don't deserve that! That kid's putting his trust in the wrong place, damn it. And it makes me feel even shittier than if he cursed me like Mari.*

Albrecht walked down the passage to the Moon Bridge room. He growled at the robed Dancer there to get him to Central Park. The Gatekeeper stared coldly at Albrecht.

"I can't," the Dancer said. "It has defenses that will not allow my pathstone to connect. Unless, of course, you could give me the proper rites…."

Albrecht growled at him. "I'll tear your head off! Don't fuck with me! I'm not in the mood. Just send me…. Hell, I don't know! To the Silver Fang Homeland in the Umbra."

The Dancer chewed his lower lip. "I can't. I can get you close, but not into the realm."

Albrecht grabbed his robe and shook him. "What's your problem? Doesn't this lead anywhere?"

The Dancer laughed. "It's a Black Spiral Dancer Moon Bridge. Do you *want* it to lead everywhere?"

Albrecht let him go. "Just open a Bridge."

The Gatekeeper began the rite. It was almost identical to the one with which Albrecht was familiar, but the names the Dancer called out to were almost unpronounceable and left a tingling in Albrecht's spine when he heard them.

A hole in the air opened up, glowing with silver radiance. Albrecht stepped into it and stepped out onto a Moon Path in the Umbra. He was in a featureless landscape under a gibbous moon. The bridge closed behind him, and he was alone.

With no idea of where to go next.

17

When the moon finally disappeared below the horizon, dimming the Moon Path, Albrecht was still lost. He had walked for hours and had seen nothing but the path and the ephemeral barrens on either side. No realms or domains to be seen anywhere. The Black Spiral Dancer had lied. He had not put Albrecht anywhere near his destination.

Albrecht sat down on the path and put his head in his hands. He had never felt so low before. Even after the exile and during the drinking bout that had followed, he had had his youthful pride to prop him up. But now…now he felt he had used up all his luck. This was the universe's revenge for his having been a self-absorbed ass for all these years. Never thinking of others, or even of Gaia really. Always concerned instead with glory.

But glory ain't worth shit if there's no one to witness it, he thought. *It's over. Arkady's going to be king and I'll crawl back to New York, packless again. I'm going to hit the bottle again, that's for sure. This time I ain't getting back out.*

He saw a light to his left and looked up to see a Lune aimlessly floating down the dimming Moon Path. Albrecht got up and stood in its way, blocking the path.

The Lune floated toward him and stopped inches away, spinning around and around. Then it floated upwards, as if it meant to go over him.

Albrecht reached up and grabbed it, pulling it back down. "I am lost, hungry and shit out of luck. You are going to take me to the Silver Fang Homeland, do you hear me? I know I don't speak your lingo, but I think you savvy mine. All right? Let's get this over with!"

The Lune began spinning about furiously, trying to break Albrecht's grip. But Albrecht only squeezed tighter.

Light exploded from the Lune and a hole opened in the air between it and Albrecht. The Lune tugged itself away, pulling Albrecht into the hole with its momentum before he could fully release his grip. He fell into the Moon Bridge.

The hole sealed up behind him, shutting out the light, as the Lune continued its enigmatic journey down the path.

Albrecht fell. He had come out on the other side of the Moon Bridge to find himself in mid-air. Looking down, he saw the ground far below. He figured the distance to be about one hundred yards as he plummeted toward the ground. The green, autumn-leaf-strewn ground.

The ground rippled, and became water. Albrecht crashed into it, shattering its wavy mirror and plunging in. He was swinging his limbs about wildly, trying to resurface, when the water turned into sand. His legs were buried in the white particles, and he spat out a mouthful of it.

He pulled himself out and looked around. He was in a desert. From horizon to horizon, all he saw were sand dunes, slowly shifting in a light breeze.

I'm in a Wyld realm, he thought. *That's gotta be it. A field becomes a lake which becomes a desert. What else could it be?*

He stood up and looked for landmarks of any kind. There was nothing.

I hope like hell it turns into a beautiful tropical island soon, he thought. *'Cause I'm awful thirsty already. Much more of this and I'll dry up here, king of an empty, forlorn patch of desert.*

Having nothing better to do, he started walking. The sun was bright and burning, so he pulled his trenchcoat off and draped it over his head to shade his face.

He walked like that for hours, until the sun went down and the moon rose. It was full enough for most humans to have called it a full moon, but, being a Garou, Albrecht was more sensitive to such things. He knew it was still gibbous. The full moon was his moon, an Ahroun's moon, and he knew he'd feel it in his soul when that phase took to the sky. He also knew that when it was full, two nights from now, Arkady would be crowned.

He had found no food or water. He was exhausted. Without some sustenance soon, he would start feeling the consequences. He could last longer than most humans or animals deprived of food or water, but he knew that the more active he was, the weaker he would get.

He lay down next to a smoothly rising dune and closed his eyes. In seconds, he was asleep.

He woke with a start. Something was wrong. He looked around, gripping his klaive. The landscape had changed again. He was now in a wood, surrounded by white birches. The ground was flat and even, a carpet of green grass between the tree trunks. It was eerily pure. Just the trees and the grass, in all directions. The trees even seemed to be lined up in rows, but Albrecht couldn't be sure of this. The moon was high in the sky. He had slept for at least an hour, if not more.

A voice came from behind him. "The ghosts of dead armies."

Albrecht was on his feet instantly, turning around with klaive in hand. An old man stood a few feet away, leaning on a birch. He was thin but looked like he once had carried a lot of muscle. His white hair grew long, well past his shoulders and almost to his belt. He wore a gray robe adorned with silver pictograms—Silver Fang pictograms—representing honor, wisdom and glory. And there, on his chest, was the symbol of kingship.

"Who are you?" Albrecht asked.

"Aaron Ever Stone," the man said. "I saw you notice the trees. They are not trees. They are the ghosts of my dead army. My loyal army."

"Your name…. It's familiar. But I can't place it," Albrecht said.

"In my time on Gaia's flesh, I was king of the Esk River Protectorate in northern England. In the seventeenth century, by human reckoning."

Albrecht stood looking at the Silver Fang king, unsure what to say or do. He had never been in the presence of such a powerful ancestor before. "How…did you get here?"

The old man looked at Albrecht, puzzled. "This is my death domain. It is you who have come here. And who are you?"

"I am Lord Albrecht, scion of the House of Wyrmfoe. I was thrown into a Wyld realm. I don't even know where this is."

The old man nodded, understanding. "Ah. You are in the Silver Fang Homeland. You have passed through the Wyld zones along the edge. They come and go, but seem to get closer every few…years. If they *are* truly years, the time I reckon by the changing of the seasons. But time moves slowly here, does it not? So say the living who visit me."

"I don't know," Albrecht said. "Umbral lore was never my specialty. I can't believe I'm here. That damn Lune did send me where I wanted!"

"Why have you come?"

Albrecht thought for a minute, trying to figure out how to bring up the topic. He decided just to say it. "I'm looking for the Silver Crown."

The old man's eyes widened. "Why? Why do you seek such a thing? Are you vain?"

"No! I need it. It's the only thing that will allow me to take the crown from Arkady. Let me explain: Arkady is Wyrm-corrupt. He has allied with the Wyrm's minions. And he's set to take the throne on the cusp of the full moon—"

"Stop! I will hear no more. A king corrupt? Never! You must be mistaken. And you seek the crown? Listen to me, then: the crown is a thing of vanity and pride. It brings only pain and ruin. I know this, for I wore the crown. I was its last bearer. It was I who hid it from the world, to save the tribe from its terrible power. A power which destroys just as surely as it raises its wearer on high."

"You know where the crown is? I can't believe this! Finally, some answers. Look, you may have had problems with the crown, but I have to have it. Regardless of the consequence to me. The consequences to others will be much worse if I don't."

"You are not listening to me! Whelp cub! I tell you, it is an evil thing. I know this! You wish the crown? Then listen to my tale, and if the wanting of this thing is still in your heart afterwards, I will reveal its location to you."

"You've got a deal."

The old king wearily lowered himself to sit on the grass, leaning his back against a birch. He motioned for Albrecht to sit also. Albrecht went to a birch nearby the old man and sat down, leaning against it.

"I ruled a war-ravaged land. The Black Spiral Dancers, born in the fens and bogs and moors of Scotland, had their power to the north of my protectorate. Filthy place. From some deep pit in the earth they crawled forth to harry my lands, to steal our flocks and to corrupt our rivers with their filth.

"And the humans were ignorant of all this. They only knew that the border wars between England and Scotland were fierce. The border reivers were indeed a hard people, cruel and cunning, with no sense of honor or decency except to their own kin. Under the cover of such havoc as they wreaked, the Dancers raided our lands and ravaged us sore.

"I knew something had to be done. I had to get the Garou to the west and east of me to band together and take the fight to the Dancers' own lands. But they would not listen to me—Fianna and Get of Fenris. Getting them to work together against a common foe was nigh impossible. And that's when I heard of the Silver Crown.

"A wandering minstrel sang its tale, telling where it was hid, in the land now known as Pangaea. I knew this crown was the answer to my questions. It would allow me to forge an alliance of all the tribes and return rack and ruin to the Dancers.

"So I set off on the quest with my loyal pack, the King's Own. It was a hard journey, for the Umbra was a wild and furious place in those times. Not like now. It is empty now. Devoid of life.

"We reached Pangaea with only minor wounds, and searched and searched for the crown. It was at Table Rock we found it, the holy rock. There, in a hole under the rock, the crown was hid. It took all our might to move the stone, but move it we did, for our need was dire.

"I beheld the shining crown and placed it upon my head. And I knew what I had to do. I was Falcon's chosen, the one true king of the Silver Fangs. Nothing could stop me from saving my kingdom and ending the reign of terror the Dancers had begun.

"We returned to my kingdom and the news soon spread of the crown. I sent for the leaders of the Fianna and Get of Fenris septs, my closest neighbors, to discuss a war party. They came, although they did not want to. But they could not resist. It was as if the crown called to them to heed my request, giving them no peace until they listened and did as I said.

"Do you begin to understand the tyranny of the crown? Its power over others? Its ability to steal choice away from them, to force them unto a course of action? I did not realize this then, believing they came because they wanted to.

"We supped together and I entertained them with my best Galliards. A fine evening it was. But they seemed to feign enjoyment, covering their fear of the crown. I believed they were subtly insulting me, and grew angry with them. I sent the Galliards away and commanded them to give me packs from their septs to go to war against the Dancers.

"The Fianna bowed, cowed before my authority, and said she would deliver them in a fortnight. I was pleased.

"But the Get. He steamed and shivered, fighting some inner demon. Or so I told myself. He was in actuality fighting the power of the crown. He won the battle, and cried that he would not send his packs to die for such a tyrant as I was.

"I was furious. Not only had he stained me with that insult, but he had stained Falcon also, implying that the crown had made a petty dictator. In an instant, I drew my klaive and cut him down. His head flew across the room and thudded against the chamber door.

"The Fianna stared at me in shock and dismay. She begged to leave, to return to her lands to begin the preparations for war. I gave her leave, pleased that she, at least, would join my endeavor.

"But the fortnight passed, and no sign of her packs was seen or heard. I was furious again. How dare she slight me? I knew I would have to teach her a lesson. I would have to war on her.

"I rallied the troops and led them out across the moors, to the lands of the Fianna. They were expecting us, and they put up a valiant fight. But we were masterful in war, and I was most masterful of all, for the crown bore me well through that battle. My cries and commands were as bolts of lightning against the Fianna. They could not resist my will. Eventually, they all fell before me.

"But the Fianna did not fold before my army easily. They delivered a dread accounting upon us: only I and my pack survived. I sat upon my horse in the field of battle, surrounded by my pack, staring at the lifeless bodies of the Fianna. And at the lifeless Silver Fangs. In a fit of anger and wounded pride, I had killed the elite of two septs, the heart of a generation of Garou.

"The Dancers did not wait long to take advantage of the disaster my vanity had caused. They came down in greater numbers against the lands, the lands so newly depleted of warriors. Only the Get withstood them, bulwarked in their caern to the east.

"The Esk River Protectorate is no more. Dead. They are all dead.

"Do you see now why I warn you against this fetish? It is the cause of two septs' downfall!"

Albrecht was silent. He thought about everything he had been told about the crown. So many conflicting stories. Was the crown a gift from Gaia or a fetish like any other, but one which had become cursed over the years? Would its retrieval only doom the North Country Protectorate, as it had this old king's land?

But no, Albrecht thought. *It wasn't the crown that did this, it was the old man. It was his vanity. How can he blame the crown for backing up his commands, for lending force to them? The choice of how to use the crown was his.*

"I am sorry to hear your story. It grieves me. It is a tragedy; one which I will never forget. But…I still need the crown. I have to save my protectorate. While the crown may damn it in the end, it is the only thing which can save it now."

The old man looked at him. "It has only brought me sorrow. Deep, unyielding sorrow. Do not seek it. Stay here with me. Brighten my days with new tales of honor and glory, tales of how the Fangs succeeded without the crown. I am so lonely here, in my place of exile, with only my dead people near…." He looked at the trees.

Albrecht felt a chill up his back. *Things are not what they seem to be,* he thought. He remembered something about this famous king, Aaron Ever Stone. Something he had forgotten, about this king's name in the tales. There was one thing said in the legends: his lineage.

"I remember you now…. What royal family are you from?"

The old king looked at Albrecht quizzically. "I am a son of the House of Winter Snow."

And then Albrecht knew for sure. He stood up, stepping away from the king. "I lived up to my end of the bargain. I heard your tale. Now, where is the Silver Crown?"

The king looked up at Albrecht, exasperated. "You still want it? After all I have said?"

"Yes. You agreed to tell me where it is."

"But I would only cause your ruin by doing so. No, I cannot."

"You are going to go against your word? Where is the honor in that?"

The king looked stricken. "Honor? It has been…so long. Please, stay here with me. I can teach you much of the old ways. I even know Gifts lost to the world today. I could teach them to you…."

"No. Tell me where the crown is."

The king grabbed the birch he was leaning against and pulled himself up. "If you stay for one moon. One moon is all I ask! I will then tell you where the crown is. On my honor as a king!"

Albrecht thought. He knew he wouldn't be able to force the answer from the king by violence. The king was just an emanation, a shadow of the dead. He was a spirit. If Albrecht killed him, he would never get the answer, since the spirit would depart to re-form elsewhere in the Umbra. But who knew where? He knew that time worked differently in the homeland. One moon here could be months in the real world, or only hours.

"One day then!" the king cried, his hands out in supplication. "One day is all I ask. Is this too much? I offer you secrets forgotten in the world of flesh, secrets which could empower you more greatly than the damned crown!"

Albrecht chewed his lip. He didn't know what to do. This was the only clue he had to the crown. The old king could be lying. But what choice did Albrecht have? There was no place left to go. And these secrets, these Gifts he was offered….

"You can give me something to overthrow Arkady without the crown?" he asked.

"Yes! Stay with me and I will give you all the royal rites of old, the words that are power when spoken from the lips of kings. And I will give you the Gift to win any challenge, and to call a challenge for any reason. You could return to your sept and challenge this pretender at your leisure! With these Gifts—true powers taught to my family by spirits long ago—you could rule any sept."

"How long? How long would it take to learn them?"

Aaron stood taller. "Two moons. Perhaps three. There are no spirits here to instruct your soul directly, so I must show you in the slow manner in which flesh learns. After this time, you can come and go from here freely, to return for more powers if you so desire."

Albrecht closed his eyes. He had to think. Calmly. Without the old man pleading with him. Two moons! That was too long. Arkady would be king by then. But if what Aaron said was true about these Gifts, he could march up to Arkady anytime to demand his true right. But what if it were too late? What if Arkady turned the sept over to the Wyrm on his coronation day?

Falcon! he thought. *Why is this so hard? I have done everything in my power here to find the crown. My packmates are in the hands of the Wyrm, probably dead by now. My protectorate is about to become Wyrm-corrupt. What else am I supposed to do? I've done everything I can, damn it! But I'm failing. It's in your hands....*

He heard a screech up in the sky. He opened his eyes and looked up. A falcon wheeled above him, and let out another screech.

"No!" the old king said, looking up fearfully at the bird. "Don't heed it! It is a servant of the crown—the evil crown! Stay here! Please!"

"I can't listen to you!" Albrecht said. "I've listened to you too much already. You're lost! I recognize Harano. Your whole family has succumbed to it. Every generation! It wasn't the crown that did you in, it was your own sorrow. This isn't the tribal homeland, is it? It's some small realm somewhere you've built to house your grief. I won't be any part of it. I've got a protectorate to save!"

Albrecht looked up at the falcon. The bird flew off to Albrecht's right, and Albrecht moved to follow it.

The old king stepped in front of him. "Please! I am lonely! Carry my memory at least! Don't let my legacy die!"

"Get out of my way," Albrecht said.

"It's in the North Country!" the old king said. "I fled from my lands to the New World, and hid the crown with the Silver Fang sept there. It lies under the royal house in New Amsterdam."

Albrecht stared at the king, barely believing his ears. "You're lying! It's not in the North Country—Greyfist would have said so! I'm from North Country, damn it! New Amsterdam is the old name for New York City, and New York is not even in the North Country Protectorate!"

The old king stepped back, flinching at Albrecht's anger. "I swear! I swear that is where I hid it. I tell you, the city of humans was in North Country when I hid the crown! It was the only place far enough from home that I could get to before...before I...I was too tired to go on. The grief, you see...the grief overtook me. Swallowed me. It has left me here, all alone. Alone and weeping."

The old king began to fade, to shift shapes, but not into a wolf. He grew tall and thin, his skin becoming deathly pale, whiter than snow. He became a birch tree, silent as the rest. But not alone any longer. He was one of many birches, testaments to sorrow.

Albrecht realized that he stood in a graveyard. A graveyard for an entire royal line. A birch for every cub of the Winter Snow family lost to Harano.

He looked into the sky again and saw the falcon wheeling about, waiting for him. The falcon again flew off, and this time Albrecht followed unhindered.

18

Fengy strolled through the park, content for once. He had just eaten a fresh fast-food meal, bought with the five-dollar bill he had found. This was working out to be a great day.

A light exploded in the air in front of him, and a hole appeared. A falcon flew from the glowing Moon Bridge, inches over Fengy's head. Fengy stared at it, aghast. This wasn't a proper Moon Bridge. It didn't open in the caern center, approved by the Gatekeeper. Was this an attack? But what could a bird do to harm the caern?

Lord Albrecht jumped out of the Moon Bridge, almost colliding with Fengy. The Moon Bridge sealed shut behind him, leaving no trace of its ever having been there.

"Watch out!" Albrecht said, running past Fengy, who was holding his hands over his head, readying himself to be run over by a pack of Garou.

Fengy looked up to see only Lord Albrecht and the bird, streaking off into the park.

"Hey!" Fengy yelled. "Where's your pack? What's going on? That wasn't a legal bridge! You're going to get in trouble with Mother Larissa!"

"Don't have time to chat!" Albrecht yelled over his shoulder, turning down a lane and running out of sight.

"Huh!" Fengy said. "Then you don't have time for me to tell you that your friend is here looking for you?" He waited, but heard no response. Albrecht was out of hearing range. Fengy shrugged his shoulders. What did he care? If Albrecht was going to be rude, always treating him like a second-class citizen, then he could damn well find his friend on his own. Wasn't everyday someone came looking for you from North Country.

Fengy continued his walk, a bit flustered, but with a full stomach.

Albrecht had stopped running to catch his breath. He stood on a street corner, watching the falcon disappear into a closed subway station. He waited a few seconds, then bolted after it. No one was around—at least no one he noticed—so he shifted into Glabro form, tore the chain lock off the gate and ran down the stairs.

It was dark in the station, so he shifted to Lupus form and called upon one of his Gifts, honing his senses sharper than any animal's. He padded along on the cement, following the falcon. Albrecht knew this was a spirit he followed, not a real falcon, but it was still strange to see something and yet not smell it.

The falcon landed on the floor next to another fence, this one blocking the entrance into the subway tunnel. The tunnel had intermittent lighting, as if this area had not been closed off for long and the electricity not yet shut off, letting the old bulbs burn.

Albrecht shifted to Crinos and tore the fence down. As soon as it was down, the falcon took wing again and shot off down the tunnel to the right. Albrecht again assumed Lupus form and ran after it.

The tunnel went down for about a quarter mile before dead-ending. A few feet before the end, on the left side of the tunnel, was a passageway, carved into the cement and stone. Unnaturally carved.

The falcon flew into the passage. Albrecht hesitated. This was not human-made. That meant that one of New York's various supernatural residents of the sewer had carved it. He was on good terms with none of them.

He jumped into the passage anyway and ran after the quickly disappearing falcon. It was pitch black now, but his magically enhanced senses more than compensated. He could smell sewer, somewhere far ahead. But before that, he heard the falcon turn right, down a side passage. Albrecht followed. He hoped there were not too many turn-offs, since he could easily get lost down here if something were to happen to the falcon.

The passageway smelled old. He could pick up no scent on it: a sign that it had been long disused. The only sign of the falcon now was its screeches. He could not see it or smell it. The next screech he heard echoed longer than the rest. The falcon had entered a larger room. Albrecht hurried ahead, then stumbled out into the room as the passageway suddenly ended, giving him a short fall.

He heard the falcon screech from the far side of the room. From the echoes and distance, he judged the chamber was maybe thirty yards across. As he padded across the floor, he felt marble beneath him. Marble tiling.

He reached the falcon, who was perched on a large, box-like object. Albrecht realized he would need eyesight here. He concentrated and lit the fires of his inner being, igniting his fur into a glowing lambent flame—the same Gift he had used against Nightmaster.

As light flooded the chamber, Albrecht looked around. It resembled an old mausoleum. The floor was marble, as were the columns holding up the ceiling. Gargoyle shapes sat at the top of the posts, staring blindly out at the room. Oddly colored dust lay along the base of the walls; Albrecht realized it was the remains of tapestries. Double doors stood open on the far wall from the passage, but they revealed a wall of dirt on the other side. It looked as if someone had begun a digging project there, but had abandoned it before ever really beginning.

The passageway by which Albrecht had traveled was not natural to the room, but a later addition. Someone had burrowed his way past the wall and into this room.

It was obvious to Albrecht where he was: in the throne room of an ancient Silver Fang sept, perhaps the first in North America. The place had fallen pretty far from its early days of glory. No court had convened here for centuries. He figured this must be the basement of an old mansion; one that probably didn't exist anymore on the surface. Most likely, it was bulldozed and new foundations had been laid across it. He wondered what was up there now. A tenement? City Hall?

The falcon screeched and he turned back to look at it. The box it stood on was a chest. It was iron, and rusted badly, but still relatively intact.

"Is that it?" Albrecht asked. "Is the crown in there?" He shifted to Glabro form and ran to the box. The falcon screeched and fluttered off, to land on the ground next to it. The lock had long ago rusted, and it flew apart easily as Albrecht threw back the lid. He looked inside.

Nothing. The box was empty.

He looked at the falcon, which screeched and bumped into the box. Albrecht frowned, then understood. He shoved the box back, revealing a marble tile with writing on it.

A Garou pictogram had been carved there so long ago that it would surely have been worn down except for the box that had covered it for all these years. It was the symbol of kingship. A rite had been performed over this tile, sealing it with power. A rite of protection of some sort? Or a spirit binding? He had seen the sort before, and knew that only Silver Fang royalty could break such a seal and not suffer the consequences intended by the ritemaster.

Albrecht shifted to Crinos form and thrust his nails between the cracks. He grunted and pulled, and the tile slowly yielded. He pried it up and placed it aside, then looked at what was beneath it. The light from Albrecht's pelt shone down a small, maybe one-foot-square shaft, revealing a wooden box. A wooden box perfectly preserved, as if it had been made yesterday, except for the ancient manufacture. It appeared to be a strongbox from the Middle Ages.

Albrecht reached in and pulled it out. He placed it on the ground and examined it. There was a catch, but no lock.

Powerful, sharp jaws clamped down onto his right forearm. Albrecht screamed in pain and tugged his arm away. It slipped free of the white wolf's grip, but his muscles were practically flayed. His arm was almost useless.

He stared at the white wolf, who had come from nowhere and was growling angrily at Albrecht. The wolf shifted forms into Crinos. A black leather battle harness appeared over the huge werewolf's torso, contrasting with the pure white fur. Fur Albrecht would recognize anywhere.

"How the hell…?" Albrecht said, drawing his klaive with his left hand.

"It is mine, Albrecht!" Arkady said, stepping forward and standing over the box.

"The fuck it is! Just step back, Arkady, and I'll let you live. At least until you're banished from the tribe!"

"Shut up, you stupid cur! How dare you try to steal the kingship from me! Moving around behind my back and plotting with that traitor Greyfist!"

"Traitor? He's the most loyal Silver Fang in this hemisphere! If you've done anything to him—"

"Like kill him? Kill him for conspiring against the crown? I have. I will kill you next!"

Albrecht stood stone-still in shock. "You…killed…Greyfist? He was my best friend in the sept!" Rage caused him to tremble and he tried to control his temper, but immediately lost the battle. He howled and lunged at Arkady, who easily jumped back.

Albrecht was like a rampaging torch as he chased Arkady across the room, the light from his fur throwing Arkady's shadow large against the wall.

Arkady drew his klaive as he ran. He slipped to the right and then spun around, stabbing at Albrecht, who was an easy target, glowing as he was.

Albrecht ran onto the klaive, which went through his right lung but did not exit his back.

He fell down, coughing up blood and coming to his senses. The pain had knocked the frenzy from him. Arkady did not follow through. Instead, he ran over to the box.

Albrecht looked for the falcon spirit, but could not see it anywhere. He got to his feet and walked resolutely toward Arkady, ignoring the pain from his chest. "How did you find me?" he snarled as he walked.

Arkady, box in hand, turned to face Albrecht. He held his klaive out defensively. "You idiot! I've been here in New York for three days, waiting for you to return! Lucky I was. I did not know you would return here first. But I could not wait at the caern—wait for you to steal my birthright from me?!"

"Birthright? You forget, *I'm* Morningkill's grandson. Not you."

"But I am scion of the Clan of the Crescent Moon. We are a better family."

"I wouldn't put too much faith in this family stuff if I were you. Not after what I've seen. But you didn't answer my question. How the hell did you find me *here?*"

"The Rite of the Questing Stone, fool! Any cub could have found you. All they would have had to do was wait for you to show up!"

"Well what are you going to do now? Put the crown on? Go ahead. Put the crown on. I want to see this."

Arkady smiled at Albrecht, a twisted grimace. He shook his head. "Oh, no. I would not do something so stupid as that. This is not for me to wear. But I shall keep you from wearing it."

Albrecht growled. "You're going to have to kill me to do that." He slashed his klaive at Arkady and actually surprised the Garou, who did not parry Albrecht's left-handed attack well. The klaive sliced the tendons off his right arm. His hand went limp and the klaive fell to the ground.

Arkady howled in rage and stepped back. He dropped the box under him and crouched low, waiting for Albrecht to approach.

Albrecht moved forward warily. They were equal now. Each had only one usable arm. But he had the klaive. He knew he could finish it with one blow if he were good enough. But if he let Arkady get too close, then Albrecht would have to drop the klaive and fight claw-to-claw. And he knew Arkady was the better hand-to-hand fighter of the two.

Before he could choose his move, he heard grunting and scuffling from the passageway. He stepped back, out of Arkady's range, and stole a look in that direction.

Black Spiral Dancers crawled their way up the tunnel, toward the room, bearing balefire torches.

Albrecht turned back to Arkady. "Damn it! If you were ever a real Silver Fang, think back to that time now. Do not let them get the crown! We can fight our way out of here if we do it together."

Arkady looked at the Black Spiral Dancers, who were almost into the room, and then at Albrecht, trying to decide. He looked at the box beneath him. "No! I can't let you have the crown. The Black Spiral Dancers promised me the kingship. It is my crown."

"They want it to pervert it! You can't let that happen. Not if you call yourself king!"

"Don't listen to him!" a voice cried out from the passageway. Black Spiral Dancers now jumped into the room and spread out to form a line, preparing to charge Albrecht. Behind them, Dagrack climbed from the passage. "He wants the crown for himself, Arkady. He can't stand the idea of you being king!"

Arkady growled at him. "What are you doing here? How did you find us?"

Dagrack smirked. "Oh, I've been watching you, Arkady. You can't go anywhere without my knowing about it. As soon as you entered the tunnels, I was alerted. Who do you think dug this passageway? Black Spiral Dancers—my cousins. I was but a Moon Bridge away from you."

Albrecht almost jumped past the Black Spiral leader when he saw Evan and Mari being pushed toward the room from the passageway. The line of Black Spirals surged forward at Albrecht's move, so he stepped back again.

He watched his packmates as they were pushed into the room. They looked terrible. They had bruises all over and seemed weak from hunger, but they both met Albrecht's gaze. Mari nodded at him, as if she approved of his being here. Evan actually managed a weak smile, happy to see Albrecht.

"Put them in the corner," Dagrack said. The Black Spiral Dancers pushed and shoved Evan and Mari into the far corner of the room, away from Albrecht.

Dagrack looked triumphantly at Albrecht. "I brought these two in case I had to bribe you with their lives. But I find that, after all your journeys, it is not you who has the crown. It is Arkady. My friend Arkady." He walked over to Arkady, who growled low as he approached, but did not move away from him. "Arkady who is to be king of the Silver Fangs. And this without the Silver Crown! Arkady does not need the crown. He has me instead."

"I need no one but myself!" Arkady yelled. "I am not your puppet. I am master here! The next king of the Silver Fangs."

Dagrack stared at Arkady, and then bowed slightly. "Of course, my lord. Excuse your servant that he spoke otherwise. I wish simply to advise you in the matter of your antagonist here."

"What?" Arkady said. "What do you have to say?"

"Revenge, Arkady. It is your time for revenge. Revenge against those who wronged you long ago, who denied you and forced you out."

Arkady shut his eyes, holding down anger. "Damn them! But they matter not now! They are gone many years while I stand here, soon to be king."

"Oh, no, Arkady, they are not gone. You think that your oppressors existed in body alone? No! Their spirits still thwart you. Their servant stands before you, defiant, ready to run any obstacle to prevent you from succeeding. Lord Albrecht, scion of a royal line. He is just the same as they were, Arkady. Remember the Motherland and what they did to you there? What royals just like Albrecht did to you?"

"No. Do not warp this. He is like me—an exile. But he is wrong to defy me!" Arkady turned to glare at Albrecht. "He should have bowed down when he could. It is too late now."

"Yes, too late," Dagrack said. "He must be punished."

"What the hell are you talking about, you asshole?" Albrecht growled. "Arkady, why are you listening to him? He's a Black Spiral Dancer!"

"You will be quiet!" Arkady said. "Dagrack, fetch my klaive."

Dagrack smiled and went over to pick up Arkady's klaive, walking back to stand next to him with it. All the while, he smirked at Albrecht. Arkady concentrated, crooning low, calling on his Gift to heal his arm.

Albrecht fidgeted, uncertain what to do. Arkady was distracted; he might be able to grab the crown. But what if the Dancers did something to Evan and Mari? He couldn't decide how to act.

Arkady finished his healing and flexed his right arm. He took the klaive from Dagrack and looked back at Albrecht. "What to do with you, Albrecht?"

"Shit if I know," Albrecht said. "How about giving me the crown and letting my packmates go?"

Arkady snorted. "You will stop treating me like a fool! I have beaten you on all occasions. Bend knee and I will consider letting you live."

"My lord," Dagrack said. "I have a better punishment. One which will prove whether Albrecht is worthy to live or not."

"What do you say? Spit it out!"

"I have heard the *Lay of the Silver Crown*, the legend Albrecht doubtless followed in his quest. It speaks of a punishment placed upon the first Garou to seek the crown, a punishment for his impudence."

"Eh? What happened to him?"

"His claws were cut off, his fangs pulled and his pelt removed."

Arkady wrinkled his brow in disgust.

"Is this not what you swore to do to Albrecht? To flay his hide and hang it from a tree? I say if he survives this punishment, he can live. I will even let his packmates go free to help him crawl from the room."

"What do you gain from this?" Arkady said, staring at Dagrack.

Dagrack's demeanor did not change at all. "Why, the pleasure of helping you mete out your first royal edict and setting you on the course of kingship. You need to learn that a king must have a hard hand, lest he be dethroned by upstarts such as Albrecht."

Arkady looked at Albrecht and seemed to think on this.

"Don't listen to him, Arkady," Albrecht said. "Don't let him tell you what it is to be a king. That's your choice. Get rid of him! You know this isn't fair. My hands are tied as long as he has my packmates captive. Let them go and we'll settle this one-on-one."

Arkady sneered and shook his head. "Now who is giving kingly advice? You, who tried to snatch the throne from me! Dagrack at least helped me to get it. You must learn, Albrecht, that packmates are secondary to rulership. If you truly wish the crown, you will forsake them. Come at me! Let them fall as they may. We shall fight and decide the affair!"

Albrecht shook his head. "No. I'm not going to abandon them. I did that once already. I won't do it twice. You gotta decide: what are you going to do about it?"

"I will take my advisor's advice. I shall exact the traditional punishment for treachery against the crown. Yield your claws and fangs, Albrecht. Your pelt also. Or watch your packmates die and you with them."

Albrecht growled low.

"Arglach! Cut the boy!" Dagrack ordered. One of the Black Spiral Dancers swiped a claw at Evan's head, slicing his left ear clean off. Evan yelled and clutched his head. Mari stepped toward the Dancer, growling, but the other Dancers gathered menacingly about her. She backed up a step, putting her hand on Evan's shoulder. The Dancer who had cut off the ear picked it up from the floor and swallowed it, looking pleased.

"An incentive," Dagrack said to Albrecht. "Think hard on this."

Damn it! Albrecht thought. *What can I do?* He measured the odds against him and knew they were too much. Arkady was healed, and was more than a match for him even when wounded. Add Dagrack and his pack to that, and he didn't stand a chance against them. He looked at Evan and Mari.

Mari glared at him, giving him a look he knew. It said that he would be a fool not to try to fight his way out. Evan looked at him, but he couldn't read the kid's intent.

I wish I were a Get of Fenris, he thought. *They think nothing of dying gloriously in combat as long as they can take a few bodies out with them. But I'm not a Get. I'm Morningkill's grandson, and I owe it to the Fangs to live up to my heritage.*

He looked for the falcon spirit, but it was gone. This was his choice alone. It was one thing to suffer declawing in a story: another thing entirely to have it really happen to you. He looked up at Arkady.

"Do you swear, on whatever honor you have left, that if I survive this, my packmates can leave unharmed?"

"Yes," Arkady said. "I can be merciful also. I bear them no ill will."

Dagrack's eyes narrowed as he looked at Arkady. He obviously did not like the promise.

"Then make sure your lap dog knows that," Albrecht said.

Arkady looked at Dagrack. "You will heed me in this. If one of your mongrels harms them, I will kill you first and then all of your horde."

Dagrack nodded. "Of course. I have no need to disobey you."

"Drop your weapon, Albrecht. Let Dagrack perform the punishment."

Albrecht gritted his teeth and placed his klaive on the ground.

"Kick it over here," Arkady said.

Albrecht shoved the sword with his foot and it slid across the marble floor to Arkady. Dagrack stepped forward, drawing out a small klaive of his own. Like all klaives, it was silver.

"Please put out your hands, noble lord."

Albrecht glared hatefully at him and looked at Mari and Evan. Mari was giving him a wide-eyed 'you idiot' look, while Evan was stone-faced. Albrecht turned back to Dagrack and slowly raised his arms, palms up.

Dagrack smiled, and in an flash swung his klaive down. Albrecht grunted as the tips of his fingers fell to the floor. The pain burned him, the agonizing touch of silver. But he slowly put his now-clawless hands down and cocked his head at Dagrack.

"So fall our ideals," Dagrack said. "Like dead flesh. Now, open wide."

Albrecht opened his large muzzle, revealing sharp fangs. Dagrack pulled a pair of silver tongs from his pocket. Albrecht wondered if he had come here planning on this punishment all along. If so, he was pretty cocky about his sway over Arkady.

Dagrack placed the pliers in Albrecht's mouth and began to yank his teeth out, one by one. He grunted with exertion as he pulled the teeth, finding them hard to remove. Albrecht shut his eyes and concentrated on blocking out the pain. It was hard to do. The silver burned his gums and the blood welled up in his throat, forcing him to cough it out at Dagrack.

Dagrack smiled as the blood sprayed over him, but he did not stop his work. "Oh, I envy you in a way, Albrecht. Such an exquisite pain for those who could appreciate it. I would carry the memory of such an ecstasy with me forever." He yanked out the final fang, leaving Albrecht's blunt back teeth intact.

Albrecht spat out more blood, speaking with great difficulty. "Then why don't you give me those pliers. I'll oblige you."

"I fear I haven't the courage. I yearn so, but fear so. I envy your conviction, Silver Fang."

"Enough compliments," Arkady said. "Take his pelt. Give it to me."

Dagrack pulled his klaive out again. "I am afraid this one will hurt the most. Try not to lose control and attack me. I would be forced to kill you then. And your friends."

Albrecht stood still, closing his eyes and trying to meditate, to go deep within himself and escape the pain. But he howled loud and long when Dagrack made the first incision at the base of his throat and worked down from there, slicing through the skin of the chest and down to the groin. The Black Spiral Dancer then sliced cleanly down the inside of both legs. Albrecht nearly toppled from the pain, but Dagrack steadied him.

"Enjoying your part in the morality play, Albrecht?" Dagrack asked. "What have your morals brought you? Only this!" He carved the skin off Albrecht's foot with one swipe. "The unkindest cut of all. Do you think I chose this punishment out of sheer sadism? No, the irony is what's important here. Didn't the *Lay of the Silver Crown* teach you anything? About how important being good and cleaning your plate is?"

Albrecht growled, his eyes shut. He winced as Dagrack continued the cutting.

"Where's Gaia now? Where is your wonderful mother? The endlessly caring nurturer? Could they have lied to you, Albrecht? All those stories about the Earth Mother? She is no kind lady. I know that better than you. No, she is a cannibal with a fanged cunt. First she fucks you and then she cuts you."

Gaia! Albrecht cried to himself. *Why are you letting this happen! I have done everything asked of me! What the hell else could I do? Does it always* come down to blood and pain in the end? Is that all this equates to? And Falcon! What happened to you? You ran away as soon as Arkady showed up. You abandoned me. I called to you and you ran. I'm alone in this. I guess it's always been that way.

But the pack. I have a pack, damn it. And they are going to live because of this. This pain—aargh! It hurts! But Mari will live. Evan will live. He'll write me up in the Silver Record, won't he? He's a good kid. I'm sure he wouldn't forget me. I'll be famous for this. A martyr.

I don't want to die. Not here. Not torn up by some damn Black Spiral Dancer. But we don't always get what we ask for....

Dagrack peeled the hide off Albrecht, starting from below and sliding the arms off like sleeves turned inside out. As the hide slid across Albrecht's raw and bloody muscles, he screamed again in pain. Only his Garou nature kept him alive. Only the regenerative power given the werewolves by Gaia allowed him to live to endure such pain and torture.

"This is the lesson of the crown, Silver Fang," Dagrack said. "No noble sacrifice. No reward for your ideals. Only a grand guignol of pain and humiliation. Ultimate degradation. Serves you right. Serves all your kind. How dare you lecture my tribe on our ways! But where are your ways now? I'm stripping them away with your pelt. That is the moral of your damn crown! It's not about honor, you fool. It's about power. It always has been."

"Shut up!" Arkady said. "Just finish it."

Dagrack walked away from Albrecht with the pelt, which no longer glowed now that it was flayed from Albrecht's body. He dragged the wet, bloody thing over to Arkady, who took it in his hand.

Albrecht collapsed to the floor, shivering and barely conscious through the haze of pain.

"Let them go," Arkady said, signaling the Black Spiral Dancers. They moved away from Mari and Evan, who both bolted to Albrecht's side.

Evan bent down and immediately called on his Gift to heal Albrecht, but while it sealed up some of the oozing blood, it did not regrow the fur, claws or fangs.

"You sick bastard," Mari said, seething at Arkady. "You're pretty damn proud of this, aren't you? Why don't you try doing that to me? I'll carve you up!"

"Tend to him and then get out of here," Arkady said. "I am being gracious in letting you live. You conspired against Silver Fang leadership rites. No tribe will defend you on that."

"Wanna bet? Wait till Alani Astarte hears about this! She'll have every tribe turn against you. No one will recognize your rule."

"Oh? If she will not, then others in your tribe will. She is old and will die long before I leave the throne. Her successor will surely ally with my causes."

Mari fumed and bent down over Albrecht. "How is he?" she asked Evan.

Evan sighed. "Alive. But—Gaia! How are we going to get him out of here without killing him?"

Dagrack stepped in front of Arkady. "I have given you Albrecht's pelt. Now I ask one thing of you in return. A simple thing. One well within your power to grant."

"Tell me," Arkady said.

"I want the Silver Crown."

"No! You are joking! I would not dare give this to you!"

"Why not? In my hands, it is safe from any enemy to your crown. I certainly cannot use it to dethrone you. Do you think I would be stupid enough to wear it? No, Arkady. I need it to overthrow Azaera."

"Your queen? Why?"

"Why not? She is a tyrant. She uses you as a puppet. I work with you out of respect. She wants only power. If I have the crown—not even to wear it, but to possess it—the Black Spiral Dancers will come to my side. Rumor alone of the crown will bring them to me. With such an army of sycophants, I could easily overthrow the bitch!"

"No...don't...." Albrecht choked out, from his prone position on the ground.

Arkady looked at him, amazed. "Do not give Dagrack the crown? Why? Because you still labor under the illusion that you can have it? Oh, no. I will give the crown to whom I see fit. In his hands, it is at least as far away from yours as it can get."

Dagrack beamed. "Thank you, my lord! I am deeply honored." He reached his hands out for the box beneath Arkady, but Arkady put his foot on the box. Dagrack looked up questioningly.

"You must swear to hide it away, and to let none of the tribes know where you put it. Is this clear? If I hear rumor of it from any of the tribes, I will kill you and take it back."

"Of course. I will be most occult concerning its hiding."

Arkady removed his foot, and Dagrack picked up the box.

"Mari...." Albrecht whispered, trying to rise. "Get it...don't...."

Mari was already moving. She was next to Dagrack before he knew it, and reaching for the box. Arkady leaped in and punched her full in the face. She was knocked back, giving Dagrack time to scurry over to his pack.

Mari moved in on Arkady, but the Silver Fang placed his klaive between himself and her.

"Do you wish to be carved up as was your friend?" he said.

"No, Mari!" Evan yelled. "They've got the crown. There's nothing we can do."

Mari glared at Arkady and over at Dagrack, dropping into an attack stance.

Albrecht stood up, grunting loudly, startling everyone. "No. Don't, Mari." He swayed but kept his balance. "It's over."

Mari quivered in anger at Albrecht but then sighed, and stepped away from Arkady. "Damn you, Albrecht. I hate you for giving in."

"Sorry," Albrecht said. "I'll make it up to you later." He almost fell, but Evan caught him. Mari ran over to help steady him, concerned now. "Heh. Not too good on my feet here."

Dagrack was ignoring them now as he opened the box. A silver radiance came forth, lighting his awestruck face. "It's beautiful. It's so…noble." He reached in and pulled out a silver headband, simple and unadorned. He let the box drop to the floor.

That's it? Albrecht thought, gritting his teeth in pain. *A band of silver? No jewels or stuff?*

Dagrack turned to show the crown to everyone in the room, beaming with pride. He then turned toward Arkady and held the crown over his own head. "Power, Arkady. Power. Only cowards fear the taboos of their elders."

"What are you doing?" Arkady cried, running toward him. "Put it away! You'll die!"

Dagrack put on the crown.

And smiled. "You see. I am the true king here. No ethical retribution. No moral finger-wagging. Your stories were wrong. Your lies about the Wyrm are also proved wrong, Arkady. We are not corrupt. Just—"

He broke off into a scream as the crown began to glow brightly. It seared itself onto his head, fusing with the skin. Smoke rose from his singed fur, stinking up the room. He frantically shifted to Lupus form, trying to knock it off, but it was part of him now. He danced around, yelping in pain.

The Black Spiral Dancers stared at him, aghast, not sure what to do.

Dagrack's head was melting. The skin caught fire and burned away, revealing red and oozing musculature underneath, which itself burned away to reveal bone. The bone blackened and bubbled, cracking into shards.

Dagrack still screamed.

His eyes pooled to jelly and ran out of the sockets, smearing across his chest fur. He fell to the ground as the bone cracked away, blackened and charred, falling from his face to reveal a cooking brain, bubbling in its own juices. The crown seemed to shrink to constrict the brain, but the gray matter quickly liquefied and spilled across the floor.

The crown hit the floor with a gentle clang.

In the next few seconds, nobody moved. They all stared at the sizzling mass of flesh that once had been Dagrack's head. His body was perfectly intact.

Then Albrecht bolted toward the crown. Calling on reserves of energy he hadn't known he had, he ran with all his might toward the crown. He was followed a mere fraction of a second later by Arkady. The Black Spiral Dancers were too stunned to react to this explosion of blinding speed from the Silver Fangs.

Albrecht reached the crown first by a palm's width. He held it up and away from the grasping Arkady.

"Give it!" Arkady growled, and dug his claws into Albrecht's exposed abdomen, puncturing the stomach wall, spilling out guts and blood.

Albrecht grunted but concentrated on one thing: dropping the crown on his head. In the moment it took the crown to settle—a measureless moment, lasting an eternity for Albrecht and Arkady, but mere fractions of a second for the others in the room—Albrecht wondered what it would feel like when his brain melted away. He prayed that he could die with more dignity than Dagrack had. *Please Gaia, let it be a quick death.*

The crown fitted itself to his head, tightening about his skull. The silver band seared into his furless flesh, causing more pain than Albrecht would have believed possible. More pain than he had known when the fur was flayed from his flesh and the teeth yanked from his jaws. More pain than could possibly exist. The silver burned into his skin and melded with it, becoming part of it, an inextricable piece of his body and being. Albrecht shut his eyes, tears flowing down his cheeks.

Visions danced in his head, images of the past. King Morningkill bent down over Albrecht, a child of twelve, and patted his shoulder. The king dipped his hand in paint and drew a pictogram across Albrecht's face. The sign of the chosen. At twelve years old, before even his Firsting, Albrecht was chosen heir to the throne. Morningkill smiled at Albrecht.

The images swirled in his mind. His first kill, a simple Bane. But it had been his first and he had done it well. The admiration of his young packmates, the other Fangs who had undergone their rites with him, becoming Garou together. The praise and cheers for the boy who would one day be king.

And the growing vanity from such praise. Albrecht saw again the scene of his exile. He dragged the Wyrm carcass behind him, beaming with pride.

But Morningkill stood up on his throne and commanded Albrecht to kneel. Albrecht refused and was banished by the king. He lost his temper and leapt at his grandfather, but Greyfist pulled him back.

New York. He wandered the streets, alone. The Bone Gnawers had been pleased to welcome him, but he disdained their company. As the days passed and soon the months, he grew more and more like them, fishing his meals from garbage cans. He drank bottle after bottle of increasingly worse alcohol. Every day made him more cynical, more gutter-mouthed. He had once spoken only as a high-born Fang was expected to, but his speech soon devolved into curse word after curse word.

Then Evan ran into him, colliding with him in the street, running for his life from Black Spiral Dancers. He had his Firsting right there, tearing into the Spirals and killing them. Albrecht took him in and helped him get to the northern spirits who taught him his heritage. And in the process, he climbed out of the gutter. He had been saved by Falcon then. He had been considered worthy by the great bird. But now...?

The pain was gone. Albrecht blinked and opened his eyes.

A golden light came from behind Albrecht, and before he turned to look at its source, he heard the flapping of huge wings and the clack of talons on marble tile.

He turned his head and beheld Falcon. Not the tiny spirit that had led him here, but Falcon himself. The totem of the Silver Fangs stood incarnate in the room. The great bird emanated golden light from his shining feathers and an even brighter radiance from his eyes. He looked down at Albrecht.

And bowed his head.

Albrecht let out a sigh. He had survived. He had been judged worthy by the greatest judge of honor there was. By the totem which stood for honor; the totem which, in a deep, mystical way, *was* honor incarnate.

Arkady whimpered and withdrew his hand from Albrecht's guts. He crawled back a few feet, staring in fear at Falcon.

Albrecht stood up, holding in his intestines, and Falcon opened his wings wide. A golden glow blinded everyone in the room. The Black Spiral Dancers screamed and clutched their eyes, scuttling into the corner. When the glow subsided, Albrecht blinked, staring down at his body. At his fur and claws. He gnashed his teeth and howled for joy that he now had teeth to gnash. He was whole again, his stomach sealed and his arm usable.

He looked around the room. Everyone was staring at him. Albrecht turned to Arkady, who was still on the floor. The Garou did not meet his gaze. He instead stared at Falcon, trembling. Albrecht turned back to Falcon.

Falcon spoke in a deep, rumbling voice. "He is yours to command, King Albrecht. You wear the Silver Crown. You are king of the Garou, as ordained by Gaia at the Dawn. What is your command to him?"

Albrecht looked back at Arkady. He knew this was his most important moment. His first royal edict. His ruling would be a reality, no matter what Arkady wished otherwise. The crown would ensure that. It would force Arkady to do his bidding. And that was a terrible power to wield.

Albrecht thought. He could kill Arkady outright. Or worse, he could force the Garou to suffer what he had: loss of his pelt. He savored that thought. But then he realized what it would do to him if he went through with it. He would be Arkady. In many ways, they were reflections of each other already: both exiles, both royals, both contenders for the crown. But he wanted nothing to do with Arkady's style of rulership as displayed by what Albrecht had just gone through.

But was mercy proper here? Did Arkady deserve it? He had killed Greyfist, Albrecht's oldest friend and a trusted Seneschal. Didn't Greyfist deserve revenge? To be weak here, to fail to dole out the proper justice…. Who would that ruling harm in the future?

Albrecht felt the full weight of the crown: not a physical weight, but one of responsibility. Arkady's life was in his hands. Arkady, who could go on to harm other Garou as he had his own sept. But Albrecht had always hated the sanctimonious leaders who so casually handed out life or death sentences, never seeming to care for the consequences of their edicts. He knew that he could not let hate rule him. He had to rule his own rage before he could rule others.

Damn it, he thought. *I don't want to become what I most hate. I don't want to be a despot. I don't want to be the strong arm of authority.*

"Get up, Arkady," Albrecht said.

Arkady looked up at him suspiciously, trembling. But he stood up, as if he had no choice. The power of the crown compelled him.

"I am not going to kill you, although you damn well deserve it."

Arkady's eyebrows rose. He stared in utter shock at Albrecht.

"But you are now an exile. Not just from the protectorate, as I was, but from the tribe. You are no longer a Silver Fang."

Arkady lowered his head. "No. Kill me. Don't make me walk alone. Kill me."

"No. Your punishment is to wander alone. Tribeless. No one will take you in. You deserve worse, you asshole. But I won't kill you. I'm not going to start playing that game. I ought to thank you, in a twisted way. You helped me shed my skin here. Literally. A friend of mine says that's what the problem with the world is: the Wyrm's not shedding its skin."

Arkady looked at Albrecht with contempt and a sneer on his face.

WILLIAM BRIDGES

"And just for that grimace you're wearing," Albrecht said, "you can bow down and acknowledge your punishment."

Arkady growled but seemed unable to resist Albrecht's command. He bowed.

"Get out of here. Get out of the city, out of the state. Get out of the fucking country. Go back to where you came from."

Arkady looked up at Albrecht with fear in his eyes. "No. You can't. Not back to Russia. You don't know how things are there. You don't know the power of the Hag—"

"And I don't give a damn. Just go."

Arkady rose, all his will useless before the power of the true king's commands. He walked to the passageway, trembling with anger.

"One more thing," Albrecht said. "You are forbidden to deal with Black Spiral Dancers. Not even they can help you now."

Arkady looked at Albrecht. All the hate and anger in him had drained away. All that was left was sorrow. "You do not know what it is to walk alone, Albrecht. Even you, who have known exile, do not know the terror of the ronin. Do you think this fate I will now suffer is unknown to me? It was my life in Russia. A hard life. Only the Black Spiral Dancers offered aid. But when I arrived here, in North Country, I was accepted. No communication could escape Russia to reveal my past there. I swore never to lose that acceptance. Being king would have allowed me to keep that and eventually to betray the Black Spirals who had so beholden me to them. But you have ruined that."

He turned and crawled into the passageway. Albrecht said nothing else to him.

Albrecht looked at the Black Spiral Dancers. He then looked at Evan and Mari. "All right. You're my advisors. What do we do with them?"

"Kill them," Mari said, staring murderously at them. "Kill them all."

Evan lowered his head and said nothing, but Albrecht could see the hate he had for them, and his shame at that hate.

"I want you to go back to your caern," Albrecht said, addressing all of the Dancers, who tried to avert their gazes but could not. They were, after all, Garou, and Albrecht wore the Silver Crown. "And kill everything you see there. If you don't get killed in the process, I want you to fall on yourselves and kill each other. If one of you is left after that, that one may live. But I want the survivor to tell this story to all your kind. Let them know that they better not fuck with me. Get out of here."

The Black Spiral Dancers ran for the passageway, bloodlust already in their eyes. They were looking forward to the coming blood-bath. All except one, the last one out of the room. Arglach. He stared back at Albrecht with fury.

"I am now leader in Dagrack's place," he said. "Leader of my hive. And you make me destroy it. From one leader to another, if I survive, I will kill you some day." He then crawled into the passage to follow his grunting and howling war party back to their Moon Bridge.

When they were gone, Albrecht turned to Falcon.

"I want to thank you for everything you've done. It seems you're always getting me out of a mess."

"You govern your own actions. I only act to aid my children when all else has failed. You had to complete the quest as far as you could; but it was impossible to complete it without me. I led you here, but only you could make the final sacrifice."

"Look…. I am a bit worried about this kingship thing. This ultimate power scares me a bit."

"Have no fear. Your ability to command the actions of others is no longer a trait of the crown."

"Huh?"

"It was a test, Albrecht. As everything else has been. The first command is the most important. It will hallow or taint your days forever after. The test is over. The crown's powers are no longer so great."

"Did I choose right, then? Should I have killed Arkady?"

Falcon was silent.

"Look…. If the crown isn't so powerful anymore, what good is it?"

"It is the symbol of Gaia's unity. One king over all the tribes. One law for all the tribes. The Litany. You wear the crown, so you must support the Litany, even when it harms your tribe. The other tribes may not immediately recognize your position, but if you rule wisely, they will learn by example."

"So all those legends about the crown's amazing powers were just tall tales?"

"No, they were true. But that was another age. The time of the king is fading, Albrecht. Gaia willing, there will come a time when each of Gaia's creatures will be able to rule themselves with no guidance but their own hearts."

"But wait a minute. The crown is from the Dawn. Everything was perfect then. Why did they need the crown?"

"Perfect? What age has ever been perfect? Things were newly born then, Albrecht. Unformed. Their purposes under Gaia had not begun to be fulfilled."

Falcon then spread his wings wide. "Enough instruction. You must return to your caern. Tomorrow is Coronation Day!"

A golden light suffused the room and blinded them all. When they again opened their eyes, they were standing on the field outside Morningkill's mansion, before the throne of the Silver Fangs.

Garou nearby sprang into action, anticipating an intruder, but they stopped dead in their tracks when they saw Falcon and his passengers.

Then Falcon raised his wings once more and was gone.

Albrecht stood there, whole again, completely healed by Falcon. The crown was on his head, a plain silver band. He looked at the Garou, running from all over and pointing at him, staring in awe. *Well*, he thought, *this sure is a change from the last time I was here*.

Mari and Evan turned about, looking in all directions.

"Is that the throne?" Evan asked, pointing at the Grand Oak and the seat carved into it.

"Yeah," Albrecht said, eyeing it. He wondered if it were comfortable to sit in.

"All this for that hunk of oak? It doesn't look like much," Mari said.

Albrecht looked at her frowning face and started to laugh. "After all this, that's all you have to say?"

"I'm entitled to my own criticism," Mari said.

Albrecht shook his head and walked up to the throne. He sat down on it. As he sat in the seat of his grandfather, he looked out over the Garou gathering around, staring at him with expectant faces, waiting for him to speak.

And he realized that the hardest part was just beginning.

Epilogue

The rites had been performed. They had taken the entire day and most of the night, but they were done. Lord Albrecht was now King Albrecht, invested through the rituals of his people.

There had been a special guest for the investiture, one Albrecht had invited personally. One who had not set foot within the caern for a longer time even than Albrecht's exile. Loba Carcassone stood proudly to the right of the throne, the position of the king's chosen, his favored warriors. The Silver Fang pariah had long been ignored for her campaign against the Wyrm's child-abuse plots, but now she was honored for them, recognized as the hero she was. Albrecht knew that, if everything she said about the Defiler Wyrm was true, there would be an accounting soon—even if he had to lead the charge himself. But that was a matter for the future. For now, Loba once again stood in her tribal protectorate. The exiles had come home.

The feast lasted for a week. Celebrants were invited from all over, even from the other tribes. Antonine Teardrop was there for the Stargazers. Mother Larissa came for the Bone Gnawers. Others came, too, leaders of their own protectorates or septs: Alani Astarte, the wise old matron of the Black Furies;

Pearl River and True Silverheels of the Children of Gaia, two level-headed ex-hippies; the somewhat rowdy but entertaining Riordan Cliffgrazer of the Fianna; and Nepthys Mu'at of the Silent Striders, who didn't stay long.

The Get of Fenris sent no one. Their leader, Arn Guth Stormbright, had never been a friend to Albrecht. The same for the Red Talons and the Shadow Lords, all nursing sour thoughts about the Silver Fangs in general and Albrecht in particular. The Uktena and Wendigo were also absent. They did not recognize the Silver Fangs' rule, and so stayed away.

This was the first time in many years that so many tribal leaders had come together. It was an occasion for true celebration. Albrecht couldn't believe it himself. Two days ago he had been just an uncouth, prideful Garou to them. Now, they came to wish him well and to discuss the future between their tribes.

Albrecht had hidden in Greyfist's library for most of the first day, nervous and unsure of how to receive them. He had never done anything remotely like this before.

There was a knock on the door, and Evan poked his head in.

"Hey, kid," Albrecht said, pacing before the desk.

Evan walked in. "You're going to have to go out there. We told them you're still suffering from your wounds, but that you'd be out soon."

"I can't do this! I'm not a diplomat. I can't schmooze with these guys."

"You don't have to. Just be yourself. They'll respect that more."

"Oh, yeah. Right. They'll respect me for being myself? For cursing and spitting out cynical homilies at every turn? They'll love me. I'll be a hit."

"Albrecht, quit whining. You've been through much worse than a simple party. You know how to do this. What did your grandfather use to do?"

Albrecht stopped pacing. "I remember once, long ago, when a high and mighty Garou came to see him. Bull Roarer, I think, of the Uktena. I don't know what he was doing here. But he's old and respected. Jacob stepped down from the throne and greeted him in Lupus form, which seemed to please the old wolf."

"See? You've got a good example to follow in your grandfather."

"Ha! Then there was the time, much later, when Kleon Winston came. You know, the Glass Walker Don? Morningkill made him wait out in the rain for an hour before he finally saw him. And then Winston left angry anyway. It's funny, but the electricity in the mansion didn't work too well for a month after that. We figured the Walker had left a gremlin behind for his troubles."

"So? It's still an example. It's just what not to do. You've got both angles now."

Albrecht looked at Evan. "Always looking on the bright side, huh?"

Evan looked back at him. "Even when we were getting kicked around by those Dancers, I knew you'd succeed. I don't think Mari had such faith, but I did. I knew I might die. But I knew you would succeed so you could take the throne and unite the tribes—those tribes out there on the field waiting for you. If I had died, what would you have done now?"

Albrecht was silent for a moment. "I'd have gone out there and made peace. For your sake."

"Good. And now that I'm alive, you're not going to?"

Albrecht smiled. "All right, Master Po. I'm going out there." He punched Evan in the arm as he walked past him. And then he went out to greet the dignitaries.

The feast was over. The guests had gone home, satisfied that the king was someone they could deal with. They did not universally recognize his rule over their tribes, but they did realize that he was a fair judge who could help them work through their own disputes.

The Silver Fangs of the North Country Protectorate all beamed with pride. The grandson of King Jacob Morningkill now sat on the throne. Things were as they should be. The low had again been raised high.

Albrecht sat on the throne, watching the Kin families clean up the field of litter left after the feast. He smoked a fat, smelly cigar and had his feet up on the armrest of the throne as he leaned back over the other armrest. He belched.

The party had been over for a few hours now. He had changed back into his old clothes, a T-shirt and jeans. His klaive hung from its shoulder holster on his left side. His long hair was no longer tied back, but flowed loosely down his shoulders. He hadn't shaved for a few days, and his beard was coming back. And the crown was on his head, immovable.

Seeing Evan and Mari walking across the field toward him, Albrecht sat up straight and put out the cigar. They were only his packmates, but he had learned from the last few days that he needed to clean up his act if he was going to lead the tribe.

Mari shook her head as she approached. They came and stood at the foot of the throne, looking up at him.

"We're going back to New York," Mari said.

"What?!" Albrecht barked, sitting up. "But you've got great digs here!"

"We live in New York, Albrecht."

Albrecht frowned and slouched again. "Yeah. I guess. Hey! I can visit anytime I want. I'm king, aren't I? No more waiting in line for Moon Bridges. No more greasing the palm of the Gatekeeper. Anytime! You guys can come back anytime, too. Sure."

"Of course we will," Evan said. "We are packmates. That hasn't changed."

"Speaking of which," Mari said. "I don't know if I'm comfortable with this king thing of yours. You're already getting an ego about it."

"Hey! Hey, now. I've been a perfect gentlemen here. We are a pack, Mari. We are equals."

Mari shook her head. "For now. But how soon till you start trying to pull rank? A male does not boss around a Black Fury!"

"Whoah! I won't. I don't even rule the Black Fury tribe. Alani Astarte made that clear. But she does recognize my position as a unifier. The Furies still make their own decisions. I'm just a figurehead, really."

"But an important figurehead," Evan said. "We're not humans. Symbols mean something for us. And that's why you're important, Albrecht. Don't let the other tribes tell you otherwise."

"Don't worry. I'm not going to push them around, but they're not going to push me, either. I *am* the king of the Silver Fangs, after all. Like it or not, the other tribes need to recognize our precedence."

"Hmph. This is just too weird," Mari said. "But don't you ever forget that I can kick your white-furred ass around this field. You just got lucky the last time."

"Luck?! Luck, was it? I don't know about that. I got in a pretty good lick—"

"Stop it!" Evan said. "What is this? A sitcom? You guys return to normal at the end of the episode? Haven't you learned anything from this?"

"I still owe him for this scar," Mari said, pointing at the scar on her belly.

"I'm sorry already!" Albrecht said. "How many times do you want me to say it?"

"Mari, you did attack him first, you know," Evan said.

Mari fumed silently for a moment. "He was trespassing in my territory. But I guess I overreacted."

"Well…." Albrecht said. "I guess I should have watched where I was going. But I didn't expect you to attack me."

"Wait a minute," Mari said. "You told me you didn't know it was my territory."

"Uh…well, I might have lied."

"You bastard!" Mari yelled, stepping toward him.

"Will you two stop!" Evan said, stepping between them. "I am getting really sick of pulling you off each other!"

"I'm sorry," Albrecht said to Mari. "I've said it before. What do you want? A free shot at me?"

"Yes," Mari said. "I'll take that as an apology."

Albrecht tore his shirt in half down the front, revealing his chest. "There. There it is. Go for it."

Mari stepped up, but then stopped. She looked at the ugly scar on his right pectoral, the one Arkady had made with his klaive. The wound was healed, thanks to Falcon, and the lung had already grown back, but the scar would be permanent. She stepped away.

"It's too easy," Mari said. "I know I can take you. I don't need you to sit there for me. It's over."

"Apology accepted?"

"Yes."

Evan smiled. "Thank Gaia that chapter is over! Well, Albrecht, we'll catch up with you soon. But we've really got to get back home. Mari has classes to teach."

"I know, I know. You just get going. Maybe I'll drop by next week, once things have calmed down here."

"Good," Evan said.

"Farewell, Albrecht," Mari said.

"Good-bye, Mari," Albrecht said. "And thanks for your help. I couldn't have done it without you."

Mari smiled. "I know. You would have failed miserably without me. What else is new?" She turned around and walked off.

Albrecht's eyes narrowed, but he smiled. He waved at Evan as the boy followed Mari.

The new king sat back on the throne and watched Eliphas open a Moon Bridge for his packmates. When it closed and they were gone, he sighed. It was kind of lonely here. The only person he really knew anymore was Eliphas. With Greyfist gone, he had few good friends here. Regina was all right, but he barely knew her. His family had lightened up toward him considerably, although he knew some of that was simply kissing up to the king. Sutter still wouldn't speak with him, though.

No, it was going to be a lonely place. He'd have to bridge back to New York now and then just to stay sane.

He saw two people coming toward him from far across the field. And he knew then that it wouldn't be too lonely.

His father walked with young Seth. They were coming over to him, and his father waved. Seth waved also, beaming at his uncle, the king.

Albrecht smiled and waved back.

Mister Magick

EDO VAN BELKOM

DEDICATION

To my parents,
Frank and Romana van Belkom
who worked hard to make sure
both their sons turned out all right.

ACKNOWLEDGMENTS

This novel took flight with the help of several key people. I'd like to thank my editors at White Wolf Publishing, Stewart Wieck and Laura Perkinson; writer and Las Vegas resident Bob L. Fleck; National Circus School of Canada artistic director Anatoly Butko; fellow White Wolf author Don Bassingthwaite; my good friend and SF author Robert J. Sawyer; and of course, my wife Roberta.

"Within all of us there is an elusive melody which when heard and followed leads to the fulfillment of our fondest dreams."
— Siegfried and Roy

PROLOGUE

MONTREAL, MAY 198—

The school's scratched and chipped blue metal doors burst open and a flood of screaming children emptied into the yard.

"I'm Guy Lafleur!"

"I'm Mats Naslund!"

"I'm Mario Tremblay!"

"Last one there's a rotten egg!"

The large gravel yard behind St. Raphael's suddenly came alive with the scurry of feet and the sounds of innocent voices at play.

Most of the girls headed for the hilly parts of the yard away from the school. In minutes they would be jumping ropes twirling in doubletime, and moving to melodic strings of words spoken in rhyme. Elsewhere there would be chains of elastic bands stretching from knee to knee, hip to hip, and ear to ear, and by the end of recess there would be a new champion leaper declared.

Closer in, nearer to the school, boys ran off into dark corners where hockey cards swirled and spun in games of topsies and knock-downs. Traders were active too, their chants of "Need-em, need-em, got-em, need-em," serving as a faint background noise to the schoolyard's main event.

The foot hockey game.

Just to the right of the school's rear doors stood a broad chimney. Standing ten bricks wide and jutting out from the rest of the building, it served as the perfect goal. Across the gravel "rink," a wooden porch leading into one of the school's portables served as the opposing goal.

In between the two makeshift "nets," at "center ice," two boys were busy splitting a group of eight others into two teams.

"I'll take Jean-Louis."

"Okay, Alan."

"Sean."

"Harvey."

And on and on it went until just two boys remained.

Yves Bouchard, one of the captains and the biggest boy in all of Grade Six, looked at the last two and laughed. "Maurice," he said, curling a finger at his final choice.

That left one last boy.

"Aw, c'mon," whined the second team's captain, Daniel Sernine, who like Bouchard was almost a head taller than the rest of the boys in the class. "I had *him* on my team last time…and the time before."

"Too bad. You should have picked first, then," Bouchard laughed, turning away to face his teammates.

"We get to be the Canadiens, then," Sernine shouted.

"All right," Bouchard said. "We'll be the Bruins. Now, let's go, recess is already half over."

Sernine nodded, then turned back around to look at the last, unwanted player.

Romano Minardi was a skinny kid who dressed in funny clothes and absolutely stunk at foot hockey. Nevertheless, he always had a scuffed-up tennis ball in his pocket and, as a result, always got to play in the game at recess and at lunch, even if nobody really wanted him on their team.

"Just try and stay out of the way, okay?" Sernine said as he made his way to the net next to the portable.

Romano just nodded as he watched Sernine take off his jacket and hold it out in front of himself, protecting the net against opposing players like a toreador facing a bull.

Romano turned and saw that Bouchard was likewise playing goal, his scuffed and dirty coat kicking up dust as it was dragged across the gravel in front of him.

If I could only score a goal, thought Romano, *Bouchard wouldn't be so quick to pass me over next time.*

"Look out!" It was the voice of Sernine.

Romano spun around in time to see two players coming toward him. They were kicking at the ball, their feet acting as hockey sticks, the ball serving as a puck. In an attempt to get out of their way, Romano took a step to the left…too late. He was bumped hard and knocked to the ground by his own teammate.

"Ha-ha! Keep your eye on the ball, *Min-ar-di*," Bouchard shouted from the other end of the rink. The insult was obvious. Romano was an Italian living in St. Urbain's, a neighborhood of Montreal that was made up primarily of Jews and poor French Canadians. Although his family was about as poor as they came, with two Italian immigrant parents, Romano identified with neither the Jews nor the French Canadians. Likewise, none of them identified with him.

Romano picked himself up off the ground, rubbing his sore behind. It stung a little, but didn't hurt half as much as his wounded pride.

The game continued, but not before Bouchard took the opportunity to have a good long laugh at Romano's expense.

Romano gritted his teeth and ran to catch up with the play. He ran and weaved as quickly as he could, but no matter how hard he tried he was always a step behind the rest of them. For one thing, his black dress shoes—shoes he wore out of his own preference rather than that of his mother, as had been suggested on numerous occasions by the other boys—slipped too much on the gravel. Then there was the physical aspect of the game. Although he possessed a delicate touch and could finesse the ball as well as anyone, there were just too many brutes on the playground to make it a very practical way to play the game. Still, he wanted to be liked, and providing a ball for the others to play with made him *feel* like he was part of the game.

"He shoots!"

Romano watched one of his teammates kick the ball at Sernine. Sernine slid across the gravel and captured the ball in the folds of his coat. That done, he fished the ball out with his hand and looked up-ice for a teammate.

There was an opposing player standing in front of Sernine, making it hard for him to find someone to pass to, especially since every one of his teammates was similarly covered by an opponent.

Everyone that is, except Romano. After the shot had been taken, Romano had wandered in the direction of the school. Now he stood free and clear just five feet in front of Bouchard. He raised his hands to signal to Sernine that he was in the open.

With no other options, Sernine fired the ball at Romano.

Romano caught the ball, but as he turned to drop it onto the ground and take a shot, he decided to try something different.

Romano's hobby was magic, card tricks and other sleight of hand. It had never occurred to him to use the tricks he knew in the schoolyard...

Until now.

Just as he was about to drop the ball, he back-palmed it, making sure Bouchard saw nothing but the empty palm of his open hand. Then he looked around at his feet as if searching for the dropped ball.

Bouchard laughed at Romano's clumsiness, then moved forward, coming away from the net in search of the ball.

With his heart pounding in his chest like a thunderclap, Romano calmly placed the ball on the ground and kicked it into the open net.

"He shoots! He scores!" he shouted, the words coming in machine-gun-like rapid fire. He threw up his hands and ran around in triumphant circles.

Romano's teammates, the Canadiens, threw up their hands and cheered. Bouchard continued to search for the lost ball, but looked up when he heard the laughter.

"Hey Bouchard, I hear the California Golden Seals are looking for a goalie..." Romano shouted to the delight of everyone in the schoolyard.

Bouchard's face flushed red. The National Hockey League's Golden Seals had been a mockery of the game. With green and yellow skates, the team was embarrassing to watch. To suggest someone should play for them....

"Cheater!" Bouchard shouted.

Romano just turned his back on Bouchard, shaking his head. He wanted to laugh and laugh, but figured it was best to keep the delight he felt hidden from view. He'd just made the biggest and toughest kid in school look stupid in front of everyone and he wasn't going to ruin it by getting into an argument.

"Look out!"

Romano turned around and saw Bouchard charging toward him. He tried to run, but his shoes slipped on the loose gravel. A moment later a pair of hands slammed into his back, pushing him roughly to the ground.

The schoolyard was silent, as if everyone there was holding their breath in anticipation of what came next.

Romano opened his eyes, spit gravel from between his lips and got up onto his knees. Bouchard was there, towering over him, fists clenched and ready to fight.

Romano wasn't much of a fighter. Even at the ripe old age of twelve he was fond of saying, "I'm a lover, not a fighter." But here was a situation he could not avoid. If he backed off he'd be finished in the schoolyard. Hell, they were already calling him a sissy. No, this time he'd have to fight.

"Get up!" Bouchard ordered.

Romano stood.

Only to be shoved back down by Bouchard.

The surrounding kids laughed.

"I said, get up!"

Again, Romano got to his feet.

And again he was pushed back onto the ground.

The laughter rose.

Bouchard began to smile as his place at the top of the schoolyard's pecking order was slowly restored.

This time Romano remained on the ground, hesitant to get up, knowing that if he did Bouchard would just put him down again.

"What's the matter, little boy? Are you chicken?"

Anger began to roil within Romano. He was better than this bully. So he couldn't play a stupid game, so what! He could do plenty of things the other kids couldn't. There was something different about him, he could feel it, especially when he performed. He could do magic tricks and dance as well as any of the people on television could and some day that would mean something to people.

Some day...

He looked up at Bouchard.

Bouchard could push people around; that's all he was really good at. He was so good at it that one day he might end up in jail for pushing somebody too hard. *Well,* thought Romano. *He can push people around all he wants, but not me. Not anymore.*

Romano stood up, looked Bouchard in the eye, and said, "Canadiens 1, Bruins 0."

The boys behind Romano laughed and whooped.

Bouchard moved forward, ready to push Romano back down.

Romano prepared for the blow, tensing his body like a tightly coiled spring.

But then something curious happened. Bouchard's movements began to slow down, slower and slower until it looked as if he were hardly moving at all.

Romano glanced around and saw that the other kids had slowed down too, their hands and mouths moving at a fraction of normal speed, like people in the slow-motion scenes you sometimes saw in the movies.

Strangest of all, however, was the fact that Romano hadn't slowed down a bit. He was still moving at what to him felt like normal speed while everyone around him had almost ground to a halt.

Romano looked back at Bouchard. He was still inching forward, but from the look on his face it seemed like he planned on doing more than just pushing this time. He looked mean and angry, as if he planned to jump on Romano and punch him until he cried.

"No!" Romano shouted, swinging his fist at the almost stationary nose of Bouchard.

There was a loud *crack!* and a spurt of blood.

And then the world sped back up and the schoolyard was once again filled with the sharp cries of the children.

But almost immediately, the noise died down...

As everyone watched Bouchard, blood running freely from his broken nose, stumble backward and fall to the ground.

The school bell rang.

Everyone was suddenly in a hurry to get back inside.

Romano, still somewhat dazed over what had just happened, stepped around the prone body of Bouchard and hurried along on his way back to class. As he looked at the bigger boy lying there, people began to slap him on the back, again and again until his shoulders became sore.

"Hey, Minardi," Sernine said. "You want to play with us after school?"

Romano looked at Sernine, and smiled. Suddenly, here was the acceptance he'd wanted for so long. Only now, he really didn't want it anymore.

"No," he said. "I've got something better to do with my time."

PART ONE

NOVICE

I

Franco Minardi opened his eyes, blinking away the veil of sleep that shrouded them. The living room was dark and the soft glow from the hockey game on the television set in the corner painted the dirty white walls with a faint blue light.

With a groan he lifted his head off the couch. His sleep-stiffened joints snapped and popped with each movement, the effects of another hard day's work. It was a good feeling, especially when he knew that, because of the fruits of his labor, his family had eaten under a roof for another night. Tomorrow morning he'd wake up at 6 AM, be at work at the packing plant by seven, then work ten hard hours before trudging home to prepare for the never-ending cycle to begin again.

If he'd had his choice in life, he might have taken another job, but something inside him told him he probably wouldn't have. Given an infinite number of possibilities, he most likely would have opted for just what he had. A regular shift, steady work, and most importantly a paycheck every Friday afternoon. With no other ambition than providing food and shelter for his family, Franco Minardi was well-suited for the work.

After a final stretch to get the blood flowing, he lifted himself off the couch, shut off the television and shuffled down the hall toward the bedroom.

Up ahead a faint sliver of light shone out from under the door of his son's room.

He smiled at the thought of his son studying hard to graduate from high school with good grades. High marks in his final year at school would look good on his application at the plant. Surely Mister Albert Levinson, the personnel manager there, would hire Romano on in a minute.

He stopped at the bedroom door and listened. Then, seeing that it was slightly ajar, he gently pushed it open further with the dirty tips of his fingers.

The room was like the rooms of most boys his age. But instead of being decorated with posters of hockey players like Bobby Orr, or Jean Beliveau, it was adorned with theater posters advertising people with strange names like Mandrake, Ching Ling Soo, The Great Rantiki, and Harry Houdini.

Houdini, he had heard of. As for the others…

Romano stood at the foot of his bed wearing blue pajamas, his sleeves rolled up past the elbows. He was a tall, skinny kid who was just starting to fill out, the muscles of his exposed arms lean and well-defined. His hair was thick and black like his father's, but his fingers were long, soft and nimble, more like his mother's. On top of the bed were several decks of playing cards, some still packed in their boxes, others scattered across the bedspread.

Over and over again Romano snapped his arm outward and each time a card appeared between his fingertips, as if out of thin air. Again and again he moved his arm and snapped his fingers, as cards fluttered onto the bed like so many autumn leaves.

Franco watched his son with a mixture of awe and disappointment. While he was good at his tricks, he wasted too much time with them. Like now—when he should be studying, or getting his rest, or thinking about girls, he was playing with cards.

For what? So he could be good at playing poker? So he could entertain the men at the plant during lunch break?

He shook his head and continued watching his son for another few moments.

Romano rolled the sleeve farther up his left arm and began making cards appear in the fingers of his left hand. The first few attempts were awkward as the cards came up bent or else fell away before he could present them properly. But he continued on undaunted, never dwelling on an unsuccessful move. Soon, his fingers moved more nimbly until their movements were virtually a mirror-image of those made by his right hand.

Franco sighed. If only he could work so hard at something that he could make a living at.

Romano produced cards with both hands, first the right, then the left. Right, left, right, left, until his arms moved with a single smooth and continuous motion.

Now, suddenly confident in his ability, Romano began firing the cards into the air, as if he were shooting off a pair of card-loaded pistols.

Franco slowly let the door close, then said sternly, "Get to bed!"

There was a sound of cards being gathered up, and then of the light being switched off, and then nothing….

Franco shook his head again, and continued on down the hall, the floorboards creaking and moaning beneath his feet despite his best efforts to step lightly.

The kitchen was warm and full of the smell of cooked meat and potatoes, and tomato sauce simmering in preparation for tomorrow night's meal.

Franco Minardi pulled his suspenders off his shoulders and sat down at the supper table in his dirty white undershirt. It was black around the collar, yellow-grey under the arms and reddish pink above the waist. All his work shirts were similarly stained, something Romano had become acutely aware of after sitting across the table from his father every night for most of his eighteen years.

Romano's sister Louise and his mother Romana were busy preparing the table for supper. It was Wednesday night and that meant they'd be having shepherd's pie. Had it been Monday they would have had chicken. Tuesday meant meatloaf. Thursday and Saturday were pasta, and Friday was leftovers. Sunday was the only day that was left to chance, with no regular meal or mealtime, and as a result was Romano's favorite food-day of the week.

Romano's father held his knife and fork in his fists and waited patiently for the Minardi women to serve him supper. Louise put the serving bowl of shepherd's pie on a dishtowel folded neatly in the center of the table. As she set it down, Romano watched his father give his usual nod, a subtle motion which meant he approved of the timely way dinner had been prepared and served. The gesture was just about the most he'd ever done to show his approval of anything in his life. Once, when Romano won a high-school talent contest, his father had nodded in that same way, then patted him on the back and said, "Good boy." Romano had often wondered when he might please his father in such a way again, but after years of trying he realized that that one night was an aberration and could be just as easily explained by his father having drunk too much wine as the man having an abundance of pride in his son.

At the other end of the scale, his father's disapproval could manifest itself in a wide variety of ways ranging from a simple stern look to a well-placed slap of the hand, something Romano was more than a little familiar with.

Louise took her seat to Romano's right and his mother began to ladle out the soup, a food they had every night except for pasta nights. Romano had wondered why they had soup so often since no one but his father seemed to like it. When he asked his mother about it one time she simply said, "Because your father likes it." And that was the end of that.

"I talked to Mr. Levinson today," Franco Minardi said as he crushed bits of days-old bread into his soup.

No one said anything, and for the longest time all that could be heard was the tink of soup spoons against soup bowls and the occasional slurp. Eventually the silence became awkward enough to force Franco to repeat his words. "I said, I talked to Mr. Levinson today."

Romano looked up, noticed the smile on his mother's face and then glanced over at his father. There was a similarly approving smile on his face, but it was mixed in with something else, a highly focussed gaze bearing down on him from across the table.

Romano then realized his father had been talking to him.

"Oh, that's great, papa," Romano said with a nod. "Did he offer you a promotion or something?"

His father's smile slowly waned and disappointment began to creep in from the corners of his face. "No, he didn't offer me a promotion. I talked to him about *you*." The man punctuated the final word by shoveling a heaping spoon of soupy bread into his mouth.

"Oh," Romano said, getting a bad feeling in his stomach about what was coming next.

"That's right. He was very interested in you. When I told him how smart a boy you were, he mentioned he might have something for you in the shipping department."

"That sounds great, papa," Romano said, trying to put some excitement into his voice, but failing miserably.

"It *is* great. The shipping department." He said it as if it were located just south of Oz. "That's the cleanest part of the plant. You could almost go to work every day wearing a tie."

"A tie? Wow!" Romano didn't want to sound patronizing, but he couldn't think of anything else to say.

"It's a good job for a boy your age."

"Oh, I know, I know."

His father just looked at him. "Then why don't I think you want it?"

Romano put off answering the question by taking a spoonful of soup into his mouth. He chewed on the beans and vegetables of the minestrone as if they were made of gum.

His father soon lost patience. "Eh?"

Romano looked at his mother. Her head was down, her eyes fixed on the hands folded across her lap. He looked at his sister. Her eyes were wide open to make sure she didn't miss a thing.

He took a deep breath. "Maybe working at Canada Packers isn't the right thing for me."

His father's hand slapped hard against the table, making the forks and spoons bounce into the air. They landed on the table with a crash, and for a moment, everything was silent.

"Why not? It's not good enough for you?" The man's voice was growing louder.

"No, no, it's not that," Romano said, his voice flat and insincere.

"Then what? What is it?"

He took another deep breath. "Maybe I'd like to try something else, something different."

His father nodded slowly, a mocking gesture suggesting he'd let the boy have his say before telling him no.

Romano looked to his mother for help. She'd always believed in him, always encouraged him to be the best he could be. But now, at this pivotal moment, she just sat there with her head down as if she'd pulled herself away from the table, or perhaps had long ago bowed to her husband's stronger force of will on the matter.

"Maybe I'd like to be a professional magician...."

There it was, his lifelong dream, laid out on the table alongside the soup and shepherd's pie. He thrust out his chin, pressed his lips together in a thin line and looked at his father with unblinking eyes in an attempt to give his resolve an outward appearance that would do justice to its inner strength.

His father looked at him for the longest time...

And laughed.

"A *mago?*" He said the word in Italian and it came out sounding as if it were something dirty. "A *mago?*" He laughed again, this time shaking his head. "That's something that's good for fun, to show your friends, impress the girls, but not for a man to raise a family."

Romano's jaw went slack as the insult hit him like a punch in the stomach. "A lot of famous magicians are very rich men," he said, trying to keep his voice even. "They can make as much as ten thousand dollars in one night."

"My son the famous magician, heh!" Franco folded his arms over his chest as if to emphasize his point. "What are you going to do while you're not so famous? Are you going to make food appear out of thin air?"

Romano looked at his father with an ache in his heart. Here was a man who could thoroughly enjoy watching dancers and magicians on television shows like *Circus* or *Stars on Ice*, but who could never imagine that his son might one day be one of those very same performers. To him, the people on television were from New York or California, not the poor neighborhoods of Montreal. But Romano knew better. He knew that, just like with hockey players who dreamed of wearing the red, white and blue of Les Canadiens, a poor Montreal suburb was exactly where the next great master would come from. And if not from Montreal, then from Chicoutimi or Sherbrooke or Kingston or any one of a thousand small towns across Canada or the United States. Anywhere there was a young boy who dreamed of something better, then that was where the next great one would come from.

"I can make money doing magic," said Romano. "I already have."

"You call a couple of dollars here and there doing birthday parties *making money*? That's not making a living, that's pocket change so you can make jingle bells when you walk down the street."

"How do you know how much I make?" Romano said, feeling the volume of his voice rising in anger, but not doing anything to stop it. "You've never come to see one of my shows. You don't know how good I am…. You don't know anything about what I want to do."

His father paused a moment, and when he spoke his voice was surprisingly calm. "I know you're good. And I know you have great dreams, all young boys do. And they should. But the world is a hard place. Life is hard. So you work at the plant, you can still do magic at night and on weekends."

Romano shook his head. "No," he said. "No, no, no. If I start working there, *maybe* I'll keep up with my magic, but after a while I'll come home exhausted and just want to sleep so I can make it through the next day. And eventually I'll forget about my dreams and I'll become—" He stopped himself from saying another word.

"You'll become what?" His father pushed his chair back from the table. "Become what? Become *like me*?"

Romano didn't answer. He couldn't answer. Of all the things in the world he was afraid of, becoming like his father was the thing he feared most. But how could he tell his father that?

He looked down at his soup bowl, silent.

"Let me tell you something," his father said, his voice rising to a shout. "I might not have been a fancy magician wearing sissy costumes, but I worked hard for the things I have, for the things I gave you. So I gave up on my dreams. At least I put a roof over my family's head and food on the table every night. You look at me and tell me how that can be bad?"

Romano was losing some of his fight. His father's life wasn't such a bad one, it just wasn't for him. He wanted to say as much, but knew it would probably come out wrong. So instead of answering the question, he got up from the table and turned to leave the kitchen.

"Don't turn your back on me!"

Romano sighed, but kept on walking.

Behind him he could hear his father getting up from his chair. "Come back here! No son of mine walks out on me!" There was rage in his voice.

"No, Franco, please!"

That was his mother's voice.

Romano turned around.

His mother was putting herself between her husband and her son, trying to avert an inevitable fight between the two men in her life.

"Get out of my way!" he said. "The boy's had this coming to him for a long time now."

His mother stood firm. "Your supper's getting cold," she said. "You can talk about this later."

"I told you to get out of my way!" he said, grabbing her by the arms and pushing her aside.

Louise screamed.

"Mama!" Romano shouted, as he saw his mother stumble toward the wall.

Anger and something else, something stronger and more powerful rose up within Romano, washing over him in a wave.

His father stepped toward him with blind rage in his eyes, ready to teach his son a lesson.

He drew his hand back to give the boy a slap....

"No!" Romano said forcefully.

And then a strong, unseen force stopped Franco's hand in mid-air. He glanced at his hand wondering why it wouldn't move, then suddenly found himself moving away from Romano as if he were being *pushed* backward into the kitchen. He continued to backpedal, just barely managing to maintain his balance until he slammed heavily into the stove. On impact, his hands automatically moved behind him to steady himself. His right palm pressed flat against one of the still-hot burners.

The man wailed in pain as the same force that had pushed him kept his hand on the burner until the flesh began to blister.

And then it was over.

Whatever it was that had held him released its hold.

He fell to the floor, grasping his right hand at the wrist and writhing in pain.

Louise was crying.

Romano's mother looked down at her husband and then at her son, an expression of stunned amazement on her face.

Romano turned his back on the scene and headed up to his room.

EDO VAN BELKOM

The house was quieter now.

After an hour of weeping, a terrified Louise had finally fallen asleep.

After applying salves to his hand and wrapping it in bandages (and after drinking a liter of homemade wine), his father was fast asleep on the couch.

And after everyone else had been taken care of, his mother still shuffled about the house, opening cupboards and closet doors as if searching for something that she'd lost. She wouldn't be going to sleep anytime soon. She was the emotional heartbeat of the household, and would no doubt be up half the night tending to her broken heart.

As Romano packed his clothes into his one canvas bag, he realized it would be his mother he'd miss most. She was the one who had approved of his magic, who had encouraged him along the way, teaching him the few card tricks she'd learned as a girl in Montecastello, and sewing costumes for him so people would know he was a magician even before he showed them his tricks.

As he crammed his playing cards into the last few open spaces in the bag, he vowed to keep in touch with his mother, once a week or so just to let her know he was alive.

There was a faint knock at the door. "Romano."

Romano's hand lingered in his bag. It would pain his mother to see him packing his things, but he couldn't let that stop him.

"Yes, mama," he said, zipping the bag and sitting on the edge of the bed.

The door creaked open. His mother stood there with a forced smile on her face. After an awkward moment, she stepped into the room. As she neared, she looked at him, and then her eyes fell to the packed bag on the bed. If she was surprised at seeing it there, she didn't let it show.

She gestured for Romano to make room for her on the bed. Romano moved over and she eased herself down next to him. For a few seconds she was content to look about the room, admiring all the decorations and posters Romano would be leaving behind.

"You know," she began. "Sometimes, when you're at school and your father is at work, I come in here and just look at everything. These places…" She gestured at the posters. "They all seem so far away from here, so exciting. Almost like a schoolgirl, I wonder what it might be like to see one of these shows, or to be in one."

"Mama, I never knew that—"

She raised her hand to cut him off.

"When I was a little girl, I remember stealing a magazine belonging to one of the American soldiers stationed near our town. It was a movie magazine and was full of pictures of American movie stars like Montgomery Clift and Elizabeth Taylor. I treasured that magazine, but I never showed it to anybody. I just kept it with me wherever I went until one day it finally fell apart in my hands."

She looked at Romano, looked into his eyes. "Do you know why I loved it so much?"

Romano shook his head.

"Because like you have now, I had dreams. I wanted to be a model, an actress, maybe even a movie star." She smiled a little at her foolishness. "But who could think of being such things when there wasn't any food to eat? When I married your father and he brought me to Canada, life was better here, but it was still very hard. We both had to work to earn money for a house. Then you came along and I stayed home to take care of you while your father went off to work. The dream," she shrugged her shoulders, "slipped away and was forgotten."

A pause.

"Sometimes I read advertisements in the paper for auditions for plays at some of the churches, or even downtown, and I feel myself wanting to try it." A sigh. "But I know your father would never approve. So I stay home and clean the house, cook dinner, and all the time I hold on to a new dream of the stage. But now, the dream's not for me, it's for you, my son."

Romano was stunned.

"I've watched you do magic, Romano. You are good. Very, very good. Maybe you could be great, maybe not. But at least you should try and find out. If it doesn't work you can always come back here. No matter what your father says, you can always get a job at the plant. But you'll only have one chance to be a *mago*."

Romano took a breath.

"I want you to have this." She reached into the pocket of her smock and took out a wad of folded bills.

"Mama, what's this?" Romano whispered.

"Your father doesn't know about this money. I've saved it over the years for when something like this might happen. It's not much, but I don't want you to fail because you didn't have a good chance."

She handed him the money.

Romano tried to refuse it, but his mother pushed it harder into his palm. He didn't count it, but just at a glance there looked to be hundreds of dollars there.

"Thank you, mama! I'll make you proud."

She shook her head. "You've already made me proud."

Romano smiled.

"Just promise me one thing."

"Of course."

"Promise me you'll be the best *mago* you could be. Call it a mother's pride in her son, but something in here," she tapped at her heart, "tells me you are going to be famous."

They came together in a long hug that neither of them wanted to end.

Finally, Romano said, "I have to go."

"I know."

He got up from the bed, went down the hall to look in for a few moments on his sister, then walked past his sleeping father and out the front door.

Into the night.

Into a world of darkness.

2

He saw the city's lights long before he reached it.

As the bus lumbered westward down the 401 into Toronto, the thing that struck him most was the sheer number of lights stretching out in every direction as far as the eye could see, as if a blanket of stars had been laid upon the ground.

Toronto was a big city, the biggest in Canada. Surely there would be some sort of work for a talented young magician here. And even if he couldn't find work, he could always do some busking on the sidewalk. With the summer coming there would be scores of entertainers working the downtown streets. In fact, Romano had heard stories of jugglers and street artists who made very good livings working Toronto in the summer then moving on to southern U.S. cities in the winter. It wasn't what he had in mind as a career, but it was a possibility. A place to get started.

The bus skirted the south end of the city and then turned north, heading away from the lake. A few minutes later it pulled into the noisy bus terminal in the middle of downtown.

Romano picked up his bag and wearily made his way off the bus. As he stepped onto the pavement outside the terminal he saw a dirty and disheveled old man with long white hair and a salt-and-pepper beard lying on a bench asleep. Romano looked at the man and frowned; the sight wasn't the kind of first impression he'd wanted from this city.

Still, he was in Toronto. More importantly, he was out of Montreal. While he strongly doubted his destiny lay in Toronto, or in Canada for that matter, he had taken that all-important first step toward the pursuit of his dream.

It felt wonderful.

He took a deep breath…and choked on the diesel exhaust coming from a bus exiting the terminal.

When he finished coughing he went inside the building. The place was filled with a variety of travelers, from those rushing to catch their bus to those asleep on benches awaiting their connection.

Romano considered his options, reveling in the feeling of absolute freedom, but wishing he'd had a better plan before walking out on his family. He sat down and gave some thought to his predicament.

Toronto was a metropolitan city with plenty of venues for live entertainment. But the trend seemed to be moving toward big productions and Broadway-style shows. Sure there would be circuses and carnivals coming through town, but none of those shows were based here. Perhaps it would be better to move on.

But where?

For a brief moment he let his imagination soar and considered traveling to London, Brussels, maybe even Paris. The dream was short-lived. Even if he could overcome the language barrier, he hardly had enough money to get to any of those places. Perhaps New York, or even Los Angeles. Plenty of opportunities in both cities for actors and singers, but what about for magicians? He shook his head.

Then it struck him. Why not Las Vegas? There were probably more magicians there than anywhere else in the world. And if there were magicians, maybe there were apprentices, young men and women like himself eager to work for and learn from a master.

Yes, Las Vegas. It was where The Great Rantiki did most of his shows. Why not go there?

He got up off the bench and headed for the ticket booth.

"I'd like a ticket to Las Vegas, please."

The cashier shot Romano a look of bewilderment. He leaned forward toward the glass for a closer look at him. "You want to go where?"

"Las Vegas, please."

The cashier was an older man, bald on top and more than a few crow's feet around the eyes. Upon hearing Romano's words, those crow's feet deepened and came together as his face lit up in a smile. "You're not kiddin' me, are you?"

Romano shook his head. "No."

"Well, you can't get there from here." A pause. "I mean, you can, but you'd have to take a bus to Detroit or maybe Philadelphia first. From there you'd need a bus to Indianapolis or St. Louis, you get the idea. By the time you get there, if you ever got there, it would almost cost you as much as an airplane ticket."

Romano nodded, a little embarrassed by his own naïveté. "I see. Well then, how much is a plane ticket?"

"Maybe a few hundred bucks," the cashier said, shrugging his shoulders. "I don't know, kid. I sell bus tickets."

Romano nodded. "Right, thank you anyway." Romano lingered at the booth a few seconds, then turned away.

A *few hundred dollars*, he thought. It was almost as much as he had in his pocket. If he were to spend everything he had just getting to Las Vegas, then what would he live on those first few days after his arrival?

For the first time in his life, he began to have a better understanding of his father's view of the world. Maybe there was something to be said for having a steady job and a stable home life. Maybe so, but it still wasn't for him. Although he was figuratively and perhaps even literally stranded halfway between his home and his ultimate destination, he'd already passed the point of no return. The only way he'd be returning to Montreal was as the headliner of a full evening show.

And so, with his resolve reaffirmed and his goals in sharper focus, he unzipped his bag, placed an open box on the floor in front of him, and began doing card tricks for the people passing by.

No one paid any attention to him for several minutes, but then a middle-aged woman with a child in tow stopped to watch. They were soon joined by a young man with long black hair and three earrings in his left ear. Then an elderly woman stopped to have a look.

Soon there were a dozen people standing there watching cards appear and disappear from his hands with both speed and flair.

By the time he'd exhausted all of his card tricks there were more than twenty people in the crowd. As the gathering dispersed he collected the coins that had fallen into the box over the course of his impromptu show.

Six dollars and thirty-seven cents.

Not much, but enough for a bite to eat and a cup of coffee.

His stomach rumbled at the thought.

He grabbed a burger and fries at the terminal's lunch counter, ate them quickly, then spent the next twenty minutes sipping his coffee.

He hated to admit it, but now that the full magnitude of what he was doing was setting in, he was scared. He'd never been so far from home, nor felt so alone. Yet, as much as he was scared, he was also exhilarated. Despite his fear, there was still something inside him eagerly pushing him further from home and wanting him to isolate himself from the rest of the world so he could pursue his dream with as few distractions as possible. Magic, he realized, wasn't just something he *wanted* to do, it was something he *had* to do, *needed* to do.

It was getting late. He also needed some sleep.

He finished the last of his coffee in a gulp and got up from the table. He asked the cashier where he could stay overnight cheap, and the man answered by giving him photocopied directions to the Youthlink hostel less than a block away. It was obvious that the hostel was close to the bus terminal in order to give the runaway teens that streamed into Toronto every day a chance to reconsider their situation, maybe even call home. And while Romano was running toward something rather than away from it, he didn't have a problem accepting free lodging under false pretenses. If it helped him to achieve his goal, how could it be wrong?

The directions were good ones and Romano arrived at the hostel just a few minutes after leaving the bus terminal.

After being asked a few questions by the young man at the desk just inside the lobby, Romano was brought to a room containing six beds, three of them occupied by young men like himself, the other three empty.

"You're lucky we're not too busy tonight," the man said. "It's a pretty warm night out."

Romano smiled politely and took the empty bed by the door. When the young man was gone and the room was filled with the regular breathing of the three sleeping teens, he slipped off his shoes, lay down on the cot…

And fell asleep in seconds.

The hostel didn't suit him.

First of all he had to be wary of everyone around him since he had a bag with him containing valuables. How valuable his card decks, handcuffs and other assorted tricks were to the street kids, he didn't know, but they sure showed an interest in them every time they thought his back was turned.

Secondly, he couldn't get comfortable around these teenagers. Although they were all roughly the same age as he was, they seemed to be from a different world. While he knew he was destined for better things, knew he was going somewhere, they seemed to be going nowhere fast. After his second night in the hostel, with the boy in the cot next to him crying himself to sleep, he knew he had to get out before he was sucked down into the bottomless pit that was the runaway's world.

In the morning he left, vowing not to return.

He spent the early hours looking for work, starting out in the hopes he might find a job as a magician or entertainer, but he soon realized that at this point any odd job would suit him just fine.

He was still unemployed by mid-afternoon, but he was lucky enough to find a room. It cost him money to stay there and it wasn't much better than the hostel, but it was cheap enough for him to live in while he continued searching for work.

That night, his lucky star was shining brightly. At the third restaurant he tried, he got a job washing pots. The place was called Torchy's, a middle-of-the-road kind of place with a clientele that looked as if it was from both sides of the tracks, and on both sides of the law; a place where both cops and robbers hung out. But the best thing about the place to Romano's mind was that they featured nightly live entertainment. While Romano wouldn't be seeing much of the inside of the restaurant, or the entertainment for that matter, there was an air of show business about the place that he liked. Besides, the kitchen was clean enough and at fifty dollars a night, meals included, he'd have enough for the trip to Las Vegas in a couple of weeks.

"So, who do you like?"

Romano hadn't paid much attention to the man working the sink next to him, and up until now the man hadn't paid much attention to Romano, each of them content to wash their pots in silence. But now on Romano's third night on the job, it seemed like the guy wanted to talk.

"What do you mean?" asked Romano.

"Who do you like, Van Halen, Aerosmith?"

"Oh, well…" Romano said, a little stunned by the man's choice of ice-breaking topics. He wasn't all that familiar with the pop-rock scene, but he did recognize the name Van Halen from one of the tattoos on the man's right arm. "I, uh, hadn't thought about it much."

"Mmm," the man mumbled, apparently at a loss for something else to talk about.

Romano busied himself with the task of cleaning the pots in his sink. There were four of them, all covered in baked-on tomato sauce and melted cheese. If he was lucky, he'd be out of this place by midnight with his arms sore and the raw skin on his hands and fingers the texture of sun-dried raisins.

He scrubbed harder against the pot, feeling the bristles of the steel wool pad biting into his hands, shredding them and making them sting under the hot, soapy water in the sink.

Perhaps he wasn't so lucky getting this job after all, he thought, flexing his aching fingers.

Just then, the door coming in from the restaurant burst open and Nick Torchia, the restaurant's owner, stepped into the kitchen.

Romano took a break from his work and looked at the man. His usually jovial face seemed troubled. "Anybody here can sing?" he said, loud enough to make everyone in the kitchen stop what they were doing.

"What happened?" asked one of the cooks.

"I got no singer tonight, no piano player either."

"So what." The chef shrugged his shoulders.

"So what?" Torchia said, slapping his hands together as if he were praying. "Since I opened, the sign outside says live entertainment. Tonight for the first time in forty years I got nothing."

Romano couldn't believe it. Not only was his luck still holding out, it was stronger than ever. "Uh, Mr. Torchia?" he said, meekly.

"What is it?"

"I can do some…I do a…"

"Spit it out, kid!"

"I do a magic show."

The big man looked at him for several long seconds. "What do you mean, like cards and coins and things like that?"

Romano nodded.

"You any good?"

"Yes."

He looked him over for several more seconds, top to bottom, then said, "All right. Finish washing those pots, then get your stuff ready."

Romano was all smiles. "Thanks, Mr. Torchia."

"Don't thank me, kid. You might stink."

Romano continued to smile. "Not a chance."

"Yeah, right," Torchia nodded. "Now take your time, but hurry up, if you know what I mean."

Romano returned to his pots, four of them as dirty as pots could get. He closed his eyes for a moment, concentrating on the task at hand, then began scrubbing the pots again. Although he wasn't doing anything different from before, the baked-on food came away with a single pass of his hand, as if the pots had been soaking in scalding hot water for days.

"Hey!" exclaimed Mr. Van Halen. "How'd you do that?"

"Uh, I don't know," said Romano, wondering what the hell had just happened. But as he started thinking about it, he decided it was best not to ponder the incident. He had a show to do, after all.

As Romano hung up his apron and washed up, Mr. Van Halen examined the four pots drip-drying in the rack over the sink. When he was done, he dropped his pots into Romano's sink and began scrubbing at them with Romano's steel wool.

"What do you call yourself, kid?" asked Nick Torchia. "You got a stage name?"

"No, not really."

"All right, what's your name again?"

"Minardi," he said. "Romano Minardi."

"Good, fine. Get ready."

Torchia stepped up onto the tiny stage set into one corner of the restaurant and blew on the microphone. "Ladies and gentlemen," he began, even though the customers were mostly young to middle-aged men. "Beverly Reno won't be singing tonight. She, uh, came down with a chest cold…and with a chest like hers you know what that means…." He paused, even though there was no drummer present to snap a rimshot for him.

"So tonight we have something a little different for you, a young magician who will leave you utterly amazed. Here he is, Armando Rizzardi."

There was a smattering of applause.

"Thank you," Romano said, his small voice lost in the large room. He put his bag down on the stage and began to work his way around the room.

At the first table he stopped at he produced a few ribbons, handkerchiefs and flowers. They were standard tricks, but Romano knew he performed with a confidence and flair that made them look different from those of other magicians. The couple at the table smiled politely, but hardly seemed impressed.

He moved on. At the next table he did several coin and cigarette manipulations. Again, polite applause, nothing more.

He moved on, now doing card tricks. Then, just as he was doing his most difficult card trick, making the cards appear in the fingers of both hands in rapid-fire succession, he actually saw a young man yawn....

Romano's heart sank into the pit of his stomach.

He couldn't understand it. The card tricks had taken him years of practice to perfect, and some of them were distinctly of his own invention. But here people were bored with his performance. Yawning.

He decided to cut short his close-up magic routine and do an on-stage handcuff release instead. He stepped up to the microphone. "For my next trick I will require the assistance of someone from the audience. You, sir!" He pointed at a young man with long hair, a beard and several earrings.

Reluctantly the man made his way onto the stage.

Romano produced the handcuffs and held them up with a single finger. "You look like you may be familiar with these." No one in the room laughed at the joke. In fact, the man onstage seemed slightly offended by the comment. Romano did his best to carry on. "I'd like you to examine these and verify to the audience that these are regulation handcuffs."

The man locked the cuffs, then opened them with the key. "Looks okay," he said.

"Very well, then," Romano said. "Would you be so kind as to snap them to my wrists?"

The man did so. And then when he was sure they were secured, he turned away and headed back to his seat. But before he got down the first step, Romano tapped him on the shoulder. "Excuse me, could I trouble you to lock me up again?"

The man turned to see Romano standing there with the cuffs hanging loosely from his finger.

Shaking his head, the man again stepped back onto the stage and relocked the cuffs, only to have Romano ask him to do it again seconds later. Once more the man shackled Romano's wrists.

"Are you sure they're secure now?" Romano asked.

The man checked them and nodded.

Then in full sight of everyone present, Romano instantly freed himself from the handcuffs.

The applause was faint.

"Trick cuffs," someone shouted.

"I assure you they are not," said Romano, infuriated at being called a cheat. He had practiced this escape for years in order to be able to do it so quickly. And, as far as he knew, no single magician or escape artist in the world, not even The Great Rantiki himself, could do it any faster.

"Hold on, hold on," said a man in a plain blue suit. "I'm Sergeant Joe D'Alessandro." He flashed his badge around the room. "I happen to have my cuffs with me…." A pause. "*If* you're up to the challenge?"

"Of course I am," Romano said.

The room burst into applause, this time genuinely enthusiastic applause.

The officer stepped onto the stage, a smile on his face.

"May I inspect the cuffs?" Romano asked.

The man turned to the crowd. "Sure, sure, look all you like."

People laughed and snickered.

Romano took hold of the cuffs and looked them over. They were a common model of handcuff made by the Peerless Handcuff Company of Springfield, Massachusetts. This particular type was in use by police forces across North America and featured a double-lock mechanism to ensure a suspect couldn't cut off circulation to his hand by closing the cuff too tightly during a struggle. Romano was familiar with the cuff and knew the secret to opening it without a key or pick. "All right," Romano said. "Lock me up!"

"You asked for it," said the officer. He snapped the cuffs onto Romano's wrists, tightening them a little more than was comfortable. When he was done, the officer turned to face the audience, a self-satisfied smirk on his face.

And then the room burst into laughter as Romano casually stood behind the policeman swinging the cuffs in circles around his fingers. When he was done, he draped the cuffs over the policeman's shoulder. "I believe these belong to you," he said.

Everyone cheered.

Later, back in the kitchen, Romano was met by Nick Torchia. "That was great, kid. Especially the part with the cop. You think you could do it again tomorrow night?"

"How much?"

Torchia appeared to be somewhat taken aback by the brashness of the youth. "Same as before, fifty bucks a night, but you don't have to wash pots anymore."

There it was, his first professional job offer as a magician. It was a proud moment, but somewhat tainted by the experience of doing that night's show. Sure they had cheered after he'd almost been upstaged by a policeman, but when he'd shown them his best tricks, they had failed to recognize them as being the pinnacle of the art form. If he continued to work here for pocket change he'd have to endure yawning patrons and those who dared to call him a fake.

His tricks were better than Torchy's. They deserved to be presented in a room that complimented his artistry, not masked it. His resolve to travel to Las Vegas was suddenly renewed within him.

After just one show, he knew he was destined for better things. Still, performing magic was a lot better than washing pots.

He decided on a compromise.

"I'll work seven days," he said, and then, thinking what the hell, added, "Sixty a night, plus meals."

Torchia held up his hands as if Romano were holding a gun to his chest.

Romano didn't bother waiting for an answer. He was fully prepared to walk out on the job if his demand wasn't met. "Okay," he said. "Maybe somebody else—"

"All right, all right," Torchia said. "But two shows a night."

Romano nodded. That was fine. It would help him get some practice working a live audience.

"You're a real ball-breaker, kid. You know that?" Torchia said, turning and walking away.

"Yeah, I know," Romano said, smiling broadly.

If only his father had been there to see him negotiate that deal....

3

The lights were out of this world.

Romano lit a cigarette—a foul habit he'd picked up working at Torchy's—and walked down Las Vegas's famous Fremont Street, or Glitter Gulch as it's sometimes called.

And he'd thought Toronto was full of lights.

As he walked westward past the Four Queens Hotel and Casino, and the Fremont Hotel, all he could do was turn slowly on his feet while he craned his neck and looked at the flashing, pulsing, blinking, flickering lights that turned night into day, capping the city like a glitter dome of man-made stars.

With each step he became more and more convinced that he'd made the right decision in coming here. And he knew why, too.

This was a place where people came expecting wonders.

This was a place where anything was possible.

This was a place where magic was meant to be performed.

When he'd first done his routine at Torchy's, no one had expected a talented magician to be performing in some downtown Toronto hole-in-the-wall. What they expected was a down-and-out no-talent bum who couldn't pull a rabbit out of a hat. In that setting, people weren't able, or perhaps ready, to recognize true talent when they saw it and were more apt to dismiss a performer as a fake than recognize him as the real thing. But here in Las Vegas, people paid good money to see a show, just about any show, and when they paid so dearly they expected those shows to be good, and as a result were more likely to believe that the performer's talent was real.

Yes, this was the place he belonged.

This was the place that would do his talent justice.

This was the place where he'd become a star.

As with so many visitors to Las Vegas, the luck that had seen him through so many rough spots in his life was suddenly nowhere to be found.

After a week of searching, Romano was still without a job.

He'd visited several of the big hotels on the strip, as well as a few of the smaller ones off it, but it soon became obvious that no one was going to give him the time of day without an agent. And after he'd visited a dozen or so of the agents listed in the Las Vegas Yellow Pages, it soon became obvious that a week at Torchy's wasn't much of a professional engagement to brag about.

Only one agent, Jay Bilmes, had been kind enough to take a look at some of his stuff.

Thinking it might prove to be his big break, Romano eagerly dug out his coins, cards, cigarettes and handcuffs and presented each trick with all the flair and showmanship he'd refined during his week-long engagement at Torchy's.

When he was done, he stood before the agent with a hopeful smile on his face.

"Not bad, kid," Bilmes said. "What else you got?"

Romano wasn't sure what the man meant, but did his best to answer the question. "Well, I can do a few variations on the card tricks and I do a few rope escapes."

"No, no, no. I mean what else you got in your show? What kind of fakes do you work with?"

By fakes, Bilmes meant what kind of trick boxes and other equipment he worked with on stage, but Romano had never been able to afford any of those things. Besides, he liked to keep his magic pure by working exclusively with real items. That had always sounded good and virtuous, but somehow Romano didn't think Bilmes would see things quite the same way.

Romano looked at his worn and scuffed bag containing everything in the world that he owned and suddenly felt incredibly small-time. "I have a few other handcuffs," he said, "but I really don't use any fakes."

The optimism that had been so evident on the agent's face quickly faded. "You don't have *any*, do you?"

Romano shook his head.

Bilmes let out a sigh. "Look kid, this is Vegas. The big leagues. You don't come here to build up a show, you bring an already high-class polished show here. You got some real talent with the cards, but there are a dozen guys in this town who've been doing that stuff longer than you've been alive. You've got to come up with something different, something unique, because people here want to see more than just talent, they want to be wowed, amazed, shocked. If you're interested in a little free advice, kid, I'd suggest you go back to Appleton, Wisconsin, or wherever the hell you're from and work up a real pisser of an act. Then, when you're ready to come back, you give me a call and I'll take a look at what you've got."

Romano was disappointed, but not upset with the agent. How could he be angry with the one man who'd given him a chance, then honestly told him he didn't have what it took to play in Las Vegas?

He'd just have to prove him wrong.

But now, sitting in his flea-bag of a motel room, reading through the classifieds of the *Las Vegas Daily News*, proving the agent wrong didn't seem all that easy a thing to do. In fact, working a regular gig at Torchy's was starting to look better all the time.

He had exactly one hundred and six dollars left in his pocket, enough for two more nights in the motel and maybe a meal or two. He could try to gamble with it since he was good with cards, but he couldn't stand the thought of possibly losing money—hard-earned money his mother had scrimped and saved for years—in a few minutes at a card table. Gambling was for people who could afford to lose, and Romano couldn't. Besides, he was never one to look for an easy way out. Hard work had never scared him. So if he didn't find work soon, magician's work, he'd be washing pots again by the end of the week.

He turned the last page of the newspaper over and was startled by what he saw.

WHERE THE POSSIBILITY CEASES
THE IMPOSSIBILITY COMMENCES
THE *GREAT* RANTIKI
MASTER OF MAGICK

The price of a ticket was there in the bottom right corner of the ad. When he read the numbers he sighed heavily. At thirty-five dollars for one seat he'd be giving up almost half of what he had—not to mention a night's sleep indoors—just to see a magic show.

Ah, but this wasn't any ordinary magic show. This was The Great Rantiki, his boyhood idol. The way his fortunes were going, there might not be another chance to see the aging magician perform.

Romano took out his billfold and counted his money again. As he slapped the sheaf of bills against his palm, he decided that there couldn't be anything more worthwhile to spend his last few dollars on than a ticket to see the great one's show.

He tore the ad out of the newspaper and put on his jacket.

The Stardust Hotel and Casino.

The show began at eight, but Romano was standing in front of the ticket booth by six-thirty waiting for it to open. He stood patiently for the next half-hour hoping it wasn't too late to get a ticket for the performance.

"One, please," he said, before the large, elderly woman in a multicolored polyester blouse could even get the cash register up and running.

"Just one?"

"Yes."

"You sure?" she said, looking at him strangely, perhaps to see if someone might be hiding inside his jacket.

Romano nodded. "One's all I need."

The woman took his money and gave him a ticket.

He held the ticket in his hand as if it were a hundred-dollar bill and headed toward the showroom.

He stopped at the entrance and took a look around. The place was filling up, but not as fast as he might have thought for someone as internationally famous as The Great Rantiki.

A few moments later, he was met at the door by a middle-aged usher who looked at Romano's single ticket and promptly led him to a seat in the second row of the balcony. Once there, Romano sat down and watched the room fill. At the door, he could see money changing hands between new arrivals and the usher. The more money that flowed into the usher's hand, the closer people got to the stage. At first Romano was upset by it, but he quickly realized that money talked in Las Vegas and he was practically a mute. Besides, he was content just to be here, to have a chance to take in the surroundings and soak up some of the atmosphere pervading the room.

And it was a magnificent room, the kind of theater Romano always imagined great magic was meant to be performed in. Dark swatches of red velvet adorned the walls, framing plaster reliefs of the masks of tragedy and comedy. Overhead, the ceiling was covered by an intricate design of interlocking squares set into the plaster and painted in a mesmerizing pattern of red, gold, blue and yellow. And down front, shining onto the gold-accented, dark scarlet curtains was the visage of The Great Rantiki himself. It was an inexpensive little gimmick, costing no more than a custom-made gel and a spotlight, but the effect was haunting for Romano, as if Rantiki's piercing dark eyes were looking out at him and challenging him to believe in the impossible.

Yes, this was a place worthy of great magic.

Romano could hardly wait for the show to begin.

By showtime the room had filled up considerably with high-rollers with free tickets and line passes, but as the ticket lady had promised, there were still plenty of empty single seats down front.

When the lights went down, the crowd grew silent and the small orchestra in the pit in front of the stage began to play somber music featuring string and reed instruments. The curtain slowly rose, the red material gathering in large, elegant scoops as it was lifted off the stage.

Then the stagelights came on, first one, then another, and another, all coming from the foot of the stage, lighting Rantiki's one female assistant from below and giving the show a spooky and mystical quality.

As the music continued to play, the assistant suddenly looked up and a moment later The Great Rantiki floated down from above, gently landing on the stage as if he were no heavier than a feather.

Romano watched closely to see when and how the wires would be disconnected, but Rantiki went right into his act without hesitation. If he'd been wired up, he wasn't anymore.

Romano was awed. If this was merely The Great Rantiki's entrance, it was no wonder he'd been hard pressed to find work in Las Vegas. Compared

EDO VAN BELKOM

to Romano's few card tricks and coin manipulations, Rantiki's show was somewhere in the stratosphere.

Romano rolled forward onto the edge of his seat, knowing he'd made the right decision in buying a ticket.

After the dramatic entrance, Rantiki settled down into a more conventional magic act, performing old standards like the Chinese Linking Rings and a few simple levitation tricks, all done with his trademark seriousness, stern face and piercing eyes that told the audience that each feat required the utmost concentration.

As he continued to watch the show, Romano began to feel strange, queasy in the pit of his stomach. He tried to explain the sudden onset of it as simply excitement over seeing his idol performing live, but it was a different sort of feeling—like nothing he'd ever felt before. But curiously, the feeling passed as quickly as it had come and he forgot that anything strange had happened.

The show was a far cry from the glory days of The Great Rantiki, when he would electrify audiences with two solid hours of incredible magic and death-defying escapes, but it was still an impressive show for one so old. And even though Romano knew the secrets behind each of the tricks and could do most of them himself, he was still captivated by the show, caught up in the truly magical atmosphere that rippled through the room upon the completion of each trick.

"For my next trick, the first escape of the night," said Rantiki in an authoritative voice, "I will require the assistance of some people from the audience."

Romano had no idea what the trick was, but he nearly jumped out of his seat volunteering. "Me!" he shouted. "Pick me! Pick me!"

A slight laugh coursed through the room as people below looked up to see what all the commotion was about.

"You sir, and you sir," said Rantiki, pointing to two burly men sitting in the front row.

Seeing the two men heading toward the stage only made Romano's pleas more urgent, not to mention louder. "Me!" he shouted again. "Pick me!"

Rantiki was obviously reluctant to bring someone down from the balcony, but too many people in the audience were looking at Romano for the magician to ignore him any longer. "All right, young man. Come down here if you like, but be quick about it."

Romano leaped out of his seat and headed for the aisle.

On stage, Rantiki was continuing the show without him.

As Romano ran down the stairs, he could hear Rantiki talking over the theater's public address system. "Now, I'd like to assure the members of the audience that I've never met the three people I've asked up here to help me prepare for this escape…including the boisterous young man from the balcony."

The audience laughed just as Romano, slightly breathless, ran up onto the stage.

Rantiki smiled and bowed slightly in Romano's direction, then continued.

"I challenge them to tie me up with rope—" He held up several pieces of rope of varying thicknesses. "And close me in this box, where I will attempt to extricate myself within a specified limit of time. The longest I've ever been held inside this box was six minutes after being tied up by three men at a performance in Boston. If I am confined inside this box longer than six minutes tonight, the ticket price of these three good men will be refunded in full."

Romano was impressed, not by the trick but by the reward being offered if the challenge proved successful.

He knew most of the tricks to rope-tie escapes, and the escape was pretty straightforward. Rantiki offered several thicknesses of ropes to the trio on stage, knowing that a person's first inclination would be to use the heaviest rope, which in fact was easier to escape from than light, thin rope. Second, each length of rope was roughly six feet long, more than enough to obtain the necessary amount of slack for an escape. Finally, he'd only have to worry about the first few knots, since most people tired after tying their initial knots tightly. And, even if Rantiki was still unable to untie the knots, he would likely have a small blade inside the case with which he could cut a few inches off the rope, since a missing length that short would usually go unnoticed by the crowd.

"You may begin," Rantiki said, holding his hands together at the wrist behind his back.

"All right," said one of the men, picking the thickest rope off the table.

"No," said Romano. "This one." He picked up the thinnest rope there, hardly thicker than a skate lace, and strung it between his outstretched hands. It went from fingertip to fingertip, meaning it was exactly six feet long. "All right, go ahead."

The big man took the rope from Romano and began tying up Rantiki. After the first couple of knots, Romano tapped him on the shoulder. "Let me do one now."

"Go ahead."

Romano took hold of the rope and tied several tight knots, even looping the rope through two of Rantiki's belt loops in the hope of preventing him from getting the proper slack. He was determined to keep Rantiki in the box for longer than six minutes; the refunded ticket price sure would make a big difference in his finances.

When he was done tying his knots, he passed the ends of the rope along to the other man. "Your turn."

The man tied a few knots, but he obviously felt Rantiki had already been tied well enough, since he hardly bothered to make the knots secure.

"Satisfied?" Rantiki asked when they were done.

"No," said Romano. "I want to check the box."

"Oh, the young man wants to check the box," Rantiki bellowed for the sake of the audience. "Go ahead, be my guest."

Romano stepped into the box, looking not for a blade—that would be too hard to find, or would be concealed on Rantiki's person—but for some evidence of alternate ropes. Since it was Rantiki's own box, there was nothing to stop him from keeping duplicate lengths of rope inside and presenting them as the whole uncut rope after he'd sliced the original one to shreds.

But the box was empty.

"I'm satisfied," Romano nodded.

"Good," Rantiki said, making an exaggerated face for the sake of the audience. "I was beginning to have my doubts."

The audience laughed.

Rantiki stepped into the box and his assistant, a beautiful older women dressed in a tuxedo and flashing a smile as bright and as warm as a neon sign, closed the box.

The orchestra played a tune much like the "thinking music" from the television show *Jeopardy,* and his assistant did a few sleight-of-hand tricks at the end of the stage to keep the audience entertained.

Romano made it a point not to watch the woman doing her tricks lest she should be a diversion to what was happening inside the box. He also kept a close eye on his watch, noting that they were rapidly approaching the five-minute mark.

For a moment, Romano felt a little strange. It was the same thing he'd felt while in his seat, but it was stronger up here on stage. Thankfully, the sensation didn't last long.

As he watched the seconds, then minutes pass, Romano had a fleeting notion that he had bested the master, but just as his watch approached the six-minute mark, the door to the box fell forward and Rantiki stood there holding the length of rope in his hand.

The crowd cheered enthusiastically, but Romano held back his applause, wanting to check the rope first.

He took it from Rantiki's hand and measured it again between his fingertips. It was exactly the same length as it had been before, neither end showing any evidence of having been cut.

Romano was stunned.

How in the world did he do it? he wondered.

And then he dropped the rope onto the stage, applauding louder than anyone else in the theater.

After Rantiki left the stage for intermission, Romano spotted a still-empty seat down front and took it. Then he sat there for several minutes wondering over and over again how he'd done it.

It had to be some skill Romano hadn't learned yet.

Either that or magic.

Real magic.

Romano laughed at that. It had been years since he'd believed in magic, but now he was almost ready to believe in it all over again.

The lights went down, the stagelights came on, and Rantiki took to the stage once more.

The magician went through all of his most impressive tricks, including the metamorphosis or "trunk trick," and the infamous milk-can escape, a trick pioneered by Harry Houdini himself. Each trick was a magnificent piece of illusion and showmanship, but Romano knew how each of them was done. When the show ended Romano remained in his seat, still wondering how the rope-tie escape had been possible in such a short period of time without the rope having been cut.

As the audience began to file out of the room, he decided to find out. He would just have to ask Rantiki how the trick had been done, magician to magician.

He got up from his seat and went against the flow of the departing crowd until he was at the door leading backstage. The only problem was that the doorway was guarded by a big security guard with a square jaw and matching crew-cut.

"Can I help you?" the security guard asked after noticing Romano lingering in front of the doorway.

"Uh…I'd like to see The Great Rantiki. I have a question to ask him."

"Sorry kid, no uninvited backstage visitors after the show," the man said with a forced smile. "And if you want to know how it's done, it's all smoke and mirrors."

"Yeah, right," said Romano, forcing a smile of his own. He turned to walk away, taking a few tentative steps in the direction the rest of the crowd was moving in.

He needed some kind of distraction, something to get the security guard away from the door.

And then it happened.

"Oh, *Dio*," a woman suddenly screamed, her shrill call to God cutting through the air like a knife.

Maybe someone's having a heart attack? Romano thought. He hated to think it, but what a lucky break!

The security guard bolted from the doorway to the middle aisle, where a small group of people had gathered around a fallen woman.

Then, with the backstage door clear, Romano turned back and slipped unnoticed through the doorway.

Backstage was a far cry from the ornately decorated interior of the showroom. It was dirty, in need of a coat of paint, and the smell of greasy food cooking in the kitchen next door lingered in the corridors like smoke.

Romano stopped in front of several small doors in search of Rantiki's dressing room, but they all had signs reading "private" or "employees only." Certainly The Great Rantiki would have a shining star above the name on his dressing-room door. He checked two more doors and then found it.

THE GREAT RANTIKI
ENTER, IF YOU DARE

He read the message on the door, smiled, and decided that yes, he would dare.

He knocked on the door sharply.

"Yes?" came the voice from within.

Romano almost caught himself saying, "It's Romano Minardi from Montreal," but decided that deception was probably more appropriate, considering who was on the other side of the door.

"Telegram," he said at last.

"The door's open."

Romano put a hand on the doorknob, opened the door, and was a little disappointed by what he saw. The room was just as shabby as the outside hallway, and certainly not the sort of room he'd expected for someone of the stature of The Great Rantiki. Even so, the room had little effect on the larger-than-life image Rantiki held within Romano's mind. This was an informal meeting with his idol, a man he'd studied and revered for years. All he could do was stand in the doorway and gawk with an open mouth.

"If you're waiting for me to guess the contents of the telegram you'll be waiting an immeasurable amount of time, my boy," Rantiki said, his back to Romano. "I'm a magician, not a mentalist. I'm afraid you'll just have to deliver it the old-fashioned way."

Romano closed the door behind him. "Uh, there's no telegram, sir," he stammered.

Rantiki turned around in his chair, his face looking somewhat less mystical away from the glare and shadow of the stagelights. He looked almost friendly here, like a grandfather.

"It was the best way I could think of to get through the door," said Romano.

Rantiki didn't seem to be angry, or even surprised by the deception, for that matter. But he did look closely at Romano, stroking his white beard as if thinking. "Ah, yes, you're the boy from the balcony. You seem to know your knots," he said. "You gave me a nervous moment or two."

"How did you do it?" Romano asked, knowing he was being rude, but not caring. He had to know.

"I beg your pardon?"

"You didn't have any substitute ropes in the box, and you didn't cut the rope. The rope you came out of the box with was the same one I used to tie you up."

"Of course."

"So how did you do it?"

"I admire your persistence, but you must be aware that a magician never reveals his secret."

"Yes, but with the rope I chose, and the knots I tied, there was no way for you to get out without cutting it...not in less than six minutes. How did you do it?"

"Why the curiosity?" Rantiki was smiling now, his deep, penetrating eyes alight with a curiosity of their own.

"I'm a magician too," said Romano, his voice wavering at the presumptuousness of the statement made in the presence of a master.

"Are you?" Rantiki said the words slowly.

Romano took a deep breath, then said proudly, "Yes!"

"And you know a thing or two about rope tying, do you?"

"Yes."

"Well, apparently there's still a thing or two you *don't* know."

Romano looked at the floor, suddenly humbled. "I guess so."

Rantiki was silent a moment, then said, "Sit down. Let me show you something."

At one point the security guard came into the room and saw Romano sitting next to Rantiki. "I'm sorry sir," he said, approaching Romano as if he were an intruder. "A woman had a heart attack on her way out of the showroom and I had to call for a doctor." He put his hand on Romano's arm. "I won't let something like this happen again."

Rantiki waved his hand at the young man. "If it happens again, then I suggest you let it," he said. "I haven't had this much fun since I don't know when. This boy knows the ropes."

The security guard nodded apologetically and backed out of the room.

They continued on for the better part of an hour, showing each other an assortment of knots and rope ties, starting with the simplex and thumb ties and moving on to the North American Indian Tie and the Russian Transport Tie. Each time Rantiki showed Romano a new knot, Romano showed Rantiki a more difficult one.

"Very impressive!" Rantiki said. "One more. Hold out your hands."

Romano eagerly obliged and held out his wrists, watching Rantiki closely. After the first loop was made around his right wrist, Romano realized Rantiki was testing him with a "Full View of Audience" release. Romano made sure he caught the center of the rope with his left little finger and made a loop with it, then concealed the loop between the pressed-together heels of his hands.

Romano was pleased with himself. He'd practiced the trick so many times with his younger sister Louise that he was able to make the subtle movements almost undetectable.

Rantiki finished tying the knots, then pulled hard on each end of the rope. Almost instantly, Romano's hands came free.

Rantiki beamed. "Bravo!"

Romano smiled, breathing a sigh of relief for being able to perform the trick so smoothly under the master's watchful eyes. "Thank you," he said with a slight bow of his head.

Rantiki glanced at his watch. "Where has the time gone?" he said. "You must excuse me now, but it's time for me to be going home. I'm not as young as I used to be and I'll need my rest if I'm to do another show tomorrow."

"Oh, of course," Romano nodded. He'd been having such an enjoyable time it had never occurred to him that it would eventually come to an end. He got up to leave, but before turning for the door he realized that, in true magician's fashion, Rantiki had avoided answering his original question by creating an elaborate distraction. He looked at Rantiki again. "How did you do the rope trick so fast?"

Rantiki looked surprised, then curious. "You are a persistent one, aren't you?"

"And some say, confident to the point of being cocky."

"An admirable quality in a stage performer."

"I like to think that it isn't bragging if you can do it."

"Indeed."

Romano was silent. "You're not going to tell me, are you?"

Rantiki shook his head.

"All right then," he said, hesitating before turning to leave. "You wouldn't happen to know of any jobs in this city for a good young magician who's just starting out, would you? I've been looking for work for a week now without any luck."

Rantiki looked at him for the longest time, an almost admiring gaze on his face. At last he said, "You could come and work for me if you like."

Romano stood there, stunned.

"What did you say?"

"I'm offering you a job," he said, matter-of-factly. "Do you want it or not?"

"Yes," he said, barely managing a whisper.

"Fine, then go find my assistant, Martin Kraas. Tell him I've just hired you on. He'll get you squared away."

"Thanks."

"No, thank you."

272   **EDO VAN BELKOM**

"For what?"

"For reminding me of myself when I was your age."

Romano turned for the door again. As he stepped out into the hall, he was struck by a thought. Even though he hardly had a dollar to his name, he couldn't help thinking that he was the luckiest man in Vegas.

He walked down the hall looking for Martin Kraas, a lively new spring in his step.

4

Rantiki's engagement at the Stardust Hotel and Casino ran for another week. Each morning Romano left his motel room, packed his bag and walked six miles to the theater where he was given such glamorous tasks as cleaning out the rabbit and dove cages, or warming the water in the milk can so Rantiki wouldn't catch his death of cold while performing the escape.

On the last day of the engagement, Romano was finally assigned what he thought was his first important job. He was given two complimentary tickets to that night's show and told to take them to the MGM Grand Hotel at the other end of the Strip and deliver them to Tony Curtis, the actor who'd played the great Harry Houdini in the 1953 film *Houdini*. It was a film which, despite its erroneous depiction of Houdini's death occurring while performing an escape from the Chinese Water Torture Cell—he actually died in hospital in 1926 of a ruptured appendix—Romano had found quite entertaining. As a result, he could hardly contain himself at the prospect of meeting the famed actor, a man with some connection, however tenuous, to the most famous conjurer and escapologist the world had ever seen.

After receiving the tickets and cab fare from Rantiki's manager, Arthur Gardner, Romano told the driver to take him to Harrah's Hotel and Casino, which was only halfway to his ultimate destination. From there he'd walk, pocketing the rest of the money for himself.

He didn't like being such a sneak, but Rantiki hadn't mentioned anything about a salary yet and he needed his last few dollars to pay for his room.

When he finally arrived at the MGM Grand, Romano walked up to the front entrance in awe. The MGM Grand was the world's largest hotel, complete with a casino and theme park. The front entrance was shaped like a large lion, albeit a lion only Picasso might have recognized, but a lion nonetheless. After entering the "lions's den," Romano walked proudly through the impressive marble foyer and past the wall of monitors behind the check-in showing larger-than-life ads for the shows being presented at the hotel. Judging from his gait, people could only assume Romano was at the hotel on a matter of tremendous importance. In the elevator, he pressed "P" for the penthouse and looked around to see if anyone had noticed he was on his way to the top.

By the time he reached the penthouse the elevator was empty. He stepped into the hallway and knocked on the lone door in front of him.

While he waited for someone to answer, Romano thought about what he was going to say to Mr. Curtis. He decided he'd just tell him how much he enjoyed his performance in *Houdini* and how he hoped to see the actor backstage at Rantiki's show later that night.

But when the door opened, a middle-aged woman was standing in the doorway. "Yes?" she said in a tired voice.

"I'm here to deliver tickets to Mr. Tony Curtis for tonight's show at the Stardust, compliments of The Great Rantiki." He said the words proudly, enunciating each one as if he were summoning the actor to a Roman feast.

"That's fine," the woman said. "I'll make sure he gets them."

Romano was stunned. He'd thought all along he'd be meeting Mr. Curtis personally. The sudden realization that the delivery of the tickets would be made assistant-to-assistant came as a complete and utter shock.

"Will Mr. Curtis be attending tonight's show?" he asked, still hoping for a chance to meet the man.

She pulled the tickets from Romano's hand. "Maybe, but I'll have to check his itinerary." And with that she closed the door.

Romano stood there in the hallway for a long time trying to imagine someone passing up the opportunity to see The Great Rantiki. The best seats in the house…free!

As he pressed the button for the elevator, Romano realized that Las Vegas wasn't just a long way from the poor Montreal streets that he'd grown up on—it was an entirely different world altogether.

Outside the hotel, Romano walked past the taxi stand and continued on, walking all the way back to the Stardust.

The final show was a sellout. Every seat in the house was filled except for two seats up front, the same two seats Rantiki had generously set aside for Mr. Curtis and a guest.

EDO VAN BELKOM

Romano just shook his head, thinking how much those tickets would have meant to someone who couldn't afford them. Someone like him.

That night's show was Rantiki's best performance of the week, but even though everything went off like clockwork there was little time following the show for congratulations and back-slapping. Everything had to be off the stage by 6 AM so the next night's act could have the day to set up for their show.

The pace was hectic, but Romano found the work fascinating and fun. He wasn't just carrying boxes and packing away equipment, he was getting the chance for a close-up look at some of the best fakes in the business. More than once he had to be chased out of the truck by others bringing in more equipment behind him.

And the more equipment he was able to inspect the more he was in awe of Rantiki's ingenuity and ability. The tricks to most of the fakes weren't apparent to him and several times he was convinced that there was no trickery to the devices whatsoever.

There was just so much for him to learn.

When the truck was fully loaded, and a final check of the stage and dressing rooms revealed nothing was left behind, Romano felt a sudden wave of worry wash over him.

What was going to happen to him now that the show was over? Did he even still have a job?

He walked slowly out to the truck, wondering if that was where he should be.

"C'mon, hurry up!"

He looked around. The voice belonged to Martin Kraas. He was climbing into the driver's side of the truck.

Romano looked at him as if to say, "Me?"

"Get in the truck, let's go!" said Kraas.

Romano needed no more prodding. He'd checked out of his hotel earlier in the day in anticipation of the show changing venues. Now he eagerly threw his bag in the truck and climbed into the passenger's side, wondering where in the world he was going.

"Thought you were going to be left behind," said Kraas, putting the big black Peterbilt tractor in gear and pulling away from the Stardust loading dock.

"Not me," said Romano.

"Good, because I wouldn't have come back for you."

Romano was unsure what he'd meant by the comment. Kraas looked over at Romano. "Relax, it was a joke."

Romano laughed then, taking a closer look at Kraas. He figured Kraas to be in his early to mid-thirties, and judging by his name and mild accent, probably of German or Austrian descent. His blond hair was cut short on top and left long in back, almost to his shoulders. He had a thin blond mustache and a bit of hair on his chin. Whether Kraas was growing a beard or just hadn't shaved in a while, Romano couldn't be sure. But if he didn't know better, Romano might have thought Kraas was a rock musician. And while he was friendly enough and had treated Romano well, Kraas's eyes were dark and brooding, as if there was something dangerous about him. Romano knew it was silly, but he decided to be wary around this man.

At least until he got to know him better.

Kraas guided the truck easily through the lot, then pulled into traffic on Las Vegas Boulevard, heading north. The sun was just beginning to crest over the eastern horizon, but there were still dozens of people wandering the streets; people who, like the city itself, had been awake all night.

When Kraas turned the truck onto the Las Vegas Expressway and headed west on I-95, Romano's curiosity had become too piqued to ignore any longer. "Where are we going?" he asked.

Kraas smiled. "Home."

Romano didn't understand. "Where's home?"

Kraas looked at him, his face slightly distressed by the question. "I guess I haven't filled you in on much, have I?"

Romano shook his head.

"Well, we're taking all this equipment back to Rancho Rantiki," he said. "Then we'll spend the next couple of weeks making sure everything works, before putting it in storage till it's needed again for a show."

"Really?"

"Well, we don't really put stuff into storage as much as on display." Kraas took his eye off the road for a moment. "You do some magic, don't you?"

Romano nodded.

"Then you're in for a real treat. I remember when I saw his collection for the first time. It's like no place else on earth."

"You do magic too?"

Kraas leered at Romano as if the question had offended him. "I guess you've never heard of me, then."

Romano shook his head, a little embarrassed. "No."

"I was doing an act for about five years when I got a job up in Reno, close-up stuff mostly, cigarettes, coins and cards, but I did a couple of box escapes as well. One night, about six years ago, Rantiki came up to Reno to see my act. When the show was over he asked if he could see my fakes. 'I'd be honored,' I said.

"He looked at them for a long time and was impressed by the variations I'd worked out on them. Well, I never had a better compliment in my life. But then, he topped it by saying he'd been looking for someone like me to look after his equipment for him, help him design his shows, and he offered me a job, right there on the spot."

Romano smiled, thinking he must have impressed Rantiki in much the same way to be offered a job under similar circumstances.

"So, here I am, six years later, Senior Technical Advisor and unofficial apprentice to The Great Rantiki."

"You're his apprentice?" Romano said in a voice edged with wonder and admiration.

"Well, not exactly," said Kraas, his eyebrows knitting together to suggest the matter wasn't quite cut and dried. "He and I don't always see eye-to-eye on magic. I'm more into lighting and illusion props while he's more into the mystical side of magic, only he spells it with a K on the end, like that makes it something different. He calls himself a mage too, and babbles on about the Traditions, the Technocracy and their Pogrom, but it's just a lot of eccentric mumbo-jumbo. He also claims to be able to do real magic, and sometimes he *can* do things that are so fantastic that even I can't figure out how they're done. He says it's magick with a K, but I say it's just a trick whose cleverly concealed secret I'm not yet aware of."

"And you're his apprentice?" Romano asked again, trying to keep the skepticism out of his voice.

"Well, he hasn't said so in as many words, but it's sort of understood that I'll take over his collection when he's gone. And if I'm going to have access to all his stuff I might as well use it in a show."

Romano thought about it.

"Right?" Kraas prodded.

"I guess."

Kraas nodded and adjusted himself in his seat. "Almost there," he said.

"Mind if I smoke?" Romano asked.

"No, go ahead."

Romano lit a cigarette and scanned the horizon, looking for a house of magic.

Rancho Rantiki was a sprawling ranch-style house just off
I-95 on the slopes of Mount Charleston, about forty-five miles northwest of Las Vegas. Because of its elevation, Mt. Charleston was a local skiing haven in winter while in the summer it offered a respite from the searing 115 degree heat of the Mojave Desert.

The long white house featured a bell tower at one end, countless windows along each of the walls, and a gracefully swirling stairway leading up to the entrance way and the largest pair of doors Romano had ever seen.

"That's where Rantiki lives?" Romano asked.

"Sort of," said Kraas. "He only uses a couple of rooms. The rest is for guests and storage space for his equipment. You'd be surprised how much room this stuff takes up when it's all set up at the same time."

Romano nodded. "And where do you live?"

Kraas guided the truck through the huge front gate. "Over there," he said, pointing at a group of tiny bungalows next to a larger building, each of them as white as the main house. "A few of us have rooms over there next to the workshop in case we have to work late rehearsing or fixing some piece of equipment."

"We?"

"Me and the other assistants."

Romano was silent.

"I guess I really haven't filled you in on much. Sorry about that."

Romano shrugged. He'd been wanting to ask Kraas and Rantiki a million questions, but the Canadian part of him had been too polite to ask.

Kraas slowed the truck to a stop, then spread his arm out toward the cluster of buildings set back from the main house. "Romano," he said, "this is your new home."

"Really? For how long?"

"That depends on you."

Kraas put the truck back into gear and drove it behind the mansion. There was a big heart-shaped pool in back complete with its own waterfall, as well as a smaller building that looked to be an aviary. Kraas stopped the truck again and shifted it into reverse, backing it slowly up to the loading dock built into one end of the house.

When he gently bumped the dock wall, he engaged the truck's parking brake and shut off the engine. The truck died with a rattle, the air compressor letting go with a final *whoosh!*

"We better get some sleep," Kraas said with a yawn. "C'mon, I'll show you your room. We'll unload the truck this afternoon."

Romano frowned. Even though he'd worked through the night helping to pack up the show, he didn't feel much like sleeping. If the inside of Rantiki's house was as good as Kraas had made it out to be, he wouldn't be able to sleep until he at least had a quick look around.

Kraas must have noticed Romano's disappointment because he smiled and said, "All right, you can have a quick look inside, but then we've really got to get some sleep."

Romano hurried out of the truck and around the other side where a door led into the house. He waited there for Kraas to unlock the door, then followed him inside.

"Wow!"

It was all he could say.

"I told you it was something."

Romano took a few tenuous steps inside, as if he were afraid of disturbing some kind of inner sanctum. Every available inch of floor space held some sort of magical device or apparatus, every square foot of wall displayed an ancient showbill or photograph.

Romano stepped closer to the wall and read one of the framed advertisements. It was for a performance at the Cardiff Empire Theater for Monday, January 6, 1913.

THE WORLD-FAMOUS SELF-LIBERATOR

HOUDINI

Presenting the Greatest Performance

of his Strenuous Career

liberating himself

after being locked in a

WATER TORTURE

CELL

Romano reread the showbill and wondered if the Water Torture Cell was part of Rantiki's collection.

It certainly was possible.

To his left was an array of trick milk cans in varying sizes and colors. To his right stood a row of oblong cabinets all designed to create the illusion of sawing a woman in half, compressing her into half her original size, or god knew what else. Overhead, a levitating mirrored ball floated motionless without the aid of any visible wires or supports. Behind him, an entire wall was covered by a display of hundreds of different handcuffs and shackles, some standard issue, some custom-made by the manufacturer, some homemade by tinkerers, but all quite formidable constraints.

Romano sucked in a breath and felt his knees go weak.

It was like being in church. No, it was better than that. It was like a visit to the holy land, or some higher plane of magical existence.

"Seen enough?" asked Kraas from where he stood waiting by the door.

Romano's head rotated and pivoted on his neck as he tried to absorb the room's countless wonders all in a few scant seconds. "No," he said. "I want to see more."

"Don't worry," said Kraas. "You'll have plenty of time to see everything up close. More than enough time." He pushed the door open and held it for Romano.

Reluctantly Romano turned to leave.

They walked across the compound toward the buildings that made up the assistants' quarters and workshop.

Romano's new home.

Kraas showed him his room. It was about ten by eighteen feet square with one window, a bed, phone and desk. It wasn't much, but it was far better than his motel room had been, even better—he was sorry to say—than his old room back in Montreal.

"Now get some rest," Kraas said. "You're going to need it."

Romano thanked him and stretched out on the bed.

He tried to doze off, even forced his eyes closed for a while, but he couldn't fall asleep.

And as he lay there staring at the ceiling, he wondered if angels ever slept in heaven.

Because this was the way he'd always imagined heaven would be.

5

It wasn't much of a job. But at least he was in the magic business.

He spent a lot of his time doing things like washing cars, or cleaning out the pool, the kind of jobs he didn't have to travel clear across the continent to get.

But at other times, he was able to work with Kraas and the others inside the workshop. And even though he might be pushing a broom or carrying out the garbage, he was given every opportunity to see how the illusions came together, from conception to design, from construction to presentation. Another benefit of the job, the best part of it as far as he was concerned, was that he was allowed to spend as much of his free time as he liked inside the main house.

This was where his real education took place.

Every morning and every night he'd wander through the museum-like displays, trying out some new apparatus until he was able to perform the illusion or escape as smoothly as the master himself.

In a way he was just like the kids from the neighborhood he'd grown up with who'd had dreams of playing in the National Hockey League. They'd wake up early or stay up late, playing shinny on frozen ponds and rivers, or at the local arena, honing their skills in preparation for the day they might step onto the ice of the Montreal Forum, Maple Leaf Gardens or Le Colisée. It was no different for Romano, except his Forum and Gardens would be the stages of Caesar's Palace, the Tropicana, the Aladdin and Sahara.

And he *would* make it, he was sure.

"Romano!" called Kraas.

Romano dropped his broom and hurried over to where Kraas stood at the entrance to the wardrobe room. While Rantiki mostly wore tuxedos, the room was also filled with an array of shoes, assistant's costumes, and props.

"Take these to the dry cleaners in the Fashion Show Mall," he said, holding up several tuxedos. "It's right on the Strip, across from the Desert Inn and next to the Frontier. We've got an account there, so you won't need any money."

Romano nodded. He still wasn't familiar with Las Vegas, but he knew the Strip well enough. He took the clothes and a set of keys from Kraas and went to get a car. He took the Toyota, since it was the only car Kraas had trusted him with since he'd arrived.

It was a short drive into the city and he circled the mall once before finding the small dry cleaners near the American Museum of Historical Documents, a store that sold framed autographed letters written by the likes of Abraham Lincoln, Marilyn Monroe and other famous people.

Romano entered the cleaners, carrying the tuxedos casually over his right shoulder. "Hello," he said, cheerfully.

"Hi," said the young woman behind the counter. She had bright blonde hair, a pretty white smile and an ample, curvy figure, all of which made Romano wonder if she moonlighted as a showgirl.

"These are tuxedos belonging to The Great Rantiki," he said proudly, as if the name was a secret password that magically opened doors wherever he went.

"Are you working for him now?" she asked.

"Yeah, for a couple of months now."

"That's good to hear."

Romano looked at her, not quite sure what she'd meant by the comment. From the way she'd said it, it sounded as if she were happy for herself, not for Romano. Finally, curiosity got the better of him. "I don't know what you mean."

"Well," she began, taking the tuxedos from him and processing them, "usually Martin Kraas is the one who delivers the stuff and I don't like him at all."

"How come?"

"Every time he comes in here he lingers, sometimes making small talk for over an hour. That's not so bad, lots of customers do that, it's the way he looks at me and the things he says…" she shivered. "He just gives me the creeps."

"I don't know all that much about him, but he's treated me okay so far," Romano said, which was true. Even though he hadn't got a real sense of the man yet, he hadn't done anything to cause Romano to form a strong opinion of him either way.

"That's because you don't have, how can I put it delicately…feminine charms."

Romano smiled. "I guess not,"

She hung the tuxedos on the rotating track behind her. "They'll be ready Wednesday," she said. "*You* can pick them up in the morning if you like."

"Okay, sure," Romano said, realizing she was telling him she wanted to see him again. "My name's Romano, by the way. Romano Minardi."

"Is that your real name?"

"Yes."

She looked impressed. "My name's Rhonda Mazey; on stage it's Roxanne May."

"You're an entertainer?"

"Isn't everyone in this town?"

Not knowing the answer, Romano shrugged his shoulders.

"Sometimes I sing in a lounge off the Strip called the Bohemian Embassy."

Romano hadn't heard of it.

"It's way, way off."

"Maybe I should come see you sometime."

"That would be nice."

Romano stood there…lingering, he realized. "I better go. See you Wednesday."

"See ya."

Romano left the cleaners wondering if he had any dry-clean-only dirty clothes in his bag.

When he got back to Rancho Rantiki, Kraas was waiting for him. "Did you see her?" he asked.

"Who?"

"You know," Kraas said, holding his hands out in front of himself as if he were carrying two beach balls.

"Oh, yeah. I did," Romano said, wondering if Kraas knew Rhonda's name.

"Did she ask about me?"

Romano looked at Kraas closely, as if he had just gotten a peek through the curtain. "As a matter of fact, she did."

The months passed quickly for Romano, his knowledge of magic increasing almost exponentially with the passage of time. Rantiki kept busy by appearing at a few small events, a charity event here, a single illusion or effect on a television show there, while the rest of his crew worked on designing his next big stage show.

When Romano wasn't working in the shop, or taking care of the animals, or keeping up the grounds or maintaining equipment, he was free to study in the library, a room crammed full with thousands upon thousands of volumes on magic. Some nights he would join Rantiki himself in the library and the two of them would read for hours, neither disturbing the other's study.

It was while looking through one of the books in the library that Romano came up with one of his best ideas for increasing Rantiki's fame and celebrity.

Hundreds of people wrote to Rantiki each month, most of them tourists who had caught his show while visiting Las Vegas and had written to the Stardust saying how much they'd enjoyed his performance. Romano's idea was to keep in touch with these people by way of a fan club. When he approached Rantiki about the idea, the magician tentatively approved, but not before asking that Romano do two things for him. One, he wanted it to be called the Consor's Club, and two, he asked that Odele Walsh, a woman who had seen over eight hundred of his performances, be given the fan club's first membership.

Romano wasn't sure why Rantiki wanted it to be called the Consor's Club, since he didn't know what a consor was and he couldn't find the word when he looked it up in the *Deluxe Encyclopedic Edition of the New Webster's Dictionary of the English Language*. Nevertheless he called it the Consor's Club and was happy to have the chance to correspond with so many magic fans.

When he'd looked up the word *consor* and found it absent from the dictionary, he called up Delair, the company that published the book and asked why. No one there knew anything about the word *consor*, but they said they would consider including it in their next edition if Romano could provide them with a definition.

Of course, Romano couldn't.

Romano wet his finger and placed the damp fingertip against the iron. It was hot and ready.

He pressed the iron down on the black tuxedo pants, giving the trousers a final pressing before Rantiki would wear them to the Academy of Variety and Cabaret Artists function later that night. Romano was doing the pressing because the pants contained several special pockets in which Rantiki could conceal a few tricks which he would use to liven up the party.

Kraas would be going to the function too, as would Rantiki's assistant Susie Wand, but Romano would have to stay home. Rantiki had told him that the party was for members only. Romano wasn't sure if that were true or not, but he did know that he didn't want to attend any academy function until he was a fully active member, deserving to be part of the group as opposed to being a wannabe hanger-on.

But despite his convictions, Romano couldn't help feeling a little like Cinderella. The irony of the situation was that there was magic all around him, but none to provide him with a horse-drawn coach, or transform him into a party-going Academy member. *At least I wouldn't have to be home by midnight*, he thought, finishing the final crease in the pants.

"Romano!" called the voice of Rantiki.

"Yes sir," he said.

Rantiki came into the room, holding a pair of black shoes in his hands. "Look at this!" he said, pointing.

"What?" Romano had just polished the shoes an hour ago and they'd looked fine to him then.

"This!" Rantiki was pointing to a scuff mark over the toe of the left shoe.

The mark hadn't been there when Romano had finished with the shoes. "Somebody else must have done that. They were shining like mirrors when I was done with them."

"Were they?" Rantiki asked, his tone of voice suggesting he didn't believe Romano.

This kind of condescension wasn't anything new coming from Rantiki, but it was just too much to take tonight. "What do you want from me?" he said. "Blood? I polished your damn shoes and when I was done, they were nice and shiny!" He let out a sigh and shook his head. "I'm not a shoe-shine boy, anyway. I got a job here to learn the craft of magic. And, while I'm on the subject, I'd like to know if you're ever going to teach me any, or am I going to have to learn everything myself just so you can take the credit for being my mentor when I finally break the big time?!"

Romano was breathing hard, knowing he should keep his mouth shut, but too upset to act on the knowledge.

"And another thing—"

Rantiki held up his hand as if he were a mentalist controlling Romano's thoughts. Romano saw that hand and his mouth clamped shut.

"Enough, enough," said Rantiki.

Romano expected his next words to be "you're fired," but Rantiki smiled and said, "Sit down."

Romano took a chair. Rantiki remained standing.

"I've been hard on you, haven't I?"

Romano did his best to backpedal, to take back his words. "Well, not rea—"

"The truth."

"Yes."

"And I've made you do a lot of things you never thought of as being apprentice's work, right?"

"Yes."

"Do you know why?"

Romano shook his head.

"You like reading science fiction and fantasy stories…"

"Sometimes."

"Then you must be familiar with a writer named Harlan Ellison."

Romano was surprised that someone like Rantiki knew who Harlan Ellison was. "Of course."

"Good. Then you may know that in addition to being a brilliant story writer, Harlan Ellison has also worked as a writing instructor."

"Yes."

"Well, Ellison's philosophy on teaching creative writing is simple. He says that if he can convince someone *not* to become a writer, then that person was never meant to be a writer in the first place. Do you understand?"

"I guess."

"So, if I could make your life so miserable here that you forgot all about being a magician and wanted to go home to Bremen—"

"Montreal."

"—whatever...then I could be sure you wanted to learn magic and weren't just in love with the thought of being a magician."

"But I want to be a magician more than anything."

"I know that now," Rantiki said. "You've done well, very well. In fact, you've lasted twice as long the last one did, three times as long as the one before that."

Romano smiled proudly. "So, now that you know I'm sincere and dedicated, will you teach me? I mean, really teach me?"

"We'll see."

Romano felt light and giddy after suddenly finding out that all the hard months he'd worked for Rantiki had merely been a test of his resolve, a test which he had apparently passed with flying colors.

"And could I go with you tonight, then?"

"No," Rantiki said. "Members and guests only."

Romano's spirits sagged and his eyes dropped down to the floor.

"Hmm, but maybe tonight you could be my guest."

Romano leaped to his feet and ran out of the room. "I can be ready in a second," he said.

"I know you can," whispered Rantiki in the now-empty room. "Maybe even faster than that."

6

Things didn't change all that much. Romano was still doing odd jobs, only now he was allowed to sit in on development sessions for the upcoming show. Here he got to watch the master and his assistants at work, creating new illusions or devising new ways of presenting old ones.

Romano seldom spoke at these meetings, choosing instead to listen carefully, absorbing like a sponge every little thing that went on around him.

During this particular session, Rantiki had been pushing to do some variation on the "Sawing Through a Woman" effect, which was an old trick originated by P.T. Selbit around the turn of the century.

"That trick is almost a hundred years old," said Kraas, who for years had been urging Rantiki to do a newer-style show with big cats and other animals.

Rantiki nodded slowly at Kraas's words, then turned to Romano. "What do you think, Romano?"

Romano was stunned by the question. So was Kraas.

"I don't think I should be—"

"Never mind that," said Rantiki. "You're a part of this show now. Your opinion counts."

Romano shifted in his chair and cleared his throat. He looked over at Kraas, but the scowl he got in return forced him to keep his eyes on Rantiki. He wasn't quite sure how to express what he felt, so he decided instead to quote a few lines from one of his favorite books. "Don't lose confidence in an effect because it has been done many times before. An old trick in 'good hands' is always new. Just see to it that yours are 'good hands.'"

Rantiki nodded in approval. "An excellent outlook," he said. "Whose fine words are those?"

Romano glanced around nervously. "Yours," he said. "From Chapter Two of *Rantiki on Magic*."

Rantiki gave a little laugh. Across the table Kraas stewed. "So Romano, what do *you* think then about sawing a woman in half?"

"I think it just needs a newer stage presentation."

"Such as?"

"Well, how about something like a mad scientist/reluctant assistant presentation? The mad scientist has to practically force her into the box, then after she's cut up you put her back together wrong, sort of like the Mismade Girl effect, but instead of making her whole before she walks off, why not let her walk off stage with an arm where her leg should be and a leg where her arm should be."

It was as if a light had gone on inside Rantiki's head. His eyes shone brightly as he imagined the possibility. He turned to Kraas. "Can it be done?"

Kraas didn't seem to be too impressed with the idea, especially since it had come from Romano. Nevertheless, if they pulled it off, Kraas would likely receive a partial credit as the variation's developer. "It can be done, but it would need a special costume and sleeve to make the woman's leg look like an arm."

"Can you do it?"

From the way Rantiki said the words, Romano realized that this was an altogether different question than "Can it be done?"

Kraas nodded.

"Good, perhaps we'll open with it." And then Rantiki looked off into the distance, as if pondering the subject further. "We could even call the show '*Weird Science*' and run with the theme. Oh, wouldn't the Technocracy just love that?"

And then he started to laugh.

Romano didn't understand what Rantiki was talking about, or what was so funny. Then he looked around the table. Judging by the looks on the faces of the others, they didn't know what he was talking about either.

"Pick a card, any card!" Romano said, fanning out a fresh deck of cards in his right hand.

A young boy stood in front of Romano dressed in a pair of Power Ranger pajamas. He looked at the perfectly spread cards in Romano's hand in awe, as if the simple and smooth movement of fanning them out had been the trick itself.

"Go ahead, they don't bite...."

The young boy reached for a card.

"At least not yet," Romano said, causing every second card to rise up slightly, making the deck appear to have teeth.

The kids in the ward laughed, including the one in front of Romano.

"Okay, try again. And I promise no tricks until we're done."

The boy picked out a card and looked at it.

"Remember what it is."

The boy looked at the card again, closed his eyes and nodded.

"Now, place it back into the deck."

He did.

"And think of a friend here in the room you'd like to send that card to, you know...sort of like a 'Get Well Soon' card."

The boy closed his eyes and concentrated.

"Did you send the card to your friend?" Romano asked.

The boy shrugged, unsure. "I guess so."

"All right, let's see. Look for your card in the deck."

The boy started looking through the upturned faces of the cards, unable to find his card.

"Who did you send it to, then?" Romano asked.

"Linda," said the boy.

"Who's Linda?" asked Romano.

A young girl, not more than five years old and sitting in a wheelchair, raised her hand. "I'm Linda."

"Where's the card, Linda?" Romano asked.

Linda giggled. "I don't know."

"Is it in your ear?"

"Noooo!" cried Linda, sending ripples of laughter through the room.

"I bet it is."

"No it's not."

"Let's see," said Romano. He went over to one of the doctors taking in his show and borrowed a small penlight. Then he knelt down beside Linda and looked in her ear. "There's a lot of dirt and potatoes in there, but no card."

Everyone laughed.

"Wait a minute! Wait…a…minute! I think I see it." And then Romano rolled up his sleeves and produced the card, actually making it appear as if he were pulling it out of Linda's ear. "Is this it?" he asked, unrolling the card and showing it to the room.

No one answered for a few moments as all their mouths were gaping in silence.

"Is this the card?" he asked again.

"Y-yes!" said the young boy.

"How did you do that?" asked Linda.

"It's ma-ha-ha-ha-gic," Romano sang, moving quickly onto the next trick, exhilarated by the knowledge that he now held the children in the palm of his hand. Over the course of the next half hour they would be entertained, and most importantly of all, their pain and suffering would be forgotten.

Romano had never felt better about doing magic, not even at Torchy's.

Dressed in an old UNLV sweat suit, The Great Rantiki hobbled into the lobby of the University Medical Center on W. Charleston Boulevard. Unsure about where he was going, he headed for the reception desk just inside the doors. "The children's ward?"

"Fourth floor," said a grey-haired woman dressed in white. "The elevators are down that way and to your right."

"Thank you."

Rantiki hurried down the hall, glancing at his watch. It was ten after the hour and he hoped he hadn't missed it. The others had mentioned Romano had done a few shows for the children here in the hospital, but none of them had ever seen him do any magic. Rantiki had meant to come to the hospital to see Romano perform on several occasions, but some commitment or another would always get in the way.

The elevator was waiting for him when he reached it.

Today he was free, and was determined to see Romano perform in front of a crowd. There was no better way in the world to judge his talent.

When he got off on the fourth floor he didn't have to ask where he might find the magic show. There were nurses and doctors crowded in the hall just outside the door. He headed for the crowd, hearing Romano's voice as he neared.

"Pick a card, any card!"

Rantiki boldly forced his way through the door, finding an inconspicuous spot just inside the room.

"Remember what it is?" asked Romano.

Romano looked comfortable in front of the children, around the adults as well, and Rantiki guessed that the young man's confidence was in evidence in every facet of his life. His style was also smooth, and maybe just a little bit flashy. He knew how to play to the audience, how to manipulate them so as to leave them spellbound.

"Wait…a…minute!"

Rantiki watched Romano pull the card from the girl's ear and found himself having to blink. It was a close-up effect as good as any done by the likes of Jimmy Grippo, the long-time close-up "magician-in-residence" at Caesar's Palace.

Rantiki applauded, happy that he at least got to see the end of Romano's show. But as the applause died down Romano kept performing, doing a more impressive effect, this time with coins.

When he'd first met Romano backstage, Rantiki had sensed there was something special about the young man. How special he didn't know; but he could find out.

As Romano continued to perform, Rantiki took a pair of Ray-Bans from his sweat-suit pocket and cast a rote over them, an innocuous little spell that he alone would see the effects of. Then he put on the glasses…

And was utterly amazed.

The glasses now gave Rantiki the ability to see a person's Avatar. Most people's Avatars were dormant, and could never be seen, even through devices like specially prepared glasses. However, the Avatars belonging to Sleepers—people potentially capable of magick, but who weren't yet aware of its existence—usually showed up as a faint blue glow surrounding the body like an aura. The brighter the glow, the better the chance that person had of some day becoming a mage.

But Romano's Avatar was something else altogether.

Even through the crude focus of the sunglasses, Romano's Avatar was an incredible sight, burning brightly around him in soft hues of blue, orange and gold, and at times firing sharply out from his body like solar flares.

Rantiki removed the glasses, rubbed his eyes and caught his breath. Romano, he realized, was on the verge of Awakening. And when he did come through the Curtain, he'd be more powerful a mage than Rantiki had ever dreamed possible.

He considered the prospect.

With Romano's natural affinity for magic, and potentially unbridled power to perform magick, Rantiki came to the realization that he just might be looking at the greatest stage magician the world would ever know.

"Thank you!" said Romano, taking his bows. "Thank you!"

Rantiki applauded loudly for a moment, then slipped out the door before he was noticed.

As he stepped onto the elevator, he could still hear the applause echoing out of the room and down the hall.

The greatest stage magician the world would ever know.

That night Rantiki called a meeting of the Las Vegas cabal. The cabal was an informal association of mages belonging to the Tradition of the Cult of Ecstasy who lived and worked in Las Vegas. Most of the cabal's members were magicians, but there was also a small assortment of gamblers, jugglers, singers and other various performers. They met in the back room of a nondescript little bar called the Magic Box located downtown on the corner of Las Vegas Boulevard and Stewart Avenue just behind the block of big downtown hotels.

The Magic Box was appropriately named. It was a squat, square building, the structure of which had been magickally fortified and enhanced to protect it from outside forces, especially the forces of the Technocracy, whose Pogrom—a systematic purge of all who opposed them—made the Chantry a prime target of Technomancers.

Since the Magic Box was also situated on a highly mystical site called a Node, the mages of Las Vegas visited it almost daily, drawing on its Quintessence—the stuff of magick and the source of their power. But while the Chantry was always full, tonight it was especially so since Rantiki's meeting had brought together all the mages in the area at the same time.

The first mages began arriving just after six, giving them about an hour to mingle before leaving to perform their various shows throughout the city. Since the cabal was a purely social group with only the loosest of internal structures, the mages spent their time catching up on news and showing each other their latest tricks. A small stage at one end of the room was just large enough for small illusions, and the room itself was just cozy enough to give every customer a good view whenever a close-up specialist took the stage. It was the stage on which many magicians worked out the kinks in their illusions before presenting them on the Strip.

At one table, Clayton Hines was giving a clinic in close-up magic, a skill which had given him a fifteen-year (and still going) engagement at the Desert Inn. At the bar, David Kotkin was explaining his idea for a new illusion involving a chainsaw, a bucket of blood, and a handkerchief. And at the far end of the room, several young men were flirting with Leslie Kay—a former Siegfried and Roy showgirl who had gone on to become one of the few solo-performing female magicians on the Strip—wondering when she might be requiring the services of a partner.

At six-thirty, Rantiki opened the doors to an adjoining room and began ushering the mages into it. In a few minutes the room filled with about thirty men and women, leaving the Magic Box itself conspicuously empty, save for the few hopeful young mages and magic fans who patronized the bar in the hopes of rubbing shoulders with the top magic makers in Vegas.

Rantiki closed the door behind him and moved to one end of the meeting room, conscious that he was expected to conduct business quickly.

When the room was quiet and he had all of the mages' attention, Rantiki looked over toward Harry Reddington Jr. for a sign that he might begin. In addition to being a second-generation mage and one of the most famous magicians in the world, Harry Reddington Jr. was also Deacon of the Chantry, meaning he was a founding member and one of its unofficial overseers.

Reddington nodded.

"First of all, thank you for coming together this evening on such short notice," Rantiki began, "but I think the matter I wish to discuss is of the utmost importance.

"As some of you may know, for the past few months I have had a young magician in my employ by the name of Romano Minardi."

A couple of the mages nodded, the rest just looked bored.

"When I first met him, I was immediately impressed with his knowledge of magic, all of which was self-taught. And since he's been with me he's continued studying voraciously and now can even quote me whenever I ask for an opinion."

A polite laugh coursed through the room.

"There's no doubt in my mind that he has more than enough confidence, talent and desire to be one of the greatest magicians this town has ever seen."

The room went silent. Such words of praise were never said lightly, especially by such a master as Rantiki.

"But there was something else about him that I sensed in that first encounter with him. From the very beginning I had the feeling that there was something different about this young man, something familiar.

"This afternoon I watched him give a performance at the University Medical Center. I watched him through focus-rote glasses…and his Avatar was burning brightly enough to power the neon down one side of the Strip."

A collective gasp.

"It is my intention to take him on as an apprentice so that, as his mentor, I can teach him the fundamentals of magick. At the same time I can provide him with a legacy of stage magic which would ensure that he remain in Las Vegas after my passing. His presence might also ensure the survival of this Chantry for years to come; he is *that* strong."

The room was silent, considering Rantiki's words.

Over the years, the Technocracy had made several token attempts to infiltrate the Magic Box and break up the Chantry, each one slightly more spirited than the one before. The Las Vegas cabal had been able to defend the Node easily enough, but the mages all knew it was only a matter of time before the Technomancers made a more concerted effort to destroy it.

Reddington shifted in his seat. "This isn't the first time you've addressed the cabal concerning apprenticeships. Wasn't Martin Kraas slated to be an apprentice as well?"

Rantiki nodded. "It was my intention that Kraas take care of my estate, perhaps even continue presenting my show after my passing—"

"It's a dangerous thing to promise something to someone, then give it to someone else. This could turn Kraas against you, against all of us."

"I have never specifically informed Kraas of my intentions. If he has expectations, it is not because I have led him on."

"Still," said Reddington. "There's an understanding."

Rantiki nodded. "Yes, but Romano Minardi is too powerful a Sleeper to let get away. With his devotion to magic and illusion, he could just as easily be trained as a Technomancer. But, as a mage of the Traditions, he could be so much more than a stage magician. He could become a fellow of the Chantry, a mentor…perhaps even a pedagogue for the Cult of Ecstasy itself."

Reddington thought it over, talking to several of the cabal's fellows surrounding him. As they conversed, a low murmur of voices spread across the room.

While it was true that Rantiki was looking out for Romano's best interests and those of the Cult of Ecstasy, he was also aware of the fact that, if he successfully inducted as powerful a mage as Romano promised to be, he would garner a fair bit of fame as the young man's mentor, both in the mundane world and in the world of mages.

"Very well, then," said Reddington. "You may take Romano Minardi on as an apprentice, provided you agree to take full responsibility for his initiation, and agree not to take on any more apprentices."

"I agree."

"It's done, then."

Rantiki smiled, and waved his hand in the air dramatically, producing a bottle of champagne where there had not been one before. "To Romano Minardi, the next great mage of the Las Vegas stage!"

"To Romano Minardi," the mages said in unison, each producing a champagne glass with a wave similar to Rantiki's.

Rantiki popped the cork.

And the Chantry drank a toast to its newest member.

"You wanted to see me?" Romano asked, poking his head inside the door of Rantiki's master bedroom.

"Yes, yes," Rantiki said, sitting up on the bed. "Come on in."

Romano hesitantly stepped into the bedroom. He'd been in the room before, hanging up clothes or dropping off shoes, but never at night and never while Rantiki was in the room as well.

"It's all right, you're not in any trouble," said Rantiki. "Far from it."

Romano sat down in a chair next to the bed.

"I went to see a group of my colleagues today—"

"The Academy of Variety and Cabaret Artists?" Romano asked hopefully.

"No not that stuffy old band of has-beens and want-to-bes…. A less formal group, and a group that is, in many ways, more important than any academy or association could ever be." There was a flicker of light in Rantiki's eyes.

Romano sat up in his chair, listening even more intently.

"As I was talking with some friends about you, one of them looked me straight in the eye and said, 'Sounds like the boy would make a damn fine apprentice.'"

Rantiki paused, giving Romano time to understand.

"So I thought about it, and after a while I came to the conclusion that yes, you would make a fine apprentice. A *damn* fine apprentice, as my colleague so aptly put it." Rantiki's mouth curled upward in a rare smile.

Although Romano's heart was pounding, his body felt weak. "But I thought Kraas was—"

Rantiki put up his hand, cutting Romano off. "That is no concern of yours. Your only job from this point on is to learn."

Romano nodded.

"I am the master, you are the student. You are the apprentice, I am your mentor. Is that understood?"

Romano nodded.

"Good. I will expect you to listen to every word I say, study every book on magic and magick I place in your hands, practice every trick, spell and rote I show you until you have mastered not only its performance, but its concealment as well."

Romano wasn't sure he comprehended everything Rantiki was saying. He thought he heard him say the word *magic* twice, and he didn't have a clue what a rote was, but he still nodded as if he understood it anyway. If he was going to be an apprentice, there would be plenty of time to understand later.

"You will walk in my shadow, live under my wing. Then, when you're deemed ready to be Awakened, you will arise from your sleep and you will be a mage…a master of magick in your own right."

Romano's head felt light and airy, as if he'd been made punch drunk by Rantiki's words. "When will that be?" Romano asked, doing his best not to sound impatient.

"Perhaps sooner than you think."

By morning, news of Romano's apprenticeship had made its way through the ranks of Rantiki's employees. Most of them were happy for Romano, recognizing themselves that the young man had talent and maybe something else, something more.

When they began work on a new illusion that morning, Susie Wand, Rantiki's on-stage assistant for many years, came up to Romano and gave him a great big motherly hug. "Congratulations," she said. "You've been working hard at it, kid. You deserve a break."

"Thanks," Romano said, a word he'd been saying a lot that morning.

"Now, you listen to what he has to tell you. As long as you respect him, he'll never let you down. Got it?" She gave him a wink and flashed him a charming smile.

"Got it."

"What's going on?" asked Kraas, just entering the workshop.

"Didn't you hear?" Susie said.

"Hear what?"

"Rantiki just made Romano here his apprentice."

Kraas stood there, saying nothing.

"Isn't that great?" Susie asked.

Kraas looked at Romano with a glare hot enough to burn flesh. Romano tried not to, but was forced to look away.

"Yeah, that's great!" Kraas said. "Just great!" He turned and left the workshop.

Romano went to the window and watched Kraas walk across the compound toward the house.

A curtain shifted in the window of Rantiki's main-floor bedroom, and Romano wondered if the old man was expecting company.

There were three rapid knocks on the door, sounding more like the pounding of a fist than the rap of a knuckle.

"Come—"

The door burst open and Martin Kraas stepped into the room.

EDO VAN BELKOM

"—in," Rantiki finished, speaking slowly. He crossed his legs and shifted in his chair to make himself more comfortable.

"I just heard something interesting," said Kraas. "And I can't believe it's true."

"And that thing is?"

"Susie just told me that you've made that little wop Minardi your apprentice."

"That's correct."

"You said I was going to take over for you when the time came."

"Not quite, Martin."

"You told me—"

"I said I would entrust you with the maintenance of my equipment, custodianship of my collection."

"But when you hired me on, you said you were looking for an apprentice and you never told me I *wasn't* the one."

Rantiki sighed. He was a master of on-stage deception, but realized that personal deception, with all the emotional baggage that goes with it, was a far more difficult task. He decided it would be best to tell Kraas the truth. "When I offered you a job I wasn't lying about looking for an apprentice, because I was. But after you began working for me I realized that you and I are too different in our approaches to magic. You're ingenious when it comes to devising illusions and effects, but you don't have the imagination or soul to perform real magick."

"Magick with a *K*, right?" Kraas asked the question as if he'd just run up against a wall he'd slammed into many, many times before.

Rantiki nodded. "As a technical assistant and back-room boy, there are none better, Martin. In fact, I wouldn't hesitate to put you in the same league as Houdini's most-trusted assistant, Franz Kukol."

Kraas let out a sigh of exasperation.

"But you just don't have what it takes to be the kind of magician who can take over for me when I'm gone. You know all the secrets of the trade, but it's not enough to know how to do the tricks, you have to have something in here…" he tapped a thumb against his chest. "Romano has it, you don't."

"After all these years." Kraas shook his head.

"You must understand, it's nothing personal. I just think Romano is better suited for the responsibility of carrying on with the Rantiki name."

"But he's still wet behind the ears…."

"A diamond in the rough, Martin. He has the potential to be one of the greats."

"After all the effects and illusions I've designed…" Kraas said, obviously not listening to what Rantiki had to say.

"All of which were spectacular," Rantiki said honestly. "Which is exactly why I want to keep you working for me. Of course, if you wish to go out on your own, or work for someone else, I'll match their salary offer and then some, but I won't stand in your way."

Kraas turned and stomped off.

Rantiki watched him leave, figuring it was the last he'd ever see of him.

After Kraas slammed the bedroom door on his way out, the room fell silent and Rantiki slumped back in his seat, physically drained by the confrontation. Kraas was an excellent assistant and one of Rantiki's most valuable assets. He'd hate to lose Kraas, but something told him that his long-time technical advisor would be back before long.

And that might even be worse than losing him altogether.

PART TWO

APPRENTICE

7

Kraas was nowhere to be seen the rest of the day, but work on the new illusion seemed to go all right without him. Maybe even better than all right, especially for Romano.

They worked on the reluctant-assistant version of the sawing through a woman effect. While the trick leg and arm had originally been made to fit Susie Wand, Rantiki suggested Romano get his proverbial feet wet by taking an active role in the illusion by playing the part of the reluctant assistant.

No one seemed to object, especially Susie, who was perhaps getting a little old for such a physically demanding illusion. She gladly gave the trick over to Romano.

And Romano ran away with the part.

Although he'd never gone in for acting before, he played a convincingly reluctant assistant, so much so that the other on-stage assistants almost had to carry him onto the stage and push him into the box.

"Very good," laughed Rantiki. "I've never been known for comedic magic, but I certainly can play the part of a straight man." His eyes grew large as he stroked his white beard—the quintessential mad scientist.

Romano was enjoying himself immensely, and although he didn't want to upstage Rantiki in his own show, he had an idea on how to make the illusion even better.

"What if I was secured inside the box with a handcuff or two?" he said. "I could escape, and then be bound by even stronger shackles, two or three times until you have to nail me into the box. It would give the final part of the trick a better effect."

"Yes, it would," said Rantiki. "And it would really *get* them, wouldn't it?" He looked at the others standing around the shop. "All right, then. Get two sets of cuffs and a pair of leg shackles. We're going to have some fun with this."

"Where are we going?" Romano asked, getting into Rantiki's black Lexus, his favorite car and the one he always used for personal transportation.

"We're heading into town," Rantiki said. "To a special place. There are some people there I'd like you to meet."

"Friends of yours?"

"Yes."

"Fellow magicians?"

"Yes."

"All right!"

Rantiki took his time behind the wheel and drove cautiously eastward along the expressway heading toward Las Vegas.

Romano enjoyed the slow ride through the city, but nothing could compare to the drive through the neon tube that was downtown Las Vegas after the sun went down. Whenever they drove along Fremont Street there was color all around as the lights dazzled their eyes. Beginning with greetings from the tall neon cowboy, Vegas Vic, and sexy neon cowgirl, Sassy Sally, it was like entering another world, a veritable playground.

Disneyland for grown-ups.

"Is it around here?" Romano asked, his eyes still dazzled by the glow of colorful neon.

"Just behind the downtown casinos," Rantiki said. A moment later he turned onto Stewart Avenue. "Here it is."

Romano read the sign above the door, a small, innocuous little lighted sign (and not neon light either) that told the world that this place was just another bar. "The Magic Box," he said. "I've heard of this place." He looked at Rantiki. "Isn't this where most of the Vegas magicians come to talk shop and try out new tricks?"

"That's right."

"I've always wanted to come here. This place and the Magic Castle in Hollywood."

"Well, you're here," Rantiki said, parking the car. "And my guess is you'll get to the Magic Castle soon enough."

They got out of the car, walked to the Magic Box and stepped inside.

At first Romano was a bit disappointed by the place. It was dark and a little dingy. It looked more like Torchy's than a place where some of the best magicians in the world got together.

But then he saw something, or more correctly *someone*, that immediately changed his mind about the place. Sitting alone at a small round table close to one wall was an old man wearing a faded red fez. The man had several decks of cards on the table in front of him and another deck in his right hand. Without looking at his hand, and seemingly without any conscious thought, he was manipulating the cards, fanning them, turning them over, and cutting the deck in a continuous series of smoothly flowing movements.

"That's Jimmy Platt!" Romano said. "I read his book."

Rantiki smiled proudly.

Romano hurried over to the old man's table. "Mind if I sit down?"

The old man stopped what he was doing and looked at Romano. "It's a free country!" he said.

Romano waited for him to continue his card manipulations, but he just sat there staring into his glass.

"I hope you don't mind if I watch you?" Romano asked.

Platt looked annoyed. "I usually get paid for doing my act, kid."

Although Romano was almost twenty now, he didn't mind being called a kid by the likes of Platt. The man looked so old everybody had to be a kid in his eyes.

"He's with me, Jimmy," Rantiki said, taking the third seat at the table.

"Oh, so you're the one, eh?"

Romano looked from Platt to Rantiki, then shrugged. "Yeah, I guess I am."

"Then you watch closely, kid," said Platt. "Maybe you might learn something."

Platt rolled up his sleeves and picked up a deck of cards. After making the cards vanish, he began presenting them one by one, then in a split fan, followed by more single cards.

While Platt performed, people at nearby tables took notice and began to watch.

None more closely than Romano.

Platt was a skilled performer, there was no doubt about that. But his fingers were old and stiffened by the passage of time. While he still performed the trick well enough to fool the layperson, Romano could clearly see the man's back-palm movement. Romano was impressed, but he wished he could have seen the man perform in his prime.

"How's that, kid?" Platt said when he was done.

The people around Platt applauded.

"That was great," said Romano. "Mind if I try?"

"No, go ahead. Let's see what you can do."

More people gathered around and Romano realized that he was about to show up an old master; perhaps it would have been better just to keep his big mouth shut.

But more and more people gathered round, and with a captive audience waiting, Romano's natural instincts toward showmanship and style kicked in. He couldn't walk away from the table now even if he wanted to. So he picked up two decks of cards from the table, stood up, and after a moment's preparation began doing the exact same manipulations Platt had done a moment before. But instead of using one hand like Platt, Romano used both hands, the fingers of which were nimble and dexterous with youth. His back-palm and split fan movements were so clean, so fluid that there was no question he was performing the technique with the level of skill and presence required to create a sense of pure magic, as opposed to Platt's exhibition of age-old skill.

When he was done, a slightly louder round of applause spread through the room.

"How's that…" Romano said, resisting the temptation to say, 'Grampa' and settling on, "Mr. Platt?"

"Please," he said. "Call me Jimmy." He extended his hand and shook Romano's firmly. Then he looked over to Rantiki. "He is good, isn't he?"

Rantiki nodded.

"You're good, kid," Platt said, still shaking Romano's hand. "Just remember who your friends are. Okay?"

"I will," Romano said, not knowing why it was important.

"Come on, Romano," said Rantiki, "there's someone you have to meet before you butt heads with anyone else in here." He grabbed Romano by the arm and led him to a table at the other end of the room.

There, a middle-aged man sat alone at the table, sipping a drink from a highball. He had a full head of black hair cut short and parted on the left as well as a neatly-trimmed van dyke mustache and beard. His glasses were plain and made with thin wire rims. If Romano hadn't known better, he might have guessed the man was a high-school English teacher.

"Harry Reddington, Jr." he said.

"And you are?" Reddington asked politely.

"This is Romano Minardi," Rantiki said before Romano had a chance to answer. "The young magician I was telling you about."

"Oh really," Reddington said, looking Romano over.

"It's a pleasure to meet you, sir," Romano said, offering his hand. "I've read almost everything that was ever written about your father, and I never missed you on any of the talk-shows you appeared on when I was a little kid."

Reddington smiled. "Was it that long ago? Thanks for reminding me."

Once again Romano wondered if he hadn't put his foot in his mouth. "I'm sorry, I didn't mean—"

"That was a joke, young man," Reddington said, offering Romano and Rantiki a seat. "The great one here—" he gestured to Rantiki "—has told me a lot about you, but I want to hear it from you myself."

"Me?"

"Yes," Reddington said, making himself comfortable. "Tell me all about yourself. Start from the beginning and don't leave anything out."

"I'll get us something to drink," Rantiki said, getting up from the table.

Romano just sat there, amazed that someone of Reddington's stature— a magician on the same level as Rantiki—would show so much interest in a no-name apprentice from Montreal. It was too strange and just a little too good to be true.

"Go ahead," Reddington prodded. "Talk to me. Where were you born?"

Romano took a deep breath and began. "My parents emigrated from Italy in the early 1960s. They settled in one of the poorer neighborhoods in Montreal...."

Reddington listened intently, his attention never wavering. Apparently, he truly did want to hear it all.

So Romano told him.

Martin Kraas sat alone on a stool in the bar at the Gold Spike Hotel and Casino in downtown Las Vegas. The place was cheap—the kind of place the cabbies and locals called a grind joint—and he could get loaded here and not have to worry about ending up without enough money for cab fare home.

Besides, the Gold Spike seemed like an appropriate place to get hammered in since that was just the particular item Rantiki had screwed him with. All those years of hard work, all the illusions he'd created, all the refinements he'd made to the act, turning Randall Wynne into The Great Rantiki.

For what?

So a little wop from Montreal could come along and take his place as Rantiki's successor. So a kid who didn't know his ass from a hole in the ground could come along and steal the money, fame and glory that were rightfully his.

The golden spike all right, right up the you-know-where.

He still couldn't believe it.

"Bartender," he said. "Anoffer one. No, make it two."

The bartender looked at him a little strangely. People didn't usually come to the Gold Spike to get wasted. It was a place for blue-haired old ladies to play penny slots and dime roulette so they could feel like high rollers without losing more than a couple of bucks.

"You sure you're in the right place, buddy?" asked the bartender. "Maybe you should try the Las Vegas Club or the Golden Nugget down the street."

"I said two mores," demanded Kraas, lifting his hand off the bar and making a twenty-dollar bill suddenly appear between his fingers.

"Whatever you say, pal," the bartender said, beginning to mix a couple of drinks.

"And while you're at it," said Kraas, "bring me the telephone, will ya."

The bartender brought him two drinks and a black cordless phone.

Kraas took a sip of his bourbon and water and picked up the telephone. He'd had a standing offer from Jerry Baker, the Christian fundamentalist talk-show host based in Las Vegas, for several years now, but he'd never really given it much thought.

There had never been any reason to.

Until now.

He fished inside his wallet for a slip of paper with a phone number on it. The paper was old and the writing smudged, but he could still make out the number. He dialed it and got a sleepy female voice on the other end.

"Hello?"

"You work for Jerry Baker, right?"

"I'm one of his producers."

"My name's Martin Kraas. I work for The Great Rantiki."

"Yes." The voice suddenly seemed awake.

"Tell Jerry I'm interested."

"Are you sure?"

"Yeah." He took a sip of his drink. "I'm sure."

It was well after midnight when Romano and Rantiki left the Magic Box. The visit had been so much fun that if it hadn't been closing time the two of them would still have been inside.

Romano had never seen Rantiki so animated. He'd strutted around the room like a proud father, ushering Romano from table to table and introducing him to everyone as if he'd just finished a stint of military service and had a shoe-box's worth of medals across his chest.

"Here he is," he'd say presenting Romano to yet another table of magicians and illusionists.

"Isn't he something?" he'd say after Romano did a close-up trick in honor of his new acquaintances.

He hadn't minded it all that much at first, but after a while he couldn't help feeling as if he were on display like a new trick or gag. A moment later he dismissed the thought. Perhaps it was to be expected. After all, he was Rantiki's new apprentice and maybe the man was simply proud.

Then what was it that bothered him?

He gave it some further thought.

The single strangest thing about the evening had been the way everybody had treated him as if he suddenly belonged there, as if he were one of them, their equal. Romano knew—with a knowledge he was more certain of than anything else in the world—that, as a magician, he would one day be their equal, perhaps even their better, but for now he was still just an apprentice and worthy only of being treated as such.

The way things had gone lately had all been *too* right. He thought about that a moment, and suddenly began to have bad feelings about the way it was all speeding forward.

Things were not as they appeared.

Perhaps something was amiss, maybe even terribly wrong.

"What's going on?" Romano said when they were about halfway to the car.

"What do you mean?"

Romano stopped on the sidewalk and waited for Rantiki to stop and turn around.

"First of all, Martin Kraas."

"What about him?"

"He works for you for years and is under the impression that he's your unofficial apprentice. And then suddenly he's not, and I am. Why? I don't know. Then he walks out on you and you don't really seem to care all that much."

Rantiki said nothing.

"And then in there." He gestured in the direction of the Magic Box. "Everybody's treating me like *I'm* The Great Rantiki; no, better than that, like I'm Jesus H. Christ."

"What do you mean?" Rantiki said, his tone of voice suggesting that Romano was more than a little out of his mind.

"Like Jimmy Platt…. That guy was working clubs when I was still in diapers, but I showed him up in front of everyone and he's patting me on the back saying 'you're good, kid.'"

Rantiki remained silent.

"He should have told me off, I had it coming to me. What the hell is going on here?"

Rantiki let out a sigh. "You're a smart young man, Romano. Obviously too smart to be deceived for long by an old mage like me."

"What are you talking about?"

"Come on," Rantiki said. "Let's go for a walk."

Rantiki turned and starting walking.

Reluctantly, Romano followed.

8

They turned south on 3rd Street, heading toward the Lady Luck Casino.

"Tell me something, Romano," Rantiki began. "Have you ever noticed that things have happened in your life that sometimes defy explanation?"

"You mean magic?"

"No, not magic, things during the course of your normal everyday life, astonishing coincidences…." He paused as if thinking of a new tack. "Did you ever wish something would happen and then by some miracle it did?"

Romano thought about it. There'd been plenty of things that had happened that he couldn't explain, but those sort of things happened to everybody now and then. And as far as wishing for something and then having it happen, well, he'd always been lucky that way, that's all. "I guess so."

"Give me an example."

"Well, I got a job working for you. That's something I've always wanted."

"No," Rantiki said patiently. "Something smaller and much more specific."

Romano thought about it. There had been that fight with his father just before he left home. The way his father had fallen backward and put his hand on the stove had been uncanny. It was a good example of what Rantiki was talking about, but he'd rather not get into his troubled homelife. He tried to think of something else, and then it occurred to him. "After I saw your show for the first time and wanted to get backstage to meet you, the security guard wouldn't let me by."

"Yes."

"So I figured I needed some kind of distraction to get him away from the door. A second later, a woman exiting the theater started having a heart attack in the aisle and the security guard was forced to leave the door unattended in order to see what was going on."

"Exactly!"

"But that was just a lucky break, a coincidence. Wasn't it?"

Rantiki stopped on the sidewalk, the neon glow of the Lady Luck giving his face a strange, fiery hue. "It was a coincidence, Romano. But luck had nothing to do with it."

Romano just looked at him.

"It wasn't luck. You *made* it happen."

Romano's eyebrows rose up in a high arc.

"Yes, I know," said Rantiki. "It's a difficult concept to accept and I've never been able to introduce it to someone without getting that kind of response."

Romano continued to look at Rantiki skeptically.

"Perhaps a little demonstration is in order," said Rantiki. "Come, I'll show you."

They turned into the Lady Luck.

The lobby was full of tourists, old women, retirees and a few others who looked like the type who spent most of their lives tiring out their arms on the slots.

They walked casually through the room, Romano following Rantiki's lead, the older man appearing to be looking for something in particular.

"Okay, here," he said at last.

They were standing at a three-dollar blackjack table where a heavyset black woman in a T-shirt and pants was the only one playing the dealer. She was sitting to the dealer's right at Third Base and had a five and a three showing.

"Her next card will be a three," Rantiki said with certainty.

Romano felt a quiver.

The dealer placed a three on the table.

"Her next card will be a ten."

There was that same strange feeling again, and then the dealer dealt the woman a ten, giving her twenty-one in all.

"Praise the Lord!" she cried.

Romano looked at Rantiki suspiciously. "How did you do that?" he asked, his voice barely a whisper.

"Magick."

"Oh, come on."

"Magick…with a *K*."

"There's a difference?"

"Yes."

"You can't predict—"

Rantiki silenced Romano as the dealer dealt another hand. The woman was looking at a five and a seven. "What card would you like her to have next?"

"How about a six."

Rantiki nodded. Again there was a quiver, and the woman was dealt a six.

She had eighteen showing, but her success with the last hand had made her greedy. She foolishly asked for another card.

"What should it be?" Rantiki asked.

"A three," Romano said, not wanting the woman to lose on account of him.

Another quiver, and the woman was dealt a three, giving her another twenty-one.

"Hallelujah!" she whooped.

Rantiki's body suddenly stiffened as if it were racked by an intense pain. He was short of breath and had to struggle in order to remain upright.

"Are you okay?" Romano asked.

"Find me a chair. I must…sit down."

Romano put his arm around Rantiki and the two of them limped toward a comfortable-looking peach-colored couch without attracting too much attention from the people in the casino. They sat down and after a few moments Rantiki regained some composure, but still looked for all the world as if he'd just received a hard punch to the stomach.

"Are you all right?" Romano asked.

"I'll be fine." He was already breathing easier.

"What happened back there?"

"All the threes must have already been played."

Romano just looked at Rantiki.

"Let's get out of here," Rantiki said, lifting himself off the couch and heading for the front door.

Romano followed, knowing more but understanding less than when he'd first come in.

"You see, Romano," Rantiki said as they made their way west along Fremont Street, past the Fremont and Four Queens Casinos. "I am a magician and illusionist, but I am also a mage. There's a difference, a big difference. A stage magician performs magic, does parlor tricks and illusions, but a mage has the power to perform real magick—" he said the word in a way that put an emphasis on the second syllable "—which is far more than tricks; it is the act of altering reality itself."

"Is that what you were doing in the casino, altering reality?" Romano couldn't help but be skeptical.

"After I told you what the next card would be, did you feel something odd? Did it feel as if something passed through your body?"

Romano thought back to the scene in the casino and remembered the strange sensations rippling through him. "Yeah, it was like a shiver or something."

"That was Quintessence you felt, the raw stuff of magick, flowing from me to the deck of cards, changing the face of the next card being dealt from the deck."

Romano thought about it for a while. The feeling had been familiar, as if he'd felt it before dozens of times. And then he remembered he'd felt the same thing the night he'd first met Rantiki. "That's how you got out of the ropes so quickly, wasn't it?"

Rantiki smiled. "That's right."

Romano slowed his pace, thinking about the possibilities of having such amazing abilities. "But if you can change things like cards and ropes with magick—" Romano pronounced it like Rantiki had "—then why aren't you working the tables, or playing the slots? You could be a millionaire in a couple of hours."

Rantiki laughed. "Unfortunately, Romano, nothing in life is so easy, and magick is no exception to that rule."

"Why not?"

Rantiki took a deep breath. "There are two kinds of magick, static and dynamic. Dynamic magick is more of the kind you usually associate with wizards and warlocks. You know, blazing fireballs and lightning bolts. Spectacular, but very, very dangerous. That kind of magick is more commonly called vulgar magick because it is an obscenity to the laws of reality.

"Static magick on the other hand, a magick which is also known as coincidental magick, is more refined, intelligent, and easy to conceal, because it insinuates itself into the fabric of reality. Everything done via coincidental magick must fit within the limits of reality, remaining indistinguishable from the events of normal everyday life."

He paused a moment to see if Romano was following him.

Romano's intense gaze remained unwavering.

Rantiki continued.

"When you told me what the woman's next card should be, I made it so. I changed the next card into a three. It was coincidental magick because who could know what the next card would be? It might as well have been the one you suggested as any other card in the deck."

"But what happened at the end, when you suddenly felt ill?"

"Ah, you see, you asked for another three. It's likely that all four threes in the deck had already been played, therefore making the next card a three wasn't coincidental anymore. Suddenly the magick became vulgar because I had to alter reality in order to make it a three. When that happened, there was Paradox."

"You mean something that couldn't be explained?"

"Precisely. It was something that couldn't be explained as a coincidence."

"But there might have been an extra three in the deck," Romano said. "Maybe the manufacturer made a mistake."

"In any other part of the country I might have gotten away with it because of just such an explanation, but this is Las Vegas. If a card company put five threes in a deck just once, it wouldn't be selling cards to the casinos."

"So there could be no explanation for an extra three other than the use of vulgar magick."

"That's right, and when that happens, the forces which preserve reality were moved to punish me for unraveling it, even so slightly. That was the pain I felt after the final three was dealt. I used to be able to handle Paradox better in my youth, but God knows I'm an old man now…too old."

Romano nodded. It all sounded so fascinatingly mysterious, but he still didn't understand where he fit in to all of it. "Forgive me for being so self-centered, but how does all this relate to me and the way I was being treated at the Magic Box?"

"Patience," Rantiki said. They were in front of Binion's Horseshoe Hotel and Casino, home of the World Series of Poker. "Let's go in and get a coffee. I'll explain the rest to you inside."

"All right."

They found a coffee shop at the far end of the hotel, away from the casino. Romano ordered a decaffeinated coffee, Rantiki an espresso. When the two coffees arrived, Rantiki began to explain.

Romano lit a cigarette and listened.

"I'm a mage," Rantiki said. "I can perform magick, both coincidental and vulgar, because I have been Awakened. You, Romano, are currently a Sleeper, but you will Awake very soon, and when you do, you will be more powerful a mage than any that have come before you. Including me."

Romano was stunned. He'd always felt he was different, but he'd always felt it was because he was such an oddball. But here was Rantiki telling him that he was different because he was special, more special than he could ever imagine. It was all too…incredible. "How do you know that?"

"I've seen your Avatar."

"My what?"

"Your Avatar. It's something each human possesses. It's a measure of your ability to perform magick. On some people it's dim, barely even detectable."

"And mine?"

"Burns brighter than any I've ever seen."

Romano was beginning to understand. "So the people at the Magic Box were all being nice to me because they figured I might be a powerful mage some day and they didn't want to piss me off?"

"Not *might* be a powerful mage," Rantiki said. "*Will* be." A pause. "And yes, that was part of the reason for it."

Romano wasn't sure whether to be flattered or offended. "And was that also the reason you offered me a job so quickly, then took me on as an apprentice?"

Rantiki nodded. "You're a very special young man, and I didn't want to lose you to the Technocracy."

Romano sighed. "Don't tell me there's more to this stuff."

EDO VAN BELKOM

"Yes, I'm afraid there is," Rantiki said, his eyes growing wide. "Much more."

They ordered two more coffees and something to eat.

They talked for hours.

Rantiki explained to Romano that he was apprenticed to become a Traditions mage and, like everyone else in the Magic Box, a member of the Cult of Ecstasy. He told him that the Magic Box was more than just a meeting place, that it was a Node, which collected and stored Quintessence. That it was a very special place, to be revered, respected and protected.

He also explained to Romano why he'd started smoking.

"Every Cult of Ecstasy member requires a vice in order to work his or her magick. It helps to keep it focussed. You are slowly becoming a heavy smoker, and your vice is nicotine."

Romano nodded in realization. It had seemed strange to him at the time and as if there were no possible connection between the two, but Romano had felt that his magic had improved, become smoother and more polished, since he'd taken up smoking. Now he knew why.

"In my younger days I drank far too much alcohol," Rantiki continued, giving a little laugh. "Certainly far more than was required for the purposes of magick. That's why these days I prefer caffeine. I don't sleep all that much, but I always know where I am." He pointed to Romano's cigarettes. "You might want to think about quitting those sometime too."

At the end of their talk, Romano's head ached from the sudden influx of data. Funny thing was, they'd only scratched the surface. There were so many questions he wanted to ask. Where to begin?

"What about Houdini?"

"What about him?" Rantiki said, seemingly annoyed.

"Was he a mage?"

"Yes, but he was a Technomancer, and admittedly a great one. Perhaps even the Technocracy's greatest."

"Really?"

"Yes. He began life as a Traditions mage, but his career never really took off until he gave up magick and became solely concerned with the manipulation of physical reality. After becoming a Technomancer, he spent much of his time seeking out and discrediting as many mages as he could. Every time he denounced a mage and was able to explain their performance by purely physical means, their career was over, while his fame soared ever higher."

"Is that why you don't see too many spirit mediums today?"

"One of the reasons," said Rantiki. "Houdini almost singlehandedly wiped out the profession. But I don't think that kind of thing would fly today anyway. These days people are too sophisticated to be fooled by parlor tricks, even if they are performed with magick."

Romano was silent. Learning that his idol had not been exactly what he appeared and was an enemy of what Romano was destined to become left him with a hollow feeling of disappointment that almost soured the knowledge that he would soon become a mage.

After a moment he asked, "Are there any Technomancers performing as stage magicians today?"

"A few, the most notable of them being Penn and Teller. The way they've 'exposed' the secrets behind several classic tricks hasn't made them very popular among magicians, or mages for that matter. A few of us can't wait until they head back to New York City."

Romano nodded.

"C'mon," said Rantiki. "It's late." He glanced at his watch. "Really late."

Romano got up from the table a changed man, literally a different person from the one that had sat down. Suddenly there was an even bigger world of opportunities open to him and he was eager to take up its challenge.

Rantiki let Romano drive home. By the time they reached Rancho Rantiki, Romano had to nudge the older man awake. "Good morning," he said.

Rantiki's eyes fluttered open. The sun was indeed peeking over the eastern horizon. "Get some rest," he told Romano. "I'll see you at lunch."

They went to bed, Rantiki to the main house, Romano to his quarters on the compound.

Romano tried to sleep, but he couldn't. It was all so new and fascinating...not to mention hard to believe. Here he was, Romano Minardi, the poor son of a factory worker from Montreal, destined to be the next great Las Vegas mage.

He stared at the ceiling, dreaming with his eyes wide open. After a bit, when he knew his father would be out of the house on his way to work, he decided to give his mother a call.

"Hallo?"

It was the voice of his father.

Romano was speechless, stunned that his father—as punctual as a Swiss clock—was still at home and apparently very late for work.

"Hallo?" his father said again.

A second ticked.

"Papa!" Romano said at last, the word popping from his mouth like a pair of firecrackers going off. "It's Romano."

"Who?" Years of work in the packing plant had left the man a little hard of hearing. Or maybe his hearing had gotten worse in the last year or so.

"Romano! Romano!"

The phone clicked dead.

There was nothing but silence for several moments, then the hum of a dial tone. He hung up the phone and lay back in bed, sick to his stomach.

How different a feeling would he have had if his mother had answered? Like night and day.

He thought of his mother, longing to talk to her and tell her that he'd made a success of himself, that he was going to be the best *mago* he could be, the best anyone could be. If only she had answered the phone instead of him.

Maybe if he waited a few more hours he could—

The telephone rang.

Romano picked it up. "Hello?"

"Romano?"

"Mama?"

"*Si.*"

"How did you get this number?"

"Your father wouldn't tell me who called. I had a feeling maybe it was you, but he wouldn't say yes or no. So when he went to work I pressed the button on the phone that says redial and then you answered."

Romano thought about it. Pressing the redial button on a telephone only dialed the last number dialed out on that phone. There were such things as call-back features, but for that you had to dial *69 or something like it in order for it to work. It was virtually impossible for his mother to get a connection the way she said she had.

Impossible, or an incredible coincidence.

A coincidence.

Like coincidental magick.

He had been thinking hard about his mother calling him, maybe even wishing that she might. Maybe he'd had something to do with making it happen.

He shook his head in disbelief and resigned himself to being happy that he had his mother on the line to talk to.

"I guess it was just a lucky connection or something," he said at last.

"Yes…so, are you still alive?" she asked.

Romano smiled at that. It was the same thing she said when he called her after being late for supper. The words had always annoyed him before, but now they felt good to hear.

"Yeah, I'm still alive," he said.

"What have you been doing?"

"A lot of things, Ma," Romano said.

"Like what?"

Romano lay back on the bed and told her.

9

"That's not quite right, is it?" Rantiki said as he looked at Romano wearing the fake arm and leg that were supposed to cap the reluctant-assistant illusion.

"I could try and do—" Romano began, only to be interrupted by Rantiki.

"It's not the presentation, it's the prostheses. They don't look real enough."

Everyone fell silent, as if Rantiki's point had been obvious but no one had wanted to be the first to say it.

The only way the trick could work was if the fakes were indistinguishable from the real thing so that it actually looked as if Romano's leg and arm had been put back incorrectly. There was a lot they could do with lighting, but the fakes had to be good to start with or the whole illusion wouldn't work.

"I think I could do better with another set," said Graham Chambers, a former underling of Kraas's who had been thrust into the role of senior technical advisor a little before his time.

"Very well, try again," said Rantiki. "This is too good a showpiece to give up on."

Just then the door to the workshop opened, and standing in the doorway was Martin Kraas.

Everyone stopped what they were doing and looked at Kraas as if he were a dead man just washed up on shore.

Rantiki, however, didn't seem all that surprised. "You're back," he said, as if Kraas had just returned from a drive into town to pick up pizzas.

"Yes."

"To collect your things, or to stay?"

Kraas glanced about the workshop, looking everyone in the eye. When he looked at Romano he broke the connection after a second, quickly moving on to the person next to him.

"To stay," he said at last.

Something akin to relief swept the room as everyone slowly let out their breath. Chambers looked most relieved of all, since now he could resume the role of student and didn't have to worry about the success or failure of the illusion riding squarely on his shoulders.

Romano didn't feel so good about Kraas's return. While he was an invaluable member of Rantiki's stage show and his knowledge of equipment and apparatus would virtually ensure the new show's success, there was something wrong about him coming back. He should have been out finding work with one of Rantiki's rivals, or putting together a show of his own, anything that would show Rantiki that he'd made a mistake choosing Romano over him. That's what Romano would have done. That's what any ambitious performer would have done. By all rights the setback should have been a turning point in Kraas's career. But he was back, making the incident little more than a bump in the road.

It just didn't feel right.

"Good, good," Rantiki said, shaking Kraas's hand and slapping him on the shoulder. "Now…" he picked up the fakes and brought them to Kraas, talking to him as if he'd never gone away. "You see the problem Graham had with these."

Kraas looked them over, then turned to Chambers. "You still have the molds?"

Chambers nodded.

"You'll have a new pair in a couple of days."

"Excellent," said Rantiki. "I'm glad to have you back."

Romano wasn't so sure.

Despite Romano's initial misgivings about Kraas's return, things went smoothly for the next couple of months. Rehearsals were well executed and Kraas seemed genuinely interested in the show's success. If he was still bitter about Romano's position as apprentice, Romano wasn't aware of it. Although they didn't talk to each other much, they were able to interact on a professional level, something they both seemed grateful for.

Away from rehearsal, Romano was immersed in his study of magick. Each night Rantiki would instruct him in the Protocols, the codes of honor followed by all mages of the Traditions. He also gave him several simple rotes, or magickal effects, to practice over the next couple of days. Although the rotes Romano first tried were basic things like creating balls of light, and levitating objects, he was still unable to perform any since he hadn't fully Awakened yet. Nevertheless, he continued to practice them, never becoming frustrated at his failure to produce an effect.

Rantiki was pleased, realizing that Romano's years of isolated practice of magic tricks and illusions—sometimes practicing a certain trick for years before getting it just *right*—had prepared him well for the rigors of being a mage.

Soon, Romano began learning about the more difficult rotes, especially those having to do with Time. As a member of the Cult of Ecstasy, much of Romano's study was concentrated on Time rotes because Time was the sphere of magick most closely linked with the Cult. Eventually, Time would become Romano's own sphere of magick, the type of magick he would specialize in.

As his studies continued, he learned the mechanics behind more specific Time rotes, and much to Rantiki's surprise and delight, he also asked to learn about rotes in the other spheres of magick such as Correspondence, Entropy, Force, Life, Matter, Prime and Spirit.

Rantiki was somewhat leery of teaching Romano too much too fast, but Romano was so inquisitive and insistent on knowing everything Rantiki could teach him, that the lessons continued on at an accelerated pace. After a while, it was Rantiki who found it difficult to keep up with his protégé, as if the fountain of his knowledge was barely enough to quench his student's thirst.

One thing was for certain, they were both looking forward to his Awakening so he could put into practice the rotes he'd so far only been able to learn in theory.

He would have to Awaken sooner or later.

More likely sooner than later.

It was only a matter of time.

The first sign of it came one day when Romano was consciously able to slip a bit of coincidental magick into his everyday life.

Kraas had sent him looking for a Phillips screwdriver in the workshop. He'd looked for one for more than five minutes, but all he could come up with were the slotted kind. Then it occurred to him that there was nothing to say a Phillips screwdriver couldn't be hidden beneath the group of slotted screwdrivers.

And then, as if by magick…

The screwdriver just happened to be there.

"Got it," he said, bringing the screwdriver to Kraas. Rantiki looked at him curiously, somehow knowing he'd used coincidental magick to find the screwdriver. Romano smiled, as if to ask if his harmless little bit of magick had been okay.

Rantiki nodded.

And he handed the screwdriver to Kraas.

Opening night at the Flamingo.

Weird Science.

Rantiki had insisted on the name. Although no one else understood Rantiki's reasoning, Romano understood it perfectly. Rantiki was making a statement, a commentary…he was thumbing his nose at the Technocracy. And he was having more fun with his stage show than ever before. But as much as Rantiki was enjoying himself, Romano couldn't help but feel that he was tempting fate. Making a mockery of science was a sure way to draw the attention of the Technocracy, perhaps even their ire.

He'd expressed his concern to Rantiki, but Rantiki said he was too old to be of concern to the Technomancers. He was past his prime, well past. Technomancers were more concerned with younger mages, the ones with the ability to really rip into the fabric of reality.

"You mean, mages like me?"

"That's right."

All of a sudden Romano didn't feel worried for Rantiki anymore. Now he was worried for himself.

"Relax," said Rantiki. "You haven't even Awakened yet."

The show began slowly with solemn pipe organ music playing as the curtains rose up onto a Doctor-Frankenstein-like laboratory complete with bubbling beakers and jumping sparks.

Rantiki made his entrance by emerging from a coffin. He was dressed in a blood-stained white labcoat, his white hair sticking up wildly from his head like flames, giving him a look of absolute madness.

The audience spent a few moments taking in the set, then applauded heartily.

Romano looked on from backstage. If they were applauding for the set alone, then it was a good bet that the show would be a hit. Romano took satisfaction in knowing he'd had a small part to play in the show's success.

He'd made his contribution.

Now he couldn't wait to get onstage.

The first illusion in the show brought Susie Wand onto the stage dressed in a costume that made her look like an early experiment in reviving the dead. Rantiki set her onto a platform at one end of the stage, wrapped her in paper, then used the pulse of a huge strobe light to set the paper ablaze. When the smoke cleared, the resurrected-from-the-dead monstrosity was gone and Susie was now her usual lovely self. And even though she was dressed in rags, the rags were torn in all the right places, giving the act a bit of sex appeal.

This was Las Vegas, after all....

After the first illusion was completed, the show's pace never relented. Each spectacular illusion was followed by an even more spectacular one.

The penultimate illusion of the first act was a variation of the age-old spike cabinet invented by P.T. Selbit. However, in keeping with the weird-science theme of the show, the cabinet's spikes were replaced by multi-colored neon tubes.

While Romano had been on stage helping with equipment throughout the first act, he'd never had a pivotal role to play in the show. But with the spike-cabinet routine, it was his turn to step into the spotlight.

They worked the illusion like this: After Rantiki decided that Susie was too lovely to risk in the cabinet, Romano played the eager assistant, getting into the cabinet quite willingly. Then, when he was apparently impaled by the lights, he shrieked and howled in mock pain. After a few tense moments in which Rantiki gave the impression that something might have gone wrong, Romano was released from the cabinet unharmed. However, since a set of lights had been sewn into the lining of his lab coat, it looked as if he'd been made radioactive by the lights passing through his body.

All of which was an elaborate set-up for the final illusion of the first act, the reluctant assistant. After the upright box was brought on stage, Rantiki went looking for Romano. When he couldn't convince him to get into the box, he had him forced inside and handcuffed to the walls of the box.

Romano wailed louder than he'd ever wailed before.

Some people in the audience even gasped in terror.

And then Rantiki locked up the box and cut it into four pieces. After shuffling the pieces of Romano about (never putting him back together as he should be) he settled on a combination that was close enough, but which the audience knew was incorrect.

The box was opened slowly. Romano stood there, an arm where his leg should be, a leg inside the sleeve of his coat.

Romano slowly hobbled off-stage, leering at Rantiki, who placed a hand over his mouth as if to say "Oops!"

The crowd loved it.

And Rantiki was pleased enough by the response that he called Romano back out in order for him to take a bow.

When he came back on stage, this time in one piece (with everything in the right place), the volume of the applause doubled.

The show was going to be a smash.

Romano bowed deeply, drinking in the applause as if it were water to a thirsty man.

He'd never felt more alive in his life.

"That was great, Romano," Susie Wand said, the first to congratulate Romano.

"They loved it!"

"I smell extended run!"

The others all congratulated Romano as he made his way to his dressing room. He was almost there, when he stopped dead in his tracks.

Kraas stood in front of the door to his room. "The show is a hit," he said.

"So far, so good," said Romano.

"They love the set, the equipment I created. It's what's making the show a success."

Romano wasn't sure how to answer. It sounded as if Kraas were trying to dismiss the performer's part in the show, but he didn't have the time to argue with the man. "They love everything about it."

Kraas remained in front of the dressing room door, blocking Romano's way. "But they love the look of it most."

The seconds were ticking away. Romano had to get ready for the second act. He decided to humor the man. "Yeah, they loved your equipment best, man...."

Kraas moved out of the way, and started down the hall with a self-satisfied smirk on his face.

Romano stepped by him. When he was safely inside the room, he muttered loud enough for Kraas to hear, "Especially what Rantiki and I did with it."

Kraas stopped, spun around on his heels.

Romano could hear him approaching, but he closed the door before Kraas could get to it.

Kraas lingered on the other side of the door for a while, then finally walked away.

"Asshole!" Romano mouthed the word, not making a sound.

Still dressed as the mad scientist for the second half of the show, Rantiki did a series of time-honored illusions such as rice, orange and checkers, the floating light bulb and zombie balls, all updated to fit within the weird-science theme. Romano—still playing a somewhat reluctant assistant—was handcuffed to a water pipe on the set and acted as a captive audience for Rantiki's illusions—a literally captive audience.

The audience enjoyed the illusions, but their applause wasn't as enthusiastic as it had been during the first half. The show just didn't have as much spectacle to it in the second half.

As the show neared its end, Susie made several dramatic attempts to free Romano from his confinement. At this point Romano was supposed to free himself from the cuffs, as well as several other restraints which had been added after each time he made an attempt to flee.

Rantiki caught Susie helping Romano and put her back on the platform she'd been on earlier in the show. Rantiki then wrapped her in paper and set her alight.

At this point Romano was supposed to free himself from the final set of handcuffs in order to be well away from the flames when they went up.

But something was wrong.

Although he applied the pressure to the correct point in order to effect a release, the cuffs would not open.

Rantiki saw that Romano was having trouble, but by then it was too late. The paper had been ignited. The flames licked their way up the cone of paper.

EDO VAN BELKOM

Romano concentrated on the cuffs, concentrated....

The heat began to sear his flesh.

And suddenly the cuffs popped open, freeing his hand.

He ran to safety.

The flames died down, and out of the smoke, Susie appeared once more, back in her back-from-the-dead costume.

Romano breathed a sigh of relief.

Rantiki rushed to his side. "Are you all right?"

"The cuff wouldn't open," said Romano. "I'm not sure, but as I was trying to get out, I think I used magick to get it open."

Rantiki nodded. "You did. I felt it."

Romano looked up at him. "Does that mean I'm..."

"Yes, you've Awakened."

Romano smiled.

Rantiki just gave him a pat on the back and turned to face the audience. There was no time for further congratulations now. They still had a show to finish.

Up next was the finale, Rantiki's opportunity to take center stage.

In continuing with the theme of weird science, Susie and Romano acted as if they were conspiring against Rantiki, exacting their revenge against the mad scientist.

Susie, still in costume, snuck up behind Rantiki and gave him a needle in the behind, which apparently rendered him unconscious. After that, she and Romano slipped him into a straitjacket and hung him up by his feet above the stage. Then Susie set fire to the rope from which he was suspended.

After watching the rope burn for several moments, Susie and Romano left the stage. The stage then darkened and a single spotlight fell upon Rantiki.

Milking the situation for as much tension as possible, Rantiki remained unconscious. Only after a few strands of rope began to snap and the rope dropped an inch did he wake up.

He looked around, realized his predicament and feverishly began to make his escape from the straitjacket.

As the rope burned hotter, the spotlight dimmed, until only the burning rope could be seen.

Several seconds later the fire cut through the rope and the flames separated, one set burning above the stage, another set fluttering down onto it.

The crowd gasped.

The next moment the spotlight opened up on Rantiki standing on the stage, straitjacket in hand.

The audience cheered and applauded in a mix of relief and astonishment. It was a truly spectacular end to the show and almost made up for the slow start to the second half.

Rantiki bowed deeply, once, twice, three times.

Then he called for Romano and Susie to join him on the stage.

They ran out and bowed.

Kraas watched from the sidelines.

The mood was festive backstage after the show and plenty of Las Vegas celebrities as well as fellow magicians gathered for the opening-night after-show party. The consensus permeating the room was that *Weird Science* was going to be a huge hit, with a run that would likely be measured in years.

But while Rantiki was eager to celebrate the success of the new show, he avoided the party. Part of it was because he wanted to make a big entrance, but more importantly there was a business matter to attend to.

He walked the halls in search of Kraas.

After a few minutes, he found him onstage, checking out the set.

"Can you explain this?" Rantiki said.

Kraas didn't bother turning around. "Explain what?"

"This!" he said, holding out the handcuffs, the latches on each side broken and looking as if they'd been pried apart with a pair of pliers.

Kraas finally turned around. "What about them?"

"They were the wrong pair," Rantiki said. "These were standard issue, not the trick cuffs we'd used all through rehearsals."

"They opened all right."

"Yes, by some miracle. If it hadn't been for Romano's skill as an escapologist, I might have had a very dead apprentice on my hands. Not only that, but this show would have closed after a single performance and you would've been out of a job."

Kraas took the handcuffs from Rantiki and gave them a closer look. There was an expression of surprise on his face as he inspected the damage Romano had done to them in order to free himself.

EDO VAN BELKOM

"Chambers must have given you the wrong pair," Kraas said, placing the blame on his underling without a moment's hesitation. "I'll give him his walking papers as soon as I find him."

"No you will not!" Rantiki said. He suspected Kraas of negligence, but he couldn't prove it since there was virtually no difference in appearance between regulation cuffs and the handcuffs prepared for the stage. Furthermore, he wasn't about to let some promising young employee go simply in order to have a scapegoat. "What you will do is take full responsibility for the apparatus and equipment used in this show. If something doesn't work, it's *your* fault."

Rantiki remained standing there, silent.

Kraas looked at him, the anger and resentment at Rantiki's words slowly ebbing from his face. Finally, he sighed and nodded.

"Now, can I be confident that something like this will not happen again due to any negligence on your part?"

"Yeah," Kraas said. "It won't happen again."

"Good," Rantiki smiled. "Now, go join the party. Have yourself a good time. You've earned it."

Kraas smiled. "Thanks."

Rantiki avoided the party for another few minutes, checking the dressing rooms in search of Romano. Luckily he found him alone in the first room he tried.

"Are you all right?" Rantiki asked, closing the door behind him.

Romano nodded. "I'm a little spooked."

"Yes, that was a close one, wasn't it?"

"The cuffs wouldn't open. If I'd have known the hasp wasn't going to open, I could have picked it, but I didn't have any picks on me. I didn't think I'd be needing any." Romano's voice was apologetic, as if he thought he'd let Rantiki down.

"Look, if you're going to use magick, saving your life is one of the best reasons I know for using it."

"Is that why I didn't feel any Paradox?"

"No," Rantiki shook his head. "You didn't feel any Paradox because none of the Sleepers in the audience recognized what you did as vulgar magick. You see, everyone was expecting you to release yourself from the cuffs. How that release was made wasn't all that important. That's one of the benefits of being a stage-magician mage. You can sometimes perform vulgar magick right under people's noses. Because they're expecting something magical, the Paradox spirits are rarely notified about the vulgar magick that's been used."

"But if I'd been arrested by police and had broken the handcuffs in a similar way..."

"That would have been vulgar magick," Rantiki said, finishing Romano's sentence. "Enough about that episode now. Kraas figures a real pair of handcuffs were substituted for the special ones. An honest opening-night mistake, perhaps, but one which he assures me will never happen again."

Romano looked at Rantiki as if contemplating Kraas's role in the mix-up.

"Enough of that, now. We put on a fantastic show, and now it's time to enjoy the accolades. There's a party waiting for us to arrive in order for it to begin. Let's go."

Romano stood up. "It was a good show, wasn't it?"

"Best of my career," Rantiki said.

"Mine too," echoed Romano.

The two mages laughed.

Then Rantiki put his arm around Romano and together they headed for the party.

Despite what Rantiki had said about the party, it was in full swing by the time they arrived. Still, the room stopped dead when they entered and then erupted into heartfelt applause, a standing ovation.

Rantiki put up his arms to quiet them down. "Thank you," he said. "But I hope that most of your applause is for the people who really made this show work. By that I mean Martin Kraas—" Kraas raised a glass to Rantiki "—Susie Wand—" she blew him a kiss "—and Romano Minardi." Romano just waved. "Without their help, this show never would have been possible, never mind being any good." There was a little more mild applause, then silence. "Now, ladies and gentlemen..." he paused a moment, raising a fisted hand. A second later, cut paper and streamers shot out from his hand as if from a gun. Then he opened his hand, revealing it to be empty. "...It's party time!"

The room erupted in laughter, applause and general noise.

Romano made his way around the room, saying hello to people he knew. He didn't get very far before Harry Reddington Jr. came up and shook his hand.

"Rantiki is the one you should be congratulating," Romano said. "It was his show."

"You're being modest, young man," Reddington said with a smile. "I've seen all of those illusions dozens of times before. Believe me, it's not the trick that's important, it's the presentation of it that matters."

Romano tried to get a word in, but Reddington kept talking.

"Rantiki told me what parts of the show were your idea and from where I was sitting, those were the parts that made the show."

Romano wasn't about to try to convince the man otherwise anymore. He looked at Reddington and simply said, "Thanks."

"You're a born showman," Reddington said, as if poking Romano in the chest with the words.

"People have been saying I'll go far," Romano said idly.

"Not too far, I hope," Reddington said good-naturedly.

And suddenly it clicked. Reddington was thinking of the Chantry, the Magic Box, and making sure Romano would be a frequent and long-time patron.

"No," Romano said. "Not to worry. I like it here."

And he did.

After all, what was not to like about Las Vegas?

10

After the first three shows, Rantiki decided to make a few minor changes to the act. Instead of opening the second act with his solo illusions, he moved them up to the start of the show. He also decided to shorten the intermission, which pleased the management at the Flamingo to no end since they were considering adding another show to each weeknight and a third on Saturdays.

A younger magician would have jumped at the chance, but Rantiki was an old man who didn't want for money and there was little benefit for him in doing more than one show a night. He was already a star in Las Vegas, if not around the world. Doing twice as many shows wouldn't make him twice as famous.

He put the matter to his employees and assistants.

After hearing Rantiki's manager, Arthur Gardner, lay out the offer of a second show, Romano had only one question: "Will we get twice the money we're getting now?"

"Yeah," the others chimed in around him.

"I'm afraid it's not that simple," said Gardner.

Romano was sure it wasn't, but he couldn't help feeling the same way he had at Torchy's when the bar owner Nick Torchia offered him a job performing magic. The man had been trying to get something for nothing. "What's so difficult about it?" Romano asked. "If they fill up the room twice, then they can pay us all twice as much."

Gardner shook his head, slightly exasperated. He looked at Rantiki as if asking him to do something, but he remained firm in his decision to leave it up to the others involved in the show.

"Look, just about everyone else in town does two shows a night…."

"The Great Rantiki isn't everyone else," Romano said.

Rantiki smiled at this, while everyone else stood silent, no doubt amazed by Romano's cockiness.

"This show's only on a three-month contract. Do you know what you're going to be doing in four months?"

"Yes, I'll be doing this show. If not here, then at another hotel." Romano was beginning to get annoyed with this man, an agent who was supposed to be convincing the Flamingo management Rantiki was worth more, not convincing Rantiki he should settle for less. "Double or nothing, take it or leave it."

"That's right," a few people called out.

He looked once more at Rantiki. Rantiki nodded.

"Double or nothing," Romano repeated.

Gardner left, shaking his head. But he came back a half hour later with a broad grin on his face. "Double it is, then," he said.

Doubling the number of shows required that a couple of illusions be pulled from the act. Romano rode on the truck with Kraas as they brought the few pieces of equipment no longer needed back to Rancho Rantiki.

Neither said a word to each other the entire way.

The buzz swept through the compound like a hot desert wind.

Rancho Rantiki had a visitor.

And not just any visitor either. Jerry Baker was a Las Vegas icon; one of the few people who were immediately associated with the city, like showgirls, like Wayne Newton, like Liberace before his death.

But when news of Baker's visit reached Rantiki, he was hard pressed to be as excited about it as his staff was. Baker was a Bible-thumping Christian fundamentalist with radio and television talk shows that helped him preach his views to a mass audience. Rantiki had a feeling that after the early success of the *Weird Science* show Baker might want to have him appear as a guest on *The Jerry Baker Show*. That in itself might not be a bad thing, since Baker's show was syndicated to television stations all through the Bible Belt, and a good percentage of people in the area made the trek to Las Vegas each year, some more than once.

The problem was that Jerry Baker wasn't interested in advancing the career of anyone other than Jerry Baker. If there was a reason he wanted Rantiki on his show, it was probably so he could shoot his star right out of the sky.

Rantiki decided it would be best to be cautious.

"Jerry Baker's here," Romano said, escorting the talk-show host into the big front room.

Rantiki nodded and Romano stepped aside to let Baker enter.

Rantiki had been expecting Baker to be dressed in his trademark white suit and boots, but instead the man appeared in tailored grey silk with a white shirt and striped tie. The boots were still there, but thankfully they were dark grey instead of white. The only thing that was the same as Rantiki had remembered was the man's hair; it was parted on the right and combed to the side in the shape of an ocean wave, not a single white strand out of place.

"Mr. Baker," Rantiki said, extending his hand and gesturing for Romano to leave the two of them alone.

Romano nodded and backed out of the room.

"The *Great* Rantiki," Baker said.

They shook hands. It all seemed friendly enough, but there was something in the way that Baker said *Great* that told Rantiki this wasn't a social call.

"What can I do for you?"

"Well, last week we signed up two more independents, giving our talk show blanket coverage throughout the southern United States with a total of twenty-five stations."

"That many?" Rantiki said, wondering why he should care.

"Yes, that many." Baker smiled, an almost forced smile that showed off most of his perfect white teeth. Caps probably. "As you can imagine, with that many stations signed on, there's been growing interest in national syndication."

"Congratulations," Rantiki said, graciously. That might explain the switch from all-white suits. White suits didn't play well in Chicago or New York. Then again, he might be saving his whites strictly for television. Too hard to clean.

"Thank you." A pause. "But I'm not here to boast, I'm here to invite you to be a guest on my show. Just you, for a full hour."

Rantiki was flattered. Full hours were usually given to big-name celebrities and movie stars who could carry that much time alone. Rantiki was a celebrity, but not the big-name variety. Sure he could do an illusion or two to fill up some time, but a full hour? Something was fishy.

"I've been performing in Las Vegas for over twenty years, and you've been on the air for five—"

"Seven."

"—seven years. Why the sudden interest in me now?"

Baker smiled again, but this time his grin was just a little bit devilish. "Have you ever seen my show?"

"A couple of times," Rantiki said, then, knowing he couldn't pass up the opportunity, he added, "but never all the way through."

Baker's eyes narrowed and some of the charm was gone from his manner. "Well, if you had been watching lately you'd know that I've renewed my solemn pledge to fight the devil in this Satan's Temple of a city."

"That's very righteous of you."

Baker paused, looking at Rantiki as if sizing him up. "You are a magician."

"Some people think I am."

"The word is derived from the ancient Persian sect of the Magi and means a practitioner of the occult arts, a possessor of supernatural powers."

"Who are you trying to fool? That's the archaic definition of the word. Today it's generally accepted to mean a stage performer who simulates a magician for purposes of entertainment."

Baker raised an admonishing finger. "But in the past you have professed to have the ability to perform true magic."

It was true. He had boasted about his abilities early in his career, and had now lived long enough to regret it. "I've said I can do *magick*." He pronounced it with a hard emphasis on the second syllable. "It's spelled with a *K* on the end. It's something else entirely."

"Magic, or magick. It makes no difference to me. You've said you can perform magic, and the only one who possesses that kind of power is God himself. I'm afraid in your case, it's time to call a spade a spade."

Rantiki laughed. "I assure you, I am not a god, nor do I profess to have any godlike powers."

"But you admit to having the ability to perform real magic...uh, excuse me, *magick*."

Rantiki felt he'd painted himself into a corner. "That's right."

"So if you can do magick, what do you have to fear by appearing on my show? Why don't you come on the show and make a believer out of me?"

"I fear nothing, Mr. Baker. Not you, or your television show. I don't watch your show regularly, but from what I've seen I can tell you that I'm not interested in being treated like a convicted criminal by you, or in suffering the verbal abuse of the angry mob you call a studio audience."

Baker let out a little laugh. Rantiki thought he was becoming angered, but he couldn't be sure. The man was just too hard to read. "You're an old man, Rantiki. If you did possess the power to do magick, you should be ashamed of yourself for wasting those powers performing parlor tricks like some cheap dime-museum magician." He huffed a pitying laugh. "Tricks you're not even doing that well anymore."

Rantiki knew the man was being confrontational in an attempt to bait him into appearing on the show, but he still felt the sting of the man's words. Maybe he could have done more with his life, but he'd loved the stage too much to do anything else. He sighed deeply, strengthening his resolve not to get suckered into doing something he didn't want to do.

"What's more pathetic, my good man, an old dog doing old tricks, or looking for a gangster's vault on live television only to end up getting just what you deserve?"

Rantiki was referring to the live prime-time special Baker had done early in his career, opening up the alleged secret vault of famed Las Vegas mobster Bugsy Siegel on the grounds of the old Fabulous Flamingo. Instead of finding a secret vault, work crews broke through the side of a main drain and were flooded by hundreds of gallons of the city's raw sewage. Baker had been a running joke on late-night television for months (*He was looking for the dirty underworld of Las Vegas—and he found it. Boy did he find it!*) and his career took several years to recover.

The mask concealing Baker's emotions suddenly vanished and anger flared across his face for the first time. "If you don't do my show, I'll do a show on you anyway, exposing you for the fraud that you are."

"If you can do it without me, why should I dignify your show with my presence?" Rantiki realized he was sounding pretentious and condescending, but he'd had enough of Baker.

"For one," Baker said. "If you really can do magick, you can come on the show to defend yourself by proving it."

Rantiki shook his head. "I have nothing to prove, nor do I wish to defend myself or my profession against the likes of you. I'm sorry, Mr. Baker," he said, saying the man's name as if it left a bad taste on his tongue. "But I'll have to decline."

"Suit yourself," Baker said, smiling brightly with his internal charm generators back on line and firing on all cylinders. "I just thought you'd appreciate the chance to save your good name and your profession before they both go to hell...pardon my language."

"Again, thank you for the offer," Rantiki said, gesturing toward the door. "But as far as hell goes, I don't think *I'll* ever be running into you there."

The insult wasn't lost on Baker. His smile soured for a moment, then he spun around and headed out of the room.

When Rantiki heard the front door open and close, he slumped back in his chair and sighed. His body shivered, his hands trembled, and there was a sharp pain in his chest.

"I'm too old for this," he muttered. "Too old."

That night, Rantiki was still feeling the effects of Baker's visit. As he drank his coffee, his cup clinked and clattered against the saucer as if he were a doddering old woman.

Perhaps it was the price of fame, or at least of success.

With the acclaim of his newest show, he'd once again become the most prominent magician in Las Vegas. And now that he was representative of his profession, he was a target for those who would like to bring about its downfall.

It was like the situation that existed between the publishers of men's magazines and feminists. The feminists always went after *Penthouse* and *Playboy*, trying to get their sale banned as being offensive to women even though there were plenty of worse offenders out there—magazines with the names of body parts for titles, that didn't even bother trying to balance their spreads of naked women with insightful articles and interviews, or even words for that matter.

There were plenty of other mages working the casinos on the Strip using vulgar magick in their shows as casually as if it were just another way of lighting the stage. But mages who used magick in their stage shows usually rose rapidly in the ranks, then vanished from the business in a year or two. Some mages, especially those in the music industry, rose meteorically to superstardom, only to suffer quick deaths. People like Jimi Hendrix and Jim Morrison. The only benefit to such a short existence was that the mages left the world at the pinnacle of their existence, ensuring their name would live far longer than would be possible otherwise.

Rantiki, on the other hand, had kept his magick use to a minimum, both on the stage and off, allowing him a slow rise to the top and enabling him to remain there for many, many years.

And now here he was, The Great Rantiki, at the top, the *Playboy* of Las Vegas magicians, except unlike the magazine and its stream of gorgeous women, this *Playboy* was showing signs of age. Arthritis, rheumatism, a bad heart and a network of brittle nerves that could be frazzled by a few words from a self-righteous Bible-thumper with his sights set on a national television deal.

He'd been thinking about the confrontation with Baker all day, even during that night's performance. The thing that bothered him most about it was that part of what Baker said had been true.

He was an old dog, doing old tricks.

He knew that was the real problem. Without question.

In his younger days he never would have backed down from such a challenge. In his youth he would have gladly accepted Baker's offer and shown up for the show like a pit bull straining against its leash, claws sharpened, teeth bared and fully prepared to take a chunk out of Baker's hide.

But television was different now. It was no longer the innocent entertainment box it had been in the days he'd appeared on *The Ed Sullivan Show*. Now it was a powerful medium, a tool used to sinister purpose by the Technocracy.

And even though Baker had no apparent connection to the Technocracy and was nothing more than a loudmouth preacher who thought the Bible made him bullet-proof, Rantiki was scared to death of him.

That's how he knew his Avatar had lost its spark.

That's how he knew it was time for him to move on.

This was a battle that couldn't be won by one so old. It required youth, strength, energy and skill, all the qualities which Romano had in abundance.

Rantiki picked up the phone and called the Magic Box. He asked for Harry Reddington Jr. and waited.

"Hello, Harry."

"James, are you all right?"

"I had a visitor today. Jerry Baker."

"Yes." Reddington sounded as if he knew what was coming.

"He challenged me…" Rantiki said.

They talked for hours.

II

Weird Science had been running for three weeks with a near sell-out for each show. Rantiki had never been more popular at the Magic Box and Romano found himself being treated more and more like a colleague by the patrons with each visit he made.

Tonight they'd gone to the Magic Box directly from the show at the Flamingo, but after just a single coffee for Rantiki and beer for Romano, Rantiki suggested they leave the lounge and go for a walk downtown.

Romano eagerly accepted the invitation. There was something about the pulse of the neon lights and the movement of people from casino to casino that made the trip interesting no matter how many times he'd walked the length of Fremont Street.

When they reached the Fremont Hotel and Casino, they turned right and began walking northwest along Fremont toward Binion's Horseshoe Hotel and Casino.

"Did I ever tell you about the time I was on *The Ed Sullivan Show?*" Rantiki began.

Romano tried to recall. Rantiki had never been one for stories about the good old days. "I've seen some clips of it, but you've never mentioned anything about it to me."

"Perhaps I should."

"I'd love to hear it."

Rantiki took a deep breath. "It was in the fifties and I was an up-and-coming magician working a few nightclubs in New York City. One night Ed Sullivan showed up at the club I was playing. After watching my act he invited me onto his show. Two weeks later I was on national television, just like that." He snapped his fingers to emphasize the point. "They wanted me to do five minutes of my club act, but I gave them six, a lot of which wasn't even in the act I did at the club."

Romano looked away from Rantiki for a moment and moved to the left to avoid a woman searching the inside of her purse for some change.

"See, I wanted to give them a real bang-up act, so I put a lot of magick into my routines. Nothing fancy, no thunderbolts or fireballs or anything like that. Just little stuff to make myself look better than I was…. Like I would start out with a poker chip in my hand, close it up in my fist, then open it up again and make a dove appear in my palm. Vulgar, vulgar magick, but it was spectacular, especially when they did clear close-up shots of my hand."

"Weren't you worried about Paradox?"

"Perhaps I was being a little naïve, but I didn't think there would be any, at least not for one single performance. But by the end of a week of rehearsal after rehearsal I'd done far too much vulgar magick. It ended up that each time I did my act I was forced to run to the dressing room so I could throw up from the pain. Everyone thought it was nerves, you know, stage fright, which was fine by me."

He paused as if the recollection had brought back a sliver of that terrible pain from so many years ago.

Romano waited patiently for him to continue.

"Well, Friday night came and I did the show perfectly. I was a smash. Ed even came over to talk to me and everything, but instead of waiting around to chat with him, I ran to my dressing room to heave into the toilet. It was an hour before I could get back on my feet again, but it was worth it. My career took off, with offers coming in from theaters and agents all over the country, even a couple from here in Las Vegas."

"Sounds great."

"Well it was great in two ways, but not in the way you're thinking. True, it advanced my career, but more importantly it taught me to restrict my use of vulgar magick to only when it was safe, or absolutely necessary. It also taught me first hand how dangerous Paradox is, how deadly its forces can be. It's a power to be respected and avoided at all costs."

Romano was silent, listening attentively.

"But the most curious thing about that night was that the next day and all through the next week incredible feats and happenings were reported all across America. It rained fish in New Mexico. In South Carolina a hurricane devastated an entire city block but left one house with an elderly man inside unscathed. In California a surfer rode a wave for over thirty minutes. No one made a connection between these kinds of events, but I did. None of these things could have been explained by anything other than magick, and since they all followed my appearance on *The Ed Sullivan Show*, it was obvious that my use of magick had Awakened Sleepers all across the country, hundreds of them, maybe even thousands."

"Wow!" Romano said. It was a strange word coming from Romano, but it was all he could manage.

"I'm telling you this because it has a lot to do with your Ascension— the enlightened state of being to which all mages aspire."

"I'm still a little fuzzy on that concept."

"Well, Romano, I'm sorry to say that I've never actually achieved Ascension myself, and I don't think I ever will. I do know this, however…that night on *The Ed Sullivan Show* I brought a small amount of enlightenment to a large number of people. I Awakened more Sleepers in those few minutes than I could ever hope to Awaken during the normal course of my lifetime. It was the closest I've ever come to achieving something that felt like Ascension. I've tried to get it back many times over the years until I finally realized I had become too old for the pursuit."

They passed Binion's Horseshoe Hotel and Casino and continued on toward the Las Vegas Club Hotel and Casino. There was a man slumped against the wall of a restaurant, crying. No doubt he'd lost his life savings to the temptation of just one more pull on the one-armed bandit.

Rantiki walked past the man without giving him a second look. "And that's where you come in," he said.

"Me?" asked Romano.

"Yes. You have the power to achieve Ascension, and to achieve it fairly early in your life. You're destined for greatness and I wouldn't be surprised if you eventually wound up as a great and powerful pedagogue, surrounded by dozens of students."

Romano shook his head. There was *so much* people expected from him. Too much, it seemed. All he ever wanted was to be a famous magician, but from the way Rantiki talked about things, that was a goal of secondary importance. "Why are you telling me all this?" he asked.

Rantiki stopped on the sidewalk and turned to face Romano. "I'm getting old, Romano. My time is near, I can feel it. I wish I could take you farther along your path, give you a better start toward your Ascension, but I don't think I'll be with you long enough to see it happen."

"What's wrong?" Romano said. "Are you sick?"

"No, nothing like that," Rantiki said, smiling as he placed a comforting hand on the younger man's shoulder. "Let's just say it's time for me to be moving on, time to leave the stage to make room for some younger, fresher, *stronger* blood."

"You're talking like you know you're going to die soon."

Rantiki was silent for several seconds. Finally he said, "Let's just say that in a short while I'll be gone."

"But—"

"And when that happens, when I'm out of the way, you will be able to become stronger and more powerful on your own than you ever could become under my wing."

They reached the end of Fremont Street and stood facing the Union Plaza Hotel, one of the largest of the downtown casinos, with a working train station inside which dropped off passengers in the casino.

"How about another drink?" Rantiki asked. "You look like you could use one."

"Yeah, I probably could."

"Come on, then. I'll buy."

They crossed Main Street.

Neon signs in front of the Union Plaza encouraged patrons to "Live it UP!" Romano read the signs but didn't feel all that much like partying.

They settled in at a corner table in a coffee shop away from the noise and smoke of the casino. Rantiki ordered an Irish Cream coffee and Romano a rum and Coke. They sipped their drinks slowly, neither saying a word.

Romano lit up a cigarette.

"There are a lot of dangerous people in this town," Rantiki said at last.

"Are you talking about the Mob?"

"No, nothing like that."

"Then who do you mean?"

"There a lot of people to be wary of. First of all, be careful of the women here, especially the showgirls. They're ambitious, sometimes ruthless, willing to do anything just to get ahead. They don't call them 'two-legged cats' for nothing, you know."

Romano let out a little laugh. He'd been out on the odd date with women Susie had fixed him up with, and there had been a few one-night stands, all of which had been pleasant enough. Some even a little more than pleasant, but nothing he'd wanted to evolve into a regular relationship.

"Then there are the people who will always be there to try and knock you down. And the more successful you get, the harder they'll try to hurt you."

"Who do you mean?"

Rantiki hesitated.

Romano prodded him. "From the way you're talking it sounds like you've got somebody specific in mind."

"Yes, I suppose I do. Have you heard of Jerry Baker?"

Romano laughed. "That guy's a joke."

"To you and me maybe, and to anyone else with half a brain, but nevertheless he's got his fans, or maybe followers is a better word. He asked me to appear on his show, wants to expose me to the world as a fraud."

"Is that what he came by for?" Romano asked in disbelief. "What did you tell him?"

"I told him no, of course. But with people like him that's never the end of it. He's looking to go national with his show and thinks he can score big ratings points by gunning for me. So, no matter how many times I tell him no, he'll keep trying."

"Is there any way to stop somebody like that?"

"Yes. You either face them head on, or you become so big and famous and powerful that people like him look pathetic when they come around to bother you. Then, no matter what they have to say, people automatically think they're just trying to steal a little bit of your spotlight."

Romano thought about that a moment and the realization came slowly, leaving him with a sickening feeling in the pit of his stomach. Baker was the reason Rantiki had been talking so morbidly about his end, about how it was time to move on.

"Are you going to face him head on, then?"

"No, I'm too old for that, I'm afraid."

"If you're not going to do it, then who is?"

Rantiki took a sip of his drink, then nodded in Romano's direction. "You are."

"Me?"

"Yes. You've got the strength and imagination that's required to beat these sorts of people at their own game."

Somehow, knowing that didn't make Romano feel any better.

Romano crushed out yet another cigarette, leaving the ashtray on the night table filled to overflowing with butts and ashes. He was about to light another one, but decided he really didn't need it.

He lay back in bed, eyes wide open and staring at the ceiling as if he were looking at the stars hanging over the Nevada desert. For the first time in his life he was afraid. It was a strange feeling for him, one he'd never thought he'd experience. After all, he had left home, traveled to strange cities, even moved to another country, but none of that had struck fear into his heart. Up until now everything had been a grand adventure to be embraced, a minor obstacle to be overcome, or a troublesome problem to be tackled.

He wasn't afraid of the people Rantiki had warned him about. Those people, especially guys like Jerry Baker, were just more obstacles along the way. They would either be avoided, knocked down or trampled upon when their time came.

Then what was he afraid of?

In part, he was afraid for Rantiki. The man had never been more successful than he was right now, but for some strange reason, now was the time he felt his life was coming to an end. Sure, he was an old man, but the way he talked about his death it was as if he could see it coming. What was worse, if he could in fact see his end coming, he obviously couldn't, or perhaps wouldn't, do anything to prevent it.

That was an unsettling thought, even for Romano.

The only positive thing that Romano could see in all of this was that if Rantiki did indeed die soon, then at least he'd be going out while on top and at the pinnacle of his career.

Leaving Romano alone.

The thought sent shivers through his body.

Romano had lived much of his life hoping that his father would be proud of him and encourage his pursuit of a career in magic. And here, thousands of miles from his home, he'd found that father in Rantiki, a man who'd literally taken him by the hand and guided him along the path to becoming a stage magician, a man whose every second word wasn't merely one of encouragement but one telling him he would be the *greatest* mage the city of Las Vegas had ever seen.

With that kind of support and positive reinforcement, how could he fail?

Without it, how could he succeed?

Romano rolled onto his side and took another cigarette from the half-empty pack. He cast a rote which caused a flame to leap out from the tip of his thumb and used it to light the cigarette. After a few puffs he sat up in bed, held out his hands palm up and began sending an arc of yellow neon light from one hand to the other, and then finally around the room at ever-increasing speed until it seemed to be a continuous yellow ring around him, sheltering him from the outside world.

He inhaled deeply, the smoke of the cigarette combining with the rote he'd cast to make him feel somewhat more relaxed than he'd been moments before. Somewhat, but not all. Tension still bit into the muscles of his back and shoulders, anxiety still gnawed at his stomach.

He got up from the bed, put out his cigarette and began doing a series of exercises that to all outward appearances looked like an offshoot of t'ai chi or some other martial art.

But as he moved about the room, his bed rose up from the floor, books dropped off the shelf and flew about the room like bats, and the hands of the clock on the wall stood still.

He was at peace.

For the moment.

Martin Kraas picked up a pay phone in the lobby of the El Cortez Hotel, the oldest standing casino in Las Vegas. The hotel was opened in 1941 when cowboys still rode up and down Fremont Street…and it showed. It was an old casino in every sense of the word, with low table minimums, cheap drinks, and not a lot of charm.

Kraas felt at home here.

"You wanted to get in touch with me?" he said when the producer answered.

"Who is this?"

"Kraas, Martin Kraas."

"Oh yeah, right." There was a pause as the woman on the other end collected her thoughts. "We've decided that we're going ahead with plans for the show."

"Did Rantiki agree to appear?"

"No."

"But you're going to do it anyway."

"We were hoping you might appear on the show."

"That's a possibility."

"But Jerry says we'll need some tape for it, you know, some backstage stuff."

Kraas laughed. "I can't walk around backstage with a video camera. It might look just a little suspicious," he said, shaking his head and finishing his drink in a gulp. "When I leave Rantiki I want it to be a clean break."

"We'll pay for it. And I do mean *pay*."

"And I'm telling you that you don't even need to have a camera backstage during the show."

"No? What do we need, then?"

"You tape a performance from the audience, preferably a seat up front. Once you have that I'll be able to tell you what to look for."

"When's a good night to tape a show?"

"Let me think," Kraas said, ordering another drink.

12

Saturday night.

The last of the day's three shows.

The crowd standing in line for the show outside the hotel looked to be large enough for another sellout.

At the front of the line a security guard in grey pants and blue jacket stood before the entrance to the theater, feet firmly planted, arms folded across his chest in a show of strength.

"I'm telling you, we have permission to set up our cameras," said a shapely brunette, pretty enough to be a showgirl, but dressed in a white blouse and tan skirt and blazer. "If you let us in we can start setting up our cameras so we can be ready when the show starts."

"Look, ma'am," the security guard said. "Nobody told me about allowing any cameras inside, and until I hear something, you can just wait right there like the rest of the good people who've bought tickets to the show."

"Yeah!" "That's right!" the people at the front of the line chimed in, thankful for the extra entertainment they were getting before the show began.

Just then the door to the theater opened up and Martin Kraas was there. "What's going on here?"

The security guard turned to him, looking glad that somebody involved with the show had come to take the matter out of his hands. "These people—" he gestured to the woman and cameraman "—say they have permission to set up inside and tape the show."

"And you are?" Kraas asked the woman.

"My name's Daria DePaul. I'm a producer for *The Jerry Baker Show*."

"I'm Martin Kraas, pleased to meet you."

She hesitated a moment. "Likewise."

"And who gave you permission to tape the show?"

"The Great Rantiki himself."

"Well, then," Kraas said, shrugging his shoulders and stepping back from the door. "Let them in."

The security guard nodded, and moved to open the door.

"Hold it! Hold it!" It was Romano. "What's all this about a Jerry Baker camera crew wanting access to the show?" He was addressing Kraas, but spoke loud enough for everyone to hear.

"They say Rantiki okayed it," Kraas said.

Romano shook his head. "I doubt that very much." He turned to look back into the theater where Graham Chambers was looking on from a distance. "Call Rantiki!" Then he turned to the woman and cameraman. "Let's just wait and see."

Minutes passed.

Romano, Kraas and the security guard stood in silence waiting for Rantiki to appear. Daria DePaul paced back and forth, sighing like she'd just been dealt an outrageous insult. The cameraman began setting up his tripod, no doubt to catch the confrontation with Rantiki on tape.

At last Rantiki arrived at the door. "What's all this, then?"

Kraas and the television crew remained silent, leaving the job of explaining the situation to Romano. "They're with *The Jerry Baker Show*, and they say they have your permission to set up their cameras and tape some of tonight's show."

"They certainly do *not!*" Rantiki said. "While I'm impressed with your tenacity, Miss—"

"Daria DePaul," she said, extending her hand.

Rantiki ignored it. "—I told your Jerry Baker, and in no uncertain terms, that I did not want to be a part of his vile little program."

People in line who had been craning their necks to see what was going on cheered. Perhaps they were fans of Rantiki. Or perhaps they'd caught a few minutes of Jerry Baker's show.

Rantiki turned to face the security guard, who by now had been joined by two other guards as well as plain-clothed members of the Casino's security staff. "No one carrying a camera or any sort of recording device is to be allowed into the theater. If I ever give permission to anyone to tape my show, you'll know about it before they do. Understood?"

"Yes, sir!" said the security guard. He looked at Miss DePaul and her cameraman. "You heard Mr. Rantiki." The security guards moved in unison, forming a wall of bodies that ushered the two of them out of the casino.

Before the cameraman was too far away, Romano cast a simple rote erasing the footage he'd shot of Rantiki confronting the producer.

Rantiki must have felt a ripple of Quintessence because he looked over at Romano and said, "Thanks."

Kraas looked at both of them as if he'd just been left out of a hushhush inside joke.

"Now," Rantiki said, the word edged with an uncharacteristic nervousness. "Let's go. We've got a show to do."

It was just another show, one of dozens they'd performed since the beginning of the month, but the incident in the lobby before the doors opened had put Rantiki off his mark. He was a step slower, a second behind, his gestures were automatic and he was working without any sense of style and flare.

Luckily, Rantiki was rarely on stage by himself for long, and Romano and Susie managed to keep things moving along by being just a little more animated and playing up to the crowd a little more than usual.

When they got to the reluctant-assistant illusion, Romano had to practically pull Rantiki through it, waiting a few extra seconds for each of his cues and having to remind Rantiki to undo the last latch on the cabinet so he could climb out of it and finish off the illusion—which went over poorly since the surprise effect of its finale was lost while Romano struggled to get out of the still-locked cabinet.

When they got a short break backstage, everyone had a long, worried look on their face. A few more shows like this and they'd all be looking for work when the contract ran out.

Romano wanted to talk to Rantiki.

"Is he in his dressing room?" he asked Susie as he passed her in the hallway.

"I knocked on the door, but he sent me away. He said he doesn't want to talk to anybody."

Romano continued on, hoping that *anybody* didn't mean *him*.

When he got to Rantiki's dressing room he found the door locked. He tapped lightly.

"Go away!"

"It's Romano," he said softly.

The lock in the door snicked and Romano tried the knob again. This time it was unlocked. He opened the door and saw Rantiki sitting in a chair at the far end of the room. He was looking into his mirror, holding his head in his hands.

"Is everything all right?" Romano asked, taking a seat at the other end of the room. Although all the lights were on, the room seemed dark.

"It's been years since I've visited the Umbra."

Like a lot of Rantiki's talk of late, his words were a riddle to Romano. "What are you talking about?"

"But it's not really like dying is it?"

It was a question that didn't need to be answered. Rantiki was mumbling now, more as if he were thinking aloud than talking to Romano. Romano listened nervously, fear creeping over his body like spiders.

"It's just another place, another reality, somewhere to watch from. And maybe I can visit. There are ways...." Rantiki's face was losing some of its color, as if he were fading away and *already* at that other place he was talking about.

"I'm going to get the hotel doctor," Romano said at last, getting up from his chair.

"No!" Rantiki shouted.

Suddenly the door locked, and Romano knew he wouldn't be able to open it unless Rantiki allowed it.

"Sit down!" said the mage. "There are a few things I want to tell you."

Reluctantly, Romano sat down.

Rantiki smiled at him, the kind of proud, fatherly smile that Romano had never seen as a child. "You're not only a good mage, Romano, you're a good person too."

Romano felt uncomfortable sitting there. Thankfully they were on a short break and it would end soon when they were called back onto the stage.

"I want you to do something for me."

"Anything."

"I want you to make sure my name lives on, make sure it keeps its dignity. I don't want to be remembered like Elvis Presley...."

Romano nodded, understanding.

"He and I became good friends when he played Las Vegas. He deserves better." Rantiki turned around to look Romano in the eye. "You will do that for me, won't you?"

"Of course."

"Come here," he said, rising up from his chair.

Romano walked over, stood awkwardly in front of Rantiki, and then suddenly found himself in an embrace. At first he was shocked by it, since he'd never been held like this by a man before, not by any of his uncles and certainly not by his father. Even his mother had hugged him rarely. But as the moments ticked by Romano felt himself drawn closer to the man until he finally wrapped his arms around him and hugged him back.

There was a knock at the door. "We're waiting!" It was Susie.

Rantiki was the first to let go. "Come on," he said. "Let's get this over with."

Romano let out a sigh of relief, thinking Rantiki was referring to the show.

The second part of the show went off much better than the first. Rantiki's performance was smoother, and he was more sure of himself than he'd been in weeks. The crowd seemed to notice the change too since their applause was louder and livelier than it had been earlier.

As the show neared its completion, Susie did her bit to rescue Romano from the exposed water pipe to which he'd been handcuffed, and together they conspired to exact their revenge on the mad scientist.

But this time as they tied him up, Rantiki neglected to put up much of a struggle. Usually he twisted and shouted in an overly dramatic attempt to hamper their efforts to restrain him, but tonight he was helping them as if he were doing a straight escape and not one as part of a larger themed show.

Then, just as they were about to tie him up in the straitjacket and suspend him over the stage by his feet, he turned to each of them and said, "Wish me luck!"

Romano and Susie looked at each other, a little confused.

He'd never said anything like that before.

In fact, he was never one to believe in luck at all.

But despite the odd nature of his comment, there was no time to ponder the remark. The show continued on and Rantiki was hoisted up over the stage. Then the rope was set alight and the stage lights dimmed.

Romano remained where he was, going through the steps to the escape in his mind as if he were performing it right alongside Rantiki.

The seconds ticked by as the fire gnawed at the rope.

The lights slowly dimmed.

In Romano's mind, the escape was finished. Rantiki should have been standing on the stage, straitjacket in hand, waiting for the lights to come up again.

But he was still in the jacket.

And the jacket was not moving.

Romano remained motionless and silent while he rigorously debated whether to call for Rantiki to be brought down, or to leave him up there a few more seconds.

That's when he felt a ripple of Quintessence.

Suddenly the flame on the rope flared and the fire began burning *down* toward Rantiki as if the rope was not a rope at all, but a fuse or a wick.

Romano's first thought was to stop the flames.

He cast a rote against the fire to put it out, but instead of extinguishing the flames it had no effect. In fact, it felt as if his rote had been repelled by something, as if it had run into a brick wall.

Could it have come up against another rote?

He turned to the audience, scanning it quickly for a Technomancer. If there was one out there attacking Rantiki in the name of the Pogrom, then he would likely be sitting in the first few rows.

It was nobody out there.

"Get him down!" Romano shouted to Graham Chambers who was operating the winch. He'd already been working at it, and looked at Romano with outstretched hands. "It's jammed."

Romano tried another rote on the flames and this time realized that the counter rote wasn't coming from the direction of the audience but rather from somewhere on the stage.

He tried one last rote, this one slightly different from the first, and learned that the counter rote was being cast by Rantiki himself.

He had fanned the flames.

He had inhibited any chance of rescue.

The realization hit Romano like a punch in the gut. Rantiki was killing himself onstage, in front of a live audience, at the height of his popularity.

And then everything began falling into place. Everything Rantiki had been saying these past few weeks began to make sense. He was too old to confront Jerry Baker, and if he didn't he'd end up humiliated, his career as a magician ended. This way, his career was still over, but his spectacular death would ensure that the Rantiki name—the name entrusted to Romano—would live forever, just as it did for Hendrix and Morrison.

The flames had reached his legs.

His pants began to burn, the burgeoning flames the color of a cloudless sky.

The audience and everyone on stage drew in a collective breath.

Held it.

And then the straitjacket went up in a fireball, great gouts of blue and orange flame reaching up for the catwalk high above the stage.

People began screaming.

A couple of stagehands were trying to put out the fire with extinguishers, but Rantiki was too high up, the flames out of range.

Finally the rope burned through and the fireball crashed onto the stage, flames shooting out in all directions upon impact.

The fire was out in seconds.

"Drop the curtain!" Romano shouted.

Slowly, the curtain began to fall.

And then in seeming silence amid all the confusion, Romano stepped up to the charred black husk of a body that the flames had left behind.

And sucked in a gasp.

Although many of the features of the head were unrecognizable, there was an unmistakable, almost hideous, smile on the lips.

Romano hoped that was a sign that Rantiki was happy.

Wherever he was.

An hour later the theater was filled with people who had nothing to do with magic, as well as a few who did.

There were police officers everywhere, as well as firemen, ambulance attendants and the coroner.

Nobody involved with the show was allowed to go home, which was just as well since nobody really wanted to be alone right now.

Like everyone else, Romano waited his turn to be questioned by the police. After a few questions about Romano's background and his relationship to Rantiki, the detective—a bulldog of a man with a bald head, mustache and dark blue overcoat—asked a question Romano could not answer with either the whole truth or a blatant lie. He decided half the truth was better than nothing.

"Had Rantiki been acting peculiar lately?"

"What do you mean?" Romano said, stalling for time.

"Any changes in his character or mannerisms?"

"Well, he'd been talking in general terms about how he was getting old and how it was time to move on, but he'd been saying stuff like that ever since I'd met him."

"You were his apprentice, right?"

"Yes, he took me on."

"And you were in his dressing room during the break."

"That's right."

"And what did you talk about?"

Romano began to see where the detective's questions were leading. "He thought the show was going well, but there were a few things that could be improved."

"Like?"

"Minor things, costume colors, lighting."

He made a few notes. "Did he mention any personnel changes, or anything like that?"

"No."

The detective paused again, as if planning a different tack.

"Now that he's gone, will you be taking over for him?"

"I haven't a clue—" Romano said, cutting the last word short. He'd had about all he could stand of this. "Look, detective. I loved the man. He took me in and taught me everything I know and would have taught me more if he'd lived longer. I owe everything to him—just like everyone else involved with his show—and I would have had the most to benefit if he had lived twenty more years."

"But now that he's gone…"

Romano decided it was time to cast a Mind Rote over the detective. The rote was a variation of the Blissful Discipline rote he'd studied in one of the Akashic Brotherhood textbooks in Rantiki's library. The rote would simply alter the detective's thought patterns every time he considered Rantiki's death to be a murder. The effect of the rote would last a week or so, but by that time Rantiki's death would be forgotten and several real murders would have occurred to occupy the detective's thoughts and time. It was a dangerous bit of magick, but it was probably the best thing for everyone involved, including the police.

"Now that he's gone…" the detective repeated.

"Yes?"

"I think a lot of people are going to miss him."

"I would think so, yes," Romano said. "Now, if you won't be needing me any further…."

"Yeah, that's fine," the detective said, closing his notebook.

When he reached his dressing room, Romano found Kraas sitting in his seat in front of the mirror. He turned around when Romano entered, his face as white as a sheet.

"I didn't do it," he said, a strange mix of terror and apology in his voice.

"What?"

"The fire. Rantiki. I checked out the rope and the straitjacket before the show like I always do. They were both fine. I…I don't know what happened."

Romano thought it was odd that Kraas was denying any wrongdoing when no one had accused him of any. But he'd already seen a half-dozen different reactions to Rantiki's death; maybe blaming himself for it was just Kraas's way of handling it.

Whatever the reason, he had nothing to worry about. Even the police wouldn't be thinking foul play anymore.

"Relax," Romano said. "I know you didn't have anything to do with it." For a second he considered telling Kraas the truth, but decided against it. "It was an accident, that's all. No one could see it coming, and no one could have stopped it."

"You really think so?"

"Yes," Romano said. "Shit, maybe it was even destined to happen."

Upon hearing the words, Kraas looked relieved.

Which, for some reason, bothered Romano.

13

Romano lay back on his bed with the television remote in one hand, a cigarette in the other. It had been two days since Rantiki's spectacular onstage death. The telegrams, phone calls and e-mail had finally slowed to a trickle, but the television tributes were still going great guns.

Last night it had been all the local stations who did special features on Rantiki at the end of their Sunday news broadcasts and weekend round-ups. It was interesting for Romano since many of the pieces showed clips from Rantiki's early years in Las Vegas, as well as local interviews and testimonials from Las Vegas celebrities like Wayne Newton and Siegfried and Roy, the latter hinting Rantiki was one of the reasons they had pursued a career in magic. Romano didn't really believe that. He knew enough about the two German illusionists to know that their success was largely the result of their being individual stylists rather than emulating any one magician. They had turned down several lucrative offers over the course of their careers just so they could do their own thing. Still, they were top, world-class magicians and the gesture was greatly appreciated, prompting Romano to make a mental note to send something special for one of their infamous white tigers to play with.

And after a hectic day of phone calls, visits by camera crews to Rancho Rantiki, and a search through Rantiki's video collection for rarely seen clips, now it was the national media's turn to pay tribute to Rantiki. From network news to CNN, from *60 Minutes* to *48 Hours*, and from *Hard Copy* to *Entertainment Tonight*, every news show in the country had prepared a piece on Rantiki, who was now being described by the likes of *PM Magazine*'s host Dan O'Doyle as "one of the greatest magicians and illusionists of our time."

Romano had been trying to tape as many of the shows as possible, but most were airing in the same time slot, so his only hope was that Kraas, Susie and the others were trying to tape the shows as well.

At seven-thirty, after channel surfing up and down the dial, he happened upon *Inside Affair*. A beautiful blonde-haired reporter named Cynthia Keegan promised to close out the show with a special report on the life and death of the Great Rantiki, but first…

The screen switched to a shot of three catatonic Forrest Gump wannabes spraying a cleaning solution onto a car tire.

Romano quickly set up the VCR, lit up a cigarette and waited. The half-hour show seemed to drag on and on as he smoked three cigarettes— each time lighting a new one from the dying butt of the old one—before it was time for the piece on Rantiki.

He was in the middle of lighting up yet another cigarette when the piece started. He was caught slightly off guard, but managed to press *REC* before Keegan finished her newsdesk intro to the piece.

The feature began with a picture from Rantiki's yearbook from Oak Forest High School in Oak Forest, Illinois. The name under the boyish photo read *Randall Wynne* and under that in brackets was the name (*Mr. Magic*). Keegan's voiceover said Rantiki performed magic in high-school talent shows and at local fairs, winning several prizes. When he had finished high school he traveled the country in an old Ford, doing shows anywhere people would let him.

"It wasn't until he was discovered by Ed Sullivan in a New York nightclub that Rantiki's career really took off...."

And then, there was Rantiki, barely in his twenties but already in his trademark tuxedo. The funny thing about seeing him so young was that he hadn't changed all that much over the years. Sure, his skin had sagged and wrinkled some, his moves had slowed and become more refined, but his youthful blond hair looked as white on the grainy black-and-white footage as it had in his later years. He'd aged gracefully, Romano thought. He'd embraced the onrush of years, rather than fought them, and as a result the years had been kind to him.

Romano moved forward to sit on the edge of the bed in order to watch the performance more closely. Rantiki was making things appear out of places they had no business appearing out of. And even though he was watching the performance on tape years after the fact, Romano could still feel a twinge of something flowing through him following each trick.

It was a marvelous performance, Romano admitted that, but it had depended far too heavily on vulgar magick ever to work on a consistent basis. No wonder he'd become so sick from Paradox.

The tribute continued with a montage of newspaper headlines and clips of the man performing onstage at bigger and bigger venues, until he finally "arrived" in Las Vegas.

And then there was Harry Reddington Jr. being interviewed inside the Magic Box.

"We're all shocked," Reddington said, just the right amount of quiver in his voice. "He was one of the best there was, an inspiration to everyone who knew him. He did a lot to make magic a respected art form." A pause. "The profession won't be the same without him."

Romano nodded. Yes, things would never be the same.

The piece ended with a shot of a billboard promoting the *Weird Science* show, and an old black-and-white photo of Rantiki. The publicity photo was a simple head-and-shoulders shot, but made interesting by the hypnotic look of his eyes, eyes that were mesmerizing to look at even now, and the strategic placement of his open right hand, the back of it against his left cheek, looking as if he were about to cast a sinister spell on the watcher.

Looking at that photo, who could *not* believe that magic was possible? It was a great, mystical image and a wonderful way to have Rantiki remembered for generations to come.

Romano was pleased.

In fact he was more than happy with all the tributes that had been done. All of the short memorial pieces on television were fine encapsulations of Rantiki's life, and certainly as good a review of one's life story as you could expect in just a few brief minutes of air time.

But most importantly for Romano, they had all been dignified portrayals of his life. Just the sort of thing Rantiki had wanted.

Rantiki would have been proud.

When *Inside Affair* ended, Romano got up from the bed, switched off the VCR and headed to the main house for a bite to eat.

It was the second night they wouldn't be doing a show, and Romano was already feeling something akin to withdrawal. It wasn't so much that he missed the applause, but rather that he missed having something occupying his mind so totally that he couldn't think of anything else.

With the death of Rantiki, having something to occupy his mind would have been a godsend. As it was, every minute of his day was filled with thoughts of Rantiki, and even when he did manage to think about something else, there was always a reporter calling up to ask, "What's it like there without him?"

Casting rotes helped, but magick wasn't always possible because of the close contact with the others on staff. Most of the time Romano ended up casting innocuous little rotes which no one would ever notice if they weren't looking for them.

Like now, as he walked across the sandy ground toward the main house, his shoes kicked up no dust. It was a silly thing to waste his Quintessence on, but it helped him cope.

Inside the house, Susie and Kraas were on the phone with the last few reporters who wanted quotes to fill out their stories and features that would probably appear in next month's newsstand magazines.

Romano had spoken to the people from all the magician's publications like *Juggler's World*, *Linking Rings* and *GENII*, while Kraas had fielded the calls from *People*, *Time*, *Maclean's* and *Newsday*.

Romano didn't mind Kraas taking all the big-name magazines for himself, since he was articulate, cordial and honest in his responses to the questions; Romano didn't think he could have done a better job himself. Besides, he would rather talk to people from the trade magazines since they were the ones whose readers would be most affected by Rantiki's passing. The best you could hope for with the big circulation publications was a reaction like, "Hey, hon, you know who died?" over the dinner table.

Furthermore, Kraas was doing double duty now that Rantiki was gone. In addition to handling the media, he was also making all the arrangements for Rantiki's Wednesday afternoon funeral, which was a chore that didn't appeal to Romano in the least. It occurred to Romano that Kraas might be trying to slide into Rantiki's place, but he was familiar enough with the old mage to know that Rantiki had more than likely already taken care of those arrangements and no amount of up-front or back-room wrangling was going to change a thing.

Still, Kraas was a different man now, and for a moment Romano wondered if it would be possible for them to work closely together in the future, as partners perhaps.

He decided to keep the idea on the back burner for a while and watch how things developed.

"Is there anything to eat?" Romano asked, moving through the front room on the way to the kitchen.

"There's a tray of sandwiches in the fridge, love," Susie said, cradling the phone in the crook of her neck. "Some salad and cold beer too. Be a darling and bring me one, will ya?"

"Will do. How 'bout you, Martin?"

Kraas continued talking into the phone and didn't bother looking up.

"Martin," Romano said. "Do you want a beer?" He punctuated the question by acting as if he were holding a bottle and drinking from it.

Kraas looked testily at Romano, waving his hand as if he didn't want to be disturbed.

Romano looked at Susie and shrugged.

"Maybe he's talking to Rantiki," Susie said.

Romano looked at her sternly, then saw the faint smile on Susie's face and couldn't help but start to laugh. It felt good. "All right," he said, returning Susie's smile. "Two beers it is, then."

"Coffee. Double-double." Martin Kraas waited for his coffee, shifting his weight from one foot to another. When the woman behind the counter was about to ring the sale of his coffee into the till he said, "And a cruller too."

She gave him a look, then went to pick the cruller off the shelf behind her. "Anything else?" she asked when she had his order ready for the second time.

"No thanks," Kraas said. He paid her, picked up his tray and scanned the interior of the donut shop looking for Daria DePaul. He found her sitting at a table near the windows at the far end of the room. She was dressed in a black skirt and jacket with her hair tied up in a bun. Although she was dressed for a funeral, Kraas found the cut of her clothing flattering to her shapely form.

Kraas was dressed in a black suit he'd bought especially for Rantiki's funeral. It was an expensive suit, made-to-measure, and as good as you could get without going for tailor-made. As he approached her, he wondered if she thought he looked as good as he thought she did.

"Glad you could make it," she said as he slid into the seat across the tiny table from her. "I know how busy you are today."

"Couple of minutes won't hurt."

Now that he was closer, Kraas noticed a strange look about her. She looked like she felt out of place here, her eyes darting around the room as if she were afraid someone might recognize her.

"The deal's off," she said, stirring a bit of artificial sweetener into her pale yellow tea.

Kraas took a bite of his cruller and nodded. "I figured as much."

"Look, Jerry's not interested in dead men. If you haven't noticed, his show is *live*."

That wasn't the real reason and she knew it, thought Kraas. He looked at her skeptically. "Rantiki has become quite popular these past few days, hasn't he?" he said, doing little to keep the contempt for her out of his voice. "A little too popular, I would say."

Daria DePaul's face soured.

"And I bet defaming the dead doesn't play well in New York or L.A., right?"

"It doesn't play well anywhere," she said, putting down her tea. "If you haven't noticed, Rantiki suddenly has more fans now than he could have ever hoped for while he was alive. People who die the way he did become larger-than-life. Going after him now would be like trying to tell people George Washington was a child molester."

"All right, all right, so the deal's off. Will I still be getting some of the money?"

She just looked at him with wide eyes and a slightly open mouth.

"You know, like a kill fee."

She continued to stare at him.

"What? What is it?" He searched the lapels of his jacket for crumbs or dandruff.

"I can't believe you," she said.

At last Kraas understood. "Look, honey. I took a helluva chance for that show of yours. If Rantiki had ever found out I'd been talking to you, I'd be out on my ass right now and there wouldn't be anyone in town willing to give me a job."

She considered that a moment and some of the disbelief that had been on her face faded. "I'll talk to Jerry and see what I can do."

Kraas smiled. "I'd appreciate that."

She sipped the last of her tea and gently patted her lips with a paper napkin.

"Listen," Kraas said. "The funeral isn't until this afternoon. If you're not doing anything between now and then, maybe we could go somewhere."

She looked at him sharply. Although she was smiling, the same look of disbelief had returned. "No, I don't think so." She got up to leave.

Kraas watched her leave the donut shop, admiring the cut of her skirt.

The Guardian Angel Cathedral was a church unlike any other.

Located on Desert Inn Drive, right on the Strip, the Guardian Angel was the busiest church in Las Vegas, a city which ironically happens to be one of the most religious in the world, with more churches per capita—one church for every three hundred residents—than any other city in America. Local residents tended to be avid churchgoers while visitors usually came to pray for better luck. With so many churches, Sin City also just happened to be one of the greatest places for those seeking redemption.

Daniel Dafoe, author of *Robinson Crusoe*, wrote in *The True-born Englishman* that "Wherever God erects a house of prayer, / the devil always builds a chapel there…."

In the Las Vegas, those words held true, only in reverse.

For every new den of iniquity that went up over the years, a new church project was never far behind, maintaining the town's delicate state of equilibrium between the combative forces of evil and good.

But while the Guardian Angel was a different sort of church, its peculiarities seemed unremarkable to the people of Las Vegas. For example, donations at the Guardian Angel were more often made in casino chips than cash, and once a week the priest, Father Quintino Marucci, took them to Caesar's Palace to cash them in. Furthermore, Sunday masses were seventy-five per cent tourists, and the late-afternoon mass on Saturday was always overcrowded.

It was the perfect place for Rantiki's memorial service, even though he wasn't Catholic and had never had any inclination toward organized religion. In addition, it was a convenient place for celebrities to attend and "be seen" without having to travel all the way out to the cemetery. The motorcade to the burial would take Rantiki through the north end of the strip past many of the casinos he'd performed at over the years and then through downtown and finally past the Magic Box.

Kraas had arranged it all and it seemed to Romano like everything was proceeding just the way Rantiki would have wanted it.

Father Marucci kept the ceremony moving, realizing that he and many of the performers inside his church were on a tight schedule. When it came time for a eulogy, Harry Reddington Jr. gave a brief but endearing speech which ended with him calling Rantiki a "master magician and even better friend who enriched the lives of all who knew him."

That seemed to sum Rantiki up nicely for Romano. Everyone he knew that had known Rantiki would have agreed. Even Jerry Baker might've said the same thing now that the man was gone.

Reddington finished the eulogy, walked down past the casket—the same underwater casket Houdini had used to break Rahman Bey's "underwater burial" record of nineteen minutes by staying at the bottom of the Hotel Shelton swimming pool in New York on August 5, 1926 for one hour and thirty-one minutes—and produced a bouquet of flowers in his hand, which he laid down on top of the big, brown box. It was a silly bit of stage magic, but the non-mages and magicians in attendance all thought it was a fitting gesture.

After that, the casket was wheeled down to the edge of the altar where Romano and the other pallbearers, Martin Kraas, Harry Reddington Jr., Graham Chambers, Jimmy Platt and Arthur Gardner, carried it out of the church to the back of the waiting hearse.

From across the street, camera crews recorded the solemn moment in silence.

Once the casket was inside, Romano went to the second black Lincoln provided by the funeral home and rode along in the procession with Reddington and Susie Wand.

When they reached the Magic Box, the procession slowed as most of the regulars were lined up on each side of the street holding card fans made up of multiple decks. As the hearse passed they showered the car with cards. The cards all fell like autumn leaves, creating the perfect front-page photo for the Thursday edition of newspapers all across North America.

After exiting downtown, the procession drove north on Highway 15 for several miles to the Las Vegas Showman's Memorial, where many of the city's greatest entertainers were buried.

When they arrived at Rantiki's plot, Romano saw that there was already a battery of camera crews waiting to get a few last feet of tape. Included among the group was a crew Romano recognized as being from *The Jerry Baker Show*, the same man and woman who'd been trying to get in to tape Rantiki's last fateful performance. Romano was suspicious about their motives for being there, but the cemetery was a public place—a tourist attraction in fact—and they had as much right to be taping there as any of the other crews did. Besides, if he used magick to damage their tape again, he might be risking Paradox, since it was unlikely that a professional cameraman would lose video images twice in the same week.

Romano decided he'd keep an eye on them, nothing more.

The sun shone brightly down on the grounds and everything about the burial went smoothly.

Romano had to give full credit to Kraas for pulling it off. He'd done a marvelous job.

When the assembly began to break up there were plenty of photo and interview opportunities for those who'd made the trek to the cemetery, and out of respect for Rantiki few requests were denied.

Kraas got more than his share of the spotlight, but it wasn't surprising since he'd been the first contact most media had had when trying to arrange their schedules. And he was, after all, Rantiki's most senior technical advisor and had known the man longer than most. And finally, he was getting adept at providing reporters, especially television and radio people, with perfect ten-to-fifteen-second sound-bites, any one of which were suitable for broadcast.

Romano watched Kraas being interviewed for perhaps the dozenth time that afternoon and was impressed with the man's continued coolness under the hot mid-afternoon sun.

Sure, he was acting like a bit of a publicity hound, but he'd worked hard to do Rantiki proud and he deserved whatever attention he could get for himself.

He'd earned it.

Furthermore, with his apparent flair for planning and execution, Romano was again thinking that they might work well together as partners.

Kraas and Minardi.

Minardi and Kraas.

There were a few things about the man he still didn't appreciate—his attitude toward women, for one—but at least now there were more things about the man to like rather than dislike.

They'd have to sit down and have a talk.

And soon.

With Rantiki interred and the last of the camera crews packing up and heading home, Romano glanced around to see if anyone was watching, then casually walked over to the plot and looked down at Rantiki's casket. It sounded a little silly, but with all that had been going on these past few days, Romano hadn't had the chance to spend a moment "alone" with Rantiki.

Now was his chance.

His last chance.

He crouched down at the edge of the rectangular hole and took a deep breath. "I'm sorry you're gone, Mister Magic," he said, remembering the words under the photo in that high-school yearbook. "I believe in everything you told me and I want you to know that I'll do everything within my power to make you proud."

He shook his head. Coming from a family devoid of practically every emotional display save for anger, this kind of thing proved more difficult for him than he'd thought it would be. It was as if he was saying the words he should have told his father upon leaving Montreal more than two years ago.

Finally, he said, "Thanks...for everything. I won't ever forget you. And I won't let you down."

Then, after glancing around to make sure no one was looking, he put his clenched fists together at the thumbs and began pulling his hands slowly apart. Between them, a length of rope appeared, the exact same type of rope Romano had used to tie up Rantiki the night they first met onstage at the Stardust. When the rope was the right length, he pinched off the ends and held it tightly between his hands. Then he tied the rope in the most complex series of knots he knew.

"There, that should keep you busy for a while...."

He threw the rope on top of the casket, where it landed with a thump. Then he rose to his feet and gestured to the workers waiting off to the side. They came forward, eager to fill in the hole and finish for the day.

Romano turned for the car, felt the sun's warmth on his face and realized he was sweating. He took off his black jacket and a sudden gust of desert wind sent a chill down his spine.

God, I'm going to miss him, he thought.

As he walked toward the Lincoln, Arthur Gardner came up from behind and fell into step on his right.

"Hello," Arthur said. His smile was strained.

Romano nodded acknowledgement.

"This is probably the worst time I could bring up something like this…but I've got to make a few calls to some investors when we get back and I need to know what I can tell them."

"About what?"

"Well, I want to know when you can have a show ready."

"What are you talking about?"

The two men stopped at the side of the long black car and Romano lit up a cigarette.

"I've got contract offers for a new 'Rantiki-style' show, the most lucrative of which begins in just under four months."

"What about *Weird Science*? It's a great show. It sold out just about every performance."

"It *was* a great show. But if we continue to do the show the hotel will lose out on its insurance claim. They don't want to risk a poor box-office without Rantiki himself performing in the show."

The hotel and casino's owners didn't want to risk it? Romano thought sardonically. They'd rather go with the sure thing? The irony of it was too much. Obviously there was still a lot to show business and Las Vegas that he didn't know a thing about.

"Okay, so what's this new 'Rantiki-style' show got to do with me?"

"Well, somebody's got to do it and since you were Rantiki's apprentice, the job is yours."

The realization that he was being given the opportunity to simply step into The Great Rantiki's shoes—and try his best to fill them—left Romano stunned.

He fumbled with his cigarette pack, trying to fish a fresh one out.

"Here," Arthur said, handing him one of his. Arthur didn't smoke, himself, but he kept cigarettes handy to give to business associates who did. He offered Romano a light as well.

Romano inhaled deeply and let out a long, thin stream of smoke.

He began to nod.

"Okay," he said at last. "I'll do it."

PART THREE

14

Romano and the others were all allowed to remain on the grounds of Rancho Rantiki as long as a suitable amount of the proceeds from their next show went toward its maintenance and the payment of property taxes. Arthur Gardner and some of the others encouraged Romano to move into the main house, but he'd become comfortable in his room near the workshop and decided to stay there.

That's what he told everyone.

Truth was, he didn't feel like he deserved to make the move. Not yet. Maybe after their first show was a hit he'd feel like he'd earned the move into the larger quarters, but until that happened, he'd remain in his room and work on the new show.

The first thing he did was have a talk with Martin Kraas.

After everyone took the week following Rantiki's funeral to do what they liked, he met with Kraas in the workshop, handing him a beer as a sort of peace offering and making sure their talk remained light and casual.

"So, Artie asked you to take over for Rantiki, did he?" were the first words out of Kraas's mouth.

Romano was surprised by the question and wondered for a moment if it was asked rhetorically. Nevertheless, he appreciated Kraas's straightforwardness since it made things easier knowing he wouldn't have to beat around the bush.

"Yeah, he did." A pause. "Sorry."

Kraas shrugged. "That's all right. Can't say I'm surprised, but I didn't really expect so soon." He took a sip of his beer. "When *did* Artie tell you anyway?"

Romano was a little embarrassed to say it. "About five minutes after Rantiki was in the ground."

Kraas shook his head.

"He said he had some contract offers from people who needed to know if there was going to be a new show in the works."

Kraas looked at him. "Is there?"

"Yes, and that's what I wanted to talk to you about."

Kraas said nothing.

"I'd like you to keep working with me as you did with Rantiki." Romano was careful to say "with me" rather than "for me." He felt as if he were putting together a team, rather than hiring employees, and would feel more comfortable in the position of team captain rather than boss.

Kraas took another pull on his beer, then looked at the floor, considering the offer.

"If it's more money you want, you can have it, but you're already making more money than I am." This was true. Romano was still drawing his meager apprentice's salary, but that was sort of misleading since he had full access to Rancho Rantiki and if he needed to make any large purchases he could do so with a check drawn on Rantiki's 'professional' account, the very healthy checking account with which he'd bought new equipment and magic supplies.

"No, it's not the money."

"Well, what is it then?"

Kraas went silent again. After several long seconds he said, "I used to be a magician too, you know."

"I know," Romano said softly, remembering that he hadn't heard of Martin Kraas until hooking up with Rantiki.

"I'd like to develop an act of my own. You know, get my own career going again."

Romano had thought Kraas might feel this way and had figured out an offer that he hopefully couldn't refuse. "I understand that, and I don't want to stand in your way. If you want to branch out on your own, I wish you all the best. But before you make your decision I'd like you to hear me out." Romano took a sip of his beer in order to give what he had to say next a bit more weight. "How does this sound? You work with me on developing a new show. Then, once it's up and running, you hand over the day-to-day stuff to Graham. You check on things once a week or so, and the rest of the time you're free to develop a show of your own...." And here came the deal sweetener. "With full access to Rantiki's equipment."

Kraas's usually grim face brightened, then broke into a smile. "What will it cost me?"

"Ten per cent of your gate."

"That's a good deal."

Of course it was, but Romano wasn't offering it to Kraas solely for the purposes of keeping Kraas on as a senior technical advisor.

Romano had another plan in the works.

A bigger plan.

If Romano was going to become a great tutor of other mages, perhaps even a pedagogue, he'd need some sort of set-up to attract students and keep them close by. He knew that he wouldn't always be performing in Las Vegas, and since there was already more than enough equipment in Rantiki's collection to run several shows at once, it made sense to begin trying to get more than one show operating out of Rancho Rantiki.

If Kraas's show was successful, Romano intended to form a company which would produce magic shows on a variety of levels for performances across the country, from Atlantic City to Reno, from Chicago to Miami. If the plan worked as he envisioned it, Romano would be able to bring in young mages, start them with birthday and Christmas parties, move them up to trade shows and conventions, then on to nightclubs and dinner theater, before hitting the big time with a full stage act. And all along the way he could instruct them in magick in an almost classroomlike setting. He even dreamed of starting a College of Magick to help attract the best young mages the world had to offer.

He would Awaken many.

Teach a select few.

In the end, Ascension would be his.

But before all that happened, it started here with a little experiment with Martin Kraas.

"Yeah, okay," Kraas said. "You've got a deal."

They shook on it, each of their grips as firm as they could make them.

Romano soon learned that there was a world of difference between being an apprentice and being the master. Suddenly his opinion counted on everything and people came to him with questions about everything from lighting to color schemes, music and program notes—things that he'd taken for granted before, things that Rantiki had been able to handle as if by…well, as if by magic.

Nevertheless, Romano was learning to cope with each new responsibility as it came and was taking firmer control over the production of the new show.

Since the contracts had stipulated that Rantiki's name be used in connection with the show so it could be placed on the marquee, Romano had suggested they call it *The Legend of Rantiki*. It seemed dignified enough and Romano figured that if the purpose of using the master's name was to sell tickets, the least he could do was begin the campaign to make the Rantiki name larger than life and synonymous with great magic. It wouldn't be easy, but in the same way that Harry Houdini's legacy included the general perception of him as being a great magician even though he was only a magician of average skill—the two fields he excelled at were showmanship and escapology—Romano would make sure that Rantiki's reputation would continue to grow with each passing year. Hopefully, in the end, when people thought of the great magicians the list would be a short one—Houdini, Mandrake, Siegfried and Roy, Copperfield, Rantiki...

And Romano Minardi.

But such an achievement could only be the result of a career guided firmly along the path. Deviations and setbacks could not be tolerated. Failures had to be corrected immediately or overshadowed by an ensuing huge success. In the field of show business, a magician was only as good as his latest illusion.

And for that reason, Romano was beginning to feel that things were going badly with the new show. The harder he tried to pay homage to *The Legend of Rantiki* the more he felt like things were going wrong.

All wrong.

When he told Harry Reddington Jr. about what he was feeling the veteran mage didn't seem concerned, even though the new show was set to debut in less than a month.

"Listen," he said. "Rantiki wouldn't have passed you the ball if he thought you were going to drop it on the first play. You're just going through what everybody goes through in the middle of big project. Novelists call it mid-novel-angst. That's when they get to the middle of the book they're working on and suddenly think everything they've written is garbage, and what they've still got to write will be lousy. You know what they say is the best thing to do?"

"No, what?"

"Relax, keep writing, everything's going to turn out all right."

Romano didn't feel at all comforted by the suggestion.

"In your case, I'd suggest you keep working on the show. Sooner or later you'll realize what's wrong with it and you'll be able to fix it. All I know is this...it'll all work out in the end. So don't worry so much about it now."

Romano was silent.

"Okay?"

Romano nodded and tried to smile, but the churning in his stomach told him no...

Things were *not* okay.

But what exactly was *wrong*?

Opening night was fast approaching, but Romano wasn't feeling any better about the show. He was doing his best to pay homage to the master, repaying him for the kindness he'd shown the last two years, but it didn't seem to be working.

For example, he was doing the classic milk-can escape, the one first made famous by Houdini and then done by Rantiki in the early years of his career. Romano performed the escape dressed in a full-body swimsuit in order to try to recreate the style of show Rantiki presented in his youth.

He stepped out into the workshop for a full dress-rehearsal of the escape and was already looking forward to getting inside the water-filled milk can since that was the only sure way to ease the incredible amount of itchiness the old woolen suit was causing him.

Susie was there to receive him dressed in a heavily sequined dress that was cut high up on the neck and just below the knee. Her hair was done up in a bun behind her head and she looked for all the world like Barbara Billingsley standing on the front porch waiting for the Beaver to get home from school.

"It's a shame you're wearing that outfit," she said. "You've got such a gorgeous body, love."

Romano was somewhat surprised by the comment, never having thought of himself as sexy before. He began thinking about it.

Las Vegas was a town where naked flesh was as readily available as a pastor at a wedding chapel—you could see both any time of the day or night.

He had filled out over the last couple of years by eating right and working out. He was proud of his musculature, just as Houdini had been proud of his athletic prowess in his youth.

Then why was he covering up?

Why was Susie?

He got into the can. Water spilled over its sides as it was displaced by his body. He took a final few deep breaths (more for show than anything else) and descended the rest of the way into the can, under the water.

As the lid of the can was clamped down over top of him, he continued to think about what Susie had said.

And then it hit him.

What he was trying to do was wrong.

The more he was trying to be *like* Rantiki, the bigger disservice he was doing to the Rantiki name. Rantiki hadn't wanted him to follow in his footsteps, he'd wanted him to make a whole new pathway for himself. Rantiki was a stage magician from another era and if it hadn't been for Romano's ideas for the *Weird Science* show the man would have still been walking out on stage in his tuxedo and asking members of the audience to tie him up. That kind of show wasn't for Romano. He needed to develop his own style as an illusionist and escapologist. A style for the nineties.

He wouldn't do the milk-can escape dressed in a fifty-year-old swimsuit, he'd do it in a Speedo. People from the audience wouldn't tie him up, members of the Las Vegas Metro Police Department would be invited on stage every night to lock him up in exchange for an appearance fee paid to the department's victims' services fund.

Suddenly, Romano's lungs began to ache.

He'd been thinking so much he'd lost track of time.

He pushed hard on the milk can's lid and it popped off. He lifted his head out of the water and gasped. Still breathing hard, he refitted the lid onto the can.

Then the curtain that had been set up around the can fell.

Susie, Kraas and the others were looking at him strangely, no doubt surprised he'd taken so long to get out of the can.

He took a few more seconds to catch his breath, then turned to Susie. "Can I talk to you for a minute?" he said. "In the office." He gestured in the direction of the small room at one end of the workshop that had a desk, an old 286 computer, a phone/fax, and a cot.

"Sure."

Romano entered the office and sat down in front of the desk, drying his hair off with a towel. The walls were plastered with dozens of unframed snapshots pinned in a haphazard way that chronicled the career of Rantiki in an interesting mosaic. There were pictures of Rantiki and such famed magicians as Stanley Collins and Albert Goshman, as well as more recent stars like Doug Henning and Mac King.

Susie came into the office shortly after Romano, hesitating in the doorway before moving slowly through the room.

"Sit down," Romano said casually, pointing to the cot.

She sat down on the edge of the small bed, crossing her legs like a lady. From the look on her face, it was obvious she had an idea about what Romano had on his mind.

"How long did you work with Rantiki?" Romano asked, pulling open drawers in search of some cigarettes. There were none in the desk, but just before he opened the final drawer he cast a rote that put a half-empty pack on the bottom of it under some papers. A lighter too.

"This last time we were together for four years," she said.

"And before that?"

"I worked with him for a few months in the mid-eighties, and for two years in the late seventies."

Romano nodded. "Why the gaps in-between?"

"He'd take the time off to develop new illusions, or I'd have a contract with someone else and he'd have to use a different girl."

"Have you kept in touch with the others you've worked for in the past?"

"Of course," she said. "I haven't lasted this long in this business by being a shy girl."

"No," Romano smiled. "I guess you haven't."

"You're going to change the show, aren't you?"

"How did you know?"

"Well, we've been talking about how you don't seem to be very comfortable doing this style of show. We'd been wondering how long it was going to take before you realized it yourself."

"Was it that obvious?"

Susie leaned forward, reached out and put a hand on Romano's knee. "Rantiki was an old man." She gave a little laugh. "He used to get dressed up in a jacket and tie to eat dinner, for crying out loud!"

Romano *had* thought the ritual was a little outdated.

"You're a young man," she continued. "You need a young show, young girls, young music...."

"Why didn't anyone tell me?"

"Rantiki left things up to you, so we trusted your judgment. We didn't think the show would go over well, but you gave Rantiki a hit with *Weird Science*, so we all gave you the benefit of the doubt."

"Even Martin?"

"He didn't seem to have an opinion either way."

Romano nodded, realizing that now that he was in charge he would get full credit for creating a disastrous show just as easily as a smash hit.

"So you're not surprised?"

"No, not at all." She paused, as if thinking. "And maybe I'm a just a little bit relieved. I'm getting older. Maybe it's time I find me a high-roller and get married. You know, find a family that needs a mothering former showgirl and move right in."

Lucky family, Romano thought. "So you're not mad at me then?"

"No…you know me, I never would have quit myself. I would have done my farewell show from a wheelchair if they'd have let me." She paused to give him a smile. "Maybe it's better that somebody else made the decision for me. If I get out now, at least all my memories will be good ones."

She got up off the cot and gave Romano a hug.

He was sorry to have to let her go, and he was going to miss having her around, but it wasn't going to work with his being the only new blood onstage.

He was confident that he'd made the right decision.

And he knew that because he was already beginning to feel better about the show.

After letting Susie go, he'd had the unenviable task of informing the rest of the crew that Susie wouldn't be working with them anymore. When he told them, he made sure he told them that the reason for the move was that they'd be doing an all-new show that would appeal to a younger, yuppier audience.

Like Romano, everyone was sad to see Susie go, but no one seemed surprised. And if Susie harbored any ill feelings over it, she never let on. In fact, she was the perfect lady about the affair, telling them all that leaving the show was partly her idea and she was going to take the opportunity to enjoy life a bit.

Graham Chambers asked her if she'd come to opening night.

She looked at him and smiled. "I wouldn't miss it for the world, kid."

And later, after she left, everyone turned to look at Romano, awaiting their instructions for building the all-new show.

Unfortunately, Romano didn't have a clue as to what the new show was going to be. With three weeks to go until opening night, there wasn't time to do anything really "new." All there was time for was to give the current show, the current sequence of illusions and escapes, a more modern presentation. If the show went well and they were offered an extended run, then maybe they could spend a few months working on a signature illusion or escape.

He looked at everyone in turn, clapped his hands together and said, "Take the rest of the day off, go home, take in a show, and relax. We'll still be doing the same tricks, but we'll be running them all through a time machine. We'll start tomorrow by trying to give the show an all-new look."

No one was very enthusiastic about the change. Most simply shrugged and said, "See you tomorrow, then."

Romano nodded. "I'll be here."

He knew that changing the show so close to opening night was a huge gamble, but unlike most of the hotel owners and booking agents in Las Vegas, Romano was more than willing to try his luck on something different. The fact that the stakes were so high didn't bother him much. With each move he made, each step he took toward creating a show that was "his," he became more certain that he was doing the right thing, more certain that Rantiki would have approved.

After all, it was the master himself who had once said: *An old trick in a new dress is always a pleasant change.*

He would find that new dress.

And when he did...

It was going to be tight, and sexy, and it was going to make his show the hottest on the Strip.

That night, Romano went to the Magic Box. He had the Spinning Plate Special, but hardly ate any of it. His thoughts were too preoccupied with the show and the changes he'd have to introduce in the morning.

After a coffee and a final smoke inside the bar, he stepped outside and went for a walk. After strolling downtown Las Vegas with Rantiki so many times, he'd come to enjoy the lights of Fremont Street's Neon Garden.

After passing Binion's and the Fremont Hotel, Romano crossed the street in front of Fitzgerald's Hotel and Casino and continued along the south side of the street. At Las Vegas Boulevard, he made a right, walking casually along the sidewalk thinking about the show and what it would need to make it fresh and alive.

With each step he took, he recalled another one of Rantiki's bits of wisdom that he'd memorized during his studies of the man's writings on performing stage magic.

EDO VAN BELKOM

An old trick well done is far better than a new trick with no effect.

Never work to fool a magician; always work to your audience.

You may think your trick is old, but it is always new to members of your audience.

Never tell an audience how good you are; they will soon find that out for themselves.

Don't drag your tricks, but work as quickly as you can, bearing in mind the Latin proverb, "Make haste slowly."

All of it was good advice, and he would put all of it to good use in the revamping of the show. He'd so far decided that he'd speed things up considerably so that what had originally been conceived as a forty-five-minute show would now packed into thirty.

One of the problems which plagued Rantiki's shows was his insistence on doing several escapes in each performance. While turn-of-the-century audiences could sit through a single escape which might take an hour or more to complete, in the age of MTV, escapes took far too much time to be truly entertaining. Romano would still perform escapes, (the show was still to be called *The Legend of Rantiki*), but he would have to figure out a way to set them up quickly.

Speaking of quickly…

Romano looked up, saw the tall thin sign of the Sahara Las Vegas Hotel and realized he'd just walked over two miles on the Strip without even breaking a sweat.

He turned left on Sahara Avenue and came upon Paradise Road. He looked at the street sign for a moment trying to remember what it was about that street that made it sound so familiar. Hoping something along the way would jog his memory he turned right on Paradise and continued his southern trek.

When he reached Riviera Boulevard, it all came back to him.

The red, white and blue neon sign read—

The Bohemian Embassy

It looked like a sleazy little joint, the kind of place that had given Las Vegas its start, but to Romano there was a name up on the sign that gave it all the class in the world.

Now Appearing

Roxanne May

If he wasn't mistaken, Roxanne May was the stage name of the clerk who worked at the dry cleaners inside the Fashion Show Mall, Rhonda

Mazey. She was a nice girl, not to mention good looking. Hell, maybe she was even drop-dead gorgeous.

He thought about that for a moment and wondered if this was another one of those lucky coincidences that had been a part of his life since childhood. He'd thought that after learning about coincidental magick and how to control it, the sheer coincidences he'd experienced throughout his life would become a thing of the past.

He decided not to think about it on the off chance that pondering them might cause them to stop happening.

He crossed the Embassy parking lot and entered through the front door. The inside of the place was dark, dimly lit with candles and soft lighting to give the impression it was always evening inside, an important feature to have in a twenty-four-hour city like Las Vegas.

The crowd looked to be a mixed bag of Vegas residents and tourists who'd lost their way from the Strip. Both groups looked tired, burned out, as if they might as well be here as anywhere else in town.

Romano took a stool at the bar and ordered a draft. It was flat when it came, but he wasn't surprised. At least it was cold, and after his long walk from the Magic Box, it was also refreshing. He finished the beer and ordered another. When the bartender served up his beer he asked her, "When is Roxanne's next show?"

The short, heavyset blonde glanced at her watch. "In about ten minutes."

Romano nodded, sipped his beer, and lit a cigarette. He took a better look around, this time paying closer attention to his surroundings. It was a dark, gloomy, depressing sort of place where people could cry in their beer after they'd lost a lot of money at the casinos.

There are a lot of sayings about Las Vegas. One of them is that people arrive in $15,000 cars and leave on $100,000 buses. Well, this looked like the place where a lot of those people had one last drink before they went on their way.

And yet, despite the split between locals and non-locals, there was a strange commonality among the patrons. They somehow all looked like regulars, as if they'd wandered in off the street like Romano had, and wound up remaining there for an extended stay as bits of scenery, or pieces of furniture.

Romano wondered what sort of songs Roxanne May sang in a place like this. Hurtin' songs, to be sure.

"Ladies and gentlemen," boomed the lounge's public address system. Romano looked around for an M.C. but couldn't find one. The introduction must be on tape. "The Bohemian Embassy is proud to bring you the vocal stylings of Miz Roxanne May."

There was a smattering of applause, most of it the product of Romano's efforts.

A baby spotlight lit up a circle on the small stage and Roxanne May walked out in front of the black grand piano. She picked the microphone out of its holder and kindly thanked the room for their generous applause.

If Romano hadn't known it was her, he'd have had a hard time recognizing the sweet young girl he'd met at the dry cleaners.

She was wearing a low-cut sequined dress that was missing a few rhinestones here and there, and which looked too heavy to allow her slight frame to move about the stage comfortably. Her hair had been left down and hung loosely over her shoulders, and she looked to be wearing way too much make-up for such a small room.

Still…

Romano was captivated by her. She was a beautiful woman, far too beautiful to be working in a dump like the Bohemian Embassy.

The only question was, could she sing?

Sadly, the answer was no.

She started out her set playing the piano, nothing fancy, just some soft melodic stuff that people could talk over without being drowned out. Then she sang her first song, an almost ancient tune called "How Deep Is Your Love?", originally sung by the Bee Gees on the soundtrack to the movie *Saturday Night Fever*. Romano remembered the song because when the film came out every teenager on the street had gone out and bought a polyester three-piece suit like the one John Travolta had worn in the movie. By the time Romano was in his teens, he could buy those same suits for less than a dollar in every thrift shop in the neighborhood. It was enough to turn him off polyester for the rest of his life.

Unfortunately, the anecdote should have been Roxanne's because it might have distracted listeners from her limited range and poor enunciation. By the end of the song she was practically speaking the words to the song at little more than a whisper.

Romano wondered how she was able to continue playing here. The answer was either that she was performing for almost nothing, which was likely, or she had some other talent that wasn't in evidence yet.

When she finished her first song, she picked up the mike again and worked her way around the room doing the "Hi, what's your name? Where you from?" routine that was the staple of every lounge act in the city.

At this she excelled.

She seemed to have a real knack for playing the audience, speaking in a slightly exaggerated southern drawl, flirting with all the men and calling all the women ma'am. She seemed to have a sixth sense about who could take a joke and who couldn't, who she could tease and who was better left alone.

"Hi!" she said to an older woman sitting at a table with her husband. He must have been in town as part of some convention since he was wearing a white nametag that read "Roy." She, however, had none. "What's your name, ma'am?"

"Agnes."

"Agnes what?"

"Agnes Brown."

"I have a friend named Agnes. But I don't think you two are much alike. See, she's a real good woman…a genuine, god-fearing-prim-and-proper-go-to-church-every-Sunday-twice-on-Christmas kind of good woman." A pause. She put a hand on Agnes's shoulder. "Which is not to say that you aren't as well, ma'am."

The room broke into laughter.

"Anyway, Agnes got a cleaning job at one of the chicken ranches outside of town. I told her, 'Agnes, do you think that's the right kind of environment for a woman like you to be working in?'"

Agnes's husband Roy laughed at that. Roxanne took the opportunity to poke fun at him. "See, he knows!" she said. "I *heard* about what goes on there, but *he knows!*"

The room responded with more laughter.

"Anyway, I ran into my friend Agnes a week or so ago and asked if she was still cleaning and dusting and vacuuming out there at the chicken ranch. She said, 'Yes, except sometimes on the weekends there's a rush on business so I help out a little wherever I can.'"

The room roared. Romano even laughed at that.

Then Roxanne settled down at the piano to sing a song, and her act slowly slid back into mediocrity.

She needed to get out of this dive, Romano thought. If she didn't she'd eventually become a bitter, boozy, fifty-year-old barfly telling the Agnes story to the Bohemian Embassy's one-millionth customer.

Romano waited for her to finish her set. When she did, he asked her if she would join him for a drink. She accepted.

He ordered drinks for the both of them, another beer for him and a Golden Cadillac for her, and they sat down at a table near the stage.

"I was wondering when you'd come by to see me."

"Well, we were doing two shows nightly...."

"I know, I saw it three different times."

"You did?" he said, starting to feel guilty about not coming sooner as a matter of professional courtesy. "Then there was Rantiki's death and the funeral arrangements to take care of...."

"Never mind," she said, bright and cheerful, the southern drawl she'd used up on the stage all but gone. "You're here now. How did you like my act?"

Romano knew he couldn't lie to her. If they were going to have any kind of relationship he would have to tell her the truth—even if it hurt. He opened his mouth to speak and at the last second decided on a compromise. "Some parts were better than others."

Surprisingly, she took it quite well. "I'm not much of a singer, right?"

Romano closed his eyes and nodded.

"Yeah, I know. But they want a lounge act here so I do my best to sing a few songs. I've managed to keep the singing down to just four songs for every half-hour set."

While he couldn't say much for her singing ability, he had to give her full marks for chutzpah. That was a word Romano had learned in the old neighborhood. It meant spunk, and Roxanne had plenty of it.

"They pay you much here?" he asked.

"What do you think?"

Romano shook his head.

"I don't work at the dry cleaners for fun, you know."

"I didn't think so."

There was a moment of silence between them and they each took the opportunity to sip their drinks.

"Listen," Roman said. "Why don't you come work for me in the new show I'm putting together?"

"Are you serious?"

"Of course I am. I'll pay you double whatever you're making here and at the dry cleaners."

"You don't know how much that is."

"Can't be much."

She was still hesitant. "But I don't know anything about performing magic. No matter how many times I see it, I can never figure out how you guys do that stuff."

"You don't have to know any magic. I can teach you. All you'll have to do is smile, look sexy, and play up to the crowd, and at that I think you're a natural."

She was silent for a minute, obviously awed by the offer. At last she said, "Well, some people have said that the way I've lasted so long as a lounge singer has been nothing short of magical."

They both laughed.

"You won't have to sing in my act."

"Promise?"

"I promise."

"Then you've got yourself a deal."

They shook on it, Romano pulling her hand toward him and giving it a gentle kiss.

15

Diego Salerno puffed on his cigar and looked over the papers on his desk. He was a short, heavy man with a gruff voice (the result of smoking cigars since the age of eighteen) that people found intimidating. Although he was born in Las Vegas and had rarely been out of state, his appearance made people believe he had connections to the "de boyz" who'd run Vegas before the big clean-up in 1955.

Despite his outward appearance, Salerno had the unlikely job of booking entertainment for Circus, Circus, the one casino in Las Vegas that had catered to kids and families before the trend caught on all along the Strip and every casino in town started presenting shows suitable for all ages.

Martin Kraas had come here looking for a job working their free daily circus-style show. It wasn't the kind of thing he'd had in mind, but all of the other hotels on the Strip wanted him to do a show on a smaller scale to get his feet wet before they risked booking him into one of their bigger rooms. As a result, he was looking for bookings he would have turned up his nose at seven years ago.

And now, here he was trying to get work in a circus.

"So, what did you say your name was?" Salerno asked, his words accompanied by a thick plume of cigar smoke.

"Martin Kraas."

Kraas felt himself burning up inside. His name used to be up in lights. Small lights, but lights just the same.

Salerno repeated the name over and over again, snapping his fingers with each word. "Martin Kraas, Martin Kraas…"

"I worked with The Great Rantiki for seven years," Kraas said, jogging the squat man's memory.

"Right, right, so that's where I heard the name before." He shook his head. "Gee, that's too bad about what happened. I liked him…."

"It was tragic."

"So, you're a magician too?"

"Yes."

"Where have you performed lately?"

That same question again, the one that killed his chances of getting a booking at any of the bigger casinos in town. "I've been working as Rantiki's senior technician the last seven years. Before that I worked in Reno, Tahoe, a couple of places in town like the Cameroon and the Landmark."

"The Landmark's been closed for years."

"Yeah, well, when it was open, I did my show there."

Salerno smiled at that. "You know all our acts are circus acts."

"Yeah, I know."

"So, how do you feel about doing your act dressed up like a clown?"

Kraas could just picture himself in a flaming orange fright wig and big red nose, scaring the shit out of toddlers and listening to pre-teens telling him he couldn't hold a candle to Bozo. *Well,* he thought, *anything to get a foot back in the door.* "I've always wanted to be a magical clown," he said, trying to keep his voice as even as possible.

"Good, then maybe you could come work for me."

"I'd like that," Kraas lied.

Romano introduced Roxanne to the rest of the staff at 9 AM sharp Monday morning and every one of them stealthily gave Romano the "thumbs up" as soon as Roxanne moved onto the next introducee.

"Roxanne May," Romano said, showing her off almost like a teenager introducing his parents to his first real girlfriend. He'd tried to introduce her as Rhonda Mazey, but she preferred to leave that name back behind the counter at the dry cleaners. From here on out, she wanted to be know exclusively as Roxanne May. Romano didn't mind. There was something exciting about knowing a woman named Roxy.

"This is Graham Chambers," Romano said. "He's another one of our technicians…a back-room boy."

Chambers extended his hand. "Pleased to meet you." He held onto her hand, shaking it slightly as he studied her face. "Don't you work at…" he paused to think about it, "at the Bohemian Embassy?"

"Not anymore."

Chambers looked at Romano and nodded in approval. "I never did think your talents were, uh…suited to a place like the Embassy."

Roxanne smiled. "A diplomat. Thanks, that's the most polite way I've heard it said in a long, long time."

By mid-morning Romano was already showing her what she had to do for the presentation of the show's final few escapes. She was a quick study and quickly became familiarized with the mechanical part of her on-stage role. Soon she'd be adding the little bits of presentational flare and pizzazz, but that stuff would come to her naturally as they rehearsed the show a hundred or so more times before opening night.

And then there was the little matter of a costume.

Romano didn't have a clue as to what kind of costume would best suit Roxanne.

But not to worry.

He knew someone who did.

By Wednesday, Romano had gotten in touch with Susie. He felt uneasy about calling her up so soon after letting her go, but thankfully she was her usually effervescent self on the phone. "Geez, Romano. It's not even a week and you're already lost without me."

Romano laughed. "Something like that."

"All right. I've got a few days before I leave for Hawaii, I'd be glad to help you out."

Susie took Roxanne to an old Italian woman named Regina DiMaio who worked out of her home in the northwest part of the city inside the pocket between Highways 15 and 95, where she created some of the most spectacular—not to mention sexiest—stage costumes on the Strip. She did mostly custom work, individual costumes rather than entire shows, and over the years she had dressed such Vegas entertainers as Dionne Warwick, Helen Reddy, Ann-Margret, Donna Summer, even Tina Turner. It was her attention to detail that made her such a success. She wouldn't let a costume out of her house until she was satisfied that everything about it was as good as she could make it—even if the new show she was making a costume for was set to open in less than an hour.

The two women walked up to the long, flat bungalow, knocked on the door, then waited for what seemed like forever for someone to answer. At last they were greeted by an hunched-over old woman with short, salt-and-pepper hair. She wore a well-worn, faded blue smock, old red slippers that slapped against the floor as she walked, and a pair of fallen stockings that had gathered around her ankles.

"So," Susie said. "What do you think?"

The old woman nodded. "*Girati*."

"She wants you to turn around."

Roxanne turned slowly.

"*Vieni con me*" she said, closing the door and walking slowly toward the back of the house.

"Let's go," Susie said.

The two women followed.

By the following Monday Susie was off to Hawaii. She wouldn't say if she was headed there by herself, with a girlfriend, or on the arm of some millionaire. She vowed to be back for opening night and Romano and Chambers had set up a pool so everyone could place bets on who they thought she'd be showing up with. Right now, "Jed Clampett" (a Texas millionaire with nothing else to spend his money on) was leading 3-1 while "Thurston Howell III" (an anal-retentive old-money millionaire who wanted to show the world he could still attract beautiful women) and "Richie Rich" (a wealthy young man looking for a woman who would baby him) were a close second and third.

But before she'd left, Susie had spent two long days with Roxanne, giving her a crash course in how to pack sex appeal into the act without acting like a tramp.

If Roxanne was as quick a learner with Susie as she'd been with everything else, thought Romano, she was going to be a knockout on stage.

And now came their first test, a dress rehearsal of their entrance.

Kraas and Chambers had fixed the lighting in the workshop to approximate the proscenium stage they would have to work with once they moved into the Frontier Hotel and Gambling Hall for the final week of rehearsal. Although Kraas had come in for this morning's dress rehearsal, he had been somewhat conspicuous by his absence most of the last two weeks. But he hadn't been shirking any of his responsibilities, and Romano figured he was probably working on his act. Whatever the reason for his absence, there hadn't been any problems so far and Romano wasn't interested in creating any. He was here today when it mattered.

Kraas and Chambers worked the lights, turning them down low as Roxanne stepped onto the stage wearing what looked to be one of Susie's old tuxedos. Romano stepped onto the stage from the other end, similarly dressed in an old black-and-white tux. As the somber organ music played, they stood facing each other.

Suddenly Roxanne reached out, grabbed Romano's tuxedo at the shoulders and tore it from his body. Underneath he wore a second suit, this one a bright blue, studded with rhinestones and sparkles that shimmered and glittered with every move he made.

Acting as if he'd been offended by the temerity of his assistant, Romano took hold of the shoulders of Roxanne's tuxedo and pulled down.

The black jacket and pants came off easily, giving way to a skimpy red dress that had aspirations of being a bodysuit. Up top it hugged her figure to perfection, and was low-cut down the front so that her cleavage line could easily be made out from way back in the cheap seats. The suit's sequins followed her figure, swirling down past her waist, where the dress part of her outfit left one leg exposed high up on the thigh and swept down to cover her other leg like an evening dress.

Roxanne put her bare leg forward in a stance that was second nature to every dancer on the Strip, then raised her hands in a flourish.

Their entrance finished, the music faded out.

"Well, what do you think?" she asked Romano.

"Could still be improved, but I think you're going to be the most gorgeous magician's assistant this town has ever seen."

"Do you really think so?"

He nodded slowly. "I know it."

They came together in a tight embrace.

Romano kissed her full on the mouth.

Roxanne reciprocated.

Up on the scaffold, a pair of eyes narrowed, watching the two kiss.

After rehearsal Romano took Roxanne to the Magic Box for a bite to eat and a few drinks. Shortly after he began introducing her to the bar's regulars, a queue formed around the room as everyone was eager to meet Romano's new lady friend.

"She's a real looker, kid," Jimmy Platt said, gently holding on to Roxanne's hand for as long as he could. "I'd buy a ticket just to see her up on the stage." He gave Romano a wink as a sign of approval.

The introductions ended with Harry Reddington Jr. While he'd previously referred to her as his new onstage assistant, he introduced her to Reddington as his acolyte.

To that Reddington nodded graciously, and said, "Welcome."

As they sat down to eat she asked Romano about this somewhat strange introduction.

"What did you mean when you called me your acolyte?"

Romano figured this was as good a time as any to introduce Roxanne into the world of mages, and he attempted to explain it all to her in a way that might help her understand.

"The Magic Box isn't just a gathering place for magicians, it's a place where a special kind of magicians meet."

"You mean like a secret society."

"Yes and no. The magicians who come to this place are also known as mages. In addition to their stage magic, they can also perform magick," (he made sure to put the emphasis on the second syllable), "or what you might think of as 'magic' in the classic sense of the word."

"Oh, come on," she laughed. "You don't expect me to believe that...." Her voice trailed off. When Romano's expression remain unchanged, she said, "Do you?"

"Not right away, but eventually, yes...Perhaps after a demonstration."

"That would be nice..." she said a little skeptically. "But if it's like a secret society, why are you telling me about it?"

"Because I want you to become a part of it."

She sat there in silence, a little stunned by Romano's admission. Finally she said, "So being an ac-o-lyte—" she said the word slowly "—is more than just being an assistant?"

"Much more," Romano said, his voice sliding into a low, seductive tone.

"Oh, really," she said, flattered and flustered.

Their conversation was cut short just then as the waiter arrived with their prime-rib dinners and a bottle of Mateus. When they began talking again, it was all about the show and how it might be improved.

"I was thinking you could do with some better music."

Romano nodded. "I think you're right. I've been concentrating so much on staging the illusions, I haven't gotten around to considering new music yet."

"I could help you."

Romano just looked at her.

"I know I'm not much of a singer, but I do have an ear for music. I even have some friends with access to recording studios and mixing boards. If you tell me what you'd like, I could put together the music for the show."

"That's a wonderful idea. Yes, please."

"What did you have in mind?"

Now here was a problem. Romano wasn't "into" music and while he knew a good tune when he heard it, he didn't have a clue as to musical styles or the names of groups. This was one part of the show that was best left up to someone else.

"I'd like the music to be for young people, with a hard pounding rhythm that will constantly push the show forward."

"Hard rock with a beat."

Romano wasn't sure, but he said, "Yes."

"Any particular bands you have in mind?"

Romano didn't know any. He could name the top one hundred and fifty magicians and illusionists from the past one hundred and fifty years, but he didn't know the names of five musical groups other than the Beatles and the Rolling Stones.

"Who do you like?" she asked.

That was a familiar phrase. He tried to recall where he'd heard it before and suddenly remembered the potwasher at Torchy's. He'd asked the exact same question. Then, like now, Romano didn't have an answer. But the potwasher had mentioned groups named Van Halen and Aerosmith and those names sounded as good as any. "Van Halen and Aerosmith?"

Roxanne looked at him strangely, as if he'd said Lawrence Welk. "Well, I suppose that kind of music would make for an interesting stage presentation. Give me a couple of days. I'll see what I can put together."

"I know you'll do a great job."

They finished their meal and sipped the last of their wine.

"When will I see that demonstration you mentioned before?"

The wine had warmed Romano's insides and he was feeling more than a little bold. "Not here," he said.

"Then where?"

"Your place."

She looked at him, smiling coyly. "All right."

Romano raised his hand and pulled two twenty-dollar bills out of the air. He put it down on the table and said, "Let's go."

Martin Kraas sat on a stool at the bar in Ralph's Diner inside the Stardust Hotel. "Fucking hotshot with his big-tit bimbo…" he mumbled as he hoisted another highball full of scotch and water.

He'd spent the late afternoon under the big top over at Circus, Circus getting his costume designed and fitted. They'd named him Blinkles, since the Casino's mascot clown was named Blinko and they'd already gone through Blinky, Blinker, Blinkette, Blinkster, Blinkaroo, Blinkidink, and Blinkus in their free circus act. He would be performing in white pancake make-up with a huge red, shit-eating grin on his face. His costume was fitted with blinking lights and was so big it made him look like a circus tent, never mind a circus clown. To top it all off, his shoes were the size of mailboxes and flopped around so badly he couldn't take more than three steps in a row without tripping.

All of this after he'd had to watch Romano Minardi, a no-name punk from Butt-Fuck Nowhere, play tongue-hockey with a woman he'd fantasized about for years.

"I bet he's doin' the nasty with her right fucking now!" he said, slamming his drink down on the bar top and ordering another.

It just wasn't fair. *He* was supposed to be the one taking over for Rantiki. *He* was supposed to be the one to have his name up in lights. *He* was the one who was supposed to sweep the women off their feet.

Instead, he was the one doing free shows for the kids at Circus, Circus. Blinkles.

No matter how good a show he did, everyone would remember him as Blinkles. Not Martin Kraas.

Blinkles the Clown.

God, it made his stomach turn.

The bartender slid another drink onto the bar in front of him and he downed half of it in a gulp.

If it hadn't been for Romano Minardi…

He interrupted the thought in midstream. Maybe it wasn't too late. He considered it, then slowly began revising his thinking.

If it wasn't for Romano Minardi…

Yes, that was better.

If Romano Minardi was out of the way…

Better still.

If Romano Minardi was out of the way…it would leave the spotlight open for Martin Kraas.

Wonderful, but how to do it?

If he were to die…

No, too much. Especially after Rantiki's curious demise.

Perhaps if he were to fail.

No, he was too good a magician for that.

What if…he were exposed? Yes, exposed as a young no-talent hustler exploiting the legend and good name of an acknowledged master.

It was prime-time tabloid trash, enough for a movie-of-the-week and then some.

"Gimme the phone, will ya," Kraas said to the bartender/soda jerk behind the counter.

An old black dial phone was brought in front of Kraas. He fished inside his wallet and pulled out a familiar slip of paper. He dialed the number.

"Hello?"

"Hello, Daria. This is Martin Kraas. I think I've got a new angle for Jerry."

"Look, I told you Jerry's not interested in—"

"It's got greed, exploitation, and sex…and I can get you tape."

"All right, maybe I'm interested."

"I thought you might be."

Romano and Roxanne went to her apartment on South Chapman. It was a one-bedroom apartment on the top floor of a three-story low-rise. It was decorated with secondhand furniture and a few new pieces, and everywhere you looked there were books on shelves made out of wooden planks and cinder blocks. It had the feel of a university student's apartment, but Romano hadn't known enough university students (or any, for that matter) to be sure.

"Did you go to UNLV?" Romano asked, sitting down on the couch in the living room. It looked as if it had been pulled out of the garbage, but it was comfortable as hell.

"Yes," Roxanne answered. "Hotel and Restaurant Management. Graduated at the bottom of the class, hence my job at the dry cleaners."

"So you sang your way through college?"

"That's what it says on my C.V., but unfortunately I waited on tables more than anything else…which wasn't too bad since it was sort of like studying." She went into the kitchen and opened up the refrigerator. "Red wine okay?"

"Sure."

She began pouring their drinks.

"Listen," he said. "You're welcome to come stay out at Rancho Rantiki. There's plenty of room and it would save you your rent and travel expenses, food too."

She walked into the living room carrying a tray with two wine glasses on it. "Are you inviting me to move in with you?"

Romano wasn't sure if she was flattered or offended. "Oh no, there are plenty of rooms for everyone. You wouldn't even have to stay in the main house if you didn't want to. I don't."

She slid into the seat next to him on the couch and handed him a glass of wine. "But that wouldn't be any fun."

A mixture of excitement and relief washed over Romano. "No, I suppose it wouldn't."

"It would be much more fun if we, you know, came into close contact with each other." She moved closer to him and he could smell the floral scent of her hair.

"Yes, it would."

She put down her glass, then wrapped her arms around him and kissed the nape of his neck, working her way slowly toward his lips.

"That would be—" Romano's words were cut off by her kiss. He still had his wine glass in his hand. Not wanting to spill anything on the couch, he released the glass and cast a rote that floated it gently over to the end table.

Then, with the glass safely at rest, he turned his attentions to Roxanne and put his full concentration toward returning her kiss.

They adjourned to the bedroom.

Romano made sure they took their time, making love rather than simply having sex.

And while they made love, Romano heightened the experience for both of them by applying just a touch of magick.

The more he'd studied magick, the more he'd come to realize that his sphere of magick—his area of speciality—was magick having to do with Time.

It was just as well since time was a sphere of magick that was particularly suited to a stage magician and escape artist. He could slow down time around him, making a second of real time take up to ten seconds or more for him. This came in handy for escapes, and could give him as much time as he needed (even an hour or more) to complete an escape during which only a few minutes would have passed for the audience. It was the same magick Rantiki had used to escape from the ropes Romano had tied him up in on the first night they'd met. Rantiki had probably spent half an hour getting out of the knots, but from Romano's perspective and that of the audience, he'd escaped from the bonds in just under six minutes.

But magick didn't only have its uses on the stage. There were also more practical, and perhaps more satisfying, applications to be considered.

Like now.

Romano used his talents sparingly, but in such a way as to give Roxanne the most satisfying sexual experience of her life.

Each time she'd let out a slight moan or some other sign that she was experiencing a pleasurable sensation, Romano slowed down time around her, stretching out that one moment so she could experience the pleasure longer and more intensely than she would have otherwise.

When she orgasmed, he slowed down time almost to a standstill, making the intense pleasure of the moment of her climax last as long as he could. The effect for her was like having a shuddering half-hour orgasm, one that left her absolutely satisfied and utterly exhausted by the time it was over.

"That was wonderful," she managed to say, a little out of breath.

Romano took a cigarette off the night-table and lit it. "Yes, it was." Even though he'd concentrated on pleasing her, he'd enjoyed it almost as much as she had.

She rolled over and wrapped her arms around him, rubbing her damp, naked body against his. She ran her fingers in circles over the thick dark hair on his chest.

"Everything's been so wonderful these past few days."

"Hasn't it?" Romano said, holding her in his arms. He thought about it for a moment. Everything had been going extremely well this past week—too well, in fact. There hadn't been any personality clashes between staff members, Susie had been a great help even after she'd been dropped from the show, all the equipment worked perfectly, the dress rehearsals had gone off without a hitch, the costumes looked stunning (especially Roxanne's), and now this...a night of slow, sensuous lovemaking, bonding mage and acolyte and hopefully ensuring her loyalty to him forever.

It was all too wonderful.

Too good...

Too good to be true.

Something *had* to go wrong.

But what?

16

They had moved the show onto the stage at the Frontier Hotel three days before opening night. After a day and half of preparations they had gone through their first full dress rehearsal without incident. Romano performed each illusion expecting something to go wrong, perhaps even hoping it would go wrong so that it wouldn't go wrong when the curtain went up in front of a theater full of people.

Like all magicians, he was prepared for his magic to fail. His line was, "Ladies and gentlemen, mistakes sometimes happen, and that was one of them," but he hoped he'd never need to use it.

And now he sat in one of the casino's meeting rooms four hours before the show's opening in order to give interviews to local newscasts, and freelancers working for the tabloid and digest television shows like *Inside Affair* and *Entertainment Tonight*.

"You're calling the show *The Legend of Rantiki*," said a short Asian woman, stringing a segment for *ET*. "But from what I've seen of the show in rehearsal, it doesn't look much like a show The Great Rantiki would have been a part of."

Romano smiled. "That's right. While this show is to honor one of the greatest illusionists and escapologists that ever lived, it's also my show. I tried to perform it as Rantiki would have performed it, but that was like asking Picasso to paint like Norman Rockwell. I'm doing the exact same escapes and illusions Rantiki did over the course of his career, but I've given them an updated package, or a 'new dress' as he might have said."

"You're also calling yourself Mister Magick. Is that all part of *The Legend of Rantiki?*"

Romano let out a little laugh. He was beginning to cultivate the name as a subtitle to his own. If hockey fans and broadcasters could call Wayne Gretzky simply "The Great One," and the previous generation could call Gordie Howe "Mr. Hockey," then maybe he could come to be known as Mister Magick. If all went well and the name caught on, Mister Magick would become the name of a magic company that would produce shows all over Las Vegas. It would also become the name of a company which would make small illusions and magic tricks for retail sale to kids. All of this from the two words he'd seen under Rantiki's picture in his high school yearbook—Mister Magic.

"That's my way of paying homage to The Great Rantiki. It was a nickname of his. I've adopted it, but like everything else, I've updated it to make it my own."

Romano was distracted by some sort of commotion outside in the hall. He paused for a moment and looked over the woman's shoulder.

Just then the door to the dressing room burst open and Jerry Baker stepped into the room, followed by not one, but two cameras, a sound man with a big boom mike and an assortment of other people who looked like Baker cronies.

Baker paused a moment before speaking, no doubt to give the other cameramen in the room time to swing their lenses around and focus on his perfectly coiffed hair, white suit and boots, yellow carnation and black bolo tie.

Graham Chambers ran into the room. "I tried to stop him, told him he wasn't on the media list, but one of his thugs held me back."

Romano waved at Chambers in a way that told him that everything would be all right.

The Asian reporter who had been interviewing Romano turned to see what all the commotion was about. Baker's crusades against the seductive side of Las Vegas must have been garnering plenty of national press of late, because as soon as she saw Baker and his war party she got up out of her chair and told her cameraman to keep rolling tape.

Romano had a hunch that Baker wasn't here to do some puff piece on the show's opening. From the way he'd burst into the room, it looked as if he'd arrived wanting to pick a fight, and Romano vowed to do everything in his power to avoid one.

"Well, you wanted something to go wrong," Romano whispered under his breath. "Careful what you wish for...you just might get it."

He got up from his seat.

Roxanne came over and stood by his side.

"Mr. Baker," he said graciously as he walked across the room. "How nice of you to drop in on the opening night of our new show. If you'd like an interview I can accommodate you in about twenty minutes. Then we can chat for as long as you like." Romano was doing his best not to sound abrupt or condescending, but it was a difficult task knowing Baker had been one of the forces behind Rantiki's untimely onstage death.

"I'm not interested in sitting down and having a chat," Baker said, already into his television-pulpit style of oration. The words were bellowed rather than spoken, and the pauses were drawn out as long as possible for effect. "Not yet, anyway. What I'm here for is to call a spade a spade."

Romano smiled politely. "I'm afraid I don't follow you."

"You, Romano Minardi," he thrust his index finger forward as if it were a knife, "are nothing more than a parasite, living off another man's good name. That's right. The Great Rantiki was perhaps one of the finest illusionists this town has ever seen…and now you are set to make a fortune from his name with a show that represents everything that's corrupt and evil about this devil's spawn of a city."

Romano couldn't believe how Baker was able to change his opinion of Rantiki so totally. It was as if his personality was simply an extension of his television show and beneath that spotless white suit there was absolutely nothing of substance.

At that moment Romano realized that in death Rantiki had beaten Baker more completely than he ever could have while alive. But while death had been a viable option for Rantiki, it wasn't for Romano. He'd have to try diplomacy first, and then if that didn't work, he'd fight the man tooth and nail. "I was his apprentice. His wish was that I continue on in his place."

"With a show featuring the severing of body parts? The decapitation of women? Bondage? Impaling?"

Apparently Baker hadn't bothered to take in one of the open dress rehearsals put on for the benefit of the media. "I don't know where you've come up with things like severed body parts, or impaling…none of those things are in my show." Romano felt he was going on the defensive and checked himself against it. "But if they were, they'd be mere illusions for the purposes of entertainment…." He did his best to keep his voice calm, an increasingly difficult task.

"Entertainment? These aren't entertainments, they are the amusements of men who are the sworn enemies of God…the perverted foes of our Lord Jesus Christ! How else could you explain such acts performed in a titillating orgy of naked flesh, pounding rock music, and light and shadows commanded by the Prince of Darkness?"

It was now obvious to Romano that Baker wasn't particularly interested in anything he had to say. Nevertheless, the cameras were rolling and he had to say *something* to balance out Baker's diatribe.

"Nothing more than simple magic," he said. "Stage tricks and illusions."

"Yes, magick," Baker said, pronouncing the word correctly with emphasis on the second syllable. "Spelling it with a K doesn't fool me or anybody else. You profess to be able to perform magick and whatever way you want to spell the word it still reads B-L-A-S-P-H-E-M-Y. Blasphemy against God, the church and all the good God-fearing people of Nevada and the United States of America, the greatest country on God's green Earth."

Baker's rant had stirred up several of the shills he'd brought into the room with him and they had now begun to cheer him on.

"Praise the Lord!" said one.

"Hallelujah!" cried another.

No doubt about it, Baker was a force to be reckoned with. He was charismatic on cue, a gifted public speaker, and from the way he called upon the power of God he almost had Romano believing he could summon a thunderbolt and direct it anywhere he pleased.

For a moment, Romano wondered if Baker was a Technomancer. It was possible—he certainly knew how to use the technology of television to his advantage—but somewhat unlikely since Romano had never felt any Quintessence in his presence and no one ever spoke of him as being dangerous in that way.

Still, he now understood why Rantiki had opted out of a confrontation with the man. Even with Romano's knowledge of magick, Jerry Baker was a formidable opponent. The man understood the power of television and used the television cameras as both a weapon and a shield. With the cameras rolling he could attack Romano almost with impunity, since retaliation, either verbal or physical, would result in lawsuits and even more adverse publicity. And if Baker was ever dragged into court on charges of defamation of character, there'd be even more publicity, and then the First Amendment would suddenly kick in, making it look as if he, Jerry Baker, were the victim.

Romano realized he was in a no-win situation. The best he could do was to remain strong and perhaps put Baker off for another time, a time when they might meet on neutral ground.

"It seems that you've come here to make a little speech. Now that you've made it, I'd appreciate it if you would leave so I can continue with these *respected journalists—*" he said these words so that it was clear Baker was not considered to be part of their group "—who have graciously and patiently waited for an interview."

"I didn't come here to make any speeches, only to state the God-honest truth, and..." Baker said, drawing out the word to capture everyone's attention, "I've come here to invite you to be a guest on my television show so that you may have the opportunity to defend yourself against my charges that you, sir, are a no-talent fraud, exploiting women, playing the devil's music, and claiming to have godlike powers which you call *magick,* but which everybody in the world knows are merely parlor tricks and devilish deceptions."

Romano stepped closer to Baker, deciding that the best way to handle him was to beat him at his own game. If Baker was putting on a show, Romano would put on a better one. He stopped just inches in front of the man, ensuring that they'd both be in the same tight shot. Curiously, Baker smelled of alcohol.

"First of all, I wouldn't dignify your show with an appearance if it were the only one on television, so you're going to have to obtain respectability for it some other way. Secondly, I'm not sure I've ever *claimed* to be able to perform magick since I haven't set foot on the stage as a solo act yet. But since you are so keen on defaming me for my ability to perform magick— an ability which I assure you I possess—you leave me with no other choice than to admit to it."

He looked into one of the cameras that bore a logo of *The Jerry Baker Show.*

"Yes, I can perform magick," he said, staring directly into the lens. "And if there any doubts as to whether I can or cannot, perhaps a little demonstration is in order." He rolled up the sleeve of his right hand and twisted his wrist three times as he cast a rote. On the fourth rotation a small sign connected to a short stick appeared in his clenched hand.

He turned the sign toward the camera so that the big red block letters would fill up the screen.

The sign read—

The Jerry Baker Show...

He turned the sign around to expose the other side to the camera.

SUCKS!

Then he turned the sign around again to expose the side he'd first shown to the camera.

BIG TIME!!

For a moment the room was silent. Then everyone began to laugh. It was a light chuckle at first, but as Romano made sure everyone in the room read the sign, the laughter grew.

Then as he continued to display the sign, he felt a slight jab of pain as Paradox flowed through his body. He flinched, but nothing noticeable to anyone looking on.

Soon the chuckles grew into loud, roaring laughter.

Baker was not amused, which seemed to make everyone laugh even harder. "That little stunt will never make it onto my show."

"Maybe not yours," Romano said. "But there are lots of cameras here, still photographers too. I'm sure your viewers will get to see evidence of my magick one way or another."

"You mean your clever little hoaxes, your ingenious little lies, your spurious attempt to honor a legend."

Romano had heard just about enough. Roxanne placed her hands on his shoulders in an attempt to calm him, but it was too little too late. "Listen, Mr. Baker…instead of targeting me, why don't you just find some neo-Nazi transvestite party clowns to denounce, or have you already done that show idea to death?"

Baker moved closer, his smile somewhat sinister, his breath laced with liquor. "You're a game one, aren't you?"

"I don't play games, Mr. Baker."

"Good, neither do I."

They stood there for several seconds, staring each other down. Baker was the first to move, spinning on his boot heels and leaving the room, his entourage following him closely as if there were something to be gained by traveling in his wake.

Romano remained standing in the middle of the room for some time afterward, a little surprised that Baker and his crew had left so quickly, not to mention so willingly.

Obviously, this little incident wouldn't be the end of it. More likely it was the prelude to some future battle, a set-up for things to come.

The confrontation had left Romano pumped, psyched, and ready to fight.

He would have to settle down somewhat by showtime, maybe do a few relaxing rotes backstage before the curtain went up.

Hopefully, once that happened, the rest of the evening would go smoothly.

Something told Romano it wouldn't, but he could still hope.

EDO VAN BELKOM

Martin Kraas lingered by a concrete light standard in the parking lot in front of the Frontier Hotel. From that spot, he had a clear view of the large column of neon that was the Frontier's sign, and the big lighted sign announcing the opening of *The Legend of Rantiki*. His only consolation about the sign was that while Romano Minardi's name was up there in lights, it was in tiny letters near the bottom.

Kraas had been inside the hotel watching the meeting between Romano and Baker from the edge of the doorway. After Baker left the room, he'd headed for the parking lot to meet him there.

Minutes later Baker pulled up in a van driven by Daria DePaul. Baker was not a happy man. The look on his face was mean enough to kill.

"Who the hell's side are you on?" Baker said.

Kraas wrinkled his nose at the foul stink of booze on Baker's breath, then took a nervous look around. "What are you talking about?"

"That sign of his had to have come from somewhere. He had to have known we were coming and somebody had to have told him." His eyes narrowed. "Are you playing both ends of the field?"

"I didn't tell him a thing. I didn't tell anybody." He shook his head. "He's a good magician; sometimes he's even as good as he says."

"I don't give a rat's ass about how good he is. I just want to show the world that he can no more perform magick than you or I can shoot bullets out of our butt. If we do this right, *The Jerry Baker Show* could go national and then we can give that Geraldo fellow a run for his money."

Kraas nodded.

"Now we're going to need that tape."

"You'll get it."

"Damn right I will."

The van pulled away with a faint screech of rubber, leaving Kraas to choke on the dark, foul smoke left by its exhaust.

He watched it pull out of the parking lot and head south along Las Vegas Boulevard. Then, after taking another look at the huge neon sign towering over him, Kraas turned to face the Frontier, took in a deep lungful of dry and dirty desert air, and headed back inside.

"Here goes nothing."

17

One hour to showtime.

The media finished with their photo opportunities and were politely ushered out of the room as fresh finger foods, wine and cheese were brought in. Then the doors were re-opened and Romano welcomed friends and guests to a informal reception.

The first to enter were Romano's parents, whom he had flown in from Montreal to celebrate the occasion. They had left his little sister Louise in Montreal with Zia Yolanda, saying Las Vegas was no place for little girls. Romano knew that Vegas was a perfect playground for kids and had already arranged for her to fly out when school let out for the summer.

When the Frontier Hotel had heard that Romano's parents were coming for the opening they made a suite available for them at no charge and gave them all sorts of other comps for free shows, meals, as well as free pulls on selected slot machines.

Romano regretted the fact that he'd had so little time to spend with his parents, but he was still glad they'd come out to Las Vegas so they could see for themselves that he'd indeed made it as a *mago*.

"Romano," his mother said, coming toward him with her arms open. She looked different dressed in the black nylon jacket embroidered with the Frontier name they'd given to her upon check-in, but it was a good kind of different. She looked younger, vibrant, and she was smiling a lot. Most of it had to do with "her son the famous magician," a phrase he'd heard her say more than a few times these past few days, but another part of it was that she was in her element. If she were forced to move to Las Vegas tomorrow, she'd have no trouble adapting to her new environment. This was a place she could thrive in, and Romano had a feeling he'd be seeing a lot more of her in Las Vegas over the next few years.

She hugged him long and hard, then told him, "*Bona fortuna*," before heading back out the door to play a few more slots before the show began.

But while his mother was having the time of her life, his father was another matter entirely. He wandered the halls of the hotel and gambling hall with a long face, refusing to gamble away money—even someone else's—and was constantly asking what the catch was to all the free things people were offering him.

But more than anything else, he was embittered by the fact that Romano had forced him to admit that he'd been wrong. Two short years ago he'd tried to convince Romano that working in a meat-packing plant was the best thing for his future. If Romano had followed his advice, he'd be making an annual salary equal to what he might clear in the first two sold-out days of *The Legend of Rantiki*. So instead of enjoying his son's success, Franco Minardi was haunted by it.

Romano realized the situation his father was in and had steered clear of mentioning the circumstances surrounding his leaving home the entire time his parents were in Las Vegas.

As the two men came together, his father extended his hand and they shook.

"You've done well," he said.

Romano nodded thanks.

And then his father said something Romano had thought he might never hear from the man.

"I'm proud of you."

Romano pulled his father close and the two men hugged. It was a long, heartfelt embrace.

"Thanks, papa."

When they were done, Franco Minardi stood awkwardly by his son's side. Finally, he said, "I better go check on your mother," and he hurried out of the room and into the anonymity of the crowded gambling hall.

The smile on Romano's face remained there for a long, long time.

After his parents left the room, the rest of the visitors passed through in a blur of bodies. Harry Reddington Jr., Jimmy Platt, and a half-dozen other members of the Las Vegas cabal dropped by to say hello and to offer their support.

Other Las Vegas performers followed, like Tom Jones, Wayne Newton, and Don Rickles. The cream of Las Vegas entertainers were all coming to check out the new kid on the Strip.

Even actor Tony Curtis paid a visit, wishing Romano luck.

Romano was surprised to see Curtis there—especially since he hadn't even bothered to invite him—and somewhat awed by the presence of the others, but he never let down his guard, maintaining an air of confidence right up until showtime.

"There he is!"

The voice was loud and shrill. And familiar.

Romano looked up and saw a welcome sight.

She was a bronze-tanned, bottle-blond wearing a skin-tight red dress, who looked as if she'd done more than all right for herself these past few weeks.

Susie Wand rushed across the room, nearly bowling Romano over with a hug and a kiss.

"Hi, Susie," Romano said. "Who's your fella?"

To Susie's right was a tall, barrel-chested man with a full red beard and a black cowboy hat. He wore a tan blazer, brown corduroy pants and big black boots. If he hadn't been so tall, he might have been a dead ringer for Yosemite Sam.

For a moment, Romano wondered if good ole Sam had been on the list for Susie's marriage pool.

"This is Ed. Ed Treasure."

Ed tipped his hat. "Howdy."

Romano looked up at him. "Howdy, Ed."

"Ed's from Texas," Susie said.

"You don't say."

"We met two weeks ago at the Hacienda and I invited him back for your opening night."

"Glad you could make it, Ed."

"Mah pleasure," he said in a thick drawl.

Susie looked across the room at Roxanne. "Oh, Ed darling, there's someone you have to meet." She grabbed Ed firmly by the arm, pulling him across the room as if he were on wheels.

"Nervous?"

Roxanne looked at Harry Reddington Jr. and shook her head in answer. A moment later she exhaled and said, "Yes!"

"Well, don't be." Reddington took Roxanne's hands in his. "Romano is a talented young man, and a powerful young mage. With you by his side...I think you'll do very well together."

Roxanne breathed easier. "Thanks."

"Now, I'd tell this to Romano, but I don't think he'd listen." A pause. "If you're ever in trouble, or you need any kind of help, either you or Romano, I want you to call me first."

Roxanne wasn't sure why Reddington was telling her this, or what he could do for them, but she knew enough to know that he wasn't offering his help lightly. "What kind of trouble?"

"Don't worry about that now. You'll know what kind when you come up against it." He fished inside his jacket. "Here's my card. You can call me at that number at any time of the night or day."

"All right," she said, slipping the card into an inconspicuous spot under her dress, a dress which couldn't afford to have its lines marred by something as trivial as pockets. "I'll do that."

"Good, good." He patted her hand. "Now, break a leg, you two. I'll be rooting for you."

Half an hour to showtime.

The showroom was filling up nicely. In another few minutes there wouldn't be an empty seat in the house.

Martin Kraas headed backstage for one last check of the equipment, making himself look busy with a piece of apparatus as a few people shuffled across the stage.

"Everything okay?" asked Graham Chambers as he carried a recently delivered bouquet of flowers backstage.

"Oh, yeah. Not to worry," Kraas said. "Just opening-night jitters, I guess. You can never be too sure."

Chambers nodded, and continued on across the stage to the backstage dressing rooms.

Kraas took a quick look around.

The stage was empty.

Quickly he got off the stage and climbed the ladder that led to the catwalk hanging over it.

He reached inside his jacket pocket, then stopped suddenly as Chambers walked back across the stage. When the young man was gone, he continued to move. From inside his pocket he took out a palm-sized 8mm video camera. It had already been fitted with a mounting bracket and was easily clamped to the railing of the catwalk.

Kraas adjusted the direction and focus of the camera in order to get an unobstructed view of the stage. Once that was done, he took a roll of black electrical tape from his pocket and taped short strips over the camera's LEDs, making it virtually invisible from the stage below.

One last check through the viewfinder and he was satisfied everything was set. He pressed the *record* button and walked off the catwalk. He hurried down the ladder, slowing near the end and trying to land as softly as possible.

"Martin?" came a voice.

Kraas froze, thinking he'd been caught.

"Martin, are you there?"

Kraas breathed a sigh. The voice belonged to Chambers. Evidently he was in the process of looking for him. "Over here," he said, inspecting the hinges on a giant box of Jumbo Size Rantiki Playing Cards.

"Susie's looking for you backstage," Chambers said. "She says there's somebody she wants you to meet."

Kraas tried to look annoyed, his usual response to such a summons, but the truth of the matter was that he eager to get off the stage. "Let's not keep the woman waiting, then."

Ten minutes to showtime.

Romano slipped yet another cigarette between his lips. He rubbed his fingers together, produced a slight flame, and held his fingers to the tip of the cigarette. It was an innocuous little rote that helped calm him down. Even though he'd never prepared his fingers to produce such a flame, people had come to expect such surprises from him and Paradox was never a threat.

"Nervous?" Roxanne asked, echoing the words Reddington had asked her minutes before.

"No," he said. Then, "Well, maybe."

"Don't be. Everything's been so wonderful so far. I just know the show's going to be a smash."

"I hope so." Romano sucked on his cigarette and glanced around. "Where's Martin? I don't think I've seen him all night."

Hearing the remark, Graham Chambers stepped forward. "He's been around. I saw him checking out the equipment about twenty minutes ago. When I found him I told him Susie was—"

"Was he alone on stage?" Romano said, cutting Chambers off.

"Uh, I think so. Yeah."

Romano had no reason to think anything was wrong, no reason to distrust Kraas, yet something was setting off alarm bells in Romano's mind.

EDO VAN BELKOM

"Where is he now?" Romano's voice was rising in volume and he was beginning to sound frantic.

"I don't know," Chambers said. "I told him Susie was looking for him."

"I haven't seen her for a while," Roxanne added.

The commotion had caught the attention of Arthur Gardner. He walked over to Romano with his arms raised as if he were trying to keep the peace. "All right, now. What's the problem?"

"Where's Martin?"

"He's in the reception room getting a bite to eat. Why?"

"He was on stage a while ago, fiddling with the equipment."

Gardner nodded calmly. "That's because that's his job, that's what you pay him for. Now, I know this is a big night in your career, the biggest so far, but let's not get paranoid over it. Everything's going to be fine, and you're going to be a big, huge star. Okay?"

Romano realized he must've looked foolish. Kraas's job, after all, was to care for the equipment. Perhaps he was just doing his job, making sure that everything was okay. Still…. "I want to check all the equipment before we go on."

"Are you crazy?" Gardner said. "There's less than five minutes."

Romano shook his head. "Something's wrong, I can feel it."

Gardner sighed. "All right. We'll delay the show ten minutes. That'll give you fifteen for one last check. But after that, you've got to put on a show. If you've forgotten, let me remind you that some people have paid a lot of money to watch you perform, and it's not a good idea to disappoint them, especially on opening night."

"Thanks." Romano turned away from his manager. "Roxanne, Graham. Check all the apparatus. If you notice anything odd or out of the ordinary—and I mean *anything*—you let me know."

They went to the stage and quickly began examining the equipment, as closely as was possible in the short amount of time they'd been given. But in the end, everything was found to be in perfect working order and ready for the show.

Romano shook his head, trying to dismiss his misgivings as opening-night jitters. Perhaps, but considering Jerry Baker's appearance earlier in the evening, something had to be up.

Something.

But what?

Reluctantly, Romano gave Gardner the go-ahead to start the show.

"What's going on?" Kraas asked, arriving backstage with a cup of coffee in one hand and a donut in the other.

"Nothing," Romano said. "Just running a little late is all."

"Ladies and gentlemen," said Jackson Zwinge, a popular local radio personality with a nightly music show ('Swing with Zwinge') whom Arthur Gardner had asked to emcee the opening night show. "The Frontier Hotel and Gambling Hall is proud to bring you a young showman, a respected illusionist and escape artist, and a one-time apprentice to The Great Rantiki." A pause. "Accompanied by his lovely and beguiling assistant, Roxanne May...Mister Magick, Romano Minardi and *The Legend of Rantiki!*"

The house and stage lights suddenly dimmed, and the solemn organ music that had been droning on throughout the introduction closed out with a final drawn-out chord.

Then the guitar intro to the Van Halen song "Panama" began to play, louder and louder until the rest of the band kicked in. At that point there was a burst of white light in the center of the stage and Romano appeared through a magical apparatus called a Flash Appearance Portal, dressed in a black tuxedo.

The audience, thinking they would be seeing old-style illusions performed by a Rantiki impersonator, was a little hesitant to applaud. But as Romano stepped upstage, walking in time to the music, the applause grew louder. Then, as they realized they were going to see something new and different, the applause became an ovation.

Romano bowed, then gestured across the stage.

A scale model of the Frontier Hotel set on a platform and complete with flashing neon was wheeled onto the stage by Kraas and Chambers, who were both dressed in black.

Romano opened the model hotel, showed it to be empty, then closed it again. Then, as he turned away searching the stage for his assistant, the roof began to rise at one end and Roxanne made her entrance from within the model of the hotel.

Like Romano, she was also wearing a tuxedo, except hers was deep royal blue. He helped her down onto the stage and both bowed slightly.

The music changed then, but the pulsing rhythm of the beat remained and would be a constant driving force behind the act throughout the rest of the show. With the music change, they faced each other and tore away the other's tuxedo. Romano now wore a blue, skin-tight, rhinestone-studded spandex jumpsuit that hugged his thighs and buttocks and covered his upper body like a muscle shirt. Roxanne was wearing her red dress, an item of clothing that brought whistles and cheers from the audience all on its own.

From there they did a quick sword suspension, which Romano turned into a levitation illusion by removing the large broadsword supporting Roxanne's head.

Then it was on to an illusion called "Shooting Through a Woman." In this one, Romano fired a neon arrow at a target while Roxanne stood dangerously between his crossbow and the target. Roxanne acted reluctant to stand in the line of fire, but Romano convinced her everything would be all right. She tried to move several times, but each time Romano would move her back into position. Finally, he gave her a blindfold and she stayed put.

And then he took aim.

The music died out for one of the few times in the show.

Complete silence.

Romano fired.

Roxanne screamed and fell to the stage.

The neon arrow hit the target, scoring a perfect bullseye. Romano admired his marksmanship for a moment, then followed the bright yellow ribbon connected to the arrow's shaft and found that it was threaded *through* Roxanne's body as if the arrow had passed right through her. Realizing what had happened, Romano revived Roxanne, and pulled the ribbon from her midsection while making a few overly dramatic gestures in an attempt to apologize.

But Roxanne would have none of it.

She took firm hold of his hands and led him toward a large box. There she cuffed his wrists, placed him inside the box and pulled a colorful bag over his head, tying off the bag with a short length of rope. That done, she secured the box with two locks and climbed on top of it, crossing her arms defiantly as if to say "that'll teach him." But as she was doing this a curtain slowly rose up around the box. She tried to keep the curtain down, but it continued to rise. Then, the second after it rose above her head, it fell down, leaving Romano on top of the box, now dressed in a red jumpsuit.

Romano then opened the box to find Roxanne now dressed in a blue dress identical to the red one she'd been wearing. Her hands were bound by cuffs.

The "metamorphosis" was always a spectacular illusion and the audience applauded appreciatively.

Romano released Roxanne from her bonds and made an attempt to reconcile their differences, but Roxanne was still having nothing to do with it.

As she turned her back on him, a large grey milk can was wheeled out onto the stage. She turned back around and looked at Romano, pointing suggestively at the milk can.

Romano shook his head, pleading. But to no avail.

She pointed at the milk can again.

Finally, Romano reluctantly slipped into the can. Fresh white milk spilled over the brim onto the stage. He lowered himself inside, pausing at the last moment as if begging for his life. But Roxanne shook her head and pushed Romano under the milk.

In seconds the can was capped and locked up tight with four heavy-duty padlocks.

A curtain came up around the can and again Roxanne crossed her arms over her chest in her "that'll teach him" pose.

But seconds later the curtain fell and there stood Romano on top of the can, dripping milk from head to toe and panting as if out of breath.

She looked at him, stern-faced.

Fearing he'd have to do another escape to please her, Romano jumped down off the milk can and began waving his arms with a flourish, producing one gorgeous bouquet after another until flowers were falling onto the stage like rain.

Roxanne stepped toward Romano and gave him a hug. The embrace ended with a kiss and then a deep final bow.

Sure, the show was corny as hell, but it was a safe, crowd-pleasing show geared toward Las Vegas-type crowds. And this audience—a typical one by Las Vegas standards with middle-aged to elderly tourists—was eating it up.

It might not have been as good as *Weird Science*, but he would revive that show in a few years when he had the experience and confidence (not to mention an apprentice) to produce it convincingly. For now, *The Legend of Rantiki* was a fine beginning, an excellent starting point for a long and successful career.

And the show wasn't even over yet.

Edo van Belkom

As the audience applauded, Romana Minardi leaned to her left and shook her husband's arm for what must have been the hundredth time in the past half-hour. "That's my son up there," she said.

Franco Minardi nodded, then turned to the man sitting to his left. "That's my son," he said.

The man smiled politely, then turned to the woman next to him. His wife. "That's his son up there."

"Oh, very nice," said the man's wife.

And now it was time for the finale.

In true honor of Rantiki, Romano had decided to close his show with the escape which had taken Rantiki's life.

The rock music was gone, as were the flesh-baring costumes.

The darkened stage was lit by a single spotlight.

Romano stepped into it.

"Ladies and gentlemen…in honor of my good friend and mentor, I'd like to conclude tonight's entertainment with a very difficult and dangerous escape. It's a more difficult variation of the illusion known to magicians simply as *Gone!*, but I'm sure most of you will recognize it as the escape which took The Great Rantiki's life."

A hush fell over the audience.

"To help me with this escape we've invited two orderlies from Las Vegas's fine Humana Hospital Sunrise to strap me into one of their own regulation straitjackets."

Roxanne escorted two men dressed in white onto the stage. They waved to the crowd, then immediately began strapping Romano into the jacket. In two minutes he was being placed into a oversized mail sack, adding a degree of difficulty to the escape.

But before they tied up the sack, Romano stopped and turned to address the audience.

"Ladies and gentlemen. I dedicate this escape…as well as this entire show…to the memory and legend of The Great Rantiki."

There was a small round of applause.

"Wish me luck."

And with that they stuffed him into the sack, hoisted him up over the stage and set the rope he was hanging from alight.

Romano immediately began to work his way out of the straitjacket. He'd avoided using magick throughout the show and didn't want to resort to using it now, but the orderlies had secured the jacket tightly, too tightly, leaving him little slack to play with.

He'd worried about something going wrong.

Apparently, this was it.

Above him he could hear the flames eating away at the rope.

As she watched her son struggle to free himself, the thumb of Romana Minardi's right hand counted off another bead of the rosary that was tightly wound around her fingers.

It was taking too long.

Romano had no choice but to resort to using magick. He cast a rote that slowed down time around him.

The fire eating away at the rope stopped burning as realtime suddenly pulled off the expressway and onto the back of a snail. The flames curled out from the rope as pretty and as harmless as the petals of a flower.

He now had as much time as he needed, but even so, the straitjacket was proving harder to escape from than he'd anticipated throughout rehearsals. He gave it another try, frantically twisting and turning within the bag.

From the audience's perspective, they would merely see a flurry of movement inside the bag, almost as if a venomous snake had suddenly been dropped into it for effect. There was no danger of Paradox, but it was disappointing to Romano not to be able to get through his first show without resorting to magick.

He consoled himself with the thought that perhaps he'd get quicker over time.

At last he freed himself from the jacket, and then he was out of the bag. He brought realtime back up to speed and leaped behind a blackout curtain placed halfway up the stage.

Seconds later, the flames chewed through the rope, and the sack fell to the stage…

EDO VAN BELKOM

Empty.

The crowd gasped.

Romano walked onstage.

The audience looked on in stunned amazement, then began applauding, not stopping until they'd given him a long, well-deserved standing ovation.

"You had me worried there for a minute," Roxanne said, as they took their bows. "I didn't think you were going to make it."

"That's good to know," he said. "I thought I was the only one who thought that."

A look of fear crossed Roxanne's face…

He gave her a wink.

And her fear was erased by a smile.

2 AM.

The soul's midnight.

The stage at the Frontier was dark and desolate. Martin Kraas walked across it, the click of his shoes echoing as if he were walking through the dungeon of some medieval castle.

When he was halfway across the stage he stopped and moved upstage until he was front and center. From there he looked out over the expanse of empty seats fanning out from the stage. Although it was dark, and the individual red seats were barely distinguishable in the blackness, he was able to imagine them full of people.

He closed his eyes and in his mind the stage lights came on, a spotlight picked him up and thousands of people were cheering….

A standing ovation for the great Martin Kraas.

He stood there for some time, breathing deeply, breathing in the sweet smell of success.

And then he opened his eyes…

To utter darkness.

Complete silence.

And instead of Martin Kraas, grandmaster magician, he stood there as Blinkles, the magical clown. His stomach turned at the thought, and the anger he'd been harboring for weeks roiled within him once more.

He walked off stage toward the ladder and climbed it two rungs at a time. He ran across the catwalk, not caring that the metal structure clanged loudly with his every step.

The video camera was still there. The tape had ended and the machine had shut itself off.

He peeled the black tape from the outside and pressed *rewind*. After letting the tape rewind halfway, he stopped it, pressed *play*, and then pressed *rewind* so he could watch what he had taped as it rewound.

Most of the illusions would look just as mysterious from above as they had from out in the audience. For example, the *Gone!* escape would be nothing more than a white blur of motion as Romano fought his way out of the straitjacket.

Kraas continued to watch the tape rewind, wondering if he'd promised Jerry Baker something he couldn't deliver.

But then there it was.

The trick.

The gimmick.

The fake.

Caught on tape.

"Yes!" Kraas said, his eye pressed hard against the tiny camera's eyepiece. He stopped the tape and played it back at normal speed.

"Say good-bye to your career, Mister Magick."

He rewound the tape and played it back again.

And for several minutes, the Frontier's stage echoed with the sound of laughter.

18

The phone wouldn't stop ringing.

At first he thought it was part of a bad dream. It was, but there was no way he could know it at the time.

Romano slid a pillow over his head in the hopes that whoever was calling would give up and call back later. With the pillow covering his ears, the irritating noise was somewhat muffled, but the phone just kept on ringing...

...and ringing...

...and ringing.

He opened his eyes and glanced at the clock.

It was ten after ten, for crying out loud! Whoever it was had better have a good excuse for calling this early in the morning after an opening night. He picked up the phone, brought the receiver up to his ear and mumbled, "Hello."

EDO VAN BELKOM

"Romano!" It was the voice of Arthur Gardner and it sounded frantic. "Turn on the television to Channel 45. Jerry Baker's doing a show about you today."

Romano suddenly came awake, leaping out of bed and hurrying to the television. Shaken by the sudden movement, Roxanne looked over and asked, "What is it? What's going on?"

Romano didn't answer. Instead he stared at the gray television screen, waiting as it took *forever* to warm up.

Roxanne pulled aside the sheets and slid down to the end of the bed, sitting down beside him.

They could hear the audio part of *The Jerry Baker Show* before they could see any pictures. But the sound coming from the television was bad enough.

"He claims to be able to perform magic," Baker was saying with all the fire and brimstone he could muster. "He'll tell you it's the art of producing illusions for entertainment. But magic is also the art of producing a desired effect through the use of incantation and other techniques which presumably assure human control over supernatural agencies or the forces of nature."

So far Romano didn't have a problem. Baker could blather all he wanted. The end result would likely be more people lining up for that night's show at the Frontier.

The television picture finally came into view. There was Baker, walking back and forth across the small chapel that doubled as the show's set. He was dressed in a white, double-breasted suit, so clean it looked to have been washed by the hand of God. In fact, everything on the screen was white, with crosses, candles and flowers strewn about, more as decoration than symbols of religion.

"A writer once said, 'Any sufficiently advanced technology is indistinguishable from magic.' Well, friends, let me assure you that Romano Minardi is *no* scientist. In fact, he has no formal education whatsoever. That's because he's been schooled solely in the art of deception, of trickery. He is, plain and simple, a deceptor, a deceiver…a man who claims to be able to perform magic, real magic, or mag-*ick* as he calls it, spelling it with a *K* on the end as if that made all the difference in the world."

Baker picked up a leatherbound Bible and struck a pose with the book slightly raised in his clenched right hand. It was an image suitable for framing.

"There was only one person who walked this Earth that could perform what a lay person might consider to be magic, only when he did it…they called it a miracle! I'm talking about the Son of God, Our Lord Jesus Christ!"

A wave of "Praise the Lord!" and "Hallelujah!" swept over Baker's studio audience.

"Turning water into wine. Now that's what I call *magic*. Feeding hundreds of hungry people with just a few loaves of bread...*Magic!* Healing the sick with just a touch of a hand..." Baker shook his head in dismay. "That, my friends, is magic. The power of the Lord, his power alone...is magic."

There was a slight tremor in Baker's voice now.

"The deceptions, frauds and fakery..." Baker said, almost to the point of tears. "This prestidigitator...this con-artist named Romano Minardi, is making a name for himself by exploiting women in a show that is laced with violence, the devil's music, and all manner of blasphemy against the laws of the Christian faith...

"God's laws!"

Baker turned to face the camera.

"And in a moment, we'll show you just how he does it." A smile. "We'll be back right after this."

The Jerry Baker Show logo popped up in the bottom right corner of the screen while the show went to commercial, showing a ten-second bit from the previous afternoon when Baker had confronted Romano at the media reception prior to the show.

"...a show featuring the severing of body parts? The decapitation of women? Bondage? Impaling?" Baker was saying.

Then the camera angle changed and Romano was caught answering Baker in mid-sentence, leaving out the part where Romano cited Baker for getting his facts wrong: "...mere illusions for the purposes of entertainment..."

"Entertainment?" Baker barked incredulously. "These aren't entertainments, they are the amusements of men who are the sworn enemies of God...the perverted foes of our Lord Jesus Christ! How else could you explain such acts performed in a titillating orgy of naked flesh, pounding rock music, and light and shadows commanded by the Prince of Darkness?"

And finally, mercifully, they went to commercial. A cheap-looking spot for some sort of life insurance—*everyone eligible, no questions asked, nobody refused...and your rates will never go up*.

For a fleeting moment, Romano considered taking out a policy, seeing as his fledgling career appeared to be at an end thanks to one Jerry god damn Baker.

The phone rang.

Romano didn't move.

Roxanne went to the nightstand and answered it. She brought the phone to Romano. "It's Art."

"Yeah," Romano said, eyes still glued to the television.

"What the hell did you say to him?"

"That wasn't everything I said. They cut some of it out."

"This is not good, not good. We're going to have to do damage control for the next month."

"Settle down, Art. I can handle this guy," Romano said. At one time he might have been sure of that statement, but now, watching Baker on television, he realized how incredibly powerful a weapon it could be in the right—or perhaps *wrong*—hands. Baker wasn't a Technomancer, but he might as well be.

"*Handle* him?" Art was going ballistic. "I don't want you to *handle* him, I just want you to slap a muzzle across his big fat—"

The Jerry Baker Show was back from its commercial break.

Romano hung up the phone.

Studio G.

G for God and God's favorite television show.

The Jerry Baker Show.

The studio was a-buzz with electricity. Jerry was in fine form and several people from regional networks and superstations had so far been impressed. National syndication was a cinch, especially since Baker had come up with the unique marketing strategy of offering his show as a weekly *Sunday Morning* talk show. He'd clean up against all the local church shows, then work his way into a daily format where he could ask for donations to help him fight the good fight.

And it was all coming together, thanks to Romano Minardi.

"We now have with us a children's performer named Martin Kraas who performs as 'Blinkles The Clown' at that most wholesome of Las Vegas entertainment establishments, Circus, Circus."

The studio audience gave Kraas a warm round of applause.

Kraas nodded to Baker, waved to the audience. "Thanks Jerry," he said.

"Kraas," hissed Romano. "Since when did he find God?"

Romano lit a cigarette, and watched as Kraas talked about how Rantiki's apprenticeship was stolen out from under him by Romano Minardi, a conniving street-rat from Montreal.

"It was my idea," said Kraas, "to present *The Legend of Rantiki* in the manner in which Rantiki would have presented it himself, not as a carnal glitter show unsuitable for family entertainment."

Romano couldn't believe it. Martin Kraas, suddenly holier-than-thou, the man who'd known Roxanne, no…who'd known Rhonda Mazey as "the girl with the Big Ones!"

It was so pathetic it was almost funny.

Almost, but not quite.

"You've brought a tape along to show us just how *human* Romano Minardi is, is that right?"

Kraas nodded.

"No special powers."

"None."

"No ability to perform magick."

"Nope."

Baker smiled. "All right, then. Let's roll it."

And suddenly, Romano's heart fell like a stone into the pit of his stomach. There was the stage at the Frontier Hotel, seen from above; the perfect vantage point to see the tricks behind some of the illusions.

Sure enough, there was the milk-can escape.

Romano was locked inside.

The curtain rose up around the can.

And then Romano was seen pushing open the false lid of the can, a lid which fit snugly over the upper rim of the large liquid-carrying part and looked to all observers as if it had been riveted into place. After stepping out of the can, he set the lid back in place, pressing it down hard onto the exposed lip until he'd restored the perfect metal seam. Then he lifted the can by the lid, making sure that the friction between the pieces was more than enough to keep everything securely in place.

The locks had never been opened.

And then the curtain fell and Romano took a bow as if he'd just performed some feat of spectacular derring-do.

The audience at the Frontier cheered.

Jerry Baker's studio audience laughed.

Then the dark, grainy tape faded out and Jerry Baker appeared in close-up, looking into the camera and shaking his head.

"Magic?" he said.

The question was answered with chuckles.

"Mag-ick?"

More laughter from the audience.

"I don't think so."

Romano was livid.

With the fingernails of his clenched fists cutting into his palms, he began to mutter a string of strange words, the formula to the force rote called "Unseen Arm."

The glass ashtray that had been sitting next to him began to move, then suddenly flew off the bed and slammed into the television screen at high velocity.

For a brief moment, Jerry Baker's face was a shattered, disjointed image. It looked good that way.

And then the television imploded with a loud *Thwok!*

Sandlike grains of glass filled the air.

Roxanne threw up her arms to protect herself from the flying glass. When the broken shards of television screen tinkled their last, she scrambled over to the night-table and looked in the drawer for a card.

Reddington had said she'd know when to call.

Now seemed as good a time as any.

Romano's phone kept ringing all morning.

Some of the calls were from radio talk shows that suddenly had a hot topic to talk about. Romano tuned into one of them and learned that callers' reactions to what Baker had done was about fifty-fifty for and against.

On the one hand were a few vocal members of the silent majority, the ones who weren't all that into religion and who'd never given magic shows a second thought. These people wondered why Baker had bothered with Romano when there were plenty of other, not to mention more deserving, "sinners" he could go after.

"If Jerry Baker's so eager to expose corruption, why doesn't he try and take out a few of the more disreputable casino operators in town? Or how about city hall? I hear there are plenty of liars and cheats down there."

And then, on the other hand, there were the people who lauded Jerry Baker for taking a stand against one of Satan's minions. It was time, they said, that somebody did something about this festering cesspool of a city, and performers professing the power to do magic was as good a place to start as any.

"Mando Rizzardi had it coming. Anyone who dances around to the devil's music, thinks shooting women with arrows is entertainment, and claims to have the power to do magic, needs to be taught a few lessons about the power of God. That...and he needs to have his head examined too."

Those in favor of Baker were about equal in number to those in favor of Romano. But the numbers might have been deceiving, since Baker was known to use shills to good effect and had probably instructed his followers to make those calls as often as possible. They might have only gotten on the air once, but while they weren't on the air, they were clogging up phone lines and preventing pro-Romano callers from getting through. Romano had thought of using Rantiki's rather large fan club, the Consor's Club, in the same way, but decided it was probably better not to stoop to Baker's level. Besides, Consor Club members were fans, not fanatics.

At noon, when Romano was contacted by WKLV's Grant Stirling for a comment on the whole affair, he was as diplomatic as possible under the circumstances, avoiding making any wild accusations or defamatory comments about Baker until he'd had a chance to meet with his lawyers later that afternoon.

"I'm shocked, hurt and a little disappointed, not so much with Jerry Baker, because people have come to expect these kinds of cowardly attacks from him, attacks which really serve no purpose other than to boost the ratings of his show. No, I'm more saddened that Martin Kraas has joined forces with Baker. He was a long-time friend and employee of Rantiki, and had worked with me on putting together my new show. All I can say about him is that I hope he has a second career lined up for himself because I don't think he'll be working as a magician for very much longer."

He hung up the phone knowing some of his anger had seeped into his voice, making his words a thinly veiled series of insults and threats.

But he didn't care.

If Baker wanted a fight, then Romano would give him one.

He could hardly wait to take off the gloves.

"What if we haul his ass into court?" Romano asked.

He was seated at one end of the long oval table in the main dining room of Rancho Rantiki. At the other end of the table was Arthur Gardner. To his right was Ehrich Weiss, one of the top entertainment lawyers in Las Vegas, from the firm of Burns, Weiss and Manning. At Romano's left was Graham Chambers, his new senior technical advisor. And sitting to Romano's right was Harry Reddington Jr. Romano hadn't called him, but he was glad he'd showed up. His advice might be needed.

"There's no doubt you'd win a slander case, Mr. Minardi—"

"Please, my father's name is Mr. Minardi. Call me Romano."

The lawyer began again. "There's no doubt you'd win a slander case, Romano. The thing is, it would take months to get the case tried, and by then the whole situation might have blown over. The other drawback is, of course, cost. Trials are very expensive and you might wipe out the Rantiki fortune simply by trying to prove legally that Jerry Baker is an ass."

"But it would cost him money too, wouldn't it?"

"Of course it would," Weiss answered. "But you're not seeing the whole picture. If you take Jerry Baker to court, he'll plead the First Amendment, and then go on a crusade telling everyone he's being persecuted by 'one of Satan's own.' Until you finally got into court, it would be like banging your head against a brick wall."

Romano sighed and allowed himself to be distracted by the sight of Roxanne entering the room. She'd been on the phone with yet another reporter and from what Romano had heard of the conversation, she'd handled the call perfectly. He watched her circle the room and take the seat between Gardner and Reddington, then he looked in turn at everyone sitting at the table. At last his gaze fell upon the lawyer. "So what you're telling me is that if I don't do anything about this, I lose. And if I sue his ass, I lose. I know I'm not American, but I fail to see where justice comes into play in this system."

"Uh, Ehrich has come up with a plan," Gardner said, his voice sounding hopeful.

"What is it?"

"The first step is to take a full-page ad in tomorrow's *Las Vegas Daily News*. The Frontier Hotel has agreed to split the cost."

Romano rolled his eyes.

"Then," the lawyer continued, "you make yourself available to every camera crew and newspaper reporter who will listen to you, and you refute Jerry Baker's claims until your tongue gets tired. Then…"

Romano sighed in disappointment. This must have been what Gardner had meant by "damage control." Romano had another way of putting it— "Rolling Over and Playing Dead."

When the lawyer finished, Romano looked around the table again and shook his head. "That's the best you can do. A battle of words fought through the media."

"It would generate a lot of publicity."

"You call name-calling publicity?"

"In this business, Mister…uh, Romano, there is no such thing as bad publicity."

"No such thing as bad publicity," Gardner chimed in, scared shitless that the career of one of his top clients was about to go down the tubes.

Reddington cleared his throat. "There is an alternative."

Everyone at the table looked Reddington's way.

"What is it?" Romano asked.

"Well, you could fight fire and brimstone with fire and brimstone, so to speak."

"I'm listening."

"Well, he's asked you to appear on his show to defend your claim that you can perform true magick. You quite rightly refused, but after what we saw today I suggest *you* challenge *him* to prove that you *cannot* perform magick. By putting the ball back in his court, the next move automatically becomes his. He will, of course, take you up on the challenge. Then, once you've proven yourself, he'll fade away like a one-hit wonder."

Romano beamed. This was more like it, going head-to-head with Baker and grinding him into the desert sand like a cigarette butt under his heel.

Although riskier, it sat better with Romano than calling each other names in the papers and on television.

Besides, it was what Rantiki would have wanted.

In fact, that was what he'd died for.

"I like it," Romano proclaimed.

"Wait a second," Gardner sputtered. "I know you're a good magician and all, but you're talking about real magic here. Not carefully prepared escapes and illusions, but real magic…right?"

"Yes," Romano said, his voice unwavering. "That's right."

"Are you out of your mind?"

"Arthur, are you doubting me?" Romano said, staring hard across the table at his manager so that the message was clear. If Gardner answered "yes," he'd be out looking for new clients in the morning.

"No, no. If you say you can do it, then you can do it."

"He can do it," Reddington said.

"I can do it," Romano nodded.

"All right, Romano. You tell me what you want out of the deal, and Ehrich and I will make some calls."

"All I want," Romano said, "is to see Jerry Baker squirm."

19

Romano Minardi had never seen the Frontier Hotel's parking lot more full. It was totally congested with cars, some even parked in spots not designated for parking. It was as if the slots inside the Casino had begun paying out on every pull and word of it had been carried through the town on a hot desert wind.

But of course, that wasn't the case.

The sudden jump in business was all due to Jerry Baker's broadcast. Like high-school kids showing up to watch an after-school fight, people were showing up to see if any sparks were going to fly between Baker and Romano.

Romano had the feeling that sparks would indeed be flying tonight.

As they walked through the packed gambling hall, they were met by the casino pit boss, Mark Garland. He was a tall, handsome man, well into his forties but looking barely older than thirty. His "Ken doll" features did not betray his black-belt in karate and the .45 he always carried "close to his heart."

"Mister Minardi, Miss May," he said, escorting them through the hall. "I hope your show goes well tonight."

Romano nodded. "So do I."

As they made their way through the scattered, and crowded, gaming tables, Romano noticed people staring at him, then pointing, saying things like, "There he is," and "That's him."

"Now I know locals don't usually gamble in Las Vegas," Garland said. "But you come and see me after your show tonight and I'll set you up with some chips…you know, make sure you have a real good time."

"I've never really gambled much," Roxanne said, her smile telling Romano that she'd love to give it a try.

"That's a very kind offer," Romano said.

"Listen, with all the people you brought into my casino tonight, it's the least I can do."

They reached the backstage entrance door.

"Thank you, Mark."

"No, thank *you*. And remember, after your show you come see me. I'll make sure you have a good time, everything comp."

"All right, then. We'll do that."

They entered the theater and Romano was suddenly reminded of a comment Ehrich Weiss had made that afternoon.

There's no such thing as bad publicity

Apparently there wasn't.

Before the show, Romano made himself available for interviews, and several freelance camera crews took advantage of the opportunity by doing interviews for the networks and syndicated entertainment shows.

After each interview, Romano invited the reporter and cameraman to set up their camera in a specially prepared pit just below the foot of the stage. From that vantage point they would be allowed to tape the first half of the show.

"You're letting them tape the act?" Arthur Gardner asked incredulously as the last of the camera crews left the dressing room.

Romano was surprised Gardner hadn't told him he was out of his mind yet. Perhaps he was learning to go along with Romano's schemes and to trust him despite his better judgment, a better judgment that had taken fifteen years in the business to develop. Then again, he might be turning into a yes-man and would allow Romano's career to self-destruct just so he could hang on to his meal ticket for a little bit longer.

Romano hoped it was the former.

"Just the first half of the show."

"And what are you going to do when *The Legend of Rantiki* shows up as a bootleg video at Sunday-morning flea markets across North America?"

"Hadn't thought of that," mused Romano, inwardly glad that Gardner hadn't opted for the yes-man route. "All right, you go down into the pit with them. If Baker doesn't show up after the first few illusions, send them all packing."

"Baker? You think he'll be here?"

"You saw the crowd on the way in, right?"

"Yeah."

"Well, in some respects Baker is a lot like God."

Gardner looked at Romano strangely. "How do you mean?"

"Whenever two or more of you are gathered in his name…"

Gardner's face brightened in a smile.

"…Jerry Baker is there."

"All right," Gardner said. "I'll tell security to keep an eye out for him."

That night's show was somewhat different from opening night. Instead of appearing onstage through the Flash Appearance Portal, Romano decided to warm up the crowd first with some traditional magic.

He did the Chinese Linking Rings, the zombie ball and a small-scale rice, orange and checkers effect. The illusions were old standards, but Romano had learned to perform them with such originality and flare that they were like all-new tricks.

But the real reasons for the simple illusions were threefold. One, since the milk-can escape had been taken out of the show, he needed something else to fill up the time. Two, Romano wanted to give the cameras some good shots of some smaller illusions so viewers would associate Romano with traditional magic and make Baker's claims seem even more outlandish. And three, he wanted to give Baker time to show up before he began his show, since it was unlikely he'd stop the show in the middle just to confront Baker.

He finished the orange, rice and checkers to a rousing round of applause. After taking a bow he remained onstage to give Baker the chance to make an appearance. When he didn't, Romano took the opportunity to address the audience.

"Ladies and gentlemen," he began. "As I'm sure most of you are aware, today televangelist and talk-show host Jerry Baker slandered…oh, excuse me, *exposed* me as someone who claims to have magical powers, but who in reality has none."

He couldn't resist punctuating his remark by drawing his hand over his head and creating a brief comet-like arch of fire above him. The magick was partly for the cameras, partly to show the world that Baker didn't have a clue what he was talking about.

"Since Baker professes to speak to God on a regular basis, such accusations have to be taken seriously."

A slight chuckle rippled through the audience.

"But I'm not interested in waging a war of words against a man who knows so many small ones…you know the ones I mean, 'Praise the Lord,' 'Glory to God,' 'Hallelujah'…. Oh, excuse me, that last one was a big word."

The laugh this time was bigger, and lasted longer.

"What I'm interested in is ending this war of words. And as you know, actions speak louder than words…. So what I propose is some action. You people in the audience are witness to it. If Jerry Baker is so all fired up to claim that I can't perform true magick, then I challenge *him* to prove it."

Romano paused to give Baker a chance to show his face. He knew he was in the room, he could feel it in his gut.

"I challenge him to prove his contention that I can't perform magick without the use of trickery or fraud. And in order to put this matter to a final and definite rest, I agree to undertake this challenge live on his television show."

Romano knew that what he was proposing was dangerous, that he'd be risking Paradox, not to mention attracting the attention of the Technocracy, by going through with this challenge. But he had to do it in order to defend Rantiki's honor and ensure his future success in the magic business. He was a young and powerful mage *now*, and if he wanted to ward off such accusations, *now* was the time to do it, since a successful defeat of any challenge now would protect him against similar claims in the future.

He scanned the audience for Baker, but saw no sign of him.

"I accept!" came a faint voice from the back of the room.

The heads of the audience members turned around in unison. The cameras at the foot of the stage swung around. The showroom fell silent.

Romano looked out over the audience and, through the glare of the stage lights shining in his eyes, he could just make out the movement of a white body coming down the aisle followed by a camera crew.

It was Baker, waiting until the last possible moment to make his appearance.

"I accept," he said once more, this time addressing the entire audience. "If you want to come onto my show and show the world exactly what kind of phony, lying, cheating, con artist you are, then you name the day and you've got a full hour to prove to the world that Jerry Baker speaks nothing but the God-honest truth."

"A week today," Romano said. "You devise the challenge and I'll meet it."

Baker smiled a devilish sort of grin. "You've got it!"

The crowd broke into applause with plenty of hoots and whistles mixed in.

When the noise died down, Romano looked at Baker and said, "Now, if you'll excuse me, Mr. Baker…I have a show to do."

Again the audience cheered.

As Baker left the room, his exit was marked by several boos and catcalls to which he answered, "God Bless."

Confident everything was going according to his plan, Romano walked off stage, eager to get on with the show.

"Did you get that?" Arthur Gardner asked each of the cameramen in the pit.

"You bet!"

"Thumbs up!"

"All right, then," Gardner said. "Show's over. If you need any more footage or interviews, give me a call. Here's my card."

The show went off without a hitch.

Romano felt sharper and more focussed than ever and managed to do the final escape without the use of magick.

When the show was over, Romano and Roxanne earned themselves a standing ovation.

Later, they gambled the night away.

At one point, Romano was up fifty thousand dollars. But, since he'd won the money using magick, he quickly lost it all and ended up the night breaking even.

Pit Boss Mark Garland looked relieved.

20

The Legend of Rantiki was suddenly sold out three weeks in advance as people planning on visiting Las Vegas called to find out if tickets were available.

The war between Jerry Baker and Romano Minardi had become big news, bigger than Romano had ever anticipated. Most of his mornings were taken up with interviews with radio and print reporters doing features previewing the upcoming challenge.

"How are you preparing for the challenge?" asked that morning's reporter, a man named Barry who had a daily chat show on the Toronto AM radio station, CFRB.

"I really can't," Romano answered. "They're still working on the challenges, so for the time being I'll just have to rely on my skill as a magician."

"I've heard that Martin Kraas, a former employee of Rantiki who also worked closely with you, is helping Baker devise the challenges. Does that worry you?"

It did worry him, but Romano would never let on.

"No, not at all. Martin Kraas isn't trained in the ways of mag-ick—" he exaggerated his enunciation of the word for added emphasis "—and I'm confident that I'll be able to defeat whatever they come up with."

It was his standard line, but it was wearing thin.

Kraas would no doubt devise escapes which couldn't be escaped from by traditional methods. He could rely on people's expectations of him to beat the challenges, or at least come very close to doing so. But even so, he'd probably have to rely heavily on magick and would likely be racked by Paradox.

How much Paradox depended on how elaborate the challenges were and how much magick he'd have to use to beat them. Either way, he'd need plenty of Quintessence to see him through and for that reason he spent every moment that he wasn't giving interviews either practicing rotes, smoking cigarettes or visiting the Magic Box. As a Node, the Magic Box was his only source of Quintessence.

He was building up a good supply.

But would it be enough?

"There's more of them this morning," Roxanne said, looking out the front window of Rancho Rantiki. "A lot more."

They'd moved into the main house two days ago to get away from the media scrum that showed up every morning outside the compound, just on the other side of the fence from the guest houses and workshop.

Romano lit a cigarette and moved toward the window. There were indeed more reporters out there this morning, far more than there had been any other day that week. One of them was quite attractive, tall with long, slim legs and long blonde hair that fell down around her shoulders like West Coast sunshine.

"Hey, isn't that Cynthia Keegan from that show *Inside Affair?*"

Roxanne took a closer look at the woman as yet another news van pulled up outside the front gate. "Yeah, I think so. But doesn't she usually do 'green' stories, stuff on the environment and recycling and stuff like that?"

Romano didn't answer Roxanne's question. He just scanned the collection of vehicles and people and said, "Wow, I thought I'd get more of them out here, but I didn't expect the response to be this good."

"What are you talking about?"

"You don't think this many news teams showed up to tape me stepping out of the house, do you?"

"No," she laughed.

"I invited them."

"And what, now you're going to serve them all breakfast?"

"Nope, now we're going to go on a little trip."

Romano stopped the Lexus about twenty-five yards from his final destination. He got out of the car, leaving Roxanne to get out whenever she liked.

After straightening his tie and buttoning his black, double-breasted suit, he began walking across the grass.

The grounds of the Las Vegas Showman's Memorial were immaculately kept, making it look more like a theme park than a cemetery. And in some ways it was more like a park, albeit a morbid one, with picnic tables and trash containers scattered about the grounds at strategic locations near the plots of famous Las Vegas entertainers and more than a few gangsters.

As he strolled casually past the elaborate tombstones, he glanced at a few of the names and their stories which were printed on small cards set in the ground in front of the gravesites:

George "Burger" Reynolds, one-time owner of the Havana Club casino who was shot while opening his garage door in the driveway of his Las Vegas home in 1952.

Aldo Izquierdo, an illusionist from a distinguished family of magicians who was killed by a drunk driver while driving home from a late-night performance in 1985.

Fred Kaps, a blackjack dealer at the Sahara who was shot dead by Jorge Zhebrovski, an unemployed steel worker who'd lost his life savings while playing Kaps in an effort to win enough money to support his family in 1972.

No wonder this place is a big tourist attraction, Romano thought. *I might even pick up a guidebook on the way out.*

Finally he came upon the familiar tombstone of Rantiki, a solid block of quarried redstone capped by a stone sculpture of an upside-down top hat, a magic wand sticking out at an angle and a pair of gloves hanging limply over the rim—a classic image associated with magic and magicians. This rendition also happened to be a fine work of craftsmanship.

Romano read the inscription…

James Rantiki

The Great Rantiki

1926-1995

"It's not how you start,

it's how you finish!"

…and smiled. Show business was a way of life, and you never really stopped entertaining, even in death.

Then he looked at the little card the groundskeepers had set into the ground.

James Rantiki (Randall Wynne), AKA The Great Rantiki, a Las Vegas legend and master illusionist who died while performing a death-defying escape onstage at the Flamingo in 1995.

Romano knelt down.

And from behind him the battery of cameras clicked and whirred as each of the camera crews bumped and shoved in order to get a better vantage point to shoot from.

Romano remained on his knees for a long time, making sure all of them had enough time to get the shot. Then he leaned forward, getting closer to the ground as if he were going to speak to Rantiki.

Which, of course, he did.

"Well," Romano whispered. "It looks like you checked out just in time to leave me holding the bag." He gave a lighthearted sigh. "I don't mind, and I don't blame you for it. Hell, I might have even done the same thing in your shoes. I just would have appreciated it if you'd have stuck around a little longer to teach me more about being a mage. I don't mind learning everything by the seat of my pants, but I'd like to be able to get through a day without being afraid my ass is going to get singed."

He was about to smile at that, but remembered a dozen cameras were trained on him in time enough to turn the smile into frown.

Still on his knees, he straightened his back and looked up at the sun.

Then he waved his right hand in an elaborate flourish and produced a huge bouquet of flowers. It was a startling bit of magick and caused some of the reporters and cameramen to gasp in amazement. Paradox was not a problem since he'd arranged the junket and would be expected to have prepared for such a trick even though he hadn't.

"I'm going head to head with Baker in two days. It would be nice if you could be there at least to watch, you know…if you don't have anything else to do."

Romano paused, just on the off chance that Rantiki could contact him from wherever he was. But the only sound was that of the wind whistling between the tombstones.

"See you around," Romano said, getting up from the ground. He turned to head back to the car, but was blocked by the mob of reporters wanting to get a new interview to go along with the piece on "Romano Minardi visiting the grave of the fallen master on the eve of the toughest challenge of his fledgling career."

Romano stopped halfway to the car and waited for the mob to swarm around him.

That afternoon Romano made arrangements for Roxanne to get a ride to that night's show at the Frontier with Graham Chambers so he could make a little trip down the Strip alone.

He gave Chambers the keys to the Lexus in exchange for the use of Chambers's gray Chevette, a deal Chambers was more than willing to transact.

With inconspicuous transportation secured, Romano quickly fashioned a simple disguise for himself, pasting a pair of bushy brows over his eyes, a van dyke mustache under his nose and around his mouth, and a pair of 1960s-style rose-colored glasses from Rantiki's wardrobe room.

Satisfied he wouldn't be recognized, he hopped in the Chevette, drove into Las Vegas, and cruised down Las Vegas Boulevard.

He turned in at Circus, Circus Lane and parked in a spot close to the exit, just in case he was recognized and needed to get away in a hurry. He checked his watch under the light of the 125-foot neon sign of "The Clown" who stood watch over the tent-shaped casino while sucking a huge neon lollipop. It was five minutes to the hour. If he hurried he'd be able to catch the next free Circus, Circus showing, a production which featured trapeze and high-wire artists, unicyclists, and a clown named "Blinkles" every twenty minutes from eleven AM to midnight.

It was always more crowded in Circus, Circus than in any other casino in town, and tonight was no exception. Romano had to bump and jostle his way through the crowds in order to reach the midway where the seats for the circus show were located. At first this arrangement seemed a little impractical to Romano, but as he watched several parents dumping off their kids while they went downstairs to pull the handles on the slots, the set-up suddenly seemed ingenious.

After buying a bag of popcorn from a walking vendor, Romano settled down to watch the show.

The first few acts were standard circus fare, entertaining to be sure, but somewhat mild compared to what was being offered along the rest of the Strip. Nevertheless, the crowd, which was always large, loved every minute of it.

The show ran almost fifteen minutes before Blinkles the Clown was introduced. If Romano hadn't known it was Martin Kraas under all that make-up he might not have recognized him. But, after watching him perform a few simple tricks, he realized there was definitely something familiar about the man's walk and mannerisms.

When he was sure it was Kraas, Romano prepared himself.

Kraas's next trick was the Linking Coat Hangers, a variation of the Chinese Linking Rings. Romano recognized the coat hangers as the set missing from Rantiki's collection and simply shook his head. He'd allowed Kraas to use whatever he wanted from the collection, but seeing as Kraas hadn't been around since his spot on *The Jerry Baker Show*, Romano had to consider the equipment stolen.

After Kraas connected the coat hangers together, seemingly slipping steel through steel, Romano cast a matter rote sealing the coat hangers up so they could not be separated again.

And then he sat back and watched as Kraas struggled with the hangers, trying to pull them apart and being dumbfounded by his inability to do so.

Kids in the front row laughed.

Romano snickered.

Finally, Kraas discarded the coat hangers with a shrug as if not being able to get them apart was part of the act. Then he moved on to the Floating Ball illusion.

Romano wondered why he'd chosen to do this illusion since it was so well known that the layman usually recognized the effect as "that ball on a stick thing." But despite the non-existent mystery element to the trick, Kraas performed it well enough to keep it fresh.

But not for long.

Romano cast another matter rote, causing the ball to jump off the lightweight silk foulard it was resting upon and fall to the ground, where it shattered into dozens of tiny pieces.

Even through his make-up Kraas looked astonished at what had happened.

The audience howled with delight.

Romano joined in, laughing hard.

Kraas quickly moved on to another trick. Apparently he ended his act with some dove magic.

Romano sat back and watched Kraas produce his first dove from a colorful silk handkerchief with the Circus, Circus clown and logo emblazoned on it. Kraas released the white dove and it flew to a platform a few feet away. There it waited to be collected at the end of the act.

When Kraas made his second dove appear, Romano was ready.

Kraas held the dove on his gloved finger, then gave it a gentle toss toward the first dove sitting on the platform.

Just as the dove took flight, Romano cast another matter rote, this one making the dove's wings inoperable.

The bird fell to the ground like a dead weight.

Kraas's hand went to his forehead in exasperation, nearly knocking off his bright orange wig.

This time, Romano was the one howling with laughter as the kids in the crowd were all silent, afraid that the dove was dead.

Kraas went to the bird.

Romano removed the rote from its wings and the bird fluttered up to join the other dove, unharmed.

Kraas looked at the bird.

The birds looked at Kraas, their heads moving jerkily from side to side.

Finally, Kraas turned to the audience, bowed once and bolted off stage as if he couldn't get away fast enough.

End of show.

Romano laughed hard, holding a hand over his mouth to keep his mustache and beard from flying off.

The juggler riding a unicycle came out for a second time,

probably so the show wouldn't close on such a downer.

Romano took the juggler's appearance as his cue to leave.

In the parking lot, a single, raucous laugh cut through the warm night air.

People looked at the bearded man stumbling through the parking lot as if he were drunk, or insane, or both.

It had been such a simple and childish sort of revenge, Romano thought.

But it had been so much fun.

He'd be back.

In a week or so.

Whenever he felt Kraas needed to be taught a lesson.

Or whenever Romano needed another good laugh.

21

"Hi, Roxanne," Arthur Gardner said as he stuck his head in through the kitchen door of Rancho Rantiki. "Is Romano around?"

"Hi, Art," she said, still in her silk kimono. "He's in the collection room. Do you want some coffee?"

"No, thanks." He walked through the kitchen and headed for the collection room with a purposeful stride.

"Good news or bad?" Roxanne asked.

"Won't know until I hear what Romano has to say."

Romano walked through the various apparata in the collection room still feeling like a kid in a candy store. The emotion surprised him, since a kid in a candy store feels a certain way because he knows he can't have the candy behind the glass. That was what Romano had felt the first time he'd stepped into the room. The equipment was just so much candy, stuff that he could only look at and admire, but never touch and certainly never use. Now it was virtually his to do with what he pleased, but he still felt like a kid—a kid who'd grown up and come to own the candy store. The candy was still something to admire from afar, yet if he consumed too much of it, he'd be eating into his profits.

He'd been looking for an illusion to replace the Milk Can Escape, but he was having trouble deciding on one. He'd narrowed the choices down to the Chinese Water Torture Cell or the No Feet illusion invented by Joe Karson and featured by magicians like Doug Henning and Andre Kole.

He was leaning toward the Cell.

"Romano?" It was the voice of Arthur Gardner.

"Over here."

He listened to the footsteps approaching, then turned to face Gardner. "What do you think I should replace the Milk Can with, the Chinese Water Torture Cell or No Feet?"

"What the hell is No Feet?"

"Thanks. Torture Cell it is."

"You're welcome," Gardner said, looking a little perplexed. "Listen, I got a call from one of Jerry Baker's producers, a woman named Daria DePaul."

"Yes, and...?"

"Interest in the show is in the stratosphere. They want to move the show to the Circus Maximus Showroom at Caesar's Palace...."

"Really?" Romano was impressed. The Circus Maximus Showroom was one of the top rooms in Las Vegas and had featured such stars as Bill Cosby and Sammy Davis Jr., the equivalent to Las Vegas royalty. "How were they able to set that up?"

"I don't know, but in addition to Caesar's Palace, they've also got a deal for prime time on thirty-six independent stations."

"So what's holding up the deal?"

"Well, I didn't want to agree to anything without running it by you first."

"Good man," Romano said, pleased that Gardner had come to respect Romano's opinion in addition to trusting his judgment. "So what is the deal?"

"If you agree, they pay you twenty-five thousand as a sort of honorarium."

Romano's mind was slightly awed by the sum. It was more than his father took home (after taxes) in a year and a half at the plant. And here he was making that money in one night. He was glad to have it, but somehow it didn't feel right, taking money for something he would have gladly done for nothing.

"All right, I agree," Romano said, then quickly added, "provided you do three things for me."

"Name 'em."

"One, take five thousand and divide it equally among the staff. Two, take another five thousand and donate it to the Las Vegas Showman's Memorial. And three, take the remaining fifteen, and establish a scholarship fund for young magicians."

"What school will these young magicians study at?"

"When I build it, I'll let you know."

"You got it," Gardner smiled.

"Then it's a deal." Romano said.

"All right. I'll call Ms. DePaul and tell them it's a go."

When Romano arrived at the Circus Maximus Showroom on the night before the challenge, Jerry Baker was there to greet him.

"Mr. Minardi, how good of you to show up. I've seen so much of you on television lately I thought you'd be too busy to drop by."

"I haven't been the only one who's been on TV lately."

"No, but you might as well be."

Romano was a little unsure what Baker was complaining about. Then again, the man might be a bit tipsy. He sure smelled like it. "Don't tell me you're having trouble sharing the small-screen spotlight?"

"With a no-talent, devil-loving blasphemer—"

"All right, all right," Gardner said, stepping between the two men. "Let's save some of this for the show." He turned to Romano. "We've come here to take a look at the challenges, and that's what we're going to do."

Romano nodded, walking away from Baker and toward Graham Chambers, who along with Roxanne had been examining some of the tests.

"He's gonna have you bending keys," Chambers said, holding up several small brass keys and two silver spoons. He pointed to the cameras set up to the front, left and right of the table the keys were on. "And it looks like he wants to catch you bending them against the table top."

Romano smiled at the simplicity of the challenge. Obviously Kraas had figured that he would bend the keys by the same means in which former stage performer Uri Geller had bent them decades earlier. Geller had achieved worldwide fame in the 1970s by claiming he had psychokinetic powers and could use those powers to bend spoons, keys and other metal objects. The truth was that Geller was simply a skilled close-up performer who'd made untrue statements to achieve publicity and fame. In many ways Romano's situation was similar to Geller's, but with one major distinction—Romano's claims of possessing special abilities were true, while Geller's were not.

"Well, he won't," Romano said. "I'll do the keys."

"And the cameras?" asked Chambers.

"Can stay right where they are."

Chambers looked at Romano with wide eyes, as if he suddenly realized that this was going to be a showcase for Romano's talents unlike anything he'd ever seen before.

They moved onto another challenge. It was a paper bill, in this case a one-hundred-dollar bill, suspended on top of a pin, inside a glass case.

"I'll do this one too."

"Miked?" asked Chambers.

Romano was pleased that Chambers knew the trick behind the challenge and that a microphone was likely the way Kraas would try to expose him as a fraud.

"Of course. The most sensitive they can find."

"This is going to be great."

In all, Romano agreed to four tests of psychokinetic powers and one escape involving wet bedsheets—an item stronger and more difficult to escape from than ropes and/or chains.

"Is that it?" Romano asked.

"No," Baker said. "Just one more." He gestured offstage and moments later Martin Kraas wheeled a large apparatus covered by a white sheet onto the stage.

Roxanne, Gardner and Chambers all glared at their former colleague. Romano just smiled at him. "Hi Martin," he said. "How are things going over there at Circus, Circus? I heard you've been all thumbs lately." It was one of those rare sort of moments that people only dream about. Here was Romano about to perform in the Circus Maximus Showroom asking Kraas about Circus, Circus. *It's true what they say about living well*, Romano thought. It was by far the best revenge.

Kraas avoided looking Romano in the eye, and once the apparatus was on the stage, he quickly left, leaving Baker to the task of unveiling the apparatus.

As he pulled the cover off the piece, people on the stage sucked in a gasp.

"It's a Table of Death!" Chambers said.

"Indeed it is," said Baker.

Romano looked at the piece. The Table of Death was an escape illusion invented by Andre Kole in which the magician is chained to a table above which is suspended a board with downward-pointing spikes. As the escape is performed, a curtain is drawn in front of the imprisoned performer. Soon after, the board falls with a crash and the spikes penetrate the table, the tips being clearly visible beneath it. Then, when the curtain is pulled aside, the performer is lying *on top* of the board, unharmed.

It was a thrilling illusion and popularly used in television shows and movies whenever magic played a part in the plot.

Romano didn't recognize the apparatus as being from Rantiki's collection and it looked slightly dissimilar from other Tables of Death he'd seen.

"There's no catch, no gimmick," Chambers said, after looking the piece over closely. "This isn't a fake. When these spikes fall, they *really* fall."

Romano nodded, betraying no emotions.

"He's correct," Baker said. "The spikes do indeed fall with no tricks or gimmicks. For the challenge, I propose that you be cuffed at the hands, bound by ropes at the feet, and placed under the spikes from where you will try and make good your escape. To place a time limit on the escape the spikes will be suspended overhead by a rope, which will be set alight by a single flame, here…." He gestured to a spot on the rope. "Above the flame will be a pail of water. Now, if you in fact possess the powers you claim to, you will A) simply be able to escape before the flames eat through the rope, or B) be able to put out the flame with the pail of water, thereby giving you all the time you need to escape your restraints." He looked at Romano, an eyebrow raised inquisitively.

"I don't like it," Chambers said.

"It's too dangerous," pleaded Roxanne. "You can prove everything with the other challenges. Say no to this one."

"Are you out of your mind, Baker?" Gardner asked. "Romano's a magician, not a daredevil." He turned his back on Baker, shaking his head.

Romano cleared his throat. "I'll do it."

22

Romano and Roxanne pulled up in front of Caesar's Palace in the Lexus in the middle of the afternoon. Romano was a little disappointed that he wasn't arriving at dusk when the lights would be on in the world-famous fountain and the bright yellow, orange and white lights of the *porte-cochère* would be beckoning him in through the front doors.

But their arrival time did have the advantage of allowing them to slip into the hotel unnoticed and therefore unbothered by reporters, tourists, fans, or any of Jerry Baker's loyal followers.

After they entered the hotel, the concierge immediately recognized Romano and personally took care of their bags, escorting them to their suite overlooking the Garden of the Gods pools and spa situated behind the hotel.

"Want to go for a dip?" Roxanne said. "I've got a new bikini I've been dying to show you."

Romano smiled and took her in his arms. "As much as I'd like to see you in strategically placed dental floss, I've got to go down to the Showroom to check on things."

"When are you expected?"

Romano looked at his watch. "In about twenty minutes."

"Then you can at least let me model it for you."

He kissed her full on the lips, his tongue darting deep into her mouth. "I'd like that."

"Sit down," she said. "I'll be right back."

"Where have you been?" Arthur Gardner said, giving Romano his you're-giving-me-gray-hairs-way-before-my-time look.

"Sorry I'm late," Romano said. "Something came up."

"Yeah, well…something's come up here too."

"What?"

"Baker's bringing in even more cameras. At last count he was set up with sixteen with four more on the way from the television station."

"So?"

"So, with so many cameras he's gonna catch you doing some sleight. It's just too many eyes up on the stage for my liking."

"He's going to set them up on the stage?"

"On the stage and just about everywhere else in the room."

Romano looked around, counting off the cameras. He could see twelve and he assumed the other four that were in place were out in the audience or hidden from view. It was all quite comical. The *more* cameras there were on stage, the *less* evidence Baker would have against him, since every one of them would produce the same result—irrefutable proof that Romano could do magick.

Romano lit a cigarette. "Tell him he can put as many cameras on stage as he wants…he can put one over my shoulder if he likes, it won't make the slightest bit of difference."

"Are you sure?" Gardner asked.

"Sounds like you're doubting me, Art," Romano quipped.

Gardner stood up and straightened his tie. "Me? Never." He turned to the technicians waiting to get the word. "All right, all right, what are you guys waiting for? Bring them in and put them where you want. Let's go!"

"Romano!"

He turned around and saw Harry Reddington Jr. making his way down one of the aisles toward the stage. Waving his hand in greeting, Romano stepped down off the stage and met Reddington halfway.

"If I don't see you between now and the show, I want to wish you the best of luck," Reddington said, patting Romano affectionately on the shoulder.

"Whatever happened to 'break a leg?'"

Reddington just looked at him. "All right, break your *neck* then, as well as both your legs."

"Thanks," Romano smiled. He looked up at the stage, and tried to look at the challenge from Reddington's perspective. Finally he said, "I guess I'm going to need all the help I can get."

"That's why I brought you these." Reddington fished inside his jacket pocket and took out three small objects that looked a lot like used tea bags.

"What are these?" Romano took one from Reddington. Not only did it look like a used tea bag, it felt like one too—damp and spongy. But no matter how hard he squeezed it, he couldn't get any moisture out of it. Strangest thing of all was that it felt very warm in his hand.

"It's a Dram," Reddington said. "Most mages call it Tass."

"What's Tass?"

"It's a physical form of Quintessence. Very rare."

"Where did you get it?"

"The Magic Box. Nodes can sometimes produce Tass when they haven't been tapped for a while. When the Quintessence builds up quickly, it overflows into the physical world. These three pieces took me over eight months to collect."

Romano suddenly took great care with the malleable lumps.

"Keep them close to your body. You'll start drawing on them when you need to."

"You mean like magick batteries?"

"Sort of."

Romano placed the pieces of Tass in his shirt pocket where they could stay close to his heart. He didn't really think putting them there would help the stuff work any better, but then again, it couldn't hurt. "Thanks," Romano said. "And I mean for everything."

Reddington smiled humbly. "Don't worry about it. Rantiki asked me to look out for you, so I am…. Speaking of which, is there anything I can do for you while the show is going on?"

Romano thought about it. "As a matter of fact, there is. We don't have anybody in the control room. Maybe you could watch the show from there just to make sure everything's on the level. If there's one thing I've learned from this whole situation it's that television people can perform a style of magic all their own."

Reddington nodded. "Right!"

They shook hands once more and Reddington headed for the control room.

As he watched the man walk away, Romano patted a hand against his shirt pocket.

The Tass was getting warmer.

It was a good feeling.

"How about dinner in the Spanish Steps Restaurant," Roxanne said, gazing out the window overlooking the pool.

Romano sucked deeply on his cigarette, then used the glowing embers of the butt to light a new one. He'd been smoking almost continuously for the past hour and more heavily than usual the past few days. All the smoke and tar were wreaking havoc on his lungs, but he needed the extra indulgence in his vice in order to hone the focus of his magick to razor sharpness.

"No thanks, I'm not hungry." Besides, if he went down to the restaurant there would be Art and Graham to deal with, and reporters asking questions and a whole slew of other people who meant well and just wanted to say hello, but were still a considerable distraction. Better to stay isolated in his room with his acolyte until just before showtime.

"All right," she said, a little disappointed. "Promise to take me tomorrow?"

Romano looked over at her and smiled. "Sure thing."

She returned his smile and picked up the phone. "Want anything from room service?"

Romano didn't hear her. He was busy casting innocuous little rotes that helped him to relax. Presently, he was floating coins on the rising smoke coming off his cigarette, letting a penny be carried aloft by the rising grey tendrils before fluttering back down to the heater when the smoke became too thin to hold it.

"Romano," Roxanne called.

"Huh?" The penny fell noisily onto the table.

"Do you want anything from room service?"

"No," he said abruptly. Then, looking around, recanted. "Yes, get them to send up another carton of cigarettes…and put in the order for the post-show party."

"What party?"

He cast a rote and lifted the penny off the table as easily as if it were connected to a string in his hand. Then he manipulated the coin to dash and loop through the air to spell out the letters M-A-G-I-C-K.

"The wake we're going to be hosting for Jerry Baker's career."

23

Daria DePaul lowered her head and looked over the tops of her glasses at Jerry Baker. "They say that with all the hype on TV and in the newspapers this past week they're expecting over a million people to be tuned in tonight."

"Jesus," Jerry Baker muttered, taking a stiff drink from the forty-ounce bottle of gin on his dressing-room table.

The producer kept talking. "And considering the news value of the show, it's estimated that more than ten million people will know who Jerry Baker is by this time next week."

"Praise the Lord." He took another swig, put down the bottle and showed off his perfect white teeth with a smile. "Now, let's do some of God's work."

There was a knock at the door. "Ten minutes, Mr. Minardi."

Roxanne turned toward the door and said, "Thank you, we'll be there in a minute."

Romano lit one last cigarette and buttoned up the front of his shirt. He decided on a pair of black slacks and a plain white shirt, rolled up at the sleeves and two buttons left undone at the collar. Nothing flashy this time out, he just wanted to show that he was relying on nothing other than his skill as a magician to get through the challenge.

"Do you think they'll let me smoke in the elevator?"

"Worst they can do is say no."

He nodded, tucked the cigarette into the corner of his mouth and headed for the door.

Outside in the hall a doorman was holding the elevator for him, part of the hotel's arrangements to get him to the Circus Maximus Showroom just as the show began.

He nodded hello to the doorman and stepped onto the elevator, followed by Roxanne.

"Good evening, Mr. Minardi."

Romano took a puff on his cigarette.

The doorman coughed once, but didn't say a word.

Romano stepped backstage just as comedian Alvin "Laugh if you Love Jesus" Wheatley was finishing warming up the crowd.

"Sean O'Regan, a Protestant, made the trek to St. Patrick's Cathedral in Belfast to ask Father O'Malley a very important question.

"'Father,' said Sean. 'With all the bombings and fighting between the Protestants and Catholics here in Northern Ireland, where in the world can I find peace?'

"'Quick, look behind you!' said Father O'Malley.

"Sean O'Regan turned around, and Father O'Malley smashed him on the back of the head with a brick. 'There,' the priest said, adjusting his collar. 'Is that peace enough for you?'"

Admittedly, his humor wasn't for everyone, but the joke did get a big laugh and Wheatley left the stage to a healthy round of applause.

During the break, Romano paced backstage, moving and stretching his fingers in a series of limbering exercises.

Then they were back live with the opening theme music to *The Jerry Baker Show* being played by a twelve-piece orchestra.

Romano watched Baker stroll onto the stage resplendent in his familiar white suit. His hair was just as perfectly white, and not one strand out of place.

The crowd applauded his entrance and for a moment Romano wondered if Baker hadn't checked audience allegiance at the door.

"Thank you! Thank you so much!" Baker said. "You all know why we're here," he said to the Circus Maximus crowd, "but for those of you at home who are tuning into *The Jerry Baker Show* for the very first time—God bless you!—allow me to fill you in on the history of this co-conspirator of Satan who masquerades as a Las Vegas entertainer named Romano Minardi." Baker said Romano's name as if his mouth were full of slugs. "Roll tape."

There was a short break as a quick recap of how the challenge came about was played for the home audience. It was a biased piece of telejournalism slanted in Baker's favor. Romano had seen it during set-up, and although he didn't like the way he was portrayed in it, there was nothing he could do about it. Nothing, except defeat each of Baker's challenges and show the world what kind of fool the man really was.

"Now, here he is, the Grand Deceptor of Sin City...Romano Minardi."

Romano walked onstage. The applause was so thin and unenthusiastic that he wondered if they'd remembered to flash the "Applause!" sign to remind the crowd about what they were supposed to do. Probably not.

"Right this way," Baker said, escorting Romano to an empty chair in front of the table which held an assortment of keys and spoons.

Romano sat down without saying a word. He was going to try to get through the evening by saying as few words as possible. For one, he didn't want to give Baker any material to ridicule him with, and two, actions spoke louder than words, and his actions tonight would speak volumes.

"One of Satan's greatest con-men, Uri Geller, made a fortune deceiving people into believing he could bend keys and spoons with the sheer force of his mind. Eventually, his psychokinetic powers were exposed to be nothing more than clever deceptions, and the forces he invoked were nothing more than brute force and ignorance.

"Mr. Minardi, if you possess the ability to perform magick, as you say you do, then I challenge you to bend these keys with nothing more than that power."

Catcalls and a smattering of applause.

The cameras moved in on either side of him, filling up the television screens of viewers with nothing more than his hands and the keys.

Romano simply nodded to Baker, picked up a key and held it delicately between his thumb and forefinger as if he were making the sign for "OK." Then he began rubbing the key between his fingers. After a few seconds he cast a matter rote on the key, and slowly, its ends began to droop down toward the table.

People gasped.

Baker blinked.

Romano continued rubbing the key until it curled around, its ends almost touching, to form a sort of ring around his finger. Then he dropped it onto the table where it clinked loudly.

A shiver of Paradox passed through Romano, but it was nothing he couldn't handle.

The stage was silent.

Baker looked at Romano suspiciously. He looked as if he'd been instructed by Martin Kraas where the deception would be and was dumbfounded when there was no deception in evidence.

Finally, Baker spoke. "Well, Mr. Minardi. You're a clever manipulator, but I know there was some of the devil's trickery at work. We'll be studying the tapes closely, friend. Perhaps you'd like to try that same stunt with this here spoon."

Romano took hold of the spoon. It was a quality piece of cutlery made from a heavy gauge of steel that was presumably hard to bend. No matter, he'd bend it as easy as a piece of solder wire. He turned his hand palm up, held out his index finger and laid the spoon across the pad of the fingertip. Then he cast a rote and watched as the spoon drooped toward the floor like a hot piece of plastic.

Again, people gasped.

Audience members whistled.

Baker's jaw dropped in amazement.

Romano lifted the spoon off his finger and placed it on the table, where it rocked back and forth before falling onto its side.

Another wave of Paradox flowed over his body. Romano closed his eyes to stave off the pain. It lingered a moment, then was gone.

"A masterful piece of deceit."

Romano nodded smugly as if to say *thank you*.

"Now if we could move onto the next test?"

Romano got up and followed Baker to another table. There was a hundred-dollar bill on it and a pin. Baker set the bill onto the pin so that it was perfectly balanced. That done, some stage hands placed a glass case on the table, encasing the bill within the glass.

"Now, Mister Minardi," Baker said. "As you agreed to yesterday, we will be placing several microphones on your shirt, each of which can detect the slightest sound or movement of air."

Romano nodded. The trick to this illusion relied on the fact that the four walls of the glass case never sat perfectly flat on any table top. Since there were minute cracks between the glass and the table, it was possible to blow a small breath of air through the crack in order to move the bill. The microphones would supposedly detect any "wind" coming from Romano's mouth.

Romano held his breath and raised his hand. Rotating his hand clockwise, he cast a rote on the bill, sending it turning slowly and evenly on the pin.

The audience gave Romano a round of applause. A small amount, but genuine.

Baker shook his head. "You're blowing air under the glass. I know, because I used that method to move the bill just this afternoon." Baker's voice had risen slightly, but he paused a moment to compose himself. "Apparently we aren't picking up the sound of your breath because of a technical problem. I'd like to make a slight modification to the case…if I may?"

Romano nodded.

Martin Kraas came onto the stage with a caulking gun and spread a bead of white silicone caulking around the base of the glass where it butted up against the tabletop, sealing the case off from any drafts.

Again Romano held his breath and cast a rote that started the bill turning. Baker looked absolutely vexed. Romano saw the look on the man's face and sent the bill spinning even faster until it took flight, rising up inside the case before fluttering back down again.

People began cheering.

Romano's body shuddered with Paradox, but he tensed his muscles and hid his grimace until the pain passed. Finally, he exhaled and smiled.

Baker's face was turning a pale shade of red, which despite its paleness was in striking contrast to his all-white suit. He turned to a camera. "Well, ladies and gentlemen. The Lord works in mysterious ways, but so too does the devil. We'll be back right after this brief commercial message."

The cameras panned over the audience.

And they were finally at commercial.

"What the hell is going on here?" Jerry Baker was shouting at the top of his voice. Several veins were bulging up from his forehead.

"I don't know," Martin Kraas said, shrugging his shoulders.

"You don't know! You don't know!" He took a pull from his bottle of gin. "I'm watching my career go down the toilet and you don't know."

"Look, he had a day to figure something out. Maybe he treated his finger with a chemical to bend the keys, or figured out some way to heat the air inside the glass case."

"Are those things possible?"

"I don't know…maybe."

"Maybe's just not good enough."

"When are you going to realize that he's a good magician? He wouldn't have agreed to the challenge if he didn't think he could beat you. Maybe he did those things to win the first two challenges, maybe he didn't. Check the tape. If you can't find anything on the tape, then maybe, just maybe, you'll have to admit that this magick of his is for real."

"Never!" Baker took one last swig, then slammed the bottle down onto his make-up table. "He's a fake, he's a con man. And I'm going to expose him tonight on live television."

"Suit yourself," Kraas said.

Baker looked at Kraas a moment, as if weighing his options.

At last he turned to leave the dressing room, shouting to the others backstage, "Check the tape! Check the tape! There's got to be something on it."

"How do you feel?" Arthur Gardner asked.

Romano puffed on his cigarette and nodded. "I feel good."

"Great, just great." Gardner clapped his hands together. "You should have seen the look on that guy's face when that bill flew around inside the case."

"Arthur…" Roxanne said, as she worked the muscles of Romano's neck and shoulders in an effort to keep him relaxed.

"Yeah?"

She nodded her head toward the door.

"Right, I'm sorry." He started toward the door. "Break a leg, buddy."

Romano touched the fingers of his right hand to his temple in a casual salute. Gardner left the room.

"Thanks," Romano said to Roxanne.

He closed his eyes and began casting rotes, causing things to begin lifting off the tables. After the ravages of Paradox on his body, the rotes calmed him.

"I feel good," he said.

"Excuse me, are you Ms. DePaul?"

"Yes." Daria DePaul turned away from the stage to see a short man with a bald head and black thick-rimmed glasses standing behind her. "Who are you?"

"I'm Doctor Lyle Laughlin from UNLV. Jerry Baker asked me to come on the show to talk about paranoid delusion."

"When?"

"After Mr. Minardi fails."

That wasn't the *when* she was asking about, but it told her enough.

"Sit down, Doctor Laughlin. I'll let you know when we need you." She turned back around and watched Jerry Baker walk back onto the stage.

If *and when*, she thought.

"Welcome back," Jerry Baker said, looking more than a little haggard following the extended commercial break. "So far, Romano Minardi has succeeded in defeating the challenges prepared for him by myself and renowned Las Vegas illusionist Martin Kraas. However, we are not about to admit that some sort of fraud or trickery was not responsible for the bending of the key or the movement of the bill."

He looked at Romano, hoping his words would goad him into speaking.

Romano remained silent, his lips pressed together tightly. Truth was, he wasn't even listening to Baker anymore as all his thoughts and concentration were sharply focussed on the next challenge.

After a brief pause, Baker droned on. "…An escape worthy of the great Harry Houdini himself."

The bedsheets were brought onto the stage. A little water dripped from the corners, which was a bit of showmanship on Baker's part since the sheets weren't required to be wetted down until after they were tied.

Romano moved to the center of the stage and allowed himself to be tied up in the sheets.

"As you most likely know, Mr. Minardi, but which our audience may not, the wet-bedsheet restraint was devised by asylum attendants decades ago as a means of subduing dangerously maniacal inmates. So, needless to say, it is an effective means of containment and one of the most difficult escapes of all to perform…especially if you don't have the devil's magick to work with."

Romano remained still as a piece of cloth was wrapped around his body, binding his hands to his sides. Then he was eased down onto a sheet laid out on the stage and rolled up tightly inside it. After the first sheet was rolled up, a second sheet was wrapped around him, and then finally, a third.

"Comfortable, Mr. Minardi?" Baker asked, smugly.

Romano didn't answer. He was already preparing the magick he'd need to make good his escape.

"Now, normally with this type of challenge, the escapee is placed upon a bed with a strong frame so that heavy cloth bandages can be wound around his ankles, knees, waist and neck, and secured to the permanent irons fitted to the sides of a bedframe. But we thought that, seeing as you might be too familiar with that escape, we would lock you in a safe and give you a time limit in which to perform the escape…. Perhaps fifteen or twenty minutes would be enough. If not, you can have until the end of our hour."

A huge safe, the kind that is usually built into the walls of banks and other financial institutions, was wheeled onto the stage. The heavy wheels rolled like thunder against the floorboards of the stage.

Romano was angered, but not surprised, by the sudden change in plans—the safe had not been part of the agreed-upon challenge. Romano realized that since he was defeating Baker so thoroughly the man had to do something in order to save face, but this was despicable. Still, Romano was just as glad to know that he'd be locked inside the safe, since it would allow him to use his magick freely out of the sight of any Sleepers who might be in the audience.

"Do you agree to the conditions of the challenge?"

Romano nodded; to say no now would be akin to admitting defeat.

"Very well," Baker said. "Complete the challenge."

Romano was then drenched in buckets of hot water, around one-hundred and ten degrees Fahrenheit, which soaked the sheets so that they stuck together. Then he was lifted off the stage, carried to the safe, dripping a river of water from each of the low points on the sheet, and placed inside. Then the door was slammed shut, leaving him in...

Absolute darkness.

The first thing he did was cast a rote over time, slowing time outside the safe to a crawl. He wanted to make his escape appear to take only minutes, and this would allow him that.

Next he concentrated on the problem of the sheets. Since they wouldn't give, there was no slack to play with. Therefore, he had to turn the water into oil. He did this with a combination of Time and Matter rotes, the Time rotes accelerating time within the safe and the Matter rotes changing the water's chemical composition to that of baby oil.

With the rotes invoked, Romano waited.

It was a slow process.

He sped it up a little.

And noticed for the first time that the Tass in his pockets had begun to sizzle like drops of water in a hot frying pan.

The realization shocked him. First of all, it meant that he'd already used up all of his own Quintessence, and second of all, it meant there was a possibility that he might not get out of the safe before he'd used up all his Tass.

He began to struggle against the sheets, deciding he couldn't wait until they were completely oiled to attempt the escape.

The Tass continued to sizzle.

It felt hot against his skin.

The air inside the safe was also getting hot.

Hot and fetid.

But at last the sheets were slick.

And then, he felt something give. He wriggled forward and out of the outer sheet. Then he managed to get a hand free, slid it up and out, unraveling the second outside sheet. After that, both hands were free and it was only a matter of untying the final few knots.

Which left the locking mechanism of the safe.

If he had slipped some tools into the safe with him, he might have been able to manipulate the mechanism manually from inside. But all he had with him was Tass.

He checked his supply.

He'd begun with three lumps. Now, two were gone, evaporated into nothing, leaving less than one lump to escape the safe and make it through the final challenge…

The Table of Death.

He hoped it was enough.

He cast a Matter rote on the inner workings of the safe and heard the tumblers click and fall.

He pushed the safe door open a crack and inhaled the dry, ice-cold air that was sucked inside.

Then he pushed the safe door open…

"Let us pr—"

…interrupting Baker in mid-sentence.

Romano squinted at the sudden brightness of the stagelights. Then he glanced at his watch. According to the timepiece, less than two minutes of real time had elapsed while he'd performed the escape.

Baker's face had suddenly turned as white as his suit.

Romano crawled out of the safe, his slick body exhausted and racked by an excruciatingly painful wave of Paradox.

While he had performed his magick in the darkness inside the safe, it was still virtually impossible for him to have escaped the wet bedsheets *and* the safe in such a short period of time. He could never have escaped the safe without risking Paradox. Now he was paying the price.

He writhed around on the stage, his body tensed and twisted by the needle-sharp spikes of pain.

People in the audience weren't sure whether to scream or cheer. They did a little of both.

Arthur Gardner and Roxanne ran onto the stage.

"Romano," Roxanne cried. "Are you all right?"

The Paradox ebbed from his body and he was left feeling exhausted, like the morning after a rare day of hard physical labor. "I'm okay," he gasped. "I'm all right. Lift me up."

Together they pulled him to his feet.

He looked like a mess, but he smiled and raised his hand to the crowd, then to the cameras.

Everyone cheered.

"Let's go to a commercial," Baker said.

"You don't look too good," Arthur Gardner said when they got Romano back to the dressing room.

Judging by the way he felt, Romano wasn't surprised.

"You've done enough," Gardner said, the tone of his voice telling Romano he was speaking as a friend, and not as his business manager. "You've already beaten this guy at his own game. If you want to stop it here, no one's going to think anything less of you."

Roxanne lit a cigarette for Romano and placed it between his lips. "No," he said softly after a couple of puffs. "I'm not going to give him an excuse to claim victory."

"All right, whatever you want." Gardner looked at Roxanne, then back at Romano. "Do you want me to leave?"

Roxanne looked at Romano.

He wouldn't be doing any rotes during this break. The last escape had burned up far too much Tass and he had to save what little Quintessence he had left for the stage.

"Stay, Art," he said. "And tell me a story. Tell me a story…about Rantiki."

"How the *hell* did he do that?" Baker shouted.

Kraas shook his head. "I haven't got a clue. Even when Houdini did the escape it was a test of endurance. He should have been spending the night in that safe." He shrugged his shoulders.

"Well he's not spending the night in there, he's going to be spending it as the toast of Las Vegas." Baker was frantic now, like an animal caught in a cage who knows that the end is near. "What can you do to the last escape to make sure he doesn't make it?"

"What?" Kraas asked.

"I said, what can you do to make sure he doesn't get out of it?"

"It's already tough enough to get out of as it is. If I make it any tougher, it'll probably end up killing him."

There was an extended moment of silence between them.

"What can you do?" Baker said.

Kraas looked at Baker, eyes narrowing. "You're out of your mind, do you know that?"

Baker turned and took a swig of gin.

"And this has nothing to do with God, does it?" Kraas rose up from his seat. "This is all about Jerry Baker…. Romano's done everything you wanted him to do. I don't know how he did all of it, but he did it. And you *still* have to win, even if you have to kill the man to do it."

"Get out of my sight!" Baker shouted.

"Don't worry," Kraas said, opening the door. "You won't be seeing me again."

Kraas slammed the door behind him.

Baker took another gulp of gin.

He looked at the bottle a moment, watching the swish and swirl of the clear liquid inside…

And it gave him an idea.

When they came back from commercial for the finale, Romano looked a little better, having changed his clothes and combed his hair.

A little better, but not much.

For the most part, Baker still looked freshly pressed, although he was perhaps getting a little frayed around the edges.

"Labies and gendlemen," he said, slurring his words slightly. "Romano Minardi has proven that he is one of Satan's minions tonight…. How else could you explain his miraculous escapes and manipulations? However, he is still a mortal man. And no mortal in the history of mankind has ever been able to cheat…"

A long pause, almost too long.

"Death itself. Ladies and gentlemen, the final challenge, the Table of Death."

The audience in the Circus Maximus Showroom let out a collective "Ooooo…"

At that same moment, the same sound was no doubt being made in tens of thousands of households across the southwestern United States.

Romano wasted no time preparing for the escape. He was ready, or at least as ready as he could be under the circumstances.

"To make sure there is no trickery involved, we've asked members of the Las Vegas Metro Police Department to handcuff and bind Mr. Minardi for this final escape."

Two officers stepped onto the stage to a mixture of boos and cheers. One officer cuffed Romano's wrists while the other tied up his ankles. When they were done, they tipped their hats to Romano and said, "Good luck!"

Romano nodded and the officers left the stage.

After that Romano was hoisted onto the Table of Death while Baker babbled on:

"The Table of Death is a perfect close to this live television challenge because it incorporates the forces of Earth, Air, Fire and Water. First of all, the steel spikes represent the *Earth*, hanging just a few feet over the table with nothing but *Air* between the deadly spikes and the mortal Mr. Minardi. The rope suspending the spikes will be set on *Fire* while a bowl of *Water* is secured to a platform just above the flames. If Mr. Minardi's magick can control these forces—forces upon which only God can impose his will—then escaping from the Table of Death should be as easy as awakening from a pleasant dream."

Baker paused, looked behind him.

Everything was in place.

"Are you ready, Mr. Minardi?"

Romano nodded.

"Light the flame."

The stagelights dimmed.

The flame was lit.

Romano's first inclination was to slow down time once more to give him more than enough time to escape from the table. But the moment he invoked the rote, the Tass in his pocket began to sizzle. Too fast, too fast.... Obviously, he had enough of the material to perform one more small feat of vulgar magick.

He looked behind him, saw the flame chewing at the rope and the bucket of water resting just above it.

He decided to tip over the bowl and let the water put out the fire. He cast a simple rote and the bowl tipped forward, spilling the clear liquid onto the flames...

...sending them shooting up to the ceiling as if they'd been doused with gasoline.

People in the audience screamed.

Stagehands moved to get to Romano, but Baker held them back.

"Stand back! It's God's will forbidding one of Satan's own to triumph! He's just getting a small taste of the flames of hell in which he is destined to burn for all eternity."

Romano watched as the flames burned higher.

He could hear the individual strands snapping and popping as they were eaten through by the fire.

Romano tried casting another rote, but the Tass in his pocket sizzled for a second, then fell silent.

He was without his magick.

And on his own.

He took a deep breath to calm himself, then set about the task of escaping.

He glanced at the handcuffs around his wrist.

Blinking, he took a second, closer look, and read the familiar name pressed into the metal—Peerless Handcuff Company, Springfield, Mass. The handcuffs were the exact same make and model as the ones the policeman had cuffed him with years ago at Torchy's.

An incredible coincidence, or a wonderful piece of coincidental magick.

Romano didn't care.

He was too busy getting out of the cuffs.

With a quick and easy manipulation, the cuffs popped open, freeing his hands and allowing him to untie his feet.

In seconds he was free.

A final glance up at the rope told him it was going to give way at any moment.

He rolled to the right.

The spikes fell…

Pinning his arm to the table.

The stage and audience were a mass of noise and confusion.

He looked his arm over and saw no blood.

One of the spikes had caught the sleeve of his shirt. He tore the shirt away, and walked upstage past an incredulous Jerry Baker.

The crowd rose up onto their feet, giving Romano…

A standing ovation.

EDO VAN BELKOM

Harry Reddington walked onstage, flanked by officers from the Las Vegas Metro Police Department.

"Mr. Baker," said one of the uniformed policemen, "you're under arrest."

"For what?" laughed Baker.

"Attempted murder," the cop said.

"That's ridiculous."

"It *is* ridiculous," Reddington said. "But sadly it's true. You insisted on so many extra cameras for the challenge that one of them happened to catch you replacing the water with gin. So I'm afraid, Mr. Baker, the only forces of evil here tonight were the ones working through your own hands."

The police slapped the cuffs on Baker.

The crowd cheered even louder.

Epilogue

Professor Thomas W. Tobin, a Technomancer, pressed the channel selector on his remote and allowed the cable converter over his television to surf up the dial.

He'd scanned a big news item on several stations about some goings-on in Las Vegas, but had been unable to catch a full report from beginning to end. At last he found one on Channel Seven's *Inside Affair*.

"In Las Vegas, tonight," the beautiful, blond reporter Cynthia Keegan said. "A bizarre turn of events…"

Quickly, Professor Tobin picked up a second remote and pointed it at his VCR. The machine came to life and immediately began recording the report.

Then he watched as keys and spoons bent like paper, money encased in glass fluttered like a butterfly, and a man miraculously escaped death, not once, but twice.

Something wasn't right.

He didn't exactly feel the ripple of Quintessence coming off the television screen, but he'd felt something damn near close to it.

He let the report run out, rewound the tape, and watched it once more.

Again, something wasn't right.

He continued surfing the dial in search of other news reports on the subject.

And while he did that, he also made a mental note to follow with greater interest the career of one Romano Minardi…

Mage.

Beyond the Shroud

RICK HAUTALA

DEDICATION:

To Bonnie and Jim Moore…without whom…

"I wear the chains I forged in life"
— Dickens

"Oh, ye interminable gloomy realms
Of swimming shadows and enormous shapes,
Some fully shown, some indistinct, and all
Mighty and melancholy—what are ye?
Live ye, or have ye lived?"
— Lord Byron, *Cain*

Author's Note: If you try to use any of the descriptions in this book to find your way around Portland, Maine, I guarantee that you will become hopelessly lost. Don't say I didn't warn you!

Prologue

PORTLAND PRESS HERALD, Wednesday, July 17 LONDON (UPI)

Investigators report no further leads in their investigation of the theft from London's Riverside Museum last week of three knives reputed to have belonged to the nineteenth-century serial killer popularly known as "Jack the Ripper."

The antique surgical "post-mortem" knives with hard rubber handles and 24 cm blades were reported missing after a routine check by security guards following closing time at the museum on the evening of July 11.

Investigators have determined that no other displays or objects, some of which are of much greater value than the knives, were tampered with or stolen. Police are baffled as to why the culprit or culprits would steal only those particular items. Unofficial speculation is that the theft was planned and executed by a Ripper enthusiast, or "Ripperologist," as they are known, who wanted to personally own a small piece of one of London's most notorious crime sprees.

Not many people in Portland, Maine—or the rest of the country, for that matter—noticed this small news article when it ran on the wires on July 17th.

If the year had been 1988, the centenary "celebration" of Jack the Ripper's ghastly murder spree, more people might have paid attention to it. It might even have garnered a brief mention on the CBS Evening News.

As it was, however, the five-sentence squib on page three of the *Portland Press Herald* was either quickly read and forgotten, or else overlooked entirely by nearly everyone who read the newspaper that day.

Sarah Robinson never had much time for anything more than a cursory glance at the headlines on this or any other morning. Most days, she barely had time to gulp down her coffee and take a bite of toast or bagel before grabbing her purse and running out so she wouldn't be late for her job at the University of Maine Law Library. Ever since the divorce from her husband, David, had been finalized six months ago, she'd had a tough enough time pulling her life together—especially following the deeper and much longer lasting pain of losing her nine-year-old daughter, Karen, five years previous.

The last thing Sarah was inclined to notice or give even the slightest bit of thought to was a relatively petty theft in London, England.

That evening, after work and a light supper, she folded the newspaper in half, not even noticing that the "Ripper" article was face up as she placed it underneath her cat Bingley's water bowl on the kitchen floor.

Over the next several days, the paper would wrinkle from spilled water and turn yellow in the hot summer sun as the printer's ink slowly faded to gray.

And it begins…

1

AWAKENING

Consciousness returned slowly…like dark, heavy drapes being pulled aside by unseen hands….

David Robinson could feel his face, chest, and belly pressing down against the uneven ground. His fingers were hooked, like claws, into the loose gravel. He could feel a groan gathering strength deep within him, but no matter how hard he tried, he couldn't release it.

It was as though he had forgotten how.

The dense air blanketed him, squeezing and pressing him mercilessly down against the unyielding earth, forcing the breath out of him. Whenever he tried to breathe, he could not feel even the slightest movement of muscles and ribs, expanding his chest…no cool rush of air in his throat and lungs.

A cold, stark fear stronger than any emotion he had ever experienced before gripped David as he stared into the darkness that pulsed behind his eyes.

And then, after he had stared into that utter nothingness for a terrifying, timeless instant, patterns began to emerge—

Veined flashes of yellow and white hot light split the purple, velvet darkness….

Hazy, flickering amorphous shapes looking like huge, glowing amoebae simultaneously advanced and receded in the darkness behind his eyes….

Faces, stained by impenetrable shadow, danced and whirled around him like vagrant breezes, pulling at him from all directions at once….

Vague thoughts and dull, echoing voices flitted like phantoms through his mind. Whenever he tried to grasp any one particular thought, it would slip away from him like fine beach sand, sifting between his fingers.

Gone….

Lost forever….

Just like I am, a tiny voice whispered like hissing, spitting water in his mind.

Memories and half-remembered words drifted past him like wind-tossed sheets and disappeared before he could catch any of them until—finally— one single image burned more strongly and clearly in his mind than the others….

Lights!

Yes, twin spinning whirlpools of light…like razor-edged cyclones, zooming straight at him from out of the darkness.

David felt his body tense, and he automatically ducked to one side as though braced for the impact.

Yes, impact!

The thought was as palpable as a stinging slap across his face.

There had been…IMPACT!

A sudden rush of sound, like the tearing of old, wet cloth filled his ears, making him cringe inwardly. He remembered hearing a heavy, dull *thud* followed by a chorus of wailing voices.

And there had been something else…something about a…a river…

David struggled hard to sharpen his memory.

…Time moves like a river…and you can either sink or swim….

That's it!

He'd been looking down into the swirling depths of the Stroudwater River.

It had been night.

Late at night, maybe even almost dawn.

The sky had been overcast with no moon or stars overhead. A gray shroud seemed to envelope him where he had been standing, isolating him from the rest of the world.

In the darkness, the river had looked like slick oil, sliding with a faint, throaty gurgle underneath the cement pillars of the bridge. Whirlpools and eddies dimpled the river's surface, and something—a faint, trilling voice— had been calling his name.

David's hands had been hot and sticky against the thick metal railing that still radiated heat from the blistering summer day. The night air had been raw in his throat, thick and burning as he gulped it like water into his lungs.

Dark water…choking him….

In the distance, he remembered hearing a steady, hissing whisper. He eventually realized that it must have been traffic, passing by on the interstate.

But there wasn't much traffic out here on East Bridge Street.

Not at this hour.

David often walked out here late at night…to think, he told himself, to work through story and character ideas, and to contemplate what the hell he was going to do with his life now that—once again—it had changed so drastically.

But tonight, he remembered, he had told himself that he had done all the thinking he was going to do.

Tonight he had determined—finally—to *do* something about it!

And why not?

It was all over.

Just yesterday morning, his publisher had rejected his proposal for a new mystery novel. His editor had, in fact, informed him—as politely as he could— that he also wouldn't be interested in seeing anything else from him.

With the divorce finalized more than six months ago—compounded with the grief of losing his only child five years before that—his rapidly shrinking income and increasing depression, after destroying whatever love his wife might have once had for him, had finally broken him, too.

Over the last six months, he had withdrawn more and more into a shell of total isolation punctuated only by outbursts of anger. He had directed most of his anger at his ex-wife, but he had known deep inside that the real anger—the *pure* anger—more properly should have been directed against himself.

But what was he supposed to do?

Pick up his life, at least what was left of it, and get on with it?

Just like, for the last five years, he was supposed to work through his grief and guilt, and get on with living after Karen died?

Just like, with sales of his novels and his book advances steadily declining, he was supposed to get on with his life as a professional writer, or else find something else to do to earn a living. As if he could find anything better than pumping gas at the corner Sunoco or bagging groceries at Shop 'n Save!

No, it didn't work that way, at least not for him.

David had told himself many times that he had tried to make his life work out, but—ultimately—it hadn't.

He had failed.

So—finally—tonight, feeling as though he had absolutely nothing left—no options; no one to talk to; nowhere to turn—he had decided to *do* it.

He was going to kill himself.

His face was still pressing against the hard ground, but he was starting to remember more clearly now.

Fragmented images and memories coalesced into bigger chunks that began to have content and meaning. Some parts of what he remembered almost made sense.

He'd been standing on the bridge, gazing down into the river and wishing—no, *praying* to God that he had the strength and courage to go through with what he had planned.

He knew that it could be easy.

All he had to do was clear the railing with a smooth, easy vault, and then let himself drop.

Let gravity do all the work.

Free-fall.

Arms and legs kicking in the air. Hands tearing at the overcast night sky until finally, with a sudden, cold shock, he would hit the water.

He tried to imagine what it would feel like, and that, perhaps, was one of the drawbacks of being a writer: he could imagine violent and deadly things much too easily and vividly.

Standing there at the bridge railing, he had almost tasted the thick, choking stench of the polluted river water gushing into his nose and mouth....

He had watched the dark river's current, strong and fast, channeling between the stone pilings, waiting to pull him under....

He could almost feel the burning need for air as his lungs collapsed inward, choking him...strangling him...like huge, unseen hands that had caught him and were wringing his body like the useless dishrag his marriage, his career—his entire *life* had become.

But I didn't have the courage to do it!

That single thought burned inside David like the white hot flame of a welding torch. He experienced a misery and despair that he hadn't felt since Karen died.

He had *thought* about doing it, had planned it and imagined it in finite detail; but when it had finally come down to leaping off the bridge into the river, he hadn't had the fucking balls to do it!

But then...something else had happened.

Something had gone terribly *wrong*!

If only he could remember....

A telephone call in the middle of the night usually means one of two things—either someone has dialed the wrong number, or else there was bad news.

The sudden ringing of the telephone beside her bed, inches from her head, ripped Sarah from a deep, dreamless sleep. She uttered a strangled cry as she bolted upright in bed, one hand reaching for the phone and the other supporting her as she shifted her eyes over to the blue digital numerals of the alarm clock and tried to focus.

4:08

"Oh, *shit*," she muttered before snatching up the receiver in the middle of its third ring.

Her heart was thumping quick and hard in her neck. A sour taste flooded the back of her throat. The only semi-lucid thought she had was that it probably was David, pissed off again about something.

But maybe it wasn't so bad.

Maybe the worst that had happened was that he'd been drinking and hadn't been paying attention to the time. Since the divorce, that had happened...more times than she cared to remember.

The telephone receiver was slick and cool in her hand as she pressed it to her ear. In a raw, rattling voice, she said, "Hello."

"Is this Mrs. David Robinson?"

This isn't David's voice, was her only clear thought as she tried to force herself awake. *This could be bad!*

"Ahh—yeah, yeah," she said, her voice still ragged with sleep. "At least I used to be."

No matter how much she tried to swallow, the sour taste wouldn't leave the back of her mouth. Her stomach suddenly felt like it was full of acid.

"This is Officer Murray, down at the Westbrook Police station. Are you married to a Mr. David Robinson?"

"I *was.* We've been divorced a while now," Sarah said thickly.

She wiped her dry lips with the back of her hand, noticing how chapped they felt, and swallowed tightly. Tension gripped her with a cold pressure that centered in her chest.

She knew that whatever this policeman was going to say next, it wasn't going to be good.

In a flash, her mind registered that the only possible question was—*How bad is it going to be?*

"I'm afraid there's been an accident, ma'am. Your ex-husband was killed tonight."

"Oh, Jesus!"

Sarah let her breath out in a shuddering groan. Her mind went blank for a moment.

"Wha—what happened?"

The air seemed suddenly to have been sucked out of the room. The night was hot, and she had been sleeping in a thin nightgown outside the covers, but suddenly the room felt several degrees colder. Sarah shivered violently.

"Apparently he was taking a late-night walk—"

"Yeah, he's a writer," Sarah blurted out, grasping for something—anything to say, even though it sounded rather foolish. Her eyes brimmed with tears as they darted back and forth, scanning the darkened bedroom. "He—he takes a lot of late-night walks. To get ideas and stuff."

"I'm sorry to have to tell you like this, over the phone, ma'am. I would have sent someone directly to your place, but we've had some—uh, another situation to deal with tonight as well. Anyway, as your husband—your ex-husband was crossing East Street Bridge here in Westbrook, a trailer truck struck and killed him. The driver says he never even saw him until it was too late."

"Oh, Jesus...oh, *Jesus*! Was he—? Did he—?"

"The M.E. says it looks like he was killed instantly, that he most likely didn't suffer," the officer said.

"Umm...I see," Sarah said, staring blankly ahead. She blinked her tear-filled eyes rapidly, making her view of the room go all gray and blurry. She looked around for something to ground her, and tried to focus on the rectangle of the window where slivers of light from the corner streetlight angled through the slats of the miniblinds, but her eyes kept twitching back and forth, making the whole room dance jerkily.

"I know it's terribly late," Officer Murray said mildly, "but if possible, we'd like you to come down to the hospital morgue to make a positive I.D."

"A what?"

"We need you to identify your husband's body," Officer Murray said. "Do you think you're up to doing that?"

"Oh, yeah...sure."

"If you could be ready in a quarter of an hour, I'll have a squad car pick you up."

Sarah started to reply, but then her mind went suddenly blank. She had barely heard, much less understood, what the policeman had said. Her vision of the darkened bedroom was blurry and out of focus. For a brief, shattering instant, she thought she saw the dark silhouette of a man, standing at the foot of the bed between her and the window.

She gasped and sucked in her breath sharply.

"Mrs. Robinson? Are you all right?"

When Sarah blinked her eyes and looked again, the illusion was gone. It took her several seconds to recover. She cleared her throat and said into the telephone, "I—I'm sorry. What did you say?"

"I said I can have a squad car stop by to pick you up in fifteen minutes if you can be ready that fast."

"Yeah, I—I guess so," Sarah replied weakly, still staggered by the news. It all had an unreal cast, like this was still part of some terrible dream.

"You're at Sixteen Canal Street, correct?"

"Yes. I...I'll be ready in fifteen minutes," Sarah said, and then she cradled the phone.

For the next five minutes or so, she sat on the edge of the bed, all the while shaking her head and trying desperately to clear her mind. The ambient light in her bedroom was still shattered by the tears that filled her eyes, but as she looked more carefully at the softly glowing window, she could see that no one was there.

Of course there wasn't!

How could there be?

She took a calming breath and held it for a moment. Without looking away from the spot at the foot of the bed, she reached over and snapped on the bedside light; but even with the light bathing her small bedroom with a warm, lemon glow, she couldn't shake the thought that—for just an instant—there really *had* been someone there....

Someone who had been *looking* at her...holding his arms out to her as though pleading with her....

And she couldn't shake the feeling that—maybe—just maybe—he was still there....

Unseen...no matter how dark or light the room was.

David was still lying on the ground with his head turned to one side as he listened to the wind. It whipped and snapped like loose ropes in the darkness. The shrill whistle reminded him of a blizzard, sweeping across the land. He closed his eyes and tried to remember what had happened earlier tonight, if it was, in fact, still "*tonight.*" His mind was flooded with fragmentary images and memories which he still couldn't piece together into anything meaningful.

One of the sharpest images, though, and the one that made the least sense to him, was of a hooded figure he thought he had seen leaning over him. His vision had been distorted, making everything look almost like he was underwater, looking up at the sky. Hazy blobs of light shimmered and shattered into warped curtains of glowing energy. The face inside the hood that had leaned close to him had been lost in a dense pool of darkness.

A darkness as deep as a moonless midnight.

He also remembered either this cloaked figure or someone else speaking to him, but he couldn't recall any of what had been said.

It took a great deal of effort, but David managed to roll over and sit up. Hugging his knees with both arms, he looked around, hoping to get his bearings.

As he scanned up and down the street, he realized one thing that had been bothering him. Although the wind was blowing with a loud, flute-like whistle, he couldn't feel even the faintest trace of a breeze on his face or arms.

His sense of time seemed distorted, as well.

He had no idea how long ago he had been standing on the bridge, looking down into the dark river. It could have been minutes or days ago…maybe even an entire lifetime ago.

Am I dead? he thought, but he quickly dismissed the idea.

His idea of what *death* was didn't include self-awareness.

He had always imagined death to be pure, total oblivion, and that's exactly what he had been seeking tonight.

Oblivion!

He recalled that the summer night had been warm. The air had been close and sticky with humidity, but right now he had absolutely no sensation of temperature. Everything—even the atmosphere surrounding him—felt strangely neutral and distant. He couldn't resist the odd sensation that he was somehow detached from reality, as if he were floating outside of it in a bubble and looking in.

"Jesus, what the hell's going on here?" David whispered hoarsely to himself as he slowly stood up and brushed his hands together. His palms made a faint clapping sound that echoed oddly in the close night.

David frowned as he looked down at his hands.

He could feel them touching each other, but even as simple a sensation as rubbing his hands together seemed strangely distorted. It felt as if he were touching everything though thick, padded gloves.

A deep, lonely ache filled David when he looked around and realized that he didn't recognize where he was.

This *certainly* didn't look like anywhere near the bridge on East Bridge Street…at least, not as far as he could see.

It was still night, that much he was sure of.

He wasn't even sure if it was still the same night he had gone for a walk to the bridge.

The sky appeared too close and dense, like a low-hanging fog bank. Each streetlight lining the side of the road cast a dull glow that fragmented into deep blue and purple splinters of light that cast distorted ink-wash-thin shadows across the stony ground. When David raised his hand to his forehead, the numerous shadows of his arm coiled at his feet on the ground like a tangled nest of snakes. He took several lurching steps forward, but the effect of his multiple shadows moving along with him was completely disorienting. He almost lost his balance.

Leaning forward with both hands on his knees, he braced himself as he looked around. He realized with a dull shock that he was standing in the middle of a debris-strewn road in what looked like an ancient, abandoned city.

He didn't recognize anything.

He was surrounded by tall buildings that loomed darkly against the pressing night sky. Their square hulks looked ancient and somehow threatening. Along the fronts of every building—most of them three or four stories tall—were gaping dark windows that hung open like huge, hungry mouths. In many of the windows and shadowed doorways, David thought he caught subtle hints of motion—of people or possibly animals moving about; but whenever he looked directly at anything, he couldn't see what might have caused it.

A cold, clammy sensation traveled up his back to the base of his skull. He couldn't shake the sensation that numerous unseen eyes were watching him from the darkness, studying his every move.

He wanted to start moving, but he had no idea which way to go until he heard the soft scuffing sound of feet, dragging in the dirt behind him.

Clenching both fists, David whirled around to see a dark, hunched figure, making its way slowly toward him.

The person was stooped over. One leg—his left—dragged behind him as though partially paralyzed. Tension filled David as he cautiously watched the person approach. The light from the streetlights overlit the person's features, casting the hollows of his cheeks and neck into deep shadow.

David could see that it was a man—or at least what had once been a man. As he got closer, David could see that his features were decomposing. Wide, white flaps of skin hung from his forehead and cheeks. They swayed with every halting step he took closer to David.

"Why don't you stop right there, friend?" David said, surprising even himself by the strength of his voice.

The old man jerked to a halt. Hunching over to one side, he glared at David.

"Friend?" he said in a high, cackling voice. "I like that! Friend, indeed!"

The streetlight's glare caught the old man's right eye, making it glow with a deep, eerie gleam.

"Why don't you just back off?" David said.

"I can do whatever I like," the old man replied. "I sure as shit don't need *you* telling *me* what to do!"

The old man's voice sounded as ancient as the decrepit buildings that surrounded him and David.

A cold, clutching sensation of fear took hold of David's throat. It grew steadily stronger as he and the old man squared off, facing each other. Less than twenty feet separated them, but David had the unnerving impression that the man was somehow insubstantial…like he might not really even be there.

"Who the fuck are you?" David finally asked, once he could stand the silence no longer. "Where am I? What the hell's going on here?"

The only response from the old man was a sniff of laughter; but then, as though reacting to a sound which David hadn't heard, he stiffened and cast a wary glance over his shoulder.

"It's not safe out here at night. I can tell you *that* much," the old man said.

"And just where the hell *are* we?" David made no attempt to disguise the nervous quaver in his voice.

The old man continued to look over his shoulder for a while. Then he turned around slowly and faced David again.

"Maybe you'll see something you recognize come daylight," he said. "Although, to tell you the truth, it doesn't often get all that much lighter even when the sun's out."

David was filled with a sudden, violent urge to grab the old man by the throat and throttle him until he told him exactly where he was and what the hell was going on.

Instead, he clenched his fists tightly at his sides, barely managing to control the hot rush of anger that swept through him with surprising force. It was almost as if he experienced the pure essence of the emotion.

"Hey! No need to get all hostile about it," the old man said. "I'm just trying to help you…if that's what you want."

"I don't need your goddamned help," David snapped, his voice still tight with anger. "I just want you to tell me what's going on here."

"Why, you're in the Shadowlands," the old man said. "I'm surprised you didn't realize that. Are you that new here?"

Again the old man glanced over his shoulder, and this time David could hear something—a distant, echoing, keening sound that sounded a bit like a pack of howling dogs.

"Barghests. I think they're headed this way," the old man said. Then he chuckled. "Maybe they smelled the new meat."

David was about to ask him what he meant by *new meat* but then realized he didn't have to. He looked past the old man, trying to see what might be making all that noise, but the night was too dense and dark. All he could see were the streetlights, disappearing like a string of Christmas tree lights into the distance.

"You can come along with me if you'd like," the old man said. "But whether you do or not, I'd suggest you don't want to be here when the barghests get here."

"What are they?"

The old man snorted again with laughter and said simply, "Trust me. You don't want to find out."

With that, he began walking slowly toward one of the dark buildings, moving much faster than he had when approaching David. His left leg dragged behind him, leaving a scalloped line in the thin dirt.

"The streets aren't safe at night, I tell yah that much," the old man called back over his shoulder just before he disappeared into the darkened doorway of one of the buildings. Like an apparition, he faded from sight, leaving David with the distinct impression that he might not ever have been there in the first place.

But the sound in the distance was definitely getting closer. It sounded like a pack of barking dogs, their angry yips, howls, and growls filling the night.

David glanced toward the building where the old man had disappeared and almost ran over to it, but then decided not to follow him.

How did he know he could trust that old man?

He preferred taking his chances in one of the other buildings—alone.

Once the sun was up, he'd take a look around and try to figure out where the hell he was.

Off to his left, not more than a hundred feet up the street, David saw a darkened doorway. After casting a quick glance over his shoulder, he started running toward the building. His footsteps echoed like distant gunshots in the night.

Just before he ducked into the shadowed doorway, David looked back one last time to see—something.

At the far end of the street, huge, indistinguishable shapes as black as holes in the night appeared. Some of them ran on all fours. Others ambled on two legs, their arms dangling at their sides. The chorus of wails filled the night and was loud enough to hurt David's ears as he felt his way to the back of the building through the rubble that littered the floor. When he bumped into the far wall, he turned around and slid to the floor where he sat hunched up, his arms wrapped around his legs.

Lost as he was in the darkness, he realized that his only hope was that, whatever those things were out there, they hadn't seen or smelled him, and they wouldn't know that he was hiding in here.

2

DESERTED STREETS

Tony Ranieri smiled confidently to himself as he strode up the stairway of Bailey Hall, heading toward the University of Southern Maine's library. Through the large, plate-glass window, he could see that Sarah Robinson was alone at the book checkout counter.

Okay, so maybe today will be my lucky day! he thought.

Or maybe it'll be HER lucky day....

His smile twisted into a lopsided smirk as he ducked behind a pillar and quickly raked his hands through his hair and zipped open the brown leather jacket he was wearing. He was going for that casual, wind-blown look. After adjusting the bookbag on his left shoulder, he undid the top three buttons of his shirt to expose his curly chest hair. Then, sucking in his breath, he wheeled around the pillar and approached the library door, consciously putting a brisk, causal bounce in his walk.

As he swung the heavy door open, he glanced at his reflection in the dark glass and smiled with approval.

How could she *not* be interested in him?

Sure, she was quite a bit older than he was—maybe even ten years older, but didn't most older women like their men young and strong?

He was positive that Sarah wasn't married. At least she never wore a gold wedding band or engagement ring on her left ring finger. In the eight months since he had first noticed her, they had never spoken except for passing comments now and then at the counter when he was checking out a book. In fact, he only knew her name because of the brass plate on her desk. As far as she was concerned, he was just another nameless face in an ocean of people.

But as confident and cool as he was trying to appear on the surface, Tony was shaking inwardly as he pushed through the swinging arm of the entrance gate.

He wasn't quite sure why.

Usually, he didn't feel the least bit intimidated about approaching a woman he intended to hit on. But those women generally were undergraduates. Maybe it was because Sarah was older and seemed more settled and secure in her life.

After a quick glance at her when she wasn't looking up, he strolled over to the array of computers located beside the old card catalog. The back of his neck was burning, and his hands felt clammy as he imagined—and hoped—that Sarah couldn't help but notice him, and that—even now—she was surreptitiously watching his every step and *wanting* him.

Whistling tunelessly under his breath, Tony casually slung his bookbag onto one of the desks, leaned over the computer, and began punching the keys on the keyboard, pretending to be entering a book search. By cocking his hip to one side and angling his body, he positioned himself so he could maintain a clear view of the front desk. After clacking on the keys for a few seconds, he glanced over at Sarah again.

His heart thudded heavily in his chest, and a thin sheen of sweat broke across his brow when he saw that she was looking straight at him.

As soon as they made eye contact, she raised her right hand and curled her index finger, signaling him over to the front desk.

Holy shit! A sudden tightening took hold of Tony's stomach and groin. *She wants me!*

Pretending confused surprise and struggling to stay in control, he tapped his chest with his forefinger and raised his eyebrows questioningly.

Sarah smiled and nodded, then reached under the desk and pulled out two hardbound books. Holding them up, she tapped the top book with her finger and mouthed what looked to Tony like she was saying: "Are these yours?"

Tony let his smile widen and nodded as he grabbed his bookbag and walked quickly over to the counter. The back of his neck was prickly with heat. Chilling trickles of sweat ran down the inside of his shirt from his armpits. His legs felt like they were filled with jelly.

"The books you wanted through inter-library loan came in the other day," Sarah said, keeping her voice to a whisper as she glanced around the library. "I think the notice was mailed out yesterday."

Tony was suddenly disappointed to hear her speak to him with such an "all-business" tone of voice, but he continued to smile widely. He was satisfied that she, obviously, had recognized him.

That was a good start.

"Oh, good. Thanks…thanks a lot," Tony said, nodding and feeling totally stupid for not thinking of anything more intriguing to say. "I—uh—" He glanced nervously over his shoulder at the reference desk. "I've got to check out a couple of other books, first. I'll pick 'em up when I leave."

"No problem. They'll be right here," Sarah said without the slightest bit of interest in her voice.

Tony continued to smile brightly at her, but he was disappointed to realize that his charm was working on her. Sarah scooched down and replaced the books on the shelf below the counter. Then, without another word to him, she walked back to her desk and resumed working.

Tony hesitated another few seconds, all the while trying desperately to think of *something* to say, but his mind drew a total blank.

After nodding his thanks, he backed away from the counter and walked back to the computer he'd been using.

Oh, real smooth, there, buddy! he thought. *That'll make her want to jump into the sack with you!*

Tony's hand trembled slightly as he fished the pen from his jacket pocket, took a sheet of scratch paper from the desk, and pretended to scan the screen while writing down titles and call numbers without paying any attention to what he was writing. He kept himself busy for another minute or two, all the while taking every opportunity to glance over at Sarah to see if she was looking at him, but she was involved with her work.

Tony was crestfallen.

Figuring it was time to leave, Tony slid the pen back into his jacket pocket and hefted his bookbag. When he looked at the sheet of paper and saw what he had written there, he snorted with surprise. A young woman, standing opposite him at another terminal, glanced at him and frowned.

On the sheet of paper were the words: *She's yours if you want her!*

For a dizzying instant, Tony stared at the message, not quite believing what he was seeing. This didn't even look like his own handwriting.

Did I write that? he wondered. Or had someone else left this piece of scrap behind?

Narrowing his gaze, he looked around the room to see if any of his friends might be close by, watching his confused reaction.

He didn't see anyone he knew.

But even as he tried to dismiss it, an uncontrollable shiver rippled up his back. He looked around at the wide expanse of the room, focusing, in turn, on the students and faculty members who were seated or standing around, studying or whispering to each other.

For a single, shattering instant, Tony was acutely aware of how utterly strange everything appeared.

He felt disoriented, as if he had somehow slipped outside of reality and was looking at everything through an inches-thick plate glass window.

Dull afternoon sunlight filtered into the library through the windows between the slats of the blinds. Everything looked diffuse and dusty.

Every sound Tony could hear—even the hushed whispers of the two students closest to him—seemed oddly muffled and distant. The sound of someone turning the pages of a book was oddly magnified and sounded like tearing paper.

A quick thrill of alarm raced through Tony.

A moment later, a stronger, deeper tingle of fear gripped him.

Maybe he was getting paranoid because of the knife he was carrying in his bookbag. He had found it in the alleyway last night, while he was taking a shortcut to his apartment after work. To help with his expenses, Tony was waiting tables at the Hollow Reed, an upscale vegetarian restaurant on Commercial Street in Portland.

His throat felt suddenly hot and dry as he sucked in a shallow breath and rubbed one hand against the side of his canvas bookbag. He looked up but still didn't see anyone watching him. He could feel the handle of the knife through the thin material. It made him suddenly nervous to have the knife here with him.

What if the blade sets off the metal detector when I try to leave?

A sickening rush of panic ran through his gut.

A knife with an almost six-inch long blade certainly constituted a legal weapon.

Carrying it into the library had been a stupid thing to do. He could get nailed for carrying a concealed weapon!

How would he ever explain it to the campus cops?

Then again, how could he even explain where he had gotten the knife in the first place?

Would anyone believe the truth, that he had picked it up in an alleyway late last night?

He shuddered to remember what had happened.

It had been later than usual—a little past midnight when he had finally gotten off work. A large party of six rowdy couples, obviously on vacation, had been seated fifteen minutes before closing time. Because he had an eight o'clock class the next morning, and had already missed it too many times this session, he thought he could save a little time by cutting through the alleyway from Commercial to Fore Street. Tony was finding it tough enough just going to summer school, but working a full-time job while going to law school was wearing him down fast. And here it was, only the second week of July, with four more weeks of classes to go.

Still, he couldn't help but wonder how he had even noticed the knife in the first place, or why he had bothered to pick it up.

The alleyway had been darker than he'd expected, with only the faintest glow of light from the streetlight on Fore Street at the far end of the alley.

He had taken this particular shortcut many times before, but it had usually been during the day.

At night, Tony had a hard time feeling his way through the rubble and trash that clogged the narrow alley. But as he worked his way along, he had noticed a sliver of light as faint as moonlight, angling down the throat of the alleyway. Faint as it was, it had illuminated the knife blade like the hot center of a searchlight.

The blade had shone with an iridescent blue glow that he hadn't been able to ignore.

He had stopped and stared at the knife for a long time before finally picking it up. And he told himself he'd only picked it up because it had practically demanded his attention.

The instant he picked the knife up, it felt strange in his hand, as if it were charged with a current of energy. It was quite obviously old, maybe even an antique. Its hard rubber handle, narrow at the hilt and bulbous at the end, was cracked and worn. The blade was slim and symmetrically straight with no hilt guard. The most unusual feature Tony noticed was the small indentation on the metal sleeve in which the blade was fitted. As he gripped the rubber handle, he'd been struck by an odd sense of familiarity.

It was almost as if he had held this very knife before.

Automatically, he rested his thumb comfortably in the narrow indentation above the hilt. He realized that this must have been designed so the user—the cutter—could apply some serious pressure when using it.

Tony had lost all sense of time, but he snapped back to attention when he realized how heavily he was panting as he hefted the knife.

He was surprised by how light the knife was for its size. Turning it over a few times, he smiled as the blade gleamed wickedly in the dim light of the alleyway. He braced himself and slashed the knife back and forth a few times, smiling as he listened to the loud *whick-whick* sound the blade made as it cut the air.

He had known instantly that he was going to keep the knife, so he slipped it into his back pocket, making sure to pull his jacket down so the knife wouldn't stick out as he continued his walk home.

It wasn't until he had arrived at his apartment on Congress Street and examined the knife under better light that he noticed what looked like a thin wash of rusty streaks at the base of the blade and on the handle. Although he tried to deny it, he realized that these could only be bloodstains.

A cold shock of surprise hit him when he opened his hand and saw on his palm a faint, red smudge.

He had gone to the kitchen sink and hadn't been able to stop his hands from trembling as he washed the knife under the faucet. For some reason, he kept looking furtively over his shoulder as though expecting to see someone watching him. He'd been careful to hide the knife in his bookbag so his roommate, Alexander, wouldn't discover it.

He had no idea how or why, but Tony knew that he couldn't let Alex or anyone else know that he had found this knife.

It seemed almost silly, he thought, feeling that way about it; but just knowing that he possessed it gave him a funny sensation, almost a new and different measure of security and power.

Yes, power!

Feeling like he was in a daze, Tony shook his head and squared his shoulders before walking back to the library checkout counter. It took him a minute to catch Sarah's attention, but she nodded as she got up from her desk and walked over to him. He took his library card from his wallet and, without a word, handed it to her. Sarah smiled pleasantly as she took the two books from the shelf and began processing them.

"So, did you find what you were looking for?" she said.

Her tone seemed warm and friendly, and Tony noticed that she gave him a quick, intense look this time.

He smiled back at her, sensing that she might be interested in him after all, but he was too nervous to respond. All he could think about was how he was going to get the knife through the security gate. For an instant, he was convinced that—somehow—Sarah knew what he was carrying in his bookbag. Cold panic gripped him, making it impossible for him to speak.

Finally, though, he managed to grunt and say, "Uhh—no, I—uh, I didn't."

Sarah bit down gently on her lower lip as she nodded and then stamped the due dates in the back of the books. Before handing them to him, she glanced at the titles. Her expression revealed her surprise.

"*Inside the Criminal Mind* and *Autopsy*." She raised one eyebrow higher than the other. "What are you studying, anyway?"

Tony realized that this was his chance.

She had obviously noticed him before and had at least taken the trouble to remember his name. Now she was trying to initiate a conversation.

But Tony was feeling feverish and tense. All he wanted was to get outside and catch some fresh air.

"I'm—uh, I'm studying law. For the summer session, I—I'm taking Criminal Psych with—ah, with Professor Morgan."

He cringed, thinking how lame he must sound. He desperately wanted to say something—anything—to keep things going, but she seemed to pick up right away on his reaction. After handing him the books, she quickly started back to her desk.

"Uh—thanks," Tony said, mentally kicking himself in the seat of the pants.

Sarah barely turned to look at him as she waved one hand over her shoulder in farewell.

Jesus, what the fuck's the matter with me? Tony thought as he unzipped his bookbag, carefully shielding the knife inside, slipped the two books in between his notebooks and hurriedly zipped his bookbag shut.

For several seconds, he just stared at Sarah's back, wishing to God that he had responded to her a little more aggressively.

Why didn't he ask if she'd like to go out for a drink after work?

But he knew it wasn't talking to Sarah that had gotten him so wound up.

It was knowing that the next few steps were going to tell whether or not he would set off the alarm, and if he was going to have to open his bookbag for the campus security cop who was sitting by the exit.

He was trying his damnedest not to look guilty as he slung the bookbag onto his shoulder. Feeling like a condemned man, trudging slowly toward the scaffold, he sucked in a sharp breath and held it as he walked through the metal detector. He cringed, waiting to hear the high-pitched warning buzz and almost fainted with relief when the alarm didn't go off. He felt so relieved that he looked back at Sarah and called out to her in as jaunty a voice as he could muster, "Hey, catch yah later."

He didn't wait to see if she had heard him.

A thin, gray wash of morning light seeped into the building, slowly rinsing away the shadows.

David was leaning against the wall, as far away from the door as he could get. At first, he barely noticed the change in light, but at some indistinguishable point he realized that he could see his pale, thin hands, clasped tightly together around his bent knees. The tendons in the back of his hands looked like thin pencils just beneath the surface of the skin. It took him an indeterminate time to realize that something was wrong.

Then he suddenly got it.

His hands had never looked like this before!

They looked thin and pale, like an old man's hands.

What the hell was going on here?

Maybe it was just a trick of the light, he told himself, but when he took a quick personal inventory, he realized that other things—*several* things were definitely wrong.

For one, he had the distinct and frightening sensation that he wasn't breathing.

No matter how long he sat there and thought about it, and no matter how much he tried to *do* it, he couldn't feel even the slightest hint of motion in his chest or throat. There was no steady intake and exhalation of air— no surge of warm breath through his nostrils.

"Jesus, this is fucking *weird*," he whispered to himself, but just as quickly he cut himself off when he heard the hollow echo of his voice in the gloomy silence. His words reminded him of the scraping, skittering sound rats made, scurrying for cover.

His eyes were wide open as he looked around and tried to pierce the inky gloom.

Something was *definitely* wrong!

He felt suddenly compelled to get up and start checking things out. It was time he figured out just where the hell he was.

If he could determine that, then maybe he could dredge up other memories about what had happened.

Fragments of thought flitted through his mind, but most of them didn't make sense. The most vivid memories—especially the one of a hooded figure leaning over him and whispering to him—were too terrifying to contemplate for long. He had a vague impression of a skeletal face peering at him from within the folds of a heavy hood, but dismissed that as just his overworked imagination.

He hoped that he would forget all about those disturbing thoughts if he got up and started moving around. If he didn't do *something*, he was going to go *nuts!*

But then he started thinking about the old man he'd met last night.

Who the hell was he?

What was his story?

And those hounds or whatever those things he'd heard baying were…what had the old man called them?

Barghests?

Well, whatever they were, what if they were looking for him?

What if they came back?

The old man with the crippled leg had obviously been afraid to be caught out in the open.

After finding his way into the building, David had crouched in the darkness and listened to them, their howls growing louder and louder until he was positive they were right outside the building where he was hiding. He had even heard one or more of them sniffing and snorting around the dark entrance of the building. He didn't doubt that they had caught his scent, but for some reason they had moved away from his hiding place. He guessed they must be hunting someone else.

David groaned as he stretched his arms over his head. His muscles felt as thin and dry as paper. His bones and tendons seemed ready to snap as he shifted his weight forward and shakily stood up. As he straightened his body out, something in the small of his back popped. He let out another low groan and sank back down and slumped against the wall as a surprisingly strong wave of nausea and dizziness swept over him.

Cupping both hands over his eyes, he stared into the perfect well of darkness behind his eyes until the feeling eventually faded away. He had no idea how long it took.

Once it was gone, it struck David as strange how the sensation of pain had been more like a memory of pain than the real thing.

Something was *definitely* wrong here!

After taking a few seconds to collect himself, David stood up and slowly picked his way through the debris toward the doorway. The closer he got to the doorway the more his eyes began to sting from the gradually brightening daylight outside. When he reached the doorway, he supported himself by leaning against the rotting door jamb as he looked outside.

He was struck with utter amazement by what he saw.

The city—wherever the hell he was—looked like the bombed-out ruins he'd seen in World War II footage. The street was a mess of rubble and debris. Broken bricks and stones, piles of trash, uprooted trees, bent and rusted street signs, and other litter were strewn everywhere. A few rusted hulks of abandoned cars and trucks lined both sides of the road. The sun, hanging low in the sky, looked bloated and red as it rose above the distant tree line. Its feeble light cast thin, jagged shadows across the street and buildings.

A steady, whistling wind was blowing around sheets of yellowed newspaper and other litter that flapped like broken bird wings until they fetched up against a building or rusted chain-link fence. David half-expected to see a pack of mongrel dogs rummaging through the garbage in the alleyways, but the street was strangely deserted, absolutely devoid of any people or animals.

"Even birds," David whispered as he craned his neck back and scanned the sky beyond the bare branches of a few nearby trees.

Come to think of it, where were the leaves?

It was supposed to be July.

Shouldn't the trees be covered with leaves and filled with singing birds?

But as he looked around, all he could hear was the low, hollow whistle of the wind and the high hiss of dust being blown about.

David wanted to call out, to see if he could draw anyone's attention, but then he remembered the baying hounds he had heard the night before and, for now, decided to explore the area in silence. He wasn't sure he wanted to encounter the man with the bad leg again. There had been something about him that had bothered David. Talking to him had been like…

"—like talking to a corpse," David said.

His words were whisked away by the whistling wind like fine dust. The sound was almost like faint laughter.

David felt all but drained of energy as he started walking up the street, looking from side to side, trying to see anything that was familiar. It was only when he paused and looked back at the building where he had spent the night that a cold blade of panic sliced through him.

Above the arching doorway of the building was a sign.

The painted letters were chipped and faded, but by squinting he could still make out what was written there. He read the name out loud, then repeated it a few time before it finally sank into his awareness.

"Pine Knoll Elementary…Pine Knoll Elementary! *Jesus Christ!* That can't be *Pine Knoll Elementary!*"

For a dizzying instant, David felt completely disoriented. It had to be just coincidence that this building had the same name as the elementary school in Portland that he had attended when he was young.

But the longer he stared at the building, mentally trying to restore it by ignoring the near total decay and deterioration, the more he realized that this, in fact, *had* to be the school he had attended.

Tension gripped him.

He couldn't fathom what had happened to the school since he had last seen it, but he could see now that this was the familiar building at the corner of Deering Avenue and Prospect Street.

"How the hell…?"

His voice trailed off as he tried to absorb the sudden shock.

How had he ended up here?

The last thing he clearly remembered was standing on the East Bridge Street bridge in Westbrook sometime after midnight and looking down into the murky water. There were other, vaguer memories after that—some of them terribly frightening—but there was no *way* he could have gotten here.

And there was no way this could be Deering Avenue!

Granted, it had been a while since he had been out this way, but it had been a month or two at the most. There was no way this part of Portland could have deteriorated so quickly.

"What the hell is going on here?" he said, clenching his fists and bouncing them against the sides of his head.

"I might be able to explain it…some of it, anyway."

The voice, speaking so suddenly and so close behind him, startled David. He let out a shout of surprise that echoed from the derelict buildings as he wheeled around and saw the old man with the injured left leg, standing less than ten feet behind him.

David had no idea how the man could have gotten this close without him hearing his approach, especially with that bad leg, but there he was, smiling a grin that exposed a top row of yellowed, rotting teeth.

David was filled with a sudden burst of rage that made him want to grab the old man by the collar and throttle him until his few remaining teeth fell out of his head, but—somehow—he managed to control himself.

"That would be…yeah, I—I'd appreciate that," David finally said, once his initial shock and rage had passed, and he could speak again.

The old man smiled crookedly as he nodded to David and then turned. Looking back at David over his shoulder, he hooked his forefinger and beckoned for him to follow.

"Come with me, then, if you'd like," the old man said. His voice was as faint as the whickering whisper of the wind.

"Where are you going?" David called out, his voice sharp and demanding. He folded his arms across his chest, making it clear that he wasn't going anywhere until he got some straight answers.

"No, not out here…not out here," the old man said, shaking his head as he cast a furtive glance up and down the street. "We don't want to be seen out here."

"Who will see us?" David asked, frowning as he looked around. "As far as I can tell, there isn't another living soul within miles."

The old man smiled and cocked his head back as he laughed out loud, but his laughter sounded more like a snarl as he shook his head from side to side. When he spoke again, his voice snapped at David like a whip.

"That's it! That's exactly it," he said with a high, wavering cackle. "Not another living soul! That's rich! Still, we don't want to be seen by anyone! I can tell you what's going on—some of it, anyway, but I doubt that you'll believe me."

"Try me," David said with a forcefulness that he didn't truly feel.

"Well, then…" the old man said.

His eyes gleamed wickedly as he moved a few steps closer to David.

"For one thing—you're dead. You're a wraith now. But I'll bet you already figured that part of it out, didn't you?"

Sarah never took her eyes off Tony Ranieri as he left the building and walked away down the sidewalk.

She couldn't help but notice how uptight and nervous he had seemed, and that surprised her. Usually, he came across as totally confident and secure. That was one of the first things she had noticed about him, besides the fact that he was extremely handsome. She couldn't help but notice how many coeds kept their eyes on him whenever he came into the library. Sarah had, in fact, first noticed him right around the time the divorce from David came through, and she was pretty sure that she had picked up that he was interested in her as well.

But after he was gone, Sarah chastised herself for even thinking about him.

For one thing, he was much too young for her. Maybe not young enough to be her son, but still…

She had known before today that he was working on his law degree, so that meant he already had a bachelor's degree. That put him in his early twenties, at least. Sarah guessed around twenty-five or so.

So why was she—a thirty-six-year-old divorced woman—thinking about dating someone who was at least ten years younger than she?

The answer was simple enough.

She liked the way he looked, and the few times they had spoken, only at the book circulation desk, she had found herself attracted to his mild but confident manner.

He was a heartbreaker all right, and Sarah told herself to forget him.

Granted, these days it was tough enough for a divorced, almost middle-aged woman to find a suitable date. What was it her friend Carol was always saying? "All the good ones are either married or gay." Although the divorce was only six months old, she had been separated from David for more than five years…pretty much ever since Karen died. It had been a while since she'd had any loving.

But thinking about Karen instantly cast a cloud over Sarah's attitude. If Karen had lived, Sarah thought, they would have celebrated her fourteenth birthday last May.

Fourteen years old!

It was such a tragedy that she had been robbed of those years.

The divorce had been hard enough on her, but Sarah knew that she'd eventually get over it. She was, in fact, pretty much *over it* already.

But the death of a child—her *only* child—was a loss that Sarah knew she would never recover from. It was also what had caused the minor stresses and strains in her and David's relationship to finally destroy their marriage.

And now—as of last night—Sarah had even lost her ex-husband.

She was alone and found herself wishing she had someone she could talk to, but—maybe from living so long with David—she had gotten used to bottling things up inside her.

Sarah was surprised that she wasn't feeling more upset about David's death.

She guessed it was simply because—at least right now—she was still in shock about it. Going to the hospital early this morning to identify his body had seemed almost surreal. She was having a great deal of difficulty convincing herself that it had even happened.

Couldn't it have been some terrible nightmare?

She knew or at least sensed that, over the next few days, the true depth of her loss would finally sink in as she made David's funeral arrangements and settled his affairs.

She also knew that David's death, as terrible as it was, would never cut her to the core or shake her faith in *everything* the way Karen's death had.

The loss of a child was something she felt no one should ever have to face. There still weren't many nights when she didn't wake up crying, positive that she had heard the soft tread of footsteps or the gentle sound of breathing coming from Karen's empty bedroom.

It was the one loss she knew she could never reconcile unless she was willing to give over to the idea that the Universe was nothing but a meaningless, mindless machine that functioned purely on chance and that, in the great scheme of things, no one's life or death amounted to anything of any lasting importance.

But how else could she explain the death of a nine-year-old girl—a beautiful, bright nine-year-old girl who had her whole life ahead of her?

Sarah shook her head and straightened up, suddenly aware that she had been standing at the counter, staring out the window at the sidewalk where, quite some time ago, Tony Ranieri had walked away.

She could feel the slick tracks of her tears streaming down her cheeks. Sniffing loudly, she wiped them away with the heel of her hand. She noticed that her face was cool—almost cold to the touch.

Closing her eyes for a moment, she pinched the bridge of her nose and tried valiantly to collect herself; but powerful surges of grief twisted like a nest of snakes in her stomach. She knew that things were only going to get much worse over the next few days and weeks.

Sarah jumped and uttered a high squeal when the phone on her desk began to ring. Her hand was trembling violently as she spun around, lifted the receiver, and pressed it to her ear.

"U.S.M. Library. Ms. Robinson speaking."

"Yeah, you were married to Dave Robinson, right?"

The man's voice over the phone sounded sharp with demand.

"Uh—yes. Yes, I was."

Sarah frowned suspiciously, wondering who this was. He obviously hadn't heard yet that David had died.

"This here's Sam Lowell, his landlord over on Brown Street," the man said, still sounding edgy and demanding.

Sarah felt a sudden wave of grief for David.

"I need you to help me out with something," Lowell said.

Sarah closed her eyes, took a steadying breath, and held it for a moment before speaking. Then she cleared her throat and, as calmly as she could, said, "I'm sorry, Mr. Lowell…I don't know if you've been notified yet, but David was in an accident last night. He was—"

"Yeah, yeah, I know. He died last night," Lowell snapped. "That's why I called. The end of the month's coming right up, and his rent's already a week past due. I know this probably ain't a good time for you and all, but if you can't pay up his rent, I'm gonna have to ask you to have his place cleaned out by the end of the week."

Sarah covered her mouth with one hand and blinked her eyes rapidly to force back the sudden hot rush of tears. Another, stronger wave of grief washed through her, leaving her feeling cold and limp.

"You still there?" Lowell said, almost a growl.

"Yes, I—I'm still here. Just a minute, Mr. Lowell."

Sarah stared down at the floor and took another deep breath, struggling hard to control herself.

"To tell you the truth," Lowell went on, "he's bounced checks on me more times than Michael Jordan's bounced a friggin' basketball. You can understand my position here, can't you?"

Sarah cleared her throat and then, in a high, trembling voice, said, "Well, you know, David is—he was a writer, and you know how that is. Sometimes the money just doesn't come in fast enough."

"Look, I don't care if he wrote the friggin' Bible, as long as he pays his rent on time…which he almost never did. I ain't in this business as a friggin' charity, you know."

Anger and grief clashed inside Sarah like storm clouds. She took another deep breath and said, "I'll have a check in the mail to you by tomorrow morning at the latest, Mr. Lowell. How much does David owe you?"

"Four-fifty, plus a late fee of another fifty dollars," Lowell said. "Five hunnert even. You can make the check out directly to me. Send it to 47 Brown Street in Westbrook. You know the zip?"

"I can look it up," Sarah said.

"It's 04092. Got that?"

Before she had to listen to one more word from Lowell, Sarah depressed the cutoff button with her thumb and hung up the phone. She was vaguely aware that someone was standing at the counter, waiting to check out some books; but without saying a word, Sarah turned and ran to the staff lounge out back where she collapsed into a chair, leaned forward with her face in both hands, and began to cry.

3

FETTERS

Powerful gusts of wind buffeted the building like hammer blows. Wherever there was a crack or hole in the walls or windows, a steady breeze blew in with a high, shrill whistle that set David's nerves on edge.

For the last half hour or so, David had been pacing back and forth across the floor of a cavernous, dimly lit room, all the while keeping a wary eye on the old man who was seated cross-legged in the center of the floor. The ancient floorboards creaked horribly with every step he took. With every gust of wind, dust and fine grains of sand filtered down from between the planks of the ceiling overhead. Through the narrow windows at ground level, David could see that the sun was shining, but it had an odd, muted glow that made his view of the city street look like a sepia-tone photograph.

The old man had led David down a crumbling cement stairway into the basement of what appeared to be an abandoned factory or warehouse. The room was filled with ancient, rusted equipment. The grease and dust-laden hulks of huge lathes and drill presses, as well as radial-arm saws and other machinery that David didn't recognize, were ranged in three rows, one against each long wall and one running straight down the center of the room to form two wide aisles along either side. The wooden floor, walls, and ceiling were caked with thick black rot. Especially in the corners and under the machinery, it looked like a spreading, cancerous growth.

"Does the wind always sound like that?" David asked.

He shivered involuntarily as he rubbed his hands together, unable to get rid of the odd, dissociated feeling he had whenever he touched anything, even his own body. Every sensation seemed so far away.

Muffled was the first word that sprang to mind.

"Oh, sometimes it's much worse," the old man replied softly. "But most times—hell, it ain't so bad. Eventually you get used to it and hardly notice it a'tall."

David nodded agreement as he cast a furtive glance around the huge room. Although he hadn't seen or heard anybody else, he had the distinct impression that he was being watched by someone—maybe several someones who were hidden in the deepest shadows. The hairs on the nape of his neck tingled as though charged with a current of electricity. Once or twice, when David turned his head quickly, he thought he caught a quick flutter of motion, but there was never anything there, at least as far as he could see.

"Do you mean to tell me I'm going to be *stuck* here? That this is *it*? This is what being dead's all about?"

The old man tossed his head back and laughed heartily, but the sound was deep and hollow, more chilling than humorous.

"Christ, no! No one knows what being dead's '*all about.*' You're a wraith in the Shadowlands. Far as I know, this is just the beginning."

"A wraith...?"

"Yeah," the old man said. "A ghost—a phantom. Remember? You're dead. You don't have a body anymore."

David extended his hand and waved it. "So then—what's this?"

"Your *corpus*. It's kinda different from your body. It's what's left after the physical part...sloughs away."

"Yeah, okay, but then tell me what—exactly—are these—these *Shadowlands*?" David arched his eyebrows. He wasn't sure why, but just saying the word *Shadowlands* filled him with a gnawing sense of loneliness and discomfort.

"Well, 's far as I can figure it," the old man said, "there are dozens of levels of existence. Hell, maybe there're hundreds or even thousands of 'em that you and I'll *never* understand—probably never *could* understand. I reckon you're here now because of something that's keeping you here."

"What do you mean, *keeping* me here?" David asked sharply.

A sudden spark of anger flared inside him, but he gritted his teeth, trying hard to repress it.

"Look, I didn't ask for this, all right?" he said, his voice low and trembling. "And I *sure* as hell don't want to *stay* here!"

"Oh, but you see—you don't really have much choice about the matter. 'Least, not right away. Not unless you want to embrace oblivion."

Without even knowing what the old man meant, David shook his head firmly. He didn't like the sound of that word. His first thought was that oblivion sounded like *death* for the dead.

"But, hey," the old man continued, "as long as you're here, you might as well make the most of it. I'd suggest you consider hooking up with some of the other wraiths."

"The others? How many other wraiths are there? You're the only person—uh, wraith I've seen since I—"

He cut himself off sharply because he'd been about to say: *since I got here*, but then he realized what he really should say is: *since I died*.

"Sure. Of course there are others."

The old man seemed to be taking inordinate pleasure in David's confusion and surprise.

"There's plenty of folks who have 'passed on' but who remain here for—well, sometimes for quite some length of time. Take, for instance, them that were out hunting last night."

"You mean the dogs I heard barking?" David asked, trembling at the memory.

"Not dogs. They're called *barghests*, and believe me, you don't wanna let them catch you. Of course, there were some other wraiths hanging around, too." The old man looked steadily at David, his eyes gleaming like he was insane. "Maybe you didn't see any of 'em, huh?"

"No, I—I didn't see anyone except you," David replied, shaking his head. He couldn't shake the memory of *feeling* like other people, unseen, were watching him even now.

Another, stronger wave of anger rushed through David. At first he thought it was directed at the old man, but he quickly realized what was really happening: he was having trouble processing everything that had happened to him so far.

And who could blame him?

How could he be expected simply to accept the fact that he was *dead?*

He wanted to believe that he *couldn't* be *dead,* that this all had to be some crazy dream or hallucination.

That's it! David grasped desperately at the thought. *Maybe I did finally jump, and I'm imagining all of this while I'm drowning.*

But all of his sensory impressions so far, while oddly distant, seemed much too real, much too immediate to be simply products of his imagination, dying or not.

He had to admit to himself that he had *wanted* to die. And he *would* have jumped off that bridge…if he'd had the balls! So on some level, maybe this *was* real.

He really was dead!

"Why should I 'hook up,' as you say, with other wraiths?" he asked after a moment of silence, broken only by the fluting of the wind outside.

The old man didn't respond immediately. David watched as his eyes shifted like oiled beads first to one side, then to the other. He looked like he was keeping a watchful eye on someone that David couldn't see.

"Well…because the Shadowlands are a very dangerous place," he said at last.

"How can they be dangerous?" David said even as a coil of tension slithered through him. "We're already dead, for Christ's sake. What can possibly hurt us now?"

"Oh, plenty of things," the old man replied. "For one, there's the slavers. They'll take yah if you drop your guard. And there's lots of other wraiths who'd just as soon cart you off in chains and throw your corpus into the forges in Stygia."

Leaning forward, the old man cast another cautious glance back and forth, then in a low voice added, "And, of course, there's always the…*ferrymen.*"

The old man whispered the last word so softly David wasn't quite sure he'd heard him correctly.

"Ferrymen?" he repeated, taking a step closer to the old man. He wanted to say something more, but his voice failed him.

In the silence that followed, he began to feel extremely uncomfortable. As if on cue, the wind outside suddenly gusted much louder. It shook the building's walls and caused something on one of the upper floors to fall with a loud crash.

David jumped, startled by the sound. He looked furtively around, expecting at any moment to be rushed from his blind side. He felt as though he should say or do something, but he had no idea what. If there was anyone else around here—any other wraiths—he'd probably be damned glad to join up with them. They certainly couldn't be half as loony as this old coot!

The old man nailed David with a long, piercing stare. Then, in a low, almost accusatory voice, he said, "As a matter of fact, I understand that you were seen talking to a ferryman."

"Oh, no—no way." David shook his head in adamant denial. "That isn't possible. I haven't seen anyone here, much less spoken to them before I met you last night. I was just—actually, I have no idea how I got here. All I can think is I was transported here or something. The last thing I remember was going out for a walk and then, next thing I know, I wake up on the side of the road. I have no idea what happened."

The old man smiled at him grimly, exposing his bad teeth all the way to the gums. David shied away from him as if the old man were a rabid animal about to try to bite him.

"Well, now, maybe you don't remember it," the old man said, "but you were definitely seen with one. And I have to tell you—that ain't good. Not good a'tall."

"Why's that?"

The tension winding up inside David was almost unbearable. His chest ached as if he had been panting heavily, even though, no matter how hard he tried, he couldn't feel even the slightest motion in his ribs and chest. The fringes of his vision began to vibrate and blur, and for a single, shattering instant, he remembered—

He remembered looking up at a hooded figure that was leaning over him…and he remembered staring into the swirling black nothingness inside the heavy cowl…and he remembered hearing a grating, iron-hard voice whisper to him…whispering words that didn't quite make sense, but which, on some deep level, spoke directly to his soul.

"It ain't good because that ferryman may have put his mark on you," the old man replied, casting a fearful glance over his shoulder as though afraid they might be overheard. "If that's the case, that may have been him out last night, hunting for you, trying to collect his property."

"I'm not anyone's *property*!" David said with an angry snarl.

"That's just the thing." The old man shrugged, looking like he was enjoying this just a little too much. "That may not be for *you* to decide. Tell me—after I took off last night, where did you spend the night?"

David was about to respond, but something warned him that it might not be such a good idea to let anyone know where he'd been. He smiled thinly and shook his head, saying nothing.

"If they *were* looking for you, and you avoided them," the old man said, "then you must have found a haunt that has quite a bit of power. Usually, barghests can track down anyone pretty easily. But then again..."

The old man shrugged again and leaned back, trying to appear absolutely casual, but there was something in his manner that seemed entirely forced to David. A crazed, eager fire gleamed in the old man's eyes, and any second, David expected him to break out in maniacal laughter or to lunge at him.

"Maybe they weren't after you, after all," he said. "But you ought to tell me where you spent the night."

"Just...outside," David said with a shrug.

"Outside? Ha! Your first night in the Shadowlands, and you mean to tell me you spent it *outside*? By yourself?" He shook his head and clicked his tongue. "My goodness, you certainly *are* a brave little soul, aren't you?"

"I—ah, over the years, I've gotten used to being alone," David said, hoping that he could end the discussion. He was anxious to get outside and see if he might meet some of the other wraiths who were supposedly in the area.

"So—ah, what do you do here...in the Shadowlands, I mean? What's the point?"

The old man tipped his head back and roared with abrasive laughter.

"The point?" he said, hardly able to talk. "Shit, it's just like when you were alive. You have to *make* your own point!"

David considered this for a moment, then said, "Well then, can you give me some idea why I'm here? I sure as hell never wanted to end up here."

"It's your fetters."

David thought the old man looked more and more squirrely with each passing minute.

"There's something—maybe *several* things from when you were alive that are keeping you here. Holding you from moving on. You know what they say: 'we wear the chains we forged in life.'"

"That was Marley's ghost, in *Christmas Carol*," David said. "But look— as far as I'm concerned, I've got nothing to keep me here." He shook his head, thoroughly confused. "Just like I had nothing to keep me when I was…alive."

Even before he finished saying that, an aching loneliness welled up within David, filling him with such deep misery that he almost cried out loud. He suddenly felt as though he were falling backwards, spinning head over heels in an endless, black void. He'd felt like that before, when he was alive. Not as intensely, but now he realized with a hard jolt of fear that the endless void might be inside him.

He *had* lived an isolated life.

Even when he and Sarah were married, he had kept too much to himself, had bottled too much inside him. He had always told Sarah—and anyone else who would listen—that it was just part and parcel of being a writer and who he was. He maintained that he *had* to be self-involved to a large degree simply to create.

It was only after Karen had been born that he'd even begun to come out of his self-imposed isolation.

And then, after Karen died…

"After she…after my daughter…died…" David started to say. His voice broke on nearly every syllable until he finally fell silent.

"Yes-s-s?" the old man said, drawing the word out like a snake's hiss.

"I…I just couldn't see any…any reason to keep on living," David said, surprised by the suddenness of his confession. "It destroyed my marriage, my career…my whole fucking *life*!"

"You had a daughter, you say?"

The old man looked at David with eyes that glistened with interest. David barely had the strength to nod his head.

"So she might be here, too," the old man said, as much to himself as to David. "In fact, she might be one of your fetters—one of the things that brought you to this part of the Shadowlands. Maybe she's the reason you can't go on."

In the center of his chest, David could feel a feeble spark of hope flare up; but it was so small it quickly sputtered and faded.

Karen is dead, and that's all there is to it!

But what if she's here?

He wanted desperately not to hope.

What if she has spent the last five years, wandering around alone in this dangerous, desolate place…?

An almost overwhelming feeling of parental concern surged inside of David. He had to close his eyes tightly and try to control the storm of emotion that raged in his heart.

"Maybe you should try to find her," the old man said in a voice so low that David almost mistook it for his own thoughts. He looked at the old man, wanting to ask him if he had any idea how he could find Karen.

Where could he start looking?

But then—suddenly—he knew.

Just as, somehow without his knowing why he had ended up at Pine Knoll Elementary School, probably because of the attachment he must still feel for the place, at least as a haven of safety, he got an idea where to start looking for Karen.

He'd go out to Riverside Cemetery, where his daughter was buried.

"Is something the matter?" the old man asked, arching his eyebrows. The flaps of skin hanging from his face fluttered when he spoke.

David almost said what was on his mind, but then stopped himself.

"I have to go outside," he said, and without waiting to hear if the old man had anything more to say to him, he turned and walked up the concrete stairs, back into the world of diffused sunlight.

The tires grumbled and spit up gravel, making the car's frame rattle as Sarah took the turn into Riverside Cemetery.

It was another hot and humid July day—the fifth in a row.

Interlacing trees—mostly maples mixed with a few pines— overshadowed the narrow, rutted dirt road. Their leaves and needles hung limply in the heavy heat. Like everything else along the side of the road, they were coated with a fine layer of gray dust. The cemetery lawn and shrubbery, the flowers, even the ordered rows of tombstones all looked like they were in desperate need of a cooling rain. Along the western horizon, a dark row of thunderheads outlined with bright, white light gave Sarah hope that relief might be coming later this afternoon. Right now, though, the summer air was as heavy and warm as a wet wool sweater.

It was early Friday morning, and Sarah didn't have to be to work until two o'clock. Usually she waited until Saturday or Sunday morning to visit Karen's grave, but for some reason—no doubt because of David's recent death—she felt compelled to come out here today. She told herself that it was just to water the potted flowers she'd placed on Karen's grave last Sunday, but she knew better.

Sarah often came out here to be alone to think…and remember.

Today more than most days, she needed to sort out some things mentally before she had to deal with them head on. The next few days were going to be tough, and she wasn't sure she had the necessary resources.

It had been more than five years since Karen had died, but the terrible, lonely ache of loss still filled Sarah whenever she came out here. The pain seemed absolutely undiminished by time and tears.

It was stronger, if anything.

As she negotiated the curves in the road, she noticed that her grip on the steering wheel was tight enough to make her knuckles turn white. She also realized that she was clenching her teeth and holding her breath. Her lungs ached. But just as she was mentally commanding herself to relax a little, she looked up ahead and saw the grassy slope where Karen's grave was located.

"Oh, *Christ*," she whispered, blinking back the tears that instantly formed in her eyes.

Karen's grave and a few others were nestled at the top of a small hillock in a far corner of the cemetery. The site faced roughly east and was bordered on three sides by a dense wall of trees and shrubbery. Throughout most of the day, those trees shaded the whole area; but this early in the morning, a hazy wash of sunlight was lighting up the gravestones and grass with muted pastels.

Sarah considered this one of the loveliest spots in the entire cemetery which lined the Stroudwater River for almost a mile. She always appreciated coming out here. The spot was so private she felt as though she could be completely alone with her thoughts. She often talked out loud to Karen, telling her what she'd been doing that week, and how much she missed having her around. All the while she would stand with her hands folded in front of her as she stared at the small, pink marble headstone until her vision blurred.

"What the—"

Sarah's voice choked off when she noticed something at the top of the rising slope of land.

For just an instant, she thought she caught a glimpse of what looked like a man, standing with his head bowed beside Karen's grave.

Sarah stepped down hard on the brakes. The tires skidded in the dirt with a raw, tearing sound. The car heaved to one side, and then stopped short. Sarah was thrown forward and would have bumped against the steering wheel if she hadn't been wearing her seat belt. Panting heavily, she jammed the shift into *park* and, leaning across the passenger's seat, stared up the rise.

No. There's no one there.

At least not now.

She looked up and down the road just to make sure the person—if there really had been someone up there—hadn't walked away from the grave while she wasn't looking.

The grassy slope rippled with dense heat waves that distorted her view of the trees beyond. The sky to the west looked like hammered pewter. Sarah's stomach clenched like a fist with anxiety as she rolled down the window, cocked her ear, and listened, but the only sounds she could hear were the distant trilling of a robin and the rhythmic, flickering hiss of the cemetery sprinkler system.

Maybe he wandered back into the woods behind the cemetery.

Sarah knew that the land dropped off steeply to the riverbank not more than fifty feet beyond Karen's grave. The slope was covered with dense brush and trees where people threw old flower arrangements and other trash.

No, if someone was there, he couldn't have gone that way.

So who the hell could it have been?

And how could he have disappeared so quickly?

Sarah's body was wire-tight with tension as she switched off the ignition, undid her seat belt, stepped out of the car, and slammed the car door shut. The sound echoed dully, like a gunshot in the dense air. Her legs felt as stiff as wooden spindles as she started up the hill toward her daughter's grave. All the while, she kept scanning the area for any sign of the person she was sure she had seen there just a moment ago.

No, it must have been just a shadow or something else, she told herself, but the thought gave her little comfort.

Maybe she was so upset she was imagining things.

She paused beside Karen's grave and lowered her head. Sucking in a sharp breath, she stared at the tiny headstone until the name and dates started to blur. All around the plot, the grass was wilted and yellowed from the heat. It was too dry to leave any clear tracks to determine if someone had been standing here.

Sarah wanted to believe otherwise, but she couldn't shake the feeling that she had seen *someone.*

Usually she found the cemetery so peaceful, but right now it filled her with a surging sense of apprehension and foreboding.

She looked up at the sky again.

The thunderstorm was blowing up faster than she had expected. The horizon was purple with haze that might be falling rain. The air had the sharp sting of ozone. The leaves at the tops of the trees fluttered wildly, but Sarah couldn't feel even the slightest trace of the breeze at ground level. The hairs on the back of her arms tingled as though the air were charged with static electricity.

She shivered violently when she glanced over at the empty plot beside Karen's grave and realized that very soon—tomorrow or the next day at the latest—workmen would come out here with a back hoe and excavate a hole for David's coffin.

"Jesus, Jesus, oh, *Jesus!*"

Her voice suddenly choked off and was followed by a high, strangled moan that simultaneously seemed to be coming from the surrounding woods as well as from deep inside her. Sarah clutched her head tightly with both hands and shook it from side to side.

Unable to stand up any longer, she collapsed onto her knees and slumped forward, her face buried in her hands as powerful sobs wracked her body. The cups of her palms filled with her tears as the sun beat down mercilessly on her back. A deep grumble of thunder that sounded like tumbling boulders vibrated the dense air and made the hair on the back of her neck stir.

When did everything go so terribly wrong? she wondered as her body shook with pent-up emotions.

She'd had such a good start in life—a fun childhood and four good years of high school followed by a challenging but still rewarding four years at the University of Maine and then generally decent library jobs, doing work that she absolutely enjoyed.

But somehow, somewhere along the line, it had all gone sour.

It had happened so gradually that she couldn't really pinpoint when it had started or when she had first noticed it.

When she did notice it, it was already too late to fix.

Even during the first few years of her marriage, though, right after college, she'd begun to think that something essential was missing in her relationship with David. She thought there might be something wrong with her, but she blamed a lot of it on what seemed like his negative attitude. As much as she had tried to resist it, over the years she had found herself drifting further and further away from her husband. Instead of her spouse, she found the depth she needed from relationships with her close friends and co-workers. After Karen had been born, she had thought, briefly, that this might pull her and David back together.

For a while it had.

But then came that terrible day in February....

Karen had started fourth grade that September. It was February school vacation, and David, who still maintained that he felt guilty having the house all to himself every day, said that he wanted to take Karen and Sarah skiing. Because college was still in session that week, Sarah hadn't been able to arrange for the time off from work, but David and Karen had gone without her to Mt. Rainey, just outside of Augusta.

Then, late that afternoon, just around the time Sarah was expecting a phone call from David, telling her that they were back home after having a total *blast* on the slopes, he called her from the hospital in Augusta....

There had been an accident, David had told her, his voice breaking with sobs.

How bad? she'd asked.

Really bad!

Karen had been coming down a slope that was maybe a little too difficult for her level of ability. In fact, the slope was much steeper than either she or David had expected, but she had said that she wanted to give it a try.

She did fine until the first, sharp turn.

David said he had seen her have trouble negotiating the turn, and he had watched—helplessly—as she plowed into a stand of pines.

Over the years, David had told her—too many times, in exacting detail what had happened.

The impact had been hard enough to knock one of Karen's ski boots clean off her foot. Both skis were shattered. The poles bent like corkscrews. Karen's face was smashed and flattened. As she lay on the snow, taking shallow, raw gasps of the cold mountain air, ribbons of blood had bubbled up and run from her mouth and nostrils.

David said he had shouted out for her to slow down. Sarah had heard it so many times, she thought she *had* actually witnessed it, watching it all happen and unable to do anything to stop it.

He had kicked off his skis and, tears streaming down his face, run over to her and knelt down in the snow to cradle her head in his lap as he told her how much he loved her and that everything was going to be all right.

But everything *didn't* turn out all right.

David had told Sarah the story so many times and so vividly that she felt as though she had been there and actually witnessed it. She couldn't help but cry whenever she imagined her daughter's eyelids fluttering and then closing as she faded away with a final, shuddering groan. Worse of all, she couldn't bear the thought that her daughter had died, and she—the person who had brought her into the world—hadn't been there with her.

That had been almost five and a half years ago, but Sarah's memories of that terrible day, and the stinging, numbed memories of the funeral that followed were as sharp and painful as if they had happened just yesterday.

"I miss you, Sugar," Sarah whispered in a broken voice as hot tears coursed down her cheeks.

Suddenly she shivered and straightened up.

Even with the sun beating down warmly on her back, she felt a sudden rush of chills. She had the distinct, almost overpowering impression that someone had just touched her.

Someone had tugged at her shoulder with the faintest of touches.

Sarah's throat closed off, and her eyes were wide with fear as she turned around, expecting to see the person she had seen earlier standing there behind her. She let out a long, pained moan and almost fainted when she saw that she was alone.

The cemetery was deserted.

When she looked down at her car, parked at the foot of the slope, it looked impossibly far away, almost lost in the hazy distance. The tops of the trees surrounding the cemetery were tossing back and forth wildly in the wind, but the air around her still was absolutely motionless.

Sarah had the impression that she had somehow been transported outside of the world and was watching it like a passive observer. The air was charged with subtle currents of electricity that were gathering strength. Sarah was suddenly fearful that, with the thunderstorm approaching so rapidly, being up on a hill might put her in danger.

C'mon! Get your butt out of here! she thought, but she was too frightened to move.

She knew that she should sit in her car and wait out the storm. Usually storms that came up this fast blew over just as fast.

Or maybe she should go back home and come out here another day— sometime when she could handle it a little better.

No matter what she decided, she knew with a dull, dread certainty that she'd be back out here in another few days for David's funeral; but as she looked around the cemetery, she couldn't shake the feeling that the touch on her shoulder had been real—more than a static charge in the air, and more than her imagination.

She could easily imagine that invisible hands had reached out to her and had tried to touch her.

Maybe it was Karen! she thought.

"Jesus," Sarah muttered as she stood up slowly. She could feel every muscle and bone in her body creak like she was eighty years old. Her stomach felt like a hollow pit. The world seemed to be spinning crazily around her, and she had to struggle to maintain her balance.

The keen sense of her loss she felt was suddenly too much to bear.

As she started back down the hill, heading to her car, she took halting, choppy steps and looked all around as though she wanted to start running, but had no idea which way to go. Emotions welled up from deep inside her, and she was vaguely aware that she was crying…

Crying for Karen…and for David…and for herself.

At the moment, there was only one thing she knew with any certainty—that no matter how long she lived, her feelings of grief and loss, of guilt and despair would never, *never* be dulled, much less go away.

As if watching her in a dream, David stared at Sarah as she walked up the hill toward their daughter's grave. Her hands were clasped in front of her, and her head was bowed.

He had no idea how he had gotten out to the cemetery, or how long it had taken him to get here. He had only a hazy memory of walking down Deering Avenue and along outer Congress Street to the cemetery. He had experienced an odd sensation of time passing and of distances being crossed, but he couldn't remember anything about it very clearly. Time and distance seemed to be much more tenuous, less well-ordered and defined than they had ever been when he was alive.

Along the way he remembered noticing several other people.

Some of them seemed to have taken notice of him, and others had ignored him completely, either on purpose or because, he assumed, they were living and *couldn't* see him.

In either event, he had decided that it would be futile, possibly even dangerous, to attempt to speak to any of them. The old man had told him that the Shadowlands were dangerous, and whether he wanted to believe him or not, David could *feel* the danger like a palpable presence in the air. If he ignored everyone he met, then maybe they'd all ignore him and leave him alone.

It didn't take David very long to realize that it was relatively easy to distinguish the living from the dead.

The living, even those who looked like they might be harboring some deep-seated sickness inside them, all seemed to vibrate with a sparkling, healthy glow of energy. Some of them even appeared to be almost translucent, like "ghosts" dwelling in the dead world.

All of the dead, on the other hand, appeared to have a dull, gray pallor about them that was far more than the lifeless tone of their skin. Their "essences," maybe what New Agers would call their "auras," appeared to be wilted and faint, as though tainted by the corrupting touch of Death. Their eyes looked hollow and blank, like poorly polished marble.

Whatever the case, somehow David found himself at Karen's grave when Sarah arrived. Standing at the top of the hill, he watched as his ex-wife moved toward him in slow-motion. She looked as though she were battling her way through an invisible barrier.

David felt no exhaustion from the effort of walking all the way to the cemetery, even though he knew it was better than four miles from Pine Knoll Elementary to Riverside; but once he was at his daughter's gravesite, he felt drained both emotionally and physically.

How can I feel drained physically when I don't even have a body anymore? he wondered.

He was almost amused by the concept of actually being dead.

He assumed that everything he was thinking and feeling were his own thoughts and emotions; but being dead, now that he was free of any physical reactions or restrictions, seemed to heighten such intense feelings.

Standing beside his daughter's grave, David trembled as he watched, half-frightened and half-amazed as he clasped his fingers together tightly. No matter how hard he tried to squeeze his own hand, he couldn't get rid of the uncanny dissociative feeling that there was almost no feeling in his hands. It was like watching someone else move their hands.

Powerful, conflicting emotions almost overwhelmed him as he watched Sarah kneel down beside Karen's grave, bow her head, and start to cry.

David could experience grief, too, but no matter how strong it surged inside him, tears wouldn't spill from his eyes. The emotions felt bottled up inside him, with no way to find release.

It was pure torture.

His corpus shuddered horribly as he looked at Sarah and called out to her.

"Sarah...Sarah."

He forced his voice to rise louder and louder as he moved closer to her and reached out with one hand. He could barely stop himself from shaking as he touched her on the shoulder, but then he watched in stunned horror as his hand passed like a whiff of smoke through Sarah.

His entire being was filled with knife-sharp pangs of dread and agony when he saw Sarah suddenly startle and look around.

Her lips moved as she said something, but the air seemed too dense, and the sound was too distorted for David to hear her clearly.

"Yes!…Yes, Sarah! I'm right here!" he shouted. "It's me, David! I'm standing right beside you!"

David was convinced that she could neither hear nor see him, but he felt a slim ray of hope when he saw Sarah tense, seeming almost to respond to his voice. She stood up slowly, frowning as she looked around.

David lunged forward, seeming to move in slow motion as he grabbed at her with both hands, trying to embrace her and shake her; but it was like watching everything through a thick, dirt-filmed pane of glass. Dimensions and distances seemed oddly warped. A dark, tugging swell of vertigo surged through him, and inside his head he felt as though he were falling backwards, spinning crazily, head over heels.

"Please, Sarah!…Listen to me…look at me…" he wailed.

She was so close…so close, yet so far away!

"Please, Sarah! I'm right here beside you!" he shouted with all his strength, but even to his own ears, his voice sounded no stronger than a whisper of wind that wasn't even strong enough to blow out a candle.

Tormented beyond belief, David watched as Sarah glanced around the cemetery. Then, wiping the tears from her eyes with both hands, she started down the slope, back to her car.

David followed after her, still pulling at her, trying to touch her, but it was useless. After one last, tearful glance at Karen's grave, Sarah got into her car, started it up, and drove away. A plume of dust rose up like yellow smoke in the wake of her car.

David was left standing in the dappled shade of the trees, feeling more alone and desolate that he had ever felt before. The receding sound of the car reverberated in the dense air like the fading patter of distant drum beats.

As soon as her car was out of sight, he was filled with such a deep, lonely ache that he wished he could simply will himself to dissolve into nothingness.

The old man's words echoed in his memory, mixing with the dull, distant roll of thunder….

"Not unless you want to embrace oblivion."

Standing there alone in the cemetery, watching as the fine dust settled to the ground like gently falling snow, David would have cried if he could have.

4

THE STORM BREAKS

As he walked away from Riverside Cemetery, not really knowing or caring where he was headed, the sky rapidly darkened. Mountainous clouds the deep purple color of bruises shifted from the west across the hazy gray arc of sky. The air seemed charged with static electricity.

Because all of his perceptions, even his senses of time and distance, were severely altered, David at first thought that night must be coming on much faster than usual. After a moment, however, he realized that a thunderstorm was blowing in from the west.

David was mesmerized by the energy and power he could feel in the approaching storm. About a mile away from the cemetery, he stopped on the roadside and listened as the wind gathered strength. A deep-throated, hollow whistle sounded from the sky as strong gusts rippled like gushes of water over the trees and grass. Dust and debris blew in tiny tornadoes down the street. David found it slightly bothersome at first, then almost fascinating that he couldn't feel even the slightest puff of wind on his face. It wasn't until the rain began beating against the sidewalk, leaving wet splotches the size of half dollars, that a wave of sadness came over him.

He couldn't feel the rain hitting him!

Most people, if not actually *afraid* of thunderstorms, at least didn't *enjoy* them; but David always had—especially at night, when brilliant flashes of lightning flickered like blue strobe lights across the dark land, and the breeze was tinged with the sharp, fresh aroma of ozone and damp earth.

And now, here he was—*dead*—and it was raining hard enough to make the pavement look like it was dancing with energy, and he couldn't even *feel* it.

It was frustrating!

Infuriating!

The sky steadily darkened as the storm clouds, moving like closing drapes, clashed together. Thin veins of lightning forked across the purple sky. The ground trembled with the low, steady rumble of approaching thunder.

David was surprised to notice how everything around him seemed to be glowing with a diaphanous haze of static electricity. Trees, passing cars, road signs...everything he looked at was surrounded by shifting halos of light. He extended his hands and looked at them, amazed to see tiny curling tendrils of blue light caught like spider webs between his fingers.

Any sense of time vanished as David tilted his head back and watched the storm unleash its fury all around him.

The trees tossed violently back and forth, and the loud patter of rain on the road was almost deafening. All of the cars passing by had their headlights and wipers on. Their tires threw up fantails of spray from the wet pavement that hissed like angry serpents. Thin rivulets of runoff water washed down into the weed- and litter-clogged roadside ditches. Blankets of steam rose like twisting ghosts from the sun-baked asphalt as the cool rain washed the world.

The only other person David saw outside was an elderly woman, who was muttering to herself as she walked toward him on the same side of the road. Her "aura" looked absolutely neutral, and David wasn't able to decide if she looked alive or dead.

Not that it mattered.

When she was beside him, he greeted her with a smile and a curt nod. She glanced at him and scowled angrily.

"Hey, have a nice day, ma'am," he said.

The old woman's scowl deepened. She waved her hand once, dismissively, in his direction and continued on her way without a backward glance.

"Must be a dead one," David muttered to himself, shaking his head.

Even though he couldn't feel the chill in the air, David shivered. He still wasn't reconciled to the idea of being dead. He didn't like the way his perceptions seemed so distorted. It was disconcerting, at best. He couldn't stop wondering if he would eventually adjust to this, or if he would have to exist indefinitely in this odd state of distorted—and sometimes frightening—awareness.

But the most pressing problem on his mind was simply—*How long is this going to last?*

If he was already dead, when or how would it ever end?

He couldn't very well exist like this forever—

Could he?

If everyone who had ever died was still walking the earth, trapped here in the Shadowlands, then even a small city like Portland, Maine, should be swarming with wraiths. The old man had told him that there were other wraiths in the Shadowlands, but how many? They couldn't *all* still be here. He would have seen more of them by now.

So where did all the other wraiths go?

It was possible, he supposed, that many of them had passed on to Heaven or some other kind of paradise in the afterlife that the ministers and priests and yogis were always talking about. If the old man hadn't struck him as a potentially dangerous lunatic, David might consider seeking him out and asking him more about this. He decided not to, though, figuring that he'd eventually encounter other wraiths he could question about it all.

But the big question that he still didn't have an answer for was simply, *Why am I here?*

What was the word the old man had used?

Fetters?

So what *fetters* were keeping him here?

As the storm raged around him, David pondered this question for a while, but he concluded that he wouldn't come to any final answers on his own. After a last glance at the sky, he continued on his way. Because he wasn't able to feel the rain pelting his face or back, he felt isolated from it all, as if he were encased in a transparent, protective bubble.

Maybe he was even invincible.

Even if the Shadowlands were as dangerous as the old man had told him they were, David figured, since he was already dead, there wasn't much that could harm him. He was confident that eventually he would figure out what was going on here and, more importantly, he'd get some idea how he was going to get the hell *out* of here!

He continued to walk, not really paying any attention to the direction he was headed, hardly even aware of the activity because he no longer had a physical body that could become exhausted. Suddenly he drew to a halt and looked up, amazed to see where he had arrived.

Although it didn't look very much like it had five years ago, when he and his family used to come here regularly to picnic and play, he instantly recognized the Brighton Avenue Park.

A shock of pure, unalloyed surprise shot through David as he looked around.

The area appeared to be much larger than he remembered it, and starker, more desolate.

Maybe sometime during the last five years the city of Portland had expanded the park, he thought; but if they had, they also had allowed it to decline into near ruins.

The grassy field where he and Sarah and Karen used to throw Frisbees was now clotted with clumps of crab grass and yellowing weeds. The ball field where, in the evenings, they would watch Little League teams play now looked like a washed-out dust bowl. The rain had turned the depressions along the baselines into long, narrow quagmires of brown water. Even the trees that surrounded the park, what had once been beautiful stands of oak and birch mixed with pine and cedar, now looked scraggly, old, and diseased. The playground equipment—the swing set, slides, and climbing bars where Karen used to play with such delight—were all rusted and broken. The wooden supports were black with rot. Fitful gusts of wind caught the swings and tossed them back and forth. The sound of rusted chains scraping against each other grated on David's ears.

He couldn't believe that the park had deteriorated this much in such a short time—just like Pine Knoll Elementary, he thought.

But how could everything have fallen into decay so fast?

The longer David stared at the park, the more he became aware of how distorted his perceptions were. He wondered why some sensations seemed so distant and dull, while others, things which he might not have even noticed when he was alive, were now loud and irritating. The more he focused on any particular sound, the more it seemed to work on his nerves. The hiss of rain sweeping across the field and trees was almost maddeningly loud. The sound of traffic passing by on Brighton Avenue approached and receded with warbling, hollow *whooshing* sounds. And everywhere he looked, the world—at least here in the park—appeared to be gray, drab and desolate, as if it had all been touched by the hand of death.

Out of habit rather than necessity, David stood in the shelter of the trees and watched, enthralled, as gray curtains of rain shifted across the field. A flock of small, black birds darted across the lowering sky like wind-tossed leaves. David had the quick impression that they looked skeletal against the sky.

The sense of loneliness and loss that filled him was almost too much to tolerate. Thinking that he'd rather be *anywhere* except here, he was just about to turn and leave when he noticed a small, frail figure, standing hunched against the storm over by the swing set.

Instant recognition hit David like a thunderclap.

"Karen?"

As soon as he whispered her name, it was swept away by the wind. A hollow ache of despair and regret filled him as he stared across the field at the solitary figure, not quite able to trust his senses.

She was standing no more than a hundred yards away, her head bowed to the rain as though she could actually feel it. The features of her face were lost beneath the thin, gray shadow of her hooded raincoat.

"*Karen!*" David called out again, louder. He winced at the almost frantic tremolo he heard in his voice.

Either she couldn't hear him, or else she chose to ignore him. She just stood there, as still as a statue beside the bowl-shaped depression in the ground underneath one of the swings. Her face was downcast as though she was hypnotized by the plump drops of rain hitting the muddy surface of the puddle.

Shivering inside, David took a halting step forward. He didn't even dare to blink because he was afraid that she would vanish the instant he did.

Jesus! Can this really be her?

He was trying hard to contain the chilled rushes of excitement. A dull glimmer of hope flared up inside him when he started across the field at a brisk walk. After a few steps, he broke into a run.

Of COURSE it's her!...Yes, if she's alone and afraid, she might come here!...We used to come here all the time...ever since she was a little baby!

David cupped one hand to his mouth and shouted as he waved his other arm wildly over his head.

"Karen! It's me! It's daddy!"

When he was more than halfway to her, the little girl looked up, shifting her head slowly, almost mechanically.

David still couldn't clearly see her face beneath her hood, but he thought—no, he *knew* that he recognized Karen's red, rubber raincoat— the one with the emblem of a yellow duck holding an umbrella sewn above the breast pocket. She was wearing the faded blue jeans she always preferred and her favorite white sneakers with purple laces.

By Jesus, it is her!...It has to be her!

Rain and mist swirled across the field like the smoke of battle. The sky pressed down like a coffin lid as he ran toward her. But as he was running, for the first time since he had realized he was dead, David was suddenly gripped by complete and utter exhaustion. His arms and legs felt like they were being weighed down by iron shackles. He continued running toward the swing set, but every step he took was increasingly difficult until he was overcome with the sensation that he wasn't getting any closer to her. It felt like, with every step, he was sliding backwards in the rain-slick grass.

Then, in a blinding flash, David's vision suddenly exploded with a bright flash of white light. For a single, terrifying instant, he felt as though he'd been swept up by a powerful current of wind, and his body was being tossed around like a handful of dust. All around him the air was filled with flashing lines of blue and white light that ripped through him like a buzz saw. After a dizzying, timeless moment, there came the deafening concussion of an explosion that knocked David backwards onto the ground.

He hit the ground hard but was disoriented only for a moment.

Shaking his head to clear it, he leapt to his feet and looked over at the swing set. Somehow, he wasn't surprised to see that there was no one there.

She was gone!

He darted his glance back and forth, scanning the expansive field, trying to see where she could have gone. At first glance, he didn't notice her; but then, far across the field, at the border of the trees, he saw the small, red-hooded figure.

"No…"

David's voice was lost within the fury of the storm.

Absolute despair wrung him out. He dropped onto his hands and knees in the wet grass, knowing that he didn't have the strength to follow. He was positive that, whoever it was, even if it was Karen, she would disappear again as soon as he got close to her.

"Oh, Karen…"

He held his arms out to her in desperation.

The solitary figure tilted her head and looked up at him. David could feel her penetrating gaze focusing on him. Then, like a column of smoke whisked away by the wind, she disappeared, blending into the gray fingers of mist that swirled like rivers among the rain-blackened trunks of trees.

At least fifty or sixty people were crowded onto the small dance floor. They seemed to be happy, packed shoulder to shoulder and hip to hip as they moved about in languid, random gyrations. The room was filled with a cacophony of shrill laughter and shouted conversation that struggled to be heard above the bone-jarring music, if that's what you could call it, of the band on stage. The singer's voice was buried in a bad sound mix that pushed the bass guitar and drums up much too loud. The only time she could be heard clearly was between every song, when she mumbled what sounded like a very insincere "thank you very much" to the audience.

Thick, blue rafts of cigarette smoke swirled like ghostly strata. Thin, flickering lines of green laser light pierced the darkness above the dancers, turning everyone into an indistinguishable mass of dark, twisting bodies. Sarah's first impression when she and Tony entered the club was that they looked like tormented souls, writhing in Hell.

It didn't take long for the noise of the crowd to get on Sarah's nerves. She felt at least ten years too old for a scene like this, and she couldn't help but notice the numerous quizzical glances she'd gotten when she and Tony arrived.

But she smiled broadly as she and Tony went out onto the floor and started to dance. She smiled, wanting Tony to think she was having fun.

She had to admit that she enjoyed watching Tony move. His arms, head, and hips shifted and waved in time with the hard-edged beat. Although she had hesitated at first, she was glad she had finally accepted when Tony called her at the library and asked her out. She had almost admitted to him that her ex-husband had died the other day, and that she needed some time alone to absorb what had happened; but after feeling the way she had out at the cemetery this morning, and now that a thundershower had cut the humidity—at least for the evening—she had quickly decided that being alone was exactly what she *didn't* need.

The best thing for her tonight would be to get out, maybe have a few drinks and conversation, and then stroll around the Exchange Street area for an hour or two before...

Well, she wasn't quite sure what would happen next, but she had some ideas. If she and Tony ended up at his or her place later on, and if they made love—well then, all the better. It had been too long since she'd had sex with *anyone*. It'd be nice to feel a man hold her once again and enter her—especially a man as young and strong as Tony.

The only problem was, she hadn't been counting on something like *this*!

The song the band was playing sounded identical to every other one they had played so far. It ended with a crash of cymbals, and then the singer announced that they would be taking a short break.

Sarah leaned forward to say something to Tony, but before she got half a sentence out, the music system in the club kicked in, blasting recorded music even louder than the band had been playing. Tony took Sarah by the hand and led her through the crowd over to the bar.

"Would you like something to drink?" he asked. He had to lean close to her ear and shout to be heard above the thundering music.

Sarah considered for a moment, then shook her head. The noise was hurting her ears. Putting her mouth so close to Tony's ear that she could feel his body heat radiating off him, she yelled, "Maybe we could find someplace a little quieter."

"Quieter?" Tony repeated, his eyebrows rising like dark commas. "You mean *this* place isn't quiet enough for you?"

Sarah laughed and shook her head, then motioned as if to stick her fingers in her ears.

"What did you have in mind?" Tony asked, leaning closer to her.

Sarah was pretty sure she picked up the message he was communicating by the glint in his eyes. She told herself that she might be going too fast, that it was still too early in the evening to be thinking about having sex; but she couldn't deny the strong attraction she felt for him—an attraction she had, in fact, felt for him since the first time she had noticed him in the library.

"I dunno…maybe some other place," she said, cupping her hands over his ear and bringing her mouth close enough to his ear lobe she could have licked it. She had to resist the temptation. "Someplace we can talk."

Tony looked at her and smiled as he cast a quick glance around the room. Then, gripping her hand tightly, he led her through the crowd to the front door.

The instant they stepped outside, and the barroom door swung shut behind them, the noise level dropped, becoming almost bearable. Sarah's ears were still ringing as she closed her eyes, leaned her head back, and took a deep breath. Her face and arms were slick with sweat, and she shivered from the chill of the night air.

"I didn't realize so many young people still smoked cigarettes," she said, wrinkling her nose.

Tony smiled at her, then looked up and down the street as though unable to choose which way to go. Sarah squeezed Tony's hand tightly and he started up Exchange Street, heading toward Federal Street.

"I'd rather not go past where I work," Tony said, smiling tightly. "I see enough of that damned place during the day."

Sarah nodded her agreement and walked along slowly beside him, pausing every now and again to look at the displays in the lighted store windows. Their conversation was friendly and casual. Tony told her about his law studies, his frustrations with his job at the Hollow Reed, and his intention—eventually—to establish his own law practice. He hadn't yet decided on a specialty, but he told her that he thought he might like to do something to help protect abused children. Sarah found that admirable.

Sarah skirted around the details of her own life, talking mostly about how much she enjoyed her work at the university library. Feeling the way she did tonight, she figured she'd let Tony do most of the talking. It was best if she just avoided revealing any details about her marriage, divorce, and—especially—Karen's and David's deaths.

"So how come you're not married or anything?" Tony asked when they were standing outside the Painted Horse, gazing at the assortment of painted wooden toys and puzzles in the window.

Sarah felt a twinge of remorse, remembering how she and David had bought Karen a rocking horse from here for her second birthday. She stiffened slightly and looked away, momentarily flustered by the sudden rush of emotion. She considered not telling the truth, but then decided that it would probably do more harm than good not to.

"I was married…for a while," she said, hoping Tony wouldn't notice the dry tightness in her voice. "But—well, actually, the divorce just came through a couple of months ago."

"Umm, I see. Sorry to hear that," Tony said. Smiling, he squeezed her hand and added, "Well, not really."

Blinking back the tears that were forming in her eyes, Sarah looked at him and smiled.

"I—I've been kind of—you know, just starting to pick myself up, trying to find a new social life and all," she said. "It isn't easy for a woman my age."

"I wouldn't think so. Not for someone as beautiful as you," Tony said as he gently caressed her cheek.

Sarah looked at him for a moment and then, feeling as though the moment was perfectly right, she leaned forward until their lips met. At first they merely brushed their lips against each other, but then Tony shifted forward and pulled her close. He started kissing her with rapidly increasing warmth and passion.

Sarah closed her eyes and let herself melt into the kiss. She shivered when she felt his hands let go of hers and slide around her waist and then down to her hips. His hands felt big and strong. A wave of dizziness almost swept her away, but then she broke off the kiss, pulled back, and smiled at him.

"I sure do hope your plans include continuing to date young law students," he said. His heated breath washed like water across her face.

Sarah tossed her head back and laughed nervously.

"Well, we'll just have to see what kind of case this young law student can make for himself," she said, laughing.

Hand in hand, they started up the street again, leaning close to each other, Sarah's head resting on his shoulder.

This feels good, she told herself. *Good and natural.*

They passed other couples and small groups of people out enjoying the gorgeous summer night. High over the buildings, a nearly full moon hung suspended like a white spotlight in the deep blue sky. The rain had passed a little after sunset, leaving the air with a clean, fresh tang. She could smell the ocean not far away.

"So—ah, were you happy—being married, I mean?" Tony asked after a while.

Sarah shrugged and didn't look at him as she bit down on her lower lip and shook her head. She felt even more compelled to tell him about what had happened to David, but right now the last thing she wanted to do was cast a pall over their time together.

She told herself to be careful.

Tony was quite a bit younger than she, and getting involved with anybody this fast—and so soon after the divorce—could only complicate things. Tomorrow morning, she had to start facing the harsh realities of settling David's affairs and arranging his funeral.

Right now wasn't the time to mention any of that.

She couldn't deny the strong attraction she felt for Tony. She told herself that it wasn't just his good looks. There was something about him—his presence…something in his eyes, and in the way he carried himself that she found irresistibly attractive. She kept warning herself that this might just be because it had been so long since she'd had sex, but it felt deeper, much deeper than that.

"We wouldn't have gotten divorced if we'd been happy, now, would we?" she finally said.

Tony laughed nervously. Their footsteps clicked on the cobblestone sidewalk.

"No, I suppose not," Tony said as he gave her hand a gentle squeeze. He seemed to sense that it would be a good idea to leave it at that, and fell silent.

He looked up the street and smiled as he pointed to the yellow and white striped awning of a TCBY store.

"Hey, you wanna indulge a little?"

Happy for the moment to put any morbid thoughts about David's death out of her mind, Sarah nodded excitedly.

"Why not?" she said, laughing a little too loudly, she thought, as they picked up their pace.

As they walked up to the shop, Sarah couldn't get over how instantly comfortable she felt being with Tony. The thought crossed her mind—as it had already several times this evening—that she wouldn't mind…in fact, she was rather anxious to see if they ended up in bed together tonight.

That would be nice.

When they paused outside the TCBY store, Tony opened the door with an exaggerated flourish and held it for her.

In the sudden glare of light from inside the shop, Sarah got another good look at his dark, handsome face. Then and there, she decided that if they *didn't* spend the night together tonight, she was going to be disappointed. And she mentally vowed to do everything she could to keep this thing going until they *did* end up in bed together.

The storm ended just before sunset, and the sun came out blazing, shining with a molten glow on the undersides of the storm clouds as they raced to the east and out to sea. The puddles that had formed along the rutted baselines and under the swings flashed like polished mirrors that reflected the angled sunlight and clouds scudding by overhead. Raindrops hung from the tips of almost every leaf and blade of grass. They glowed like fat drops of mercury. The wooden playground equipment looked slick and black from the rain.

David, filled with near total despair, stood rooted to the spot in the middle of the playing field, just staring blankly ahead into the fringe of woods where the small figure had disappeared.

He was *positive* that it had been Karen, so he couldn't understand why she had avoided him.

She *must* have heard him call out to her.

Why had she run away?

The flash of lightning and clap of thunder had momentarily blinded him and left him shaken. He wasn't sure how she could have gotten away from him so fast, unless he'd been unconscious for at least several seconds.

The only possible answer was that, if she had spent the last five years alone in the Shadowlands, she must be afraid of everyone and everything here. She had been only nine years old when she died. Maybe she hadn't even recognized him. Or maybe she hadn't heard him, even though he'd been yelling as loud as he could. David had no idea how sound traveled here.

It was more likely, though, that she was too frightened to trust anyone who spoke to or approached her.

But I'm her father, for Christ's sake!

Anger and the hurt of rejection coiled inside David like a python.

She should trust me!

David felt an almost overwhelming compulsion to follow after her into the woods, but he knew that he'd never catch up with her or find her if she wanted to avoid him.

Besides, with evening rapidly approaching, he wanted to make sure to get back to Pine Knoll Elementary in case the *barghests* returned. The old man had said the Shadowlands were dangerous, especially at night. He'd also hinted to David that wherever it was he had spent the previous night, it must offer some kind of protection. David wasn't very keen about "joining up" with the old man or any of the other wraiths he'd seen thus far. The thought of spending the night in the old man's warehouse, his "haunt," as he called it, filled David with an ill-defined dread. Even in the daylight, the place had struck him as really creepy. If he hadn't been so upset about seeing Karen and not being able to talk with her, David would have found the idea that a ghost could be frightened almost amusing.

"But—*damnit!*—I *will* find her!"

He stared off into the woods, all the while helplessly wringing his hands together.

Now that the rain was over, the evening looked mild and pleasant, even though David couldn't feel any difference in the air. All of his senses still felt maddeningly distant and neutral.

Some kids, obviously relieved at the break in the heat, showed up at the park with baseball gloves, balls, and bats, ready for a scratch game. They vocally expressed their disappointment when they saw the washed-out playing field, but they started the game anyway.

Needle-sharp pangs of loneliness and loss stabbed at David's heart as he watched a young mother who couldn't have been more than twenty years old wheel a newborn baby in a stroller across the still damp field. Her large breasts bounced heavily beneath her thin T-shirt, and David felt a stirring of sexual attraction made all the worse because he knew he could no longer satisfy it.

The young mother and her baby looked so happy, so...

"So *alive!*" David whispered.

His words sounded like the wind, whisking over the rain-trampled grass.

He felt almost overwhelmed by an immense, aching sadness when he thought about what had happened to him and Karen, and he couldn't get rid of the gnawing thought that someday even this young woman and her child—so happy and full of life on this glorious, summer afternoon—were eventually going to die.

Die and end up here, lost and alone in the gray, lifeless desolation of the Shadowlands!

Jesus, what's the fucking point?

David hung his head as he turned slowly and began to walk away. He tried to forget or at least ignore the infinite sadness he sensed at the heart of everything.

Life—existence—it all seemed so pointless.

He started up the sidewalk along Brighton Avenue with the vague intention of heading back into Portland. A nearly unbroken line of late-afternoon rush hour traffic was streaming out of the city and back to the suburbs, but David paid only the slightest attention to it. He walked slowly with his head bowed. His footsteps dragged on the ground with a dull, scuffing sound.

Tall, desolate buildings lined both sides of the avenue. David knew that, in the living world, most of these buildings hadn't been—and probably still weren't—as run-down as they appeared now. Everywhere he looked, all he could see were decaying storefronts and apartment buildings with shadowed alleyways, broken windows, faded and peeling doorways, and derelict cars and trucks parked along the street. The trees and shrubs were stripped of leaves, looking like they had been blasted by a strong November gale. Wet leaves stripped from the trees by the wind and rain were pasted to the street and sidewalk like bloated, black leeches.

David realized that he would have to accept that nearly everything in the Shadowlands was just a pale, decrepit reflection of what he had known in the "real" world—if that's what he could call it. After all, this existence was just as *real* as his previous life had been, and much more unnerving.

And by the looks of things, being here might last a hell of a lot longer than his life had.

Along the way, David encountered several other beings whom he guessed must be wraiths. He chose to ignore all of them, even the few who hailed him with loud, friendly greetings. Just as he had done when he was alive, David preferred to be alone. He repeated to himself something he had always said, half in jest to Sarah and his few friends:

"Just because I'm alone doesn't mean I'm lonely."

At the intersection of Brighton and Deering Avenue, he knew that he should turn left in order to go back to Pine Knoll Elementary, but without making a clear, conscious decision or even knowing quite where he intended to go, he kept walking straight on Brighton.

When he approached the Brighton Medical Center, he stopped suddenly in his tracks and stared up at the building in amazement.

The hospital where Karen had been born was not at all the way he remembered it in real life.

On the site of the building, instead of the modern brick, steel, and glass structure he recalled, was a sprawling, eight-story Victorian mausoleum that looked like it had been built more than a hundred years ago. Dark and brooding, it perched like a vulture on the crest of a desolate hill. A tower with a corroded green copper-roofed cupola pierced the sky from the center of the building. Badly deteriorating cement gargoyles lined all of the cornices, their blank eyes staring ahead into nothingness. The front doors were heavy wood that had been weather-beaten to a dull, black sheen.

In the dying rays of the setting sun, the hospital's imposing brick façade glowed the color of dried blood. Row upon row of long, narrow windows blankly reflected the gathering night sky from glass that looked like slabs of polished black marble. Through the grimy panes of the windows, many of them broken, David caught fleeting glimpses of motion—faces and gauzy white figures that shifted in and out of sight like wind-blown swirls of dust. On the upper floor of the tower, more than eight stories above the street, an old woman whose face was as pale and wrinkled as death was leaning out through a jagged, circular hole in the glass. After staring coldly down at David, she motioned with a faint flutter of her pallid, claw-like hand.

A cold shock of fear ripped through David when he realized that she was signaling to him. He quickly looked away and picked up his pace as he continued down the street.

Just before the building disappeared from sight behind him, he turned around to look back. Stark terror hit him when he saw that the old woman was still leaning out of the window, still watching him and beckoning to him. Even after he had started down the hill, and the hospital was no longer in sight, he held in his memory an image of that old woman's steady, unblinking gaze. He could almost feel it boring like a heated drill into the back of his head.

David wasn't consciously aware of where he was going until some time later, when he arrived at the intersection of Brighton and Forest Avenue. Across the street, no more than a block or two away, was Canal Street, where Sarah lived.

"Shit, yes," David whispered. "Of course!"

His voice rasped, sounding like someone dragging their feet in loose sand.

Why *not* go visit Sarah?

She definitely was one of the *fetters* the old man had said were keeping him in the Shadowlands. Probably the only one.

At the cemetery this morning, when he had tried to touch her and speak to her, he felt certain that she had sensed his presence, however briefly. He had seen her react to his touch with a violent shiver.

So maybe it was as simple as that.

Maybe all he had to do was contact Sarah before he could move along to the next level, whatever it was.

She already knew where he kept his life insurance policy and other important papers, and he didn't have any other bank accounts or stocks hidden that she didn't know about, so it wasn't a matter of him having to settle any unfinished business he'd left behind.

True, there was *Fallen Angels*, the novel he'd been working on; but he accepted that he would never complete it now. Besides, his publisher had turned down the proposal. According to his agent, because of the dismal sales of his last two novels, no one in New York wanted his next book. That particular book wasn't going to be the one that finally blasted him out of the midlist ghetto where his career had been floundering for the last ten years or more.

Maybe—someday—he might have written that ever-elusive "breakout" novel, but he was positive *Fallen Angels* wasn't going to be the one to do it. In fact, for the last couple of years he'd begun to doubt that he even *had* a breakout novel in him.

No, his failed writing career wasn't keeping him connected to his old life, so maybe that's all he had to do—say a final good-bye to Sarah.

He had already tried once this morning, but maybe he'd do better if he visited her at night—the time when ghosts were supposed to haunt the living.

Maybe daylight was what had kept him from touching her.

The sun slowly dropped below the horizon, and night settled down on the city like a soft cushion. In the gathering gloom, streetlights silently winked on, casting distorted ovals of orange light onto the darkening sidewalk and street.

David experienced a vague inner tension as he walked down to the corner of Canal Street. Sarah's house—the house where all three of them had lived before the divorce and before Karen had died—was the third one on the right.

A dark tremor of sadness went through David, and if he could have cried, he would have when he stopped beneath the shadow of the maple tree in the front yard and looked up at the dark windows.

Here in the Shadowlands, even Sarah's house looked like it had fallen into serious disrepair. David hadn't been over to visit in several months because he wanted to avoid any unpleasant memories the house might stir in him, but he knew for certain that Sarah hadn't let the place fall apart *this* badly.

David realized with a sudden jolt that, ever since he discovered that he was dead, he hadn't entered a building other than the schoolhouse last night. Last night, the schoolhouse door had been open. The door there was hanging to one side as if someone had ripped it off its hinges.

David wasn't sure he'd even be able to enter a building.

If his hand was going to pass through the doorknob, how was he going to open a door?

Just because he was transparent, and no one in the living world could see him, that didn't necessarily mean that he could simply walk through one of the walls to enter, did it?

He hadn't done anything like that yet, and he wasn't so sure he wanted to try.

The fact that, as a wraith, he could walk down the street without falling through the asphalt indicated *something*, but he wasn't sure what. Although he was still experiencing that curious deadening of his senses, when he stomped his feet on the ground the sidewalk felt perfectly solid and real beneath him.

So what was keeping him here in the Shadowlands? Why didn't he just fall through reality into…something else?

Why would a simple wall stop him? It couldn't be that much of a barrier, could it?

Was existence here just as real to him now as "reality" had been when he was alive, or was he limited only because he *thought* he was limited?

He lost track of the time as he stood outside the house, thinking about such things.

He was distantly aware of the night sky deepening until it fairly vibrated with darkness. The small sprinkling of stars that he could see through the ambient light of the surrounding city looked like diamond dust spread against a drape of gray velvet. The bone-white moon had risen over the buildings, looking huge and bloated. It seemed to leave behind a trailing blue afterimage as it streaked across the sky. A few people passed by on the street, but none of them acknowledged David's presence.

Some time later, David heard the steady rumble of a car as it turned off Brighton Avenue. Out of habit, he ducked behind the maple tree and watched as a sleek, red Corvette turned onto Canal Street and pulled to a stop in Sarah's driveway. The glare of headlights illuminated the peeling paint of the garage door before winking out. David heard the car doors click open, and then watched as Sarah and a young man David had never seen before got out of the car. They were laughing about something. The sound of their laughter reverberated with an odd distortion in the eerily silent night.

"I *do* have to meet with my Crim. Psych. professor first thing tomorrow morning," the young man said, "so I really can't stay very long."

A slow anger began to simmer in David when he saw his ex-wife take the young man by the hand and pull him close to her. Their arms encircled each other's waist, and then they kissed, long and passionately. David could hear the low moaning sound his ex-wife was making deep in her throat. She used to make that sound when they made love.

Sudden fury shifted like scarlet curtains behind David's eyes. He clenched his fists and took a threatening step forward, more than ready to pummel this man.

"Are you sure about that?" Sarah asked, looking up into the young man's eyes when they broke off the kiss.

They stared at each other for what seemed to David to be entirely too long. Cold jealousy and blazing anger surged inside him. He was ready to explode with anger as he watched Sarah lead the young man up the side steps onto the porch. She paused long enough to fish her keys from her purse, then unlocked the side door and, stepping to one side, waved her hand for the young man to enter.

"Welcome," she said with a short, breathy laugh.

Just as the young man was about to step across the threshold, a blur of motion streaked from the darkened corner of the porch and zipped like ball lightning between the man's legs and into the house.

The young man let out a shout of surprise and jumped backwards. Sarah chuckled softly to herself as she reached inside the house and snapped on the overhead light in the kitchen.

"Oh, don't worry," she said. "That was just Bingley, my cat."

The young man's face was bathed by the glow of yellow light that highlighted the hollowness under his cheekbones as he looked at Sarah and smiled tightly.

"I...don't really like cats very much," he said, sounding more than a little annoyed.

"You don't have to worry about Bingley," Sarah said, still snickering. "He'll avoid you more than you'll avoid him. He's a loner, just like my ex used to be."

"Umm," the young man said, nodding and looking grim.

As they were about to enter the house, David suddenly realized that he didn't want to test whether or not he could open the door or walk through walls. As Sarah followed the young man inside, David leaped up onto the porch, hoping to get inside before she closed the door. Even if he wasn't able to communicate with her, the least he could do was keep an eye on her.

But Sarah went inside and swung the door shut, locking it shut behind her before David could follow her, and he was left standing outside, looking in through the door window. His view of the kitchen was horribly distorted, as if the glass were fogged. Moving about inside, Sarah and the man looked like rippling figures swimming underwater.

David was fuming with anger as he watched Sarah open the refrigerator and take out a bottle of white wine. At her direction, the young man fetched two wine glasses from the cupboard above the sink and placed them on the counter. He took the wine bottle from Sarah, worked the cork out of the bottle neck, and poured them each a generous amount. David watched as they walked off into the living room.

Feeling sad and angry and frustrated, David turned and walked slowly down the porch steps. It pained him to think that, here it was, only six months after their divorce, and already she was bringing a new man home with her.

But it didn't really surprise David.

One of the many wedges that had split them apart was the conflict between Sarah's passionate, sociable nature and what she always referred to as his "stick-in-the-mud" attitude.

With a hollow, sinking feeling deep inside him, David realized that no matter what he tried to do now, no matter how hard he tried, he would never be able to feel or regain that kind of passion.

It was only for the living.

He bowed his head, unable to stop himself from dwelling on all the things that he had missed simply because he had let them slip away from him.

And now they were gone…

Forever.

His footsteps echoed softly in the night as he walked slowly back to Brighton Avenue, heading back to Pine Knoll Elementary.

5

A Taste of Oblivion

"My mommy needs help. She's in a lot of trouble."

The fragile voice—a little girl's—came to David from out of the spinning well of darkness that surrounded him. It echoed softly, sounding like the powdery flutter of a moth's wings against the night.

After a moment of disorientation, David realized that he was sitting up, his body rigid, his eyes wide open.

He had no idea if he had been asleep or awake or somewhere in between.

All he knew was that the night had been long and dark, and filled with a penetrating cold that seemed to originate inside him. Throughout the night, the silence of the schoolhouse had often been punctuated by faint, echoing groans, low laughter, soft whisperings, and dull clanking sounds. All night long, the floorboards creaked loudly, as though possessed by tormented souls. Less frequently, from outside, David heard distant screaming and animal-sounding howls that throbbed in the night.

David lost track of time and even a sense of himself as he huddled in the darkness, leaning against the cold, plaster wall with his knees bent and pressed hard against his chest.

After wandering the streets of Portland, not even caring if he encountered any of the dangers the old man had spoken about, he'd returned to Pine Knoll Elementary. After making sure that he wasn't being watched by any wandering wraiths, he'd entered the old schoolhouse and felt his way in the darkness across the floor to the same spot where he had spent the previous night.

He hadn't thought to check out the school during the day, and in the dark it was hard to tell exactly where he was. He thought he might be in the janitor's closet, or maybe in the old supply storage closet underneath the wide stairway. If there was someone here in the dark with him, he had no idea where they might be lurking.

"What?"

David tensed as he spoke the word out loud, fighting against the powerfully unnerving feeling of dissociation. He had the strong impression that he had imagined hearing that little girl speak to him.

"What did you say?"

Even though he carefully pronounced each word, his voice seemed to be no more than a meaningless groan. If he were speaking out loud, and not just thinking this, he didn't want to frighten whoever might be here.

But there's no one there!...How could there be?

His first and most powerful impression was that the little girl had sounded quite a bit like Karen.

Quite a bit?...No, *exactly* like her!

David stared ahead into the darkness but could see nothing. He wanted to believe he had heard her speak to him, that it wasn't just his imagination. There had been a sullen dullness in the voice—a bleak emptiness, as though whoever it was had long since given up hope.

And who could blame her, being in a place like this?

A deep shudder ran through David.

"It's my…my mommy," the little girl said. Every word warbled up and down the scale in the darkness, as though she were trembling with fear.

David jumped and almost screamed out loud when he heard the voice, more clearly this time. He shook his head, trying to convince himself he wasn't dreaming this.

"I…I saw you there…tonight…at the—the house tonight…and she was there, too…she was with that man…that really *bad* man."

What she was saying bothered David, but he was still trying to decide if this voice was even real…and if it was, if it could really be Karen.

He hardly dared to hope, even though he wanted so badly for it to be her!

"Wha—what's your name?" he finally managed to ask.

He struggled to keep his voice hushed and controlled, but even to his own ears it sounded like someone hammering on metal.

"My…name?"

"Yeah. You have a name, don't you?"

David shifted forward as if about to stand up. The scraping sound his feet made on the ancient wooden floor was loud and abrasive, like a long, deep sigh.

As far as he could tell, this was really happening, and he wanted to be ready to react to anything that might happen. Staring straight ahead, he tried to pierce the darkness; but, other than the faint glowing gray light in the doorway on the opposite side of the room, he couldn't see a thing.

Not even a shadow within a shadow.

"I don't…I don't use my name much anymore," the girl said, sounding defeated.

"But you do *have* a name—"

A cold flash of worry shot through David.

"Do you remember your name?"

"Are you my…my daddy?"

The little girl's voice broke with desperate pleading.

"You sound a little like my daddy."

"I—I don't know," David said, trembling terribly inside. "I might be, but I—Why don't you tell me your name, so I can be sure?"

"If you're really my daddy, you'd know my name."

"I know what it is…*Karen.*"

The instant he said her name out loud, it felt like a sharp, metal blade had carved a deep trench through his mind and soul.

"What? What are you doing here, Daddy?" Karen asked, sounding stunned with disbelief.

David could hear her voice, hitching with anguish and fear.

"I've been here...all alone...for s-o-o long. Why didn't you come with me? You were there with me, weren't you?"

"Where's that, Sugar?"

"With me...when I...when I got hurt. I got hurt really bad, didn't I, Daddy?"

"Is it...is that really you, Karen?" David asked. His voice was high and tight, barely a whisper in the darkness.

He didn't dare hope.

From the heaviness he felt in his chest, he knew that the Shadowlands weren't the kind of place where anyone could feel *hope*.

Leaning forward and reaching out into the darkness, he groped desperately with both hands, but didn't connect with anything substantial. His fingers clawed at the night like it was a sheer curtain he could tear away. All the while, he couldn't stop thinking that he had to be imagining all of this.

It isn't possible! This has to be something I'm hallucinating! None of this is real! How can it be?

"Daddy...?"

Karen's voice still sounded flat and empty, like she was talking in her sleep, but the high, frantic edge in it tore through David like a searing knife.

"I—I'm scared, daddy...really scared."

"Don't worry, Karen. I'm right here," he whispered, even though he couldn't see her in the dark.

"Will you...hug me?"

"Oh, my God! *Karen!*"

He felt a terrible wrenching deep inside his chest as he shifted forward on his knees and flailed around with both hands like a blind man who had fallen down. He was trying not to think that, if she was dead, too, they might not be able to touch.

Weren't they both wraiths?

If they were both dead, how could the dead embrace?

A powerful chill raced up his arms to the base of his neck when his hand brushed against something that wasn't a wall. He let out a low moan as he felt her arm, just above the elbow. He ran his hand up to her shoulder and grabbed her with the other hand and pulled her to him in a tight, desperate embrace.

"Oh, my *God!*"

His voice was little more than a tormented sigh.

Raw emotions, pure and blinding, seethed in his mind. He wished he was able to cry, if only to relieve the terrible pressure that was building up in the center of his soul. Karen was trembling like a terrified bird in his arms.

"I'm right here with you, Sugar," David whispered.

He rubbed the back of her head with one hand, surprised by the solid feel of her. His sense of touch still felt weirdly distant, but just holding his daughter tightly against his chest filled him—for the first time—with the slimmest ray of hope that, even though they *were* both dead, things might turn out all right after all.

Tony Ranieri's back was slick with sweat that stung when it ran into the shallow scratches Sarah had made while they made love.

The night air was cool. Both bedroom windows were wide open, and the lacy window curtains were billowing in and out with every vagrant puff of wind. A thin glaze of blue light from the nearby streetlight cast soft shadows across the floor and up onto a corner of the bed.

Lying beside him in bed, Sarah slept with one leg draped over Tony's thigh. Her breathing was deep and even, as peaceful as a baby's. The light entering the bedroom was just strong enough for him to see the gentle swelling of her breasts beneath the sweat-soaked sheet. He felt a strong, almost painful stirring in his groin as he rolled over and started to reach for her, but then he stopped himself.

No!

He licked his lips and rolled his eyes as the tension in his groin spread to his lower stomach, like a pang of hunger.

Maybe I'll try something else…

He was glad that Sarah hadn't seen him pick up the knife from the floor of the car where he'd put it, and slip it into the back pocket of his jeans. As they walked into the house, he'd been afraid she would notice the bulge it made under his summer-weight polo shirt, but she hadn't.

After sharing most of a bottle of white wine while sitting side by side on the couch in the living room, they had started kissing.

And one thing led to another, just as Tony had hoped it would from the moment he'd first seen her.

But as strongly as he was attracted to her, Tony hadn't really wanted to do anything.

RICK HAUTALA

Not tonight.

It wasn't that he didn't feel a powerful sexual charge coming from her. The first thing he'd ever noticed about her was the size of her breasts. Large, round, and firm—just the way he liked them. Although she was considerable older than he was, she also had a look of experience that attracted him to her.

But tonight he'd been too afraid that she would discover the knife he was carrying. If she had, he wasn't sure what he would have said or done about it.

The plain truth was, he had no idea what to think about it.

Ever since finding the knife the other night, he hadn't been able to think about much of anything else. Simply possessing it bothered him, yet it also made him feel strangely attracted to it, compelled to look at it...and hold it.

And use it! a voice deep inside his mind whispered.

Yes, he liked the way it fit his hand, almost as if it had been sculpted for his grip. When he squeezed the hard rubber handle and placed his thumb on the small metal indentation just below the blade, he could vividly imagine using it to cut upward with a long, steady pressure.

The knife filled him with a sense of power and control.

"Jesus," he whispered into the darkness as the thought of using the knife to cut Sarah filled his mind.

"What the fuck's the matter with me?"

He tensed and squeezed his eyes tightly closed, but that only made the violent thoughts intensify.

He could almost hear the raw, wet ripping sound the blade would make as it sliced her throat.

He could practically smell the hot copper scent of fresh blood, gushing from her throat and down over her breasts.

And even with his eyes tightly shut, he could picture the wild, panic-filled gleam that would fill her eyes as he plunged the knife deeper into her, and he watched the life slowly seep out of her.

But no! Jesus! I don't want to hurt her!

He wedged his eyes open and stared at her until the hazy image began to blur.

Reaching out with one hand, he gently caressed the sheet-covered curve of her breast. The pain in his groin got suddenly more intense, and he was filled with a violent urge to rip the sheet away from her and force himself on her...

To fuck her until it hurt…

Yes, until it hurt so bad it fucking *killed* her!

"Fuck…*fuck!*" Tony whispered into the darkness as the violent images grew steadily sharper in his mind with every heavy throb of his pulse.

The darkness in the bedroom seemed almost alive with shifting red curtains of light.

He knew the knife was still on the floor beside the bed, sticking out of the back pocket of his jeans.

He'd been careful to hide it while they were undressing, but he knew exactly where it was.

Sighing heavily, he rolled over and let his hand hang down over the edge of the bed. An electric tingle sparked his fingertips as they brushed lightly against the knife's handle. Cold, numbing waves seemed to paralyze his arm muscles so he couldn't take his hand away.

In some crazy way, he felt as though the knife was a horrible extension of his arm, a necessary part of his hand. Something without which he wasn't complete.

When his fingers unlocked enough so he could move them, he stretched them out and took hold of the rubber handle and squeezed it so tightly spinning blue dots of light exploded in front of his eyes.

No! Jesus! You don't want to do this!

The knife blade made a long scraping sound as he slowly withdrew it from the back pocket of his pants.

Rolling over onto his back, he held the knife up close to his face. Framed by the soft glow of the streetlight shining through the windows, the blade seemed to glow with a pale, silver fire.

Tony reached out and flicked his thumb against the edge of the blade. He grunted with satisfaction at the razor sharpness of the honed edge.

Yeah, it'd do the job, all right! Quickly and cleanly.

It would slice through her skin and muscles and tendons and veins with little or no effort.

Hell, the knife would do all the work for him!

All he had to do was hold onto it, and it would do the rest.

He lay there in the dark, hardly breathing as he stared at the blade. The crazy thought occurred to him that the knife might even have a mind of its own.

Yeah, that was it!

How else could he explain the way he had found it?

It had seemed almost as if the *knife* had found *him*—as if it had been there *waiting* for him and him alone to come through the alleyway that night and find it.

It was almost as if the knife had *wanted* to be found!

Tony didn't doubt that, if he even brought it close to Sarah's neck, the blade would dart forward on its own, like a striking snake. It would seek out her carotid artery and sever it before he could even think to stop it.

And if he allowed that, the blade would thank him afterwards.

Yes, *thank* him for bathing it in the wash of her hot, vital blood.

Christ! What the fuck am I thinking?

Tony's body was rigid with tension as he twisted the knife back and forth, and stared at the blade until it seemed to be sparkling with blue fingers of energy.

You're not a killer! a voice in his mind screeched. *Get rid of that damn thing now, and stop thinking like that!*

But he couldn't stop wondering what it would be like to feel the gathering pressure in his hand, and then feel the sudden release as he drove the blade into Sarah's warm, living flesh and ripped deeper and deeper into her.

He couldn't stop wondering what it would be like to stare into the eyes of his first victim as her body slumped in his embrace, and all strength and vitality ebbed out of her body like a rushing red tide.

"No, goddamnit," Tony whispered into the night.

He was panting, his breath hissing like water being splashed onto a hot stove.

His hand was vibrating as though he were being electrocuted as he reached down beside the bed and then, forcing his fingers to open, let the knife drop.

It hit the carpeted floor with a dull *thunk* sound.

"What was that?" Sarah said, startling awake and sitting up in the bed. Her voice, speaking so suddenly and so close to him, made Tony jump.

"Jesus!" he cried out. "I didn't know you were awake!"

"I—I wasn't," Sarah said sleepily. "I thought I heard something—sounded like a door closing downstairs, or footsteps or something."

Tony could see her, sitting up and scanning the room.

"Uh—no. No," he said, trying to slow his rapidly pounding heart. "I was still awake, and I didn't hear anything."

Tony was bathed with sweat. He shivered as a cool breeze wafted over his body.

"Hey, is something the matter?" Sarah whispered, leaning forward and bringing her mouth close to his ear. "Maybe I was too much for you, huh?"

She laughed deep in her throat. "Did I give you a little too much to think about? Is that it?"

She placed one hand on his chest and began to rub ever-widening circles as she nibbled on his ear lobe.

"No, I—I was just—uh, I'm usually a pretty light sleeper, is all," he said.

Sarah slid her hand down across his belly and then, moving her fingers in delicate, lingering circles, traced a spiral path down his crotch. She took hold of him lightly at first, and then squeezed. In spite of himself, Tony felt himself getting a rock-solid erection.

"Umm..." Sarah cooed as she licked his ear passionately. "Feels to me like the little rascal might be ready for round two."

Tony was all set to tell her that he didn't feel at all like making love again, but before he could say a thing, Sarah shifted down and took him into her mouth. The sucking pressure of her lips and the soft cushion of her tongue sent waves of ecstasy surging through him. He shifted up onto his elbows and looked down at the top of her head as it bobbed up and down. The sheets made soft rustling sounds, like faint voices whispering to him. He could hear the soft grunting noises she made as she slid him deeper and deeper into her mouth with each stroke.

In spite of himself, Tony couldn't resist.

Reaching down with one hand, he wound his fingers in her dark hair like reins and guided her, up and down, up and down, letting the tingling thrill of desire roar throughout his body.

His legs stiffened and locked at the knees. His back arched. After letting her work on him a while longer, he shifted around and rolled her onto her back. Spreading her legs wide with his knees, he entered her with a sudden, violent thrust forward. As their bodies merged, and they began pumping in unison, Tony couldn't get rid of the single, sharp image that burned like white-hot metal in his mind.

He was imagining that his penis, that his entire body was gleaming like the honed edge of a knife that was ripping into Sarah, shredding her to bloody ribbons.

David had no idea what to do next.

He spent what seemed like hours, maybe even whole days and nights, trying to comfort Karen; and after a while, she did seem to settle in his arms, curling up tightly so her face was pressed against his chest. Her

RICK HAUTALA

trembling gradually subsided and then stopped. She lay still and silent in his embrace—not even breathing—but still, David felt no relief from the pressing sadness that engulfed him.

She's not even breathing!

He couldn't escape the memory of kneeling in the snow and hugging her lifeless body to him, feeling her shudder as she exhaled her final breath that turned to steam in the cold mountain air and then was whisked away.

As he held her now and stared vacantly into the twisting black shadows of night, he found himself wishing that he could cry, even if it were only a single teardrop.

He brushed his hand lightly against his daughter's cold cheek, but his sense of touch still seemed so dull that the feeling of dissociation grew almost unbearably strong. A deep, yearning ache filled him with fear when he realized how utterly *lifeless* she felt in his arms.

His mind was suddenly filled with the painful memory of her funeral, five years ago.

As if it were only yesterday, he remembered looking down at her as she lay in the small, white coffin he and Sarah had picked out for her. She was wearing a yellow lace dress, and her hands, looking so small, like tiny birds, were folded across her thin, motionless chest.

Since he couldn't see her now, in the darkness, David wondered if she was wearing the same dress she had been buried in. When he reached down and felt her clothing, rubbing his fingers over her back, his sense of touch was too distorted for him to tell with any certainty. All he could be sure of was that this wasn't a rubber raincoat, red or any other color.

In spite of the damage to her face, the funeral director had successfully restored and arranged her features in an expression David knew was supposed to look relaxed and at peace. To him, though, she had looked like she was grimacing in misery. He wondered if, in the dreary tinted daylight of the Shadowlands, her face would still show signs of the damage, or if somehow her corpus had been healed. So far, he hadn't seen her face, other than within the shadow of her hood.

With a sharp sting of memory, David recalled how both before and during the funeral, he had leaned down to kiss her on the forehead, his lips brushing against skin that felt as lifeless and cool as marble.

That's how she felt now.

Her body was as unyielding as stone.

That's because she's dead! The thought made him tremble inwardly. *We're BOTH dead!*

Beyond the sinking sadness of that thought, David also felt…something else—a deep-seated worry that gnawed at the core of his heart because of what Karen had said to him.

"My mommy's in trouble…. She's with that really bad man."

The memory of her words filled David with dread. Staring into the darkness until his vision seemed to collapse, he found that he couldn't stop thinking about—and *worrying* about—Sarah.

He had no idea who the man in the red car might have been, but there was *something* about him that David had found deeply disturbing.

He didn't think it was simply because the man was so much younger than Sarah.

It hadn't been any single thing he had seen or sensed about the man. It was more like there was a…a dark *taint* to him…some slight but undefinable indication in the way he moved or spoke or acted that set off a warning.

And Karen was worried about her, too.

David shifted uneasily, not sure if his daughter was asleep or awake. In fact, the more he thought about it, the more confused he became.

Had he slept at all last night or earlier tonight?

He wasn't sure, but he felt as though he had been in *some* kind of altered state.

But why would the dead need to sleep?

Was it merely habit, based on a lifetime of conditioning?

Or did he, even as a wraith, need a certain amount of rest?

Once again, David thought he might ask the old man about this—if he ever saw him again—but he was grateful that he hadn't seen him since this morning. He figured that, eventually, just like in life, when problems and questions arose, he'd either figure them out for himself or else make up the rules as he went.

"Should I go over to the house and check on her?" David asked. His voice sounded like a lingering sigh in the close darkness.

"Uh-huh."

The reply wasn't much more than the echo of a gasp.

"'Cause you think she's in trouble?"

"Uh-huh."

"How do you know she's even there at the house, much less in some kind of danger?"

"I was *there*, and I saw you there, too," Karen said. "Didn't you see it in the man's aura? It was as red as…as blood!"

"No, I didn't see anything. I just—I'm not used to...to being like this."

David was hesitant to use the word *dead*.

Something inside him rebelled at the idea. He wanted to believe that this was all just a dream or hallucination he was having while lying face-down beside the road after the truck or car or whatever it was hit him.

He hoped to God that he was imagining all of this; and if he was dying, he wished earnestly that he would hurry up and get it over with so the bleak agony of this experience would be over.

Yes, dear God, I want it all to be OVER!

The instant he formed that idea clearly in his mind, he felt a sudden, frigid sinking sensation in the pit of his stomach.

For a dizzying, timeless instant, a huge, black vacuum seemed to open up inside him. He could feel himself being pulled toward it like a leaf being swept away by hurricane winds.

No!...Jesus!...NO!

His mind was screaming, but the floating, tumbling feeling grew steadily stronger, tugging at him, sucking him into itself. He could feel himself expanding and dissolving, thinning out into something thinner than air, soaking into the bottomless, empty void that swirled like a tornado in the center of his being.

For an startling instant, he toyed with the idea of giving over to the feeling...of letting go and losing himself in the eternal darkness of oblivion that was threatening to engulf him.

And why not?

That's what death is all about, isn't it?

A final release...Total dissolution.

But then he heard a faint voice that didn't seem like his own thoughts. The voice gently tugged him back from the edge of infinity.

"...you have to try...you have to do something to help her..."

Somehow, David found his way out of the impenetrable blackness that filled him.

After a few more terrifying moments, each of which seemed like an eternity, the dark, crashing waves of vertigo began to subside.

Once again, he could see the faint, gray glowing rectangle of the doorway. He could feel the dead weight of his daughter in his arms, pressing against him.

Moaning softly, he slumped back against the wall, wishing that he could take a deep breath.

He very well may have, but he had absolutely no sensation of his chest moving or his lungs filling with air.

"I—I don't think you should come with me," David whispered as he raked his fingers through her hair. He wished he could find some measure of reassurance in the touch, but he still felt terribly alone. "Will you be all right, staying here alone?"

Distantly, he felt Karen nod her agreement.

He wanted to ask her where she had been spending the nights, and how she had gotten along in the Shadowlands for the last five years, but the sudden need to go back to Sarah's house and check on her was far more compelling.

He shifted away from Karen, kissed her gently on the forehead, then stood up and felt his way across the floor to the exit.

Outside, the night was dense and dark, as though the sky were filled with churning coils of black smoke. Weird, ghostly-pale lights flickered in the deepest shadows all around him, but then, just as quickly, they winked out of sight. Bracing himself for any of the unknown dangers the old man had said stalked the Shadowlands, he left the schoolhouse and started walking.

The walk to Sarah's house along the desolate streets was even more unnerving than he could have imagined. Several times he caught fleeting glimpses of other wraiths—or maybe living people—wandering alone or in small groups. He avoided contact with any of them, hiding from them when he felt he had to. He was intent on only one thing—getting back to his ex-wife's house as quickly as possible, and making sure that she was safe.

Safe from what...or who?

The gathering fear that thought generated seemed to make time and distance pass with excruciating slowness, but somehow, he eventually arrived at the house on Canal Street. The house seemed to glow in the night with an odd, shimmering purple light that was stronger than the reflected light from the nearby streetlight. David felt a dull current of dread as he looked up at the darkened bedroom windows.

"Yeah, and how the hell do I get inside?" he whispered. His voice hissed like a gentle breath of wind in the night.

Sensations of tension and gathering fear grew steadily stronger inside him as he trudged slowly up the steps to the kitchen door and looked in through the window.

The interior was filled with inky darkness, but David thought he caught a shifting motion of dark against dark, moving through the doorway into the living room.

His body was vibrating like a tuning fork as he raised both hands to the door and pressed them against the wood. All he could feel was that same muffled dullness, as though he were wearing heavy work gloves.

"Come on. *Come on!*" he whispered to himself as he stared at the door and concentrated on it.

"You're nothing. You're dead. You don't exist, so this door is nothing. It can't stop you!"

Gritting his teeth, he pushed harder against the door, but it still didn't yield. Despair and worry blossomed inside David like dark and deadly flowers.

How the hell could he affect *anything* in the living world if he was a wraith?

This is useless…absolutely useless! he thought.

But as he continued to press against the door, he got a flash of insight.

Instead of pressing harder, and thus acknowledging that the door was a solid barrier, maybe he should do the exact opposite.

Maybe he should concentrate on making that numbed sensation of touch get stronger.

Maybe he could only pass through the door if he convinced himself that it was even less solid than he was.

Closing his eyes, David allowed the deadened sensation in his hands to travel up his wrists and arms. The feeling was similar to a severe case of pins&needles, but he focused on letting it get worse instead of better. It wasn't long before he lost all sense of touch. His hands felt as though they no longer existed—that his arms ended in blunt stumps just above the wrists.

Wedging his eyes open, David was amazed to see that his hands had passed through the door.

A wave of excitement flashed through him, almost breaking his concentration, but he focused all the harder on making it feel as though his whole body didn't exist. He watched, amazed, as he pushed himself farther through the door.

Holy shit, I'm doing it!

The thought filled him with a sudden rush of discovery, the closest thing to joy he had experienced since arriving in the Shadowlands.

He closed his eyes again and tried to eliminate any sense of his body.

A thin shiver of panic ran through him when he was suddenly afraid that he might also lose the complete sense of his own identity and be swallowed up by the oblivion inside him, but—*damnit!*—he had to try!

Once again, David closed his eyes and concentrated on only one thing— moving forward without paying the slightest bit of attention to the supposed barrier of the door.

If he ended up winking out of existence…if he plummeted into the eternal blackness in the center of his soul and was lost forever, then so be it.

Strange, disturbing sensations that he couldn't even begin to describe gripped him like iron hands. He felt simultaneously as though he were immersed in frigid water and walking through a dense wall of flame.

A tiny corner of his mind was screaming that this was the end—that he was truly going to cease to exist, but he forced himself to keep moving forward.

And then, as though he had stepped instantaneously from the sweltering heat of a mid-August afternoon into the Arctic cool of an air-conditioned building, he was through.

David stumbled and almost fell when he opened his eyes and looked around to see that he was standing in the middle of Sarah's kitchen.

"Jesus Christ," he whispered.

The darkness surrounding him split his voice into dozens of echoing whispers that repeated until they gradually faded away.

David felt totally drained by the experience, and he guessed that perhaps that was why wraiths—even though they were no longer alive—needed to sleep. They needed to restore the energy they used to *do* things.

But he didn't have time to ponder this too deeply.

All he wanted to do was get upstairs and make sure Sarah was safe.

A stone-cold heaviness filled his chest as he trudged up the stairs. He didn't dare consider for long why he didn't fall through the steps. As strange and altered as existence in the Shadowlands was, he feared that, if he let go of *some* sense of reality, he would plunge into the endless, black void of oblivion.

His feet made light scuffing noises on the carpet as he walked down the short hallway to the bedroom that he and Sarah had shared until less than a year ago. He realized that he hadn't been up here since the day he'd packed up and moved to his apartment in Westbrook.

The pain of loss he felt was almost palpable.

His whole being was shaking as he approached the door and saw that it was open halfway. He stepped up close to it and looked inside.

"Oh, Jesus!" he murmured when he saw what Sarah and the young man were doing.

Deep within his chest, he could feel an agonized groan gathering strength, threatening to burst out of him. Shifting soundlessly to one side, he entered the bedroom, unable to look away as he watched the young man making love to his ex-wife.

"Sarah…oh, no, Sarah," he said, moaning as though in pain.

The light coming through the bedroom windows illuminated the young man's muscular back as he braced himself with one hand on either side of Sarah and drove his hips repeatedly forward. David could hear the dull echoes of their passionate grunts and groans. The sound of creaking bedsprings fell like hammer blows on his ears. Rage and the sharp sting of regret and loss filled him until he thought he was going to explode in rage and fury.

"Stop it, Sarah! Jesus Christ! Stop it right now!"

He shouted as loud as he could, but even to his own ears, his voice sounded flat, as though lost in the distance.

It pained him to think about how many times he and Sarah had made love in this bed. It was the same bed they had made love on the night they conceived Karen. David imagined that he could almost see a ghostly reflection of himself and Sarah writhing in ecstasy on the bed.

"Ohh…*ohhh*!" Sarah moaned.

She gripped the man's back and buried her face into the curve of his neck. She trembled as her pleasure rose, wave after wave. David caught glimpses of shimmering sheets of colored light that curled around them—subtle, shifting shades of green and blue and red that twisted and intermingled like oil and water.

He moved closer to the bed. With trembling hands, he reached out to touch Sarah, but his hands passed through her effortlessly. Agony filled him like he had never experienced before. He desperately wanted to turn and leave, but something made him stay and watch.

Was it his anger and misery? Or was it something else…

Something more?

A hint of dark motion down by his feet drew David's attention. He saw Bingley—their old cat—standing by the closet door, staring straight at him. His back was up, and his tail was puffed.

"Go on! Get outta here!" David shouted, stepping forward and waving his hands at the cat.

But Bingley did just the opposite.

Bingley's eyes widened, reflecting green in the eerie light as he hissed at David.

"What the—" the young man said, suddenly stopping and turning to look over at the half-opened bedroom door.

Raising both arms, David lunged forward and swatted at the cat while stamping his foot on the floor.

Bingley jumped into the air and took off like lightning. With a loud, trailing yowl, he leaped onto the bed and landed squarely on the young man's back.

The young man let out a piercing yell as he rolled away from Sarah and swatted with both hands at his back. In a flurry of fur and claws, Bingley hit the floor, tumbled over once, scrambled to gain traction on the carpet, and then darted out the door. The last thing David saw was Bingley's tail, puffed up to twice its size as he scurried down the stairs.

"*Jesus Christ!*" the young man shouted. "That fucking cat scratched the *shit* out of me!"

Sarah fumbled in the darkness until she found the switch for the bedside light. When she snapped it on, at least as far as David could tell, the additional light did little to dispel the murky gloom of the bedroom.

"Now, now," Sarah said, her voice low and soothing as she leaned forward and looked at the wounds. "Let's take a look at that."

The young man swung his feet to the floor. It looked to David as though he purposely kicked his discarded jeans under the bed before he sat perfectly still and angled his back to the light. Sarah grimaced as she carefully inspected the wounds. David was happy to see the man cringe when she gingerly touched him on the back.

"It's not all that bad," she said, "but I should probably put some hydrogen peroxide on it."

Moving slowly, as though chains were dragging at his feet, David walked around to the other side of the bed. He laughed out loud when he saw the deep, red gashes that raked down the man's back. A couple of them looked quite deep. The blood glowed like scarlet ribbons as it flowed down to the man's ass and soaked into the bed sheets.

Sarah suddenly stiffened and glanced over her shoulder toward where David was standing.

"What was that?" she asked, frowning as she looked around.

"The damned cat!" the man said with a snarl.

"No, I thought I heard something else," Sarah said, looking mystified.

David thought for a moment that she could see him, and he almost ducked for cover until he remembered that there was no way she could see him. He glanced over his shoulder, but all he saw was the window curtains, drifting in and out on the gentle night breeze.

"Are you gonna do something about this or not?" the young man said, scowling.

"Yeah, sure," Sarah said.

She scrambled off the bed. Still naked, she hurried out into the hallway.

Feeling a deep ache in his soul, David watched her go, wishing that there was some way he could speak to her and make her see him. He still hadn't forgotten what Karen had said about her being in danger, and he couldn't help but think that this man was the source of it.

While Sarah was out of the room, David watched the young man carefully, trying to see the "red aura" Karen had mentioned, but he couldn't see anything unusual about him.

After a moment, the young man slipped off the bed and reached down to the floor for his pants. David's first thought was that he was going to get dressed and leave, but then he saw the young man adjust something that was wrapped up inside the pants.

David moved forward, trying to see what it was.

An icy wave swept over him when he saw the black handle of a knife and a small portion of the blade.

Jesus! he whispered, and as soon as he said it, the young man tensed and looked around furtively.

He stared at exactly the spot where David was standing.

David couldn't take his gaze away from the knife. It was unlike any knife he had ever seen in his life.

The handle was dark and black, as if it had been dipped in oil. The blade seemed to glow with a sickly purple light. Even the glare of the bedroom light hardly dispelled the glow. The edge of the blade, all the way from the tip to the handle, was stained with a thick, black substance. It took David a moment to realize that this must be blood—ancient, dried blood that was still dripping in thick clots from the knife.

He watched in mute fascination as globs of the black liquid fell to the floor where they sizzled and smoked before dissolving away to nothing.

It struck him as odd that the young man seemed not to notice this as he gripped the handle and swung his arm back and forth, slicing the air with several quick slashes.

Sarah's footsteps sounded in the hall, and the young man hurriedly folded his pants back up, making sure the knife was hidden underneath them before pushing the bundle back under the bed. He straightened up on the edge of the bed and waited patiently.

Sarah entered the room with a wet washcloth in one hand and a bottle of hydrogen peroxide in the other.

Smiling, she approached the bed, looking somewhat wary of the young man.

"You know, you ought to get rid of that fucking cat," the young man said. His voice was a low, vibrating growl.

"Bingley? Oh, he's a good cat," Sarah said. "Something must've spooked him."

Sarah glanced around the bedroom again, then out into the hallway, but Bingley was nowhere to be seen. She looked like she was forcing a smile as she motioned for the young man to turn around so she could tend to his wound.

"This may sting a little," she said.

She unscrewed the bottle cap and splashed the washcloth with peroxide. The man sucked in his breath and clenched his teeth as he braced himself.

"Yeow!" he shouted, pulling away from her touch. He turned and glared at Sarah. For a flickering instant, David thought he saw a shimmering red glow surround the young man, as if his body were radiating heat; but just as fast, the light faded away, and David was left not even sure if he had seen it or not.

"Don't be such a big baby," Sarah said, chuckling softly as she gripped him by the shoulder with one hand and applied the washcloth to his back with quick dabs.

David laughed out loud again when he saw the thin streams of blood running down the young man's back turn pink.

Not dark enough, he thought, mildly surprised by the sudden violence of his thought.

He wondered if it was just because he had caught this man fucking his ex-wife, or if it was something else.

Right now, though, he didn't want to take the time to try to figure it out. He felt a need to get back to Pine Knoll Elementary and check on Karen. For now, he was content that—at least tonight—Sarah was not in any imminent danger.

Moving like wind-blown smoke, he left the bedroom and walked down the stairs. He passed through the kitchen door with must less difficulty this time, and was outside.

Without a backward glance at the house, he started walking slowly up the street. By the time he arrived back at the school, the sky was brightening with the first hint of dawn. In the thin wash of gray light, he saw to his horror that Karen was gone.

6

PREPARATIONS

Sarah figured that it was all for the best when she awoke shortly before dawn and saw that Tony was gone.

She groaned softly as she rolled over onto her back, laced her hands together behind her head, and stared up at the blank ceiling. She couldn't help but wonder if she would ever see him again, and—at least right now—she wasn't so sure she wanted to.

But then she remembered how he had made her feel last night...at least until Bingley screwed things up.

Shivering slightly, she raised her head and looked around the silent bedroom. A gauzy, gray glow was beginning to suffuse everything. A lazy, sweet-smelling breeze shifted the lacy curtains, which made faint scraping sounds as they brushed against the windowsill. Through the open window, Sarah could hear the chorus of morning birds. From somewhere far down the street, she heard footsteps and then a car door open and slam shut. The car started up and drove off, sputtering as it faded away. Then the silence fell again.

Already, the events of only a few hours ago seemed distant and strangely unreal to Sarah, as if they hadn't really happened or had been part of a dream.

A feeling of loneliness filled her, and she found herself crying as her thoughts turned to David.

She sniffed and wiped her eyes, but more tears came. She realized she'd been doing a lot of crying lately—certainly a lot more than she had after their separation. The tragedy of his death seemed to weigh down her heart like a heavy stone, rekindling the deeper grief of losing her daughter.

Sarah sighed heavily and swung her feet to the floor. When she stood up, something in her lower back popped. Stretching her arms back, she took a deep breath and twisted from side to side to loosen up. Still naked, she started down the hallway toward the bathroom; but halfway there, she stopped in her tracks.

Bingley was curled up into a tight ball on the carpeted floor at the top of the stairs. The cat narrowed his eyes to slits and shifted his head like a mechanical toy as he tracked Sarah. The cat's cool, unblinking glance made Sarah feel uncomfortable, but she forced a smile as she knelt down beside him and started scratching him behind his ears.

"So what's up with you, huh?" Sarah asked softly.

The cat started purring as he pressed his head into the warm cup of Sarah's hand. His eyes glinted like gold coins in the semi-darkness.

"Were you trying to tell me that you didn't like him? Is that it?"

Sarah tossed her head back, shook her hair, and laughed softly.

"Well, you had fair warning," she said, her voice tightening slightly as the cat's golden-eyed stare sent a tingle of fear racing through her. "He *said* that he didn't like cats. What's the matter, did you take it personally?"

Sarah continued to scratch Bingley's head until she realized that she probably should get moving. Even though it was Saturday and she didn't have to work, she had a lot to accomplish. As far as she could see, none of it was going to be either pleasant or easy.

After showering, Sarah put on her favorite faded jeans and a yellow, sleeveless T-shirt, and went downstairs to fix a light breakfast of low-fat cereal, half a poppy-seed bagel, and a small glass of grapefruit juice.

Sitting at the counter, she took a pen and clean sheet of paper from the counter drawer. She intended to jot down her plan for the day as she ate, but she knew there were only two things she *had* to get done.

First, she had to drive over to David's place in Westbrook and at least take a look around so she could start thinking about what she was going to do with everything. She had to decide which possessions to keep, and what she'd either sell, throw away, or donate to charity.

That was going to be tough enough as it was, but nowhere near as tough as going over to the Oaks Funeral Home this afternoon and meeting with Morris Green to arrange for David's funeral service and burial.

Even after five years, the memories of doing the same thing for Karen were still much too sharp and painful for Sarah to face. As she ate, tears kept welling up in her eyes. She soaked several napkins, dabbing them away. She wondered if she should call Cindy or Ruth or another of her friends and ask them to come with her, just in case things got too emotional; but she decided against it, telling herself that she could handle it. After you bury your only child, you pretty much should be able to face anything else.

By the time she left the house, the sun was up and blazing. It looked like a swollen, red ball, suspended above the heat-hazed city skyline. Back Bay looked as flat as beaten pewter. A few early morning joggers were out, obviously hoping to beat the worst of the heat, but the morning sky was already dense with humidity. Across the narrow bay, the Casco Bank building flashed the time and temperature. Any relief the thunderstorm might have brought last night was gone.

Sarah found the heat oppressive just walking down to her car. It didn't take long before her armpits were damp with sweat. Morning dew speckled the car's windshield like beads of mercury. Sarah started up her car and turned on her windshield wipers to wipe the moisture away before backing out of the driveway. She clicked on the car's air conditioner, hoping to God it would kick in fast.

There wasn't much traffic this early in the morning, and Sarah caught mostly green lights as she headed out Forest Avenue, so the drive to Westbrook took less than fifteen minutes. The chimney stacks of the paper mill in Westbrook were spewing white funnel-shaped columns of exhaust into the air, but the heavy atmospheric inversion held the vapors down. The stench of rotten eggs and sour milk was almost overpowering. Across from the mill, Sarah turned left onto Brown Street, rounded the corner past St. Mark's Cathedral, and pulled to a stop at the curb in front of David's apartment building.

A wave of sadness swept through her when she looked up at the building where David had been living ever since they separated. The building was painted a sickly yellow that David had always described as "baby-shit gold." It looked sticky and wet in the morning light. A rolled-up newspaper, drenched with dew, lay on the walk halfway up to the front steps. Remembering what David had told her about this neighborhood, Sarah made sure she locked the car after she got out.

Gripping her key ring tightly in her fist, she started up to the front door, carefully stepping over the rolled-up newspaper as if it were a sleeping dog. All the while, she had the discomforting feeling that someone was watching her, but when she looked around, she couldn't see anyone peering out of any windows at her. The entire neighborhood seemed depressed and drowsy in the thick humidity.

Sarah hadn't been to David's apartment very often—only two or three times that she could remember. After she had initiated divorce proceedings, she and David hadn't been able to spend any amount of time together without ending up in a shouting match. Mostly, she thought, he started the arguments, but she had never hesitated to jump in and defend herself. Even their occasional telephone calls quickly turned hostile. She did have a key to his apartment, though. He'd always said that she would need it, in case he got hurt or died.

Well, by Jesus, I guess that's how it turned out!

That thought made her eyes fill with warm tears.

She might have gotten used to not having any more romance in her life, but still—the realization that the man she had loved once upon a time, the man who had fathered her only child, was now dead was almost overwhelming.

Wiping her eyes with the heels of her hands, she braced herself before letting herself in through the front door.

As soon as she stepped across the threshold and closed the heavy door behind her, she let out a loud gasp. The building reeked of an indescribable stench that seemed to be a mixture of three-day-old fish, stale cigarette smoke, boiled cabbage, and something else—something wet and rotting.

As she started cautiously up the narrow, rickety flight of steps to the second floor landing, the sound of creaking floorboards set her teeth on edge. She tried to tip-toe down the dim hallway to David's door.

His name was written on a cracked and fading embossed red plastic label, which was stuck to the door marked 2-B with tarnished brass numerals.

"Two-B or not two-B."

Sarah chuckled grimly to herself as she recalled the joke David used to make about his apartment number, about how it was *perfect* for a writer! She fit the key into the tarnished door lock, but before opening it, she sighed heavily and leaned her head against the door panel. It was cool, almost cold to the touch.

"Well, Davy," she whispered under her breath. "I guess you chose *not* to be, huh?"

She turned the key slowly and, with some effort, the door lock clicked. Gritting her teeth, she twisted the doorknob.

The door hinges chattered like a braying mule, setting her teeth on edge as she pushed the door open and entered.

The instant she stepped into the apartment, a sudden rush of shivers ran through her. Sarah hugged herself as if she were outside on a January morning. After taking a moment to collect herself, she shut the front door, making sure the lock clicked shut. Just to be on the safe side, she also slid the safety chain into position.

The apartment was cool and dark and, not surprisingly, very clean. David had always been a much better housekeeper than she had been. It had turned into something of a joke among their friends. The furniture, most of which was older pieces he had salvaged from their attic, was dusted and neatly arranged. The floor and threadbare carpet looked as though they had been vacuumed just this morning. All of his published books and every collection and magazine in which he had a short story were neatly arranged on the mantle.

In the kitchen, there were no dirty dishes in the sink. All the plates, glasses, cups, and silverware had been washed and neatly stacked in the plastic dish drainer.

He must have done that sometime before going out for his late-night walk.

An aching sadness tightened like a hand around Sarah's heart.

Trembling inside, she left the kitchen and walked down the short hallway to David's bedroom.

The bed was made, and all of David's clothes were neatly folded and put away. The only thing that might constitute a mess was the stack of books and magazines on the small table beside the bed.

Sarah glanced at a few of the titles, not at all surprised to see that David's reading habits hadn't changed much in the last few months. There were several mystery and suspense novels, including the latest books by James Lee Burke, F. Paul Wilson, and Dean Koontz, along with tattered copies of *Scientific American*, *Playboy*, *Ellery Queen*, and *Cemetery Dance*. Sarah cringed when she looked at the cover of *Cemetery Dance*, which depicted a rotting corpse strung with barbed wire, crucifixion-style against a fence post in the middle of a vast, yellowing corn field.

David's desk was over by the window that looked out over a shadowed back alley. The desk was barely large enough to hold the computer keyboard and a monitor. A small laser printer covered by a plastic dust cover was on a rickety card table beside the desk. Paper scrolled into the printer, but there was nothing coming out of it.

A chill gripped Sarah's insides as she walked over to the keyboard and stared at the monitor's blank screen. After a while, her eyes began to shift in and out of focus. She couldn't help but wonder what—if anything—David had been working on before he died. She was tempted to switch on the machine to see, but stopped herself, feeling as though that would somehow be an invasion of privacy.

"Not that it matters anymore," she whispered.

It would be just as well if anything he'd been working on was left alone.

The cold, gnawing sensation in her stomach grew steadily stronger as she brushed her fingertips lightly across the keyboard. Suddenly a loud *snap* followed by a high, crackling sound made her jump back. A soft, electronic hum grew louder as the fan inside the computer began to whirl. After a few seconds, the monitor lit up. After running through the initial setup, the computer screen displayed an opening menu.

Sarah's heart was beating fast and high as she backed away from the machine, all the while staring at it in amazement.

She was sure she hadn't pressed the power button.

Maybe David had the machine rigged to turn on automatically or something.

"What the hell?" she whispered when she noticed the message flashing at the top of the screen:

...YOU HAVE 1 E-MAIL LETTER(S) WAITING...

The temperature in the apartment seemed instantly to drop several degrees.

Sarah glanced out the window above the desk and noted that, at least at this time of day, this side of the building was shaded, but that didn't account for the sudden decrease in temperature she felt. There wasn't a fan running, and the air conditioner wasn't on; nevertheless, a cool breeze was gently wafting over her back, making the hairs at the nape of her neck stir.

Covering her mouth with one hand and nibbling nervously on the knuckle of her forefinger, Sarah shook her head as though trying to clear water from her ear.

Suddenly curious, she approached the desk. Her hand was shaking as she reached out and quickly switched off the machine. The screen crackled as it went blank. The computer's internal fan slowed down with a soft *whir* and then stopped.

Maybe the fan inside the machine was making that breeze, she thought, but she wasn't convinced.

For several seconds, she just stood there, holding her breath, nibbling her knuckle, and staring at the computer. She had no idea how the machine could have switched on by itself.

Maybe there had been a sudden power surge, or there might be a defect in wiring or in the power switch.

She wondered if she should unplug the computer so it wouldn't get damaged if it turned on by itself again after she was gone, but she was too afraid to touch the computer again.

"Jesus, don't be ridiculous," she whispered to herself. "It's just a goddamned machine!"

But that didn't do any good.

Her courage failed her.

Backing up slowly, her hand still covering her mouth so she wouldn't scream, Sarah left David's bedroom.

Once outside the bedroom door, she walked quickly through the living room to the front door. Her hands felt cold and clammy as she fumbled to unlock it. She was just about to leave when she turned for one last look around.

She couldn't account for the sudden nervous feeling that had gripped her. It might just be that the sadness she felt for David was starting to sink in. Seeing his apartment and his work space, and knowing that he'd never come back here to live and work again filled her with the sadness of regret and loss.

But—somehow—it seemed more than that.

The sense of imminent danger in the apartment was almost palpable. Sarah could practically see it floating like a gray haze of smoke in the air all around her.

Besides, she didn't need to stay here long.

She had a pretty good idea what she would do with everything. All of David's clothes and most of his household items would go to the Salvation

Army and Goodwill. She didn't need or want any of the old furniture, even the portable color TV and the VCR he had set up in the living room. She might take a quick look through his books and magazines, but her and David's reading tastes had always been dissimilar. Whenever she found time to read, which hadn't been very often lately, she preferred romances and historical novels.

The only real concern she had was what to do with David's computer.

She knew that it was less than a year old. It was much too valuable simply to throw or give away. She might be able to use it at home, but she had no idea what she should do about all of David's files that still must be on the hard drive.

It would be a pity simply to erase them all, especially without reading through them first.

David's writing had pretty much been his whole life—his *only* real involvement, it seemed to her, at least before Karen was born. After encouraging him through the first two or three novels, Sarah had admitted to him one day that she never really liked any of his books or stories because they were all so dark and violent, particularly the four he'd written following Karen's death.

She was sure she wasn't up to the task of reading through any of his old files. Then again, she didn't know anyone she could ask—or trust—to do it for her, either.

She just wasn't up to doing it, at least not yet.

"I'll deal with it later," she muttered as she stepped out into the hallway and yanked the door shut. She jiggled the doorknob, making sure the door was securely locked before she walked away. She'd already sent Sam Lowell a check for this month's rent, so the place was covered at least until the end of July. If she had to pay rent for another month or two until she found the time and courage to clean it out, she was pretty sure Lowell wouldn't mind—as long as her checks didn't bounce. All she had to remember to do on Monday or Tuesday, depending on which day she chose for David's funeral, was call the electric and water companies, and tell them to switch off service to the apartment, and send her a final bill.

Sarah's footsteps echoed in the stairwell as she walked down to the first floor, and once again she had the feeling that someone was watching her.

She sighed when she stepped outside into the blistering heat of the day. The sun was still lost in a gray heat haze that made the world appear to be underwater. The instant blast of warmth chased away the bone-deep chill she'd felt in David's apartment, but she still felt as though something wasn't quite right…as if she were forgetting or missing something that was so obvious.

In the church parking lot across the street, several boys, most of them shirtless and wearing shorts, were playing stickball, using scraps of cardboard and wood for bases. On the corner next to a small "mom and pop" store, some older kids, teenagers with skateboards, were hanging out, smoking cigarettes and swearing loudly with every other word as they joked around. Several of them eyed Sarah suspiciously as she hurried down the walkway to her car. With fretful glances down the street to make sure they weren't moving toward her, she unlocked the car door, got in, and started it up.

As she drove away, she decided that the next time she came over here, she would ask one of her male friends to come along with her.

Maybe she'd even ask Tony…if she ever saw him again.

David was filled with powerful, conflicting emotions.

Cold, black agony clashed with sudden surges of terrible anger as he watched Sarah leave his apartment, practically running down the stairs and out to her car.

He was tormented, wondering if she had in any way sensed his presence, and he wondered if she was now afraid of the place.

As soon as she slammed the door shut behind her, and he listened to her jiggle the lock back and forth, he knew that he could have followed after her, but he chose not to. He wondered if he had gotten down to the street before she drove off, if he actually could have ridden in the car with her, but he was too exhausted to follow after her. What he needed was to stay here for a while and rest.

After arriving back to Pine Knoll Elementary last night, and seeing that Karen was missing, he'd been nearly frantic with fear. He wasn't sure why, but he had felt compelled to come back to his apartment.

He didn't know how to find his daughter. He had no idea where to start looking or what to do. He was positive that he had told Karen to stay where she was and wait for him, so all he could assume was that she was in some kind of danger.

Maybe serious danger.

What if someone—perhaps that old man with the bad left leg, or one of the other wraiths lurking nearby—had found her alone in the schoolhouse and had kidnapped her?

David had no doubt that the dangers in the Shadowlands were very real; but he'd lost his daughter once before, and he was determined not to let that happen again!

Before he could think of a plan of action, though, as the sun was rising in the east, turning the sky gun-metal gray and pushing the shadows back into the farthest corners of the school, he had been filled with the sudden, almost overwhelming compulsion to return to his apartment in Westbrook.

He couldn't explain it.

It was almost as if someone—or something—was calling him back, luring him.

The deep sense of loss he was feeling for his old life and his work as a writer was almost too much to bear, but this felt like it was more than that. It was much too powerful to ignore.

It was several miles from Pine Knoll Elementary to the apartment building on Brown Street, but David had already noticed how time and distance could play tricks on him. At times it seemed as though the more anxious he was to get somewhere or do something, the longer it seemed to take.

That was the important word.

Seem.

Everything he had experienced since regaining consciousness in the Shadowlands had all *seemed* so subjective.

There weren't any rules, at least as far as he could tell. Whatever rules applied to the living world certainly didn't work here. He wondered if it was simply a matter of learning the new rules…or if he could make up his own rules.

The sky was gray with haze when he started out for Westbrook. The leaves on the trees hung lifelessly from the branches. The air seemed dense, almost like being underwater. What few sounds David heard were muffled and distant-sounding. He could tell, just by the way things looked, that the day was hot and humid, but he had no physical sensation of it.

As he walked, he forced himself to remain as calm as possible. He wasn't sure how long the walk to Westbrook had taken, but when he arrived at his apartment, the sun, which had broken through the haze, seemed only fractionally higher in the sky than when he had started.

He had been inside his apartment, simply standing there, lost in his own thoughts as he looked around, enjoying the soft gray silence, when Sarah arrived.

Passing through doors and walls was no longer a problem. All it seemed to require was a strong effort of will and an intense focus and, before he knew it, he was through whatever barrier he wanted to pass. It was a little like using a part of his mind or maybe even parts of his body in a way he had never thought possible or been able to before. He felt a slight stirring of elation at the discovery of this new talent, but that feeling was quickly replaced by surprise, anger, and a painful twinge of envy for the living when he saw the apartment door open and Sarah enter.

He had watched silently, walking along beside her as she moved through the apartment, looking around. He guessed she was taking inventory of his possessions before cleaning everything out. It was only when she walked into his bedroom and walked over to his computer that he decided that he had to try to contact her.

"Sarah," he called out.

His voice had less substance than the sputtering sound a candle makes when it is blown out.

"Please, Sarah...why can't you hear me?...I'm standing right here beside you."

He made a grab at her, but his hands passed through her with no resistance. He wondered why it was so difficult to touch a living person when the rest of reality, even the pale reflection of the living world he could see, seemed so substantial.

Shivering inside, he watched as Sarah idly brushed her fingers across the computer keyboard. The faint clicking sounds the keys made rang like heavy hammer blows in David's ears.

As he watched her, he could tell that she was thinking about him. It was more than her expression or body posture. There seemed to be a direct electrical charge coming from her and filling him with subtle, unseen energy. Strong jolts of pure emotion and vitality zipped through him, but these quickly shifted to bleak desperation when he reached out again and tried to touch her.

Once again, he called her name, but she didn't respond. He wanted so badly to touch her, but she seemed totally unaware of his presence.

Then he got an idea.

If there was electricity passing between them, then maybe he could alter the flow of electricity in the living world. Maybe that's what his corpus was made of.

Reaching past her, he focused every bit of mental energy into the tip of his forefinger. He almost laughed with joy when he reached out and actually felt the slight but very solid resistance of the power button under his finger.

Staring inwardly at the eternal blackness that swirled in the center of his heart, he concentrated and tried to push the button.

It seemed to take forever, and the effort was absolutely exhausting him, but—finally—he heard the button click. The computer switched on with a low, vibrating hum.

David watched with a mixture of amazed satisfaction and hopelessness when Sarah jerked back and stared as the computer ran through its opening menu screens. A sudden fear gripped him when she stared at the screen for a moment and frowned.

"No!" David shouted as loud as he could when he saw her reaching for the power button.

He thought he detected a slight shiver run through Sarah, but he couldn't tell for sure. The energy he had felt pouring into him from her suddenly shut off. A shimmering black curtain like a cloud seemed to hover around her.

"No, please!...Please don't turn it off!...I'll write you a message!...Wait!...*Please!"*

David made a desperate grab for her hand, hoping to stop her, but Sarah snapped the power button, and the computer screen winked off. The crackle of diminishing energy in the air was as loud as a roll of thunder. He felt it prickle his corpus like pins&needles.

Filled with sudden frustration and waves of rage, David tried once again to focus his energy to turn the machine back on, but he knew it was futile. He was much too exhausted from the effort of turning it on the first time. He watched, sighing helplessly as Sarah backed out of the bedroom, walked to the front door, and left, locking the door behind her.

David would have followed, but he was completely drained of strength. The night had long since passed, but there had been no rest for him. Even knowing that Karen was missing, and wanting desperately to find her again, he could hardly move.

Besides, it was restful, here in the shadowed gloom of his apartment.

Restful and as quiet as a tomb.

David moaned softly to himself as he leaned against the wall and slid into a huddled heap on the floor. Closing his eyes didn't do any good. It didn't matter if they were open or closed; he still saw the same thing. He watched, entranced as thoughts and emotions took shape in his mind and exploded with frightening visual effects.

It's too late...too late for anything!

Turmoil raged like a beast inside his mind.

My life...my work...anyone I've ever loved...anything and everything I ever could have done is gone...gone forever....

Once again, the cold void of impenetrable darkness churned inside him, threatening to claim him.

Filled with utter despair, David let himself slip closer and closer to the darkness behind his eyes. He would have let himself be carried away if it hadn't been for one single, simple, pure thought that burned with the brightness of an acetylene torch. A voice that didn't even sound like his own mental voice kept whispering in his mind—*Before you go...you have to see Karen...just one last time...*

Tony had never really liked night and darkness, but right now darkness served his purposes.

Since leaving Sarah's house sometime in the predawn stillness, he'd been alternately filled with rage, frustration, and jealousy.

The rage was perhaps the easiest for him to understand.

His back still stung from the claw marks Sarah's cat had left. They sliced at an angle from the top of his left shoulder to the middle center of his back. It had hurt like hell when Sarah cleaned the cuts with hydrogen peroxide and bandaged them. Tony was positive that he could feel the infection spreading like a brush fire, inflaming every nerve in his back, neck, and shoulders.

But he told himself to bottle up all of the pain and rage because he wasn't going to let matters just sit there the way they were.

Oh, no.

He was going to *do* something about that, by Jesus!

That's why, about an hour after sunset, he'd left his car parked in a restaurant's parking lot on Forest Avenue and walked the mile or so down the street to Sarah's house.

The frustration he felt was the result of other, more complex things, particularly his embarrassment at his own sexual performance last night.

True, Sarah had *seemed* satisfied, and she had told him repeatedly that he made her feel things she hadn't felt in a *long* time and, in fact, had begun to wonder if she would ever feel again.

But Tony prided himself on his sexual staying power, and last night...he wasn't so sure about last night.

Maybe it had been too much wine before getting down to business.

Or maybe his own nervousness that he was actually in bed with Sarah had gotten in the way of his performance. Maybe he'd been intimidated because she was so much older than he was.

Or maybe there were other, less definable things.

Whatever it was, Tony didn't think he had performed the way he should have even before that goddamned cat screwed things up. He wished Sarah was home right now so he could go in there and *show* her.

But there would be time for that, too.

He'd show her what kind of lover he really was!

The jealousy was probably the most difficult thing for Tony to understand.

Although he was a bright and very personable man, he wasn't exactly introspective. Long ago, through the trials of his own childhood and adolescence, he had convinced himself that *feelings* only got in the way of success, particularly for anyone who wanted to be a successful lawyer.

But something last night had filled him with an aching sense of his own lack of worth or ability. He'd thought about it all day while working at the restaurant, but he couldn't pin it down.

Maybe it was as simple as feeling jealous because Sarah had been married before he met her.

It wasn't as though Tony hadn't fucked a married woman or two in the past, but last night had seemed...*different*, somehow.

He wasn't sure how or what it was, and he wasn't sure he cared to know, as long as what he *did* about it got *rid* of it!

In fact, the more he thought about it, the more he felt as though there had been another person in bed with him and Sarah.

While they'd been drinking wine in the living room, before they went to the bedroom, she had told him that her ex-husband had died recently. She didn't specify exactly how recently or how he had died, but that had put a blanket over everything. The entire time they were fucking and, especially, afterwards, once she had bandaged his wounds and he was getting dressed to go home, he'd had the distinct impression that she was still emotionally attached to her ex-husband and that she had been completely shattered by his death.

There weren't many things Tony knew for sure, but one of them was that you could never, *never* compete with a dead person for someone's affections.

No, not with a dead man!

He'd already tried that once before with his mother when he was thirteen, and his father died on an air mission over Vietnam. Once his father died—a hero, defending his country—there was no time or emotion left for little Tony.

So now, as he clung to the shadows outside Sarah's house on this humid summer evening, Tony was more bothered than confused by the conflicting thoughts and emotions inside him.

He knew that he had to *do* something. He had to strike out, and maybe not just at Sarah, but at the whole fucking world!

Swirls of darkness filled his vision whenever he squeezed his eyes shut and tried to force himself to stop thinking and feeling. But it had never worked for him in the past, even when he was thirteen years old, and he didn't expect it to work for him now. The only thing that made him feel even marginally better was when he reached under his shirt to his hip pocket and felt the hard rubber handle of the knife. Even the slightest brushing touch against the knife's handle filled him with an indescribable energy and a feeling of purpose that he couldn't even begin to understand or explain.

Not that he wanted to.

The knife made him feel powerful, and he had a pretty good idea he knew why.

If life is a mystery, and death is the doorway, then the long-bladed knife he had found in the alleyway the other night was the key to unlocking the door.

And he intended to try it out.

Tonight!

The blade was practically crying out for blood!

Ever since he had found it, Tony couldn't understand why it felt so good when he held it. He received an almost electric charge when he pressed his thumb against the metal thumb rest and slashed the air with the blade. He reveled in the rush of scarlet images that filled his mind and imagined the power of life and death that it wielded.

The key to the doorway between life and death.

Chuckling softly to himself, Tony stepped out of the shadows. As he was starting up the side steps, a car rounded the corner onto Canal Street. For a blinding instant, the pale wash of headlights froze him in mid-step, like a deer caught in the sudden glare.

If that's Sarah, I'm fucked! he thought, shivering in spite of the humid night. But the headlights swept over him, and the car passed down the street without any hesitation.

Tony stared after the car to make sure it was gone. Chances were that the driver, whoever it was, hadn't noticed him.

And even if he had, so what?

Tony reached under his shirt and slowly withdrew the knife, squeezing the handle so tightly the palm of his hand began to ache.

But he smiled.

This was a *good* ache...

A *comforting* ache.

It was the kind of ache that he knew could only be satiated when he saw the blade slice into warm flesh and release a gush of hot, vital lifeblood.

And he knew just where he was going to start.

With his other hand, Tony took a small plastic bag from his shirt pocket and shook it open. He wrinkled his nose at the rank smell of the fish fillet he had stolen from the restaurant earlier today. He laughed softly as he knelt down in the shadow of the porch and clicked his tongue several times.

"Here Bingley. Com'on, kitty, kitty," he called out into the night.

His hand holding the knife was trembling terribly, as though a steady electric current were trickling through him.

"Here kitty, kitty, kitty…"

As Tony glanced around into the surrounding darkness, he thought he caught a reflection of bright blue light glancing from the long blade. His smile widened until it started to hurt his cheeks.

The moon was lost behind the haze. Not even the slightest breeze stirred the humid night. Tony listened to the sounds of traffic passing in the distance. Closer to the house, but lost in the darkness, he could hear crickets buzzing and the soft rustle of insect wings, like short, breathy whispers against his ear. He realized with a start that he had a rock-hard erection.

Still kneeling and looking around, he opened the plastic baggie wider and waved it about, fanning the strong aroma into the night.

"Com'on kitty, kitty," he called softly. "I have a special treat for you."

A sudden shifting of motion at the end of the porch caught his attention. He felt his body tense as he squeezed the knife handle. Spinning white dots of light tracked like comets across his vision, so Tony couldn't see very well, but he knew that it *had* to be Bingley.

Clicking his tongue softly as he wrinkled his nose against the strong stench of fish, he carefully dumped the fish onto the porch floor.

Still using a high-pitched, pleasant-sounding voice, he called out, "Come on, Bingley. Come and get it, you furry little fuck."

7

BURIAL

Two days later, David couldn't figure out why he felt a sudden, urgent need to go back out to Riverside Cemetery. Until he found out otherwise, he desperately hoped that it was because Karen was there, waiting for him.

After spending close to twenty-four hours at his old apartment, recuperating and losing himself in the pure, unbroken silence, he had spent the next two days—Sunday and Monday—and most of the nights searching the Shadowlands for Karen. More times than he cared to count or could remember, he searched the area around Pine Knoll Elementary, Riverside Cemetery, Sarah's house, and the Brighton Avenue Park where he had first seen her.

All to no avail.

He had no idea where else she might go.

Although he encountered numerous other wraiths, many of them in small groups that he approached and questioned about Karen, none of them would say if they had seen her.

At least none of them would *admit* to it.

David got the distinct impression from several of them that they weren't being entirely honest with him. He couldn't help but notice how most of the wraiths he encountered acted extremely furtive or skittish around him. A few even appeared to be genuinely afraid when he approached them. One wraith—a young man with a horribly mutilated face—muttered something about the "death-mark" David carried on him, but David had no idea what he was talking about.

David spent at least part of each night huddled in Pine Knoll Elementary, alone and afraid. He couldn't help but be frightened more for Karen than for himself.

He couldn't stop thinking about how, when he was alive, he had contemplated suicide—almost daily, in fact—following his daughter's death.

He wished he was able to cry as he took a quick mental tally of his failed life.

He'd destroyed his marriage, for one.

He'd lost his daughter through what he saw as largely his own negligence, for another.

And he had been trying with steadily diminishing success to patch together a writing career that had been floundering ever since it had started.

He had no friends to speak of, at least locally, so there was no one he could have talked to about what he'd been going through.

How many areas of his life did he have to fuck up and lose before he finally lost the will to live and found the courage to cash in his chips?

Three strikes and you're out, buddy!

He had wanted to die, and he had gotten his wish.

He was beginning to think—or at least hope—that here in the Shadowlands he might be able to accomplish the same thing.

If only he dared to let himself slip into the endless void that he could feel at the core of his being—that cold, limitless black nothingness that called to him, continually pulled at him, dragging him down…deeper and deeper…into…

Oblivion!

"No!" David said in a harsh whisper that joined the chorus of voices and laughter inside the schoolhouse.

He wasn't going to give in to it.

Not yet!

Not until he found Karen or at least learned what had happened to her.

On Tuesday morning, when he awoke shortly before dawn and felt a strong impulse to go out to Riverside Cemetery, he decided to follow his instinct and go there immediately.

Maybe Karen's there…maybe she's haunting her own grave…maybe she's trying to reach out to her mother…or find me….

It was almost too much to hope for, but he couldn't stand the thought of his daughter being alone and afraid in this terrifying realm of existence.

The anxiety he felt made his journey out to the cemetery seem to take forever.

The sun was just coming up over the city when he started out. The day looked to be much brighter and cooler than it had been for the last few days, but David couldn't feel a thing. His last memory of any physical sensation was how sticky and humid the night air had been the night he died. But now the sunlight was high and strong. It lit the world with a vibrant yellow glare that made it appear as though he were wearing yellow-tinted sunglasses. The leaves of the trees, while still looking pallid and gray, fluttered in a gusting wind that David wished to God he could feel on his face.

As he walked along the roadside, contemplating how much he missed the warmth of the sun on his face and the sweet smell of growing things, he was filled with a deep, inexpressible sadness. He decided that being deprived of any sensations—even the physical aspects of the emotions he was feeling—was a perfect definition of "Hell."

David was so involved with his own thoughts that he barely noticed the solid line of cars that streamed past him as he approached the cemetery. All of the cars had their headlights on and were moving in a slow, stately procession. He finally took note of them when they pulled in at the cemetery gate, slithering around the curve in the road like a huge, black snake. Thin dust that glittered like flecks of gold in the slanting rays of the sun rose in their wake.

"Must be a funeral," David muttered to himself, but he barely spared a thought for the poor person who had died and was being buried today.

Without even thinking about it, he passed easily through the stone wall that surrounded the cemetery. It was only when he was cutting across the cemetery lawn, passing like a wisp of gray smoke between the trees and marble headstones, that he looked up and saw that the funeral procession had stopped at the base of the hill where Karen was buried.

"Oh, shit," he whispered.

A fear that he didn't dare identify gripped him.

A cold uneasiness filled him as he drew to a stop beneath the shade of a tall maple tree and watched as the mourners parked their cars and got out. The sound of car doors opening and slamming shut sounded like the dull popping of distant gunfire in the still morning.

The mourners, looking themselves like ghosts, moved silently up to the crest of the hill. Some of them walked hand in hand. Most of them bowed their heads, and all of them spoke in hushed tones. A group of young men wearing black suits, none of whom David recognized, opened the back door of the hearse and pulled out the long, dark mahogany box. Their knees buckled and their shoulders sagged as they hefted the weight.

The gnawing fear inside David grew steadily stronger, but he tried to keep the stark, terrifying realization at bay.

No! That can't be ME in there!

There were mostly young to middle-aged men and women attending. Some of them were alone; some were in couples. A few had one or more children. Even in the summer heat, almost everyone was wearing dark suits or dresses. As David watched the people stream up the rise to the area next to Karen's grave, he had the distinct impression that some of those attending were wraiths, moving about unseen by the living mourners. Like ghouls, they seemed to be enjoying the spectacle of another funeral— another member joining their ranks. Several times one or more of the people looked down the hill to where David was standing in the sun-dappled shadows. One of them—an old woman David thought he recognized but wasn't sure from where—waved a thin hand at him, signaling for him to approach.

Filled with caution, and feeling a cold darkness grip the center of his chest, David stepped out into the sunlight and started up the hill. His body looked insubstantial in the blazing summer sun. He felt both wary and tense because he knew for certain that this was *his* funeral!

When he was halfway up the hill, he stopped short in his tracks as though he had walked into a solid, invisible wall. He finally recognized the old woman who was beckoning to him.

It was Mrs. Burke, his second-grade teacher. She had died more than fifteen years ago!

Shaking his head, he took a step backwards in spite of the angry glare Mrs. Burke gave him.

David cried out loud, a low, tortured moan, when he saw Sarah. She was wearing a black ankle-length dress and was standing close to Karen's tombstone. The fingers of her left hand were brushing lightly against the polished pink marble as though she didn't quite know what to do with her hands.

As the men carrying the coffin approached, she bowed her head slightly and clasped her hands tightly in front of her. David could see, beneath the black veil she was wearing, that her face was slick with tears, but he had the distinct impression that she was thinking just as much about Karen as she was about him. He could no longer feel that subtle, invisible charge of energy coming from her that he had felt a few days ago in his old apartment.

If he could have cried, he would have.

Avoiding Mrs. Burke, he slowly approached the group, certain that some of them, at least, could see him. He got close enough to the hole in the ground to look down into it. The gaping, rectangular hole looked flat and black, like a doorway leading…someplace else. A pile of dirt and thick clumps of sod covered by a tarp were stacked neatly over to one side. At the head of the hole were several arrangements of white and red flowers adorned with ribbons that fluttered in the gentle breeze.

"Oh, Jesus," David muttered. "Oh, *Jesus!*"

In the pressing silence, his voice sounded with a hollow echo, like a sudden rush of cold wind. Several of the mourners closest to him turned and looked around, frowning curiously. Mrs. Burke clicked her tongue and shook his head, making him feel once again like an unruly schoolboy. Another one of the mourners looked steadily at him while nodding his head in silent acknowledgment.

The minister—Reverend Harry Grant, from the Lutheran church in Portland that Sarah and Karen attended—was reading from the open Bible in his hands. His voice was lost in the high-pitched rushing sound that swirled like tugging hands all around David.

It took a long while for the impact of what was happening to sink in as David glanced at the faces of the people who had gathered.

He recognized most of them, but not all.

There were friends and relatives, many of whom he hadn't seen or spoken to in years. He saw a few local writers and other "book people" he knew from around town. Mrs. Abbiati from the Warren Library, who had always been so supportive of his books, was there. Her eyes were swollen and her cheeks were flushed red from crying. The biggest surprise was that Bill Relling, his literary agent, had actually bothered to fly up from New York. David figured he had to be on vacation, because the commission from his last novel sale certainly wouldn't have covered airfare.

David's insides were wrenched with sadness, but he also found it slightly amusing that all of these people, many of whom seemed not to have given him a second thought when he was alive, were now gathered to see him buried.

Oily, black waves of fear and grief and anger washed through him when he finally found the courage to look squarely at the coffin that was resting on cloth-draped supports next to the open grave. Sunlight glinted like white fire from the brass handles and fixtures, leaving trailing afterimages in his vision. He could hear the wood creaking and snapping as it heated up in the sun.

Jesus! How can I really be the one who's shut up inside that box?

The thought made the blackness inside him surge with almost unbearable strength. For a dizzying instant, David imagined that—right now—he *really was* inside that closed box, staring up with lifeless eyes at the solid wall of eternal darkness that surrounded him. No matter how much he tried to resist, he could feel himself being sucked into the bottomless well of darkness inside him.

Maybe that's it after all! A tight thrill of terror filled him. *Maybe as soon as my coffin's lowered into the ground and covered with dirt, I'll just fade away...dissolve into nothingness.*

Maybe I'm only hanging around like these other wraiths I've seen until I'm six feet under, and then I'll move on to the next level...whatever it may be.

Feeling both fascination and dread throb through him, he watched as the pallbearers shifted the coffin onto the lowering mechanism. The minister took a handful of dirt and sprinkled it onto the coffin. Once again, David had the distinct impression that he was lying *inside* the coffin, listening to the dirt rattle on the wood like rain on a metal roof.

Then they began to lower the coffin into the ground.

Each *click* of the ratchet felt like a hot spike being driven into David's head. His vision blurred and then shattered into a million hazy fragments that merged and separated like a kaleidoscope as he watched the wooden box containing his last mortal remains lowered slowly out of sight.

click...

Click...

CLICK!...

Down into the pure, impenetrable darkness of eternity.

The fear was too much to bear.

David slouched forward and covered his face with both hands as he let out a long, agonized wail that warbled crazily up and down the scale. Even with his hands shielding his eyes, he was able to see the faces of the mourners floating like pale, bloated balloons in the darkness behind his eyes. Their eyes were open wide and unblinking, spearing him with their lifeless stares. Their mouths gaped open. Their thin lips moved as though they were trying to tell him something, but their voices were so low, and the words they spoke came so slowly, that whatever they were saying was lost in an incomprehensible babble of voices.

Strong, trembling, surges of darkness passed through David like earthquakes. The whole world—inside and outside his head—was spinning out of control. It no longer mattered if his eyes were opened or closed—he knew he would be staring into the same eternal blackness...

Forever.

David had the sudden feeling that his body was lighter than a feather and was spreading out, thinning until he was less substantial than the air.

Powerful, irresistible forces took hold of his soul and stretched him out in all directions at once.

"...trusting in the strength of the Lord...assured that David is now at peace with the Lord...so as we commit his earthly remains to the ground...believing in the resurrection of the body and the life everlasting..."

These words, which he barely heard, much less understood, echoed all around him and—somehow—cut through the raging confusion he was feeling and drew him back, screaming, from the edge of the void.

Clenching waves of nausea gripped him, but he knew that these were not physical sensations. His mind was trying desperately to process and accept the pure emotion of this ultimate loss.

He was dead!...Forever!

Vibrating pulses of red and violet light throbbed in his vision when he opened his eyes to look at the gathered mourners.

A cold shock hit him when he saw that he was alone on the hill.

The cemetery was entirely deserted.

A rounded mound of fresh-turned earth and sod covered the place where, mere moments ago, it seemed, he had seen his coffin being lowered into the ground. The wind sighed like someone in agony as it swirled among the headstones. Long, knife-edged slashes of shadow streaked across the neatly trimmed cemetery lawn. The sky was the dense color of lead and looked just as heavy as it pressed down on him.

They're gone!

The thought left him with a deep chill.

They're all gone now, and before long I'll be forgotten.

Less than a memory.

The shadows visibly lengthened and deepened as he stood there staring at his own grave.

He knew that he wasn't crying, but his vision was distorted as though he were looking at the world through the wrong end of a telescope. Everything appeared distant and blurred.

It's all for nothing!

David tried to block out the thought as wave after wave of misery washed through him.

It's all absolutely useless!

But then a single, burning spark flared up in the darkness inside him.

...but I'm still here...

The thought was the merest whisper in the back of his mind.

...it was close, but I didn't fade away...

For the second time, now, he had felt the chilling embrace, the seductive lure of oblivion; and he had almost yielded to it, but ultimately he had resisted.

And he knew why.

Karen!

Before he let go entirely, he *had* to find her!

He had no idea how, but—somehow—he was going to figure out exactly what realm of the afterlife they were trapped in, and he was going to do anything and everything he could to help his daughter find some measure of peace.

He told himself he didn't care if he never found it for himself.

That didn't matter!

Even if he had to spend the rest of eternity in this gray, hallucinatory state of being, he didn't care as long as he could find his daughter and do everything—absolutely *everything*—to help her find release.

David braced himself, suddenly filled with purpose.

The funeral was over.

Good!

Let the mourners go back home. Let the living return to their daily lives. Apparently death *wasn't* the end of it. In due time, they'd find themselves here.

All of them!

And they'd deal with whatever they encountered in their own way. He had his own problems to deal with.

As a new sense of courage and purpose filled him, his vision gradually cleared. David saw to his amazement that time had passed, and evening was already falling.

Could a whole day have passed that quickly?

He looked around the cemetery and knew that he was ready to begin his search for his daughter. But as he started down the hill, he noticed a dark figure standing in the shadows at the fringe of woods.

David drew to a halt and stared at it.

It was so silent and motionless David couldn't be sure it was really there.

When he first saw the hooded face and slouched shoulders, a feeble spark of hope that this might be Karen filled him, but he quickly realized that the figure was too thin and too tall. Even in the dying daylight, he could see that the person—whoever it was—was wearing a long, dark cloak. The hood was pulled forward like a monk's cowl, creating a long, narrow tube that hid the person's face from sight; but David could sense cold, unblinking eyes staring at him within the shadow of the cowl.

He had no idea what to do.

He wanted to call out to the figure, to determine first of all if it was even real. Chances were it was just another wandering wraith that had come out to where its body was buried.

But the sight of it filled David with unreasonable fear as well as a vague sense of recognition.

For a flashing instant, he had a memory of acute, physical pain—the sensation of something iron hard slamming into his body.

The darkness around the figure seemed to swell and pulsate with subtle energy as the memory teased David's mind. He moaned softly, filled with fear when he saw the figure raise one arm and, extending a bony finger, beckon to him.

"No...no, I—"

David shook his head and took a step backward as the figure continued to motion to him. Deep within the blackness under the figure's cowl, he was sure he could see a dull red glow of eyes, burning like angry embers.

"I...I have to find her first," David said in a high, trembling voice no louder than the wind, swirling among the tombstones.

He was suddenly sure, now, that this had to be Death, come at last to claim him.

"Just…just give me a…a little more time," he pleaded, his voice stammering and breaking on nearly every syllable. "Let me…let me find her first. That's all I ask. Let me…I have to—to find her and…and help her before I…before I go."

The figure shook its head ever so slightly from side to side. David thought he could hear the rough scratching sound of heavy cloth and something that sounded like a deep rumble of laughter.

"Please…please, just let me find her."

And then, having no idea what the figure might do, David turned away from it and started walking toward the cemetery gate. With each step, he expected to hear a dark rushing sound of wings behind him and feel a chilling tap on his shoulder, but he kept walking.

He left the cemetery, moving as fast as he could, even though his feet felt like they were dragging behind him like heavy chains. His footsteps echoed dully in the still night air.

Sarah had a vague sense that she was dreaming, but she couldn't shake the feeling that it was all somehow very real too.

She was in David's bedroom, kneeling on the floor beside his bed and searching through the teetering stacks of magazines and books that were stacked up on the floor. The light through the small window was pale and gray, hardly strong enough to see by. The air in the room seemed dense. Motes of dust swirled around her like a heavy suspension in liquid.

A feeling of desperation verging on panic filled her.

She knew that she was looking for something very specific, but she wasn't exactly sure what. Her hands moved with agonizing slowness, and every book she lifted seemed thicker and heavier than the last. The piles of books seemed to be continually growing taller, pushing up toward the ceiling like the slow-motion gush from an oil well.

"I'll know it when I see it…I'll know it when I see it," she kept chanting to herself as she worked feverishly, shifting arm-breaking stacks of books and magazines from one side to the other.

One stack of magazines beside her fell over and fanned out across the floor like a spread-out deck of cards. She imagined hearing a man's voice, low and sonorous, like a magician's, say, "Pick a magazine…any magazine…."

"Shit, shit, oh, *shit!*" she muttered as she leaned forward on her hands and knees, and scooped the magazines back into a stack. Once again, she began chanting, "I'll know it when I see it…I'll know it when I see it."

A thrill of discovery went through her when she looked down and realized she could see her own hands.

She remembered reading that you weren't supposed to be able to see your own hands in a dream, but there they were, pawing and shuffling through the books and magazines. Her fingers looked too pale and thin, almost skeletal. She was filled with the sudden unnerving idea that these might not even be her own hands. She had the disconcerting impression that someone else was reaching around from behind her, moving things around.

Cold, prickling waves of panic filled her stomach.

She groaned out loud, wishing to God that she dared to turn around to see who was standing there behind her.

Instead, she just watched, feeling oddly disembodied as her hands rifled through the magazines at the top of the stack. She picked one up and held it at arm's length.

It was an issue of *Cemetery Dance*—the one depicting the rotting, crucified corpse. Only now the cover painting looked as though it had been done in rich sepia tones, and the face of the corpse looked frighteningly familiar.

It was David's face, staring back at her, his mouth open in silent, frozen agony.

She tried to look away but couldn't as the corpse's head in the illustration began to toss slowly from side to side. David's lipless mouth was moving as his body writhed in agony.

The illusion was so real Sarah thought she could hear the rattle of dried bones and the stretching of desiccated muscles and tendons. Craning her head forward, she listened, positive that she could hear the creaking, breathy rustle as the skeleton that had once been her husband tried to speak.

No! Wait just a goddamned second! This can't be happening! This is too vivid to be just a dream!

She was mildly surprised that she could be consciously aware that she was dreaming and still not wake up.

Almost against her will, as if her hands were no longer under her conscious control, she watched as she put the issue of *Cemetery Dance* down and then continued to shuffle through the stacks of books.

Looking from side to side, but not quite daring to glance over her shoulder, she saw the piles of books looming higher and higher above her head until they teetered back and forth like buildings swaying in an earthquake.

"It's in this pile, here, someplace," a low voice whispered softly, close to her ear.

"I'll know it when I see it. I'll know it when I see it," she answered automatically, but she still didn't have the courage to turn to see who was behind her.

It had been a man's voice, she knew that much. The tone and pitch had sounded vaguely familiar, but Sarah couldn't quite place it.

Or maybe she didn't *want* to place it.

She had no idea which pile he might have meant; but her hand, moving as if it had a will of its own, reached out and touched one of the stacks to her left. The fingernail of her forefinger clicked like a ratchet as she ran it down along the spines of the books.

None of the titles seemed to make any sense.

Words and titles were strung together in meaningless non-sequiturs.

"I'll know it when I see it...I'll know it when I see it..."

Her finger hesitated, pressing against the side of one book so hard she almost pushed the whole stack over.

James...Moore's...Complete...Encyclopedia...of...Mass...Murderers...

She had the distinct feeling that these words were somehow connected, but, at least in the dream, they didn't seem to make any sense whatsoever.

"Yes, that's the one," the man's voice whispered from behind her, so close that Sarah thought she could feel the cold draft of his breath against her neck.

She shivered and felt a mild shock of recognition.

It could be David's voice, she thought, but he usually didn't sound even half as mellow as this voice sounded. Especially during the last few years they'd lived together, there had always seemed to be a hard, almost frantic edge in his voice—a sharp timbre that grated on her nerves.

"This one?" Sarah asked, still not daring to look behind her.

She had the impression that, as she moved her head, the person behind her also moved, always keeping out of sight.

Tingling with steadily rising terror, Sarah watched as a thin hand and bone-white arm reached around from behind her and tapped the spine of the book. The curled, yellowed fingernail clicked like an insect's wings against the ragged paper cover.

Convinced that she wouldn't see whoever this was if she turned around and looked, she watched as her own hands reached out and touched the spine of the thick, green book. The dust jacket was frayed from use, and she could barely read the title.

"Page one hundred and thirty-seven," the voice that sounded uncannily like David's whispered inside her head. "I just thought you might like to know."

Why? thought, but she didn't dare ask out loud. *What's on page one-thirty-seven?*

The steadily tightening pressure twisting inside her suddenly spiked sharp enough to make her cry out as she jerked backwards.

She knew that she wouldn't be able to get the book out without toppling over the stack, but she had to try. There was something on page one-thirty-seven. Grabbing the top and bottom edges of the book, she tried to wiggle the book out, but the stack started swaying heavily from side to side. Before she got the book, everything started to collapse in slow-motion, like a house of cards.

Sarah lurched forward, hoping to stop it, but falling books started raining down all around her. Like tumbling dominoes, stack after stack fell with a prolonged, thunderous roar. The book she had been trying to get was lost in the sudden avalanche.

Sarah clapped both hands over her mouth to stifle the scream inside her as her body snapped into an upright, sitting position.

She found herself staring wide-eyed at the soft, gray glow of light that was filtering through her bedroom windows. The air in the room was dense and hot, but she was left with the vivid impression that David's bedroom in her dream had been as cold as a refrigerator. Her throat felt hot and raw as she inhaled sharply and shook her head, trying desperately to clear it.

It was just a dream…. It was all just a dream, she told herself, but that didn't make the cold, slithery feeling inside her go away.

With bated breath, she looked around the room, waiting anxiously for her eyes to adjust to the darkness. When she saw the mounded lump on the bed beside her, she jumped and uttered a soft cry. Once the initial surprise passed, she let out her breath in a long, soft *whoosh.*

It was just Tony, asleep beside her. It was a miracle she hadn't awakened him.

After another moment or two, she remembered everything that had happened earlier that evening.

On Monday, Tony had called her at work. After apologizing for the way he had acted the other night, he had asked her out for a movie that night. Sarah hadn't wanted to tell him that she had to attend visiting hours at the funeral home for her ex-husband, so she had graciously declined.

When Tony called on Tuesday afternoon shortly after she returned home from David's funeral and asked her out again, she decided with some hesitation to accept. She told herself that she needed to do *something* to get her mind off the sad events of the day. David's funeral had stirred up too many dark remembrances about Karen's death, and she was finding it difficult, if not impossible, to shake them.

Even though she had vowed not to let it happen again, after going to a movie, they had ended up back at her house. After a drink and casual conversation in the living room, they had gone up to her bedroom.

Sarah glanced at the alarm clock beside her bed.

It was almost three o'clock. She and Tony had been asleep for at least a couple of hours.

She rubbed her face and let out another long sigh as she crossed her legs and shifted forward. The memory of the dream was already dissolving like cotton candy in the rain. She tried to catch a few wispy fragments before they disappeared entirely, but all she could remember was a number.

137.

It didn't make any sense.

She had no idea why that number would pop into her mind.

Squinting, she glanced around the darkened bedroom and shook her head in wonderment.

"I'll know it when I see it," she whispered into the darkness.

"What the hell are you talking about?" Tony asked.

His deep-pitched voice, speaking so suddenly in the darkness, made Sarah jump. Her breath caught in her throat with an audible click.

"Huh—? Oh, oh, nothing…I was just having a—it must've been a dream."

"Umm…a dream," Tony said, smacking his lips sleepily.

Rolling over to face her, he shifted up onto one elbow. The mattress creaked beneath his weight. "You wanna tell me about it?"

Sarah considered for a moment, then shook her head even though she knew the motion was wasted in the darkness. Reaching out with one hand, she touched him lightly on the left shoulder. The memory of their love-making earlier that night filled her with a warm glow that almost—but not quite—dispelled the chills the dream had left inside her.

Tony shifted closer to her, then flopped onto his back again and reached for her with both hands. He gripped her shoulders tightly as he pulled her down to him. His lips made soft clicking sounds as he kissed her passionately on the mouth, neck, and shoulders.

"Sounds like it was a doozy," Tony said between kisses.

His breath was hot in the shallow of her shoulder as his tongue flicked out like a snake's and started tracing a warm, wet line across her collarbone and down to the tips of her breasts. He began to lap and suck greedily on her nipples.

Sarah couldn't answer him.

She tilted her head back and moaned softly as she clutched his head with both hands. Wave after burning wave of passion swept through her, making her whole body tremble.

"Yeah, it…it was," she gasped.

Rushes of heat swept like a brushfire through her, radiating outward from her stomach when she felt Tony's hands start rubbing against the small of her back, applying pressure as he pulled her closer to him.

"Think you can handle round two?" he asked. His voice was muffled against her flesh.

Almost swooning, Sarah was about to say *yes*; but then in a sudden flash she remembered at least one part of her dream.

She tensed, almost overwhelmed by the sudden certainty that she and Tony weren't alone…that someone else was in the bedroom with them, watching them…silent and unseen.

Her body went as stiff and unyielding as wood. She pulled away from Tony and clenched her fists, poised to hit him if he didn't let her go.

"Hey," he said, grabbing playfully at her.

"No!" Sarah shouted as the fear inside her spiked stronger.

The darkness in the bedroom seemed to be pressing in on her from every direction at once. She found it difficult, almost impossible, to take a deep enough breath. A cold sheen of sweat broke out over her body.

"What the fuck?" Tony said.

Sarah couldn't help but notice the angry edge in his voice.

"I said *no*," she said. "It—it's just that I—I don't really feel like it. That's all."

"Why the hell not?"

In the darkness, Tony's voice sounded like flint striking iron. She expected to see sparks fly.

Tony shifted closer to her and reached for her, but she swatted his hand away.

The tension inside her was becoming almost unbearable. She had the distinct feeling that someone was standing behind her, watching them; and that no matter where she looked, she would never be able to see who it was. Sitting naked on the bed, she felt suddenly weak and vulnerable.

Totally exposed.

"Hey, you need to relax a little. Take the edge off," Tony said, softening his voice. "You're probably just stressed out from work. Come on, lie down. Let me give you a massage."

Sarah was in no mood for a massage, but she relented after a moment and lay down on the bed, flat on her stomach. Tony shifted around to straddle her. She could feel the hot pressure of his balls against the soft mound of her butt. The way she was feeling, that sensation was the furthest thing from sexual.

"Hey, wait just a second," Tony said. "I got something for you."

Sarah felt him lean forward and heard him feeling around for something down on the floor beside the bed, close to where he had dropped his clothes.

The tension inside her wasn't letting up. She was filled with a strong urge to leap up off the bed and run through the house, turning on all the lights. It took a great deal of effort just to lie there and wait.

Once again Tony straddled her, and then Sarah felt a light touch on her back. For an instant, she was confused; then she realized that he was massaging her with something soft—a glove of some kind.

"There now, is that better?" Tony asked. He was moving his hand in wide circles that swept from the base of her neck to the tip of her spine.

Against her will, Sarah allowed his touch to soothe her. It was almost ticklish, but she focused on letting it make her feel languid and sensuous. A cascade of warmth and well-being flooded her, pushing away all the frightening thoughts and images that had gripped her. With her head cocked to one side, she took a long, shuddering breath and then let it out slowly as Tony's touch drew the tension out of her body.

"Umm...that feels *really* good," she said in a breathy whisper. "What's that you're using?"

"Huh? Oh, nothing," Tony said.

For just a second, Sarah thought she detected a slight chuckle in his voice, but she chose to ignore it.

"Just a little piece of fur I picked up. I think it's—ah, rabbit fur or something."

"Oh, yeah...that feels unbelievable," Sarah said. She moaned softly, telling herself she had to unwind.

Her body felt like it was turning to mush as Tony continued to rub the swatch of fur up and down the length of her back. He shifted to one side and ran it all the way down her thighs to the bottoms of her feet, and then back up to her shoulders and neck.

"If you keep this up much longer," she whispered, "I'll be sound asleep in no time."

"Well, I was kinda hoping for something else," Tony whispered.

This time he did laugh out loud, but Sarah was feeling much too relaxed to notice.

The night vibrated with unseen dangers as David walked along strangely deserted streets, heading back to Pine Knoll Elementary. His footsteps clicked softly on the pavement, sounding like the steady ticking of a clock as he crossed the bridge over the Stroudwater River where it joined the Fore River before entering Casco Bay. The dark water below gurgled a soft, sad song beneath the pilings. It reminded David of another night—a night which now seemed like an eternity ago, when he'd been poised on a bridge some distance upriver, trying to find the necessary courage to jump.

If he'd had the courage to end his life that way, he thought, his drowned body might have floated all the way downstream to this bridge before finally being discovered…if it ever would have been discovered.

Maybe he would have floated all the way out to sea.

But that was idle speculation and, like everything else in his past life, long past repair.

Time and distance were still playing tricks on him, and it seemed to be taking much longer than he thought it should to walk the few miles back to the schoolhouse.

Along the way, as he passed deserted storefronts, vacant apartment buildings, and what looked like abandoned houses, he could hear faint echoes and voices from the surrounding darkness. Sometimes piercing screams and anguished wailing sounds rose in the night and were punctuated by deeper, wrenching moans that sounded like souls groaning in misery.

David remembered the warnings the old man had given him about the dangers of the Shadowlands, but he couldn't decide if it was his own fearful mindset, or if there was something he didn't know anything about, something terrible and dangerous that was gathering strength in the Shadowlands.

The night was a deep, pulsating purple energy that seemed about to rip the sky open at any moment. The line of streetlights cast ghostly blue ovals onto the sidewalk at the base of each telephone pole. As David walked from one small pool of light to the next, he could feel distinct temperature fluctuations that made him shiver inwardly.

Just as he was cresting the hill at the turn onto Deering Avenue, he heard a rising chorus off in the distance that sounded like barking hounds. The baying sounds echoed hollowly in the night, sounding both far away and much too close.

A ripple of fear raced through David as he looked around, hoping to find someplace to hide, but the shadowed doorways and windows seemed even more threatening than the surrounding night.

After listening for what seemed like much too long a time, David realized that—thankfully—the sound was moving away from him. The howling cries reverberated in the darkness as they gradually faded. David's body was tingling with apprehension as he continued on his way, all the while poised and ready either to run or fight to defend himself, if he had to.

He crossed Capisic Street and was no more than half a mile from Pine Knoll Elementary when, off to his left, a sudden flurry of activity in the shadows beside one of the derelict buildings caught his attention. Wheeling around with his fists clenched, he stared into the dense shadows inside the ruined buildings.

There was nothing there…nothing that he could see, anyway.

But then something much darker than the shadows moved so fast that he had no time to react to it. With a high peal of laughter, it rushed out of a darkened doorway and slammed into David.

Even though he experienced the impact only as a distant shock, it knocked him off his feet. His body felt like a useless sack of grain as it hit the ground. He felt oddly detached from reality as he tumbled over backward, and the person or creature or whatever it was leaped into the air and landed on top of his chest.

The world was spinning crazily out of control.

David felt a strong jolt of fear when he realized that he was flat on his back, and that someone—a creature with rotting tatters of flesh hanging from its face, and hollow, wide-set eyes that blazed with a savage red glow in the sullen light of the night—had him pinned to the ground. Its bony knees were grinding painfully into his upper arms.

"You're *mine* now," the creature whispered as it leaned close to David's ear. Its voice crackled and snapped like cold water splashed onto a hot stove.

There was no way David could think of this thing as ever having been human. Thin strings of dark hair hung in loose clumps from its head. Wide, ragged patches mottled its face where the rotting skin had pulled away, exposing grayish-yellow bone that was decayed and crawling with worms. The creature's lips peeled back, exposing teeth and gums that were black with rot.

Nearly insane with fear, David struggled to free himself, but it was useless.

The creature straddled his chest, pinning him down firmly to the hard ground. Bony fingers dug like spikes into the sides of David's head as the creature gripped him and, leaning forward, brought its face so close to David's that they almost touched noses. Thick, looping strings of drool ran from the creature's mouth as it cackled with deep, rattling laughter. An insane light shone deep within the creature's eyes.

Unable to believe that this was really happening, David tried to resist, but the creature was much too strong for him. He cringed inwardly when he felt the creature shift its weight, and then heard a loud, clanking sound. Glancing down, he saw that the creature was holding a coiled length of chain with metal clamps on the ends that looked like leg irons. The rings of the chain flickered with a curious light that made them appear dull yellow.

With a quick flick of its wrists, the creature snapped open one of the cuffs and started to force David's wrist into it.

The pain David felt the instant the metal touched his forearm and the cuff snapped shut was indescribable. Searing hot flames and powerful surges of numbing cold ripped through his body and mind. He listened to the shrill chorus of agonized screams that seemed to be coming from inside the chain links.

The creature tossed its head back. Glaring up at the thick night sky, it let loose another gale of insane laughter.

"Mine! Mine! You're all *mine* now!" it howled, its voice warbling higher and higher until it finally cracked. This was followed by another burst of maniacal laughter as the creature snapped open another cuff and shackled David's other arm.

For a moment, David was immobilized by his fear, but he quickly discovered that he couldn't resist even if he wanted to. The mere touch of the strange metal—so cold that it burned white hot against his body—drained him of all strength and resolve. The weight of the chains pinned him to the ground with a crushing heaviness that was like nothing he had ever experienced before, either in life or in the Shadowlands. His body felt as though it were encased in molten iron. Every fiber of his being shrieked with pain and anguish, but no matter how hard he tried, he couldn't move.

"Wha—what do you—"

"Shut up, slave!" the creature squealed.

Sitting back on its haunches, it hauled back and slapped David across the mouth. The impact was dull and nowhere close to the intense agony of the chains, but it knocked David's head back against the ground hard enough to daze him. Explosions of brightly colored light flashed across his vision. His view of the night sky shattered into a thousand mirrored fragments.

The creature swung off David's chest and then, reaching down, snapped open the two remaining cuffs. It was just about to clamp them shut on David's ankles when a sudden rush of dark motion against the night sky drew David's attention. He tried to lift his head enough to see what it was, convinced that it must be one of the creature's accomplices, but he couldn't move.

A hopeless, sinking sensation filled him when he saw—and recognized—the hooded figure that he had seen earlier this evening at the cemetery. The long, dark cowl masked its face in shadow, but David could feel its cold, savage stare boring into him with almost unbearable intensity.

The creature had its back to the hooded figure and seemed completely oblivious to its presence.

"Oh, I'll get a good price for this one, I'll bet. Yes, sir, I will," it babbled to itself between cackling laughter as it forced one of David's legs into the cuff and snapped it shut. "This here's a good, strong corpus, it is. And he's all mine! *All mine!*"

"Release him at once."

The hooded figure's voice boomed in the night like a cannon shot that echoed from the empty buildings across the street.

The creature froze instantly, its expression fixed in a startled, horrified grimace. The fiery glow in its eyes seemed to die instantly. If such a terrifying creature could itself be scared, this one was. It cringed like a whipped animal as it turned around slowly and looked at whoever—or whatever—was standing behind it.

"Right *now!*" the hooded figure commanded, slowly raising one hand and pointing a forefinger at the creature.

"But I...I caught him, fair and square, Ferryman," the creature said. There wasn't very much strength or conviction in its voice. "He's...mine!"

"No, he's *mine!* I removed his caul. My mark is upon him," the hooded figure replied in a deep, sonorous voice that seemed to come from several directions at once, as if the night itself had found a voice. "Release him *immediately*, or be prepared to suffer the consequences."

"But I...I *want* him," the creature said, its voice rising an octave or two. "I *deserve* him! I *tracked* him here. I found out where he stays, and I *caught* him. By all rights, Ferryman, he should be *mine*."

"*I'm* his reaper!"

The hooded figure said nothing more as it stared at the cringing creature. After a long, tense silence, he extended both hands above his head and clapped them once. The sound was like a crack of thunder that split the night sky.

The creature kneeling beside David was trembling horribly. It glanced furtively from side to side, as though looking for help that obviously wasn't going to arrive. After another long, tense moment, the creature slumped forward. Reaching into the back pocket of its tattered clothes, it produced a key. Its hands were trembling horribly as it leaned forward and began to unlock the leg and wrist cuffs.

David couldn't describe the sudden, intense relief he felt the instant the heavy chains fell away. The searing pain immediately dissolved, and the faint chorus of screams slowly faded away to nothing.

The chains clanked heavily together, and the light seemed to bleed out of them as the creature hastily gathered them together. With head bowed as though it didn't dare glance at the hooded figure, the creature stood up shakily. Hunching over as though withered with age, it scuttled off into the night. The last David heard of it was the distant clank of its chains.

Then silence settled down, thick and solid.

David was too stunned to move.

The surprise attack had caught him completely off guard. His body still felt drained of all strength. He realized that those chains must be forged of some magical material to have affected him so dramatically. He wasn't sure he could move, much less stand up.

The hooded figure regarded David with a long, steady stare.

Once again, David felt the cold intensity of its unseen gaze boring into him. He wanted to say something—to thank his deliverer, if nothing else, but he wasn't at all convinced that his situation had improved.

He tried to speak, but the only sound he could manage was a stammering "Thank you."

Without a word, the hooded figure reached out and silently flicked his fingers, urging David to take hold of his hand.

David wasn't sure he wanted or dared to touch this person, whoever he was, but he reached up and grasped the mysterious figure's hand. The touch wasn't nearly as cold as he'd expected. In fact, he felt a mild charge of rejuvenating energy infuse his being as their hands touched.

"Come with me," the figure said after David stood up.

David still felt oddly disoriented. It took him a moment or two to regain his balance. He glanced at the darkened buildings on either side of the street, convinced that he could see numerous pale faces watching them from the shadows. A deep, trembling fear gripped him.

"Who…who are you?" he asked. "What do you want with me?"

His voice sounded faint and raw, but David was amazed that he could speak at all. A steadily tightening pressure clutched his chest like huge, unseen hands.

"We have much to talk about," the cowled figure said in a deep voice that reverberated in the night. "You already have a safe place to stay. Let's go there."

8

FERRYMAN

After making love for a second time that night—something Sarah told Tony she hadn't done with David or anyone else in *years*—Sarah drifted off to sleep; but here it was, well past two o'clock in the morning, and Tony was still wide awake.

He was naked, lying flat on his back on top of the sheets which were still damp with the sweat of their lovemaking. With his hands clenched tightly at his sides, he stared up at the ceiling as a cool breeze wafted through the open bedroom windows and washed over his body like a refreshing mountain stream.

But it did little to calm Tony down.

His mind was whirling with disturbing thoughts, some of them even crazy, and all of them centered around the knife.

What that hell was he going to do about that goddamned knife?

Better yet, what the hell was he going to do *with* it?

It seemed as though, ever since he found it that night in the alleyway, he hadn't been able to stop thinking about it.

It was like a sickness—a fever that burned deep inside his brain.

He carried the knife with him wherever he went, and it seemed as though every few seconds or minutes he was compelled to feel for it underneath his shirt or in his jacket pocket, if only to reassure himself that it was still there.

That it was still *his*.

So what was the problem with that?

So what if he liked the way it felt?

It made him feel confident, more secure.

He liked the smooth touch of the hard rubber handle. He liked flicking his thumb along the razor-sharp edge.

There was nothing wrong with that, was there?

Every time he touched it or even thought about it, the image of the knife seemed to infuse his body and mind with a hot, coursing energy that generated strange and powerful thoughts and emotions.

Whenever he gripped the knife, squeezing the rubber handle so tight that the palm of his hand hurt, violent images too fleeting and insubstantial to grasp would fill his mind and make him shudder with pleasure and expectation.

Especially at night, when he lay in bed, trying to drift off to sleep.

Rage...

Anger...

Fear...

And hatred.

But all of these words were too mild, too mundane even to begin to express how the knife made him feel.

He wasn't sure there were words in English or any language adequate to capture how the knife made him feel. Sometimes he would even imagine that he could hear soft voices whispering to him in the dark.

And these voices, whether they were in the room or inside his head, would grow louder and more insistent the more firmly he gripped the knife's handle.

Some of the voices sounded desperate, wracked with grief and pain. He listened to their shrill shrieking and bubbly gasps, and tried to imagine the horrible images that accompanied them.

But there was one voice in particular that Tony heard, and this was the one he listened to.

This was the voice that he had come to think of as the *true* voice of the knife.

It urged him to do things.

Terrible things.

Tony had no idea how the knife could be influencing him like this. He didn't want to know, but especially at night, he listened intently to its secret urgings. Up until the time he had found the knife, he had never entertained such thoughts, and he had certainly never given in to any violent impulses.

But that seemed to be what the knife wanted.

It was telling him that it wanted to be used...it *needed* to be used.

As if it had a mind or a will or a purpose of its own, it whispered to him that its one, clear purpose was to slice into living flesh and feel the hot gush of blood bathe its metal edge as, like a fleeting vapor, life drained away.

Tony tried to convince himself that using the knife once, as he had on Bingley last night, would maybe satisfy the blade; but even then something told him that he was kidding himself.

As he lay in the darkness of Sarah's bedroom and listened to the deep, steady rhythm of her breathing, he knew that wasn't the case at all.

The blade had tasted blood again after a long time, and now, after such a long period of abstinence, it wanted more.

Much more!

Only this time, it wanted a different *kind* of blood.

It wanted *human* blood.

At least subconsciously, Tony knew what the knife was asking, was *demanding* of him, but he struggled against the savage impulses that seemed to radiate from the knife.

Christ, no! I can't kill anyone!

Powerful emotions coiled like snakes inside him, making him shiver as though in the grip of a fever.

He wasn't a cold-blooded killer!

What he had done to Bingley had been just a...just an experiment. That was all. He had simply wanted to try out the blade to see how well it worked.

If he *ever* thought—even for a moment—that he might use the knife on someone else—on Sarah, for instance—then he would have to get rid of the knife.

That would be simple enough, wouldn't it?

Just throw it away.

Toss it back into the alleyway where he'd found it.

Let some other asshole come along and find it.

Let someone else deal with it.

He had more than enough problems in his life as it was. He sure as hell didn't need this kind of shit!

A cold sweat had broken out over his body. Rolling his head from side to side, he gritted his teeth and clenched his fists, trying to stop himself from thinking like this.

He didn't want to hurt Sarah or anyone else.

He would *have* to get rid of the knife before it made him do something he'd regret.

Or even if he didn't actually get rid of the knife, he was determined that he could control the bloody impulses it stirred inside him.

He would have to.

RICK HAUTALA

He was studying to be a lawyer, for Christ's sake! As far as he was concerned, he was a law-abiding citizen who valued the law above everything else…everything, that is, except success and maybe a nice piece of pussy every now and then.

He was *never* going to *use* the knife on anyone or anything!

Killing Bingley had been a mistake, he now realized, and he deeply regretted that he had ever given in to the impulse.

But the knife was as much to blame as he was.

Maybe more.

Tony imagined that he could see things as he stared into the darkness. Gauzy figures rose up like smoke and swirled in the gentle breeze that blew through the room. He watched in amazement as faces formed in the darkness—mostly women's faces. Their eyes looked hollow and gaunt, their faces pale and stretched in the throes of agony. The dark ovals of their mouths opened wide in silent screams. Hands as white as bone reached out for him…grasping…clawing….

Tony covered his face with both hands as a deep, wrenching sob shook him, but even then the images didn't vanish.

"Jesus, make it stop," he whispered into the cup formed by his hands. "I didn't have anything to do with it…I just couldn't…couldn't control it!"

But as much as he tried to deny it, Tony knew that killing Bingley hadn't been totally on impulse. He had carefully planned the whole damned thing. He had, in fact, actually been looking forward to it with a great deal of anticipation.

How impulsive could it have been if he had hidden outside Sarah's house and waited until he saw her leave?

How spontaneous could it have been if he had stolen a piece of fish from the restaurant the night before to use as bait?

Yes, bait…to catch that little bastard!

And then, the most calculated thing of all—how could he excuse or explain skinning the cat and using its pelt to massage Sarah before making love to her?

Tony couldn't help but chuckle in the darkness as he thought about it. The sound of his laughter was so close to him that it sounded like someone else leaning close to his ear and snickering.

He had to admit that it had been pretty goddamned funny, almost inspired.

And it had worked, too.

Sarah had gotten so horny they had screwed for almost an hour solid before he finally couldn't hold back any longer.

Now she'd gone back to sleep like a goddamned baby, and he was wide awake.

Wide awake and thinking.

But maybe—in the long run—what he had done to Bingley had been all for the best. It had let him try out the knife, and it had given the knife a taste of blood.

He couldn't feel much regret for Bingley. He owed the little motherfucker a big payback for clawing his back the other night. The wounds on Tony's back still stung.

So Tony decided that the bottom line was, he didn't feel the least bit of guilt or remorse for what he had done.

And he had no intention of ever getting rid of the knife.

He *liked* the way it made him feel, even when the thoughts that filled his mind seemed so out-of-control compared to how he usually thought and felt.

And he liked knowing that if anyone else messed with him—anyone at all—even Sarah—he wouldn't have to put up with any shit.

No shit from *anyone*, anymore.

And he wouldn't hesitate to use the knife again, either.

After all, the knife would like it.

It would *enjoy* it!

He could use it for what *it* wanted just as much if not more than what *he* wanted.

Again, Tony chuckled softly to himself as he rolled over onto his side.

He felt better, more relaxed.

He lazily draped one hand over the edge of the bed, letting his fingertips brush against the rubber handle of the knife.

Instantly, he felt reassured.

Everything would be all right, he told himself, as long as he never lost possession of the knife.

Owning it made him feel good...almost like it was something he had owned once before...long ago...and now, after so many years, they had been reunited.

He'd never realized how incomplete his hand had felt until that first night when he held the knife and had *used* it.

RICK HAUTALA

David was filled with a cold, twisting apprehension as he and the hooded figure silently entered the darkness within Pine Knoll Elementary School. They hadn't spoken another word to each other throughout the walk to the schoolhouse. David had hardly dared even to look at the mysterious figure. If this person—or whatever it was—had been carrying a long, curved scythe, he would have been a perfect incarnation of Death.

David guessed that's exactly who he must be.

Without exchanging a word between them, they made their way through the pitch darkness to the far wall. Their feet scuffed softly on the wood. The floorboards groaned like something in pain.

David still couldn't figure out how he could be feeling so nervous and exhausted without a living body. No matter what the reason, he knew he was close to collapse. The darkness around him was vibrating with a raw, dangerous energy. He could almost imagine two huge, dark arms reaching out of the darkness, eager to enfold him.

Groping blindly in front of him, he felt around until he found the rough, plaster wall, then turned and, leaning his back against the wall, slowly slid down into a sitting position with his knees pressed up against his chest.

He had no idea where the hooded figure might be or what it might be doing, but he hardly cared.

Here in near total darkness, he couldn't see anything except the dull, gray rectangle that was the door leading outside. It was faint and looked impossibly far away.

The silence was so thick it seemed to ring like a deep-throated bell in the night. If it hadn't been for the low, whispering voices he heard coming from somewhere upstairs, David would have been absolutely convinced that he was alone.

And that's how he wanted to be.

All alone.

Just him with his own thoughts.

Shivering deep inside, he crouched in the darkness and waited. He wished he could rest, but his mind was whirling with too many disturbing thoughts and emotions.

He couldn't stop thinking about the verbal exchange between the hooded figure and the creature that had attacked him. The creature had called him "Ferryman." David wondered if that was this individual's name or his title.

He also couldn't stop wondering what the Ferryman had meant when he'd told the creature that he was David's "reaper," and that his "mark" was on him.

Could he really be the Grim Reaper, come to collect his soul?

David sensed that there were too many things going on here in the Shadowlands—too many dynamics that he couldn't even begin to understand.

He sensed that this person—this Ferryman—certainly should be able to explain many things about existence in the Shadowlands, but he didn't dare ask. He wanted desperately to know what was going on, but near total exhaustion was weighing him down.

All he could think about was rest, so he closed his eyes—at least he thought he did; it seemed not to make the slightest bit of difference in the darkness if his eyes were open or closed—and leaned his head back against the rough wall.

A deep shudder ran through him as the memory stirred uneasily within him of how those chains had made him feel so powerless. Stark flashes of fear filled him that he might slip and lose himself in the void of darkness in the center of his soul, but he couldn't stop himself from drifting further and further away.

"So why did you help me?" The question sounded like the soft rustle of coarse cloth in the darkness. David wasn't even sure if he or someone else had spoken. The darkness behind his eyes throbbed, dense and impenetrable.

"I think we might be able to help each other," came the reply in a voice so deep David knew instantly that it wasn't his own.

"Help...each other?" He was trembling inside, unable to dispel the impression that he was simply listening to himself speak, and that his voice was coming from a great distance away. "But I—I have no idea what's going on. I don't even know where I am."

"You've already been told that. You're a wraith in the Shadowlands." The reply was barely above the threshold of sound.

"Yeah, but...but *how did I get here*? And what's *keeping* me here? If I'm already dead—"

"Your fetters are what's keeping you here."

"Fetters?"

A soul-deep chill ran through David as he spoke the word, and his memory stirred.

"You mean like...like those chains that creature put on me?"

He was dimly aware that he was rubbing his left wrist with one hand as though trying to massage away the pain, but he could still feel the dull, burning collar of pain where the metal clasps had touched him.

A soft, sniffing laughter filled the darkness.

"No," the Ferryman said, "those chains that reaper had were forged in Stygia. That's another matter entirely."

"So what the hell are these…these fetters you say are keeping me here?"

"There are more fetters than there are people who have died," the voice said soothingly, almost laughing. "Generally, they're unfinished business you have in the land of the living or attachments to someone who is still alive. Then again, they could be as simple a thing as that it wasn't your time to die yet."

"My time to —"

David's voice choked off as the memory returned of seeing his ex-wife, relatives, friends, and acquaintances gathered at Riverside Cemetery to watch his coffin as it was lowered into the ground. The emotions that single memory stirred were terrifying in their purity and power. They almost overwhelmed David, but he clung desperately to his awareness.

"—die," the voice from the darkness finished for him.

The word echoed in the darkness, seeming for several seconds to intensify before it finally faded away.

"So that creature—you called it a—a 'reaper,'" David said, almost too frightened to speak. "He referred to you as 'Ferryman.' Is that your name?"

Again, a low rumble of laughter filled the darkness.

"No, that's my…function here."

"You mean like in ancient Greek mythology, how—what was his name? Charon. How Charon ferried dead souls across the River Styx?"

David didn't know how, but the darkness suddenly seemed to change. He could feel a stirring energy, like the subtle static charge just before a thunderstorm breaks loose. Even the voices whispering in the schoolhouse fell silent.

"Be *very* careful about when and where you speak that name!"

The Ferryman's voice ripped like a blade through the darkness.

"What, you mean Char—?"

"Be advised! It's not wise to speak of things about which you have no knowledge."

David was burning to ask the Ferryman what he meant, but he didn't dare speak. The dark silence lengthened, closing in around David with a steadily rising pressure.

"So what about my daughter?" he finally managed to ask after what seemed like too long a time. "Do you know anything about her? Why is she here?"

For a long time, no reply came out of the darkness. David was almost convinced that he was alone—that he had been alone all this time and had imagined the entire conversation. Maybe he'd even imagined everything he had experienced since coming to the Shadowlands. Cold fear slithered like a large black snake inside him.

"Can you...tell me why she's still here?" he finally asked.

"It's not for me to say," the Ferryman replied. His voice echoed with a hollow reverberation that made it sound like several voices combined.

A sudden desperation filled David. He was worried about Karen and couldn't stop wondering where she had gone and if she was in some kind of danger. He wanted desperately to see her again and decided that, if seeing her again was one of his fetters, he would gladly embrace it if only it meant that he *would* see her...at least just once more before death claimed him.

"Do you know where I can find her?" he asked, his voice twisted with emotion. "I *have* to find her! I have to help her if I can!"

"As I said," the low, resonant voice replied from out of the darkness, "perhaps we can help each other."

"Help...*how?*"

David found it almost impossible not to shout, but his voice—the faintest of whispers—echoed as softly as a flutter of wings in the close darkness.

"There's someone you're connected to, someone who is still in the land of the living—what we call the *skinlands*—who has something that I want. Something that I need."

"Oh, yeah? And what's that?"

"A very valuable relic," the voice answered.

"A relic? What kind of relic? I don't know what the hell you're talking about, so what makes you think I can help you get it?"

"I *did* say *perhaps*," the Ferryman said simply.

Red, blazing anger filled David as his fear for his daughter's safety grew sharper.

"Don't start talking riddles with me!" he shouted. "Tell me straight out what you want! Are you saying, if I do something for you—"

"—then perhaps in return I'll be able to do something for you. *Perhaps.* It's that simple. Even here in the afterlife, that's how things work."

The sound of the low laughter filled the darkness, but David wasn't entirely sure from which direction it was coming.

"So what is this...this relic you want so badly?" he asked.

For a long time, no reply came; and once again he began to feel as though he were utterly alone in the dark—that he always had been and always would be alone. But he could sense if not actually see that the

Ferryman was close by. David was surprised that he didn't feel the creature's cold breath against his skin.

But we're all dead here, he thought. *No one here has any breath!*

"There is a knife…a knife that is—how can I put it?—invested with great power. I need your held to obtain it."

A sudden and inexplicable anger flashed like lightning inside David's mind. He wanted to reach out into the darkness, grab the Ferryman by the throat, and throttle him.

All he cared about—all he could think about—was Karen's safety. He remembered seeing the knife the young man had hidden beneath his clothes at Sarah's house. That had to be what the Ferryman was talking about. But all that mattered to David right now was finding Karen and helping her in any way he could.

He didn't have time for bullshit like this!

"I don't know anything about any goddamned knife!" he wailed, filled with frustration.

He knew that he was lying, and he was positive that the Ferryman could tell that he was lying because of the warbling edge in his voice.

"And even if I did, I wouldn't know how to go about *getting* it for you or for anyone else. I don't know how it is for you or anyone else here, but I'm finding it just about impossible to touch anything in the real world—the…the *skinlands*, as you call them! I can't talk to anyone. I can't touch anything. I can't make anyone see me because I'm dead! Get it? I'm not part of that world anymore!"

"Oh, but your fetters keep you in contact with the skinlands," the Ferryman said softly. "That's what I've been trying to explain to you."

"Maybe, but still—all I can do is watch it like…like it's some kind of sideshow or movie or something!"

"It's difficult to reach through the Shroud, I'll grant you that, but it's not impossible. There are *always* ways."

The voice was low and soothing, but it did little to calm David.

"There are many skills you can learn here," the Ferryman went on. "Unfortunately, most of these skills take time and practice, and I'm afraid that you—and I—don't have much of either in this matter."

"Why?" David said, trying hard to shout but hearing his voice only as a whisper. "What's so important about this knife?"

David still couldn't entirely rid himself of the impression that this entire conversation was a dialogue going on inside his own head, but he struggled to understand what the Ferryman was saying to him.

"This knife is…very special," the Ferryman said. "It's a relic of awesome power that once belonged to a man you may have heard of. His name was Jack the Ripper."

"Jack the—"

"Does that name mean anything to you?"

David couldn't help but laugh out loud even though the sound was as faint as the flutter of a moth's wings.

"What the fuck are you talking about? Jack the Ripper lived in London, England, over a hundred years ago. What the hell has he got to do with anything here in Portland?"

"For almost a century, now, that knife and two others of its kind were in safekeeping, but recently all three of them have been stolen. The person who first took them has already used them again, too, as others have. Quite against their will, you understand, but there have been several wraiths seen wandering in the Shadowlands that have the deathmark of those blades on their souls."

The mention of the mark on their souls made David think to ask the Ferryman about the mark he had said was on him, but he stopped himself and let the Ferryman continue.

"I haven't yet learned where the other two knives are, but I'm sure they'll show up eventually. They have a way of making their presence known. I *do* know that someone who lives near here has one of them and has already used it."

"Jesus, you're right," David said as a dim memory sparked within him. "A couple of months ago, there was something on the news about a young woman who was murdered here in Portland. I think they said it was with a knife."

"What you have to understand," the Ferryman said, "is that whoever it was didn't really do it. It was the *knife*. I've already found the man responsible for that particular woman's death. He's a wraith here, but he no longer possesses the knife. Someone else has it now. Someone who has a connection with you, and the knife's power is beginning to influence him."

"Influence him? How?" David asked, already dreading the answer before he finished asking the question.

"Whoever possesses any one of those knives is also possessed *by* it. Eventually he'll do whatever the knife wants. Make no mistake about it. He'll use it soon—if he hasn't already. No matter how hard he tries to resist it, eventually he will have to use it."

"To kill," David said, his voice almost breaking, "like Jack the Ripper."

"Exactly!" The Ferryman clapped his hands together. "All three of those knives are strong instruments of puppetry."

"Puppetry?" David echoed weakly. This was all too much. He was finding it almost impossible to process any of it. "Look, I don't like you talking circles around me like this, okay?" he said. "Just tell me straight out what it is you want from me."

"I want your help to obtain that knife," the Ferryman said from the darkness. "Haven't I already made that perfectly clear?"

"Sure you have," David said. "But how?"

He wished he could protest more forcefully, but he was in the grip of total exhaustion that was dragging him down, deeper and deeper. He could feel himself fading away like a whisper into the night.

"For now, you need rest," the Ferryman's deep voice said almost soothingly. "Close your eyes and relax. The touch of those Stygian chains has drained more out of your corpus than you realize. You need to restore yourself."

David groaned softly, wanting to say more, but he couldn't. He settled his head against the wall and rolled it back and forth, all the while groaning softly. The sound created a steady vibration inside his head that he found soothing. A light touch caressed his forehead, but rather than frightening him, it sent waves of calmness washing through him.

"Relax now. Just relax."

"Yeah, but I…what about my daughter?"

David could hear his own voice echoing in the darkness.

"You said that you could…that you would help me if I helped you."

"I said I will…if I can."

"Then can you help me find her…my daughter?" David asked.

"I'm sorry," the Ferryman's voice replied, sounding faint and lost in the distance, "You'll have to find her yourself—"

A mild spark of anger filled David, but he was much too exhausted to react. He could feel himself drifting further and further away…dissolving into nothing…fading like a gossamer dream into the dense, vibrating darkness that surrounded him.

He imagined that his whole existence was little more than a tiny candle flame, sputtering until it finally burned itself out.

"—and after you find her," said the Ferryman's sonorous voice from an even greater distance, "if you get that knife for me, I promise that I'll do whatever I can to help you…and her…"

Leaning out the kitchen door with one hand braced against the door jamb, Sarah frowned as she looked up and down the side porch. Already the day was heavy with humidity.

"Hey! What'cha doing?"

Sarah squealed when Tony spoke so suddenly behind her. Spinning around, she stared at him for a moment, her breath caught like a hot coal in the center of her chest. Her hands were clenched into tight fists.

"*Jesus*, you scared the *shit* out of me!"

A vague sense of danger filled her as she watched Tony saunter past the kitchen table toward her. All he was wearing were his boxer shorts. He was smiling broadly, but Sarah could sense that something wasn't quite right.

Clutching the collar of her thin bathrobe to her throat, she came back into the house. The screen door swung shut behind her, slamming loud enough to make her jump again.

"I was just…calling Bingley," she said tightly. "He's usually at the door, first thing in the morning. You know, now that I think about it, I don't remember seeing him yesterday afternoon either."

"Hmm," Tony said, cocking his hip to one side and stroking his cheek. He covered his mouth with his hand, but Sarah thought she caught a glimpse of a faint smile behind his hand. Her frown deepened as she stared at him, wondering what the hell was up with him.

There was definitely something, but she couldn't quite put her finger on it.

A slanting ray of sunlight shot through the window above the kitchen sink and illuminated Tony's bare legs. The curling black hairs on his thighs made his skin look pale. She wondered why he didn't get out in the sun more often but figured, between work at the restaurant and studying at law school, he probably was too busy to indulge in much recreation.

"I—I've been calling him for more than ten minutes," she said, feeling tight and trembling inside. "I'm afraid something might've happened to him."

She kept staring at Tony, all the while thinking, *Jesus, something is really wrong here!*

"Aww, he's gotta be around somewhere," Tony said.

This time there was no mistaking it. A big smile was playing at the corners of his mouth as he came close to Sarah and wrapped his arms around her, pulling her close.

When he tried to kiss her, she turned away. She wasn't feeling very cuddly right now. Her body was ramrod stiff, unyielding in his arms.

What the hell's wrong? she thought. *What is it about him that's giving me the creeps?*

"So what do you have on tap for today?" Tony asked casually as he nuzzled his mouth against her neck. His kisses were wet and cool on her skin. They made her shiver.

"I have to go to work at—" She glanced past him to the clock on the kitchen wall and saw that it was a little past eight. "At nine o'clock."

"Really? I thought the library didn't open until ten o'clock during the summer session."

"Yeah, it doesn't, but I—I'm supposed to get there early today. I've got a lot of computer entries to make."

She hoped the lie wasn't *too* obvious. Blinking her eyes rapidly, she stared up at the ceiling and nibbled nervously on her lower lip, not even sure herself why she had lied to Tony. She really wasn't due at work until one o'clock; but for some reason, she wanted to be alone this morning. In fact, she regretted letting Tony spend the night.

But then again, why *not* spend the morning with him?

She couldn't deny how great it felt to have a man in her bed again, ready and willing to give her pleasure.

"You probably don't have the time for a little quickie, then, huh?"

Tony grunted as he thrust his hips forward, bumping against her. The solid lump of his erection pressed like a roll of quarters against her thigh, but the thought of making love to him right now almost nauseated her.

She tried to convince herself that it had to be because she was still so upset about what had happened to David; but for some reason, that didn't exactly strike her as what was wrong.

She still hadn't even told Tony that David's funeral had been yesterday.

Why was she keeping it such a big secret?

He was a great lover, and he seemed genuinely interested in a relationship with her; but there was something else about him, something in the way he was acting this morning that bothered her deeply. Now that she had slept with him a few times and was getting to know him, he seemed almost like a different person—like someone she didn't know in the least, and she found it a little bit scary.

She wished she could put her finger on *exactly* what it was.

Tony continued to kiss her neck passionately as his hands slid up and down her back, massaging the stiff muscles. She felt a warm, pleasant gush of blood in her lower abdomen and wished she could just give in to the feeling, but it was no good.

She was too worried, and it wasn't just about Bingley.

Something was different…

Something was very wrong!

9

Rip Her

The touch was light, almost feathery.

For a timeless moment, David thought it must be the Ferryman, still gently massaging his forehead as he drifted deeper and deeper into sleep.

But do the dead really sleep? he wondered vaguely.

He found the thought almost amusing, but then another, more frightening thought intruded.

And if they do dream…what do they dream about?

He was seized by a deep, sad longing for the life he'd lost. It amazed him how much he missed such simple things as being able to open a door, or feeling the wind and rain in his face, or smelling the strong, damp earth smells after a rainstorm, or feeling his daughter's kisses on his cheek.

Knowing that he would never experience any of these things again filled him with intense, almost unbearable agony.

But after another indeterminate length of time, as such thoughts swirled in his mind, David realized that the touch was no longer tracing light circles across his brow.

Someone was holding him by his shoulders and shaking him roughly.

Very distantly, he could feel his head, lolling back and forth and grinding against the pitted surface of the plaster wall. Numbing cold radiating from the wall immobilized him.

For what seemed like an agonizingly long time, David struggled to pull himself out of the dream—if it was a dream—and back to consciousness. He vaguely hoped he would discover that everything he had experienced in the Shadowlands had been a dream.

Maybe I'm still alive…. Maybe I'm back home in bed, sleeping and dreaming that I took a late-night walk and was hit by an oncoming truck…. Maybe I never really wanted to die! …Maybe… Just maybe….

A shallow, desperate hope filled him with emotion. He would have cried if he could have.

Besides, how can I be dead and still be aware of what's going on in the world?

Rick Hautala

No, I can't be dead! I have to be alive! This isn't what it's supposed to be like to be dead!

As these and other frantic thoughts crowded his mind, the touch grew stronger, more urgent and demanding.

Either that, or else he was coming to.

As he struggled back toward consciousness, David felt oddly detached from his own body, as though it were nothing more than a useless dust rag being shaken out. It took an immense effort, but he focused his attention into a narrow beam and concentrated only on trying to figure out who was shaking his shoulder like this.

He had no idea when—or *if*—he opened his eyes.

The solid wall of darkness in front of him looked like it was no more than an inch from his face. But slowly, gradually, his mind cleared.

Shifting shadows whispered as they separated like heavy drapes.

Memories of what had happened earlier that evening started to come back in sharper detail. One predominant image was of a hooded figure, leaning over him. He recalled looking up into the darkness inside the hood—into a darkness that was deeper and colder than anything he had ever experienced before.

"Who—?"

His voice made a choking sound deep inside his chest, and he could say no more. That single word echoed and then faded away as if someone were gradually turning the volume control down to zero.

"I need you," came a faint, quavering voice that sounded impossibly far away. "I need you to help me."

"But I—"

Consciousness was returning, but the process was still maddeningly slow.

Fleeting images and vague memories flapped like wind-blown sheets through his mind.

The hideously decaying face of the creature that had attacked him loomed at him out of the darkness. The peal of the creature's insane laughter rang sharply in his ears, and the clank of heavy chains. Their freezing touch felt like nails being driven into his arms and legs. He imagined that the chains pinned him as though he had been crucified.

David struggled to move his body, but it was like trying to flex a hand that was padded in a thick glove.

He was totally paralyzed.

With returning consciousness there also came jolting red currents of fear and hot spikes of anxiety.

What if this isn't *all a dream?*

The fear inside him was growing steadily stronger.

Or maybe—even if it is a dream—what if it hasn't ended yet?...What if it will never end?

Suddenly the darkness both inside and outside of him seemed to open up. He experienced a moment of rushing vertigo.

Total panic swept through him.

He cried out and made wild, frantic grabs with both hands, but there was nothing to hold onto. The whole universe was spinning insanely out of control, and he was at the center of it all.

Icy rushes of fear roared like demons inside his head, and he knew that his sanity would snap like a dry twig if he allowed the fear to take over.

No!...NO! he screamed inside his head as he tried desperately to resist the gathering fear, clinging to the few shreds of personal identity and sanity he still had left.

Dead or alive, there were things he had to do.

He had fetters that bound him to the Shadowlands, and he was more than willing to embrace them.

"Where have you *been?*" the faint voice called out.

It echoed all around him as if he were inside a huge metal tube.

"I've been looking all *over* for you."

David tried to focus his attention, concentrating hard on keeping the fear at bay and resisting the inexorable pull of oblivion.

He thought he recognized the voice, but it was too much to hope for. It couldn't possibly be—

"Karen?"

In the roaring darkness, his own voice had the harsh sound of tearing paper. His panicky thoughts screamed louder than his voice.

"Please! Daddy! Please wake up! I need you to help me!"

The shaking grew more intense, more insistent; but at the same time, it also seemed to become somehow more muted, as though the more he concentrated on it, and the closer he got to it, the further away it moved.

"*Karen!*"

When his eyes suddenly snapped open, he couldn't believe what he was seeing.

Everything was all gauzy and vague, like in a dream. Dull, diffused gray light that bled the life out of any colors was seeping like smoke into the old schoolhouse. All dimensions seemed oddly distorted. The perspective of the room was totally wrong. Walls and ceiling met at crazy angles that didn't make sense, like an Escher drawing.

David shook his head as though dazed and groaned loudly when he saw Karen kneeling on the floor in front of him. She was wearing a long, rumpled gray dress. Her pale face floated in and out of his view like a sad, wrinkled balloon. Her facial features appeared strangely flat and dimension-less. The dark hollows of her blank, staring eyes drew him in like sucking whirlpools. The expression on her face was emotionless, absolutely lifeless as she leaned forward, planted her hands firmly on his shoulders, and shook him with all her strength.

"I was afraid you were going to leave me again, Daddy!" Karen said.

Her voice was high-pitched and nervous-sounding, and seemed out of synch with her blank facial expression.

"I....you know I'd never do that," David managed to reply with a gasp. He couldn't decide if he was speaking out loud or just thinking the words. "I...couldn't find you," he said. "I was afraid that I—that I'd lost you again."

"Don't ever leave me again, Daddy. Please, Daddy! Don't!" Karen pleaded.

David wanted to convince himself that he could see a deep sadness in her eyes, but it was disconcerting that she wasn't crying. She sounded frightened enough to be crying, so why wasn't she? He still couldn't get over the impression that none of this was really happening.

It couldn't be!

Karen looked much too thin and pale. He skin was almost transparent. For the briefest instant, David thought he could actually see the dark plaster wall directly behind her, as if she were a movie projection on the wall.

"I won't leave you ever again, Sugar!" he said. "I promise you!"

The false hope that everything so far had all been a dream was quickly extinguished when he looked around, and the dank ruins of the old schoolhouse came into sharper focus. Shifting shadows clung like dark clots to the floor, ceiling, and walls. Slanting shafts of diffused sunlight, looking like sickly gray columns of smoke, caught and illuminated the dense, dust-filled air. The silence of the room was so total it made David's ears ring.

There's something really wrong with her! David couldn't help but think as he stared into his daughter's vacant eyes.

He knew that he couldn't expect to see even a hint of life there.

She was dead...just as he was dead!

But the glazed coldness in Karen's eyes seemed to be more than the dull glaze of a dead person's eyes. There was an infinite distance inside her, a lifeless void that, for the first time David realized with a shudder, he could never breach or even begin to fathom.

He wondered if his own dead eyes looked as frightening to her as hers did to him.

"Did you see her?" Karen asked. "Did you talk to her yet?"

Although he thought he should hear at least a hint of desperation in her voice, David noticed that her tone of voice sounded curiously flat. He nodded his head slowly, unable—or not daring—to break eye contact with her.

"Yeah, I—I did."

His voice sounded raw.

"I...I saw her and I tried to talk to her."

"Did you warn her? Did you tell her about the man with the knife?"

A sudden surge of panic made David reach out and grab his daughter's arms tightly. His sense of touch was still deadened, but her shoulders felt as fragile as dried bones in his grasp. He had the brief impression that there was nothing to her—no body at all inside her rumpled dress.

"How do you know about the knife?" he asked, unable to mask the tension that was winding up inside him.

For a long time, Karen didn't reply.

She just knelt there in front of him and stared at him with those dark, hollow eyes that looked like two bottomless pits. Her mouth hung open, exposing her small, flat teeth. It made her look somewhat feral. Against his will, David realized that he found her face and expression unnerving, almost repulsive.

"I...I saw it," Karen finally replied in a shattered whisper. "I was there...at the house...last night...and I saw that he had a knife and was...he was gonna use it on her!"

She has to mean the knife the Ferryman was talking to me about, David thought with a deep, internal shudder, *the same knife I saw that night in Sarah's bedroom*.

"You have to stop him, Daddy!" Karen pleaded. "He wants to *hurt* her! He wants to *kill* Mommy! I *know* he does!"

David almost told her everything he knew about the knife, but then decided it was probably better not to mention anything about it or his conversation with the Ferryman. She was afraid enough as it was for her mother's safety. He saw no reason to add to her distress.

"Don't you worry, Sugar," he said, his voice softer than a hushed whisper in the eerie silence of the room. "I'm gonna do everything I can to help her. I promise you."

David wished that he believed that himself. He wished earnestly in his heart that there *was* something he could do…*anything* to help Sarah, but he had no idea what. The Ferryman had told him that there were powers he could master in the Shadowlands, but he didn't have time for that.

"Have you ever tried to talk to her?" he asked Karen, peering intently into her dull eyes and trying to ignore the lifeless expression he saw there. It pained him not to see even the slightest hint of the young, vibrant person she had once been. It tore his heart to realize that all of those youthful, passionate qualities that he had so much loved and admired in his daughter had been ripped out of her—destroyed by Death.

"*Me?*" Karen said, sounding astounded.

She shook her head slowly from side to side and didn't stop as she back away from him.

David released his grip on her. His hands fell uselessly to his sides.

"But I—I can't," Karen said in a trembling whisper that seemed to be echoed by other, fainter voices from upstairs.

"I tried. Lots of times I tried, but I—I don't know how to do it."

All the while, she continued to shake her head.

"Besides, I—I'm just a kid. I'm not strong enough. But I know you are, Daddy. You'll get through to her and tell her about that bad man with the knife, won't you?"

"I sure as hell intend to try," David said. "You can count on it!"

And then, for the first time, Karen's expression changed.

Her lips pulled back in what David supposed was a grin; but her expression looked like nothing except the silent, horrible grimace of Death.

The steady clacking of the computer keys was starting to get on Sarah's nerves.

Then again, *everything* today seemed to be getting on her nerves.

After she and Tony had eaten a light breakfast together—just orange juice and toast with jam—Tony had gotten dressed and left with a promise to call her at work later that afternoon.

Sarah wasn't sure she knew how she felt about that.

After he was gone, Sarah, still dressed in her bathrobe, spent the next half hour or so walking around outside the house and yard, clicking her tongue and calling to Bingley.

He never showed up.

This wasn't at all like him, and as much as she didn't want to admit it, she knew deep in her heart that something must have happened to him. She tried not to imagine him getting hit by a car while crossing the street last night and crawling off into the bushes somewhere to die.

If that was the case, all she could hope was that he had died quickly, without much suffering. She checked in the garage and peered underneath the porch, but there was no sign of him anywhere.

On the drive to work, tears kept filling her eyes as she couldn't stop wondering if she would ever see Bingley again. Even then, she realized that she was crying more for David and Karen and herself than she was for her poor old cat.

She hadn't been lying to Tony about the data entries she had to make at work, so as soon as she got to the library, even though she was more than an hour early, she sat down at her desk, switched on the computer terminal, and started typing the entries.

As she worked, the steady click-clicking of the keys quickly started to work on her nerves.

She found it difficult, almost impossible to concentrate on her work. As her mind drifted, she found herself continually thinking back to David's funeral yesterday…and Karen's funeral five years before that.

Her vision blurred with tears that made the terminal screen look fuzzy green. Her eyes stung, and her cheeks were slick with tears. Every now and then she would glance down at her hands and marvel at how slim and pale they looked. The tendons shifting beneath her skin as she typed looked like thin pencils that could break with only the slightest amount of pressure.

This is no damn good!…This is no damn good!

She kept repeating this to herself, unable to stop thinking about the life she and David and Karen used to have together before it had been so horribly and tragically ripped apart.

She fought hard to control her emotions, but she knew that she was losing.

Earlier that day, Elizabeth McDonald, her boss, had offered for her to take a few days off; but Sarah had refused, saying that probably the best thing for her would be to keep working, to stick with some part of the regular routine of her life.

But now she was starting to think that that might not have been such a good idea.

Maybe what she really needed was a complete break from everything. She had some vacation time due in August. Maybe Elizabeth would let her take it now. A trip somewhere—anywhere—might be just what she needed, if only to get away from Tony for a while so she could try to sort out exactly what she thought about him.

But other things were bothering her as well—deeper things, like grief and despair and guilt, and she knew they weren't simply going to fly away.

She realized that she should probably start cleaning out David's apartment soon. There was no sense paying another month's rent for an unoccupied apartment.

That was something she wasn't exactly looking forward to. She wondered who she might call to ask to help her with it.

A wild shiver suddenly gripped her, shaking her so badly that she glanced nervously over her shoulder to see if anyone had noticed.

The library was almost deserted. A few students were slumped over their books in the study carrels and at the tables. One young couple, sitting on a couch in the periodicals section, seemed to be spending a lot more time gazing at each other and kissing than they did looking at their textbooks. Three people were using the card catalog computers, and Marilyn Crosby was busy re-shelving books. Elizabeth was in her office with her head bowed as she concentrated on the sheaf of papers that was spread across her desk.

No one had noticed her, but Sarah frowned as she craned her neck to look around, unable to dispel the discomforting feeling that someone *was* watching her.

Maybe Tony was lurking nearby, watching her.

He hadn't seemed the slightest bit mistrustful of her when she'd told him she had to work today, but maybe he was the jealous, suspicious kind who would follow her to work and spy on her anyway. She couldn't deny that there had been *something* weird about him this morning—something that she couldn't quite define but which she felt nonetheless.

As soon as she turned back to her work, another, stronger shiver raced through her veins like a surge of icy water.

Covering her face with both hands, she leaned forward with her elbows on the desk, closed her eyes, and took a deep breath. The air rushing between her cupped fingers whistled like a blustery winter wind. Cold, prickly sensations raced up and down her back as she stared into the darkness behind her eyes and calmly started counting to ten.

One…two…three…

She stared into the darkness that pulsated with two inward turning spirals of yellow and gray zigzag patterns. She found the whistling sound of her breathing almost soothing.

Almost…

Tension coiled like a tightening spring deep within her stomach.

Four…five…

Amorphous blobs of deep purple and radiant blue light appeared in her field of vision, seeming to advance and retreat at the same time, keeping time with her breathing.

Six…seven…eight…

The sounds in the library were muted and distant. Sarah had the momentary impression that she was listening to them from a great distance away. She kept breathing steadily, noticing the faint stinging smell of ozone. As she pulled the air deeper into her lungs, the smell got stronger.

Nine…

A shiver flickered like cold lightning through her. Her body instantly tensed when she heard a soft *click* that sounded a bit like one of the keys of the keyboard being depressed.

Ten…

Her insides were trembling terribly as she slowly opened her eyes, but she didn't quite dare take her hands away from her face.

Not yet.

Then another *click* sounded close to her—a short, sharp *pop*.

Cold sweat broke out over her forehead and neck. Her whole body went rigid. The muscles in her legs and arms felt like they had hardened into knots as she slowly pulled her hands away from her face and looked down at the computer keyboard.

She watched in utter amazement as another key—the letter *P*—clicked down as though being pressed by an invisible finger. She would have screamed if she'd had the air in her lungs. Something popped in her neck as she slowly raised her head and looked at the computer screen. She couldn't believe what she saw written there.

R I P

Her breath felt like a hot lead weight in the center of her chest. She wanted desperately to get up from the desk, but she couldn't move a muscle—she couldn't even blink as she watched and heard more keys click in rapid succession.

P E R

The world around her suddenly went all hazy and out of focus. She could hear herself whimpering softly, but she found it impossible to get enough air deep enough into her lungs to make any other sound. Faster now, the keys continued to clack, and letters spilled across the screen.

R-I-P-P-E-R-R-I-P-P-E-R-R-I-P-P-E-R-R-I-P-
P-E-R-R-I-P-P-E-R-R-I-P-P-E-R-R-I-P-P-E-R
R-I-P-P-E-R-R-I-P-P-E-R-R-I-P-P-E-R-R-I-P-

Wave after wave of sour nausea swept through Sarah. She wanted to stand up, to get away from her desk, but everything in the room seemed so distant, so otherworldly. Strong, icy gusts of wind swirled around her, snatching her breath away and making her shiver wildly. All she could do was watch the glowing square of the computer screen and the letters as they appeared there.

RIPPER RIPPER RIPPER RIPPER RIPPER RIPPER RIP
PER RIPHER RIPHER RIPPER RIPPER RIPHER RIPHER
RIPHER RIPHER RIPHER RIPHER RIPHER RIPHER RIP

Sarah forced herself to look down at her hands, if only to reassure herself that she wasn't doing this. Her fingers were laced together and clenched tightly in her lap. The clicking sounds of the keyboard was so rapid now it sounded like a string of firecrackers, going off inside her head.

RIP HER RIP HER RIP PER RIP PER RIP HER RIP
HER RIP PER RIP PER RIP PER RIP HER RIP HER
RIP PER RIP HER RIP PER RIP HER RIP HER RIP
HER RIP PER RIP PER RIP PER RIP HER RIP HER

"No...no...oh, sweet Jesus, no!" Her voice was low and strangled, and sounded completely detached from her body. Panic and confusion raged inside of her. She moaned softly, only distantly aware that she was rocking back and forth in her chair.

She wished she could find the strength to get away from the desk, but every muscle in her body felt unstrung, every nerve was wire-hot and tingling. She unclasped her fingers, raised her hands, and placed them on the edge of the desk. When she did finally manage to push herself back, she felt something *pop* in her lower back.

Thick, salty pressure was rapidly building up inside her head, and she was suddenly afraid that she was going to burst a blood vessel in her brain.

Maybe it's already burst! Maybe I'm dying right now!

Her eyes moved spasmodically as she scanned the computer screen, finding it impossible to make any sense out of the jumble of words and letters. Her lips moved slowly, as if she had been drugged, as she sounded out the combinations of words until—finally—the meaning hit her like the blast of a shotgun.

"Ripper…Rip her," she whispered hoarsely. "What the hell does—"

"Everything okay here?"

Sarah spun around so quickly to see who had spoken that she almost blacked out. The room seemed to slip to one side like the deck of a storm-tossed ship. It took her a moment to realize that Elizabeth was standing close behind her. Feeling embarrassed and absolutely flustered, Sarah tried to say something but found she couldn't. Instead, she just stared blankly up at her boss and shrugged as she bit her lower lip and shook her head.

"Problem with the computer, huh?" Elizabeth said, frowning as she planted both hands on the desk in front of Sarah and leaned forward to look at the screen.

The hard coldness in Sarah's stomach tightened as she turned back around to face the terminal. She gasped when she saw that the screen was blank except for the blinking green rectangle of the cursor in the upper left corner of the screen.

"What was scrolling by there a second ago?" Elizabeth asked, her frown deepening.

All Sarah could do was shrug as she inhaled sharply. It didn't feel like she got anywhere near enough air into her lungs. Her throat felt dry and scratchy, as if she had just swallowed a handful of hot sand. She wanted to say something, but was afraid even to try to speak because of the sound she might make.

"Damn computers!" Elizabeth said, gently swatting the monitor with one hand. "I hope you didn't lose any of the work you'd already done?"

"Maybe a bit of it," Sarah said, shaking her head numbly.

She almost didn't understand what her boss was saying to her, and she couldn't stop wondering what had happened to the words that had been scrolling across the screen. They were gone now as if they had never been there.

"That's too bad," Elizabeth said.

She tapped the *Enter* key several times, but nothing happened.

"Maybe the hard drive's fried. I have no idea. I hope you had it all backed up?"

Tight-lipped, Sarah nodded and managed to say, "Yeah, I got most of it saved…I think."

To her own ears, her voice sounded like a croaking frog.

Elizabeth tapped rapidly on the keys a few times. The clicking sound was like hot spikes to Sarah's nerves, but she tried her best to ignore it.

"Well, I have no idea what the hell's wrong with it," Elizabeth said.

She reached over and pressed the power button. The screen winked off with a crackle of static, and the computer powered down. Sarah half-expected to see the words GAME OVER appear on the blank screen.

"I'll have Janice take a look at it tomorrow," Elizabeth said, standing back and brushing her hands together as though dismissing it. When she looked at Sarah, her perplexed expression softened.

"You know, you don't look so good, Sarah," she said in a mild, understanding voice.

"No, I—I'm all right," Sarah replied tightly.

"Think you could use the rest of the day off?"

Sarah started to protest, but before she could say anything, Elizabeth waved her hand and pointed at the front door.

"Go on," she said. "This has got to be a really tough time for you, and—" hands on her hips, she glanced around the nearly deserted library and smiled. "We're not exactly swamped here today."

Sarah wasn't at all sure that she had the strength even to stand up, much less walk all the way to the front door, but she managed to get up from her chair while nodding her thanks.

"Yeah, I—I think I'll go home and take a nap or something," she said dazedly.

"You do that," Elizabeth replied.

Sarah put the papers away, grabbed her purse from the bottom desk drawer, and walked to the door and out into the blistering heat of the day.

But as it turned out, she didn't go straight home.

She had no idea why, but she drove out to David's apartment in Westbrook.

Still feeling all wound up and tense inside, she parked her car at the curb, made sure to lock it, and walked up to the apartment. Her hands were shaking terribly as she unlocked the door and entered.

Although she had no specific idea what she was doing, she sensed on some deep level that she had come here for a definite purpose. At times, it seemed almost as if she could hear a voice, whispering to her, telling her what to do; but it was always too faint for her to make out exactly what it was saying.

She told herself that it was just her imagination—her intuition or something. So maybe it was her intuition that directed her into David's bedroom.

For a long time, she just stood there in the doorway, leaning against the door jamb as she tried to orient herself. The heat inside the small, closed apartment was stifling, but she could feel numbing chills deep inside her.

Try as she might, she still couldn't accept the fact that David really was dead. How could he be gone forever?

The drab, cramped rooms of his apartment still seemed imbued with his presence. She closed her eyes and inhaled deeply, almost catching a lingering trace of his aftershave.

A pang of loneliness and loss filled her, and she realized that, in spite of the problems they'd had and the divorce, in many ways she still loved him. For a silent, fragile moment, she could almost imagine that he was standing close beside her, and she found the thought comforting; but when she tried to imagine hearing his voice, the only sound she could hear was the soft hiss of traffic passing by outside.

When she opened her eyes, the lighting in the room seemed to have changed subtly. A muted yellow glow filled the bedroom. The air seemed heavy and dense.

Sarah gasped out loud when her vision cleared, and she realized that she was staring straight ahead at the books and magazines that were stacked on the table beside David's bed.

There was something about them…something that struck her as vaguely familiar.

What the hell was it?

A vague memory…or possibly something from a dream.

For some reason, she thought of the irritating clicking sound the keyboard at work had made, and that reminded her of something else…another sound that was very similar.

What the hell is *it?*

Feeling as if she were moving in a dream, she walked over to David's bed and sat down on the edge. The bedsprings sagged and creaked beneath her weight. A wave of tiredness swept over her, and she was tempted to lie down and fall asleep. She had the unnerving feeling that she might be dreaming all of this as she watched her hand reach out as if it had a will of its own toward the drawer of the bedside table.

The metal latch was cold to the touch as she hooked it with her forefinger and snapped it up. When she pulled it open, the rough scraping sound the drawer made set her teeth on edge.

She gasped again, louder this time, when she looked down and saw the small revolver inside the drawer. Without even thinking, she picked it up and hefted it.

The gun was compact and surprisingly heavy for its size. She didn't know the first thing about guns, so she had no idea what kind it was or even if it was loaded, but feeling it in her hand made her suddenly feel…different, somehow.

"Safer," she whispered as if in answer to an unasked question.

Squinting one eye shut, she raised the gun with a trembling hand and sighted along the short barrel as if aiming to shoot. She let out a sharp gasp when her focus shifted from the tip of the revolver to what she was aiming at—

The faded, torn spine of a book.

Once again, the feeling came over her of knowing something but not consciously realizing what it was. Chills skittered like tiny hands up her back as she read the title out loud.

"James Moore's Complete Encyclopedia of Mass Murderers."

The gun suddenly felt too heavy to hold. It weighed down her hand and made it drop.

"Oh, Jesus," she whispered.

What is it about that title? she wondered. It rang a distant bell in her memory, but she couldn't say what or how. She didn't think it was simply that she had noticed the book from when she and David were married. Always casting about for plots and background for his novels, David often bought and read books like this.

No, it was more than that.

Much more.

The pit of her stomach tightened like a fist. Her hand was shaking as she slowly placed the gun on the bed beside her. She found it almost impossible to swallow or even breathe as she reached out to the stack of books. When she ran the tip of her finger down along the book spines, the faint *clicking* sound it made filled her with a discomforting feeling.

"One," she whispered softly.

She listened to her voice as if it were someone else, speaking to her from another room.

"One-thirty."

A cold, tight pressure filled her chest as she tried to grasp the thought that was dancing elusively in her mind, just out of reach.

"One-thirty-seven."

She couldn't keep her hands from shaking as she shifted the book out from the middle of the stack and hefted it. She grunted when she placed it in her lap. Her fingers were tingling as she opened the book and idly rifled through the pages. Her vision of the room blurred when she cast a nervous glance over her shoulder, then stared back at the book and flipped pages until she got to page 137.

"Is this it?…Yes, this is it," she whispered raggedly.

There was a small block of text at the top of the page, but what instantly drew her attention was the grainy black and white photograph of a knife that took up the bottom half of the page. Beside the knife was a metric ruler which indicated that the blade was slightly more than twenty centimeters long. Sarah wasn't sure what the equivalent was in inches, but the thin blade with what looked like a rounded rubber handle looked absolutely wicked. The caption identified the knife as one of the surgical postmortem instruments from the Victorian Era. This particular knife was reputed to have been used by Jack the Ripper.

"Jack the—" Sarah whispered as a searing spark of panic leaped inside her.

"—Ripper…"

She moaned softly and closed her eyes.

Instantly, her mind filled with the mental image of her computer screen scrolling the words *RIPPER…RIPPER…RIP HER.*

"Jesus, what's going on here?" she muttered.

With a sudden surge of energy, she slammed the book shut and threw it to the floor. It hit with a *thud* that seemed as loud as a gunshot.

Shivering wildly inside, Sarah squeezed her head tightly with both hands as though trying to contain an imminent explosion. The salty pressure pounding like hammers behind her eyes was intolerable, and it seemed only to get worse when she opened her eyes again and looked around the room.

The weird yellow glow in the room seemed to intensify, making everything appear as though she was looking through a thick, transparent barrier, like a plate-glass window. Feeling as though she were watching herself in a movie, she once again reached out and picked up David's revolver.

She grunted with satisfaction as she hefted it, but the sound seemed to come not from inside her, but from far away.

Knives aren't anything against a gun!

The sudden violence of her thought surprised her. Although she had never liked guns, and had always hoped that David would get rid of his, for some reason it now felt good to hold.

It felt *right*!

Knowing that she now possessed a gun made her feel a bit safer.

Every muscle in her body was still wire-tight as she snapped open her purse and slid the gun underneath her wallet to hide it.

She had no idea why she was doing this. It made her feel like a thief, but she told herself that David sure as hell didn't need it any longer....

And she might.

She couldn't have explained why.

She didn't even want to try.

It just seemed like the right thing to do.

It was late in the afternoon.

Golden bars of sunlight shot through the living room windows and cast thin, gray washes of shadow across the carpet and furniture. The air in the room was dense and quiet, a lot like being underwater. David felt drained with exhaustion as he leaned back against the wall and slowly lowered himself to the floor. His back made an abrasive hissing sound as it rubbed against the plaster. With no better idea of what to do, he had decided to wait here until Sarah came home.

Early that morning, he had left Karen at the schoolhouse with strict instructions not to go anywhere or do anything until he came back. He had guessed that Sarah would be at the university library, and had gone there to wait until she showed up. He had watched her reaction while he tried to type a message to her on the computer, but he knew that he had screwed it up.

His fingers had fumbled with the keys, sometimes passing clear through the keyboard and desk top as he concentrated hard, trying to focus all of his energy so he could type. Under different circumstances, he might have even found it amusing that he, a professional writer, was having so damned much trouble pressing even a single key, much less forming complete words or sentences.

After he'd gotten the first few letters on the screen, though, he had either hit the wrong key or else his presence was somehow messing up the electrical signals inside the computer. Whatever the reason, he hadn't been able to stop the words once they'd started scrolling crazily across the screen.

Sarah had, understandably, been frightened, and David had watched helplessly as she and her boss tried to figure out what was going wrong with the computer. The static charge that filled the air when Elizabeth switched off the power had given him a mild shock, and he was left feeling absolutely drained and hollow.

A mere ghost of my former self, he thought, and almost found the thought amusing.

David was most upset because he hadn't intended to scare Sarah. He wanted to find some way to warn her about the man she was seeing…and the knife that he owned. The danger that knife presented to Sarah seemed so real and immediate that it was almost palpable in the air.

He couldn't forget how he'd been watching that man make love to his ex-wife. That memory had left traces of bitter jealousy in his heart and soul. He knew that he couldn't forget or forgive—either one of them.

And it filled him with sadness to realize something else.

He realized, now that it was much too late, that he still loved Sarah.

He loved her and he knew he always would, even beyond death.

And worse than watching the woman he loved make love to another man was knowing that he had seen the knife that night.

It *had* to be the knife the Ferryman wanted.

David was irritated that he hadn't recognized its power. He might have done something about it then.

He had watched the young man take hold of the knife and swing it back and forth quickly several times, as if warming up, preparing to use it.

When Sarah had returned to the bedroom, the man had hidden the knife beneath his clothes; but now David knew—or at least sensed—what the man intended to do with it.

He was going to kill Sarah!

Maybe he didn't want to.

Maybe, as the Ferryman had said, the knife was controlling him as much as he was controlling it.

Maybe it was something else, but David really didn't care.

The important thing was, it was just a matter of time before the man worked up his courage or rage or whatever it was going to take for him to use the knife on another human being. For more than ten years, in fourteen novels, David had made up stories about murderous passions and twisted minds. It was terribly unnerving to be confronted by such forces in real life.

If you can call this 'real life,' he thought bitterly, *but I guess I really can't if I'm already dead!*

It was too bad he hadn't seen the danger of the knife that night…too bad he hadn't tried to do something about it when he had the chance. But what could he have done? Even if he had tried, how could he gain possession of something that he couldn't even touch, much less pick up?

When Sarah left the library that afternoon, David had felt much too drained to follow after her immediately, so he had made his way back to Pine Knoll Elementary. After checking to make sure that Karen was all right, he had walked over to Sarah's house.

He'd expected to see that she was already home when he got there, and was surprised to see that her car wasn't parked either in the driveway or in the garage.

Something was wrong.

He could feel a sense of impending danger like a subtle electrical charge in the air. His worry blossomed into stark fear when he passed through the closed door and walked into the kitchen.

The house was empty and as silent as a tomb except for a faint scratching sound just at the threshold of hearing.

David couldn't identify it. He wasn't even sure where the sound was coming from, but he chose to ignore it as he walked into the living room and sat down on the floor beside the TV to wait for Sarah to return home.

She would eventually.

He watched the sun slide smoothly across the floor, edging the furniture with a fine line of yellow fire. He leaned against the wall with his knees tucked up tightly against his chest and watched tiny dust motes drifting in the air. Like minuscule planets, they were illuminated for a few seconds by the narrow shafts of light, and then they winked out of existence and were gone.

Forever.

Just like our lives, David thought, transfixed by the barely perceptible fall of dust. It must have been his imagination, but he thought he could actually hear the dust hit the floor.

As he sat there, letting his thoughts drift like the dust, sad, poignant memories of the few short, happy years he had spent living here with Sarah and Karen filled him. At the time, those years hadn't seemed all that happy. He'd been struggling so damned hard to get his writing career going that he'd been fairly miserable to live with most of the time. He knew and acknowledged that at the time, but Sarah had made no bones about telling him so, anyway.

His frustration and anger at not making it big as an author was probably the single biggest contributing factor to their marriage falling apart. Karen's death had been the final straw.

In retrospect, however, maybe his life back then hadn't been all that bad.

It certainly wasn't as bad as things were now, and—at least as far as he could tell—this existence was never going to end!

Mired in his own depressing thoughts and wallowing in useless regret, David lost track of the time.

He suddenly jolted to alertness when he realized that the sun had long since set. A hushed, expectant darkness filled the room. Deep shadows stretched like groping hands across the floor, and Sarah still wasn't home.

David listened to the snapping and creaking sounds the house made as it cooled from the heat of the day. He hadn't heard any other voices whispering in the dark, so he felt slightly reassured that there were no other unseen presences—no other wraiths haunting the house. The only other sound he heard was that faint scratching sound which seemed now to be coming from underneath the floor in the kitchen…or maybe it was coming from upstairs….

David couldn't get a direction on it, but he didn't spend much time worrying about it.

He was much more concerned about Sarah's safety.

As he sat there in the gathering gloom and waited, a deep sense of futility and frustration mixed with an ineffable sadness. These feelings built up inside him and almost tore him apart. He could feel the dark, eternal emptiness in the center of his being swelling larger, reaching out for him as he wondered what had gone so terribly wrong with his life that it had come to this.

Sometime later—he had no idea when—the sound of footsteps and the doorknob being turned drew his attention.

"Sarah," he called out, even though he knew that she wouldn't be able to hear him.

Moving like a raft of thin smoke, he got up and walked into the kitchen where he saw a shadow shift across the closed window shade.

Then the door began to open slowly.

A brilliant flash of rage filled David when he saw that it wasn't Sarah. It was the young man she had been dating!

Moving cautiously, the man stepped into the house and then carefully eased the door shut behind him, locking it before glancing around.

He didn't turn on any lights as he moved stealthily into the kitchen. David heard him swear softly under his breath when he bumped into the kitchen table on his way to the living room. Moving close behind him, David noticed the slight bulge under the man's shirt just above his back pocket and realized with a sudden jolt that it was the knife.

Jesus! He's come back to hurt her!

Sudden, desperate fury filled David. He lunged forward and swung his arms around the man, hoping to tackle him, but his hands passed through the man like fleeting shadows.

The young man shivered at David's touch, stopped short in his tracks, and looked around furtively and shook his head. When he spoke, his voice sounded so low and distorted that David found it almost impossible to make out what he was saying.

"Place gives me the fucking creeps."

Fear, frustration, and rage filled David as he watched the man walk through the living room and start up the stairs. He was moving a little more boldly now that he seemed assured that Sarah wasn't home.

David stayed close behind him even though he knew there was nothing he could do to stop him from whatever he was planning to do.

When the man was halfway up the stairs, he paused.

Shivering again, he reached up under the back of his shirt. He licked his lips, and a strange glow filled his eyes as he slowly withdrew the knife and stared at it. The exposed blade shimmered in the darkness with a weird, flickering purple glow that cast fuzzy, swaying shadows on the steps and walls when the man moved the knife back and forth.

He's going to use it! Jesus! He's going to kill Sarah!

The man's footsteps clumped heavily on the stairs as he started moving again. Beneath that sound, though, David could hear something else—that same faint, scratching sound. He was trying to figure out where the sound was coming from and what it might be when he caught a hint of dark motion at the top of the stairs. He cried out in surprise when he saw a small, dark, deformed shape, standing directly in the path of the man.

At first, David had no idea what this thing was.

It looked like an animal of some kind, but instead of fur its body was composed of a network of stringy pink and red muscle, and white tendons that made it look like an anatomical diagram. Glistening white knobs of bone stuck out through the flesh, and a coiled piece of meat that looked like an intestine was hanging from underneath it. The wrinkled flesh made the animal look like a large, freshly peeled rat, but after a moment, David realized that it was—or at least it had been—a cat. Its round eyes reflected the night with a wicked green glare as it curled back its raw upper lip, exposing needle-sharp teeth.

"Jesus! *Bingley?*" David said in a hushed whisper.

The cat turned its head mechanically and glared down at him, but only for a moment before it shifted its unblinking gaze back to the man, who was still making his way slowly up the stairs.

The man seemed totally oblivious to the cat that waited for him at the top of the stairs.

David watched, both sickened and amused as the monstrosity that had once been his and his wife's pet hunched up its back and hissed loudly. The sound was harsh, like the hiss of escaping steam, but the man didn't seem to hear it. His step faltered, however, and he stumbled and might have fallen if he hadn't reached out quickly and caught the banister with one hand. He looked up and down the stairs as though momentarily confused by something, but then continued up the stairs. Hunching up, the cat hissed again—a wild, piercing squeal. Then it scampered off, disappearing into the darkness of the hallway.

Jesus, he must have killed Bingley…and now he's coming after Sarah!

David was frantic with helpless fear. He knew that he either had to stop the man or else warn Sarah, but he had no idea how to do that.

He watched as the man walked past where the cat had been and down the corridor to Sarah's bedroom. He entered the room and closed the door quietly behind him.

A sudden, loud rumbling sound from outside drew David's attention. He looked down the stairs as the harsh glare of headlights rippled across the living room walls.

A car was pulling into the driveway.

Jesus, she's home!

Frozen for a moment, David was unable to decide which way to turn.

Could he warn Sarah somehow, or should he follow the man into the bedroom and try to stop him from what he was preparing to do?

Panic as clean and sharp as a stainless steel blade ripped through him when he heard Sarah's key rattle loudly in the door lock.

Then the door opened, and he heard her enter. She sighed heavily before slamming the door shut behind her. A flood of warm, yellow light came on downstairs.

Standing poised halfway up the stairs, David watched and listened as Sarah walked into the living room, turning on lights as she went. She was whistling a tune under her breath, but David could sense that she was tense, nervous.

Finally, without any better idea what to do, he moved as fast as he could down the hallway to the bedroom, but the hall suddenly seemed to telescope outward. He had the unnerving impression that he walked past dozens, maybe hundreds of doors before he finally arrived at Sarah's bedroom. Trembling wildly, he entered the room by walking through the door.

The young man was naked and sitting on the edge of the bed in the dark. In his right hand, he was holding the knife and smiling sickly to himself as he twisted it back and forth, flicking it with quick snaps of his wrist. The blade made sharp whickering sounds as it cut the air, and this seemed to please the man no end. The strange purple glow emanating from the knife blade lit the man's eyes. His tight, lop-sided grin made him look positively insane.

"Get the hell out of here! Right now!" David shouted, but his words seemed to fade away to nothing before they left his mouth.

He lurched forward and tried to grab the man again, but his hands passed through him. David knew, no matter how hard he tried, he wasn't going to be able to touch him.

But there had to be *something* he could do!

The Ferryman had said that he wanted David to get the knife for him, so there must be some power or talent that he could draw upon to do it.

If he only had the time to figure it out….

But *now* wasn't the time to try to figure *anything* out.

With a cold, dread certainty that settled like a lead weight in the center of his chest, David knew that if he didn't stop this man right now, Sarah was going to die tonight.

10

A Dead Man's Dreams

"Shitty day…Jesus, what a *shitty* day," Sarah muttered as she walked back into the kitchen.

She hesitated a moment before taking a glass and the bottle of burgundy down from the cupboard and pouring herself more than she thought she probably should have, but she told herself it was okay.

She needed it. After a day like today, she was going to need a *lot* of something to numb herself if she was ever going to get to sleep.

Heaving a deep sigh, she pulled a chair away from the kitchen table and sat down heavily. Grasping the glass with both hands to keep it steady, she took a big gulp and swallowed noisily.

Warm and rich, the burgundy exploded on the back of her tongue and tickled the back of her throat as it went down. After a second or two, it hit her stomach like a hard, warm fist. She gasped and nodded her approval before taking another sip. Then she leaned back in her chair and stared up at the ceiling, letting her vision go fuzzy.

"Jesus, what a day!"

After a long silence, she sat up and let her gaze drift to the kitchen counter, over by the door where she had left her purse as soon as she had entered the house. The small blue and white canvas bag looked slightly ominous to her, and she knew exactly why.

It was because of the gun she had stashed inside the purse.

A real gun! She shivered. Something designed *specifically* to kill people.

She took another sip of burgundy and rolled it around in her mouth before swallowing it. She kept asking herself why she had taken the gun, but she couldn't really say why. It had just seemed like the right thing to do.

She certainly had no use for a gun. She didn't have any idea how to check to see if it was loaded; much less did she know how to use it. If she seriously thought she needed some kind of protection, then she should find a firing range where she could learn how to use a gun properly. Better yet, she should get a dog. Now that Bingley was gone, that might not be such a bad idea.

If she ever really needed a gun for self-defense, she wasn't even sure she would dare to aim it at someone, much less actually pull the trigger and shoot.

Not at another human being!

All her life, she had despised the idea of people owning guns, even if they maintained it was solely to protect themselves. More often than not, those same people ended up killing their relatives or friends during arguments…. Or worse, sometimes they took out an innocent bystander.

What she should do, she told herself, was get rid of the damned thing…

Right now!

Tomorrow at the latest.

Before she hurt someone.

Or herself.

What kind of danger was she in, anyway?

Sure, she'd been feeling tense lately, maybe a little more on edge than usual, but it had to be because she was imagining things. The sadness and grief she was feeling about David's death was working on her nerves.

Yes, David's death was sad, but their marriage had been over years before she had finally found the courage to leave him. Dealing with his funeral arrangements and attending the burial had only opened up the older, deeper wounds of Karen's death—wounds that Sarah knew and accepted were never going to heal.

And now maybe even Bingley was gone. The house seemed so empty without him. She already missed him rubbing against her ankles and meowing demands for food and attention.

A hot, salty taste flooded the back of Sarah's throat. She knew that it was something the burgundy, much less self-pity and regret, would never wash away. Her view of the kitchen blurred as tears flooded her eyes, shattering the glow of the overhead light into hundreds of tiny yellow fragments.

She raised her glass to take another sip, but the thought of the taste of burgundy nauseated her. A cold, fluttery trembling clutched her stomach. The air in the kitchen suddenly seemed too thin to breathe as wave after wave of dizziness rushed through her. Pinpoints of bright light drifted across her vision.

Sarah knew that it wasn't just the burgundy that was hitting her so hard. It had to be the accumulated stress and pressure of the last few days finally catching up with her. She sighed, wishing that she were already lying down in bed, but now she wasn't even sure she had the strength to stand up.

When the telephone suddenly rang, she squealed and spun around, almost falling out of her chair. A hot, sharp pain lanced the center of her chest.

Her first impulse was to get up and answer the phone, but then she thought to let the answering machine take it—especially if it was Tony. She wasn't exactly in the mood to talk to him or anyone else tonight.

By the third ring, though, she couldn't stand the nerve-rattling electronic beeping sound any longer, so she heaved herself to her feet and went over to the counter. Her hand was slick with sweat as she grabbed the phone from its base in the middle of the fourth ring.

"Hello," she said, her voice tight and strangled-sounding.

She was prepared to hear Tony at the other end of the line and was surprised when she heard a familiar-sounding woman's voice instead.

"Sarah. Hi. So, you're finally home, huh?"

"Hi, Mom," Sarah replied, hearing the funny, hollow echo in her own voice. The muscles in the back of her neck instantly knotted into rock-hard lumps. She let her head sag forward and her shoulders slump, hoping to relieve the tension.

"So how are you doing? Okay, I hope," her mother said. Without waiting for Sarah to reply, she kept right on talking.

"I'm sorry Dad and I couldn't make it to the funeral, but—well, you know how we haven't been feeling exactly tip-top lately."

"I know, Mom," Sarah replied in a low, twisted voice.

"So how'd it all go?"

"Okay, I guess. About as well as you can expect. But—yeah, I'm doing okay."

"I can't tell you how terrible Dad and I feel about all of this," her mother went on as if she wasn't even listening to what Sarah said. "You know how we had always hoped that the two of you would work things out and eventually get back together."

"That wasn't going to happen, Mom, but you can definitely stop hoping for it to happen now."

Sarah cringed, regretting saying that even before the words were out of her mouth.

"Is—uh, is Dad around?" she asked, trying quickly to cover.

"He's asleep in front of the TV, as usual," her mother replied. "I was just a little bit worried about you and wanted to call to see how you were doing. That's all. I tried calling a couple of times earlier today, but I guess you weren't in. Don't you even listen to your phone messages?"

"I—I just walked in a minute ago," Sarah said, knowing that her mother wouldn't catch her in the lie.

"Well, I'm sure you have friends you can visit and talk to if you need to. I just wanted to let you know that you're not alone in all of this. You know you're always welcome here at home. That's another reason I was calling. To see if you'd think about flying down here and spend a few days with us. Maybe even a whole week. What do you say?"

"Thanks, Mom, but—I don't think so. Not right now, anyway."

"Why not? It's been hot as the dickens down here, but you could sit in the swimming pool up to your neck all day if you like. And we could go out to eat at—"

"Thanks, mom," Sarah said quickly. "I really appreciate the offer, but I think I'll stick around here for now. Maybe sometime next month."

Sarah's head was spinning. For some reason, her mother's voice sounded oddly muffled in her ear. She eyed the more than half full glass of burgundy on the table and wondered if it really could be hitting her this hard this fast.

"Well, don't hesitate to call if you need to talk," her mother said. "After what you've been through—after everything that's happened, you'll only make yourself sick if you bottle it up inside."

Sarah couldn't help but notice that, even after five years, her mother still couldn't quite bring herself to mention Karen's death directly. She was suddenly quite sure that she didn't need her mother's help to deal with the current situation.

"I'm doing just fine, Mom—honest," she said. "Thanks for calling. I'll give you a buzz sometime next week, okay?"

"Or before that if you need to talk," her mother piped in, sounding almost cheerful.

"Yeah, sure. Talk to you soon, Mom."

"I love you, darling."

"Love you, too, Mom. Say hi to Dad for me, 'kay?"

"I sure will. Bye-bye for now."

And with that, her mother cut the connection, leaving Sarah with a loud, droning buzz in her ear.

Sarah was feeling all twisted up inside as she stared at the phone for several seconds, wishing earnestly that she could have felt a genuine connection with her mother. But ever since she could remember, there had always been an odd, unspoken awkwardness between them. Sure she *loved* her mother, but she wasn't positive that she *liked* her.

Fighting back her tears, she flicked the on/off switch with her thumb, cutting off the buzzing sound before replacing the receiver on its base.

"Jesus, Jesus, *Jesus!*"

She squeezed her head tightly with both hands. Tears gathered in her eyes and flowed, leaving warm streaks on her cheeks. She sniffed loudly and then, bracing herself, walked over to the sink and dumped the rest of her burgundy down the drain. It made a funny little gurgling noise as it went down.

When she turned away from the sink, she chanced to look down at the floor and saw Bingley's food and water bowl. The rounded mound of kibbles she'd dumped into it this morning still hadn't been touched. The water was still up to the brim of the bowl. The sight of it made the cold emptiness inside Sarah spike even more.

"Oh, Bing. What the hell are we gonna do?" she said, no more than a whisper. Razor-sharp misery twisted inside her like coils of barbed wire as she walked over to the door, opened it, and stuck her head outside.

The night air was warm and rich with the smell of green growing things. Above the dark line of trees in the distance, she could see a faint sprinkling of stars. Not even the tiniest puff of breeze blew in off the ocean to cool her face.

"Bingley. Here, fella," she called out, but the only sounds she heard were the steady chirring of crickets and the hissing rush of traffic in the distance.

"Where the hell are you, you damned foolish cat?" she said in a voice that sounded as fragile as crystal.

Sniffing loudly and wiping her eyes with the heels of her hands, she looked out into the back yard, but there was no sign of him. Her tears were flowing steadily as she walked back into the house, being careful to close and lock the door behind her. Once again, she looked down at the bowl full of cat food and was overwhelmed with sadness.

Bingley was gone…just like David and Karen were gone…and *none* of them were ever coming back!

Pounding, hot pressure filled her head when she bent down to pick up the bowl. Her hands trembled, and her body was racked with sobs as she dumped its contents into the sink, then turned on the faucet and switched on the garbage disposal.

The whirring, grinding sound instantly got on her nerves.

After filling the bowl with hot water and detergent, she bent down to pick up the wrinkled, yellowed newspaper she had put on the floor underneath the bowl a few weeks ago. She was set to ball up the paper and throw it into the trash under the sink when a headline on the front page caught her attention.

POLICE HAVE NO NEW LEADS IN SEARCH FOR MURDERER

Stunned, Sarah looked at the date at the top of the page and saw that it was over a month old.

It struck her as odd that she hadn't noticed this before. She remembered hearing something about a murder in downtown Portland several weeks ago, but she had dismissed it, assuming it was related to a drug or prostitution deal that had gone wrong—something that would never affect her.

Her hands wouldn't stop shaking as she sat down at the kitchen table and read the article. As she read, the tight nervousness in her stomach grew steadily worse. Chills played up and down her back, and she found it increasingly difficult even to breathe.

According to the article, the police were still investigating the murder of Margaret Harkness, a twenty-five-year-old woman who had worked as receptionist at Dixon Brothers Oil Company. She had been found dead in her Danforth Street apartment. A wave of dizziness hit Sarah, and she felt like she almost blacked out when she read further down in the article that Margaret had been stabbed to death.

"*Jesus*.... Stabbed!"

Her hands went suddenly clammy and felt entirely too weak to hold the newspaper.

Whimpering softly, she let go of the paper. It fluttered gently to the floor as she stood up and staggered backwards, feeling blindly behind her for something—anything—to support her. She kept backing up until she bumped into the kitchen wall, almost knocking the wind out of her.

A low, strangled sound was gathering deep in her throat as she shook her head back and forth as though refusing to believe what she had just read. She had no idea why this was upsetting her so much, but she was filled with a sudden, almost desperate panic.

You're just over-stressed, whispered a tiny voice in the back of her mind. *That's all there is to it. You're on overload.*

"No, no," she muttered as she turned and staggered into the living room, her hands clawing the air in front of her as if it were a curtain she was trying to tear through.

She banged her left knee on the edge of the coffee table but, in her panic, hardly noticed the pain.

With a deep, shuddering groan, she collapsed face-first onto the couch and lay there trembling with her eyes closed. The whole world was spinning wildly out of control, like she was on a carousel and barely had the strength to hang on.

Wrenching sobs shook her body as she pressed her face against the couch cushion and tried to stop the flood of thoughts that filled her mind.

Please...stop it! Someone! Make it stop!

David couldn't even begin to sort through all of the emotions that were raging inside him as he watched the naked man pull back the bed covers, climb into Sarah's bed and drape the sheet over his waist as he lay down flat on his back. The bulge of his erection tented the thin sheet. The man chuckled softly as he clutched the handle of the knife with both hands in front of his chest. He looked like a priest holding a crucifix.

The man's eyes were shining like those of an animal that had been caught in the sudden glare of the headlights of an oncoming car. His upper body was slick with sweat and highlighted by the dull purple glow the radiated from the blade. His breathing came in sharp, ragged gulps that filled the bedroom like the sounds of someone making violent, passionate love.

The thought that this man had made love to Sarah filled David with an unspeakable rage.

The man was still chuckling softly to himself when he raised the blade up in front of his face and turned it back and forth, admiring it in the darkness of the room. David wondered if he could see the subtle glow that emanated from the blade.

Jesus, he's gonna do it! he thought with a soul-deep shudder. *He's working up his courage, and he'll do it if I don't find some way to stop him!*

David moved closer to the bed and, leaning forward, stared deeply into the man's eyes. He concentrated as hard as he could to project his own thoughts into the man's mind.

Get out of here! Now! Before I rip your soul apart! I swear on my daughter's grave, if you hurt Sarah, I'll make you suffer in ways you can't even begin to imagine! I mean it, you lousy bastard! I'll make you die a thousand deaths if you so much as touch her!

The rage boiling up inside David made the dark bedroom appear to be flashing with bursts of bright red light. He clenched his fists, squeezing them as hard as he could and wishing that—just once—if he swung at the man, he would be able to connect solidly with living flesh. David's sense of touch was still deadened, but he could feel a strong current of energy fill his being. It made him vibrate subtly, like a tuning fork.

With a sudden, anguished cry of rage and frustration, David cocked back his fist and swung it at the man's chest with every ounce of energy he could muster.

The effect was amazing!

The young man let out a sudden, loud grunt. His body snapped up into a sitting position. His chest was heaving, and his breath rattled in the dark. His eyes were wide open and staring as he looked all around the darkened bedroom, trying to figure out what the hell had just happened. He placed one hand on his chest, then put two fingers on the inside of his wrist to check his pulse.

Good! David thought when he saw that the man was shivering.

For a single instant, the man stared directly into David's eyes, and David was positive that he was able to see him; but the man's gaze quickly shifted over to the closed bedroom door. Still looking tense and frightened, he threw aside the bed covers and stood up. Crouching low and moving stealthily, he went to the bedroom door, opened it, and looked out into the hallway. A faint glow of light from downstairs lit the hard features of his face.

"Sarah!" David shouted, even though he knew it was useless. No one still living could hear him. "Please, Sarah! Listen to me! Get out of the house!"

David was moving slowly toward the door, wondering how he could stop this man, but then he looked back at the bed and saw that the young man had left the knife on the bed. It lay there in the damp tangle of sheets, glowing dully, beckoning to David like a beacon.

Without really thinking about it, David made a grab for the knife with both hands. Willing every bit of mental energy he could muster, he tried to imagine that his hands once again had real substance, and that he could touch the knife. He visualized his fingers curling around the handle and lifting the knife, trying desperately to remember how it felt to touch things.

But the memory was too distant, too hazy.

David glanced at the young man, who was still crouching by the door and peering out into the hall. He had never wanted anything more that he wanted—right now—to hold that knife—even if only for a few seconds— just long enough to slash and stab this son of a bitch!

And it was almost working!

For a tantalizing, fleeting instant, David thought he could actually feel the smooth texture of the rubber handle. The memory of touching and holding things when he had been alive grew sharper, filling him with a trembling excitement. A dark, dizzying, backward rush swept over him as he raised his hands and saw that the knife had risen an inch or two off the bed.

Jesus, it's working! I'm doing it!

A blinding rush of excitement filled David, but he cautioned himself not to get too excited; he couldn't break his concentration.

David stared intensely at the knife, moving it more by an effort of will than by physical means. He watched in amazement as the blade turned like the needle of a compass pointing north. It was aimed straight at the young man's naked back.

The knife knows what I want it to do, David thought with a shivering rush. *What IT wants to do!*

The words of the Ferryman came back to David, filling him with dread.

"Whoever possesses those knives is also possessed by them. Eventually he'll do what the knife wants. Make no mistake. No matter how hard he tries to resist it, he will use it."

Just like I want to use it now! David screamed inside his mind as he focused all of his energy into moving the gleaming knife closer to the man's back.

David's corpus was trembling violently as he strained with the effort of keeping the knife in his hands and not letting it slip out. It was like trying to clasp a stream of water or hold onto a ray of sunshine. The terrifying feeling of his own insubstantiality was overpowering. As he held the knife and stared at it in his hand, David couldn't even begin to determine which had less substance—him or the knife.

All I want to do is use it! he thought frantically.

Just once!

Only for a few seconds!

That's all I ask!

Please!

If there is a God...or an angel...or some spirit who really wants Good to triumph over Evil, then let me do this!

Let me kill him!

NOW!

From somewhere far away, David heard a low, agonized wailing sound that grew steadily louder until it throbbed in the darkness like rolling thunder.

For the longest time, he didn't have the slightest inkling that the sound was coming from him. He focused his total attention on moving the knife, willing it to come closer...and closer to the man's naked back.

In the dim light, David could see the raw scabs of Bingley's claw marks that striped the man's back. He tried to imagine each of those wounds suddenly splitting open and gaping like raw, screaming mouths as they gushed fresh blood. The blade of the knife seemed to be glowing steadily brighter and vibrating wildly as it moved closer to its mark.

David imagined as clearly as he could the dazed look of surprise and terror he would see in the man's eyes when he felt the blade jab into his back and plunge through his lungs toward his heart.

He *wanted* it...

He *willed* it...

With a sudden, high-pitched scream, David thrust forward with every bit of energy he had left.

The knife whistled shrilly in the air. For a terrifying instant, David imagined that the blade had actually screamed.

The man suddenly wheeled around as if he had heard or sensed something.

With a surprised grunt, he dropped to the floor as the knife whizzed past his ear and buried the first inch or two of its blade into the wood of the door frame. It stuck there with a vibrating hum, mere inches from the top of the man's head.

"*Jesus!*" the man muttered, looking around, confused.

He kept turning his head back and forth, staring at the blade and then at the pressing darkness around him.

"Where the *fuck* did *that* come from?"

"You bastard!" David wailed.

His voice echoed with a dull, muffled reverberation. The pit of frustration inside him was too much to take. He reached out for the knife again, but he knew that he could no longer maintain total concentration. He wished he could cry as he watched his hand pass through the hard rubber handle without the slightest bit of resistance.

No!...Please!...It's not fair!

The young man's eyes were wide with terror and confusion. His hand was shaking terribly as he took hold of the knife and wiggled it from the door jamb. Holding the blade close to his face, he checked for any damage. He smiled, his eyes glowing like lanterns as he thumbed the edge, making sure it was still razor-sharp. Then, moving quickly and silently, he got himself dressed and left the bedroom with the knife clutched tightly in his right hand.

David's panic rose as he watched the man stride down the hall to the stairs. He walked with his shoulders hunched, looking like a primitive savage on the hunt. Moving silently to the head of the stairs, he peered down over the railing at the glow of light that spilled into the hallway from the living room.

David followed along, no more than two or three steps behind Tony as he crept silently down the stairs and into the living room. He wanted to shout out another warning when he saw the man crane his head forward, looking and listening for Sarah. His nostrils flared as though he were sniffing the air for a trace of her. He looked wild, feral.

If he sees her, he'll kill her!

Pure panic gripped David when he saw Sarah, lying face down on the couch. For a shimmering instant, he thought she looked as though she were already dead, but then David caught the slight shifting of her back as she breathed steadily.

He knew that the young man must be able to see her, too, but the man didn't hesitate for even a second. Buttoning his shirt and zipping his fly as he went, he hurried through the living room and into the kitchen, pausing only long enough to unlock the door before dashing out onto the porch.

He was already halfway down the steps when the screen door slammed shut behind him.

The sound instantly woke Sarah. With a startled cry, she rolled off the couch and awkwardly scrambled to her feet. Her body was tense, her eyes wide with fear and her fists clenched in front of her as she looked around the room, trying to figure out what had happened.

David felt only a slight measure of relief when he followed her out into the kitchen and saw that the young man was gone.

"Bingley?" Sarah called out softly. Her voice was a light, fluttering sound that was difficult for David to hear.

She looked around, confused and a little bit concerned when she noticed that the kitchen door was unlocked. She threw the bolt again and then, casting a suspicious glance around the kitchen, walked slowly back into the living room. She turned out all of the lights except one, and then, rubbing her face and muttering softly to herself, she went upstairs.

David felt an aching twinge of sadness as he watched her go.

She was safe, he thought, at least for tonight; but he knew that young man would be back. He was still going to have to figure out a way to warn Sarah of the danger that was stalking her.

Somehow…

"What the hell?" Sarah whispered when she entered her bedroom, turned on the light, and saw the unmade bed.

It had been so hot over the last week or so that she had gotten rid of the blanket and bedspread, and just had a top and bottom sheet. But she was absolutely positive that she had pulled up the bed covers this morning, just as she did every morning.

But maybe, she thought, because she'd been so upset and nervous lately, she only *thought* she had done it this morning. Little personal rituals can easily become so much second-nature that sometimes you think you've done them when actually you haven't.

Leaning down, she grabbed the top edge of the sheet, shook it out, and pulled it up over the pillows. When she folded it down and was smoothing, she jumped with surprise when she felt a warm spot in one spot on the bed.

As though someone's been sleeping here, she thought, suddenly tensing. She looked around the room, not having any idea what she expected to see.

Has Bingley been sleeping here?

Maybe he's still alive somewhere in the house!

It was a futile hope, she knew, because his food and water hadn't been touched all day, but she got down on her hands and knees, and looked under the bed.

Other than a few clots of dust, the only thing she found was what turned out to be a rolled-up sock that was turned inside-out. She grabbed it and, standing up, shook it out with a quick snap of the wrist.

It was obviously a man's sock.

Tony must have left it there by mistake last night, she guessed.

Shaking her head with confusion, she tossed the sock out into the hallway where she collected her dirty laundry.

"Bingley?" she called out again, surprised by the high quaver in her voice.

"Com'on, boy. Come here, Bing." She clicked her tongue a few times, then held her breath and waited; but she neither saw nor heard any sign of her cat.

Her stomach felt all tight and fluttery with apprehension when she walked down the hall to the bathroom and washed up for bed. Once she was back in the bedroom, she undressed, put on her lightweight nightgown, and slipped in between the cool sheets. After years of marriage, she still favored sleeping on the left side of the bed. Without even consciously thinking about it, she reached over to feel the warm spot on the mattress again.

It no longer felt quite as warm as before, but it *did* feel slightly damp, as if someone had been lying there recently.

"Jesus," Sarah whispered, wondering who or what else it could have been if it hadn't been Bingley.

"Someone's been sleeping in my bed," she said softly, using a "Three Little Bears" voice.

She almost chuckled, but the tension in her stomach wasn't going away.

It was getting worse.

With a heavy sigh, she rolled over onto her side away from the warm spot and closed her eyes, feeling much too emotionally wrung out to worry about it right now.

Besides, it was nothing...nothing at all....

Staring deeply into the darkness behind her eyelids, she took several long, even breaths and commanded herself to let her mind wander.

The weight of the last few days felt like it was crushing down on her, but soon enough she started to drift off to sleep.

It wasn't a very deep sleep, and before long she slipped into a dream.

For the longest time, she had a soft, mildly disorienting sensation of floating effortlessly in that hazy borderland between sleep and wakefulness. Not long after that, vague images and fragments of thoughts began to take shape. A small part of her mind was aware that she was dreaming, but she found this relaxing, so she snuggled her head into the pillow and let herself go with the gentle, cushiony flow.

After a long, timeless moment, she realized that she was no longer floating.

She standing in a vast, dark room. The darkness all around her was so dense it was almost tangible. She listened to the faint echoes of dripping water and a soft, ruffling sound that might have been her pulse throbbing in her ear against the pillow.

A mild current of apprehension tickled her mind, but she pushed it aside as she stared into the swelling darkness.

As her vision sharpened, she realized that the darkness was seething with shifting, vaguely perceived figures.

After another indefinite time, faces began to materialize and dissolve, looming at her and then receding like wisps of smoke back into the darkness. She thought she could hear faint voices whispering to her from all directions at once, but she couldn't make out anything that was being said.

She realized with a sudden start that two faces—both pale, lifeless— were resolving much more clearly. They stared at her with blank, sightless eyes.

At first Sarah was only mildly curious, but then she became a bit apprehensive.

Finally, with a violent jolt, she recognized both of them.

"No…" she whispered.

Her voice echoed weirdly in her dream, warbling up and down the register as if someone were playing with the volume control.

She watched as the two faces resolved out of the darkness like slowly developing photographs.

She was transfixed by the unblinking eyes that stared at her, cold and emotionless.

"David? Karen?"

She wasn't sure if she said their names out loud or not, but it didn't seem to matter. Neither one of them responded to her voice.

They just kept staring at her, their steady gazes drilling into her.

Sarah realized that the light around her was growing steadily brighter. The darkness was thinning like the gradually brightening light of dawn.

She could see that her ex-husband and daughter were standing side by side. Their hands were clasped tightly together. Sarah couldn't tell what kind of room they were in. It looked like some kind of large, deserted room—maybe an abandoned factory or schoolroom that had fallen into disrepair.

With mounting horror, Sarah realized that David and Karen appeared as stiff and pale as they had looked in their coffins.

Stinging grief ripped through her like a silver blade.

When she tried to turn away, she realized with a tremendous jolt of fear that she was looking down at her own hands.

She was holding a gun.

She recognized it immediately. It was the small revolver she had stolen from David's apartment.

Icy panic surged inside her like a tidal wave as she watched, feeling detached from her own body and absolutely unable to control it as she slowly raised the gun to eye level and aimed it squarely at her daughter's face.

No! ...Stop this! ...I don't want to be doing this!

Sarah had no idea if she said this out loud or simply thought it, but it didn't matter. No matter how hard she tried, there was no way she could force her arm to turn the gun away. A deep, steady, trembling pressure was building up in her hand. She could feel her forefinger steadily tightening...pressing back against the trigger.

No! ...Please! ...Make this stop right now!

But she couldn't resist or stop the tension in her hand, and she couldn't make herself look away.

A sudden, ear-shattering explosion and a brilliant flash of white light split the darkness.

Sarah screamed and tried to turn away, but she couldn't help but watch as her daughter's face exploded in front of her in vivid slow-motion. Bright red gouts of blood along with clumps of tangled, pink flesh, gray brain matter, and shattered bone splashed into the air.

Karen's left eye vanished instantly, as if it had been vaporized, but her right eye kept staring at Sarah from the bleeding hole that had appeared in the middle of her face. A wide sheet of blood was gushing down over her chest. It fell to the floor with sickening, plopping sounds.

Sarah watched as Karen's body slowly twisted to one side and then began to crumple like a marionette whose strings had been cut. Uttering a long, agonized groan, Karen collapsed into a shapeless heap on the ground, and then, in horrifying slow motion, the darkness swallowed her up.

David still stood there, his hand still extended, but now empty. He seemed not to react in the slightest to what had just happened. He continued to stare blankly at Sarah, his cold gaze piercing her like skewers. The dead-looking gleam in his eyes riveted Sarah, and she found it impossible to resist as her hand holding the gun swung around and took aim straight at David's face.

No! ...Don't make me do this!

Her voice was screaming inside her head, warbling and echoing weirdly all around her. But the gun in her hand was the only thing that was real to her now. She sighted along its barrel, drawing a steady bead on her ex-husband's face.

Please! I don't want to be doing this! Make it stop!

But she couldn't stop it. Her trigger finger twitched in a quick spasm, and the gun jumped in her hand.

Another flash and deafening explosion ripped the air. This time, Sarah managed to turn away before she had to see the effect the gunshot had on David.

She was trembling as though in the grip of a seizure as she stared into the swelling darkness. A wild, winding apprehension clutched her as she held her breath and waited...waited for something to happen next.

She didn't dare look up.

She didn't dare move.

She cringed when she felt *something* moving closer to her.

A dark, menacing presence.

She jumped and screamed when a hand suddenly clamped down hard on her shoulder and started to squeeze her.

The fringes of her vision dissolved into thick, vibrating black swirls as she slowly looked and saw—not David, but Tony.

He was grinning at her like a madman. An insane glow blazed inside his eyes. It took Sarah a heartbeat or two to realize that there was a small, black hole about the size of a quarter in the middle of Tony's forehead.

She stared at it for a moment, struck dumb with fear.

She imagined that the hole was an eye that was going to open and gaze into her heart and soul; but as she watched, a thin ribbon of bright, red blood began to trickle out of the hole. It ran down David's face, parting into two streams at the bridge of his nose.

"Why'd you go and do something like that?" Tony asked, his voice sounding whiny.

Sarah started shaking her head from side to side and tried to back away from him, but his grip on her tightened all the more, holding her there.

I didn't want to!…I couldn't help it!

Sarah wanted to scream this at him, but her voice was locked deep in her chest.

"The hell you couldn't!" Tony snarled. His tongue flicked out of the corner of his mouth and lapped at the blood that was flowing down both sides of his face. His smile widened until it looked like it was going to split his face. The wild intensity in his eyes was almost blinding.

With a sudden, violent surge of strength, Sarah jerked forward and broke Tony's grip on her. The scream that had been building up inside her finally found its way out, and she let loose with a long, trailing shriek.

When she opened her eyes and looked around, she was surprised to see that she was sitting up in bed. Her body was slick with sweat. When she took a deep breath, it burned like acid in her throat and lungs. Her right shoulder hurt terribly, as if she had wrenched it.

Or as if someone had been holding me there…hurting me, she thought.

Covering her face with both hands, Sarah slumped forward on the bed and began to cry.

11

THE SHADOW WHISPERS

"She has to kill him! Don't you understand that? And she's got to do it right away!"

David grunted and shook his head, unable to believe that he was hearing Karen correctly. Her voice maintained that flat, dead tone that bothered him so much, and he wondered if his own voice sounded as lifeless to her as hers did to him.

He wasn't sure he really wanted to know.

They were alone in Pine Knoll Elementary—at least as alone as they *could* be. Soft scraping sounds, faint voices, high laughter, and the distant opening and closing of doors echoed throughout the dark hallways. From down in the basement there came deep, reverberating groans and what sounded like the clanking of machinery or heavy chains. David felt a slight measure of relief that, at least so far, they hadn't encountered any other wraiths in the school. For now, the schoolhouse seemed about as safe a place as they were going to find.

Outside, the night was dense and pressing. A heavy overcast sky hid the moon and stars, and dulled the cold, blue glare of the streetlights. The air was charged with static electricity. Low clouds pulsated with a rippling purple light, like heat lightning that edged everything with an eerie glow.

Through the opened doorway, David could catch glimpses every now and then of faint lights, shining like candles seen through dense fog, moving from one window to another in the buildings across the street. Closer, he could hear the rustling sound of unseen wings in the dark. He wondered if it were an owl, a bat, or something else. Just once, a shrill, rising scream tore through the night like the keening wail of a siren. It lasted for only a few seconds before fading away, but it was more than enough to remind David of the numerous dangers outside his haven.

He was sitting on the floor in the darkness and staring up at his daughter, who was standing a short distance away from him. He couldn't see her very well. She was no more than a dark splotch against the shadowy background of the far wall.

He was trying his best to make sense of what she had just said to him, but it didn't register.

He couldn't get rid of the unnerving thought that this didn't sound at all like Karen—not the tone of her voice or what she had said.

"For crying out loud, Karen," he said, hearing the desperate edge in his own voice. "Listen to yourself! Listen to what you're saying!"

"I know *exactly* what I'm saying," Karen replied with a hard edge to her voice. "He's going to *hurt* her. He *wants* to hurt her, and he'll do it soon unless someone stops him!"

A deep, twisting sense of frustration stirred within David.

"But I tried to," he said, feeling regret like a cold, iron ball in the center of his chest. "I tried as hard as I could, but I couldn't get through to her. I don't know how to, and I don't have any idea what else I can do."

"You have to try harder then, because he *has* to *die!*"

The torment David felt when he heard his daughter say this was nearly unbearable.

For just an instant, he thought that one of the voices he heard whispering upstairs was now inside his head, teasing him, taunting him, urging him to *do* something. He tried, but couldn't quite make out what it was saying.

He most definitely worried about Sarah and what might happen to her, but he was just as concerned about Karen and what seemed to be happening to her in the Shadowlands.

There was something more than a little "not right" about her.

There was something plain *wrong* with her.

He wished he knew of a truly safe place where he could take her, where she could be happy and content. He didn't like the tense, empty shell she appeared to be.

Isn't there such a thing as "heaven" where the dead can dwell in eternal peace and bliss? he wondered. *This can't be all there is to the afterlife!*

He kept trying to convince himself that what was wrong with Karen was simply the result of the new state of being in which she had found herself. Just like him, she was confused and frightened. He still found it difficult if not impossible to admit—even to himself—that, unless this was some kind of prolonged hallucination or nightmare, he and she were both *dead*.

At least for now, he knew that he *had* to accept that fact at face value.

They were dead. If, as the song said, life is just a dream, then death was turning out to be a real nightmare.

How else could he expect Karen to act? She wasn't old enough to understand what had happened to her. He had no idea where she had been or what she had done during the five long years she had been here—alone— in the Shadowlands.

It pained him to remember the vivacious, fun-loving child she had once been. No matter what the situation—even when his and Sarah's marriage was at its worst—Karen had always been ready and eager to embrace life and enjoy it to its fullest. In the deep recesses of his memory, David could still hear echoes of the high, sweet ring of her childish laughter.

And where's that laughter now?

An ever-deepening sense of sadness and loss embraced him like the dark arms of night.

Maybe—somehow—she had known subconsciously that she was going to die young. The Ferryman had said that a fetter could be simply that the person had died before his or her time. Maybe something in Karen's spirit had pushed her to grab and enjoy life as much as she could in the nine short years she had been given because she had always known that she didn't have any more time than that.

But somehow it seemed to David that it had to be more than that.

The changes in her, the qualities she had lost, seemed too dramatic, too drastic.

He had lost her once before when she died in his arms on the ski slope, and he dreaded the thought that he might be losing her again. It was all too much to bear, but there was no other way to look at it. He had to admit that his daughter wasn't at all the same person or the same soul she had once been in life.

David had found existence in the Shadowlands extremely disorienting. He had tried many times to analyze himself, to determine if he, too, had changed as drastically as Karen appeared to have. At least as far as he could tell, he didn't think or feel or act that much differently from the way he had thought, felt, and acted when he was alive.

True, he experienced emotions and physical sensations very differently now, but he told himself that this was simply because he no longer had a physical body that had biological reactions to what he felt and thought. His emotions were no longer complicated or enhanced by the physical. He experienced emotions and ideas in a purer, more essential, spiritual way.

He had no idea what his corpus, as the Ferryman had called it, was made of, but he found it incredibly disorienting the way his senses of hearing, touch, and sight were distorted in this new state of being. Maybe what he thought of now as his body was just an illusion—a visual echo of the form he'd once had. It had no reality to it other than as a memory. That was the only way he could explain the way his senses seemed so distorted.

He'd lost accurate track of the time, but if his funeral had been just today—or was it yesterday?—he couldn't have been dead for very long. But no matter how long it had been, he wasn't getting any more used to it.

He wondered if he ever would.

He especially didn't like the curious loss of sensation whenever he physically touched something—even his own daughter.

Without the physical restrictions of his body, he experienced existence much differently than he had when he was alive. He was still amazed and excited that he could do things that he had only been able to imagine before—things like walking through walls with no more effort than walking through a dense fog, and walking great distances without any sense of fatigue.

And there were other powers and talents he might discover as well. The Ferryman had mentioned them, but David was afraid that he didn't have enough time to learn any of them. Certainly not soon enough to help Sarah.

A sense of emergency and impending doom filled David with a sharp sense of urgency. He knew that he had to act swiftly and decisively. The problem was, he had no idea *what* to do.

And it pained him to see and hear Karen acting this way. Shouldn't someone who had died so young and innocent end up in something at least a bit closer to the religious concepts of Heaven, Nirvana, or Paradise?

It broke his heart to hear Karen say such hateful, vengeful things. It tore him apart to sense the utter despair and hatred and fear that he could see and feel inside of her.

RICK HAUTALA

Where was there some sense of inner peace and tranquillity?

Even given their unique situation, he couldn't understand or account for the bizarre changes he had noticed in her personality. Could five years in the Shadowlands literally have drained the life and spirit out of her so completely?

Was the same thing going to happen to him?

"Listen to me, Karen," he said, his voice low and controlled. "I—I know that we didn't have much time together when you were—when we both were alive, but one thing I think your mother and I both wanted to teach you, even though maybe you were too young to fully understand it, was that we have to respect life. We *have* to!" David listened to his own voice, hearing it as nothing more than a rattling whisper in the dark. "And even though you and I aren't alive anymore, I think we *still* have to respect life."

"But *someone's* going to die!" Karen said, her voice resonating with a deep hollowness. "And *you* have a chance to choose who it's going to be— either my...my mother, or else that scumbag she's been fucking!"

"*Karen!*"

David was horrified to hear his sweet, innocent daughter speak like that. How much did she know? What had she seen and experienced in the time she had been alone in the Shadowlands?

"I'm serious, Daddy," Karen said. Coming to him out of the darkness, her voice sounded almost threatening. "When he has that knife—when he's holding it in his hand and is going to use it on her—*that's* when someone has to *kill* him!"

"*Stop* it, Karen! Please! I don't want to hear you talk like that! I don't want you even thinking like that!"

"But she *has* to do it! Don't you understand? She *has* to kill him while he's holding the knife!"

A sudden bolt of anger ripped through David. He leaped to his feet and began pacing back and forth in the darkness. His footsteps, dragging on the ancient floorboards, echoed weirdly in the dense darkness.

It's all for nothing, a voice whispered inside his head.

A deep chill sliced through David like the honed edge of a knife.

All of it...it's absolutely worthless! A useless waste of time and energy! So why not just give up? Karen's dead...you're dead...why should you care if Sarah or anyone else lives or dies.... They're all going to die eventually, anyway...everyone you ever loved will die! And in the end, everything will fade away, people, the world, the whole damned universe—EVERYTHING will be destroyed eventually.... It will all fall into the bottomless pit...the endless void of oblivion!

Against his will, David listened as the voice spoke deep inside his head. It terrified him. He had the distinct impression that someone was standing close beside him in the dark and whispering these terrible things into his ear.

"No," he said in a low, grating whisper as he clapped his hands over his ears and shook his head in adamant denial. "It's *not* like that. It can't be."

Oh, but it is, the voice inside his mind continued. *And you've always known it.... Oh, yes! Deep down in your heart, you've always understood the utter futility of it all.... So why pretend anymore? Why not just give in to it? Why not embrace the darkness fully? Let yourself go? There's ultimate peace there, isn't it? All of your suffering will end in the dark, eternal embrace of...oblivion....*

"No, stop it. Damn it! *Stop it!*" David shouted between clenched teeth as he pounded the sides of his head with his clenched fists.

"No, I won't stop it."

For a terrifying instant, David thought he had said that, but then he realized that Karen had spoken. Her voice sounded so far away, it was lost in the internal confusion that threatened to rip him apart. David was sure that, if he said anything right now, no matter how loud he yelled, she wouldn't be able to hear him.

"I won't stop it because *you* have to *do* it!" Karen said firmly. "You have to get her to kill him!"

"But...I...can't...."

His own voice sounded fainter than the grating voice that was taunting him inside his mind.

Give in to it, then! There's nothing else anyway.... Eventually everything— even the Shadowlands and the entire universe—is going to fade away into nothing...into a vast...eternal...NOTHING! You've known all along that existence is nothing but a terminal blip in the blank, meaningless, endless void.

"No...it isn't."

David's throat felt like it was burning.

"That *can't* be all there is! There has to be *some* kind of meaning or hope or...or otherwise—"

Otherwise...what?

A cold ache filled David's chest, choking off his reply.

He was dimly aware that, if he still possessed a physical body, he would have been wracked with tears as he tried to stifle the voice that was whispering inside his head. He couldn't bear to think about what it was saying.

"No, there isn't," Karen said. She sounded impossibly far away, lost to him forever. "There's no hope at all unless she kills him. And he has to be holding that knife when she does it."

Between listening to the horrible things Karen was saying and hearing that low, hissing voice inside his head, David finally couldn't take it any longer. Shaking his fists in total frustration, he focused his full attention as he struggled to ground himself as firmly as he could in the reality in which he had found himself.

He looked around at the dim recesses of the schoolhouse, at the hazy gray and purple light that filtered in through the opened door and broken windows. The distant sounds of the night faded into the background, and he concentrated only on being aware of himself, standing there, facing his dead daughter.

"I—I'm going out," he said in a low, shattered voice.

Karen started to reply, but he already knew what she would say. He hushed her angrily.

"No! You listen to me! I want you to stay right here. Do you understand? I don't want you going *anywhere* or doing *anything* until I get back."

"Are you going to—"

"Be *quiet*! Just stay here. I'll be back as soon as I can."

Without another word, he turned and left the schoolhouse, but once he was outside in the night, he didn't feel even the slightest measure of relief. He couldn't shake the dreadful feeling that somewhere in the night, somewhere in the Shadowlands or maybe on some other level of existence, a dark menace was gathering strength and moving steadily closer to him.

And Karen!

Although he tried not to think about it, he knew that, when it arrived, if it hadn't already destroyed Karen and him, it would drag both of them into a realm of terror that he couldn't even begin to fathom.

"You have to kill her! Don't you understand that? And you have to do it right away!"

The soft voice came to Tony like the hissing wind from out of the darkness, but it was loud enough to yank him out of a deep, dreamless sleep. He thought it sounded a little bit like a girl's voice, but for some reason, Tony found it neither odd nor threatening that there might be a little girl in his bedroom, talking to him in the middle of the night.

He must have been dreaming. It was just that he didn't remember it.

Sighing heavily, he opened his eyes and rubbed them. He grunted softly as he sat straight up in bed and scanned the dark bedroom until he finally saw what he thought might be her.

There was a small, dark silhouette standing motionlessly at the foot of his bed. It certainly looked like a person standing there, but he figured that it had to be a trick the darkness and being half asleep played on him.

Tony leaned forward, trying to see more clearly, but he still couldn't be sure.

All the shades in the bedroom were drawn. The only light was the thin glowing wedge of lemon light that slipped in from the hallway underneath his closed door.

It was impossible to see anything clearly.

Whenever he tried to look directly at her, trying to decide if there really could be a little girl in his bedroom, she wavered out of sight and shifted from one side of the bed to the other. Only by focusing on a spot a little off to one side of her was he able to see…

Something.

He caught the vaguest hint of a smoke-thin shadow against the darker background of the wall. But the shadow had eyes, and he realized with a deep shudder that the eyes were staring straight at him. They glowed with a steady, dull blue radiance that seemed to tear into him like claws that ripped him open, exposing the deepest secrets at the center of his soul.

"Who—who *are* you?" Tony whispered, painfully aware of the wire-tight tension in his voice.

This didn't make any sense at all.

He *had* to still be dreaming!

There couldn't be anyone else here. His roommate was asleep in the next room, and Tony had made sure the apartment door was locked before coming to bed.

"My name's Karen," the little girl replied. Her voice had an sweet, innocent-sounding quality, but it also sounded curiously flat.

"Do I…know you?" Tony asked.

She didn't answer right away, and Tony began to think that he must be alone in the room. She was nothing more than a lingering trace of a dream.

But then he caught another glimpse of her, standing at the foot of the bed. She appeared to be shaking her head slowly from side to side, and he thought he could hear her clicking her tongue as though scolding him.

"So what…what do you want from me?" Tony asked edgily. He certainly *felt* wide awake now. His scalp was crawling as though it were infested with worms. His breath caught like a hook in his throat.

"How did you—what the hell are you *doing* here?"

"You *know* she deserves it," the little girl said in a soft, hissing voice.

"Huh? *Who* deserves *what*?"

"She deserves to die. I hope you realize that you're going to have to *kill* her."

"Kill who? What the fuck are you talking—"

"Sarah Robinson, of course," came the reply in a voice so low it sounded almost masculine. "After all, she really does deserve it."

"And why's that?" Tony asked, trying to repress the wave of chills that raced through him.

"Oh, I don't think I have to tell you that," the little girl said, snickering softly. "I think you already know."

In the dark, she sounded like she was standing much too close to him. Tony shifted forward on his bed, tensed and ready to swing a fist at her if she proved threatening. A small corner of his mind was telling him this was impossible. It didn't make any sense.

How could it be happening?

How could anyone be here in his bedroom at this time of night?

And why would he be afraid of a little girl?

"She doesn't love you. She never did. Not in the least," the little girl whispered. "But I suspect you already knew that she was using you."

Her voice was starting to grate on Tony's nerves, and he didn't like what she had to say, but he had no choice but to believe her. One of his deepest fears was that Sarah—just like every other woman he had ever slept with over the years—didn't really like him, much less love him. Ever since he had first realized back in high school that he was quite good looking, and that girls were attracted to him, he had used his good looks to get whatever he wanted. Usually, at least for Tony, that meant sex without the added encumbrance of love. Over the years, it had become almost second nature for him to use women purely for his own sexual pleasure.

But his deep and abiding fear was that the joke was all on him.

All of them—every single woman he had ever screwed—had been doing the same thing to him.

Using him!

"She hasn't gotten fucked in a long time, you know," the little girl said, her voice high and taunting. "Not since she got divorced. And that's all you are for her—a good lay. She's gonna use you only for as long as she needs to, and then you're gonna be out the door on your ass like yesterday's trash."

"No, I…I don't think so," Tony whispered, shaking his head in denial. He craned forward, trying to see the little girl better, but her shadow kept shifting around the room, never standing still for very long. Her voice seemed to be coming from a great distance away and, simultaneously, so close he could almost feel the puff of her breath against his ear.

"Oh, she's using you, all right," the little girl said. "I know it because I know her. That's the way she is. She can't really help it, you know."

Tony cringed, realizing that this was one of the ways he had always justified the way he treated women. It was just the way he was.

"Oh, yeah?" he said shakily. "Well, even if she *is* using me, what's the harm? That's certainly no reason to—to *kill* her!"

Tony's chest was aching so badly he winced as he stared into the darkness. Realizing he'd been holding his breath, he let it out in a long, slow whistle.

"I know you'll do it," the little girl said, lowering her voice to a deep rumble, "because that's what *it* wants."

Tony opened his mouth, about to ask her what she meant by "it," but he suddenly stopped himself.

He knew the answer to that.

He knew it as clearly as if she had already said the words.

The knife!

That's what the knife wants!

Tony uttered a low, tortured moan as he reached out, gripped the bed sheets with both hands, and balled them up in his fists. Cold sweat broke out like fine dew across his body. A chill gripped his heart and quickly spread like poison throughout his body.

He had known this all along, but to hear someone else say it out loud filled him with an almost unbearable sense of apprehension, danger, and excitement.

Yes, excitement!

He *did* want to use the knife again.

He didn't stop to question who this little girl was or how she had gotten here or how she knew anything about the knife. On a deep, subconscious level, this all made sense.

"Yes," he whispered.

His eyes were wide open as he stared into the darkness until it started to throb with innumerable shifting figures that moved around him like wafting smoke. He could hear the faint rustle of their motion, like unseen wings in the night.

"Oh, you'll do it all right," the little girl said in a low, flat voice. "You'll do it because you don't really have any other choice in the matter, do you?"

Tony tried to speak but couldn't. His lips felt like they were glued tight.

"*Do you?*" the little girl repeated, her voice as hard as iron.

Tony's heart was slamming like a trapped animal against the cage of his ribs. Trailing spirals of light exploded in front of his eyes, and he lost any sense of who he was, where he was, or what was happening. The single clear thought in his mind was that he had the knife, and that he was going to *have* to use it…on Sarah.

"No, I…I don't have any choice," Tony replied, bowing his head submissively to the whispering darkness.

He's going to kill her! Don't you understand that? And he's going to do it right away!

That was the single, clearest thought David had as he walked along the dark desolation of Deering Avenue, away from the schoolhouse. No matter how hard he tried, he couldn't force that thought out of his mind.

The night sky was overcast and flickered with subtle energy as thin strings of lightning played like hot wires back and forth between the earth and clouds. Everything was lit up with blue flashes that left jagged traces of afterimages across David's vision. The distant, dull rumble of thunder shook the air, drowning out the dragging, scuffing sound of his footsteps that echoed from the empty buildings on either side of the street. From out of the darkness all around him, he heard faint whisperings and deep hissing sounds that might have been the wind blowing through the alleyways…or something else.

David knew that it was dangerous, and maybe even foolhardy to be out alone at night in the Shadowlands, but he was so distraught that he no longer cared if anything happened to him.

He couldn't stop worrying about Sarah and the man he was now convinced intended to kill her. The terrible thing was, he knew that there was nothing he could do to stop him.

He also couldn't stop thinking about the hard, cruel edge he had heard in Karen's voice when she insisted that her mother had to kill the man with the knife.

Karen's not herself…not anymore, anyway!

That thought filled David with the sharp bitterness of loss. He wished to God he could cry, if only to release the pent-up emotions that were building inside him, ripping him apart.

It was bad enough that five years ago he had had to watch his daughter die in his arms. Now it seemed absolutely unimaginable that he could be losing her again, and in such a terrifying, horrible way. She was losing—or had lost—the core of her humanity.

It pained him to see that his daughter had become nothing more than an empty husk of the person she had been. Five years in the Shadowlands had drained away all of her gentle goodness, her sweetness, her bright sense of humor, and her love of life. Emotionally, she was as cold and rigid and empty as the corpse lying in her coffin on the hill in Riverside Cemetery.

Is that what's going to happen to me?

A tremor of despair ran through him at the thought.

The harsh cruelty of what Karen had said to him burned in his memory, weaving through his mind like an endless mantra.

She has to kill him! Don't you understand that? And she's got to do it right away!

He knew that if he didn't stop thinking about it, this would drive him insane before very long. The only way to stop it seemed to be if he could—somehow—warn Sarah about the danger that was stalking her.

But how do I do that? I've tried everything I can think of, and I've failed!

Once again, the teasing voice deep within his mind spoke, this time loud enough to startle him.

That's right, you HAVE failed! it whispered harshly. *So you might as well just give up! You know, in the long run, that it's all useless, anyway…everything's useless! Sarah's going to die. If not now, eventually…. Everyone you've ever known and loved is going to die, not that there were all that many people you could say you loved…. And in the end, none of this is going to make the slightest difference! All existence is an illusion that's going to fade away like a dream into eternal…Nothingness….*

David halted in his tracks and looked around, suddenly convinced that someone was close and speaking those words to him.

He tensed as he scanned the shadows, but only out of the corner of his eye could he detect even the slightest hint of motion within them. The weirdly lit street and flickering night sky seemed to waver and blur like heat mirages that would vanish at any instant.

"It…it may be that way," he whispered hoarsely, "but I at least have to try."

He cringed at the sound of his own voice, echoing in the night.

But why even try? the voice whispered. *You've done everything you can, and it won't do you a damned bit of good in the end, anyway…. It's all just wasted effort! Wasted agony! You should give in to oblivion now so it will all be over…. You'll be gone, and with you goes all of your suffering….*

The void of darkness in the center of his soul seemed suddenly to open up like a hungry mouth inside him. A rush of chills raced through his corpus. He could feel himself being sucked closer to that cold, eternal embrace.

The voice is right. What good will it do for me or anyone else to resist? he thought.

Yes, that's absolutely right! said the hollow, rasping voice. *Just let go…let it all go….*

David distantly realized that he was whimpering softly to himself.

He closed his eyes and, with a deep, wrenching sob, covered his face with both hands and groaned. The feeling of his hands, pressed against his face, seemed strangely deadened.

Just let it all go… the voice rasped.

David's eyes were wide as he stared into the swelling darkness inside his hands. He was suddenly terrified, wondering if he had his eyes open or closed.

It didn't matter. The same, eternal, black void was inside him and outside him, and it would never change.

He could feel himself being pulled inexorably into it.

"No," David whispered, his voice so faint it was almost lost inside his head.

Sudden, terrible panic seized him. He was vaguely aware that he was moving—either stepping backwards or falling, but he had no sense of direction. He felt suddenly weightless…adrift in an eternal vacuum. He stretched out his arms in a vain attempt to orient himself, but he felt nothing and continued to tumble in freefall.

A strange-sounding wind was shrieking in his ears, and he had an internal sense of moving at a great speed. Strong, irresistible forces were tearing at him like cold, grasping hands, tossing him around. The darkness before him seemed impenetrable.

That's it! The ride of a lifetime! Just let go! the voice in his head wailed.

But then another, stronger voice—one that felt more centered inside him—suddenly spoke up.

No!...You can't let go!...You can't give up!

David had the brief mental image that his corpus was nothing more than a piece of cork that had been held under water, and now had suddenly been let go to pop up to the surface. Powerful waves of nausea gripped him as he struggled to clear his mind and force the chattering voice inside him to shut up.

I'm still me! That single, simple thought resounded like a cannon shot inside his mind. *I'm still me, and I can't give up! Not when Sarah and Karen still need me!*

He let loose a wild, wavering scream that seemed to originate in the soles of his feet. It tore through the night like a silver blade slashing through a sheer curtain.

The darkness in front of him coalesced into a dark, oval shape that was framed by the swirling glow of the night sky. White lines of lighting danced among the clouds. With a jolt of surprise, David realized that he was flat on his back, looking up into the darkness inside the hood of the Ferryman. He couldn't see a trace of the Ferryman's features, but he could feel his eyes boring into him like heated pokers.

"You're strong," the Ferryman said. His voice was deep and resonant, and David found it somehow reassuring. "I knew you wouldn't give in that easily to the temptations of your shadow."

"My...shadow?" David listened to himself talk as if he were someone else.

"You're new here, and there are many things you don't know," the Ferryman continued. "But you do seem to have a strong sense of yourself. That's good. Ultimately, it can only help."

David was feeling much too drained to reply—worse, even, than when the reaper had clamped Stygian chains on his arms and legs. The Ferryman leaned over him with one hand extended. David felt a numbing touch brush against his forehead.

"But he—he's going to...to kill her," David finally managed to say. It took an immense effort to think clearly, much less speak. "He's going to use that knife on her. I know he is, and there's nothing I can do to stop him!"

A low, chuffing sound like twisted laughter filled the night.

"Oh, there are things you can do," the Ferryman said in a deep, sonorous voice. "You have more abilities than you realize."

David still found it almost impossible to focus his thoughts. The sheer terror of what had just happened to him was too much to contemplate.

"You...you told me that there were skills, certain powers that I could use to...to help me," he said. "Can you teach them to me? Right now?"

For several seconds, the hooded figure remained perfectly immobile. Then, slowly, the Ferryman shook his head from side to side. The coarse cloth of his hood made a low rustling sound that seemed oddly magnified in the stillness of the night.

"I'm afraid I can't do that," the Ferryman replied after a lengthening moment.

"Why the hell not?" David shouted, unable any longer to contain his agitation and anger. "My wife's in serious trouble. I know what I have to do to save her, but I—I can't unless you help me."

"You've already done what you can," the Ferryman said. "The best you can do is to keep trying, and see what happens. You haven't even begun to learn the basic skills of skinriding, much less puppetry, embodying, or keening. But even so, without knowing any of these skills, you *have* gotten through to her. You've contacted her."

"How? I've been watching her, but I've never seen her do anything that would indicate that I'm getting through to her. Besides trying to speak to her, the only thing I could think to do was try to manipulate the computer to type her a message. But it didn't work. Something messed it up."

"There is a skill we call Phantasm," the Ferryman said. "It's the ability a wraith can develop—with effort—to influence a mortal's dreams. I know for a fact that you invaded her dreams and brought her sleeping soul here to the Shadowlands."

Frowning, David shook his head in firm denial.

"I never did," he said, feeling almost overwhelmed by confusion and doubt. "I don't have any idea what you're talking about."

"She was here," the Ferryman replied in a solemn voice. "I saw her with you and the wraith that looks like your daughter."

"No, you have to be mistaken," David said, unable to shut off the sudden rush of discomforting thoughts that flooded his mind. "I was never—"

"Well, it was either you or else that other wraith who brought her here," the Ferryman said.

"What, do you mean Karen?"

A deep chill ran through David when he pictured the cold, blank expression on his daughter's face. A desperate yearning filled him.

"No. That's not your daughter," the Ferryman replied.

His voice resonated with a deep echo. For several seconds, David stared at the Ferryman, wishing and hoping that he hadn't heard him correctly. When David was finally able to speak, his voice was so weak he could hardly hear himself.

"What do you mean?"

"That wraith—it's not Karen," the Ferryman replied simply. "Your daughter was here a long while ago. I remember seeing her, but she hasn't been in the Shadowlands for…I can't remember how long. It's been a very long time. As I recall, she disappeared not long after she first showed up here."

"What the hell are you—that's impossible! I've seen her! I've spoken with her! Don't you think I'd recognize my own daughter?"

Anger surged inside David like an electrical overload, but he also felt a sharp edge of panic because, on some deep level, he knew that the Ferryman was right.

Karen hadn't been acting like herself because she *wasn't* herself!

"I saw him take her into the Tempest himself," the Ferryman said.

"Someone took her? Who? Where did he take her?"

The Ferryman shook his head slowly, making the cloth of his hood rustle with a harsh, scraping sound.

"A reaper working for the Hierarchy took your daughter," the Ferryman said. "He has…many names, but none of them would mean anything to you. There is one way you can recognize him, though. He walks with a limp."

"A limp…?"

David heard his own voice as no more than a faint echo of the Ferryman.

"Yes, a limp. He has a bad left leg that makes him walk with a limp, at least whenever he's in his true form. I would guess that he's using the skill of imitation to appear to you in the form of your daughter. I wouldn't be surprised if he has your daughter imprisoned in his haunt. Perhaps it's somewhere inside the Tempest."

"Can you help me? Can you take me there?"

"I already told you," the Ferryman said. "You'll have to find her on your own. After that—" He shrugged and shook his head slowly.

"After that, I'll do whatever I can to help both of you."

12

THE DECEPTION ENDS

Even though she thought she was ready for it, the sound of the gun going off six times in rapid succession made Sarah jump. She was glad that she was wearing protectors that deadened the sound at least enough so it didn't hurt her ears.

She glanced over at the man with close-cropped hair standing on the firing line. His name was Sy Warner. He was wearing black wrap-around sunglasses, a tight-fitting, dark blue T-shirt tucked into the top of his dark jeans, and black sneakers. He had the body of a weight lifter. His thick, tanned arms rippled with knotted muscles and pencil-thick veins. His stomach was as flat and ridged as a washboard. Sarah thought the dark-colored ear protectors he wore made him look a bit like a comical, muscle-bound mouse.

A thin ribbon of blue smoke curled from the muzzle of his gun as he slowly lowered it and leaned forward to study the target. He glanced over his shoulder at Sarah, cocked a smile, and nodded with satisfaction.

About a hundred feet in front of him, backed by the scooped-out wall of a sand pit, the paper target of a life-sized human torso dangled from a thin, metal wire. Six holes, each of them the size of a quarter, peppered the inner white circle that marked the center of the figure's chest. The paper made a faint crinkling sound as it rustled in the hot, light breeze.

Sarah had found Sy's North Windham firing range listed in the Nynex Yellow Pages and had called him earlier that morning to ask about taking some shooting lessons. She couldn't help but wonder how he could stand to wear all those dark clothes in such heat, but he didn't seem to mind. Only a few small drops of sweat dotted his smooth forehead.

He was smiling with self-satisfaction as he reloaded his gun, then placed it down on the wooden stand next to him. Inhaling sharply, he turned to face Sarah directly.

"So, you're sure you want to learn how to handle a gun, huh?" he said, giving her a tight, lopsided grin that made her think that he found all of this slightly amusing.

"Uh...yeah," Sarah said, realizing that she didn't sound at all confident as she took off the ear protectors so she could hear him better.

"Did you bring your piece with you?"

For a second, Sarah had no idea what he meant. Then she got it and, nodding nervously, swung her purse off her shoulder, zipped it open, and withdrew David's revolver. She picked up the gun gingerly by the trigger guard, holding it with her thumb and forefinger as if it were a dead fish.

Sy chuckled.

"It's always a good idea to show respect for your weapon, but it ain't a danged rattlesnake. It ain't gonna bite you unless you get on the wrong end of it."

Flustered, Sarah sputtered an apology as she handed the gun to him, being careful to keep it pointed away from both of them.

Sy slid his sunglasses up over his forehead, where the short bristles of his sun-bleached hair held them in place. His mouth was a thin, colorless line, and his pale eyes glinted like silver coins in the sunlight as he inspected the gun carefully.

"This here's a .32 Smith and Wesson," he said, barely glancing up at her as he turned the gun over several times in his hand. With a quick flick of his wrist, he raised the gun and sighted down the firing line at the perforated paper figure. "Not a bad little piece, either. Used to be real popular with the Mob, even though it does lack a bit in stopping power."

"Stopping power?"

Sy looked at Sarah with a trace of humor flashing in his eyes.

"Yeah. Power enough to stop a man. You said on the phone this morning that you wanted to learn how to handle a gun for your self-protection, right?"

"That's right," Sarah said, nodding again and feeling like a complete idiot.

"Well, if that's what you want, I would think it'd make sense to get a gun that could really stop someone if you were being attacked, wouldn't it?"

"Yeah, I...guess so," Sarah said, nodding tightly. Her stomach felt as hollow as a drum. It churned with sour acid at the thought of learning how to handle David's gun just so she could actually *kill* someone with it if she had to.

"Did you buy this?" Sy asked.

Biting her lower lip, Sarah shook her head quickly.

"No, it was...it belongs to my husband. My ex-husband. I just thought, since I'm living alone now, I ought to learn how to use it."

"I see. Mrs....ah, Robinson, is it?"

Again, Sarah nodded. "Call me Sarah."

"Sure thing...Sarah. Let me ask you straight out: Are you sure you want to go through with this?"

"I'm sure," Sarah replied, but, not for the first time, she wondered if this was such a great idea. If she was going to back out, now was the time.

But something—she wasn't quite sure what it was—told her to stay. For one thing, although she had no reason to believe that she really was in any kind of danger, she thought that she'd feel more secure, knowing at least the basics of how to handle a gun. Sure, she'd been feeling nervous and uptight lately, and she was convinced it wasn't just because she was edgy following David's death. Although Portland, Maine, wasn't exactly New York City or Chicago, it had its share of street crime. It made sense to have some protection…at least at home, where someone might break into the house at night or something.

"You ever fire a gun before, Mrs. Robinson?" Sy asked, frowning seriously.

The cold pit in Sarah's stomach got worse as she shook her head and said, "Not really."

"Not really," Sy echoed with a half smile. "Well, you either have or you haven't."

"No, I haven't."

"Lemme tell you something, Mrs. Robinson—"

"Sarah."

"Right. Sarah. The most important thing is that you should never forget that what you're doing here is learning how to kill someone if you have to. There's a big difference…a whole world of difference…between shooting at a paper target like that one and plugging a couple of holes in a living, breathing human being. You shoot at someone, you shoot to kill. Don't you ever forget that, all right?"

All Sarah could do was nod.

"Well, then," Sy said, "there's really not much to it. Here. Lemme give you a couple of pointers first…a few safety tips."

Sarah watched, amazed at how dexterous Sy's thick hands were as he unloaded the bullets from her gun. He passed one of them to her so she could inspect it.

"This is a .32 caliber. Probably 88 grains or so. You can pick up a box of them at any hardware or sporting goods store. Shouldn't cost you more than ten, fifteen bucks tops for a box of fifty. More than you'll ever need. Just make sure you get the ones for pistols, not rifles. They're a little different."

Sarah nodded her understanding.

"Loading's pretty quick and easy, too," Sy said. "All you do is pop 'em in here like this." He slid the six bullets back into the chamber and snapped it shut. "Contrary to what you might have read in detective novels or whatever, all American-made revolvers made in this century don't have safety catches, so once this baby's loaded, she's ready to fire."

Sarah found it curious that he referred to the gun as *she* and *baby*.

Being careful to keep the gun pointed away from him, he handed the gun back to Sarah.

"Watch me, first," Sy said.

Picking up his oversized revolver that looked like a cannon compared to Sarah's, Sy quickly reloaded it while giving Sarah a quick run-down on the parts of a gun, the correct way to hold it, the proper stance and posture, and other safety pointers.

When he was done, he slid his ear protectors back on, dropped his sunglasses over his eyes, took a calm, steady aim at the paper target, and snapped off six quick shots.

Again, Sarah jumped at the sudden report of the gun, but she found herself fascinated as she watched six more holes appear in the center of the human torso.

Moving back, Sy indicated that it was her turn to step up to the firing line.

"Go ahead and give it a try," he said, shifting behind her. "It's gonna kick a little. Not much, but you have to get a feel for it."

Sarah couldn't stop the cold trembling inside, but her hands were surprisingly steady as she picked up the gun and hefted it. It didn't seem quite so heavy in her hand now. Maybe because it was less threatening, she thought.

"Take aim carefully now," Sy said. "Yeah, that's it."

He moved up close behind her…close enough for her to catch a strong whiff of his aftershave. Reaching around both sides of her, he steadied her hands until she felt as though she had a good grip. The hard knots of his arm muscles pressed tightly against her arms, making her feel like this was an awkward embrace.

"That's it," Sy said. His heated breath blew softly into her ear. "Nice and easy, now. Brace yourself. Steady both hands. Yeah, that's it."

Sarah held her breath as she drew a bead on the paper target.

"Now the most important thing to remember is to *squeeze* the trigger gently," Sy said. "Don't jerk back on it. You do that, and you'll mess up your aim. So squeeze it nice and steady. Go on."

Sarah was feeling all fluttery inside as she sighted down the barrel at the target. She tried to forget about the man standing so close behind her as she squinted her left eye and aimed.

When she let herself realize that she was aiming at the outline of a human being, and that a target had been drawn in the center of its chest, the reality of what she was doing suddenly hit her. A powerful wave of emotion swept through her. Her body started to tremble, and she almost backed down.

"Steady now," Sy said, pressing close against her from behind.

For an instant, Sarah's vision blurred as she recalled last night's dream that she was aiming a gun…not just at Karen and David, but at Tony as well.

Her legs went all rubbery when she remembered pulling the trigger in her dream and shooting first Karen, then David, who had somehow shifted into an image of Tony before he fell. In her mind, she saw the black hole that had suddenly appeared in the middle of Tony's forehead.

Shaking her head and gritting her teeth, Sarah forced herself to focus as she stared down the line at the paper target wafting gently in the breeze. The blasting heat of the sun rebounded from the ground and danced in wavering lines that distorted her view. For a dizzying instant, Sarah thought she saw a person's face appear in the center of the target. She didn't quite have time to register whether or not she recognized the features before her finger twitched back and the gun kicked hard in her hands.

The recoil brought her hands up, but she quickly dropped them, adjusted her aim as she exhaled, sucked in and held another breath, and then squeezed the trigger again…and again.

By the fourth shot, the sound of the gun going off wasn't quite so scary. It almost felt good.

Sarah kept focusing intently on the center of the figure's chest, watching as holes seemed to appear in the paper like magic. Little puffs of dirt jumped into the air behind the target.

It's just paper! she told herself. *This isn't like shooting a real person.*

She was trying to ignore the suggestion of a human face that was superimposed over the paper figure's head; but before she could stop herself, she shifted her focus up and gasped when she clearly saw what looked like Tony Ranieri's features on the target. For an instant, the face on the target took on dimensionality. Tony seemed to be staring straight at her with wide open, unblinking eyes. His mouth was twisted as if he were laughing at her.

Without even thinking about it, Sarah raised the gun and aimed at the target's forehead. She quickly squeezed off two more shots.

With the first shot, a clean, thumb-size hole appeared dead center in the figure's forehead. The second shot rang out before the echo of the first one had died away, but Sarah couldn't see where—or if—it had hit the target.

Realizing that she had been holding her breath, she exhaled noisily as she lowered the gun. Her chest was aching as though she had been underwater for a little too long. Sweat sprinkled her forehead and was running from her armpits down the inside of her blouse.

Sy cocked one eyebrow as he stepped in front of her and smiled. Stroking his chin, he glanced over his shoulder at the target.

"And you say you've never shot a gun before in your life?" he said.

Sarah took a quick, deep breath and giggled as she shook her head.

"Nope. Never."

"Well, then, I'd have to say you're one helluva natural shooter." Sy nodded his head in appreciation. "You cracked off six shots, and at least five of 'em hit in clean kill zones."

"Kill zones," Sarah echoed.

"Not many people can do that their first time out," Sy said.

"Really," Sarah replied.

She wasn't sure how she was feeling.

It was exhilarating to realize that she had done something she had always despised. And she had done it well.

It also bothered her that here she was, actually feeling a sense of accomplishment for hitting "kill zones" with at least five out of six shots.

"Yeah, really," Sy said. "And I'll bet you five to one that last shot of yours went right through the first hole you made in the forehead. As far as I could see, your gun never wavered a damned millimeter. I swear to God, Sarah, you're a regular Annie Oakley."

Sarah shrugged and gave him a tight smile.

"Thanks," she said. Suddenly stiffening, she glanced at her wristwatch and saw the time. "Well, that's probably enough for today," she said shakily. "I...I've got to be at work in less than an hour."

The overcast sky cleared sometime toward morning, but to David the sky above Portland still looked all wrong. Sickly yellow and dull brown light shimmered above the city, casting a muddy, unearthly glow over everything. Distant buildings and trees wavered like mirages in the unearthly haze.

As David walked slowly down the street, heading back to the schoolhouse, his footsteps scuffed loudly on the asphalt, sounding like matches being struck. Although he still had only the slightest sensation of feeling, he could imagine just by looking around how hot the day must be. He was suddenly filled with longing as he remembered how much he missed being able to touch and feel things as simple as the warmth of the sun on his face.

Worse than that, though, was his dread about what he might find when he got back to Pine Knoll Elementary.

He held out a slim hope that the Ferryman had been wrong about the wraith who was masquerading as Karen.

630   RICK HAUTALA

What had he called it? A "reaper" working for the "Hierarchy"? David wasn't sure what that meant, but it didn't sound very good.

Whatever the case, he was positive that Karen—or the wraith that had assumed her shape—would be gone by the time he got back.

That would be hard enough to deal with, he thought, but worse than that was the possibility that she might not be gone. David seriously doubted that he would have the courage to confront it if that *thing* was still there.

All he knew for certain was that he wouldn't be able to pretend. He'd had his doubts about Karen before this, but now he was absolutely convinced that something was wrong with her.

He had no idea why the "reaper" with the limp—or any other wraith, for that matter—would go to all this trouble to assume the shape of his dead daughter.

Was it just to try to fool him?

Try to fool him? David thought, feeling a wave of self-loathing. No, he'd been fooled, all right.

But not any more!

He wasn't sure why he trusted anything the Ferryman said, but it seemed as if the Ferryman was the only person in the Shadowlands willing at least to hint to him what was going on. There still was so much for him to learn about existence here, and David had the distinct impression that there was a whole lot more beyond the Shadowlands.

He dreaded every possible scenario he could think of, but worse than all of that...much worse...was the terrible ache of despair and loss he felt because he knew, now, that Karen was lost to him.

Forever... whispered the voice deep inside his mind.

And this loss was more immediate because it threatened even the most remote possibilities or hope he might have had regarding the afterlife. It seemed as though the pain he felt was much sharper and cut much deeper even than when he had lost his daughter five years ago.

Dark despair gripped him, making the walk back to the schoolhouse seem to take forever. With nearly every trudging step, he found himself looking skyward and silently praying that Karen wouldn't be there when he got back. He began to think that, even if this truly was his daughter, he *wanted* her to be gone.

He wanted to be alone with his misery.

Ultimately, it didn't really matter whether or not she was Karen or an impostor. He could feel that he was losing touch with himself. Without the sharp sensory input he'd had when living, he felt as though he was gradually fading away even from this shadowy existence. He couldn't bear the agony of knowing that he would never be able to really *feel* his daughter as he held her in his arms. Never again would he be able to comfort her as he had when she was a baby…when they were alive.

His daughter, his baby girl, was dead and gone.

No matter how he looked at it, she was lost to him forever, and he was positive that he couldn't stand any more pain or suffering. So if she *was* truly gone, then maybe he should do here, in the Shadowlands, what he had been trying to do but hadn't quite had the courage to follow through with when he was alive. Even though he was already dead, maybe he should truly end his miserable existence.

He knew he could do it.

All he had to do was listen to that dark voice that seemed to be continually whispering inside his mind, telling him how futile all existence was. He would let that voice carry him away and drag him down into total oblivion.

Isn't that what he had wanted all along?

He would willingly let himself dissolve into Nothingness because at least that way, even though he would lose every shred of his personal identity, the pain and suffering would…finally…be over.

Forever! whispered the voice deep inside his mind.

But this time, David listened to it and nodded his submission. He would go back to the schoolhouse, settle himself in the darkness, and then let this voice carry him away until he finally ceased to exist.

What he *wasn't* ready for was the one thing that he hadn't even considered.

When he got back to the schoolhouse and entered its shadowed, echoing hallway, he was greeted by a voice from the dark that he instantly recognized.

"So, you've finally come back, eh?"

It was too dark inside the schoolhouse to see anything more than a dim silhouette, but David knew immediately that this was the wraith who walked with a limp.

"What the hell do you want?" David shouted as blinding rage gripped him.

"What do *I* want?" the wraith asked. This was followed by a short burst of deep, cackling laughter. "What I *want* is something that I need help to get. And now, thanks to you, I just might get it."

"Where's my daughter?" David shouted, his voice reverberating with a high, keening wail. "What have you done with her?"

"Done with her?" the wraith replied. He sounded mystified and almost a little insulted by David's outburst. "Why, I've done *nothing* with her. She's right where I left her...in a place you will never find! Let's say she's my...my insurance policy to make sure you don't do anything stupid, like try to stop me from finally gaining possession of that knife."

"Haven't you done enough to me already?" David shouted. "I don't give a shit what you want! I just want to see my daughter again! My *real* daughter!"

"Oh, maybe you will...in due time," the wraith said, its voice almost breaking up with laughter. "But then again, maybe not."

David clenched his fists so tightly his hands started to tingle with hot, throbbing pressure. The hatred raging inside him coalesced into a raw, passionate power that made him feel as though he were going to explode. His view of the dark room seemed to be clearing, making it look as though he were seeing the world through a thick, red lens. A deep, resonating vibration spread up his arms and took hold of him. A scream built inside his chest as he took a single threatening step forward.

"I won't do that if I were you," the wraith said.

He sounded almost casual, but there was an edge of command in his voice that stopped David cold in his tracks.

"Do you really want to spend the rest of eternity—at least eternity as *you* perceive it—a prisoner, locked up in chains?" the wraith asked. "Or perhaps you'd rather I brought you to the smiths and had your corpus forged into Stygian steel. Is that what you want? Your body would be gone, but your spirit, your essence, would still remain, and it would be aware. Oh, yes. Even though you would no longer have a mouth, you would spend the rest of eternity wailing in agony. They say, if you listen closely, that you can hear the screams inside the metal."

"All I want is my daughter back!"

David's voice rang with a high, warbling echo throughout the dark building. From somewhere up on the second floor, there came in reply a faint ruffle of laughter.

"Didn't you listen to what I just told you?" the wraith said teasingly. "I'm keeping her where you will *never* find her. Don't even try to find her. It won't do you any good. I tried to warn you about associating with the Ferrymen. They're dangerous, you know. You can never trust them."

"And I'm supposed to trust you?" David snapped.

He cringed inwardly because he wanted to say or do something to hurt this wraith, but he was too paralyzed by the emotions that gripped him.

"Oh, yes. I have her. The Ferryman knows that. Wouldn't you think, if he knows where she is, that he'd be willing to take you there? That he'd offer to help you?"

"I just want to see her. That's all I ask," David pleaded.

The wraith clicked its tongue as he shook his head from side to side.

"I wish I could feel even a trace of pity for you," he said. "I really do, but that's one thing I never was very good at…feeling pity."

"*Please,*" David said. He felt like his insides were being torn into tiny shreds. "I *beg* you. Tell me where she is. Take me to her. That's the least you could do."

The darkness of the room suddenly swelled with the sound of the wraith's twisted laughter.

"What? You mean you want to join her? Why, how noble of you! How…how downright *fatherly*! What a marvelous display of parental love and devotion."

The wraith's laughter rose to a high, keening edge.

"Perhaps you'd even be willing to take her place in my haunt. Is that what you're thinking? Or maybe you want to suffer right there *with* her. I hadn't thought of that. Maybe that would be fun to watch."

"Anything! Just bring me to her! Please!"

"I probably should do just that," the wraith said, sounding almost sympathetic, "but you know what? Even though you've done me a great favor, something for which I'll never truly be able to repay you, I don't think I can do it."

David's fury almost exploded out of him, but he suddenly felt too drained even to stay standing on his feet, much less confront this creature. As surely as if he were being weighed down by Stygian chains, he could feel his strength seeping out of him like air escaping from a punctured tire.

"I'm not an evil being," the wraith said. "Really, I'm not, but I do have to admit that I'm rather enjoying all of this. Working together, you and I, we've set things in motion…momentous things. And I'm sure that very soon, now, I'll be able to get that knife."

"You're doing all of this for a simple knife?" David said, his voice rasping as his body trembled with impotent rage.

"Oh, it's not any *ordinary* knife, believe me. This knife is one of three that I've been seeking for a long time. And now…finally…one of them is within my grasp."

"So why don't you just take it and leave my daughter and me alone?"

Waves of exhaustion were sweeping over David, dragging him under. He couldn't help but think the wraith was weakening him somehow. Some kind of unseen magic was draining his strength.

"Look, I'm glad I could help you get it, all right?" David said weakly. "Now maybe you could do me a favor, too. It's not too much to ask, is it?"

"Not really," the wraith said, sounding so condescending it was almost insulting. "But it's just not that easy. And the thing of it is, if I wanted to cause you *real* suffering...the worst kind of suffering you could *ever* experience in your entire, pathetic existence, all I have to do is...nothing."

Nothing...

The word reverberated inside the schoolhouse and inside David's head with an odd flutter that sounded like wings unseen in the darkness, beating close to his ears.

"Don't you see it? That's the pure beauty of it all," the wraith said, stifling his laughter. "What we have here is a classic approach/avoidance situation. There's someone you love who's still alive, and someone you love who's dead, and there's not a damned thing you can do to help either one of them. You have to love it!"

He's absolutely right, you know, the voice inside David's head whispered harshly. *Haven't I been telling you this all along?...There's no goddamned point in even trying!*

"Then at least let me die."

David wasn't sure if he said this out loud or not.

Ultimately, it didn't matter. He knew that the only thing left for him to do was to extinguish himself. He could feel his soul...his life force...whatever the hell he wanted to call it...fading away like a candle that sputtered as it burned itself out.

And that's all he wanted now.

Absolutely drained of all energy and will, David sighed heavily and let himself slump to the hard floor.

"Die?" the wraith said.

That single word seemed to resonate in the darkness as though repeated by dozens of other voices.

"You're already dead. What else could happen to you?"

"Okay, fine...you win then," David said, listening to his own voice as if it were an oddly detached whisper from the surrounding darkness.

Unable even to sit up straight, he slumped to one side and moaned softly as he watched the wraith turn away from him and, dragging his left foot behind him, start for the door. The wraith's body looked almost transparent as he stepped out into the murky haze of daylight and then, like wind-blown smoke, was gone.

It wasn't until long after the wraith had left, and David realized that he was sobbing softly to himself as he leaned against the wall with his legs drawn up tightly against his chest, that David thought of something.

It wasn't much, but it did give him a slim measure of hope.

He walks with a limp!

A subtle rush of excitement filled him at the thought.

So if he walks with a limp, that must mean he's been injured somehow!

The rushes of excitement he felt got increasingly stronger as David mulled this over and finally realized something that should have been blatantly obvious…so obvious it was almost ridiculous that he had missed it before now.

If he's been injured once before…even if he carried his injury with him over into death…that must mean that…somehow…he can be hurt!

Long before she was certain of it, Sarah sensed, at least subconsciously, that she was being followed.

She was feeling a curious mixture of nervousness and exhilaration when she got into her car and drove away from Sy Warner's firing range, heading back to Portland.

Her first stop was her house, where she quickly showered after hiding David's revolver in the drawer of her bedside stand. Once she was dressed and ready for work, she went outside and walked around the house a few times, all the while calling for Bingley.

She wasn't really surprised when he didn't show up. A lonely ache filled her when she acknowledged that this had to be it. He was either dead or lying injured somewhere, and she was probably never going to see him again.

Just in case he did come back while she was gone, she put a bowl of food out on the porch and took one last quick walk around the house, clicking her tongue and calling for him.

When she got to the back steps that led up onto the porch, she stopped short in her tracks. She caught a whiff of something nearby that smelled terrible.

She sniffed the humid air and started looking around more carefully. That's when she noticed the high buzzing sound of flies that seemed to be coming from underneath the back porch steps.

Sarah's heart was pounding hard and fast in her throat as she knelt down on the grass. Bracing herself with one hand on the ground and the other on edge of the stairs, she leaned forward and stared into the cool darkness underneath the steps.

It took a moment for her eyes to adjust to the darkness, but after another moment or two, she saw...something.

A dark, formless lump.

At first she had no idea what it was. It didn't look like anything that had ever been alive once, but buzzing flies were circling around it, and it appeared to be seething with a mass of crawling, gray maggots. Sarah's first impression was that someone had spilled an order of fried rice underneath her porch, and it had magically come to life.

It didn't take long for the raw, putrid smell to get to her. Choking down a stomach-tightening wave of nausea, she leaned back on her heels and took a huge gulp of fresh air as she stared up at the heat-hazed sky and tried to collect herself.

She tried desperately to stop thinking what she was thinking. She didn't want to believe it.

It *couldn't* be true, but that rotting, smelly thing *had* to be the one thing she was afraid it was.

What else could it be?

"Oh, Jesus. Oh, no," Sarah whispered.

Another, stronger wave of nausea gripped her. When she burped, her throat and mouth were filled with a sickly, sour taste. A razor-sharp chill of grief filled her chest. Tears began to flood her eyes, blurring her vision. No matter how hard she tried, she couldn't seem to take a deep enough breath. The rotting smell clung to the back of her throat like the stench of burned hair.

There was nothing more she could do.

Sarah's knees popped as she stood up slowly and then, moving like an automaton, walked over to the garage. She went inside, grabbed a shovel, then went back outside. Her legs almost gave out on her as she walked over to the porch. Holding her breath, she got down on her hands and knees and reached into the darkness with the shovel. The flies buzzed angrily, and the putrid smell got so bad she started to dry heave, but she kept at it, working the blade of the shovel underneath the shapeless lump. Once she had it, she dragged it out into the daylight.

For one brief instant, hope rekindled inside her.

How could this...this terrible *mess* be what she feared it was?

The carcass of dark, rotting flesh and exposed bones was already more than half decomposed. Although it definitely was *some* kind of animal, it looked like a large rat or maybe a gopher, Sarah thought. She could distinguish the animal's head and legs and feet. Two round, bulging, bloodshot eyeballs that stared almost funnily in two different directions glistened like wet bone in the daylight.

The animal, whatever it was, didn't have any fur that Sarah could see, except for on its thin, crooked legs. The rest of the carcass looked like stripped, raw meat. Bones stuck out through the rotting flesh, and there was a black, tangled mass hanging like a pouch from underneath its stomach.

No! This can't be Bingley! It's too small!

But even as Sarah was thinking this, she saw something that made her heart skip a beat or two.

Around the animal's scrawny neck was a thin green and black plaid strap.

Bingley's collar.

Trembling wildly, Sarah screamed and dropped the shovel to the ground as she spun around on one foot, dropped to her knees, and vomited her breakfast onto the grass. Wave after wave of nausea squeezed her stomach, and her eyes burned with tears as she continued to retch long after her stomach was empty.

It took her several minutes to compose herself. Finally, feeling drained and dizzy, she stood up and commanded herself to stay in control; but seeing what she had feared to be true was too much to handle. Bright, trailing pinpoints of light squiggled like flying sparks across her vision. She felt all feverish and shaky as she picked up the shovel and walked over to the corner of her yard behind the garage, where she dug a shallow hole.

She had to avert her eyes when she went back to the porch and scooped up what was left of Bingley. The flies came along with her as she transported her pet to the hole. She tried to shake off the maggots that were crawling all over him, but she knew it was a waste of time. They or something else was going to eat him up as soon as she got him buried. She tried to stop thinking that pretty much the same thing was happening to her ex-husband and her daughter out at Riverside Cemetery.

She hurriedly scooped dirt over Bingley's body and tamped it down with the back of the shovel blade.

By the time she was finished, she was dripping with sweat. She thought it might be a good idea to go back into the house and take another shower, but she had an errand to run before she went to work.

Leaning on the handle of the shovel, she stared at the small mound of brown dirt that covered Bingley. It looked pitifully small and insignificant. Tears gushed from her eyes as she tried to register that it was really Bingley buried there. Every time she swallowed, she could taste the lingering sourness of vomit.

"I…I'm really sorry, Bing," she said, her voice halting and broken.

Shaking her head sadly, she turned and walked away. She leaned the shovel against the side of the garage, telling herself that she'd have to hose it down before she put it back on the tool rack in the garage. Still crying, she got into her car and started it up, making sure to turn the air-conditioner on high before backing out onto the street. Tears blurred her vision as she drove away, but she kept telling herself that she shouldn't cry now.

She *couldn't* cry now.

She had cried too much lately.

She was all out of tears.

The air conditioner quickly cut the heat in the car as she drove to the Trustworthy Hardware store over on Warren Avenue. Her hair and clothes were damp with sweat, and her eyes were red and raw when she walked into the air-conditioned store. She couldn't help but wonder what the sales clerk must be thinking when she asked for a box of .32 bullets. Her hands were clammy, and her insides were all knotted up as she paid for them, but the clerk seemed hardly to notice, much less care what she looked like or what she was buying. He took her money, slid the box of bullets into a bag, handed it to her and barely got off a curt "Thank you" before turning away.

Once she was back in her car, Sarah folded the top of the paper bag down tightly around the box of bullets and slipped it under the front seat before driving out to the university.

When she parked her car in the Bailey Hall parking lot on the Gorham campus, she worried that the hammering summer heat in the closed car might make the bullets explode. Hoping that she was just being overly cautious, she got out, made sure the windows were rolled up and the car doors were locked, and then walked up to the library.

Elizabeth, Sarah's boss, seemed surprised to see her. She commented that she thought Sarah looked pale, and asked her if she felt well enough to work. Sarah told her that she not only felt like it, she *had* to work, if only to have one thing in her life that was somewhat normal and stable.

"You know, I had your computer checked out, and everything seems just fine with it," Elizabeth said. "I can't figure out what happened yesterday."

"Must've been a fluke or something, I guess," Sarah said with a shrug. "Maybe the humidity or something got to it."

She wanted to appear unconcerned, but throughout the day she could never quite get rid of the creepy feeling that she was being watched. She tried to concentrate on whatever job she was doing; but time and again, she found herself looking around as though expecting to see a shadowy figure lurking nearby, watching her.

It wasn't until later that afternoon, around six o'clock, when she was driving home from work, that she finally became convinced that she was being followed.

As soon as she drove out of the parking lot onto College Avenue, a car she didn't recognize, a light blue Toyota, pulled up close behind her. Sunlight glared from the windshield, so she couldn't see the driver clearly; but she thought she caught a glimpse of a heavy-set man wearing sunglasses.

She couldn't be sure, but her first impression was that maybe it was Sy Warner. Maybe he had taken a little more than a casual interest in her. She tried but couldn't deny the stirring of attraction she'd felt when he stood close behind her to help her aim her gun. She recalled feeling both threatened and comforted, thinking about how his powerful arms could have crushed her with only the slightest bit of effort. She didn't remember seeing a blue Toyota out at his place, but that didn't mean anything.

Her pulse was trip-hammering in her chest and neck, and she had trouble focusing on the road as she drove. She started to worry about having left the gun back at her house, and wondered if she would have felt any safer knowing it was in her purse, loaded and within easy reach.

Calm down...Jesus, you're just overreacting! she told herself, but she couldn't stop glancing at her rearview mirror, watching tensely as the blue Toyota kept pace behind her.

At the traffic light in the center of Gorham, she turned left onto Route 25 and proceeded slowly through the small downtown area. At the fork in the road just past a Mobile station, she veered to the right onto the New Gorham Road. Sure enough, the blue Toyota turned that way, too, dropping back several car-lengths behind her.

"Jesus, it's nothing," Sarah whispered to herself, but her fear spiked every time she glanced at the rearview mirror and saw the reflection of her eyes here. She looked scared to herself, and that only made her think all the more that, whoever this was, he was following her on purpose.

This stretch of road was notorious for its speed traps, so Sarah kept checking her speedometer to make sure she was staying under the speed limit. It seemed as though every time she speeded up, the Toyota would speed up. Whenever she slowed down, the Toyota would slow down. And no matter how slowly she drove, the driver behind her held back, never getting close enough so she could see who it was.

Even with the air conditioning running at full speed, the car was stuffy and hot. Sarah found it difficult to take deep enough breaths. She felt a slight measure of relief when, up ahead, she saw the wide parking area for Corsetti's, a small "mom and pop" store. Without bothering to use her blinker, and barely slowing down for the turn, she waited until she was almost in front of the parking lot before jerking the steering wheel hard to the right. Her tires skidded on the dirt-covered asphalt as she finished the turn and pulled to a jolting stop between a parked van and a large Pepsi truck.

"You *bastard!*" Sarah hissed as she cocked her right arm over the back of the seat and watched as the Toyota sped past. Its brake lights flickered once quickly, and then the car passed by like a whisper.

Sarah realized that she was breathing much too fast and consciously made herself slow down. Once she was sure that the car had driven on by and probably wasn't coming back, she sagged forward and rested her forehead on the padded steering wheel. Gripping her head with both hands, she closed her eyes for a moment and waited as the watery rushing sound in her ears gradually subsided.

When she was feeling marginally better, she got out of the car and walked on shaky legs into the store where she bought a bottle of iced tea. The clerk at the counter joked with her about how it was as hot as a sauna outside, but she could barely manage to acknowledge him.

Once she was back on the road, she couldn't stop glancing at the rearview mirror from time to time, braced and thoroughly expecting to see the light blue Toyota pull up on her tail again.

She didn't see it and was just staring to tell herself she'd been overreacting when she turned onto Prospect Street, not far from her house and from the corner of her eye caught a quick glimpse of a light blue car far down the road.

It certainly *looked* like the same car that had been behind her, but a tractor trailer heading in the other direction got between them, and a split second later, the car was out of sight.

"You're really being too paranoid," she whispered to herself, but she still felt all wound up when she pulled into her driveway and parked in front of the garage. She fished the bag of bullets out from under the car seat. Clutching them tightly, she got out of the car and walked over to Bingley's grave.

The dirt had dried out and turned a lighter shade of brown, but the sight—and knowing what was buried there—instantly brought tears to her eyes.

She was hunched over, her body wracked with sobs as she walked up onto the porch. After a quick glance up and down the street to make sure there wasn't a blue Toyota anywhere nearby, she went inside and closed and locked the door. She hurried into the front entryway to make sure the front door was locked and then—even before she poured herself the drink she felt she desperately needed—went upstairs to put the bullets with the revolver.

Wouldn't it be funny, she thought, although she didn't laugh, *if really was Sy following me, and I ended up shooting him in the middle of the chest, just the way he taught me?*

13

INTO THE DEPTHS

The room felt like it suddenly shifted sideways, and then it began to slip away.

A sudden, roaring concussion cracked the gathering darkness, and David felt as though the world had opened up underneath him like a gigantic mouth that was going to swallow him. He let loose a wild, wavering scream as he pitched backwards, spinning crazily head over heels into a cold, pitch-black void. Panic gripped him by the throat and squeezed him as he tumbled into nothingness, twisting and turning in a wild, spastic dance.

After a while, once he realized that he hadn't just fallen over and wasn't going to hit the floor right away, the disorienting sensation of falling passed, and he felt more like he was flying or floating through a dense fog. Wind whistled shrilly in his ears and tugged at him as powerful gusts buffeted him from every side. Seemingly lighter than a feather, his corpus was tossed around like an insignificant mote of dust in the infinite darkness.

This has to be the end! he thought. *It's all over!*

Icy rushes of vertigo and stomach-tightening nausea swept through him as he thrashed about in the dark emptiness. He had no idea whether or not he was still screaming out loud. The wind that shrieked all around him with a thousand voices drowned out even his own thoughts.

All he knew was that he was plunging through a huge, shifting bank of thunderheads. Black, roiling clouds seethed with raw, flickering energy and dark, churning motion.

He lost all sense of time. He could have been falling for a few seconds or for several days.

It didn't matter.

Time had no meaning here.

All he knew was that he was alone....

Utterly alone...

Just as he had always said he wanted to be.

There was no sense of direction. No up or down. No in or out. Not even an awareness of light or dark, at least as he had understood it before this terrifying, timeless instant.

Everything was lost in a spinning chaos that could just as well have been inside him as outside.

He was lost...and frightened...and absolutely alone.

...help me...

After a while, the darkness around him seemed to be coalescing into distinct shapes.

Gripped by stark terror, David watched as huge, distorted faces, horribly underlit by flashes of red and purple light, appeared slowly from the churning clouds and then disappeared. Gigantic hands—some of which didn't even look human—reached out for him, raking the air with hooked fingers as huge and terrifying as scythes.

The roaring sound of hurricane winds filled his ears, but beneath it, David thought he could hear something else...indistinct voices that were screaming at him, calling out his name.

David couldn't possibly make out anything that was being said. The voices he heard and the panicky thoughts that filled his mind melded into a single, howling cacophony that rose louder and louder with soul-shaking fury.

...please...make this stop... the voice inside his head whimpered, sounding like a tiny, terrified child.

...just let me disappear...forever...

And then noticed something curious. For the first time since he had realized that he truly was dead, physical sensations seemed to be returning. He could actually *feel* the wind, whipping through his hair and slashing at his face and arms like stinging razors. He could imagine thick streamers of bright blood flowing from the wounds and snapping like a tangled spider web in the air as he fell.

An unimaginable cold gripped him—a cold like he had never experienced before. It numbed his mind, his corpus, his very soul.

But, he thought, *at least I can FEEL it!*

The physical sensation of cold soon became almost indistinguishable from the stark terror he experienced when, suddenly, a face he recognized loomed out of the darkness at him. David screamed and tried to turn away, but no matter where he looked, the face was there, nailing him with a steady, emotionless stare.

It was his father's face!

The expression on his father's face was truly frightening. His brows lowered like dangerous thunderheads. His jaw was set firmly either in anger or pain. Terrifying rage burned in his shadowed eyes.

"You never even liked me, much less loved me, did you, son?"

His father's voice boomed like thunder above the shrill screaming of the wind in his ears. The sound of it set David's nerves on fire and made him cringe inwardly.

"I—of course I loved you, Pop," he said in a shattered voice that was instantly whisked away by the shrieking winds. "I—I just—just didn't know how—how to—"

"How to what? How to *say* it?" his father bellowed.

When his face loomed closer to David, a blast of laughter filled the air. The hollow concussion pressed in on David like huge, crushing hands.

"Kind of ironic, wouldn't you say so, Davy? That's a writer's word, isn't it? *Ironic?* But I would think someone who professes to be a writer—if he has any *real* talent at all—would be able to think of—and maybe even *say*—four simple words like *I love you, Dad.*"

"Even if I had, you—you wouldn't have listened to me!"

Bitter agony and guilt wrung David's heart. He closed his eyes—at least he thought he closed them—but the image of his father's face floated in front of his vision like a bright afterimage burned forever into his retina and memory.

"You drove me to do it," his father said in his deep, all-too-familiar baritone. "Did you know that? I never wanted to do what I did, but I couldn't help it."

"But I never—"

Words failed David, and his father continued speaking as if what he had to say wasn't even worth hearing.

"I realize that I had a family to support—you and your sister and your mother—but I couldn't see any other way out. I suppose it just goes to prove that there's a certain kind of ultimate justice in the universe—the fact that *you* drove me to it, and *you* were the one to find me."

"I—I tried to forget all about that," David shrieked. "I never wanted you to die!"

"Oh, I realized that—afterwards, anyway," his father said.

For a moment, his voice was almost mild, but there wasn't the slightest trace of forgiveness in it.

"I was there, you see. I was still there in the garage for a couple of days after it happened. I didn't know where else to go. I was there when you came home from school and found me hanging from the rafters. I even tried to break through the Shroud to talk to you, but—well, now you know for yourself just how hard *that* can be."

David couldn't think straight, much less say anything. He watched in mute horror as his father's face suddenly darkened. His cheeks puffed out, and the lighting underneath him turned his face a deep, flushed scarlet that quickly shifted to deep violet. His eyes bulged out of his face so much they looked like poached eggs that were about to pop. After a terrifying instant, David noticed the knotted rope that was twisted in a single coil around his father's neck. The skin of his father's neck and cheeks swelled with a deep, bruised purple that steadily deepened as the rope pulled tighter and tighter. A watery gagging sound filled the air.

Wailing in utter agony, David reached out and tried to grab the frayed end of the rope that danced and snapped like a whip in the air, but either his fingers or the rope were too insubstantial. He watched helplessly as his father's bulging eyes rolled upwards into his head, and his tongue, looking like a bloated, black slug, protruded from his mouth. His father kept making that long, strangled gagging sound as blood gushed from his nose and the corners of his mouth. Then his father's eyes began to bleed red tears as he fixed David with his steady gaze.

"It won't do you any good," his father said in a high, broken voice. "It's all over now…for both of us."

"But I never meant for you to—"

"In the long run, I guess I can't blame you for trying to kill yourself, seeing as how you're the son of a suicide." His father's voice was so distorted David could hardly make out the words. "No, I can't…blame you, but I…sure as hell can't…forgive you…either!"

With those words echoing all around him in the darkness, David's father's face blended back into the darkness, leaving behind a burning afterimage in David's mind that perfectly matched the tortured expression on his father's face that he had carried in his memory ever since that day when he was twelve years old, and had found that his father had hanged himself in the garage.

"I—I'm sorry, Dad! Really sorry!" David shouted, but the vision was gone, and the wind whisked his words away the instant they left his mouth.

A sudden, random gust of wind spun him around and upside-down, and David continued to fall, screaming into the dark, endless abyss.

As he fell, numerous other faces appeared around him. Sharp voices, ear-piercing screams, and bursts of insane laughter trailed out of the darkness.

With a sudden jolt, David realized that another face was moving closer to him. It stood out in sharp detail as though etched from rock. He instantly recognized the thin, handsome features of his literary agent, William Relling.

"That's the best you can do to apologize to your father?" Relling said archly.

His eyes and words drove like red-hot spikes into David's mind.

"Well, I guess you never were all that good with words, were you?"

Relling spoke with that same sophisticated British accent David remembered hearing over the phone so many times over the years, and it immediately reminded him of how, every year, Relling had delivered increasingly worse news about decreasing sales, correspondingly decreasing advances, negative royalty statements, out-of-print books, and less than zero prospects for any foreign sales, much less a film deal.

"I—I did the best I could," David replied weakly.

"Oh, sure, I suppose you did," Relling replied smoothly, "but did you ever stop to consider that even your very best perhaps wasn't quite good enough?"

David couldn't speak. All the rage and frustration he had felt about his career over the last fifteen years choked him into silence. The disorienting sensation of falling wouldn't let up.

"I kept trying to tell you," Relling said, sounding almost snide and mocking as he narrowed his gaze at David. "I tried to warn you about how serious the situation really was, but you just wouldn't listen, would you?"

"Sure I listened," David muttered weakly in his own defense.

"Didn't I keep telling you that the boom years of the eighties were over? Over and gone. But you had to keep at it, didn't you? Because you were a *writer*, you kept telling me, and that's *all* you were. And I suppose, short of pumping gas for minimum wage at the local Sunoco, that was all you ever *could* do, wasn't it?"

"I had to try," David said, cringing inside. "Jesus! What else could I do?"

"True, true," Relling said, nodding his head as a cold light filled his eyes. "But after a while, one would think that even you would have wised up to what was happening. It was almost as though you were acting out that definition of insanity. You know, the one about doing the same thing over and over again, and expecting different results. You kept hitting the same thing, but for different reasons. After a while, it was rather pathetic."

"That's not true…that's not at all true!" David shouted, but his voice was swept away by the screaming maelstrom that embraced him. He turned away, unable to look his agent straight in the eyes.

Before long, Relling's face faded back into the seething darkness, but then other faces of friends, enemies, and business associates resolved out of the darkness and leered at him. Every one of them taunted him by forcing him to remember all the dark, secret hurts he had thought were safely hidden deep in his heart....

Alan Lindwall, the young, aspiring writer David had introduced to his agent and who had then gone on to sell his first novel for more money than David ever earned throughout his entire career. And after all his good fortune, Alan had *never* bothered to thank David for his help. Not even a brief acknowledgment in his book!

George and Ralph Rich, the twin brothers who had made his high-school years such an absolute torment because they were always picking on him and threatening to beat him up after school. Sometimes they made good on their threats and pounded the piss out of him.

Hope Parker, his "one true love" throughout all four years of high school, who had broken up with him when he came home from freshman year at college for Christmas vacation, after telling him that she had been seeing Mike Harlow, David's best friend from high school, for the last year or so. She and Mike had gotten married, had three kids, and—at least as far as David knew—were still a happily married couple.

Alexander Courtland, the investment counselor who had invested a large portion of David's earnings into a "sure-fire" money-making real estate scheme that was going to be his and Sarah's retirement. The deal had gone bust, and David ended up losing every penny he had contributed. Alex, of course, hadn't lost a dime and walked away clean.

Bernie Ryerson, the principal at Buxton High School who had fired David from his first job right out of college, teaching English. After only six months on the job, Ryerson had informed him that he had decided not to renew his contract. A gentleman's way of saying he was being fired.

Other faces appeared. They whispered or shrieked at him, forcing him to remember all the insults and injuries, all the pain and frustration he had suffered throughout his short, meaningless life.

Is this never going to end? David wondered. The thought filled him with blinding panic and a fear as stark and painful as anything he had ever experienced before in his life.

Maybe this was what had been waiting for him all along.

Maybe he would *never* find release in oblivion!

He would spend the rest of eternity plummeting through this dark void, being tormented by all the regrets and losses and fuck-ups he had ever suffered.

If so, then this was Hell, not Heaven. No fiery furnaces. No demons with pitchforks, prodding sinners into the flames. No agonizing tortures on the rack.

This was bad enough.

It was just him with his guilt and despair.

And it was just a matter of time, he supposed, before the faces of his dead daughter and his wife appeared, and he had to suffer their bitter recriminations for the sorry, final chapters of his life.

The thought of that was too much to bear.

David was positive that his mind would snap like a dried twig if he had to squarely face his own grief and guilt about Karen's death. He tried to cling to the last, few mutilated shreds of his unraveling sanity, but the icy winds were ripping through him and tearing his mind apart. He knew, before long, there would be nothing left of him except the tiniest core of his being—all that was left of his soul.

And he would have just enough sanity left to realize that he had completely lost his mind and would be in utter torment for the rest of eternity. There was no release in oblivion! He was going to end up just as the reaper with the limp had said he would—screaming without a mouth...seeing without eyes...conscious and aware without a body...thinking without sanity....

All the while he continued to fall, thrashing and clawing through the dense clouds. After another timeless moment, though, another face resolved out of the darkness.

At first, David didn't recognize it; he saw only the eyes at first—slit, golden irises, like a cat's, that sparkled like coins inside the dense shadows of dark, lowering brows.

As the light increased, the face resolved more clearly, and David felt another powerful shock of fear.

Above and below the eyes, where there was supposed to be flesh, the features looked gray and hard, like old bone. As David's eyesight cleared, he saw a thin, skeletal face, staring at him from underneath the dark folds of a heavy hood. The harsh, angular lines of bone cast deep shadows under the eyes and chin. The lipless mouth appeared to be grinning at him. The only spark of life or intelligence was in the glowing, golden eyes.

When he finally recognized the Ferryman, David wanted to scream but couldn't. The wind was pushing his voice back into his chest. He watched in mute horror as the hideous creature came nearer to him and reached out with a thin, bone-white hand.

"Can you trust me?" the Ferryman said, his teeth clacking like stone against stone as he spoke.

David wondered how such a creature could form words without lips or a tongue. He remembered what the reaper had said, something about not trusting the Ferryman; so even though he was still flailing about in freefall, and the Ferryman looked as though he was standing firmly on solid ground, David didn't dare to reach out and grasp the hand that was extended to him.

"Can you trust me?" the Ferryman repeated more emphatically. His eyes flashed like gold coins glinting in bright sunlight.

Go away! You're just another illusion to torment me! David either thought or said out loud. *There's nothing more you can do to help!...Go away! Leave me alone!*

"I know many of the byways within the Tempest," the Ferryman said simply. "Not all of them, but many."

David couldn't deny that the Ferryman's voice seemed to have the ring of truth in it. As terrified as he was, he was filled with an intense yearning for safety and release. Like a child who had awakened from a nightmare in the dark, he needed the simple reassurance of someone to touch—a hand to hold.

Do you mean there's really a way out of this?

"A way out...or a way in." The Ferryman chuckled and shrugged. "Sometimes it's very difficult to distinguish the two, wouldn't you say?"

I don't want to play word games with you!...Just help me if you can...if you can make this stop!

It took a great deal of effort, but David slowly extended his own hand. The instant he clasped hands with the Ferryman, his arm went numb all the way to his shoulder.

And something else happened.

As soon as their hands touched, the wind died away with a hollow *whoosh*. The shrill, screaming voices immediately subsided, and dim light began to bleed into the darkness like a slow-spreading stain. David could feel something solid under his feet, but he didn't quite dare to believe or trust that he was standing on solid ground. The dark clouds still churned overhead, but they seemed to be dissolving away to nothing.

When he looked down, he was amazed to see that he was standing on a hard-packed earthen surface. As his vision cleared, he realized that he and the Ferryman were standing on a flat, rocky ledge. On one side was a steep, rugged mountainside. On the other was a sheer drop down into a mist-filled abyss that shimmered with dull, gray light.

"Where—where are we?" David asked.

His voice was wrung out with exhaustion. He realized that he was still gripping the Ferryman's hand tightly, and he sensed that, if he were to let go, he would instantly be swept away again into the dark, directionless void.

The Ferryman's face was obscured by the deep shadow of his cowl, and as David watched, the darkness within the cowl deepened and expanded until it appeared to be the opening of a cave in the side of the mountain. With a sudden start, David looked down and saw that he was no longer clinging to the Ferryman's hand. The Ferryman had disappeared, and David was left alone, clasping his own hands tightly together.

"What the—" David called out, but then his voice echoed off. The only reply he heard was a reverberating echo from deep inside the cave in front of him. He shivered when he glanced down over the cliff edge and listened to the shrill hiss of the wind.

I can't take you to her. The Ferryman's voice sounded in David's memory as clearly as if he were still standing beside him on the cliff edge. *You'll have to find her on your own. After that, I'll do whatever I can to help both of you.*

Then the voice faded away like a low, grumbling roll of thunder.

Ahead of him loomed the cave opening. David knew that, if he was ever going to see Karen again or find any peace within himself, he was going to have to enter that cave.

Maybe, he thought, *just like the Ferryman said, the only way out…is in.*

Cozy little place, Sy thought as he pulled over to the side of the road and parked his car a short distance up the street from Sarah's house. He killed the engine and slipped the keys into his jeans pocket before slumping down in the front seat, carefully positioning himself so he could keep an eye on the front of the house and the side porch.

Daylight was gradually bleeding out of the sky. Thin, purple streaks of cloud stretched like claw marks across the western sky. The air was heavy and warm, but Sy thought he could detect a slight drop in temperature as the sun slowly dipped below the horizon. He sighed as he settled back and listened to the faint whisper of distant traffic. It sounded like there were a lot of cars passing by in the distance, but the road Sarah lived on—Canal Street, the sign had said—seemed perfectly quiet and peaceful. In the first fifteen minutes, only two cars went by.

Nice, quiet street to raise kids, Sy thought.

He chuckled softly to himself because he knew that he would probably never be one to settle down and raise children—not unless he and Dianne decided to adopt. That didn't seem too damned likely, so in the meantime— at least for the next day or two—he had decided to "adopt" Sarah.

He wasn't sure what it had been about her that had struck him so deeply, but there had been *something* in her demeanor, something in the way she had looked or talked or acted that had made him feel protective about her.

He was pretty sure it wasn't just some bullshit macho thing. Sy considered himself a fairly intuitive person, and out at the firing range today, he had felt that Sarah was in some kind of serious danger. Not too many women who had never handled a gun before showed up at his place so anxious to learn how to shoot—not unless they were feeling threatened by something...or *someone*.

In Sarah's case, Sy had sensed an almost desperate urgency, so he figured it wouldn't be such a bad idea to tail her for a day or two, just to see if there was anything he could do to help her out.

Sy checked the luminous dial of his watch and saw that it was already a little past eight o'clock. Dianne would have gotten home from work over an hour ago. He'd left a note telling her where he was and not to worry, but he thought maybe he should give her a call. Leaning forward, he started to reach for the cellular phone, but then decided not to and slumped back down in the seat. He'd wait another half hour or so, maybe just until night had fallen all the way, and then head on home. He tried not to think about it very much, but he had to admit that he found Sarah sexually attractive. It was making him horny, and it might be nice to get home before Dianne was asleep.

As the sky darkened to the color of soot, the streetlights lining the road winked on. One window in Sarah's house—the living room, he figured— lit up with a warm, yellow glow. Through the drawn window shade, he could see the flicker of the television. Just once, he saw Sarah's silhouette move across the window.

Sighing deeply, Sy shifted his gaze over to Sarah's car, which was parked in front of the garage. She didn't have the outside porch light on, so he guessed she wasn't expecting any visitors tonight.

Everything seemed so quiet and peaceful; he began to suspect that he must have overreacted. After taking early retirement from the Portland Police Department, where he'd worked as a detective for the last twenty years, Sy figured he was probably just looking for something to keep himself occupied on the days when it was slow at the firing range. He sure as hell didn't consider himself a super-hero who was out to save the world, but he liked to keep his surveillance skills honed, just in case. You never knew when you might need them.

The air in the car was beginning to feel stuffy, so Sy rolled down the window to let in a breeze, but there wasn't much of one. Beneath the smell of hot asphalt that wafted in, the night air was tinged with the faintly rotten scent of the nearby ocean at low tide.

The steady sound of crickets singing in the gathering darkness began to lull him. He started to consider that maybe he was being foolish. When the gun in the holster he was wearing began to dig painfully into the small of his back, he shifted around in the seat, trying to get comfortable. He was feeling so relaxed that he almost missed it when a dark shadow moved out from the thin stand of shrubbery behind Sarah's garage.

"What the fuck?" Sy said, tensing as he sat up.

His powerful hands gripped the steering wheel tightly as he leaned forward and watched the dark figure that crept along the side of the garage. It looked like a moon-cast shadow moving against the lighter background of the building.

Sy had no idea who this might be, but whoever it was, he sure as hell didn't move like he belonged here.

Without taking his eyes off the indistinct figure, he leaned forward slightly and withdrew his gun from his holster. He checked to make sure it was fully loaded—as if he'd ever leave the house without checking the load—and slipped it back into the holster.

The figure crouched low by the side of the garage, obviously scanning the house. Then, with a sudden bust, it darted across the narrow strip of lawn and leaped up to the porch. Whoever it was, he moved with a stalking, cat-like grace that Sy had to admire. Keeping low, the figure shifted over to the side door and stood up to peer cautiously into the house through the side-door window.

Sy considered calling the Portland police on the cellular, just in case he needed backup, but then decided not to in case he was misreading this situation. His hand was on the car-door handle, all set to snap it open and get out if he felt he had to.

Then things happened too quickly for him even to think about calling the police.

The figure grabbed the doorknob and, twisting his body to one side, rammed his shoulder hard against the door. Sy was far enough away so the sound of shattering wood was almost too faint to hear, but he saw the door swing open. After a quick glance over his shoulder, the figure darted inside.

RICK HAUTALA

Sy was out of the car in a flash, drawing his gun as he ran across the street toward the house. His footsteps clicked on the pavement and echoed in the dark. Within seconds, a cool sheen of sweat had broken out across his forehead, and he was trembling with a pure, sweet adrenaline rush. This was the part of his job that he always missed—the thrill of the chase!

As he was crossing the lawn, Sy saw a light wink on upstairs. He hoped that it was Sarah, that she had heard what was going on and was getting her gun out so she'd be ready for the intruder.

As he jumped up onto the porch, Sy said a silent prayer that Sarah would remember everything he had showed her this morning at the firing range. He sensed that her life depended on it.

It was dark inside the cave, but not quite pitch black.

A weird blue glow flickered like heat lightning inside the entrance, casting thin, wavering shadows across the hard-packed dirt floor and making the uneven texture of the stone walls stand out in harsh relief. Spills of dirt and small stones littered the floor. From somewhere deep inside the cave, David could hear a low-throated whistle of wind and the steady sound of dripping water that echoed loudly in the dark, sounding like an animal licking a bone.

As he stepped into the cave, sharp, winding tension filled him, compressing his chest so much that he could almost remember the sensation of breathing in and holding his breath until his chest ached. His throat felt tight and dry, and his eyes were fixed wide open, unable to blink.

I could be imagining all of this, he thought, but he pushed the discomforting thought aside, determined to accept the unreality of the situation.

With no idea what else he could do, he took several more steps into the tunnel. The darkness inside seemed to expand like a widening maw about to engulf him.

As he plunged deeper into the cave, the glowing light seemed to withdraw further into the depths, luring him on while maintaining the same distance ahead of him. After following it for a short while, David paused and looked back, surprised to see that the cave entrance was already out of sight.

How can I see in the dark like this? he wondered as he glanced up at the dense shadows above him. *I was never able to see in the dark before.*

But no matter what doubts assailed him, he knew he had to keep moving forward. He was amazed that the glowing light seemed to be leading him along, and he wondered if he could trust it, or if this was some kind of trap.

The deeper he went, though, the more his apprehension increased. He had no idea what he might find in here or what might happen to him; but as much as he dreaded the prospects, he knew that there was no turning back.

He *had* to keep moving ahead.

The single, fragile hope that the Ferryman had brought him here because Karen was somewhere nearby propelled him forward.

I have to find her myself.

With each step, his feet scraping against the dirt floor made loud tearing sounds that set his teeth on edge. To help keep himself oriented, he ran one hand along the pebbled surface of the wall. Even that little bit of contact seemed remarkably acute, and he was filled with the hopeful notion that he was experiencing physical sensations more the way he had when he was alive. He could almost feel and taste the dense, dank air inside the cave, and he thought he could actually *feel* the cool, almost chilly air against his skin. He had the distinct impression that his forehead and armpits were moist with sweat. If he dared to stop and close his eyes and listen carefully, he thought he might even be able to hear and feel the feathery beat of his pulse in his chest and neck.

No! That's not possible! I'm dead! he told himself, even as the illusion continued to heighten in intensity.

Before long, he found himself thinking and hoping that he might even still be alive.

Maybe that's what's at the other end of this tunnel, he thought with a gathering rush of excitement. *Maybe I'm still alive! Maybe I'll regain consciousness and discover that I'm still lying face-down on the side of the road after being hit by that vehicle!*

The idea sparked a fleeting rush of hope inside him, but he knew that, whatever he discovered or encountered, and whatever was going to happen, first he was going to have to make it out of the darkness of this cave...or through it!

There was no turning back.

Every sound inside the cave seemed strangely amplified. Even the slightest hint of noise—his feet scraping on the earthen floor or his hand brushing against the cave wall—set off a chain reaction of echoes that ripped through the silence, growing steadily louder, then finally fading away to faint whispers.

But the sounds never seemed to be completely gone.

The distant sound of dripping water seemed much louder now, and below that David could hear something else—another sound which, although maddeningly familiar, he couldn't quite identify.

What the hell is that? he wondered as a frantic fear blossomed inside him. The sound teased his ears just at the edge of hearing, like the barely remembered *whoosh* of blood running through his veins.

Filled as he was with fear and faint hope, David forced himself to follow the glowing blue light as it retreated deeper into the cave. He was hoping that it would lead him in the right direction, but the farther he went, the fainter the light became.

Finally, David stopped short, gripped by the panicky thought that, before too long, the light would fade away and then be extinguished entirely.

And then where will I be?

He shivered as a crushing sense of claustrophobia gripped him. He didn't like any of the answers he came up with, but he knew that he was going to forge ahead even if the cave were suddenly plunged into total darkness.

If there was even the slightest chance that Karen was down here somewhere, then he had to find her.

He had to try to save her if he could.

His life might not have had any meaning, but finding his daughter and saving her soul certainly might give his *death* some meaning.

He started walking again, but after only a few paces the scuffing sound his feet were making in the dirt suddenly drew his attention. He stopped and looked around, absolutely convinced that the sound he'd been trying to get a fix on was getting louder, but it cut off the instant he tried to focus his attention on it.

David cocked his head forward, his eyes wide open as he listened, but now he couldn't hear a thing. Not even his own breathing.

Ahead and behind him, the darkness beyond the faint glow of light was so dense that it seemed to swallow everything, even sound. The silence was so complete that David had the momentary impression that *this* was the silence of the tomb—utter and total *dead* silence!

"No," he said in a whispering voice that sounded cracked and ancient in the echoing cave. "No, by Jesus! I still *exist!*"

Even though he said this as softly as he could, his voice resounded like a rumble of thunder in the pressing darkness. His words echoed crazily and blended together until they finally faded away. The cave was perfectly silent except for that elusive sound that he still couldn't identify.

David lost any sense of how long he had been inside the cave. Just like when he had been tumbling through the clouds, time seemed to have stopped. He experienced a momentary dizzying rush of eternity, and was suddenly frightened by the thought that there might be no end to this cave.

He could be trapped here…in the darkness…alone…for the rest of eternity!

But just as he was thinking this, and fear began to sweep him away, he caught a hint of motion up ahead. He saw the distorted shadow of a person shift across the uneven cave wall. It vanished around a corner before he could even begin to react, but he thought he caught a trace of faint, trailing laughter.

Convinced now that there was someone in the cave with him, he cupped his hands to his mouth and shouted.

"Hello!"

"…hello…lo…lo…"

His voice echoed with an unnerving reverberation that trilled higher and louder before it gradually faded away to nothing.

Nothing…murmured a voice deep inside his head.

"Is anybody there?" David called out.

"…body there…" the echo repeated.

David had lost any sense of direction, but he was totally convinced that there was someone there, moving ahead of—or behind—him, someone who was watching every step he took.

He clenched his fists, poised and ready either to fight or run if he had to. He tried to push aside the unnerving thought that, all along the walls and the ceiling of the cave, bright shining eyes were opening and staring at him.

He felt suddenly, horribly transparent, almost nonexistent as though whoever—or whatever—was watching him could see right through him and easily read everything that was written in his heart and soul.

"Where am I?" he called out.

"…*am I*…" the echo resounded.

"I'm lost."

"…*lost*…"

"I'm afraid."

"…*afraid*…"

"Please."

"…please…"

"Somebody answer me!"

"…answer me…"

David was almost paralyzed with fear. Every muscle and joint in his corpus was frozen in place. He knew that he didn't have either the courage or the strength to continue, but he also knew that he couldn't turn back and that he couldn't very well stay where he was either.

He was paralyzed, his mind almost overwhelmed with dark despair.

The terrible truth was, he had no idea which way to go. The darkness at either end of the tunnel was equally impenetrable, just like the darkness he knew was inside him. Sadness and a sour, choking fear twisted inside him, filling him with an unspeakable agony.

Although he could no longer detect even the slightest hint of motion beyond the faint glow of blue light, he still felt as if he was being watched. The skin on his arms and the back of his neck prickled and crawled with the feeling that cold, steady gazes were fixed on him. He could all too easily imagine that invisible hands were reaching out at him from the darkness and brushing against him with light, feathery touches. Those touches seemed more real, more substantial than anything he had previously experienced in the Shadowlands—if that's where he still was.

He reached out with his right hand and rubbed the rough surface of the wall, amazed by how deadened his sense of touch still seemed. The most real thing—the *only* real thing here for him—was his fear, which was as solid and palpable as his living body had once been.

The light up ahead shifted, and once again David thought he caught a fleeting glimpse of a shadow, rippling like dark water across the cave floor and walls. He took a quick step forward, almost calling out again, but then drew back.

"No," he whispered.

Maybe the shadow was trying to lead him in the wrong direction.

The cold, clutching fear in him spiked stronger.

Maybe he should be going in the other direction.

With a cautious glance over his shoulder, David turned and started walking in the opposite direction. Before he had taken more than three or four steps, a voice whispered softly to him.

No, come this way.

The voice hissed in the darkness—or inside his head—sounding like escaping steam.

David gritted his teeth and shook his head, all the more determined to keep moving away from the shadow.

After a few more steps, he paused and looked back. The shadow was clearly etched against the stone wall of the cave, and whoever it was had raised one hand and was gesturing to him.

Don't be foolish…you'll be lost forever if you go that way….

David wanted to reply, but his voice was trapped deep inside his chest. The walls of the cave pressed in on him like a vise. His legs felt frail and brittle, as if they were about to collapse underneath him, but he forced himself to walk away from the beckoning shadow.

No! It's no use…you can't save her! Just like everything else in your pitiful life, you may as well give up any hope of helping her…of helping either one of them, Karen or Sarah…. It's much too late! Why can't you admit that?

David thought his eyes must be playing tricks on him, but it appeared as though the blue glow in front of him was getting steadily stronger, while behind him it was fading. The shadow on the cave wall vibrated with a solid, eternal darkness.

He kept walking away from the shadow, not at all sure if he was heading in the right direction or not. He couldn't decide which to trust—the shadow or the light.

You're a bigger fool than I thought you were! You still don't get it, do you? There's nothing you can do to help them…absolutely nothing! Karen's dead…and you're dead…and pretty soon, once Sarah's dead, it will all be over for everyone you've ever loved…. You will have lost it all!

David found it extremely difficult to keep the frantic edge of fear at bay. The rasping voice behind him was growing louder, more demanding, sounding almost angry; but David tried to convince himself that it couldn't hurt him. The shadow kept beckoning to him insistently, but no matter what it said, no matter how badly it taunted him, it was just a shadow.

"And shadows can't hurt you…not unless you listen to them," he muttered to himself, hoping that the sound of his own voice would drown out the other, more insistent voice behind him.

You'll regret it! You've already lost them, both of them…Karen and Sarah…so you have absolutely nothing left to exist for…. No hope…no future…nothing but Oblivion….

"Yes, I do!" David shouted. "I still have one thing, damnit! Hope!"

David's voice was strained and tight, not much more than a dry, crackling rustle in the darkness. As it echoed from the cave walls, it sounded like several people speaking to him all at once.

Turn back now before it's too late! You'll regret it if you don't! I swear by anything and everything you've ever held sacred or holy that you'll regret it!

But David was convinced, now, that the shadow was trying to lure him in the wrong direction. The farther he moved away from it, the fainter its voice became until it was replaced by something else—that same indistinct sound he had heard earlier and had not been able to place.

Only this time, as he got closer and listened more carefully, he *was* able to place it.

It was the strained, muffled sound of somebody crying.

Almost unbearable tension coiled inside David.

He had heard that sound before…even after he had died and arrived in the Shadowlands. It was the sound of a little child, sobbing softly to herself in the darkness. David knew that it was absolutely too much to hope for, but he was suddenly convinced that it was Karen.

It *had* to be her!

"Hello?"

He stood, tensed, after calling out into the darkness, and waited for the echo of his voice to fade into the surrounding darkness.

The sobbing stopped the instant he spoke. The silence was as solid as the wall of darkness around him.

"Is somebody there?"

David purposely kept his voice low because he didn't want to frighten whoever it might be.

"Leave me alone…please…don't hurt me anymore."

Before the first words had faded, David recognized his daughter's voice.

Hope flared within him as he started forward, looking ahead and trying to pierce the dense darkness. The blue light was glowing so dimly now that it was almost impossible to see; but after another few steps forward, David saw up ahead, huddled on the stone floor, a small, dark figure.

"Karen?" David called out, fighting the tortured flutter in his voice. "Is that really you?"

For what seemed like an eternity, he heard nothing in response, not even the reassuring whisper of his long-stilled pulse in his ears. The darkness around him swelled like a hungry beast, and he was suddenly afraid that he might be imagining all of this. This could be another illusion. It might be just a shadow, created by the dimming light against the rocks and his own desperate need.

"It's me, Karen," he whispered brokenly. "It's Daddy, and I—I promise that I won't hurt you. Nobody's going to hurt you *ever* again!"

His words echoed and then faded away to total silence.

After what seemed like much too long a time, there came a long, warbling cry from out of the darkness. It built up steadily until it resounded through the cave like the piercing wail of a siren.

"Daddy? ...Daddy! Where *are* you?"

"I'm right here, Honey," David said, as he rushed toward her and knelt down.

"How come I can't see you?" Karen asked in a voice that was faint and broken with misery. "I'm really scared, Daddy! It's so dark in here. Where am I, Daddy? What's happened to me?"

14

CROSSING OVER

Sarah leaped up from the couch and, covering her mouth with both hands, screamed the instant she heard the sudden, loud crashing sound coming from the kitchen.

The loud bang was followed by the sound of splintering wood and shattering glass falling to the linoleum floor. It made such a loud noise that Sarah's first, wild thought was that a car must have missed the turn onto Canal Street and careened into the side of the house. She held her breath and was keenly aware of her heart slamming heavily inside her chest as she took a few hesitant steps toward the kitchen.

What the hell is happening?

She cringed as she listened to the heavy tread of footsteps crushing broken wood and glass underfoot. She almost fainted when she entered the kitchen and saw Tony Ranieri, standing by the broken door, which was hanging at an odd angle from one twisted hinge.

"What the—" Sarah started to say, but then she stopped herself.

She couldn't believe how Tony looked. His clothes were dirty and disheveled. His sport shirt was torn at the left shoulder. Sweat plastered his dark hair to his forehead, making him look like he'd just stepped out of the shower. He was panting heavily through gritted teeth as he stared at her, his eyes blazing with an insane inner light.

"Just thought I'd stop in for a quick visit," Tony said in a low, controlled voice that sent a shiver racing through Sarah. He chuckled softly to himself as he looked over his shoulder at the shattered remains of the door and then kicked them with his heel. Shards of glass tinkled lightly as they fell to the floor.

"Sorry 'bout the mess," he said, snorting loudly as he wiped his upper lip with the back of his hand and glared at her crazily. "But it's your own damned fault, you know. You never did give me a house key."

"Jesus Christ, Tony! What are you—? What's the matter with you?"

Panic raced like ice water through Sarah's veins. She knew that she should get away from him as quickly as possible, get to a phone and call the police, but fear rooted her to the spot.

Tony sniffed with laughter as he turned to one side and reached behind his back with his right hand. When his hand came back around, Sarah saw that he was holding a knife. The thin, wicked-looking blade gleamed with a dull glint in the kitchen light.

"The matter? With me?" he said, panting heavily as he shifted his focus from the blade to Sarah. "Why, nothing's the matter with me. I just dropped by to fuck with you a little."

His face was flushed, and his eyes were bugging out of his head as he snapped his wrist and flicked the knife back and forth a few times. The blade made a faint whistling sound in the air.

"This has been a long time coming, don't you think?" he said hoarsely.

"I—I don't know what you—what you're—"

Sarah's voice choked off, and then she screamed. Clenching her fists tightly at her side, she turned and ran back into the living room. She almost tripped on the rug in the entryway as she wheeled around the corner and started up the stairs, taking them two at a time. The muscles in her shoulders and the back of her neck were knotted painfully as she cringed, waiting to feel a sudden impact or a sharp pain jab her from behind, but she made it up to the landing safely before daring to stop and look back.

Tony wasn't anywhere in sight.

Not yet, anyway.

But she could hear the heavy clomp of his feet on the kitchen floor as he started after her in strong, measured steps. Sarah's lungs were burning as if she had swallowed fire.

"You can run, but you can't hide," Tony called from downstairs in a teasing, sing-song voice. This was followed by a burst of crazy-sounding laughter that stripped Sarah's nerves raw.

Without waiting for him to appear, she turned and dashed down the hallway to her bedroom. She swatted the overhead light switch on as she spun around and slammed the door shut. She didn't have a lock on the door, but the large bureau that used to be David's and which she now used for her off-season clothes stood beside the door. Usually she had trouble even budging it, but the adrenaline surging through her system gave her the strength she needed to slide it over in front of the door.

She knew, at best, that it would only slow Tony down, and it would probably piss him off all the more; but she told herself that all she needed was a few seconds.

Just long enough to get out her gun!

Her hands were trembling out of control as she dashed around to the other side of the bed and slid open the nightstand drawer. When she pulled out David's revolver, her grip felt too weak to hold it. The gun seemed amazingly heavy in her hand.

Through the door, she could hear Tony tromping heavily on the stairs. He was whistling a song. Through her raging panic, Sarah recognized the old stand-by, "Strangers in the Night."

She whimpered softly when she realized that the gun wasn't loaded. She hadn't bothered to do that after getting home from work with the box of bullets. Skinning her upper lip over her teeth, she fought back her fear as she fumbled open the box of ammunition and grabbed a handful of bullets. They rattled like dice in her hands as she tried to open the gun. A few bullets made dull clicking sounds as they dropped onto the bed.

"Here kitty, kitty, kitty," Tony called out, clicking his tongue and then laughing like a madman. "Have you seen a little kitty around here somewhere?"

Sarah's eyes were watering so badly she could barely see what she was doing as she shoved three bullets into the chamber then clicked the gun shut.

A spike of fear shot through her when she heard a light, rapid knocking at her bedroom door.

"Hello-o-o-o in there…. Are you hiding from me or something?" Tony called out teasingly. "I know you're around here somewhere…."

Gripping the gun with both hands, Sarah raised it and aimed at the door panel just about chest level. Her hands were shaking so badly the gun kept weaving from side to side, but she struggled to bring it back into line.

"Come on, now. Open up the door and let me in," said the high sing-song voice again. Then, in a low, gravelly voice, Tony chanted, "Not by the hair of my chinny-chin-chin," and then laughed hoarsely.

"*Get away from me!*" Sarah shouted, surprising herself by the strength in her voice. "*I'm warning you! I've got a gun!*"

"Ohhh, so you've got a gun, do you? I'm *so-o-o-o* scared! Listen! Can you hear that? It's the sound of my knees knocking, I'm so scared."

With that, Tony grabbed the doorknob and twisted it viciously from side to side while pushing on the door from behind. The door opened a crack as the heavy bureau started to slide across the floor. Its feet made a harsh scraping sound on the wood. Sarah whimpered again when she saw the expanding darkness at the edge of the door.

"I mean it!" she shouted. "I have a gun, and I'll use it if I have to!"

"Well, *I* have a knife, and I *sure* as hell plan to use it!" Tony shouted.

The bureau shifted another few inches, and Tony's face appeared in the widening crack. The bedroom light caught and reflected in his left eye, making it gleam brightly.

With a loud grunt and a sudden shove, he pushed against the door. The bureau toppled over and hit the floor with a loud crash. The impact shook the room and rattled Sarah's teeth. Tony was smiling a wide, idiotic grin as he stepped into the room and stared at her. Fury boiled deep in his eyes, and the corners of his mouth were twitching as though he were tasting something terrible.

Sweat broke out on Sarah's brow as she stepped back, careful to keep the bed between them.

She was trying desperately to remember everything Sy had told her today at the firing range, but she was so scared her mind drew a complete blank. Whimpering softly, she squeezed the gun with both hands to steady it. She spread her legs in a firm stance, sucked in a breath and held it until it started to hurt. The aiming bead at the tip of the revolver drifted around until finally she managed to center it in the middle of Tony's forehead.

"I swear to God I'll use it," she said, trying to keep her voice low and measured.

Tony appeared mildly surprised, maybe a little irritated when he saw that she was, indeed, holding a gun. Then his smile widened even more as he raised the knife and twisted it back and forth in front of his face, all the while staring at the blade as though completely mesmerized.

"Frankly, I don't think you have the balls to pull the trigger," he said softly as he took another step closer. "In fact, I *know* you don't have the balls to do it because I've *fucked* you, and you didn't have any balls then!"

He laughed tightly at his own sick joke.

Sarah knew that he'd be able to catch her if he lunged across the bed. She braced herself, trying to control the icy flood of adrenaline that coursed through her body and made her tremble. She remembered what Sy had said, about how much difference there was between shooting at a paper target and a real human being. She knew she shouldn't hesitate. Her life depended on it.

"Fuck *you* I don't have the balls!" she shouted.

Squeezing her eyes tightly shut, she jerked back on the trigger. The split second before the gun went off, she knew that she had made a crucial mistake.

She hadn't *squeezed* the trigger the way Sy had told her to.

The gun exploded and jumped in her hands like a live animal. The bullet went wide and hit the edge of the door jamb, splintering the wood inches behind Tony's head.

Tony glanced back over his shoulder at the ragged hole the bullet had made, then turned back to her and smiled widely. His wide, white teeth glistened like a wild animal's.

"I'm impressed," he said, nodding slightly, "but you were a little wide of the mark on that one."

He shifted around toward the foot of the bed, closing in on her fast. Sarah backed up against her own bureau, feeling the edge of it dig into her rump.

"Do you wanna try again? Or was that all the bullets you have?"

"I mean it, Tony. I swear to God I'll shoot you," Sarah said, but this time there was less conviction in her voice.

Tears were streaming from her eyes, blurring her vision. The gun in her hand felt suddenly much too heavy for her to hold. The tip started to drop, until it was aiming halfway down at the floor.

Tony raised the knife and then snapped it back and forth once, quickly. The blade sliced the air with a soft, whickering sound. Chuckling to himself, he moved within striking distance.

"Get down!"

A different voice suddenly split the tension in the room.

Sarah froze where she was, but Tony reacted quickly. Dropping down into a low crouch, he started to wheel around, but he wasn't quick enough.

The deafening sound of a gun going off split the air again.

Sarah screamed and dropped her own gun. She automatically covered her face with her hands but couldn't help but watch between her fingers as Tony's head exploded like a melon dropped from a second-story window. A fan-shaped spray of bright red blood shot up to the ceiling. Chunks of pink and gray material flew everywhere. Some of the chunks landed on Sarah's chest and face, but she was too stunned to notice them. She watched, petrified, as Tony continued to spin around, looking like he was doing an awkward curtsy. His wide eyes held the glazed look of surprise, but that quickly faded as he crumpled to the floor.

Sarah saw a man's face appear in the doorway.

For a shattering instant, she didn't recognize who it was. Then she started to laugh hysterically when she realized that it was Sy Warner.

"What the hell are you—" was all she managed to say, and then her voice cut off, and all she could do was make a low, whimpering sound.

"I was just in the neighborhood and thought I'd stop by for a visit," Sy replied casually. He chuckled softly, but then his mouth fixed into a thin, hard line.

"But do you wanna know one thing?" he added. Before Sarah could reply, he said, "I was afraid that would happen."

They both glanced down at Tony's lifeless body.

Most of the top of his head was gone. Dark blood was seeping out and soaking into the rug. His lifeless eyes stared up at the ceiling as though he still couldn't quite believe or accept what had just happened to him.

"A—afraid—? Afraid of wh—what?" Sarah said, amazed that she could speak at all.

"Well, at first I was afraid that, like he said, you wouldn't really have the balls to pull the trigger. Then, when you did—you almost hit me, by the way. That was too damned close for comfort. I thought I taught you better."

Sy puffed his cheeks and exaggeratedly wiped his brow with the back of his hand.

"No, I—I didn't even s-see you there. I was—oh, Jesus, Sy!"

"Well it's a damned good thing your aim was off to the left instead of the right. Otherwise, you'd have blown *my* brains out." Sy followed this with another nervous chuckle of relief that seemed totally genuine.

Sarah suddenly felt all woozy inside. She almost fainted when Sy stepped over Tony's body and came up close to her. Her entire body felt numb, and she imagined that she was a useless sack of grain as she slumped forward into his powerful arms. She closed her eyes and let him hold her up.

"He…I didn't know what he was—what was happening," she said in a faint whisper.

She opened her eyes and looked over Sy's shoulder, down at Tony's corpse on the floor. No matter how hard she tried, she couldn't make herself turn away.

"He wanted to—I think he really was going to…to kill me!"

"Yeah, I think he was," Sy said evenly. "Good thing I just happened by, huh?"

He took a shuddering breath and held her close to him, squeezing her tightly. Sarah couldn't believe how secure she felt in his embrace.

"We probably ought to call the police, don't you think?" Sy said after a long moment.

Sarah bit down hard on her lower lip and nodded her head numbly as she clung to him. She was unable to look away from Tony's amazed, lifeless expression. She noticed that he was still holding the knife, his right hand gripping it so tightly the knuckles had turned bone white.

Then, as she was staring at him, something incredible happened.

The knife in his hand seemed to flicker like a strobe light. The blade glowed with a bright, purple glow; and then, in the blink of an eye, it winked out of existence.

Sarah leaned back and gasped. Breaking the embrace, she looked at Sy and then back at Tony. She was not ready to accept what she had just seen.

"What the hell was *that?*" she whispered.

When David got up close to Karen and looked into her eyes, he saw a deadness there that filled him with terror. Her face was nothing but a gaunt, pale white reflection of what it had been in life. The skin, especially on her cheeks and around her mouth, looked as dry as an Egyptian mummy's and was stretched paper-thin. A network of fine, dark lines like hairline cracks in porcelain marked her face. Her lifeless, glazed eyes stared back at him from within dark, bone-ridged sockets.

She seemed to register only dim recognition of her father as she slouched forward, her head lolling to one side. She would have toppled over onto the cave floor if her arms and legs hadn't been bound to the wall by heavy, clanking chains. A wave of despair swept through David when he realized that the chains and cuffs on Karen's ankles and wrists were forged from Stygian metal. The heavy links were set with thick concrete into the cave wall.

Trembling violently inside, David knelt down beside Karen and studied the chains. For a dizzying instant, he thought he could hear a faint chorus of shrill screams coming from inside the links. Remembering the pain that he had experienced when the reaper had bound him with similar chains, he didn't dare touch them; but he knew that he would have to if he was going to release her.

His mind clouded as the fear inside him intensified.

It isn't going to end like this! he thought as a sudden, savage fury ripped through him.

It can't end like this! I won't allow it!

He grabbed the chain that bound Karen's legs and squeezed it tightly in spite of the paralyzing cold and excruciating pain that tore through him like a hurricane.

The screams coming from the metal grew louder, almost deafening. David knew that, if the sound continued much longer, it would drive him insane. He wondered why Karen wasn't reacting to the sound. Maybe she had been here for too long and had gotten used to it.

Feeling his strength draining from him by the second, David wrapped a length of the chain around each hand twice and clutched it tightly.

The pain grew unbearably intense. His vision went blank, and he found himself staring into a void of Nothingness as, with a wild cry of rage, he started to pull his hands apart.

His body shuddered from the tremendous effort. He could feel his strength draining away of him like lifeblood flowing from an open artery, but he kept pulling until he felt the metal beginning to yield.

The agonized shrieks coming from inside the chain rose even louder as the links slowly separated. Bright flashes of red filled David's vision; and then, with a final burst of savage energy, he yanked his hands apart, snapping the chain like a whip.

The cave was filled with the sound of clanking metal as the links of the chain separated and fell to the cave floor, scattering like a shower of coins.

No longer conscious of the horrendous pain that seized him, David took hold of the chain that bound Karen's arms and started to pull it apart. His corpus was infused with a violent, insane strength as he concentrated every ounce of his dwindling mental and physical power on tearing the chain apart.

The screaming voices from the chain filled the cave as the links slowly pulled apart. The instant the arm cuffs fell away from Karen, David dropped the remnants to the cave floor before he lost any more strength.

He looked down at his hands and moaned softly. Although he experienced the pain only as a distant, throbbing pulse, he could see thick purple welts marking the insides of his palms and the backs of his hands. The skin sizzled like frying bacon. Thin wisps of smoke trailed upward in the still air.

Total exhaustion almost dragged him under, but then, like a cold spring breeze, a measure of relief flowed through him when he realized that Karen was free.

"Can you…can you get up?" he asked with a strangled gasp, not entirely sure that he could move, either.

Karen looked back at him with a dull, vacant stare, but after a moment she smiled faintly and nodded.

"Yeah—I think—maybe," she answered in a ragged whisper.

"Come on, then," David said, extending his hand to her. "Come with me."

He felt completely dissociated and found it almost impossible to focus on what he was doing as he took his daughter's hand and raised her to her feet. Her body felt as light and hollow as a papier-mâché mask.

Karen seemed terribly unsteady on her feet. David was afraid that he might crush her as he wrapped an arm around her waist to support her.

"I…can't believe I…found you," he said, his voice threatening to break on every syllable.

"Me neither," Karen replied, still looking at him, dazed.

As broken and lifeless as her voice sounded, David was positive that this was *really* his daughter, and not some impostor. Although he suspected that it might be just another illusion, a trick of his emotions, he was positive that he could feel tears—*real tears*—welling up in his eyes.

He almost jumped when Karen took his hand in hers and squeezed it tightly, almost desperately.

"I know you're scared and…and confused, honey," he said, trying to keep his voice low and even so he wouldn't frighten her any more than she already was. "But we really do have to hurry."

"Yeah, but I—I feel so…so weak," Karen said brokenly. "I don't have any idea how—how long I've been down here, but it seemed like…like *forever.*" She paused and for a moment seemed to be focusing on something far, far away. "And it was *so-o-o* scary!"

"I know it was, but we'll have to talk about it later," David said. He cocked his head to one side, positive that he had heard a sound from deep inside the cave. "Right now we have to get back and try to help her."

"Help…who?" Karen asked weakly.

The dim light in her eyes seemed to fade. She sagged forward and clutched her forehead with one hand as she shook her head in confusion. She looked as though she could barely stand, much less walk, but David knew that they had to get out of here fast. And he sure as hell wasn't going to leave her behind.

"Your mother," he said, and as soon as he said the word, a powerful wave of emotion filled him. "She—she needs my help."

For an instant, he thought he caught the faintest hint of a glow returning to Karen's eyes.

Side by side, with him supporting her, they started along the narrow, echoing corridor. Up ahead, the faint blue glow lit their way, but David was so exhausted that he had trouble focusing on it. Even as the echoes of their voices were fading away, another voice began to speak softly in his mind.

You're already too late! the inner voice said with a grating whisper that set David's nerves on edge.

You can't help her or anyone else! Not even yourself! Why not just give up? You're much too late....

Echoing from deep inside the cave, David thought he heard what sounded like approaching footsteps.

At first he thought—he hoped—that it might be their own footsteps, echoing in the cavern; but once he stopped and listened for a moment, he knew the sound was getting louder.

And closer!

He distinctly heard a rough scraping sound…as though whoever might be following them had a bad leg and was dragging one foot on the ground. The thought filled David with a sudden, blinding panic, but he forced himself to control it.

"We have to hurry," he said, clutching Karen tightly to support her. When he looked down at her, he almost couldn't believe that this *really* was his daughter walking beside him.

She looked so small, so thin, so frightened.

Conflicting emotions twisted like coiling snakes inside him. He didn't even want to try to imagine what the reaper might have done to her while she was his prisoner here in the dark. Everything that came to mind filled him with hatred and anger. Gripping her tightly, he urged her forward, and somehow they both found the strength to start running.

As they ran, the sound of pursuit behind them grew steadily louder.

David had no idea where they were headed, but he knew that he had no choice but to follow the faint glow of light that kept moving several paces ahead of them. He knew, but didn't dare tell Karen, what might happen if he was wrong—if the light was luring them deeper into the cave instead of out of it.

"Do you *really* think you can get away from me that easily?" a voice suddenly shouted from behind them.

David instantly recognized the shrill voice of the reaper.

He paused just long enough to swing Karen up into his arms and then, clutching her to his chest, redoubled his efforts as he ran through the darkness. The only clear thought in his mind was that, if he was going to cease to exist, then *this* was how he wanted it to be—clinging onto his daughter with every ounce of strength and love that he still had inside his dead corpus.

He had no idea how long he ran, but he was amazed that he didn't tire. He would have thought that contact with the Stygian chains would have sapped him of all his strength, but he ran knowing that his and Karen's very existence depended on getting away from the reaper.

Their footsteps and the wailing voice of their pursuer echoed wildly in the cave. The corridor twisted and turned like a huge snake, and as they ran, David once again had the distinct impression that he could see eyes opening up in the surrounding darkness. Eyes that watched them with a cold, steady stare. He could feel their piercing stares like needles, making the back of his neck prickle.

"You'll never get away from me!" the voice shouted. This was followed by high, squealing laughter, but David thought that it sounded much farther behind him. He began to feel a faint hope that they might really make it.

But where would they go?

Where did this cave lead?

Maybe he was going around in circles…or heading right back toward the reaper.

His feet pounded against the hard-packed earth floor. Every impact made his vision jump and his teeth click together. The icy panic inside him was like a huge hand had gotten a tight grip on his heart and was squeezing…squeezing….

He was so lost in the fear of his flight that he didn't at first notice when the glow of light up ahead started to fade away. The cave blended into darkness so gradually that David barely noticed the purple, trailing afterimages that streaked the corners of his vision.

But then, ever so slowly, the darkness closed in on him.

Once again, he felt a sudden rush of tumbling head over heels as he fell. He clutched Karen close to him as raging winds whistled and shrieked all around them. He could faintly hear someone calling out to him, but he had no idea if it was the reaper who had been pursuing them, or Karen, or himself.

But then, from out of the swirling darkness, he saw something—a hand, extending toward him. It was thin and bone white, and glowed with a faint iridescence.

Can you trust me?

David was so filled with terror that the voice barely registered in his brain. He saw the bony fingers spread like the framework of a fan as they reached out for him, but he didn't dare grab at them for fear of losing his hold on Karen. He chanced to look at her and saw her ghost-white face, staring up at him.

"I'm…scared…Daddy," she wailed.

He could hardly hear her above the rushing roar of the wind around them, and had to shout even to hear himself.

"I know," he said. "I am too."

Can you trust me? the voice repeated more emphatically as the Ferryman's face resolved out of the darkness. His heavy cloak shadowed his features, but David could see the steady glow in his sunken eyes, and he suddenly realized that he could—he *had* to trust the Ferryman!

He had brought him this far.

He had helped him find Karen.

As far as David could see, he had no other choice.

The fear gripped him that, should he let go of Karen, she would slip away from him and spin off into the black, bottomless depths of the raging tempest. Clutching her as tightly as he could with one arm, he reached out with the other. His hand looked pale and as insubstantial as smoke as he grabbed for the Ferryman's hand.

The instant they touched, the dizzying sensation of falling stopped.

David looked around, amazed to see that they were standing on the sidewalk of a dark, deserted street. Something made a dull concussion in the air, but when he turned to look, there was nothing there. A vague sense of relief filled David, but he still had no idea where they were or how close the reaper might be. Groaning in pain, he lowered Karen to the ground, but he still held her around the waist until she seemed stable enough to stand on her own.

"Where the heck are we? What was all of that?" Karen asked. Amazement added a faint edge to her dead-sounding voice.

"I—I'm not sure," David replied as he looked around nervously, trying to get his bearings.

The street looked vaguely familiar, but he couldn't quite place it. All around them were ruins of buildings and thin, skeletal trees that looked like hands clawing at the night sky. David could see the abandoned wrecks of a few cars lining both sides of the street. He could also sense other people—other wraiths nearby, even though he couldn't see them. Some of the densest shadows close to him shifted threateningly. When he turned and looked back at the Ferryman, he was only mildly surprised to see that he had disappeared.

"We—we have to keep going," he said to Karen, cringing inwardly as he tried to hide his own fear from her.

Holding hands, they started to run again. Their footsteps echoed with loud clicks in the silent night. For a fleeting instant, David had the distinct impression that they were still fleeing through the dark cavern.

That's right, said a voice inside his mind, although it sounded much fainter than it had in the cave. *Nothing's changed! No matter where you go or what you do, you aren't going to accomplish a damned thing...I'm telling you, you're too late!*

David tried to push the voice out of his mind, but as soon as it fell silent, he heard something else—a sound that he had heard on his first night in the Shadowlands. This time, however, he knew what it was.

A pack of barghests!

And this time, he knew that they were hunting for him and Karen.

The mournful baying sound filled the still night, broken only by the sound of their own footsteps. Karen stumbled and stopped, then cast a terrified glance down the street in the direction they had come.

"What's that?" she asked in a trembling, tight whisper. "I—I've heard it before."

"I'll tell you later," David said. "Come on. Just keep moving as fast as you can."

And so they ran through the night with the howling sounds growing louder and louder behind them, spurring them on.

The night seemed to close down around them, and David had the distinct impression that, no matter how much effort they expended, the darkness was slowing them down, making them drag their feet. Faintly glowing eyes appeared in the dark windows and deeper recesses of the buildings that lined the street. Hissing whispers filled the night, and shadows shifted, but nothing could block out the steadily rising sound of the hunting barghests coming closer.

David considered turning and confronting the pursuing beasts, but he was positive that it would mean a final death for him and for Karen—if not imprisonment by the reaper or else something worse that he couldn't even imagine.

They had no choice.

They had to keep running, but David suddenly halted and looked around. Karen jerked to a stop beside him and looked around, bewildered.

Before she could ask him what it was, David said, "I think I recognize where we are!"

Somehow—he had no idea how—they had ended up on Forest Avenue, at the far end of Canal Street, not more than a couple of hundred yards from the house where he, Sarah, and Karen used to live—

Where Sarah still lived!

"We're almost home, Honey," he whispered.

His voice was almost drowned out by the piercing howls of the barghests. David looked behind them and saw huge, black silhouettes underneath the faint glow of distant streetlights.

"Do you know where we are?"

Momentary confusion registered in Karen's eyes. Then a faint smile twitched one corner of her mouth.

"Yeah. Mommy and I used to come this way…on our way to…to that park!"

"You got it," David said.

All the while, he was looking down the street at the rapidly approaching creatures. They appeared to be a variety of shapes and sizes. Some of them ran on four legs, like huge hunting dogs; others walked with an awkward shamble on two legs, their knuckles dragging the ground.

"We'll be safe at home," David said, not really sure if he believed that himself; but it was the only hope they had.

Taking Karen by the hand, he started running again, pulling her along with him. The howling beasts pursuing them must have caught sight of them, because they raised a raucous chorus of howls that rang against the night sky. David didn't dare to look back as he ran, but he could feel their terrifying presence bearing down swiftly on them.

Ahead, almost lost in the gloom of the night, he saw the house. A few lights were on downstairs, and there was a light on in the upstairs bedroom windows. The warm, yellow glow was like a beacon that drew him onward.

As they ran, the street seemed to telescope outward. David was thinking that they should have covered the distance easily by now, but they appeared to be no closer to the house even though the barghests behind them seemed to be closing the distance—fast.

"Please…hurry," David said, having to shout to be heard above the baying of the beasts.

Somehow, Karen found the strength to scream as she ran. The sound seemed to send the pursuing creatures into a frenzy, spurring them on all the more.

With a sudden rush, the house loomed up close to them as though the ground had suddenly slipped under their feet. David stumbled and almost fell when he rounded the corner and started for the porch. He jerked to a stop when he saw something—a small, dark figure crouching on the top step. Two silver-green circles glared at him. It took David a paralyzing moment to recognize that it was Bingley.

"What's that? Will it hurt us?" Karen asked, cringing away as the cat hunched up its back and hissed viciously at them.

David cast a worried glance over his shoulder and saw that the barghests were quickly closing in on them. "Not as much as they will!" he said.

Clasping Karen by the hand, he charged up the steps to the side door. It took him a moment to realize that the door had been broken open and was dangling from one twisted hinge.

Bingley tracked them with his cold, unblinking eyes, but then he turned and looked up the street, past the single parked car, to the approaching beasts. With a loud hiss, he jumped off the porch and darted out into the street.

Just before David and Karen entered the house, he looked back in time to see that the barghests immediately turned and went after the wraith of the dead cat.

"Jesus," David whispered as he watched the dark, seething pack disappear down the street. Their cries and the loud squalling of the cat gradually faded away.

David didn't have very long to appreciate their rescue. For all he knew, the barghests would quickly tire of chasing Bingley and come back looking for them. He felt sure that they were implacable, untiring hunters who, once they had a scent, would not give up until they captured their prey.

David looked at the shattered door and instantly realized that Sarah was in danger.

There was no way of knowing when this had happened, but the voice in the back of his mind had been telling him all along that he was too late to save her. It felt to David as if he had dived into cold, brackish water as he entered the kitchen. The ceiling light was on, but it seemed hardly bright enough to light the room.

"Sarah," he called out, knowing that she wouldn't be able to hear him...unless she were dead too and had become a wraith.

Side by side, they moved through the kitchen. David glanced at Karen and was deeply saddened to see the wan expression on her face. She looked as though she vaguely remembered this house but couldn't quite place it—as though it was part of a dim memory from long ago and far away.

As they entered the living room, the muffled sound of an explosion rumbled through the house. It was deep and low, and sounded impossibly far away, but Karen screamed and pitched forward onto the floor.

David was also staggered, but he immediately looked out into the hallway in the direction from which the sound had come.

"Stay right here," he said. "Find someplace to hide, just in case those—those things come back."

Karen looked at him with mounting terror in her eyes. She started to say something, but then another explosion rang out, sounding louder. David's body drifted like wind-blown smoke up the stairs and then down the hallway toward Sarah's bedroom.

Tony was dazed.

For the briefest instant, he'd felt a sharp, searing pain in his head. This was followed by an abrupt release of pressure. He had a momentary sensation of spinning around and falling down, but then—somehow—he found that he was standing up and feeling unusually buoyant, as though he might float up into the air if he allowed himself to.

The instant the gun went off, the light in the room had seemed to dim. It cast a dull, yellow glow that made everything in the room look like an old-fashioned sepia photograph. No matter where he looked, Tony saw tiny spikes and shifting curtains of light dancing and sparkling at the edges of things. He had the frightening impression that he was looking at things through a thick, distorting lens.

Sarah and a heavy-set man who looked like a goddamned weight-lifter appeared to Tony as faint, almost transparent shadows. When he realized that he could barely distinguish their faces in the murky light, a bolt of fear shot through him.

What the fuck is going on here? he asked himself, but he didn't have time for an answer.

Another person—someone he didn't recognize—had appeared in the doorway.

For some reason, Tony could see him more clearly than the others, but he could also see by the man's facial expression that this man saw and apparently recognized him.

"You son of a bitch!" the man shouted, his voice booming like a cannon shot in the air as he entered the room. He moved fast toward Tony, who backed up and raised his hands defensively.

That's when Tony realized that he still had the knife in his hand.

He looked at the blade, amazed to see how much it seemed to have changed. Ever since he had found it, he had thought that it seemed to glow with a subtle energy, but now it was fairly vibrating with a tangle of interlacing strings of blue and purple light. The blade hummed like a tuning fork in his hand, sending a throbbing, almost painful sensation up the length of his arm.

The man saw the knife and instantly reacted, but he didn't slow down.

He hit Tony, hard and low, like a football tackler. The impact, although strangely muffled, carried them both to the floor. Before he could react, Tony felt the man grab the wrist of his hand that held the knife. By twisting and bending it backwards with a quick jerk, he loosened Tony's grip on the rubber handle.

"Oh, no you don't, buddy!" Tony shouted, trying desperately to keep hold of the knife.

He was surprised by how distorted his own voice sounded to him—as if the air had suddenly gotten thicker, or he was talking underwater.

"You rotten son of a *bitch*!" the man growled through gritted teeth.

His face loomed closer to Tony, and what Tony saw paralyzed him with fear. The man's eyes glistened like dark, wet marbles, but there was an icy, distant glow in them that shook the younger man's courage and drained him of all strength.

The man's eyes looked absolutely *dead*! His face was seamed and cracked, and the skin looked pale and dry, as if it was ready to slough off in large, flaky chunks.

"You're not going to have her!" the man said between clenched teeth as he thrashed viciously from side to side and tried to pry Tony's fingers from the knife handle. "I *won't* let you have her! It's *not* too late!"

Tony was still feeling oddly dissociated from his own body, so it was almost impossible for him to resist the man's savage strength. His hand holding the knife went numb as tingling waves of pins&needles spread like wildfire up to his shoulder. Tony thrashed from side to side, but it didn't do any good. All he could do was watch helplessly, as though distantly viewing a movie, while the man pried his fingers apart and forced the knife out of his hand.

The blade was shining with such shimmering energy that Tony found it almost impossible to look directly at it. Struck dumb with terror, he watched as the man turned the knife around and, raising it high above his head, prepared for a downward thrust.

Icy numbness filled Tony when he realized what was going to happen next.

He's going to kill me!

This was one of his last clear thoughts. He wished fervently that he could close his eyes, but he couldn't look away as he saw the tip of the knife begin its downward arc.

The motion seemed to take forever.

As the knife descended, it made a dull, rolling concussion in the oddly silent air. Then, like the stinging bite of a snake, an intense pain pierced the center of Tony's chest.

When the man pulled the blade out and raised it again, preparing to strike a second time, Tony looked down to where the knife had entered his body, amazed to see, not gushing blood, but a dull white glow of light that seemed to be radiating out of the wound.

He was terrified beyond belief.

He tried to scream, but his strength was rapidly draining out of his body. His view of the room dimmed until he and everything else were nothing more than a distorted shadow show. The last thing Tony saw before he plunged into the bottomless, eternal darkness was the looming face of a man that he didn't even know...

The face of the man who had killed him!

15

BARGAINING FOR SOULS

David was feeling utterly exhausted.

Fighting with the wraith for possession of the knife had drained what little strength remained in him. He had watched in rapidly mounting horror as the glowing knife blade, almost as if moving of its own volition, had penetrated deep into the man's chest. He had felt his own life force dissipating like wind-driven smoke as he watched the man writhe in agony while his corpus slowly dissolved away until there was nothing left except a small, dark smudge on the floor that looked like a pile of wet ashes. After another few seconds, even that disappeared, dissolving like dirty ice that was melting in the sun.

Filled as he was with anger and hatred and fear, David didn't feel the slightest compunction about destroying the man's corpus. As far as he was concerned, the stranger deserved to die a thousand deaths, if only because he had been trying to hurt Sarah.

The man's physical body still lay sprawled on the bedroom floor at the foot of the bed, but it, too, looked like it was deteriorating much faster than it normally would. Thick, dark droplets of blood and globs of brain fell like rain from the splattered ceiling. The man's face appeared to be bleaching out as it caved in on itself, looking like time-lapse photography of rotting fruit. His eyes were as cold and dead as stones as he stared sightlessly over at the baseboard beside the closet door.

David reached out helplessly with both arms as he looked over at Sarah, who was still clinging to the muscular man with the close-cropped blond hair. Neither one of them appeared to be the slightest bit aware of the terrible struggle that had just occurred in the room, practically at their feet.

As David struggled to stand, still holding the knife in his right hand, a high buzzing sound filled the room—or maybe it was in his head. He wondered if the sound might be coming from the blade itself. The knife in his hand felt as though it must weigh at least ten pounds.

His first impulse was to get rid of the damned thing, but before he even started to do that, he tensed as another thought occurred to him.

It isn't over yet!

Sarah was safe, at least for the time being, but what about Karen?

Trembling violently, David turned toward the bedroom door and stared into the deep darkness that filled the hallway. It looked like a solid wall of black stone. He wanted desperately to go downstairs to his daughter, but he was not sure that he had the strength to move.

"*Karen,*" he whispered, his voice no more than a rattling gasp.

The instant he said his daughter's name out loud, Sarah grunted as she spun around and looked directly at where David was standing. Her eyes were wide and moist with fear. Tears sparkled like diamonds on her cheeks. She licked her upper lip with the tip of her tongue.

"Did—did you just say something?" she asked, frowning as she glanced at the muscular man. Her voice sounded strangely modulated and was almost lost in the dense atmosphere of the room.

The man looked at Sarah quizzically and then slowly shook his head *no*.

"I thought I heard a—"

Sarah glanced around the room, an expression of absolute bewilderment on her face. She sucked in her breath and held it as she listened for a moment or two, then exhaled noisily. The sound filled David with sadness, reminding him again how much he missed as simple an act as breathing.

"A what?" the muscular man asked, his eyes softening with sympathy.

"My—No! I'm sure it was nothing," Sarah said emphatically. She sighed and tilted her head to one side as though trying to shake water out of her ear.

David watched as an expression of mixed worry and fear played across his ex-wife's face. He was positive that she had heard him speak, but he was also quite sure that, were he to speak again, no matter how loud he shouted, she wouldn't be able to hear him. Perhaps talking to the living was one of those skills the Ferryman had mentioned. If so, it was something David was determined to practice until he learned it.

Right now, though, his sudden fear for Karen's safety overrode any desire to communicate with Sarah.

It took an immense effort of will for him to step over the corrupted corpse of the stranger and move past Sarah and the other man to the corridor.

Thick, pulsating darkness filled the hallway.

David could tell that there was a light on downstairs, but the feeble glow seemed dimmer than that of a single match. He suspected that his own vision was fading, and not just the light. He might be so exhausted from everything he had been through recently that he was fading away.

The sound of his feet dragging across the carpet in the hallway echoed in the pressing darkness like long, weary sighs.

It seemed to take him several minutes, if not hours, to move from the bedroom to the head of the stairs. If he hadn't been so concerned about Karen, he was sure he never would have been able to descend the stairs. He would have been content to collapse right there on the hallway floor and let oblivion sweep him away.

Somehow, though, he dragged himself down the stairs and made it into the living room. The thick, murky light in the room swirled like daylight seen by a diver looking up from the muddy depths of a lake. Vague, distorted forms appeared at the edges of his vision but disappeared just as quickly when he looked straight at them. He thought he could hear hints of raw, whispering voices, snatches of conversations as well as faint laughter, but he couldn't get a fix on any of it.

But suddenly, in the center of his vision, he saw something that filled him with absolute terror.

There wasn't just one but two shadowy figures standing in the center of the living room floor in front of the couch.

David rubbed his face with his hand and shook his head, trying desperately to clear his vision, but the illusion wouldn't go away.

What he was seeing didn't seem possible.

There couldn't be two Karens!

His first thought was that he was seeing double, but as his vision cleared, he saw that there really were two figures of his daughter, standing side by side, like twins.

"Daddy?" one of them said in a voice that was low and hollow-sounding.

Before David could respond, the other Karen looked at him intently and said, "I'm *really* scared, Daddy."

David staggered backwards, overwhelmed by confusion. His right hand gripped the knife handle so tightly that a dull ache started to throb in the palm of his hand and up his arm. He looked back and forth between the two figures until it finally dawned on him what was going on.

The reaper must have arrived and assumed Karen's shape in order to confuse him. Obviously he was trying to trick David so he could gain possession of the knife.

That's what this was all about, wasn't it?

The knife!

"Please..." David said, groaning softly as another smothering wave of exhaustion swept over him. The feeling that he was drowning and looking up at the sky got stronger. "No more games. Please!"

David heard his own voice as a low, fluttering whisper. The sound reminded him of the moaning sound the wind makes, fluting inside a chimney during a blizzard. It sent shivers racing through him. The darkness at the fringes of his vision steadily deepened and began to close in from all sides with vague hints of shifting, swirling motion.

Looking like distorted mirror images, the two Karens regarded each other, then looked back at him. Their postures were as stiff as corpses lying in their coffins. Their faces were thin and pallid, absolutely void of all expression.

"One of you...one of you is an impostor," David whispered, cringing at the weakness he could hear in his own voice.

Exhaustion squeezed in on him like huge hands, crushing his head and chest. He knew that he had to find a safe place to rest—soon!—or else he would slip into oblivion.

"It's not me," one of the Karens said, stepping closer to David with upraised arms.

"Yes it is!" the other one cried out, sounding almost pitiful. "*I'm* the real Karen! Can't you see that, Daddy?"

David couldn't help but notice that both of them spoke with a terrible dead-sounding flatness in their voices, as though they were just as exhausted as he was...

Just as dead!

It made sense that Karen would be exhausted, David thought. He knew from his own experience that being bound by Stygian chains could drain everything out of a corpus.

How was he going to determine which one was the real Karen and which was the reaper?

Squeezing the knife so tightly that his hand trembled, David took a halting step forward, his eyes shifting back and forth between the two images of his daughter as he studied them carefully, looking for some slight difference between them.

But the illusion appeared to be absolutely perfect.

There was absolutely no way he could tell them apart.

If he had enough time, could wait long enough, he guessed that the reaper's illusion would eventually lose strength and fade; but he didn't have much time. He was already well past the point of collapse.

He had to figure out which one of these was really his daughter so he could get her away from the reaper. But how could he decide?

As long as he had the knife, the reaper obviously would be driven to keep pursuing him. And he wouldn't hesitate to capture or harm Karen if he thought he could use her against David to get the knife from him. As long as the reaper had his pack of barghests or whatever other allies he could summon from the Shadowlands to hunt him, David knew that he and Karen would *never* be safe.

And then it hit him.

All the reaper wants is the knife!

So why not give it to him?

What difference would it make?

David no longer had any doubts about what was so special about the knife. He had seen the power it had when it destroyed the wraith's corpus. No wonder the reaper was willing to use any means necessary to get possession of it.

But the Ferryman had said that he would bargain for it too.

"This is what you want, isn't it?" David said as he raised the knife and waved it back and forth in front of his face. He thought he saw one of the Karens flinch away from him while, at the same time, the other Karen twitched and took a tentative step forward.

"Right from the start—it's been about this, hasn't it?" he asked, knowing that the reaper couldn't be tricked so easily as to break cover and reply. "You'll do *anything* to get it, won't you? *Won't you?*"

"It's not me, Daddy!" one of the Karens wailed, pointing angrily at her Doppelgänger. "It's *him*! He's the reaper! Use the knife on him!"

"No, *I'm* your daughter!" the other Karen replied. "Come on, Daddy! Don't you even *recognize* me?"

David had to admit that whichever one was the reaper, he was playing the masquerade perfectly. There was no way he could determine which was the real Karen. He staggered backwards as heavy waves of exhaustion swept over him, threatening to drag him under.

And that's when he got an idea.

It wasn't much, but it was certainly worth taking a chance. It might be all he had left.

Raising the knife above his head, he stepped forward. His mouth was set, grim and menacing.

"There's only one way out of this for all of us," he said softly.

Both images of his daughter stared at him in amazement.

"Wha—what do you mean?" one of the Karens said.

For the first time, David thought he detected a slight tremor of emotion in the voice.

"I mean," he said, "that I'm going to have to use this knife…on both of you."

"But we're already dead," one of the Karens said, sounding nervous and a little mystified.

"Oh, I know that, but I've already seen what kind of power this blade contains," David said. "I know how truly dangerous it is."

"You have no idea," the Karen who had flinched earlier said to David.

"I'm really sorry about this, Honey," David said, addressing that one, "but it's the only way I can make sure that, whichever one of you is the reaper, you never get control of it. I can't begin to imagine the misery and pain someone could inflict with this. It has a *terrible* power here in the Shadowlands."

One of the Karens, the one that had flinched, opened her mouth as though about to speak, but then fell silent.

The other Karen slowly lowered her eyes and meekly bowed her head. David thought she looked exactly like a condemned prisoner, preparing herself for execution.

"You're right, Daddy," she said.

And as soon as she said that, David knew.

The other Karen took a quick step away from David and raised her arms as though to ward off a blow.

"It's you!" David shouted at the one who was backing away from him. He almost tripped and fell as he lunged forward at the figure, but before the knife could strike home, the figure of Karen shrieked and darted away from him. Standing with her back pressed against the wall, her body began to shimmer as though the light in the room were flickering rapidly. Her body slowly expanded and then transformed into the slouched figure of the reaper.

"It isn't over yet," the reaper snarled, his eyes gleaming wickedly as he glared at David.

The other Karen—the real one—looked at the creature with a mixture of surprise and fear registering in her expression. Her mouth dropped open, but no sound came out. Her body began to tremble violently as she clung close to her father.

"Don't worry, Honey," David said. "He's not going to hurt you anymore. Not as long as I have this." He slashed the knife through the air, satisfied to see the reaper shrink away from him.

"We'll see about that!" the reaper said, his voice rising into a high cackle. "You can run, but you can't hide!"

David lunged at him again and swung the knife, but missed by several inches. The reaper dodged to one side, moving closer to the doorway that should lead into the kitchen, but David saw something else. A dense, churning black emptiness filled the doorway.

As David watched, absolutely amazed, thick clouds underlit by a fierce red glow that flickered with sharp forks of lightning formed into faces and distinct shapes.

For a dizzying instant, David could feel himself being sucked toward the doorway. He suddenly felt ungrounded…totally off balance…uncentered. The memory of falling and floating in that vast, dark emptiness filled him with terror. It was only by a great effort of will that he focused on where he was standing and what he was doing.

"I tried to work this out with you," the reaper said, all the while edging closer to the doorway, "but now it's too late for that. You're going to be sorry."

David narrowed his eyes, fighting hard against the sense of total disorientation.

"And I swear to you," the reaper cried, "by anything and everything you ever held holy—especially on your daughter's soul—that you'll come to regret this. I'm going to make you suffer like you've never suffered before, and the beautiful thing about it is that you and I both know that it will never end!"

The reaper pointed at David and shook his forefinger angrily.

"I'll be back for you—for the *both* of you! You won't get away with this!"

With a final, nervous glance over his shoulder, the reaper darted through the kitchen door and was swallowed by the swirling clouds.

"Go after him!" Karen shouted, tugging anxiously on David's arm. "You can't let him get away, Daddy! You have to stop him even if you have to use that knife to kill him!"

But David couldn't move.

The terror he was feeling, remembering his fall through the directionless void of oblivion, rooted him to where he stood.

"*Terra firma,*" he whispered, and then chuckled softly when he remembered something his mother used to say.

"*Terra firma,* and the more *firma,* the less *terra.*"

He stared helplessly at the empty doorway as the raging tempest subsided, and once again he saw the ordinary reality of Sarah's kitchen.

Shaking his head from side to side, he looked at Karen and said, "I'm sorry, Honey, but I can't."

He wondered if his daughter had seen the same thing in the doorway that he had, or if it was something only he was able to perceive. The feeling that such a bottomless, eternal storm was at the heart of everything, just waiting for him to slip into it, filled him with dread.

Pushing aside the dark waves of dizziness and nausea that filled him, he stamped his foot a few times on the floor, grateful to hear and feel the softly resounding impact. It still seemed oddly distanced, but it was real enough for him. He only vaguely sensed that Karen was at his side, hanging onto his hand as she called out his name.

But the dizziness inside him was growing steadily stronger. He knew he was too far gone as he slumped forward, only dimly aware that he was slipping away into a twilight world where everything was muted and quiet and— ultimately—peaceful.

His last thought before he blacked out was, *If this is the end of it all, then I am truly at peace.*

Sarah let out a shrill screech when she finally realized that her face and chest were splattered with blood and wormy-looking bits of Tony's brains. Shrinking inward, she tore herself away from Sy, not even aware that she was whimpering softly as she frantically wiped at the streaks of gore. All she managed to do was smear the mess even more. Her hands slid across her breasts and arms with a sickly, greasy feel.

When Sy grabbed her wrists with both hands and held her tightly, she at first tried to resist, but eventually gave in and let him pull her to his chest. She could feel his large hand cupping the back of her head as he stroked her hair.

"Hey, now. Take it easy…just take it easy," he whispered.

His voice seemed to be coming from light years away, but—somehow— it cut through Sarah's swelling panic. She sighed and closed her eyes as she nestled against him and let her hot tears course down her cheeks.

"You…you shot him," she said between shuddering moans. "You…you actually *k-k-killed* him."

Sy's hold on her tightened, but it never got painful. His hug was warm and all-encompassing, making her feel totally secure. It was like being smothered by a huge, hard bear.

"Yeah, I had to," Sy whispered, bringing his mouth so close to her ear that she could feel the warmth of his breath against her neck. "It was either him or you. Pretty easy choice, as far as I could see."

"Umm," was all Sarah could say.

A cold, hollow vacuum opened up inside her stomach when she let herself realize just how close she had come to dying. The stark reality of that thought terrified her and made the aching grief she was feeling all the more intense.

Tony's dead! Jesus, he's really dead, and I helped kill him!

To be responsible for the death of another human being—even one as deranged and dangerous as Tony obviously had been—was too much for her to handle. But just as she was considering whether or not she would ever be able to live with herself, another thought hit her. It filled her with an icy dread that sapped all the strength out of her.

This must be how David felt when he saw Karen die.

For the first time in her life, she realized that she had been so blinded by her own grief at the loss of their daughter that she had never truly appreciated or understood how terrible it must have been for David to feel responsible for Karen's death.

Until now!

How could she have been so callous, so blind to what he was going through?

She knew that she couldn't excuse herself by telling herself that Karen was her only daughter, and that she had suffered the loss just as deeply as he had.

He had been there when she died.

He had seen it all happen.

She had died in his arms.

He had watched the light in her eyes dim and go out.

And now both Karen and David were dead…lost to her forever.

She was never going to get the chance to tell him how sorry she was for all the pain and suffering he had gone through, all the heartbreak she had caused him.

"I…I wish I could die," she whispered into the crook of Sy's neck as wrenching sobs choked her. "Right now. I—I wish I could just—just curl up and *die*!"

"Hey, you don't want to be talking like that," Sy said. His voice was edged with firmness as he stood back and held her at arm's length and stared, long and hard, into her eyes. She felt nervous and very small under his steady gaze.

"But I—I *do*!" she said, trying hard to stifle the numbing, gut-twisting rush of emotions that filled her. "I *really* mean it!"

"No, you don't!" Sy snapped. Anger flashed like lightning in his eyes. "Look, I know you're upset right now, okay? And it's understandable. Who wouldn't be upset when some guy breaks into their house and tries to kill them? But you can't let it get to you. Do you hear me? You *can't*!"

Sy was still holding her tightly by both arms as he glanced over his shoulder, down at Tony's bloody corpse on the bedroom floor. Without blood pressure, the blood was no longer flowing from the gaping head wound. It had pooled on the rug, looking like a huge splash of India ink.

"The scumbag's dead," Sy said, "and I don't feel a single ounce of pity for him. Now, I can't stop you from letting him break your spirit because of what he did—not if you want to let him; but if he does, that means he wins in the end. Is that what you want?"

Sarah closed her eyes, trying to stop the flow of tears. Gritting her teeth hard, she shook her head, rubbing her face against Sy's chest.

"No," she said, so faintly that she could hardly hear herself above the rushing whoosh of her pulse in her ears.

"You're alive, damnit!"

She looked up and saw the bright fire that lit Sy's eyes.

"And as long as you're alive, you'd better make *damned* sure you appreciate every second of it, because in the end—it'll be taken away from you just like *that*."

He snapped his fingers loudly in front of her face, but Sarah was too numbed to react. She was finding it almost impossible to register what he was saying to her. His voice echoed and modulated so wildly that she thought she might be close to passing out or something. The fringes of her vision were closing in on her like heavy curtains.

Somehow, though, she kept her balance and remained standing.

Her stomach clenched like a fist when she looked past Sy at Tony's body. It was impossible for her to believe that this was the same man she had thought she actually might be falling in love with…the same man who had taken her out to eat and out dancing…the same man who had shared her bed with her.

He had seemed so loving, so kind; but tonight he had seemed like an entirely different person.

What could have made him change like that? What could have driven him to such murderous rage?

She wondered again about the knife and where it might have gone. She was positive that she had seen it in his hand, just as she was positive that she had seen it flicker and then fade out of sight.

But that now seemed impossible.

Ridiculous.

A small part of her mind was telling her that it *couldn't* have happened that way.

Either the knife had gotten kicked under the bed, or else it was hidden underneath Tony's body. The police would no doubt find it once they investigated.

Or maybe Tony had never even had a knife. She could have imagined him holding one and threatening her with it.

"—to me?" Sy's voice suddenly broke through the spiraling rush of Sarah's thoughts. It took her another moment or two to register that he had just asked her a question.

Feeling dazed and oddly dissociated, she shook her head and looked at him. Her vision was all hazy. Everything—even Sy's head and shoulders—seemed to be edged by a shifting white glow of light. The expression she saw on his face helped her ground herself.

"Wha—what did you say?" she asked in a high, twisted voice.

"I asked if you were *listening* to me?"

Sarah bit down on her lower lip and considered everything he had said for another moment. Then she sucked in a quick breath and held it as she nodded.

"Yeah," she said. "I am."

Looking again at Tony's body, she exhaled slowly, once again feeling herself starting to collapse inward like a deflating balloon. Then she shook her head, squared her shoulders, and forced herself to smile.

"I guess we'd better call the cops now, huh?" she said.

Sy regarded her with a cautious gaze, then smiled as he nodded and said, "Yeah, that would probably be a good next step."

For the longest time—so long, in fact, that he had no idea when he first became consciously aware of it—David realized that he had been listening to two people whispering his name.

The voices blended subtly from one into the other, warbling and fluttering in the darkness like two unseen, hovering birds. Sometimes the sounds were more like colors or smells or feelings than sounds, and before long, such distinctions between any of the senses seemed futile and absolutely meaningless. The voices sounded like high, fast winds, blowing through a pine forest…like the slow, bubbly hiss of air, leaking from a punctured lung…like the soft rush of a fast-flowing river…like the distant buzz of bees in a summer field….

David wasn't sure what—if anything—they were saying, but every now and then the words *David* and *Daddy* seemed to come through like faint radio signals. Before long, every sound merged with one another until they all made a new sound that had no literal meaning, but which seemed to encompass deep, unspoken meanings.

All David knew for certain was that, for a single, timeless instant, the voices filled him with a deep sense of peace and tranquillity. He could feel his corpus getting thinner and lighter than the air as he floated above or beyond everything else. All of his worries and fears seemed to slough away like old, dry skin, and he found himself in a place where everything—even his own thoughts and feelings—were cushioned and comfortable. Rich, deep, wordless concepts formed in his mind like bubbles rising to the surface of a perfectly motionless pond. He was thrilled and almost overwhelmed by a sensation of clear and perfect understanding.

Unfortunately, this feeling of complete well-being didn't last for very long.

In fact, as soon as he became consciously aware of it, he could feel it beginning to crumble.

The image formed in his mind of a huge, elaborate sand castle that was being pulled apart by relentless, rising tides. In the center of his being, he could feel a glowing core that had density...gravity...beginning to grow.

And then it started to pull him downward, back into himself.

No, I want to stay here!

But even as he thought this, David knew that it was too late. He was already no longer in that perfectly tranquil, timeless place, and he despaired of ever finding it again.

Once more, he became acutely aware of his own essential being, of his individuality. That thought or concept or whatever it was filled him with subtle alarm and a deep, nameless anxiety.

No, wait!...I don't want to be me anymore! he thought, but the voices were drawing him back like fishhooks that had pierced his body and were pulling him down.

After another timeless moment, David heard the soft concussion of an explosion deep inside his head. He opened his eyes and looked around with frantic fear welling up like dark water inside him.

He found himself staring into a solid wall of darkness.

As consciousness returned, gradually and painfully, his vision sharpened. He caught a hint of motion off to one side—something moving against the deep darkness.

He longed to hear the soft, steady pumping of his heart in his chest, to feel the slow, steady expansion of his chest, but there was nothing. He felt as cold and lifeless as a wet lump of clay.

He realized that he was sitting splay-legged on a hard floor and leaning back against a wall.

Wait a second...this place seems familiar.

Then, with a cold rush, he knew that he was back at the schoolhouse.

A hint of hazy gray light filtered like low-hanging smoke through the darkness, but he was able to see clearly enough to recognize the two figures that were standing close beside him.

One was Karen and the other was the Ferryman.

"You gave a good accounting of yourself back there," the Ferryman said in a low voice that had a soothing, vibrant pitch to it.

The darkness filled with the soft sound of rustling cloth as the Ferryman stepped closer to David and held out a skeletal hand, palm up. The hand bones glowed eerily white, like streaks of lightning in the close darkness.

"Now, if you don't mind," the Ferryman said, sounding more peremptory. "I can't demand it, but I would like for you to give me that knife."

David's mouth dropped open as he looked down at his lap and saw that he still had a firm grip on the hard rubber handle of the knife. He had such a tight grip, in fact, that his wrist and forearm had gone completely numb. It was like looking at someone else holding something. There wasn't the slightest sense of feeling in his hand. Subtle blue light shimmered along the edge of the blade, and David thought he could hear a faint humming sound coming from it.

"I—I've seen what this knife can do," he said in a dry, shattered whisper. "And I—I'm not so sure I...that you or...anyone should have it."

"Oh, it's not for me," the Ferryman replied solemnly. "The one who might be able to harness its power and use it is far greater than *me*."

"Really?" David tried to laugh, but his throat wouldn't make the right sound. He twisted his body to one side, shielding the knife from the Ferryman.

"If it's so damned important," he said, "then why doesn't *he* come here and get it himself?"

"Because—" the Ferryman replied in a voice that sounded like something scraping against hard-packed earth. "Because he may no longer even exist. In any event, I thought we had a bargain—the knife as surety for you and your daughter's eternal salvation."

David glanced over at Karen and once again was pierced by deep regret when he saw the pale, dead look in his daughter's eyes. He wondered how— or if—those eyes would ever sparkle again with any semblance of hope or love. His hand was trembling as he reached out for her and took her hand. It felt like a small, fragile bird. Sadness filled him because their touching hands still felt so far away. He had to accept that death was a chasm that even human love wasn't able to span.

"Where can you take us?" David asked, trying his best to keep the fear he was feeling at bay.

"Someplace safe. To the Far Shores, just as we agreed," the Ferryman replied. "There you will both find eternal peace and tranquillity of the soul."

"It's a lie! It's a bloody, damned lie!"

The ragged voice that suddenly thundered in the darkness made the air throb with dangerous energy.

Karen squealed and huddled close to her father, hugging him around the neck. David scanned the darkness until he discerned the stooped figure that was moving toward them from the open doorway. The dark silhouette looked like a hole that had been cut out of the night. Only the Ferryman seemed unfazed by the sudden intrusion.

"I warned you, didn't I," the figure said, "about trusting *him* and his kind?"

The darkness was filled with the sound of approaching footsteps. David had no doubt who it was when he heard the noise of one foot dragging like a dead weight across the old wooden floor.

"And I'm supposed to trust you instead? Is that it?" David asked archly.

The reaper halted and almost responded, then caught himself and took a few steps closer, stopping a short distance away from David.

"No," he said after a long pause. "You should know by now that in the Shadowlands you can only trust yourself and no one else! Haven't you even learned *that* much yet?"

The reaper cackled with twisted laughter that set David's nerves on edge. "What does it take for you to learn such a simple fact as that, huh?"

"I—I'm not sure," David replied edgily, "but I *do* know that I can't trust *you*—not after what you did to my daughter!"

"Hey, what can I say? She was the bait—just a lowly pawn in this whole foolish game, okay? Do you actually still think that an individual—*any* individual—really matters or counts?" He laughed again, stronger now, and much darker. "If you do, then you're even a bigger fool than I suspected."

"We'll see who's the fool," David said softly.

He was trying hard to control the burning rage that filled him, but he couldn't block out his memory of everything this reaper had done to him and his daughter since his arrival in the Shadowlands. Remembering his daughter's imprisonment in that cold, lonely tunnel of the reaper's haunt filled David with blinding anger.

He was tired of being lied to and tricked. He couldn't even be sure if it had been Karen or the reaper impersonating her when he had first seen her that rainy day out at Brighton Avenue Park. He had no idea who or what to trust anymore, but he was positive that *this* reaper had more than earned his eternal hatred.

"Do you actually think that this…this *Ferryman* will do what he says he will?" the reaper asked.

Another burst of braying laughter sent a horrible chill through David.

Throughout the conversation so far, the Ferryman had remained perfectly motionless and silent, but David could feel the intense gaze from under his hood slicing into him. Once again, just as he had while fleeing the reaper's haunt with Karen, David had the distinct impression that uncountable eyes had opened up in the surrounding darkness and were staring at him with unblinking gazes.

"It—it doesn't really matter what he says or does," David said. Although he still felt totally drained of strength, he heaved himself up off the floor and stood shakily. He knew he would collapse if he didn't lean back against the wall. "Not as long as I have *this*!" He stepped forward and jabbed the knife at the reaper, satisfied to see the reaper jerk back quickly out of harm's way.

"I saw what it did to that man in my wife's house," David said between clenched teeth, "and I suspect that it would do pretty much the same thing to you or any other wraith. You wouldn't mind if I gave it a try, would you?"

"Don't be a *fool!*" the reaper snarled.

David was pleased to hear a high note of tension in his voice.

"That's exactly what I would be if I gave this to you," he said. "I have a pretty good idea how you would use it."

For emphasis, David cut the air with a few quick flicks of the blade. The reaper ducked back another couple of steps, keeping out of harm's way.

"*He'll* use it for worse purposes," the reaper said, so angry he was trembling as he pointed at the Ferryman, who remained so perfectly motionless David couldn't dispel the impression that he had turned into a statue.

"Do you *really* think that *he* won't be tempted to use a relic with that much power?"

"You have no conception of what I would or would not do with it," the Ferryman said in a low, controlled voice that resonated with strength. Even the reaper seemed cowed by it.

There was a soft rustle of cloth, and David sensed more than saw the Ferryman move closer to him. The darkness behind the Ferryman seemed to be agitated as though churning with dark energy. It looked like a kaleidoscope made of black and smoky gray glass. David had the vague impression that the darkness behind the Ferryman was thinning, as though a doorway were opening up behind him. He gasped when he saw the boiling clouds of the Tempest behind the Ferryman.

"You both may come with me," the Ferryman said. "I gave you my word that I would bring you to the Far Realms. There you will both know peace and true transcendence."

"No, you won't!" the reaper shouted, his voice so shrill it wavered and broke. "What you'll *know* is *oblivion!*"

He started to take a few steps closer to them, but David raised the knife and fended him off. The shimmering light emanating from the blade pulsated with energy, growing steadily brighter. David could almost sense the knife's need to cut—to *kill!*

"There *are* no *Far Realms!*" the reaper squealed. "They're a myth—a fairy tale—a delusion that exists only in the minds of lunatics, fanatics, and fools. Do you *really* think there's a level of existence where you can be eternally happy and at peace *forever?* A heaven where you will strum on a harp and sing hallelujah for the rest of eternity?" The walls of the schoolhouse resonated with the reaper's derisive laughter. "Can't you see? It's exactly the same thing as oblivion! You'll lose yourself. Your entire being—every aspect of your personality that is unique and individual to you—will be completely annihilated! You'll be *destroyed*—lost forever! The only place where you remain even a shadow of who you were in real life is right here in the Shadowlands! You don't want to lose what little is left of you, do you?"

"I do," Karen said in a frail voice that cut through the darkness. "I want to go there."

David looked at her and felt his heart shatter into a thousand pieces. She looked so small, so vulnerable, and he knew—as he had always known— that he would make any sacrifice necessary for the love of his child.

"I mean it, Daddy," Karen said, looking up at him with wide, glowing eyes. "I want to try."

David could feel a dull pressure gripping his hand as she took hold of it again and squeezed it tightly.

"So give the Ferryman the knife if that's what he wants. He'll do what he says. He's given us his word. We should both go, if only so we can get away from…from *him* and all of *this.*"

David didn't have to ask what she meant by "this." He knew perfectly well that she meant the darkness and the terror—the loneliness and utter despair of the Shadowlands.

He could feel the allure of wanting to go with the Ferryman to the Far Realms, even if Transcendence and Oblivion *were* the same thing; but deep in his heart, he knew that he couldn't leave the Shadowlands—not just yet, anyway.

Not as long as Sarah was still alive.

He still had at least one fetter binding him here, and if his ex-wife was a strong enough fetter to keep him, then he was more than willing to embrace it.

Powerful emotions unblocked by any physical restrictions choked him as he knelt down and stared deeply into his daughter's eyes. Conflicting thoughts and feelings raged inside him with almost unbearable intensity.

"Honey, I…I'm not sure I know how to say this."

"You mean that you're not gonna come with me?" Karen said.

David wanted to deny it, but more than that, he couldn't lie to her.

"I can't leave your mommy behind. Not just yet, anyway."

He could hear the rough catch in his voice, but he forced himself to continue.

"She—I know she still needs me to—to watch over her, to be there for her...to make sure she's still safe."

Karen regarded him with a steady, blank expression, and then nodded her head slowly. He placed the knife down on the floor by his knee as he gripped both of her arms just above the elbow. His chest ached with repressed sobs as he pulled her close to him.

"You understand that, don't you, Sweetie?"

Intense surges of emotion swelled like a storm-churned ocean inside him. His vision pulsated with wave after wave of vibrating flashes that made Karen's face waver in and out of focus. Sometimes she appeared so small she was almost lost in the darkness, but an instant later her face would loom close to him, large enough to fill his entire field of vision.

"If you want to go with him...with the Ferryman now, I promise you that I'll come along just as soon as I can, okay?"

Karen said nothing as she continued to stare at him. Her gaze pierced him to the core of his being.

"And do you know what?" David said, choking on his emotion. "I'll bet it won't even feel like more than a couple of minutes before I'm back with you. Do you think you can handle that, Honey?"

David glanced over at the Ferryman, hoping to see some sign of reassurance, but the Ferryman's face remained shrouded within the dark folds of his hood.

The torment of emotion inside David was becoming unbearable. He knew that he couldn't handle this much longer. If he was going to let the Ferryman take Karen away, then he wanted her to go soon—

Right now!

"It's all right, Daddy," Karen finally said. Her voice wasn't much more than a breathy whisper in the dark, but the reassurance David felt was immeasurable. "You don't have to cry, Daddy."

"But I'm not cr—"

Before he could finish speaking, David became aware of a thin, wet line that tickled him as it slid slowly down his cheek from his left eye. He tried to speak, but his voice choked off when Karen reached out and caressed the side of his face. She wiped the tear away with her finger and held it up to show him. A diamond-bright droplet glistened wetly on the tip of her forefinger.

David was almost overcome with emotion. He was just starting to stand up when the reaper made his move.

As quick as a striking rattlesnake, he darted forward and made a grab for the knife on the floor. David caught only a hint of motion in the darkness, but he sensed the danger immediately. His entire body seemed to prickle as though charged with static electricity. Pushing Karen roughly aside, he picked up the knife and, crouching low, swung it up in a wide arc that slashed across the reaper's face. In spite of the tight grip he had, the impact almost wrenched the knife out of his hand.

The darkness erupted with the creature's agonized wail.

Covering his face with both hands, the reaper staggered backwards, tripping over his limp foot. He shambled off into the darkness to the far corner of the room, but David knew that he hadn't left the schoolhouse, because he could still hear the creature wailing in pain.

Before he consciously thought about it, David turned and handed the knife to the Ferryman, who solemnly bowed his acceptance as he took it.

With a slow, graceful motion, the Ferryman spun around and tossed the knife into the seething darkness that had opened up like a dark flower behind him. Instead of falling or disappearing from sight, the knife seemed to float, suspended in midair as it spun slowly end over end like a compass needle going haywire.

"You fool!" the reaper shouted.

From deep inside the well of darkness, David heard a faint ruffling sound that immediately made him think of fluttering wings. He watched in utter amazement as a large bird—what looked like an owl—flew out of the maelstrom and clasped the knife with both claws. Wheeling about in a lazy circle, the bird flapped its wings and flew away. Then, with a softly fading *whooshing* sound, it flew off into the darkness.

"Are you ready to go?" the Ferryman asked, extending one bony hand to Karen.

She turned and looked at her father. For the first time since he had met her here in the Shadowlands, he saw the trace of a smile flit across her mouth.

"Go on," David said, choking with emotion as he motioned her forward. "Don't worry. I'll see you again. Real soon."

Karen looked up at the Ferryman, who was nodding his head gently. "I promise you he will," he said. "Come with me, child."

David almost shouted for her to stop when he saw Karen take the Ferryman's hand. The skeletal fingers closed around her fragile hand, engulfing it. David was burning with the desire to say something more to her. There was still so much in his heart that he had never told her.

But his voice failed him.

Tormented with doubts about this decision he had made, he watched as the Ferryman and Karen turned and walked into the swirling darkness. Their figures wavered for a moment, seeming to swell to gigantic proportions as they rose upwards in a lazy spiral. The Ferryman's cloak flapped and snapped in the gentle wind, sounding like a bird's flapping wings. And then the darkness collapsed around them like heavy, velvet curtains. Once they were gone, the only sound David could hear was the raw moan that was issuing from deep inside his chest.

"You are a *total idiot!*" the reaper said.

His voice was hard-edged, but it barely cut through to David's awareness.

"And you *will* regret this, I promise you that much!"

Shaking his head like a dazed prize-fighter, David turned around slowly and faced the reaper. He was still hunched in the far corner of the room with one hand covering the wound on the side of his face. David tried not to imagine the terrible damage the knife might have done to him, but he was satisfied that he had marked the reaper.

"I don't regret it in the least," David said.

He turned and looked longingly at the spot where, moments before, the Ferryman and Karen had disappeared.

"Even if it's like you said," he continued, feeling his strength returning as he spoke, "even if the Far Realms are the same thing as oblivion, at least I'll know that she's out of *your* reach."

"Oh, I wouldn't be so sure of that," the reaper replied threateningly, but David realized that the reaper hadn't made a move to attack him, even though he was no longer holding the knife. Either the wound had seriously weakened him, or else he didn't dare attack him because David was under some kind of protection of the Ferryman.

It didn't matter.

Whatever else happened, David thought, no matter where Karen might have gone with the Ferryman and no matter what Sarah did or what happened to her next, he was content.

He knew that he could have chosen to go with Karen, but he realized that the love he felt for his ex-wife was still powerful, too. He was determined to stay in the Shadowlands, if only so he could study and maybe even master some of those powers the Ferryman had mentioned. Maybe he could even learn to communicate with Sarah and make it so she could see him.

In any event, he was going to keep a watchful eye on her just to make sure she was safe. David was even content to wait until Sarah died, if he had to, and then…and then he would decide what to do next.

"There are two more of those knives in the skinlands, you know?" the reaper said teasingly.

David saw him as he started moving toward the opened doorway. His foot made a long scraping sound as it dragged across the floor, and he kept his hand clasped over his wounded face.

"As soon as I find another one of them," the reaper said, "if my horde of barghests haven't already ripped your corpus to shreds by then, you're the *first* wraith I intend to use it on."

David heard himself sniff with soft laughter that, in the darkness of the schoolhouse, sounded like several other people laughing as well.

Suddenly he felt much less fearful than he had ever since arriving in the Shadowlands. He watched as the reaper limped out of the schoolhouse. The creature's hunched silhouette looked like an ink stain against the dark background of the night before it disappeared.

"We'll see about that," David shouted after him.

He listened to the hollow reverberation of his voice in the big room. Then he started to laugh. And for the first time, David actually enjoyed hearing the soft chuffing sound of his laughter as it blended with the other sounds and voices he could hear all around him in the dark schoolhouse.

The Muse

JODY LYNN NYE

His friends in the bar had said the slender girl sitting by the window was mad. Alan, looking at the length and richness of her pale golden hair, her long, thin hands the color of moonlight, and dark eyes the green of ivy leaves, thought that whatever madness touched her had been placed there by the same God's hand that had given her beauty.

"I don't care," he had said. "I want to paint her."

When they laughed, he just picked up his drink and left them. The girl barely glanced away from the window when he sat down across from her.

"Lady, my name is Alan Webster," he said. "I'm an artist."

"I know," she said, showing no interest. "I'm Calemotina."

"I am sure other men have told you you're very beautiful. I would love to paint you."

"What color?" she asked, suddenly.

Alan was puzzled but intrigued. "Whatever color you'd like, although the one you've got on is fetching."

The girl looked down at her arms. "Oh, this," she said, bored again. "I've had this old thing for centuries."

It hadn't taken him long after that to seal the bargain. Over the next drink he put his proposition to her. She would come to live in the second room of his small house. On the days that were agreeable to both of them, she would pose and he would paint. When she did not feel like posing, she was free to do what she liked. Alan had other commissions, as was to be expected of an up and coming young Scottish artist who had graduated from the Academy and had his work shown in London. By the fifth drink, no two the same, she had put out one of those long, elegant hands to grasp his squarer, paint-stained fist. When her fingers touched his, Alan felt a kind of shock. He put it down to fate, for what followed in his life must surely be classed as a wonder.

The thing that fascinated Alan most about Calemotina was that she was always in motion. If she was not posing, eating, or asleep, her hands moved, she grimaced, or she swayed her long, slender body in odd, impromptu dances. Muttering to herself in a low voice, she trod ceaselessly over the fields and forest around the small house, picking up a stone here, a sheep turd there, a leaf or flower somewhere else. When once he dared to ask what she was looking for, she gave him an odd look.

"A way back," she said.

"To where?"

But that she would not answer. He was left with the perfect model, the perfect inspiration, but not really a companion, and certainly not a lover. He made sketches of her endlessly changing moods, filling pad after pad with the lovely enigma.

By the time she had been with him a month, though, he came to feel that he wanted no more from her. In fact, it was better if they did not communicate intellectually. It became a superstition with him not to speak to Calemotina unless she spoke to him first, giving him permission to interrupt her reverie. The unexpected quality of her behavior started to stir the creative juices in him. Whatever possessed her to pounce on a roosting pigeon and pull out one of its tailfeathers with her teeth he did not know, but it made a handsome crayon sketch that got him £350 from a dealer in Glasgow who really went for the wildly esoteric.

Calemotina was also unexpectedly good at fixing things. When the antiquated gas fittings in his kitchen went during the first week of July, sending ballooning clouds of stench and threatened fire throughout the house, she pushed him out of the way with a strength he'd never suspected she possessed. Through the kitchen window, he saw her grasp the pipe in her bare hands and bend it back into place. She bent her golden head down, and breathed on the break. The ends of the pipe sealed up with a bubble of white foam.

So that was how it was done! he thought, running for his sketch pad. He had never seen gasfitters at work before, but he'd heard of plumber's putty. How strange that it should melt at body temperature.

The hour after fixing the stove Calemotina spent eating grass on all fours in the field with the sheep.

The picture of Calemotina as the Dragon In the Kitchen went on to win him a prize at an art fair, and a prestigious portrait commission from a wealthy peer. He wasn't at all sure what to do with the image of her in the field. The concept of 'women as cattle' was frowned on just now. It was all this American poly-carbonate stuff, or whatever P.C. stood for. He'd always thought that as it meant "Police Constable," that was trouble enough.

Such a phenomenon as a personal muse could not go unnoticed in the art world. Alan did several interviews in his little cottage during which the reporters tried to photograph Calemotina or get her to sit still to talk to them, but she paid them no mind. Alan warned them again and again that if they drove away his inspiration he'd have the law on them under the Restraint of Trade Act. Everyone was pretty good about it except one Italian

TV news crew, and all of the Americans, to whom 'no' was just an opening point of negotiation. Luckily, when Calemotina didn't want to be noticed, she wasn't. Alan himself had seen her stand stock still between two trees, and had a whole news team in full bellow like a pack of hounds charge right by her. She was only there for him, he knew, and he for her.

Sometimes when he and Calemotina sat in front of the gas fire in his study, he would pour them each a glass of whisky, then he would lean back to watch her under his eyelids. His sketch pad and pencil were always ready at his fingertips.

The study was her favorite place in the cottage. The fire seemed to spark something in her memory. She'd reach into the dancing blue flames and play with them. Alan never questioned her immunity to the heat, nor the shadow pictures she made on the wall with her fingers: houses, castles, mountains—each with the most incredible eye to detail, as if she was projecting them from her thoughts. Sometimes he felt that he was supplying her with memories. One night in the crispness of early spring, she shaped the image of his mother's house on the wall. He sat up with a small outcry that startled her.

"You know this place?" she said.

"It's me old home," he told her, and she nodded in her enigmatic way. Between her hands, the tiny figure of a woman walked out of the door and down the front stoop. Alan sighed. His mother had been dead for fifteen years, but that was exactly the way she had come out to wave good-bye as he was leaving for the Academy for the first time. He felt tears come to his eyes and roll out onto his cheeks. Those had been happy times. His mother was so proud of him. He wished she could have seen him as he was now, famous and growing rich. He thought she might have liked Calemotina, even if each would have found the other odd.

Calemotina had watched him with a strange light in her green eyes, drinking in his emotions. Her skin seemed to grow more luminous, and when he shook his head at last, dismissing his memories, she nodded her head, satisfied. The glow remained as her eyes wandered from him, seeking who knew what. Alan regarded her with affection.

"I've been thinking, lass," he said, surprised at himself for breaking the taboo. Calemotina, swiveling her eyes back, didn't seem to mind. "We're making a deal of money now. How about if we move into a bigger place, so you can have more than one room for yourself?"

"No!" she exclaimed. Alan was surprised by the force of her voice. "We must stay here! There is a gateway here. I must stay to find it." She dropped to her knees and crawled across to the side of his chair. "Don't take us from here, Alan," she begged, putting her pretty hands on his arm. The green fire in her upturned eyes touched his soul.

He patted her shoulder. "Of course not, if you say so, my lass. But we're doing well enough to live better. This wee old cottage was supposed to be only a starting place."

She shook her head.

"It is," she said. "But not for you."

Alan realized he had missed something again. He did always feel she knew more than he could comprehend, but her mystery aroused part of that tingle that began in his spine and worked its way out of his fingers and onto a canvas. He found it strange, but he no longer wanted to move to a larger house. This one would be fine.

The next day, Alan planned to take a trip into Edinburgh to buy supplies and drop in at the Academy gallery for lunch in the private dining room. He had invited Calemotina to come along. She refused, as she always did. Before he left, he checked the fridge and the cupboard to see if she had done the marketing. She was irregular in her habits, but this time there were eggs and tea and bread. He went to say good-bye to her. She was sitting on a stone in the back garden, watching birds eat the stale crusts she'd put out for them. Even the casual, intense pose was beautiful. Alan was tempted to whip off another quick sketch of her, but if he didn't run, he'd miss his bus. He waited, and after a robin had made up with a particularly inviting crumb she turned to look at him.

"I won't be back until late," he told her.

"I'll be fine," she said. He jumped, not having expected her to speak. She smiled at him, the corners of her lips drawing outward slyly. He shook a finger at her.

"You did that on purpose," he said.

"I do everything with a purpose," she replied, and went back to watching the birds.

"Hey, rich man," his mate, Ewan Thompson, greeted him at the opulently carved walnut door of the dining hall. The two of them had been up at art school together. Thompson saved sculpting for a hobby now, having gotten rich from a few lucky guesses on the stock exchange. He didn't have to strive to survive, and Alan guessed that the safety net had ruined his creativity. Alan smiled to himself. He was lucky to have a never-dry well of inspiration in his own home.

"Hello to you," he said, slapping his friend on the back. "Let's have a drink before lunch."

"So, tell me about the mystery woman," Thompson said, when they were settled in the snuggery with a pair of whiskies. "I know what she looks like. You're turning out enough work of her I can guess everything except whether she's got a birthmark above her bum."

Alan grinned. "Ach, she's fine. She's a strange lass, but I am not complaining. She's a gift. I don't have to worry these days if I've got to skip lunch to pay bus fare, or whether it's paint or electricity I want in a month."

Thompson stroked his heavy blond beard. "But where do you think she came from, laddie? Don't you care?"

"So far as I am concerned," Alan said fervently, raising his glass to the absent Calemotina, "she was born the day I saw her in the pub with you and the lads."

"Hmph! I'm a wee bit sorry I didn't go to speak to her myself, considering she's turned you into the next Andrew Wyeth," Thompson said. "But aren't you afraid she's on the run from the law? Hiding from someone?"

"If she was, she'd hardly let me plaster her image all over the world," Alan said, finishing his glass and signaling for another round.

"Well, that's true," Thompson said, standing up. "Let's go eat. Drinking gives a man an appetite."

Late that evening, Alan walked home from the bus stop. It was a matter of three miles and two small hills, and he had parcels to carry, but he was buoyed on a wave of praise and good whisky. In the past he had no choice but to walk, but it satisfied him to know he could casually summon up the village taxi. Shocked, Alan chided himself for drunken pride. He mustn't allow success to make him lazy. If he treated gifts from God without respect, they'd vanish away, and it'd be his own bloody fault. Ah, the regents at the Academy had been generous with their assessment of his work with Calemotina. He couldn't wait to tell her all about it, though he wasn't at all sure she'd listen. She seemed to care little for things of this world. He had few ways to show his gratitude. She never let him lay a hand on her, though he'd told her how fine a lover he was. She never seemed to care what she ate or drank, and she never went away if she could avoid it. Full access to the house and gardens was all she ever wanted. Still, he had bought her the prettiest silk shawl he'd ever seen in hopes that she'd like it. He staggered on, cursing the pebbles under his feet for making him stumble. Tomorrow, he'd start that portrait of the Duke of Forbye, and make himself a rich man.

As soon as he reached the crest of the first hill, Alan could see his little cottage lit up like a beacon. Every single light was on. Something was terribly wrong. Even from where he stood, he could hear the racket, like a thousand voices shouting at once, coming from within. Clutching his packages tightly under his arm, he ran toward the cottage, yelling for Calemotina.

He found her in the study, her back hard up against the wall, staring at the gas fire with her hands thrust out before her, shoving something back. The blue flames leaped and washed over one another like angry surf. The television and the radio were both blaring at top volume. Alan dove for the controls and turned them down. There was a terrible smell everywhere, like burned flesh. Alan looked quickly at her hands, but her trick of fire pictures was not the cause of the stench.

"What's happened, lady?" he demanded.

She turned to him, her eyes wild with fear.

"Draw something!" she cried. She grabbed his sketching block and a pencil off the table and thrust it at him.

"Draw what?" he asked.

"Anything!"

His muse commanded, so he did what she said. Dropping into a chair, Alan threw off sketch after sketch of her as she ran around the room, flinging herself into strange postures.

And all around them in the room other things were happening. Alan did not dare to stop drawing, but his eyes were constantly drawn away from his pad. That was all right; he'd learned long ago to be able to keep his eyes on his subject instead of his sketch, but he couldn't believe what he was seeing.

The curtains were whipping around as if caught in a tornado. Tiny shapes made only of color zipped past his eyes in every direction. One of them flew directly toward his face. He threw up his free arm to shield it, but when there should have been an impact he felt nothing. As soon as he started to draw, he felt a sensation like a heavy force lifting off his shoulders. The room was ablaze with light, but it seemed that a window opened to a freshening breeze, and he felt brighter and cheerier. He tossed off a merry cartoon of Calemotina clambering up the wall like a spider. He noticed only then that there was a dark shadow, with nothing at all to cast it, chasing her.

"Look behind you!" he cried, pointing.

"Don't stop drawing!" Calemotina shouted, clinging to the light fixture.

"What is it?"

"The enemy," she groaned. She stopped, and swung herself up to kneel upside down on the ceiling facing the shadow. It paused at the edge of the cornice. Ornamental bits of plaster that had been there for two hundred years molted off the wall like scattered feathers. Alan was too worried about Calemotina to mourn for them. He promised himself that he'd be upset later.

His muse wound her arms in circles like the propellers of a plane. Before her, a clot of darkness formed, and grew into a ball the size and shape of the intruder. Alan's hands flew more swiftly over his sketch pad. He tossed that drawing aside, and began another. To his dismay, he found he was sketching on the cardboard backing. Calemotina must have felt the skip in the rhythm, for she glanced down, fearful.

"Oh, don't stop. Don't stop!" The ball was larger now than the intruder. She flicked her finger at its back and sent it rolling along the ceiling toward the enemy.

Alan finished the drawing on the cardboard, and flipped it over to draw on the back. The image of the rolling black ball had a yellow sticker in the center that said "£4.50." He didn't care. Let the art world think that doomsday was to be bought for a few pounds.

So it seemed. As the ball neared the enemy force, the foe ball stretched from one side to another, trying to evade Calemotina's sending. Though it was featureless, he got the clearest impression that it turned its back and fled. Down the wall it came, howling like a hound, and tore past Alan, who pulled his legs in at the last moment. Calemotina's working followed it. The two black shapes zigzagged all over the study, upsetting tables and chairs, flinging books off shelves, and finally zipping straight into the television set, where both spheres and the telly blasted into nonexistence with a deafening crash. Alan dove over the back of his armchair, and felt rather than heard shards of the glass screen shoot into the upholstery.

He heard a soft plop! and raised his head over the back of the chair to look. Calemotina had come down from the ceiling. She extended a hand to him, and helped raise him with that remarkable strength of hers. Alan sighed as he looked around him.

The study was a disastrous mess. Anything made of glass was broken, and whatever had stood on a shelf was off it. The only pieces of furniture too heavy to upset were dented.

704   **JODY LYNN NYE**

"It looks like I had a football club over for a rave," Alan said, sadly, picking up the remains of an art award he'd won as a youngster.

"I am truly sorry," said Calemotina, taking it from him and smoothing it back into shape with her lovely fingers. "I didn't think they'd attack. As a rule, they're the mannerly ones."

"Who are?" Alan asked, astonished, as solid bronze reformed under her fingertips.

"The Seelie," she said. She finished remaking his award and set it back on the shelf. "Shall I clean up the rest?"

"If you would," Alan said, stiffly. The pleasant feeling of whisky-drunkenness had faded, but if he took another drink he'd fall asleep. Still, there must have been a vestige of delirium tremens left to him. Calemotina clapped her hands like Mary Poppins, and exactly like the nursery toys, his possessions began to march back into their places. That which was broken mended itself on the way.

"What are you?" he asked, awestruck.

Calemotina looked at him with alarm. "The Glamour holds you no longer, does it? Ah, that last sending ate up the last of my power." She came towards him, her lovely hands held out to touch his face.

Alan backed away until the armchair was between them. "You bewitched me? All this time?"

"Only a little," Calemotina said, edging around, trying to come close to him. "I swear to you by lost Arcadia that I've done nothing at all to harm you. We've helped each other these last months, haven't we?"

Alan stopped sidling away, but only because he had to. He couldn't walk through walls. He suspected she could.

"That's true," he agreed warily.

"Then will you listen to me?" Calemotina turned and went to her accustomed place near the fire. The blue flames flickered gently once again, the way he expected them to. She gestured toward the seat of his armchair. Keeping a watchful eye on her, Alan edged around and sat. "I owe you a great deal."

"Then tell me all," Alan begged. He looked around him for paper, but there was none. Beside his chair was the remains of his sketch pad, with seventeen quick-draw images stacked on top of the empty covers. Calemotina reached into the air and came out with a new drawing pad and handed it to him, with a bob of her head. For the first time Alan really felt the strangeness of her actions. Before, they had never bothered him, and he hadn't questioned his good fortune.

"That's the last vestige of power I have for now, until you help me again. If you will."

And then she unfolded a tale so incredible that if he hadn't pinched himself to make certain he was still awake, he would have put it down to half a bottle of Glen Grant and a heavy meal. Calemotina sat, her animate face and hands adding detail to the story with gesture and expression.

"I was born of light and air, on the other side of consciousness that you know as Dreaming," she said. "Once, when humankind was young, it was easy for my kind to travel between Earth and Arcadia. But there came the Sundering and the Shattering, and now the ways to all the old trods are closed. Only once in a great while do they open, and always from the other side.

"There is such a way here, Alan," Calemotina continued. "I can get home again to Arcadia, if only we can pry open the gate."

"So that is why you don't want to move from here," Alan said. He was no longer sleepy. He was intrigued. A fairy maid, in his own home!

"You do understand."

"But why all the capers and japes? I'd have thought that the Fay had more, well, dignity, begging your pardon." Now that he knew he had sidhe royalty in his house, he no longer knew how to treat her. He hoped Calemotina wouldn't get mad and flit off into the darkness. After all, she was his luck. She smiled in that dreamy, faraway manner that had so intrigued him in the bar.

"It's the nature of magic," she said. "I've been questing about, trying to find the doorway, to get it open from our side. The seeking spell requires an action in exchange for each use, but never the same thing twice. Not like your human science, where an action causes the same outcome time and again. Oh, if only we could pay with the same coin over and over!" Calemotina's perfect brow wrinkled as she shook her head. "It's exhausting!"

"How can I help?" Alan asked, tentatively.

"Oh, you have already," she said. "You feed me. Your art feeds me. Oh, a soul like yours is a rare one. When you catch fire over a project, which you do nearly every day, you give off an energy I can use to create. I'd been gathering it all up, to open the gateway home. I feel the time is coming, three full moons from now, at Samhain. That would be logical, as the two worlds are closest together then. But I had to use up all the Glamour to beat away the Seelie." She pouted, and Alan was enchanted all over again by the shape of her lower lip. He felt for the sketch pad and made himself set it down again. "They'd like to put me out of the way and use the gate for themselves. But I found it first! And I shall be the one to step through to Arcadia."

"I shall miss you," Alan said, softly. Calemotina came over and stroked his cheek with her fingertips.

"Life is so short for you mortals," she said. "You'll remember enough of me to last you."

Alan shook his head. "Never enough. You've revitalized my career. I'm wealthy and famous, and all because of you."

She beamed at him. "Then you'll help me? I will need more than you may be willing to give. I need to gather enough Glamour for the largest undertaking of my life, plus enough to protect myself while I cast the opening spell, and all in a short three months' time. You'll need to reach deep within yourself to be able to produce enough."

Alan stroked his chin. "Well," he said, feeling the creative juices beginning to flow. He always did work best under pressure. "I could do a big portrait of you, full scale, in oil." He started to see it as it would be when it was finished: Calemotina, lustrous and beautiful, wearing a diaphanous gown, against a classical background of pillars and hills. He pictured the painting in a heavy gold-leafed frame and lit by three bronze spotlights. He started to see newspaper reviews, and hear the faraway chant of the auctioneer as the price grew beyond his wild imaginings....

She shook her head. "Bigger!"

The first dream popped like a soap bubble. He tried again. "Well, then, lass, how about a mural? The City Council of Edinburgh have a commission open to paint a stone wall with a series of images to promote Scotland. You could be at the center of 'The Mystic Heritage of Alba.'" His mind drifted away to the fairy tales his grannie had told him when he was a lad. Calemotina as a water spirit. Calemotina as the Goddess of Earth.

"No!" she protested. "Bigger!"

"Heavens above, woman," Alan protested, "do you want me to wrap the Grampian Hills in cellophane?"

She frowned, speculating. "I think it would lack the necessary focus," she said. "We need something that's big, but small, too. Remember that the Seelie will be watching you."

Alan tore at his hair. "We need an entirely new art form," he said, feeling the excitement begin as a tingle in his belly. Calemotina's skin took on that fabulous glow that it did when he was working hard. He knew now that she was feeding on his excess creativity, but he also realized he didn't mind at all. "I'll do it, lass. I promise you. It's the least I can do for my own personal muse."

Alan and Calemotina had little time to make all of their preparations, but they were not to be left in peace to make them. The Seelie, too, knew the deadline for the opening of the gateway, and they sent their nuisances to interfere with Alan's cogitation.

The very next morning, he awoke to the sound of an air-hammer underneath his window. He thought it must be Calemotina, paying the magic back in some strange way for another go at the seeking spell. But when he glanced out over the sill, he saw a bird pecking at the soil for insects. The noise was magnified a thousand times. The bird looked as surprised as he was.

He went looking for Calemotina.

"It's not my doing," she said. "It's the Seelie. They'll do anything they can to break your concentration, for if they can prevent you from creating, they stop me."

"Well, we'll beat them," he told her. On his next trip into town, he bought a dozen new sketch pads and a pair of ear plugs, plus a sleep mask into the bargain. The part of his mind that painted stayed alert, but the part that used to take dirty kicks at the opposite team in school football matches also came up to the surface. If the Seelie were going to interfere with his magical lady, they'd find that the path wasn't all roses. There'd be thorns as well.

Calemotina never reestablished the hold she had had on his mind. She told him it would be better if he was free to think while she turned all her attention and all of her available energy to seeking out the exact location of the sealed gate.

The notion of a gate began to coalesce in Alan's mind as well, and he went outside to pace the lawn. His cottage was not at the very top of the gentle hill. Above him was an open field that he let his farmer neighbor's sheep graze. He pictured a fine construction of pillars and arches. They should be of bronze, gold-tipped, with the most delicate leaves and vines twining around. Those should be of a green metal. He didn't know where he should find that green metal, but Calemotina had said to use his imagination, regardless of the reality.

He put his idea to her.

"But you might be putting it in the wrong place," she said.

"Does it matter?" he asked, waving his arms in circles. "God, woman, it'd be the biggest thing I've ever done! Look," he showed her the quick drawings he'd set down on paper, "the pillars would stand eight meters high, three of them on each side, in graduated size down to six meters high. The doors in the middle would be a fine filigree. Not your common-or-

JODY LYNN NYE

garden-gate tines, but like flowing Turkish arabesques. We'd have leaves weaving in and out, bright green, with touches of gold for difference, and to strike a chord with the edging on the pillars. And between the doors, I want to put a portrait of you, dressed in green. That'll be my focus."

The fairy woman's eyes glowed. "It's fine, Alan. Very fine. You've had a true vision."

Alan's own enthusiasm faded a little bit. "I've just no way to make the leaves green."

"You worry about the rest. I'll find you that green metal."

Alan started work on the gates, which he called "The Door to The Other Side." He called in his friend Thompson to help him with the metalwork. Thompson, tired of investment counselors and making lawn ornaments for stately homes, was glad to come. He brought a portable forge and a truckload of metal stock. He approved of Alan's design.

"It's a classic, lad," he said, stroking his beard. "But what's the railings around the outside here for?"

"Defensive barriers," Alan said, shading in the gray of iron on his exploded drawing of the parts. "We'll need them. I expect intruders from outside." He was thinking of that black ball of energy that had chased Calemotina around the ceiling.

"Ah, the press!" Thompson said, thoughtfully. "If you want this done by All Hallows, we'll need more help. We'll just call in the lads."

But even with a dozen artists working daily, the heavy bronze work went slowly. There were always reporters to be placated, informed, and then chased off the estate. In the end, Alan had to hire a couple of security men to watch the perimeter to keep camera crews from trying to get directly underneath the brazers while they were working with hot bronze.

"But what are you trying to do here?" a female BBC interviewer asked Alan towards the end of September, when the last of the pillars went up.

"I am trying to form a focal display point for the greatest portrait I have ever painted," he said, with complete honesty.

The interviewer glanced chummily at her camera and back at Alan. "Well, then, may we see the picture?"

"Certainly not," Alan said, suddenly losing patience with her. He'd thought of another flourish that should go at the head of each pillar, and he had to inform the master carvers before they smelted the metal. "I'll call a conference when I'm good and ready, Miss. Thank you. That's all." He crossed his arms and waited until they'd turned off the lights and went away.

But not everyone had left. Alan sensed a presence somewhere nearby. He looked around for Calemotina.

She had mostly absented herself from the proceedings. During the day, while the cluster of artists took up the whole of the hilltop, she stayed on the lower slopes, hunting here and there for the true gateway. Alan missed seeing her every hour, but the sacrifice would be worth it if he accomplished something really new for her.

In the back of his mind, he was tempted to make something go wrong in the execution of his project, so she wouldn't be able to garner all the magic she needed off him, so she would have to stay. Then he cursed himself for an unworthy fool. He'd couldn't live with himself if he deliberately spoiled such a work of beauty. *You've had enough good from Calemotina,* he thought. *Let her go. You'll paint other subjects. You were wondering just a short time ago how to pay her back for giving you inspiration. This is the payment she requires.*

She mustn't go, the whining part of his mind said.

Then he realized that the uncharitable thought was not really his own. The presence that was following him was preying on his mind. He needed to find Calemotina and see if she could give him earplugs for his brain. The Seelie were trying to pick at the weakest part of her chain of power. He realized, with no pride, that he was it. He started down the path that led to the lower slopes of the hill.

"Alan!" Thompson called. "Come here and see! We're just putting the pediment on her now!"

Distracted, Alan turned back. He'd see Calemotina at dinner.

"The gate looks wonderful," Calemotina told them all, when she served dinner. The meals had to be served in Alan's studio. It was the only room that would fit the whole group. "I am so grateful to you all." She beamed at all of them, and the men looked abashed and pleased.

"It's an honor, ma'am," Thompson said, after much nudging from the men on either side of him on his side of the long drawing table.

"Eat up," she said, with a special smile for the big blond man that made him blush. Beauty always did take Thompson by surprise. "I've been creating, too. Go on. You'll like it."

Alan wasn't sure what was in the meal. The dishes full of huge leaves and small rissoles of meat looked very strange to him, not normal like a roast joint or even a haggis. Still, he had a roaring hunger in his belly. All artists had an appetite like starving elephants.

The food did smell succulent. Within minutes, they had all gotten over their initial reluctance, and were all but fighting over the last scrapings in the vast serving dishes. Calemotina sat at one end of the table with a tiny serving of each dish on a saucer, and beamed at her guests.

"How does it go for you?" Alan asked in an undertone, as soon as the others were engaged in their own conversations. Her fabulous green eyes glowed.

"I think I've found the way," she said. "It was in the most obvious place possible for a door to be. Oh, Alan...."

At that moment, they heard a terrible rending sound coming from outside. Alan leaped to his feet, sending his napkin fluttering to the floor.

"The gates," Thompson said. He gulped down the last of the drink in his glass, and ran out the door. All the others followed, with Alan at their head.

Somehow Calemotina got there ahead of all of them. She stood in the midst of a tangle of twisted metal, wringing her hands. Alan ran to her and held her close. She trembled against him like a frightened bird.

"It must have been a terrorist bomb," Thompson told Alan grimly. "It's a mercy that none of us got caught in it."

"Philistines! Attacking the arts," Miller snorted, kicking a fallen pillar which had been his own work. He was an artist who now worked mostly in pen and ink, but had gone all the way through art school doing fine sculpture. His hands were huge and powerful.

"We can't let anyone stop us," Alan said, resolutely. It was not terrorists, he knew, but he didn't feel he could explain to his mates that their work had been destroyed by a phalanx of the Fair Folk, to keep another member of the Fair Folk from passing through the veil to the otherworld.

"Hell, no," said Miller He clenched his fists now, squeezing the life out of imaginary enemies. "They'll not stop Scottish artists. Not they!"

"We'll need protection," Calemotina said. "I'll do what I can." The others looked at her as if she was mad, but she stood resolute. Alan was proud to know her, proud to be in her service. What a woman. If she'd only been willing, and human, he'd have married her.

With only a month left before Samhain, Alan had no choice but to turn over supervision of the reconstruction to Thompson. He needed to give his whole attention to the portrait of Calemotina which was to be the focus of the arrangement.

Calemotina had woven a gown for herself out of pure moonlight, so that it matched her silken skin. To pay for the magic, Alan had sat up three nights from moonrise until moonset, sketching pictures of his muse pulling skeins of light from the full moon and wrapping them around a spindle made of a bone. Alan sacrificed his sleep willingly. He knew that he would only see this kind of wonder once, and was determined to capture it all on paper.

She stood in his studio in front of a black paper backdrop that only served to emphasize her fair looks and her gown and skin. The only real color in the image came from her golden hair, her green eyes, and the silk shawl that he had given her as a gift.

The progress he made on the portrait surprised him. It came to life under his fingertips with such remarkable speed he couldn't believe that it was as good as it was. It almost lived and breathed. He suspected Calemotina of feeding back to him some of the energy that she sipped from his creative work. He blessed his muse, and kept painting, fighting the triple barriers of the passage of time, the press, and the invisible foe.

The Seelie set to work in earnest now. There were noisy visitations every night. His friends complained of the air hammers, the motorbike gangs, and the loud teenagers with their boom boxes hovering outside the windows of the studio where they slept in sleeping bags and camp beds. Alan knew the sounds were robins, purring neighbor cats, and nightingales, but he knew that those explanations wouldn't wash. He was grateful that no one dropped out, even if they were a little groggy on the job. Thompson saw to it that there were no accidents that could be attributed to carelessness.

The Seelie also set out to annoy his neighbors into summoning the police at all hours. Calemotina's charm came in handy here. She enchanted both village constables so they no longer came out to investigate, no matter what claims the enemy put into the neighbors' heads. Perhaps it was unfair to let her play with the minds of innocent policemen, but Alan was in too much of a hurry to be scrupulous.

Then the enemy started on the artists themselves. One by one, each of Alan's friends suffered minor misadventures. With Calemotina's protections in place, the artists were only in danger if they wandered away from the hilltop site. The Seelie awaited them beyond the boundary, and took them on fast rides on pookas, robbed them of their clothes, mixed up their coordination, or put them to sleep for days on end. Calemotina said that even though they wanted to see the project stopped, the Seelie were unlikely to do worse to mortals because they were their traditional protectors. With some fast talking, Alan managed to convince his friends that the first few misadventures were drink hallucinations. Subsequently the Seelie began to get more rough. Miller was found only three days before Samhain upside down with his feet embedded in the limb of a tree. It took some careful work with a saw and a chisel to get him out again.

"All right, Webster," Thompson said that day, backing Alan into his studio with the rest of the workforce behind him. "We want an explanation of all this nonsense. It isn't terrorists at all, is it?"

"No," Alan said, giving up all pretense with a sigh. "It's the sidhe."

"Oh, yes," Miller said, hobbling up and snapping his fingers in Alan's face. "And we're supposed to believe that, are we? Like we can believe in such things as magic and miracles in this day and age." The whole group started toward him menacingly.

"All right, all right! I'll tell you the God's honest truth, lads," Alan said, thinking as hard as he could. "It's the English. They don't like us doing anything the hard, old fashioned way. They've got to stop us. We can't let them."

"Oh!" Thompson said, shaking his head. He turned to his mates. "Now, *that* I'll believe."

"Oh, aye," Miller said, sitting down heavily on a chair and rubbing his feet. "Small wonder it is. The English. Of bloody course. Well, they won't stop me. I'll show them."

"We all will," Thompson promised. The rest of the artists agreed. Alan was sorry to lie to his friends, but he'd managed to galvanize them once again. Time was very short.

Calemotina did her best to weave more effective cantrips of protection around them. She had to pay for the first day's spell by turning handsprings across the lawn. Thompson nudged Alan as he stood watching her with affection.

"Is she always like this?" he asked.

"No," Alan said. "Sometimes she behaves very oddly indeed."

With only two days to go before All Hallows Eve, Calemotina came into the workroom with her arms folded around a bundle. She beckoned Thompson and Alan to her, then she opened her parcel.

"This is to make the ivy vines and leaves. There's just enough. It will hold the glamour that we gather into it."

Formed into a rough ingot like a miniature pig of iron was a chunk of green metal. Thompson reached for it, and it glowed in his hands as if it was happy to be there.

"How beautiful! Can I have a wee bit of this?" Thompson asked, handling it. Alan touched the surface of the metal. It had the same warm, smooth feel as copper, but it was bright green, like grass. A tiny spot where it seemed to have weathered slightly was dark green, like Calemotina's eyes.

"Not a scrap. Not until after," Calemotina said, relenting a little when she saw Thompson's sandy brows go down over the bridge of his nose. "Alan will give it to you then. But I pray you, do not remove a single gram from the substance until the gates have stood complete through the night on Samhain."

"Agreed," Thompson said, with a searching look at Alan and his muse. "But look out! On November the first, I'm picking leaves."

"The more people present, the more power," Calemotina told Alan the next day. "I am sure I can get the gates to open, but I need a crowd. Excitement, joy, anticipation; I can use all of it. The purse of power is nearly full. But I'll expend it all at once. I can't afford to have too little."

Alan took her hand. "Trust me," he said. "I'll take care of it."

That very afternoon, he called a press conference in the Academy of Fine Arts.

"You've all been waiting to see my master work," he said. "Anyone who wants to come tomorrow and see the final unveiling is welcome. I think you'll agree that you've never seen anything like it."

Reporters and curious onlookers began to assemble on the lonely hilltop by the middle of the afternoon. Alan, Thompson, and the others had draped the great structure with canvas cloths, and rigged a pullcord that hung down in front, to come away with a single tug. The anticipation, the eagerness to have someone pull the cloth away, started at once, and grew into a prickle of anticipation that Alan could feel in his own marrow.

Calemotina must already be gathering plenty of magical energy from the crowd. Her eyes gleamed so much they looked like a cat's. One by one the feature reporters for the various news services took their places with their backs to the gate, talking about the beauty, the mystery of the whole project, and saying what they could about Alan Webster and his rise to stardom in the art world. They tried to take pictures of Calemotina, mincing delicately around in her moonlight gown, but she wasn't speaking to anyone but Alan. He knew she was nixing their cameras so they couldn't get clear pictures of her. The other artists, dressed in their best, were much more open. Alan had told them that they could say anything they wanted. It wouldn't matter a whit after today if anything about magic got into the papers. There wouldn't be anything left to see after today, more was the pity.

The sun disappeared in the early evening, but not before giving way to the moon, which gleamed above them like a big silver dish. As if by a signal, the crowd gathered around the bronze pillars just as the last red gleams of sunset disappeared over the breast of the hills. Alan looked out at them from the study windows. Calemotina said it was necessary to wait until the moon was at its highest point. It must nearly be there already.

"Are the Seelie here?" Alan asked her.

"They are, but they're waiting," she said, clasping her shawl more tightly about her slim shoulders. "They want me to activate the gate. They'll crowd through ahead of me if they can."

"Can I do anything?"

"No. The vines will do it all, or it will not happen."

The hubbub of the crowd got louder and more insistent, until Alan knew he must do something.

"I'd better go and speak to them," he said. "They won't wait much longer."

"I'll be ready."

To raucous cheers, she and Alan stepped out of the house and made their way through the crowd. Alan went to the center of the gates and the pullcord. He welcomed everyone and said a few, well-rehearsed words, giving praise to Calemotina for inspiring him. The crowd turned to look at the beautiful woman in their midst. She bowed, giving Alan that slight smile that never failed to send a tingle up his spine. It seemed to have the same reaction on the news reporters, who scribbled notes or photographed her busily.

The regent of the Academy of Fine Arts came forward, too, and said a few complimentary things. As everyone held their breath in anticipation, Alan went to the center of the gates and pulled the cord. The drape fell away, revealing the leafy gates, and the portrait of Calemotina. Everyone gasped and pressed forward. The bronze gates, twined with the most delicate of leaves in bright green, began to glow in a bright blue. The portrait inside was lit from all sides by the eldritch glow. Camera strobe lights went on, unnecessarily illumining the already gleaming structure.

"Oooh!" the crowd breathed.

From long experience, Alan could feel the power begin to build around him. *Gather it, lass,* he thought. *Gather it!*

And then the Seelie attacked in earnest. Above him in a clear sky, there was a roll of thunder and a tremendous flash of lightning. Rain began to fall, even though the moon was still visible overhead. Some people ran for shelter into Alan's house. More headed for the barn, arms over their heads to protect their electronic equipment or their best clothes. Some of the news reporters were still babbling into their microphones. Another fork of lightning struck the gates. The bronze only glowed more brightly.

A tremendous wind swept up out of nowhere. It drove dust into Alan's face, making him squint. Small items, including milk bottles, books, tools, and tins, became missiles thrown by the hurricane. Alan feared for the safety of his lovely portrait, but it was in the least danger of anything on that hilltop. The blue glow formed a dome inside the iron barrier that repelled anything that struck it. A bicycle tire rebounded towards Alan and Calemotina, narrowly missing them. The Seelie were trying to break through the barrier with all the strength they had in them. They wanted to pass through that gate, no matter what it took, no matter what it destroyed.

Alan was suddenly afraid. The two of them stood alone in the rain, huddled together against the magical storm in front of the great sculpture. It was the greatest work of art he had ever created, and it scared him witless to see what it was capable of. He had never believed in magic until ten months ago, and here it was on his very doorstep. Calemotina stepped toward it, pulling her shawl up around her shoulders. Alan jumped up to pull her back.

"You can't get through that," he said.

"I don't need to," she said, with a slight smile. "The Seelie think I'm passing through there. I've got to go while they're distracted. Good-bye now, dear Alan. Thank you. Know that you have a friend on the other side. I'll see you in your dreams. Remember me."

"How could I forget you, lass?" he asked, jokingly. But she looked deadly earnest. He was overwhelmed by an impulse. If this was the last time they'd meet in life…. There never had been or ever would be a more stimulating companion an artist could have. She was a source of never-ending inspiration to him. How lucky he had been to find her. As she had said, they'd fed one another. He seized her around the shoulders, and kissed her deeply. A warmth pervaded his whole body, but it seemed to center around his heart.

"Ah, why didn't I do this before?" he asked huskily.

Calemotina's eyes glowed.

"I don't know," she said. "But, like us, I suppose you have to try everything once sooner or later. Good-bye, dear one." She turned and walked through the open cottage door.

"Hey, you're going the wrong..." Alan started to say, and there was another flash of light, filling the doorway. He felt a rush of power sweep past him that knocked him sideways. Her shawl, suddenly unsupported, fluttered to the wet ground. Alan's jaw dropped. So that was what she'd meant by the 'obvious place' for a door to be. He ran over and felt the air. There was nothing there. She was gone.

Thunder cracked deafeningly over the hillside, and rain lashed down upon the crowd. Alan ran for cover in the open barn where refreshments had been laid out for the press. They all stood, drinks in their hands, watching lightning raging over the bronzework. The Seelie must have been furious to be tricked by a single Unseelie and a bunch of mere mortals, Alan thought. The storm lasted for just under ten minutes, and then dissipated. They hadn't much of an attention span, Alan decided, with a superior sniff.

"What a show, old boy!" the regent of the Academy said, congratulating Alan with a slap on the back. "What a show! What on Earth did you use for that dome of light? The effect was fascinating!"

"Oh, something the Americans thought up," Alan said. "Special effects, you know."

The regent poked him in the side with a playful elbow. "A little too modern for us old fogies, I'm afraid, lad. The other members of the board might take it amiss to have their galleries turned into rock concerts. But I liked it, oh, yes, I did. Though I think the whole arrangement's a fine thing without all the light show."

Alan looked at the gates, which now hung ajar, allowing the crowd access to the great portrait.

"I like it more with an extra wee bit of magic in it, sir," he said. "It expressed what I felt about the subject."

The papers and the television news the next day were full of the miraculous exhibition. The *Times* referred to Alan Webster's use of special effects as "a cheap way to showcase mediocre talent." The *Art Review* was kinder, and the popular press more generous still. Alan didn't read the reviews himself. Thompson had read them to him with much enthusiasm which Alan did not share. He was uninterested in the aftermath. He still had to get used to the fact that his muse was gone for good. The gate was opened, as she had wished, and she had left him. He was bereft.

"Oh, you can't sit around all day like a lump," Thompson said. "Come on, then. She said I could have some of the green metal on the day after All Hallows, and I mean to have it. Come out and help me."

Alan sighed. One had to do something, after all. Movers were coming later on to take the gates and portrait to the Academy, where it would be on display throughout the winter. After that, he could decide what he wanted to do with it. He thought he'd probably let it be sold. It had served its purpose.

The ground around the great structure looked like a scene from an autumn in a fantasy book. The grass was littered with leaves as green as grass, as green as spring. Thompson picked a few of them up and weighed them in his hands.

"As light as real leaves," he said. "I don't think I've ever done finer work. Take some for yourself, friend. There's plenty left on the gates. Do you know what? They're warm."

"Are they?" Alan said, picking up a few of the scattered pieces. "They are! How very strange." As he held the leaves in the palms of his hands, he felt the familiar tingle. So Calemotina had left him a memento. The leaves weren't a gate, of course: more of an echo of lost Arcadia, and the fairy woman who had inspired him.

"It's fine work, of course," Alan said, the beginnings of an idea starting to form in his mind. "But there's always better on the horizon, isn't there?"

His muse wasn't gone after all. With a grin to his bemused companion, Alan went into the house in search of a sketch pad.

Beyond this Book

If this was your first encounter with White Wolf's game-inspired fiction, we hope you enjoyed it. As you have seen, in the World of Darkness monsters can be heroes, and ordinary people, horrific. Those who are brave enough to further explore the personal horror and ambiguous morality of the World of Darkness may be interested in the Storytelling Games that inspired the fiction.

Each of White Wolf's Storytelling Games is a hardcover book that allows you to live the horror and glory of these creatures of the darkness. Available at most book and game stores.

In **Kindred of the East**, return from the grave in the World of Asian Darkness with a heavenly mandate to be a vampiric monster. Become one of the unique Kuei-jin, tortured with the gifts of unliving existence in order to repay karmic imbalance.

In **Werewolf: The Apocalypse**, you and your pack strive for honor, glory and wisdom as warriors against the minions of the Wyrm. Combat the ravages of pollution, heal the wounds of Gaia, and punish the evils that men do.

In **Mage: The Ascension**, join the battle for reality — control of outer space, virtual space, and the spirit of humanity. Duel to the death with techno-wizard Technocrats, insane Marauders, and corrupt Nephandi — or become them.

In **Wraith: The Oblivion**, experience the Other Side first-hand — from the grey, decaying ghosttowns in the Shadowlands to the perilous, busy streets of Stygia itself. Get to know your darker half — your Shadow — and conquer it, or fall to Oblivion.

In **Changeling: The Dreaming**, give your inner child free rein — or go Unseelie, and deal with your inner brat. One blink away from the World of Darkness the kings, courts, knights and dragons of the Fae still exist — barely — but it's far harder to stay there than they think.

STEP AWAY FROM THE LIGHT —

AND INTO THE WORLD OF DARKNESS.